WHISPER OF THE RAVENS
MANNAZ

MALENE SØLVSTEN

WHISPER OF THE RAVENS
MANNAZ

Translated from the Danish
by Adrienne Alair

This translation has been published with the financial support of
The Danish Arts Foundation

This is a work of fiction. Names, characters, places, and incidents
are from the author's imagination or are used fictitiously.

W1-Media, Inc.
Arctis Books USA
Stamford, CT, USA

Copyright © 2025 by W1-Media Inc. for this edition
Copyright © Malene Sølvsten & Gyldendal, Copenhagen 2018.
Published by agreement with Gyldendal Group Agency
First hardcover English edition published by
W1-Media Inc./Arctis Books USA 2025

All rights reserved. The publisher prohibits the use of this work for text
and data mining without express written consent. No part of this publication
may be reproduced, stored in a retrieval system, or transmitted, in any form
or by any means, electronic, mechanical, photocopying, or otherwise,
without the prior permission of the publisher and copyright owner.

Visit our website at www.arctis-books.com

10 9 8 7 6 5 4 3 2 1

The Library of Congress Control Number: 2024953138

ISBN 978-1-64690-028-2
eBook ISBN 978-1-64690-625-3

English translation copyright © Adrienne Alair, 2025

Printed in Germany

To the men in my life.
My father, my husband, and my son.
You don't always understand
what the women are up to, but your support
has never wavered by a millimeter.

This is a work of fiction. Names, characters, places, and incidents are from the author's imagination or are used fictitiously.

TRANSLATOR'S NOTE: The passages from Old Norse poems are based on the translation of the Poetic Edda by Henry Adams Bellows, which is in the public domain. They have been changed in some places to align more closely with the Danish version of the text.

PART I
MAGIC WISDOM

Necklaces had she
and rings from Heerfather
Wise was her speech
and her magic wisdom
Widely she saw
over all the worlds

Völuspá
10th century

 PROLOGUE

Hejd stopped among the trees. "This is where I want to be buried."

"Stop saying things like that."

"I mean it. It's a beautiful burial site, and I want it to be my final resting place."

Od looked around. "We're in the middle of a forest. I'll have to cut down all the trees to build a burial mound here."

"I don't need a mound. I want to go in the earth."

"In the earth?"

"I want to be down where the worms can eat me, so I become one with everything. Place me so that I'm facing east. A thousand years of sunrises await me."

"That's not funny, Hejd. I can make a place for you in Odinmont."

"An eternity next to your mother? No, thanks." Hejd turned around, but it wasn't the forest she saw. It was the future. "People will be buried there." She pointed in one direction. "And the church will be here." She gestured in the other direction, both arms outstretched.

"The church?"

"Where people worship the new god. He's on his way here, along with his son."

"The forgiving god with the son who sacrifices himself for the people?" Od's forehead creased. "No one up here will worship them."

"Not yet. But it's coming." Hejd raised her brows. "The son reminds me of you. You both love humans."

Od looked warmly at her. "I love some humans more than others."

"Your fates are also simi—" Hejd stopped herself and closed her eyes.

"This is a good place to rest." She sighed and inhaled. "I can smell seaweed and fish. People sing so beautifully, and the view of the sea is fantastic."

Od laughed hoarsely. "The sea is a day's journey to the west."

"The sea is voracious. It will eat its way into the coast." In Hejd's head, the seagulls were already screeching, and the salty wind caressed her face. She had turned a full circle around herself, eyes still squeezed shut. Without her noticing, Od had come close, so he could wrap his arms around her. She looked up at him. His dark hair shone in the way that always took her breath away, and it draped around his face in a soft curve. She brushed it away so she could get a good look at him. "Promise me you'll bury me in the ground here when I die." She leaned into his embrace.

"I promise, just as I promise to take your soul with me to the realms of the dead so we can be together forever."

"No!" she protested sharply. "No," she repeated, softer this time. "I'm not going to your wife's nor your father's home."

"Freyja will be happy if I return. She has nothing against you coming along."

Hejd raised an eyebrow. "Maybe I have something against it."

"Valhalla has just been completed. We can live there. My father—"

"You have to stay in Midgard when I'm gone. There's something you must do."

"I've already been here over a hundred years. That should be sufficient."

She didn't respond.

"You're always right," he said, defeated. "How long do you see me staying here?"

She placed her hand on his cheek, and it was hard for her to conceal her sympathy. "You need to stay here a little longer."

"But we'll meet in the afterlife, right?"

She shook her head.

"But—"

"Odin came to me yesterday," she interrupted and looked at her hand. Three gold bracelets dangled from her wrist. "I was sitting outside, alone, when suddenly the mighty god stood there. Ancient and gray, with his long beard and cloak. He looked at me with his one eye and commanded me to see the future." She clenched her fists so hard it hurt. "Now I wish I hadn't."

"What did you see?" Od asked cautiously.

It was suddenly impossible to look into his blue-green eyes, so she turned her back. "I'll tell you, and you'll put it in writing. Someone will read my prophecy in a thousand years. It's my message to the raven."

"Hejd?" There was fear in that one word.

"Will you do that for me?" Her voice was thin.

Some time passed before he replied. "I'll relay your prophecy. I will carry the Prophecy of the Seeress through time. But who is the raven? What will happen in a thousand years?"

Hejd began to speak.

CHAPTER 1

I coughed from the stench of burnt hair and flesh. Though there must have been a fire burning somewhere, it was freezing cold. Yellow lights cut through the fog in strobing flashes, and I saw dark silhouettes between the mist and the light. It resembled a brutal shadow theater. I tried to orient myself but couldn't see much more than fog.

"What is this?" The question wasn't directed at anyone in particular, nor did I get a response. I shielded my eyes with my hand. There were humans, as well as absurdly large humanoid creatures. In a jumble between them were wolves, snakes, and fingalks.

"Ragnarök is the fate of the gods." It sounded like a song in the wind.

"Serén? Is that you?" I hadn't been able to make contact with my sister in a long time, so even a nightmare was welcome if she were part of it. "Serén? Are you somewhere up there?" I shouted hopefully toward the heavens. The low cloud cover made it impossible to see the sky. The sun was a black disk behind the fog.

The mist lifted, and I looked out over the plain with horror. It flowed with blood, and there were piles of lifeless human bodies. So many that I couldn't see the ground. Crows pecked at the cadavers, and their hoarse caws blended with blasts, screams, and chops. I recognized a corpse-swallower with its long rear legs without knees, its hindquarters sticking up behind it. It chewed vigorously on a disembodied arm, and I hastened to look away.

There were long-haired, wild humanoid creatures. Their nearly naked, bulging bodies were painted with spirals, and they wore gold rings around their necks and arms. Several had cut the heads off the fallen, raising their war booty with cries of victory.

Someone came running. The mere sight of him after all these months made my heart somersault.

"Rorik . . . I mean Sverre."

He was fighting doggedly in a swarm of fingalks. His pale hair was slicked with blood, and he looked older and harsher. Maybe it was because of the war, or whatever this was, or maybe this horrible event was years in the future. Sverre pierced a fingalk with his spear. The fingalk looked like Finn, but Sverre would never hurt Finn—my own beloved fingalk had died long ago.

The creature fell to the ground, and Sverre pulled his spear from its body. The sight shocked me.

"Anna," Sverre shouted. "I know you're watching from the past. You have to stop this. Let me be consumed."

I walked forward. "Consumed by what?"

Sverre turned toward me. His brown eyes searched. "You can change this. We can be happy together."

"Can you see me?"

He ran forward, and I instinctively spread my arms to embrace him, but he continued right through me. The feeling I got when he passed through my body made me want to throw up. When I turned around, Sverre was gone.

The ground moved beneath me, and I fell to my knees. There was a loud *crack* followed by an unsettling rumble. An enormous wave of icy water swept over the battlefield, and I was swallowed in a tangle of bodies and weapons scattered afloat in the water. It closed over my head, and something sentient and scaly grabbed on to my ankles and wrists.

I screamed toward the surface, but only air bubbles escaped my mouth as the knot of serpents closed itself around my body and pulled me down into the deep.

I jerked my head back and forth and twisted my body, but the serpents held me down. Something alive and warm pressed hard against my mouth.

"Let me go," I shouted, but my words were practically shoved back into my mouth.

Whatever was in front of my lips didn't move except to tighten its grip, and I struggled to breathe. I pounded on it. An incapacitating pain shot through my arm at the same time the knotted serpent burst. Finally, I slipped free. I gulped down air, coughing, and kicked the knot of serpents away. Oddly enough, they made a loud tearing sound. Confused, I looked around, half expecting to see piles of bodies, smoke, and fighting around me, but all was still. I lay in my bed in Odinmont; it was freezing cold, and on the floor lay a ripped piece of multicolored fabric in a haphazard pile.

"Anna," Luna shouted from the driveway. "We have to leave if we're gonna make it."

I rubbed my face and cried out when I found that my skin stung. There was something wet and red under my nails, and a bruise spread across my wrist. I had apparently hit myself in my sleep. I sat up.

"Aaaannaaaaa!"

"I'm coming."

"Were you taking a nap in the middle of the day again?" I heard footsteps on the stairs outside my bedroom. Luna stuck her head in. Snowflakes sat on her brown corkscrew curls, and she was bundled up in a neon-yellow puffer coat. Her sock-clad feet stuck out beneath it. "Hey!" She gathered the ruined blanket from the floor. "That took over a week to sew."

"Sorry," I mumbled.

"It's okay. I'll fix it." She shrugged. "Why didn't you light your giant crystal? It's freezing in here."

"I forgot to." It reminded me so much of Sverre, I could barely stand to look at it.

Luna sat on the edge of the bed. "You're bleeding."

I put my socked feet down on the cold floor. My toes were already frozen solid before they hit the floorboards, and it didn't get any better when I stood up. Then I bent over and looked into the mirror. There were four red lines from my cheek to my upper lip where I had scratched myself. A little red drop trickled from the corner of my mouth.

"I saw something." I looked at her in the mirror. "There was a violent battle."

Luna studied me. "Was it a dream or a vision?"

"I think it was a vision, but it must have been of the future because I saw Sverre, and he was older."

"Did Serén send it?"

"I have no idea where or who it came from."

"Are you still unable to get ahold of her?"

I licked my finger and dabbed the blood away. It stung, but it was a minor pain. "Yep. The line is dead."

"I'm sure she'll contact you soon," Luna said optimistically and stood up. "Then she can explain what's going on."

"We'd better hurry so we won't be late." I didn't want to talk about the problems I was having contacting my sister. Downstairs, I pulled on my mother's now-quite-ragged coat. The dark embroideries on the black background had come undone, and loose threads stuck out here and there.

Luna put her thick boots on. "Are you ready? One, two, three . . ." She opened the door and raised her hand against the driving snow. The small ice crystals hit my face, and I pulled my hat down and my scarf up so that only my eyes were exposed. Together, we ran across the driveway to Ben and Rebecca's orange VW bus. My dad and Luna's parents already sat squeezed into the front, so Luna and I piled into the back. The motor whined in protest at being brought to life. Ben was bundled in a reindeer hide and black Cossack hat; Rebecca sat behind the wheel wrapped in wool shawls, revving the engine so the van wouldn't stall; and my dad looked like a green sausage in his snowsuit. I pulled my coat tightly around myself. With that, two sweaters, a scarf, a fur hat, and wool gloves, I could almost keep warm.

Almost.

"Put this under the seat." Arthur handed me a tote bag with something heavy inside. It made a sloshing noise when I set it on the floor.

"Put it a little more out of view."

I obeyed him and shoved the bag all the way under the seat. "Amazing that you've gotten your hands on some gas," I commented, trying to forget my nose, which felt like an icicle.

"Gas? The van runs on magic," Ben said in a voice so deep, it almost became one with the roar of the engine. Rebecca got the van going, and it coughed down the dirt road from Odinmont to Kraghede Road. The snow was dumping down again, and it was nearly dark. The van skidded a couple of times, but Rebecca kept us on the road into town.

The town sign was partially covered by a snowdrift, so it said only *Raven*. *Sted* was illegible, but that was fine, as all the white made it nearly impossible to see where we were. We parked and jogged from the car over to Frank's Bar and Diner. The glass door was covered in frost. It was a little warmer inside than out, but not a whole lot. Frank caught me in a bear hug.

"Good to see you," he said into my ear.

I returned his embrace but pulled back slightly and studied him. He had a full beard, but most men did now. The biggest difference was that his typical pomade hairstyle was gone. His dark hair, with its streaks of gray, hung down over his ears. Someone called from the bar, and Frank hurried over. Mathias came up to us, and his hand landed on my shoulder. I felt the cool current through all my layers of clothing. His divine powers were growing stronger every day. His skin was as golden as ever, and his eyes shone brightly.

Luna threw herself into his arms and kissed him. Mathias broke off the kiss but kept Luna's hand in his.

"What is that?" He touched my face tentatively.

"I accidentally scratched myself."

His sapphire-blue eyes glimmered.

"It's nothing," I said.

Frank's was nearly full of Ravensted locals. The back area was elevated from the rest of the bar, and where there were usually café tables was an old TV. The box framing the slightly curved screen was made of silver-colored plastic. The speakers were built into the sides, but they were covered by a fine mesh fabric. Frank pointed a large remote control at it, and a test pattern appeared.

A deep silence descended over the packed bar as a man in a suit emerged on the screen. It took me a minute, but I recognized him from the first equinox ball at The Boatman two years ago. Back then, he'd had neither a full beard nor long hair, but the bow tie was the same. He looked like a mix between a caveman and a secret agent.

Outside, the wind howled, and its pull could be felt inside Frank's. The flame of the candle on our table flickered weakly. The news anchor on-screen waited for the broadcast's intro jingle to finish.

"Daytime temperatures in Scandinavia are still between five and minus thirteen degrees, followed by frost storms reaching down to minus forty-nine degrees. The ice cap has reached northern Sweden, and there is still no contact with the rest of the world south of the border."

No one at Frank's said anything.

"The news will once again cover the cold situation," the anchor said. "We will give you an update and speak with leading experts."

He paused.

"Today is August twelfth, and this is the evening news."

CHAPTER 2

"Did you notice how the weather forecast came first in the broadcast?" Luna asked when we got back in the car. "Before, the weather was always the last thing they talked about." She rested her head on Mathias's shoulder and snuggled up to him. He tightened his grip around her, and I looked out the windshield instead of watching them. I missed both Varnar and Sverre at the same time. Maybe I just missed having someone close to me.

A gray darkness had descended over the snow-covered town, though it wasn't quite five o'clock yet. The sky was covered in clouds, as it had been for the past six months.

"Danes have always been very interested in the weather," Ben said. "That was one of the first things I noticed when I came here."

"I think this is different," I said hesitantly.

Rebecca pulled the VW bus out onto Grønnegade. The old camper van creaked and skidded on the ice. My stomach lurched in alarm, and Luna let out a little *oh*, but Rebecca course-corrected with a firm grip on the steering wheel.

"Everything is different now," she mumbled as she fought to get the van on course.

In the rearview mirror, I saw Ben and Arthur exchange a glance.

"I've experienced similar things before," Ben said.

Pensively, I fidgeted with the ring on my finger. Mathias and Luna had given it to me for my eighteenth birthday, and it was made of green crystals and witch-forged iron. The crystals were Mathias's tears—gods and demigods didn't cry salt water like the rest of us. I looked out into the darkness and struggled to make sense of our surroundings. I pressed my nose almost flat against the window.

"Hey, aren't we going home?"

"We just have to do something first." Rebecca panted as she pulled on the steering wheel to turn the van down the road to Ravensted Social Center. The entirety of the flat building was cloaked in darkness, aside from a single office where an electric light burned. I hadn't seen much artificial light in the past six months. I spotted a car parked in front of the center. In its back window, a sticker bearing the Danish government's logo told me that the DSMA was paying a visit. The Department of Supernatural and Magical Affairs.

"Are we having a get-together?" I asked Arthur.

"Niels came up from Copenhagen, along with a couple of his friends." He reached behind the seat for the bag he had given me earlier in the evening. I fished it out and handed it to him. The thick canvas had the shape of a bottle. Arthur hopped out of the van and hurried up to the glass doors, which slid aside for him.

We walked into the empty social center that had been a constant fixture of my childhood. I had come here at least once a month with various foster parents to give reports to Greta. She was the only stable adult in my life for eighteen years. Since I came of age a year and a half ago, I hadn't been here or seen her, and suddenly I missed my old social worker.

The sensors detected our movement through the dark halls, and the fluorescent lights came on one by one with crackling *pling* sounds. Right in front of an open door from which a beam of light hit the floor, we passed Greta's office. The others went ahead to the illuminated room, but I couldn't help but stop and look into Greta's cubicle.

It was so dark I had to squint, but I managed to focus my vision. The computer was turned off, the desk chair had a sun-bleached stripe where it had been facing the window, and the blue mug was full of pens, just as it always had been. I looked at the bulletin board displaying postcards, children's drawings, and a key chain made of knotted strings and beads. It had taken me several weeks to make that in art class at school number four when I was ten years old. My destructive side made it nearly impossible for me to make anything, but I worked determinedly so I could give it to Greta. I traced my fingertip across the uneven knots. For the first time, I noticed it hung right in the middle of the board. Then I tore myself away and followed the others into the somewhat larger, illuminated office.

I stopped in the doorway close to my dad and whispered to him: "A couple of Niels's friends?"

"We're going to speak with the prime minister and his wife," Arthur murmured back. "Niels loaned us this office for the meeting." Louder, he said: "Welcome to Ravensted. Good to see you. Jakob. Mardöll." He shook hands with the head of state and the first lady. Behind them stood Niels Villadsen, director of the DSMA. Ben walked up to the woman, who, in addition to being a glamorous actress, was also a mind-reading witch. They said nothing, but I sensed they were having a silent conversation. Rebecca nodded somewhat pointedly at them. The prime minister said hello at the same time his wife focused on me.

I can't wait to see what's going on in your fascinating head, seer, said the first lady, who was apparently named Mardöll.

Get out of my thoughts!

Mardöll looked intently at me, and though I tried not to think about the lack of contact with my sister and my theories about the unusual winter, the mind is a rebel, not a servant. Mardöll widened her eyes.

What visions you have. Giants, fingalks, battles, and a tidal wave of biblical proportions.

La, la, la, laaaaaaa, I tried to sing mentally, but Mardöll cut straight through my attempts to keep her out.

Sverre is warning you from the future, and your völva powers are growing.

I gave up on trying to block her. *I don't even fully understand what it means to be a völva. Could you expl—*

Mardöll examined her polished nails as if to indicate I was boring her.

The office quickly grew crowded. Everyone was talking over one another, and Niels gave out enthusiastic handshakes. Luna flung herself around his neck, nearly toppling him over, although they didn't actually know each other.

"I brought a bottle of mead." Arthur sang the word *mead*.

"I didn't hear that." Niels grinned. "The country is under rationing orders, and I'm in charge of the distribution of goods."

"Aren't you too busy keeping the supernatural world under control to get stuck with such a practical task?"

"Let's just say we have access to different distribution channels than the other agencies. The DSMA has ways of circumventing the lack of fuel." He patted Arthur on the shoulder. "But seriously. We can't drink mead outside the ration."

"There are nine of us, Niels. It would be an insult to Odin not to drink mead." Arthur gestured around.

"In that case, it's allowed." Niels bowed his head.

Rebecca poured it into glasses she took from a sideboard, and soon everyone had a cup of golden, oily liquid. Arthur handed me a glass, which smelled wonderfully of sweet alcohol.

Rebecca raised her glass. "Óðin Ullr. To the glory of Odin."

The others repeated the toast and drank ceremoniously, while I sipped without saying the Old Norse words.

"Come. You all should see this." Niels had rolled out a map of Scandinavia across the large table. I suspected he had appropriated the mayor's office, as it was spacious, with a large oval conference table surrounded by leather chairs.

We gathered around the map.

Niels cleared his throat. "The exceptional cold has now lasted six months. In continuation of the natural winter, we are approaching a whole year of frost."

"Is there any word from the rest of the world?" Rebecca asked. "They didn't say anything on the news today."

"Or any other day," Arthur added.

Niels shook his head. "We've sent out ships and drones. The drones lose signal once they're half a mile out to sea." He planted his finger in the North Sea off Denmark's western coast on the map. Then he moved his hand to the south. "The flooding down here from the Wadden Sea toward the German border cuts us off from the rest of Europe, and to the east, we lose contact in the middle of Sweden. The location of the ice cap keeps us from reaching Eastern Europe or Russia."

"What about the boats?"

Niels removed his wire-rimmed glasses and rubbed the bridge of his nose. "I've seen some of them come back."

"Survivors?" Ben spoke unusually quietly.

Niels shook his head.

I shot my clairvoyance toward him and involuntarily lifted a hand to my mouth in shock. In Niels's past, I saw ships drifting toward the coast. They were covered in ice, and their crews lay dead on the decks. It looked as though they had collapsed on the spot. A single sailor still stood frozen to the railing. I could make out her terrified expression behind the thick layer of ice surrounding her head. I blocked out the rest of the vision.

The prime minister placed his empty glass on the table. "The people are restless, but we have managed to keep society from collapsing."

"How do you do that?" Luna set down her empty glass as well.

"We maintain as much infrastructure as we can. The roads are cleared to some extent, and food is distributed. The internet and the digital TV signal for the general public are gone, but fortunately, a couple of museums had saved a few old transmitting antennae." The prime minister had dark circles beneath his eyes. We all did, after so many months without sunlight, but his were deeper. "If we didn't have the windmills, we'd all be dead by now. They produce enough energy to heat buildings and keep the electric cars running, even if it means all other energy consumption must be cut down. Plus, the windmills are tall enough that we were able to place TV masts on top. This is where you come in. We need you to help maintain calm and order, so people don't panic."

"They don't seem particularly panicked," Mathias said.

Mardöll wiggled her eyebrows. "Hypnosis. People have no idea how close they are to annihilation. The populace is better off being spared the truth as much as possible."

Rebecca crossed her arms.

Niels looked up. "You also deserve a thank-you, Benedict."

"Our hypnosis fades over time." Ben straightened. "If necessary, we can do it again. Especially if there are more cases of illness."

"What illness?" Luna and I asked simultaneously. I wondered if we, too, had been hypnotized.

"It's not serious," Niels said. There was something dismissive in his voice that made me suspicious.

"Yet," Mardöll added.

Niels flashed her a *seriously?* look, then inhaled. "There have been a handful of cases of an illness. An unknown type of influenza. The infection was contained and treated, so it never reached a critical level."

"Well, it was pretty serious for the ones who died." The prime minister scratched his forehead. It must be hard for the leader of a country to be powerless in a time of crisis.

"Death is a tragedy for the individual." Niels looked sad for a moment, before making his face hard. "But people die from this kind of infection every year. The death figures aren't much higher than those from last winter, and Od Dinesen was able to heal most of those infected using laekna."

I wanted to point out that it was Elias who had both invented and produced the potion, but I held my tongue. Elias tended not to mind others taking the credit, as long as he still profited from it.

"What do the authorities think is causing the long winter?" Mathias stepped forward and was suddenly a little larger than before.

"Most likely a meteor strike or a massive volcanic eruption that's swirled dust up into the atmosphere."

Mathias and I exchanged a look but stayed quiet.

"Is it also cold in Hrafnheim? I mean, it's pretty unlikely that a meteor would have struck both there and in Midgard." Typical Luna to think logically despite the crazy scenario.

Niels's gaze grew dark. "We have no contact with Hrafnheim. After Ragnara was killed," his eyes flitted briefly to me, "things have been a bit chaotic. The cold could also be caused by an extreme rise in global warming."

Luna rubbed her hands together. "Warming?"

"If it happens very quickly, large chunks of the ice caps break off and flow toward us. They cool everything down with alarming speed."

Luna looked doubtful.

Niels pushed his glasses up the bridge of his nose. "Those are the explanations we're hoping for."

"How can you hope that a meteor hit the earth?"

"It would only take a couple of years for the dust to settle. If this is a new ice age, it could last up to a hundred thousand years. We only have enough food for three."

An uncomfortable silence descended.

"But we've had plenty of food lately. We have meat with every meal."

"We quickly realized there wasn't enough feed for the livestock. They were slaughtered almost immediately. It's a good thing we're living in a giant deep freezer, so we can store the carcasses. In the past few months, we've had plenty of meat, but it's also pretty much the only thing we have, and our stockpiles will run out soon."

"Where are you storing the food?" Mathias asked.

Niels pointed to the map on the table. "There's a food depot in each of these five regions. Luckily, we had maintained them in case of nuclear war. With a strict distribution policy, we can make it to next summer. It'll be tough, but people are resilient."

"Hey!" I shouted across the office, and everyone jumped. "Isn't there something pretty obvious you're overlooking?"

The prime minister cleared his throat. "What might that be?"

I threw up my arms. "This is Fimbulwinter. That's what's happening, and after Fimbul comes Ragnarök. The end of the world."

Rebecca dropped us off in front of Odinmont.

"Remember to give the signal when you're home." Arthur slammed the car door, and we ran through the torrent of snowflakes. Inside, Arthur lit a candle and pushed the bench in the living room aside. I didn't have the energy to discuss his choice of bedroom again, so we just went into the kitchen, where we stared out the window in silence.

"Mathias is with them. He can get them inside quickly if a frost storm hits."

"I know." Arthur didn't look away from Ben and Rebecca's house until a light moved back and forth in their living room window. He exhaled and patted me on the shoulder. "Goodnight, Anna." He walked into the living room and disappeared into the crypt beneath Odinmont.

I went upstairs. The soles of my feet froze with each step. Warmth hit me when I swung open the door to my bedroom.

"What did they say?"

I let out a little cry, startled. "What are you doing here, Elias?"

He lay on my double bed with his arms behind his head. On the windowsill, my giant crystal shone and sent waves of heat out into the room. Elias sat up and swung his legs over the edge. "I have a key to Odinmont, remember?"

"Yes, I know, but you promised not to use it unless I said so."

"You asked me to take a look at your back. I thought that was a so?"

"Oh, right. How did you light my giant crystal?" I asked with a furrowed brow.

Elias smiled secretively. "It reacts to people you care about, so you must love me on some level or another. When I touched it, I remembered something fantastic." He focused on my mouth. "Actually, I don't need the crystal to warm myself up with that memory, but you do have to take your clothes off, so . . ."

"Elias!" I snapped, but I wasn't really mad at him. I turned my back, and it took me a while to take off all my sweaters and shirts.

"Now I hope Arthur won't come running up here and find you undressed in my company?"

"He went down to the crypt to sleep."

"He sleeps inside Odinmont?"

"He still feels most comfortable in his grave." I stopped, wearing only my bra.

Elias stood right behind me. "Take it off. I want to see what I've done."

I took it off and tossed it on the bed. My skin hadn't been exposed to air very often in recent months, so I sighed with pleasure when the heat hit my naked back. I didn't care about being undressed in front of Elias. He was over four hundred years old and had seen all there was to see of this kind of thing, including my own body on a couple of occasions. For a while, Elias said nothing. Only his breath on my skin let me know he was there. Then he traced his hand over the spot where, eight months ago, he had carved the ansuz rune into my back. I winced as his fingers brushed across my tender skin.

"If only I could take it back," he whispered.

"It still hurts really bad. I've tried to grit my teeth and ignore it for a long time, but it just won't stop. You're the only doctor I know, so . . ."

"If you had let me look at it immediately, I could have gotten rid of the wound with laekna. Now you'll have it forever."

I ran a finger along the scar on my chest, then to my shoulder, where I had small brand marks in the shape of runes, and then to my eyebrow, which was intersected by a white line. My gaze fell to my forearm, where Gustaf had imprinted the fehu rune. It looked like a tattoo, but it was made using magic.

"I already look like a pirate," I said in an attempt to lighten the mood. "One more scar doesn't really matter."

"You really have been marked by life. Both inside and out." Leather creaked, and something clinked as he rummaged in the pouch he always carried around his neck. A wet gel hit my shoulder. Then a tingling sensation spread across my back and down my arms.

"Læknir?" I asked, recognizing the soothing sensation.

"Let me see you now." He ran his hand over my back again. I didn't feel any pain shoot through my muscles. Only a pleasant warmth and the slightly rough feeling of his palm. At the back of my neck, he touched the silver chain that hung there. I felt a slight pull, after which the pendant slid up to my throat. I placed my own hand on the little silver hand that Hakim had given me for my eighteenth birthday.

"It pains me that you lost Hakim."

I turned around and looked at Elias, who was still holding the silver chain. "Does it really?"

"I know what it's like to lose someone forever."

"Did you kill him?" I concentrated on not blinking.

Some time passed before Elias replied. "No," he said finally. "I did not kill Hakim."

"Do you know who murdered him?"

Elias shook his head. His soft curls and full, dark-red lips made him resemble an angel. Sincerity itself.

"I'll find out who it was."

"How will you find out?"

"I can see ghosts, so I'll get ahold of Hakim in some way or another and I'll ask him."

"Hakim belonged to a different faith. You *can't* talk to him."

"Rules are meant to be broken." At least, that was how I saw it.

"Not this kind."

"I have no intention of following rules I haven't made myself."

"It's a law of nature, and we're all subject to them." Elias looked into my eyes, probably just to avoid looking down at my bare chest. He let go of my necklace. For a second, his face wasn't calculated, just deeply sad. "Put your clothes back on, Anna. You tempt the wrong people."

I pulled a shirt over my head.

"So, what did they say?"

I played dumb. "Who?"

Elias gave me a little smile. "I'm assuming Niels Villadsen explained away the cold with scientific phenomena?"

"I'm certain it's Fimbulwinter." The words hung between us. "But they don't believe me. It's a good thing it lasts three years, so there's time to convince them."

Elias didn't comment.

"Do you agree?" I asked.

He sat down heavily on my double bed. "This isn't the first time in history that it has looked like the end is near."

"Looks like? Seriously, it's below freezing in August." I looked toward the black square of the window. Outside it was completely dark, and the wind whistled as ice spread across the glass.

Elias gave me an overbearing look. "Sometimes I'm reminded of how young you are."

"Typical for a four-hundred-year-old to play the age card. It's not normal for it to be cold in the summer here, even for an old geezer. It has to mean doomsday is near."

"The only conclusive thing we can say about doomsday prophecies is that none of them have been true. The world has, thus far, not ended."

I sat next to him. "But I'm worried for the future, however much is left of it."

"Have you talked to your sister about it? The future is kind of her specialty."

"I can't get ahold of her," I whispered. "Something's wrong."

"Wrong?"

"I have no idea what happened, but it's like she's just . . . gone."

Elias's face took on a professional expression. He moved his head back and forth so he could study me from multiple angles. "Describe what it feels like as precisely as you can."

I shrugged. "I'm usually able to talk to her inside my head, but now it's like there's a roadblock. I don't know if clairvoyance flows more slowly in the cold. But it doesn't seem like that's it because I see all kinds of other stuff."

"Like what?"

"For example, I can see what you did last night." With a little cough, I looked away but managed to catch Elias blushing.

A few moments passed before he spoke. "You might be overwrought," he said finally.

"Overwrought?"

"Stressed. It may be true that stress isn't life-threatening, but it can be debilitating for people with supernatural abilities, and you must be affected by everything that's happened to you."

"What do you think happened to me?"

"You didn't stop even though you exceeded your limits. You

died . . ." His voice broke. "You died just over six months ago. That's very upsetting for the mind."

"How do I make my stress go away?"

"You have to find inner peace."

"How in the hell do I find inner peace?"

Elias shrugged.

"How do *you*?"

He rubbed his forearm through his shirt, and I once again caught a glimpse of the previous night's debauchery. "You shouldn't follow my example. But you can let me treat you. It's not just physical wounds I'm an expert at healing. I'm the best doctor in the country."

"Apparently, you're also the cockiest."

"I'm your best offer. Let me know if you want my therapy, and we'll agree on a good price."

I rolled my eyes. "Of course you want me to pay."

"Nothing in life is free. I'm just honest about my fee. That reminds me . . ." He held out a flat hand.

"Do you really think you're getting paid for fixing my back? You were the one who caused the injury."

A muscle in Elias's jaw twitched, but he said nothing. With a sigh, I walked to my closet and found a little ampoule I had left over from the klinte Elias had provided me with earlier. Now the vessel was filled with a red liquid. I placed it in Elias's hand, and he held it between his thumb and index finger. The giant crystal shone through it and projected a warm glow across his face. "Mathias's blood?"

"It's what's left from that time he got shot."

Elias turned it between his fingers. The red blood surged as though there were still life in it, which I suppose there was. It clearly hadn't dried up or turned brown.

"You'd better go before my dad finds you."

Elias tucked the ampoule away. "Arthur went to bed. There's plenty of time." He bit his plush bottom lip.

"Elias!"

"Do you really want to send me away? What if a frost storm hits? They're getting worse and worse."

I pointed to the door. "Maybe there's someone else who can warm you up."

"There's only one person I want to warm me." He stepped close to me.

"Elias, drop it." I inched backward.

He followed. "I want the best for you. I want the best for both of us. We go well together, and if I only have three years left of my long life, there's no one I would rather spend that time with."

"It's so typical of you to try to use the end of the world to your advantage."

He took my hand and tentatively stroked his fingertips across my wrist. It tickled pleasantly. My heart pounded as Elias came even closer and brought his mouth to my neck. His spicy scent hit my nose, and I stood completely still.

"I've been alone for more than three hundred years," he whispered.

I couldn't help but laugh. "Elias. I can see your past. You can't lie to me."

"It's possible to be alone with other people." Elias's mouth formed a small line. "Let me know if you need my assistance with your stress. I'll give you the friend rate." He said *friend* with bitter sarcasm. When he left, he closed the door behind him a bit harder than necessary. The giant crystal went dark immediately, and I was left alone in the stuffy, pitch-black room.

I fumbled my way over to the crystal in the windowsill. It was still warm but without even a trace of the light it had been emitting. I shook it, but it didn't wake up.

Oh, whatever. It was so nice to have the stinging pain in my back finally gone that I threw myself onto the bed immediately. Maybe, for once, I would get a full night of uninterrupted sleep.

But this wouldn't be the night, as I landed among piles of corpses, cackling crows, and flapping fingalks. It stank of sulfur, and the air was damp and cold. I coughed in the chaos and tried to focus.

A male figure stepped forward. He had steel-gray hair down to his shoulders, and he was naked apart from a simple loincloth. The bare skin on his body, which appeared to be carved from granite, was painted with symbols, like the other creatures of chaos, but he was significantly larger than them. He wore a necklace, but it wasn't made of precious stones. Severed human heads were strung along the cord like beads—he was so large, there were at least ten of them. In his hand, he held a burning sword aloft, and three terrifying beings followed him.

Hel, the goddess of death, touched the people she passed without looking at them. They collapsed, their skin pale and their eyes blank. On one side, Hel's skin was golden, the eye dark and deep-set with a strong brow. Her other side was rotten and crawling with maggots. Its milky-white eye bulged out. The Midgard Serpent kept its enormous head lowered, and it swallowed bodies from the ground. It was the source of the strong stench of sulfur. The wolf was as big as a cargo truck. Its fur was thick, and it looked like a supersized version of Monster. *Fenrir*, I thought, and I looked back at the man with the steel-gray hair. That must be Loki.

Someone walked toward Loki and the monsters. A tall, erect figure, who looked small in comparison. Loki said something, but the man shook his head. His dark hair swayed in shiny waves around his face. Loki spoke again, but the man knelt and bowed, so the shiny hair slid down and exposed the bare skin of his neck. Loki raised his flaming sword. It whooshed forward and cleanly separated the man's head from his body.

I screamed as the head flew through the air, hit the ground, and rolled toward me. Just in front of my feet, it slowed and spun, stopping with the face pointing up. I peeked down at it, unable to look away. Od looked up at me. His beautiful eyes were distant, and his shapely lips slightly parted.

Then the ground moved, and the earth itself rumbled loudly, as though some gigantic creature were down there. A whipping wind hit me, full of hail and bits of ice. Because the ground was tilting, I slid down in a rain of bodies, stone, and blood. My stomach contracted as though I were in an elevator plummeting down. Frigid water closed over my head, and a serpent knot pulled me down into the ice-cold waves.

Then I was torn into a thousand pieces.

"Stop it," a voice came through the darkness. "Stop it."

CHAPTER 3

Mathias's room wasn't particularly large. It was hard to imagine a demigod living in this two-bedroom apartment in the middle of Ravensted. I picked up a damp towel off the floor. It smelled a little musty.

"You're kind of a slob."

Blushing, Mathias snatched it and tossed it in a plastic laundry basket. "If I had known you were coming, I would have cleaned up." He straightened a couple of stacks of paper and kicked a pair of boxers under the bed. "We're usually at one of your places or at Frank's."

Luna threw herself down on the bed. The pillowcase's graphic print in cobalt and cherry red clashed with her orange dress, purple fingerless gloves, and turban the color of curry powder. "You can be as messy as you want. Just don't expect us to do anything about it."

I studied Mathias's wall, where a couple of posters hung. One depicted a rainbow, and another was a large grass field.

Mathias saw me looking. "Those are just something my mom bought before the winter. I don't give them much thought."

With my clairvoyance, I saw Mathias on his knees in front of the pictures as he glowed a pale verdigris green. What was he doing? *Was he worshipping the posters?* Whatever it was, it definitely wasn't true that he didn't think about them.

"What are you guys doing here?"

Luna set her batik fabric bag next to the pillow. "Sorry to just burst in like this, but Anna wants to talk to us about something."

Mathias leaned over her, and she placed her hands on his chest with a giggle. "You didn't have to come all the way here. You could have just shouted. My hearing is getting better by the day. Actually, you only have to whisper, and I'll hear it."

"I love you," Luna mouthed, and Mathias responded by giving her a big kiss on the mouth.

With my eyes squeezed shut demonstratively, I sighed. "Are you two done?"

"Not even close," Mathias said, and I heard another kissing sound.

"Ughh . . . Can you not? Nobody wants to see that."

They begrudgingly pulled themselves apart.

"Okay, then. What's going on?" Luna asked.

"Someone—possibly my sister—keeps sending me visions from the future." My other suspicion about Serén made my stomach twist. I told them about the deaths and natural disasters in the vision. "I'm pretty sure it's Ragnarök. The vision always ends with someone begging me to stop it, but how do you stop the end of the world?"

"Ragnarök? Are you sure you aren't seeing something else?" Mathias rolled onto his side and propped his head up on his hand. I didn't answer and instead looked to Luna in appeal.

She tilted her head slightly. "You want nothing less than to stop the world from ending. That's so typically you." I looked expectantly at her, and she scratched her forehead. "You can make offerings to the gods, and you can make it hard for the giants to invade."

"The first one isn't happening," I said sharply, which earned me a sour look from Mathias. "How do we stop the giants?"

"You have to be smart because they use sneaky tricks to get in everywhere. They try to fool you into running their errands. You need to be on your guard. The other thing is, you have to be frugal. Giants will take everything you throw away and use it in the final battle."

I looked at her, concerned. "Before the long winter, there was a lot of waste, so the giants must be swimming in old electronics and cheap clothes."

"I only know the legends. They say the giants keep warm with the clothes we just throw away instead of mending, they make shoes from scraps of leather, and they nourish themselves with discarded food. Ulfberht forges weapons from all the scrap pieces of iron. It probably goes back to how, in the old days, people had to utilize all their resources."

"Ulfberht." I reflected. "Tilarids is an Ulfberht sword. You know, Sverre's sword, the one he got from Eskild."

"Ulfberht is the giant who equips the others with weapons. He forges them in the eternal flames of Muspelheim. During Ragnarök, the giants kill most of the gods with those weapons."

Mathias blanched, and Luna wrapped her arm around his shoulder. "I don't think it's happening right now, babe."

"So, if I don't want to make an offering, and it's too late to not throw things away, what else can I do?"

Luna considered this. "I've read that if Huginn and Muninn are united, they can change the course of time."

I straightened. "Finally, something I can use."

Luna leaned against Mathias. "I think you're supposed to interpret it symbolically."

"There's nothing symbolic about two ravens meeting. That's pretty concrete."

Luna clicked her tongue. "Huginn is the future, and Muninn is the past. Together, they become the present. It's sort of a carpe diem thing. You can change fate if you free yourself from habitual thinking and fear of the future. The Vikings were incredibly sensible."

"It could also mean that, together, Serén and I can stop doomsday."

Luna pulled the covers over herself. "Well, yeah."

"But I still can't get in touch with her in here." I tapped my temple a few times. My stomach churned again. "There's something wrong with me."

Luna sat up fully, and the covers slid off. "Wrong?"

I coughed uncomfortably. "Do you think I seem . . . different . . . since I came home from Hrafnheim and Helheim?"

She studied me, a small crease between her brows. "You might be a little nicer."

"I'm only nicer because I died?"

Luna leaned back on her elbow. "No, no . . . You've always been nice, but you just don't chew people out as much anymore."

"I don't?"

"What do you think is wrong?" asked Mathias.

"I talked to Elias yesterday. He let himself into Odinmont while we were at Frank's."

"What?! He could have been a murderer. He *is* a murderer," Mathias sputtered.

"Not a real murderer."

"He killed Naut Kafnar and all those soldiers at Sverresborg."

"Well, yes . . ."

"And you."

I raised my index finger. "Only when I forced him to. And it doesn't matter now. Elias thinks it's stress, and apparently, that's like poison for supernatural abilities."

"It makes total sense that fate is giving you this particular challenge," Luna said. "Everything else you can fight your way out of or run away from, but this requires you to actually listen to yourself."

"Okay, but—"

"And you're *really* bad at listening to yourself."

"Hey!"

"You have to relax if you want to be reunited with your sister." Luna wiggled happily in her half-recumbent position, which made her look like a colorful eel. "Sometimes I just love the universe."

I inhaled tensely. "What do you think I should do?"

"My parents can help. They treat a lot of people. My dad hypnotizes them, and my mom does color therapy. She's actually really good."

"With all due respect, Luna, I don't think I can find inner peace with your parents in the room. Have you heard of anyone else who can help with stress?"

"There's Brenda from The Healing Tree. She specializes in treating stress. I'll ask her if she has time."

"Fine. I mean thanks. I don't want to talk about this anymore." I sat at Mathias's desk and swung in half circles on the rolling chair. "You don't seem particularly upset that Fimbulwinter is here."

"*If* it's here."

"Oh, Luna . . ."

"My parents don't think it's Fimbul, and they know the mythology really well," she said.

"Why won't anyone just consider the possibility that this is Fimbulwinter?"

"My mom and dad say you really have to be careful about yelling *Fimbul is coming*. Historically, it's bred hysteria and religious tyranny every time the population thinks the end is near. Niels knows both worlds, and he agrees."

"If it is Fimbulwinter, we only have three years."

Luna squeezed the bridge of her nose. "Habitual thinking," she said quietly.

"What?"

"I'm so tired of reinterpretations of the mythology. Sometimes, when something gets repeated enough, everyone forgets that it's not accurate. It's a little like how Freyja is the goddess of love. Yes, she rules over fertility and sex, but she's also a goddess of death and a witch, and she's highly dangerous. And she's not that much more beautiful than all the other gods."

"She's actually really tired of always being portrayed so romantically." I had met the goddess, and there wasn't much "peace, love, and harmony" about her. "So, does Fimbul not even exist?" I looked hopefully out Mathias's window at the snowdrifts in front of his apartment complex. There were a few cars in the parking lot, but they were covered in blankets of snow. Gas was almost impossible to procure, so people got around on foot or by bike, if they could find a cleared road, or in the few electric cars in the area.

"The idea of a long winter leading up to Ragnarök is a later myth," Luna said. "I think it got mixed with some old folktales. The sources only mention Fimbul once."

"Then what are the signs that Ragnarök is coming?"

"It starts with the gods' and demigods' strength increasing. And there are natural disasters, famines, and disease all at once, but it doesn't say anything about how long nature is in disarray. Friends will murder one another, and family members will fight. Oh, and there's also *whoredom* in connection with Fimbulwinter, although I don't know what qualified as whoredom in Norse society."

"What sources are you talking about?"

"The prophecy. Your friend Hejd."

I felt a strange kinship with the völva who had died a thousand years ago. Sometimes it felt as though she were speaking directly to me through a tunnel of time.

"Hejd predicted Ragnarök, but she didn't see the Fimbulwinter. There's a little about it in the Ballad of Vafthruthnir, but what exactly Fimbul is or how long it lasts, no one knows. Fimbul simply means *hard* or *harsh* in Old Norse.

> *Much have I fared*
> *Much have I found*
> *Much have I got of the gods*
> *What shall live of mankind*
> *when at last there comes*
> *the mighty winter to men?*

As Luna recited the poem, my ears rang, and the room spun around me. I gripped the edge of the desk and nearly fell off Mathias's desk chair. Both my friends reached out to grab me, but I held out my hand to signal that it would pass.

"It's a real prophecy, in any case," I panted when I was once again able to speak. "And now it makes a lot more sense why no one thinks Ragnarök is coming, but I'm pretty sure that it is."

"Wasn't there something about how you or your sister would die by Ragnara's hand before the world ends? I'm pretty sure you're alive, and Ragnara is quite dead," Mathias said.

I suddenly couldn't feel my lips. Maybe there was another reason why I couldn't get ahold of Serén. Maybe Ragnara had found a way to kill her from the grave.

"I dream about Ragnarök all the time," I said, mostly to chase the thought of Serén out of my head.

"Do the gods die?"

"There aren't any gods in my dream."

"So it can't be Ragnarök," Luna said.

"Why not?"

"*Ragnarök* means *fate of the gods*. If there are no gods, it can hardly be their fate. *Ragna* means *ruling powers*, and *rökr* means *fate* or *darkness*."

"Hmm. That sounds a little like Ragnara?"

"Her name just means that she's a female ruler. My dad says she took the name Ragnara when she became queen. Before that, she was called Melkorka."

It didn't matter because Ragnara was dead and gone, and she had done nothing but try to kill me, but it gave me an uncomfortable jolt to hear her real name. It made her more like a regular person in my mind.

"But is it not true that Ragnarök is said to be coming when the Midgard Serpent lets go of its tail and Loki leaves the cave? Both have already happened. I think Fimbulwinter is here."

"I really think we should be careful about calling this Fimbul," Luna said.

"But something is different." Mathias rubbed his eyes with a golden hand. Luna rolled onto her side and pressed herself against him. He stroked her shoulder absentmindedly, still not looking at us.

"What's different?" Luna asked.

Mathias kept his eyes closed, maybe because he was struggling to admit it. "There's something stirring." He pointed at his broad chest. "Something inside me is changing. There's a force that I have a hard time controlling."

"But you've always struggled to control your powers," I pointed out.

He swallowed. "I'm getting angrier and angrier at humans."

I glanced at him. "What are you mad about?"

"You aren't devout enough. It's my right that you should worship me." Mathias shifted uneasily.

I couldn't help but laugh. "You're a nineteen-year-old high school student, Mathias. No one wants to worship you."

"I do." Luna kissed him with exaggerated reverence, all the way up his jawline to his ear, and ended by growling into his neck and tickling him as though he were a child.

Mathias laughed, grabbed Luna's wrist, and turned her over on to her back. "A little respect, please! I am a demigod, after all." His eyes flashed at hers, and her face took on a somewhat blank expression. It lasted only a split second, and then they both carried on. But I saw it, and my heart went cold.

"How do you worship a Norse god?" he whispered.

"Each person must find their own prayer," Luna said.

"Say your prayer," Mathias said in a seductive voice.

I thought Mathias was being kind of creepy, but Luna didn't notice. That, or she was still a little hypnotized.

"Betra er óbeðit en sé ofblótit, ey sér til gildis gjöf. Sér til gildis gjöf, betra er ósent en sé ofsóit. It means something along the lines of *Better to pray than to sacrifice too much. A gift will always be reciprocated.*"

Mathias lay on his back and took in her words. I raised my upper lip uncomfortably. His divine side was gaining power, and it had to be because Ragnarök was barreling toward us. I needed to get ahold of Serén so we could stop it.

The Healing Tree, whose tagline was *We heal, you feel*, had a logo shaped like the silhouette of a branch with a cherry blossom and a nightingale on it. There was a contradiction in the black rendering of something as delicate as a flower and a bird, or maybe that was just me seeing the dark side of everything. The building's windows were large, and at one time, they must have let in large quantities of healing sunlight, but now a thick cloth hung in front of the glass on the inside, surely to keep the cold out. Under the constant gray cloud cover, there wasn't a whole lot of sunlight to let in anyway.

I shivered. There was a hollow sound as a customer left the clinic. It was a mother with her young daughter. The mother pulled their coats tight around them before they headed down Grønnegade in the strong, snowy crosswind. I clutched the bag of wood shavings that Luna had said I should bring, thinking I would have rather stayed outside in the harsh gale. The deep *clonks* sounded again as Brenda opened the door and stuck her head out.

"Ah, you're here. Come on in."

I pulled myself together and walked forward. I'd be damned if I was afraid of an alternative healer when I had gone up against both the Midgard Serpent and Hel.

Brenda was tall and slim and didn't match my idea of a homeopathic reflexologist. She had sensible, short hair, a makeup-free face, and wore comfortable dark-blue joggers and slippers. I don't know what my preconceived notion was, but after having met Ben and Rebecca, I was probably expecting henna-dyed hair, bold tattoos, and colorful robes. Inside, it smelled clean. No dense fumes from essential oils or mystical herbs overwhelmed my sense of smell. A large wind chime made of thick, hollow tubes hung over the door, revealing where the deep, melodic sounds were coming from. The room was completely white, with a couple of framed watercolors in delicate hues and a pale-green patchwork rug on the floor. In the middle stood what looked like an examination table covered with a soft, off-white wool blanket, and along one wall was a metal rack on which there sat a few books. I quickly scanned the titles.

Holistic Relaxation. The Homeopathic Alternative. Harmonic Relaxation.

I inhaled the scent of cleaning products and wondered where Brenda had gotten them. Soap was nearly impossible to come by. Above all, the room was warm. A stove in the corner sputtered, and orange flames flickered inside. I noticed immediately how my muscles relaxed. Brenda held out her hand, and I gave her the bag.

"Oh, thank you," she said with a little smile. She opened it and looked inside. "Fuel. Wonderful. Is it approved?"

"I got it with ration stamps." I automatically lowered my voice. It was like being in a church, where you were only allowed to speak quietly.

Brenda placed my bag on the shelf and wrote something in a notebook. She turned back toward me. There were smile lines around her eyes, and she held her hand out again. It took me a while to figure out that she wanted to shake mine. That was probably what she had wanted in the first place. I gave her a tentative handshake.

"Welcome, Anna," she said softly.

"Thanks for seeing me on such short notice. Luna said you're very busy."

"Please hang up your coat, take off your shoes, and tell me why you're here."

"Did . . ." My voice exploded into the room, and I quickly adjusted my volume. "Did Luna not tell you when she booked the appointment?" It actually wasn't so easy to speak quietly. As slowly as I could, I took my coat off. Nevertheless, I felt clumsy and chaotic in Brenda's stoic company. Though I tried to unzip my studded black biker boots in absolute silence, it felt like I was only making more noise as the zipper creaked. I tried to place my boots quietly on the plastic tray provided for that purpose, but they kept tipping over, and drops of gray snowmelt trickled onto the wooden floor. I wiped the mess up discreetly with my sock, making its underside cold and wet. I managed to set my boots down so at least their wet soles were on the tray, while the leather tops drooped down. Brenda practically floated across the floor to the coat rack where she hung my coat, which looked like death and destruction amid the bright surroundings.

"Luna said she gave me immunity," Brenda said and shook her head elegantly. "Luna is a sweet girl, although I don't always understand what she's talking about."

Huh, so Luna could give magical immunity now? It wasn't just Mathias's powers that were getting stronger.

Brenda pointed me toward the table, which I padded over to in my socks—one with a damp sole.

I forced myself to sit on the off-white surface of the table. "Should I lie down?"

"Just sit for now." She sat in a wicker chair with a pink patchwork seat cushion. It creaked, and she looked expectantly at me.

My jaw worked without me saying anything at first, until I finally squeaked out: "Stress." I cleared my throat forcefully. "I think I might have stress."

"I help lots of people with stress," she said in her characteristic subdued way. "It's normal for there to be times in our lives when we feel a lot of pressure."

"Pressure. Yes!" I accidentally spoke too loudly again, so I coughed to bring my voice down. "I much prefer putting it that way," I whispered.

"Pressure." Brenda smiled, and on its own, the word sounded friendly. "Let's call it pressure, then."

After that, neither of us said anything for a while. When the silence had hung between us for a long time, I realized she was waiting for me to speak.

"A doctor told me I have it." I felt like I had to defend my supposed stress—or pressure, or whatever we were calling it.

"Your doctor?"

Elias would love to know that I called him *mine*, but it was too hard to explain, so I simply nodded. Brenda sat for a moment with her eyes directed at me and looked like she was trying to formulate a very difficult question. I glanced at the little clock on the wall. I wondered when we would get started.

"How does this pressure feel to you, Anna?"

I shifted on the eggshell-colored wool throw. "I actually don't feel anything. That's the problem. It's like I'm numb."

"You feel isolated from other people."

Bingo! "I feel totally cut off. There's no way through."

"How long has this been going on?"

"More than six months."

"What about before that?"

"No problemo. Everything was running smoothly." Plus or minus a couple of murder attempts and a trip to the underworld.

"So, something happened a little more than six months ago that has you feeling blocked?"

"Well . . . I don't know. Maybe."

"Do you know what might have happened?"

"No idea!" I opened my eyes wide.

Brenda seemed like someone who had spoken with a lot of people who were in total denial. I didn't need my clairvoyance to see she didn't believe me one bit.

"Were there other signs earlier? Angry outbursts? Aggression? Did you have a feeling of helplessness?"

A laugh burst out of my mouth. "Yeaaahh . . . there was some of that."

"For how long?" She folded her hands in her lap.

"I don't know." *Approximately my whole life.*

Brenda didn't push. "What about now? Are you able to sleep?"

"It's hard," I admitted. "I always fall asleep immediately, but then I wake up in the middle of the night." The night before I had lain awake for hours, terrified of seeing Od get his head chopped off again.

"Do you sleep fitfully?" Her eyes flitted over the scratch marks on my cheek.

Embarrassed, I brought my hand up to them. "I don't know. I'm asleep."

Brenda paused briefly. "How do you feel during the day?"

"My muscles tremble, and my heart beats. I guess that's a good thing. I mean, it wouldn't be so good if it weren't beating. If it stopped. What I'm trying to say is, it beats quickly sometimes for no reason." I pressed my lips together as I wondered why I had suddenly started babbling.

There was understanding in Brenda's face, but it was a professional sympathy. "I think we should figure out what triggered this pressure. Lie on your back."

I obeyed. The table creaked beneath my weight, and Brenda tucked a pillow under my head. I didn't know what to do with my hands, so I folded them on my chest. I unconsciously twiddled my thumbs. Brenda stood behind my head. I heard a little *click*, and sound flowed into the room. The music was a combination of instruments and nature sounds. Piano and string instruments blended with crashing waves and buzzing insects. Brenda gave me a little time to acclimate to it. She simply stood behind my head without doing anything. It didn't feel unsafe. More like she was keeping watch over me. I lay there with my eyes closed and waited for her to get started. Sloshes and drips mingled with the sound of a harp.

"Breathe slowly." Brenda's voice grew deeper. "Take a moment to get comfortable lying there. You must take care of yourself."

I inhaled deeply and tried to relax. The other thing Brenda asked me to do was impossible.

"Accept the sounds and smells around you. Accept any discomfort or tension in your body. Accept your thoughts."

It reminded me of when Elias had taught me to shield my clairvoyance, so this part wasn't hard for me to do.

"Accept the cold."

"The key word is *acceptance*," I mumbled. "Got it."

"Shhhh . . ." Brenda sounded slightly fuzzy. "Slowly fill your lu—"

"Can you just tell me before you do something?" I interrupted.

"What?"

"Like, for example, if you're going to stick a needle in me. I can totally handle it," I hastened to add. "It's just easier when I know the pain is coming."

"I'm not going to stick a needle in you. In fact, I'm not planning to touch you at all."

I opened my eyes and looked up. Because I was seeing Brenda upside down, she looked strange. I couldn't quite fit her features together into a face. "Then how will you fix me?"

"I'm trying to fix you now. This is the therapy."

"Oh, no! Is this some kind of meditation bullshit?"

Brenda's mouth opened, but she said nothing. From this angle, she resembled a gaping fish. I thought she would throw me out, but she burst into laughter that mixed with the sounds from the speakers. She hiccuped.

"Never in my twenty years in the clinic has anyone ever said something like that to me. I've met my share of skeptics, but they don't book an appointment and lie down on the table." She sounded completely different. "How wonderful you are. How lovely."

The positive words stung like lashings from a whip, and I sniffed. "Okay, okay, okay."

"Let's try again. This is guided relaxation, and it's completely harmless. If you don't think it helps, I'll give you your wood shavings back. All you stand to lose is time."

I considered this for a moment. "Okay. I'll stay."

"Meditation bullshit." Brenda chuckled. Then she cleared her throat and got back into her role. "Close your eyes. Breathe slowly. Take a deep breath in. Fill your lungs with air and feel the tightening in your chest. Empty your lungs. Let the tension dissolve as you breathe out, and notice how you rest heavier on the table."

She asked me to do this a couple of times, and the tense feeling actually diminished a little.

"Breathe normally again. It's natural to breathe. Your body does it automatically. Your breathing is your best and most loyal friend. It stays with you your whole life."

I thought about how, not too long ago, I had been dead and not breathing, and my chest tightened again. Then I felt guilty for being mopey on Brenda's table with the pretty music.

As if Brenda had heard me, she said, "It's okay if you have negative thoughts. They're allowed to be there."

Yes. Acceptance. Got it. Out of respect for the mood, I didn't say this aloud but raised my hand in a thumbs-up.

She continued, asking me to relax my feet and legs. I was supposed to feel every part of my body, from my toes to my earlobes. It felt silly, but Brenda's voice was bewitching, the music was soothing, and the room felt safe.

"Good, Anna. Now we'll go on an imaginary journey together. Imagine that you're standing on a high point somewhere in nature. You can see out over the landscape."

I imagined the cliff behind The Boatman. Because my breathing was slow and my body was calm, I just dropped right down onto the ridge. I could feel the sand giving way beneath me. Blades of lyme grass prickled my hands.

"The sky is blue, with scattered clouds. You smell grass."

The salty air of summer on the west coast tickled my nostrils. I could hear the characteristic *click* of the lyme grass as the wind rustled through it. The cicadas ran amok, and the waves crashing from Brenda's speaker became the sound of the sea. To my left were the remains of the church that had been there since the Middle Ages. The churchyard, with all its headstones and skeletons, had long since tumbled down the steep slope.

"Sunbeams hit your skin. They're warm and mild," Brenda said from somewhere above me.

I nearly cried as I was bathed in warm sunlight for the first time in a year. I could see why, in olden times, people had worshipped the sun as a god. Especially after a long, dark winter.

"You walk forward. There's a descent. A staircase that leads down from the high point you're standing on. Below, you can see water. It might be the sea or a lake. A river or a spring."

I tiptoed forward and saw the stairs that led steeply down to the beach.

"You walk down. One step at a time. Breathe in. Release the air. Release the tension. Release your fear. With each step you take, the further you sink into calm."

Cautiously, like the time I actually did walk down the nearly vertical stairs to the beach beneath The Boatman, I took one step at a time. It felt like I was sinking deeper and deeper into a thick, warm substance.

"You reach the bottom. When you're ready, walk toward the water."

My bare feet touched the sun-warmed sand, and its grains crunched pleasantly beneath my footsteps. The loose sand was imprinted with the soles of my feet as I walked forward. Down here, the wind was stronger, but it was warm, and it wrapped itself lovingly around me. The waves lapped up onto the beach, and I heard the cries of seagulls. The beach was wide, chalk white, and empty apart from me.

"When you're at the point where water meets land, you're in the deepest part of your consciousness. Inhale and exhale as you go. Blow all your worries and sorrows out over the water, where they'll be carried away on the wind."

As I walked, I breathed forcefully in and out. With each exhalation, a tiny fragment of my worries slipped away.

"When you reach the water, look down into it. It will show you what's blocking you."

Boldly, I walked forward in the warm wind. My subconscious was not scary at all.

"See what the deepest parts of you are hiding. See what's standing in your way. I am with you, and I am taking care of you."

My heart was beating so slowly, I knew I was both asleep and not. I could hear it over the waves and the wind.

Thump-thump . . . thump-thump . . . thump-thump . . .

The wind came from behind and pushed me forward. I reached the water's edge and let the salt water flow over my toes. It was lukewarm and felt nice. I waded out until the waves lapped against my stomach, and then I looked down. What I could see of my feet and legs was distorted by the water. I leaned farther forward, until my nose almost touched the surface. Small fish swam over my feet, and a crab crawled along the seafloor. Maybe it was just my imagination. Maybe there was nothing wrong with me.

Then a figure glided in front of me. At first, I thought it was my reflection, or better yet, my sister. I leaned farther down to the water and stared intently. Water splashed up onto my face, so for a moment, I couldn't see. I wiped it away with my sleeve.

"Serén?" I asked hopefully.

But it wasn't my sister, as the person had black hair. When I realized who it was, I shouted wordlessly in terror.

The woman looked up at me. On one side, her skin was taut and golden. Her eye sparkled darkly beneath a pronounced eyebrow, and her full lips curved upward. Her cheekbone was high, but its mirror image was a white bone, and the other side of her head was crawling with maggots. The eye was milky white, and it appeared to be opened wide, but that was because no eyelid remained. The skin had rotted away, exposing the bone, sinew, and flesh beneath.

I leaned away with a scream, but hands reached up from the depths and grabbed ahold of me. They tightened around my forearms. One hand was slim and had beautifully shaped nails. The other was bone. Hel used my body to drag herself up from the sea. She tilted her simultaneously horrific and beautiful face. The wind rushed through me, and I felt like just as much a skeleton as Hel's rotten side.

"What are you doing in my subconscious?" I stammered.

She opened her mouth, and something twisted around deep in her throat. I saw yellowish scales and heard an sssssss sound. Hel's voice was deep like a bottomless pit, damp like a dark cave, and her breath smelled like mildew.

"I'm here because I am death," she rasped.

I twisted free from her grasp and took a swing at her. She laughed in response. I hammered my fists into her face again, and this time, there was a cracking sound when I hit her cheekbone.

"Hee-hee," she laughed, waving with her skeletal hand. "I've taken so many you care about, and I'm going to take more."

This made me see red, and I threw myself at her. My fingers squeezed her throat, and she hacked as her face changed from mocking to desperate.

"Let me go," she coughed.

"Go away, go away, go away." I shook both hands, so Hel's head dangled. "Go awaaaaaay," I screamed, standing in front of her with a firm grip around her neck. "I don't want death in my life."

"Anna's attacking me," shouted Hel. Her long black hair pulled back into her head. Everything around me tilted. We were lying down, and I sat straddling Hel's chest, still trying to strangle her.

"Help." Hel's words sounded like faint whistles. "Help."

"Shit!" I exclaimed when I realized I was on the floor of The Healing Tree. To my horror, Brenda lay under me.

Her face was red, she had a mark on her cheek, and terror shone in her bulging eyes. Her lips were turning blue, and she was flailing her arms desperately. I let go immediately, and Brenda rolled around with a prolonged cough. She crawled away from me and held out a hand pleadingly.

"I'm sorry," I said. "You have to forgive me."

"No." The word ended in a deep hacking sound.

"I'm really sorry. I didn't—" I tried to grab Brenda's shoulder, but she screamed and crawled behind the table, where she held up a book about healing as a shield.

"You're sick in the head," she gurgled.

"That's why I'm here."

Brenda shrieked in reply.

"Should I get you a glass of water?" I asked.

"Get out of here." Brenda swung the book at me, and I jumped back. "Out. Out. Ouuuuuut!"

I hurried to grab my boots and coat and yanked the door open. There were a few deep *clonks* from the wind chimes.

"Sorry," I whispered again and closed the door behind me, after which I stood on Grønnegade in my socks and sweater.

The wind and snowflakes whipped around me.

 CHAPTER 4

I was horribly embarrassed after my stress treatment and was therefore not paying very close attention as I rode my bike home from The Healing Tree. Odinmont was shrouded in fog, and I had to stand up to pedal up the hill against the strong head wind. Because of this, I didn't see the person in the middle of the dirt road until I had nearly run into him. I was so startled, I slammed on the brakes, and the wheels slid on the ice. I toppled over and landed painfully on the cold, sharp clods of frozen earth. The front wheel kept spinning with a *click-click-click* sound.

The knees of my pants were ripped, my eyes were watering, and the mist smudged everything, so I couldn't see the figure clearly. I struggled to disentangle myself from the bike.

The person looked up the hill, then turned toward Kraghede Forest. "This is where I died." The voice belonged to a man, but I couldn't place it.

I rubbed my eyes and still couldn't focus, but my eyes weren't the problem. He was simply blurry. I was still lying on the ground beneath my bike.

"Who are you?"

"It would make more sense to ask who I was."

Finally, I got myself untangled from the bike's frame. "I can't really handle cryptic ghost talk right now." The ghost swayed slightly. I struggled to my feet. *Okay—maybe without sarcasm.* "Then who were you?" I rephrased.

"Your polar opposite and your mirror image. We believed in the same thing, yet we're separated by our beliefs."

I slowly inched closer, but the person drew farther away. "Is that you, Hakim?"

The ghost stiffened. "Hakim? I know that name."

"Was it once yours?"

"Hakim, Hakim, Hakim." He tried the word on his tongue. "*Al hakim* means *the wise* in an ancient language." His contours dissipated like smoke in the surrounding air.

"Why are you here?" I asked gently. I wanted to reach out to him, but I didn't dare, seeing as how he was a fragile spirit.

"I want to warn you about Odin. He is not the god for you. You shouldn't make offerings to him." Hakim's ghost sighed, as though he had to search for the right words. "And the ravens must meet. You have to."

"Luna said so, too. I need to meet my sister." I tried to stretch my hand out, but he disappeared again.

"Tonight, there will be a message for the people. Don't listen to it. It will change—"

Just then, a black bird dove down from the sky. It cawed and flapped its wings. I tumbled backward, frightened, and the ghost lifted his arms, which were now almost completely disintegrated. Like ink flowing into water, he seeped into the air and disappeared.

The raven circled a couple of times and shrieked. I placed a flat hand above my eyes.

"Odin?"

Be careful, little seer. You are mine. No one else's. The raven floated away with a final aggrieved *caaaw*. I watched it, also searching for the mysterious spirit that was nowhere to be seen. Then I noticed that my knee hurt like hell. I picked up my bike and hobbled toward Odinmont.

Luna was sitting at my dining table when I came in. I set my bag on the floor and limped over to the table. On the way, I grabbed a roll of duct tape. Sitting down, I propped my sock-clad foot on the table and inspected my torn pants leg. My knee itself was barely scraped, but the pants had a hole. I pulled a flap of tape out and ripped it with my teeth. I carefully gathered the fabric and placed the tape over it.

"You won't believe what happened today. I attacked Brenda because I thought she was Hel. I still can't reach Serén, and I need to get in touch with her to find out if it's winter in Hrafnheim, too. And just down the road there was . . ." I looked more closely at my friend. Luna was staring out my living room window. I wasn't sure if she had even heard me. "Luna!"

With a start, she turned her head toward me. I pulled back when I saw her distant eyes.

"What's wrong?" My voice was edged with alarm.

In her hand, she clutched a piece of paper. "I read it again," she said in a slurred voice.

"Read what again?" I looked questioningly at her. "Luna, did you . . . take something?" Back when I was in Nordreslev Youth Center, I had seen several of my fellow inmates partaking in recreational drugs, so I could easily recognize when someone was tripping.

Luna ran a hand over her curls. Despite the biting cold, her hair was damp with sweat. "I took some of my mom's mushrooms."

"You took psychedelic mushrooms?" I couldn't decide what was worse: that Rebecca even had such a thing, that she had given them to her daughter, or that Luna had taken them.

Luna closed her eyes.

Hrimfaxi name they the steed that anew
Brings night for the noble gods
Each morning drops

From his bit there fall
And thence come the dews in the dales

The prophetic words of the poem struck me, and it felt like the ground was swaying. Luna breathed heavily, as though it were an effort to say the words.

"I want drops from the bit."

I went into the kitchen and got some cold water. "Drops from the tap will have to be good enough." I placed the glass in front of her. "Why, in all the worlds, did you take mushrooms?"

"A different angle." Luna smacked her lips, as though her tongue were suddenly bone-dry. Then she drank greedily. Afterward, she looked a little more alert. "I wanted to understand what it's like for you when you read the poems."

It wasn't exactly a compliment that Luna had to take drugs to understand me, but now wasn't the time to point that out. I crouched over her, pulled my sleeve over my hand, and wiped her sweaty forehead. I eased the paper out of Luna's hand.

"The Ballad of Vafthruthnir."

"I saw it all, Anna. I saw creation, I saw life, death, the worlds, and the end."

"Were you having a vision?"

Luna coughed, not self-aware enough to cover her mouth. "It was more like the poem became a movie. I saw all the living and the dead. Down to the smallest blade of grass and the vast heavens. The grains sprouted and rotted before my eyes, only to begin again."

"You were hallucinating."

"It was . . . terrifying, and it was amazing." She looked at me, and there was a little more lucidity in her eyes. "It's part of a witch's practice to expand her mind. We need to be able to travel with our thoughts."

"Okay, but you can't do that again. Not alone, anyway."

"I believe you, Anna. Ragnarök is coming." Luna blinked, and heavy tears clung to her eyelashes. "The world is ending, and we're powerless." She flung her arms around me and cried into my neck. I stroked her back.

"We're not powerless. There's still time," I whispered. "I'm sure I can manage to avert it. Serén and I just have to find a way to meet. I guess I'll have to ask Elias. He says he's the best at treating stress, but he's *always* confident in his own abilities."

A hollow rumbling sound came from Luna's stomach. "I feel nauseous."

I quickly pulled her toward the bathroom, and we made it just before Luna threw up.

"Ugh," she moaned.

"You only have yourself to blame," I said.

She leaned back on her heels and wiped her mouth. Now she looked more like herself, if a somewhat pallid version. With effort, she got to her feet and leaned over the sink.

"Here." I handed her some dried mint leaves that she had left by the sink in case the toothpaste ran out. She chewed them slowly, then spat out a couple of stems.

"I feel better, but I'm sad about the world ending."

"I'm not sure it has to happen," I said when I thought she seemed somewhat stable again. "My vision ends with someone saying I have to stop it." I put my arm around Luna and guided her back to the living room. "That must mean I *can* stop it. If only I could talk to Hejd and ask her."

"Is she in Valhalla?"

"I have no idea. I don't even know where she's buried, or when she died. It was apparently over a thousand years ago."

"Does Od know?"

I shrugged. "Hejd's death is still traumatic for him, even though it happened so long ago. I've noticed how sad he is that she's gone."

"How did your treatment go?" Luna asked as she trudged back to the living room. She plopped down heavily onto a dining chair. "I didn't really hear what you said."

"It went well." I sat down.

"What happened?"

"Brenda is very talented," I said, avoiding answering the question.

"Anna!" Luna crossed her arms.

"I went down to my deepest subconscious." To evade her gaze, I spun the ring with the green stone around my finger.

"Cool! I want to see mine," Luna said. "It's probably full of crystals and flowers. What's in yours?"

"Death."

"De—wait, what?"

"The goddess Hel." I looked down at the table.

"What is Hel doing in your subconscious?"

"We have a shared past."

"Oh no—what did you do?" Luna asked, afraid to hear the answer.

Cautiously, I looked into Luna's widened eyes. "I tried to strangle her."

"You strangled Hel?"

"At first." When Luna didn't say anything, I was forced to continue. "I can never show my face at The Healing Tree again."

The front door opened, and Mathias came in and sat at the table. Neither of my two friends seemed to consider that this was actually my home. They just came in as they pleased. I smiled to myself.

"Why weren't you guys at school?" Mathias asked.

"It's a bit silly to go to school when there's a state of emergency."

"Most of the teachers and students are still going."

Luna rolled her eyes. "My dad hypnotized them not to fear the winter."

Mathias laughed. "What were you two doing while the rest of us slaved away at our lessons?"

"We had other things to do." I pulled the corners of my mouth back in a smile and made fleeting eye contact with Luna, who ducked her head with a little giggle. There was no reason to let Mathias know that we had been busy trying to strangle death and taking illicit drugs.

"I'm looking forward to going home. My mom is making beef stew for dinner," Luna said. She must have been starving after throwing up.

"Where did you get beef from?" I asked.

"You and Arthur can come to eat with us."

"That's not what I asked."

"Paul Ostergaard gave us half a cow yesterday. He slaughtered his whole herd several months ago. My mom gave the bones as an offering."

"It sounds delicious." Mathias leaned into Luna and kissed her neck.

"You and your mom can come over. No . . . Mathias, that tickles." She ducked her chin.

"We have enough food. The prime minister and Mardöll gave me a box when they were here." Mathias opened his bag and pointed down into it. There was a package of cookies and a chocolate bar.

"Isn't it a little unfair that you're both getting food on top of the ration stamps?"

"I'm sure you and Arthur can get a box, too, if you just ask," Mathias said.

"I'm sure you think it's totally fine to get extra, Mr. Chocolate Bar. I'll bet Mads from our class isn't getting any boxes from the prime minister. You know, with his giant blood."

Mathias shrugged. "I should get more than him anyway. I *am* half god, after all."

"Mathias!" Luna spoke so sharply that both Mathias and I sat up straight.

Mathias slapped a golden hand over his mouth. "I have no idea where that came from. Of course it's not okay." The words were muffled, as he held his hand in front of his lips. "I can't control myself at all these days. The wildest things come out of my mouth. It got even worse after Mardöll came by. I don't know why I got that stupid box."

I looked into his bag and pulled out the chocolate. The gold wrapper caught the light when I turned it in my fingers. "I know why they wanted you to have it."

Mathias looked to me for an answer.

"It was an offering."

That evening, we gathered at Frank's to watch the news. The TV from the 1990s sat ready on the podium in all its silvery glory, though it was currently turned off. People sat as close to the device as possible. I, too, kept my gaze aimed rigidly at the dark screen.

"Is there no more tea?" a woman asked Luna, who stood behind the bar. Frank had convinced her to give him a hand, even though he had stopped paying us. There was nothing to spend the money on anyway. I leaned against the counter, but fortunately, my repulsion spells made it so that no one noticed me.

"We're out of tea and coffee. We might get tea with ration stamps next week. Milas is making a kind of decoction from lemon balm. He knows how to make it because my mom taught—"

"Okay, okay," the woman said with her hands raised. Luna got a mug for her. The woman sniffed it. "It actually smells good."

Frank looked at his watch. "It's time." He brought out the massive remote control with its many buttons, half of which I couldn't discern the function. I stood up straight and stared at the television, unblinking. Hakim's ghost on the road had said there would be a mass message to the people tonight, so I had to show up.

The news broadcast discussed the cold again. Everyone was watching, but no one seemed hysterical or worried about the situation. *Hypnosis!*

"Researchers are still charting the long winter," the news anchor said. The image on the screen cut to the lobby of a higher education institution. A person bundled in a hat, coat, and scarf was being interviewed.

"I'm here with lead researcher Karin Grøndal," said a male reporter. "What can you tell us about the frost situation?"

"We can rule out the idea that this is a meteor strike, as iridium levels aren't particularly elevated. We are now working with the theory of a massive volcanic eruption that is temporarily blocking light from the sun."

I shook my head.

"And how far have you gotten with that?"

"We're measuring CO_2 as high up in the atmosphere as our drones can reach with the cloud layer. So far, they are showing elevated levels in comparison to last year, but that could be due to a delayed effect of pollution before the long winter. It could also come from volcanic ash."

The camera turned, and the reporter came into focus. "There are demonstrations currently taking place around the country. Dissatisfied citizens have gathered in front of the Scientific Institute."

It cut to a group of red-nosed people. There were at most fifteen of them. Their breath turned to steam and made them look like snorting animals. A man with wild hair and a dark beard stood in the foreground.

"Look at those nutjobs," a woman in front of me said.

"The situation is critical!" the man on the television shouted. Who knew why Mardöll hadn't gotten to him with her hypnosis? "The gods must be appeased." The man's slightly manic face filled the entire screen. "That is all we can do now."

"You mean God."

"God and Jesus with their talk of palm trees." He pointed down at his winter boots, which were caked with snow. "We must seek the answer from the gods who know something about frost and cold."

"What are you suggesting be done?"

"Too much time has been wasted," the man said. "The gods are angry. We have ignored them for a millennium, and this is our punishment. We need a revolution. No, a reformation." He took a step toward the camera. "You must make offerings to the gods if you want a chance of survival. Get in touch with your local Norse Pagans."

At Frank's, there was scattered laughter. People raised their cups of steaming lemon balm decoction and appeared to be quite comfortable. Even though the snow was dumping down outside, the diner was warm and cozy. Only a handful of patrons exchanged questioning glances.

When the news broadcast was over, people dispersed. They turned up their collars and ducked into the wind outside. Frank turned off the TV, and I was left standing there with an anticlimactic feeling. The ghost on the dirt road had said there would be a message for the people, but the broadcast had discussed only the usual things. I rode my bike home deep in thought, grateful that the local authorities were still prioritizing clearing the roads of snow.

At Odinmont, my bedroom was freezing. I was exhausted after the day's many events, so I lay on my bed just to rest for a moment. With eyes closed, I fumbled my hand to the side and laid it on my darkened giant crystal. To get it going, I thought of someone I loved, and without consciously meaning to, I pictured Varnar. He smiled one of his rare smiles, and my heart skipped a beat. Because I was so in touch with the past, I felt like I was standing in front of him, even though, on another level, I was lying alone on my bed in Odinmont with my arm stretched out and my palm resting on my giant crystal. Beneath my fingers, the crystal glowed and sent waves of warmth toward me.

In my thoughts, Varnar came closer to me and slid a hand around the back of my neck. I could feel it so clearly, as if he were right next to me, and I let myself float away in his eyes.

"Ow!" I jerked my hand back; the crystal had gotten so hot that it burned my fingers.

I continued the fantasy. Varnar stood close and kissed me tentatively, and even though it wasn't real, I felt the electric current from his lips. The intoxicating scent of fresh air and forest was everywhere, and he put his strong arms around me. I completely let go of consciousness and let myself drift toward my dreams of Varnar.

I landed in an auditorium. The wooden benches sloped steeply upward and were painted pale blue and pink. The room was hexagonal, with a glass dome ceiling that let the bright daylight in. In the middle of the space was an oblong table, upon which lay a naked person, but the blinding light made the body hard to make out. Next to it stood a woman in a floor-length white dress, giving a lecture. Because both she and the motionless naked person on the table were bathed in harsh sunlight, I couldn't see who they were.

"I want to go back to my Varnar dream," I said aloud, but no one reacted. The narrow benches around me were filled with men in black jackets, all of whom sat hunched over thick sheets of paper. With quills and ink, they filled the paper with spidery handwriting. The scraping sound over the parchment was interrupted by the woman's voice.

"Suffocatur," she said. "Cum sanguine."

The men wrote this down. Dipped their pens in ink and kept writing.

"That's how we have to do it. The instructions can be found in this operating theater."

I turned my head when I recognized the voice next to me. "Elias?"

He had much longer hair and wore the same dark jacket as the other men in the auditorium. From his ears to his jaw grew impressive sideburns. He dipped his quill and wrote. Dipped and wrote. Dipped and wrote without looking at me.

"Can you hear me?"

Elias continued writing unimpeded, while occasionally casting a curious look down at the body in the center of the auditorium.

"Oblatio," the woman said far below us.

I leaned back on the narrow bench. "You can't hear me." It was just a lifelike dream. At that moment, a cloud moved in front of the sun outside, and I was able to see what was happening on the auditorium floor. The woman wore a white mask over her mouth, and the man on the table was unmistakably dead. Very dead! His face was covered in a blue-black bruise, there was a red line on his neck where it had been cut, and at his side lay a noose.

The woman continued in her monotone voice. "Apokalyptein."

"We must preserve the peace," Elias said. "Even in times of fear."

The words reached down to my marrow. It was so important to stay calm, even if the world was collapsing around you.

The cloud must have passed, because a harsh light once again bathed the room. I squinted and slipped away from the sharp dream. Everything became incoherent and fuzzy again. Unfortunately, I was not sent back to my Varnar fantasy.

Instead, there was smoke that stank of burnt wood, along with an iron-rich, sickly smell. Lightning flashed, and a deep rumble traveled up my legs as the ground shook. My fingers were covered in rough, reddish-brown clumps. Clay?

Od was there. His beautiful head was firmly attached to his neck, and he stood with a young Odin with raven-black hair. The only thing that marred him slightly was the empty eye socket.

"It's time," said Odin.

Od straightened his neck. "I want to do this to save you."

Odin looked back at him contentedly. He raised his arms. "You must sacrifice your blood for the gods." Lightning flashed on the undersides of clouds that spun wildly like huge tornadoes. Large, hard hailstones fell. Even though I shouldn't have been able to feel them in a vision, it hurt when a golf ball-sized chunk of ice hit me.

"Stop it," came a voice from above. "Raven, stop it."

The whole night continued in this manner, with glimpses of nightmares and the same voice beseeching me to stop Ragnarök. I slipped in and out of sleep, unable to really rest, but also not awake enough to get up and avoid the awful dreams.

The next morning, there was a banging at my door. Arthur hadn't come up from the crypt yet, so I stumbled half asleep down the stairs, but Luna had already come into the hall. Her knit hat was covered in snow.

"We have to go to school."

"What's the point of going to school when the world is ending anyway?" I whined. "I don't have time. I have to find another way of contacting Serén."

Luna cast persuasion magic over me, and before I knew it, I was on my bike and halfway to Ravensted High. I cursed, but I was unable to turn around.

"I'm certain we need to maintain the peace," Luna said. "Although one might well suspect that some teachers would still be teaching, even when doomsday *has* come and gone. But I know it's important. It just is." She turned into the parking lot, and I followed. "I had a dream last night that made me see it clearly," she confided.

"Hmm." I parked and rubbed my eyes with a yawn. In front of me, Kamilla and Thomas from our class were talking.

"It was so lifelike," Kamilla said. "He said we must preserve the peace, even in times of fear."

"It's funny we had the same dream," Thomas said. "What a coincidence."

I stopped and tried to kick-start my sleep-fogged brain and dispel Luna's persuasion magic. While I was thinking, she put down the kickstand of her cargo bike.

"What exactly did you dream last night, Luna?"

The kickstand was so rusty, it took a few kicks to get it to stand in a position to support the long bike.

"I dreamed that I was in this old auditorium. Elias was there. He said we had to preserve the peace even in—"

"—times of fear," I finished.

"How do you know what I dreamed?" Luna put a hand on her hip. "Have you been sneaking around in my past again?"

"I had the same dream. *Everyone* had the same dream." Just then, it dawned on me. The message to the people that Hakim's ghost was talking about was not delivered via television. It was delivered in dreams.

"Did you also dream that Od was decapitated?"

The skin of Luna's forehead tightened. "Decapitated? No! Afterward, I dreamed of fresh fruit. Soooo good. What I wouldn't give . . ."

I pulled my bike out of the stand.

"Where are you going?" Luna asked, confused, but I was already heading in the opposite direction. She struggled with her own bike but got it straightened up and swung out after me.

I stood up on the pedals. Luna groaned behind me as she pushed the ancient bike forward.

"You don't have to come."

"Yes, I do!" She inhaled effortfully. "If a frost storm hits, I can cast heat magic on you."

"There are no frost storms in the morning."

"Just because there haven't been frost storms during the day yet doesn't mean they won't come."

Snowflakes stung my eyes, and the air I inhaled forcefully

threatened to freeze me from the inside. I shivered, reminded of when I was in the realm of the dead. My breath formed a cloud around me, and my fingers were starting to freeze to the handlebars, even though I was wearing thick gloves. When we arrived at The Boatman, we parked our bikes against a wall of dark wooden posts. The air was oddly still on the otherwise storm-swept west coast. Only a faint breeze rustled the frosted lyme grass. On the coast, there was usually too much wind for high snowdrifts to form. There were only wave-shaped tongues of snow licking up the walls. I studied the building. It was unbelievable that I hadn't noticed how exotic the bar was the first few times I had been there. The walls were thick beams; the roof was made of overlapping oiled planks; the wood was carved with snakes, cats, and horses; and the handle of the large wooden door was cast in the shape of a boar's head. I pulled it, but the door was locked. This was the first time I had seen The Boatman closed. I peered through one of the few windows, but it was completely dark inside. Still as a grave, although in my experience, graves tended not to be as still as they made themselves out to be. I used my sleeve to wipe sea spray and sand off the glass.

"It seems completely abandoned," Luna said from the other side. She stood at a different window, looking in at the empty bar.

A foreboding feeling made the back of my neck prickle, and I crept toward The Boatman's back entrance. It was dark along the side of the bar. When I was almost around the corner, I heard something.

"Od?" For some reason, the sound of my own voice made it even more unsettling. The sand crunched beneath my feet, and I trailed my hand along the rough wooden wall. A splinter pierced my glove and bore into my palm. "Od," I called again, slightly louder.

A woman chanted through the still night. The sound made a different kind of chill spread across my body; I had heard Ragnara's herders chanting the same way. It was nasal and monotonous, and the words she repeated in a loop sounded like Old Norse. A light flickered from the private parking lot. There were piles of white snow everywhere, but something dark had sprayed across the drift closest to me.

"Od!" I ran toward the voice. I got so close to the cliff that I nearly tumbled over it. Gravel sprayed over the edge, and a moment passed before it hit the beach below with faint *plock-plock* sounds. A cloud of sand got picked up on a little squall.

When I shifted my gaze, I saw that the spatters closest to the door were more intense. A salty, iron-rich smell spread through the air.

A woman dressed in a long, pale cloak stood in the middle of the parking lot with her eyes closed. In several places, the cloak was smeared with a red liquid. What was worse, she held a glinting knife in her raised hand.

An erect figure stood with his back to me. He turned around.

"Anna?" It sounded like a plea.

I stared, and Od looked back at me.

He was smeared with blood.

CHAPTER 5

Without thinking, I threw myself at the woman.

She opened her eyes with a cry of surprise and fell backward with me straddling her chest. I squeezed her ribs with my knees, and she gurgled loudly. She swung the knife around, but with one fist, I punched her in the jaw, then the nose, and with my other hand, I squeezed her wrist so hard the knife fell into the snow with a soft thump. My blows were dampened by my gloves, but blood ran from the woman's nose. Someone else grabbed me from behind and pulled, but I pounded the back of my head into my unseen opponent's face in a reverse headbutt.

"Aghhh," they moaned.

I was free again, and I grabbed the knife and held it to the woman's throat. Bubbles of blood formed in her nostrils, her eyes wide.

"If you move, you die," I said in a low voice.

"Help," she whispered. In addition to the sacrificial blood, she was now dripping her own into the snow.

"Hey, that's Jytte," Luna said weakly, but my instincts had taken over, so I didn't understand what she was talking about.

"Why are you hurting Od?" I pressed the blade closer against the woman's neck. The vision of Od's disembodied head rolling toward me kept running through my mind. I knew Odin was ready to let his own son die. There was a connection between Od being sacrificed and the impending Ragnarök, even though I wasn't quite sure what it was. Unblinking, I lowered my face close to the woman's and shook her. "Why?" Thin, red streams trickled from her throat, where I was slowly pressing the knife in.

"Enough!" The shock wave of a metallic voice struck me. Gigantic fingers, each the size of my entire arm, closed around my body and lifted me off the woman as though I weighed nothing. I kicked my legs as the ground vanished beneath me. In a flash, I was transported into The Boatman and plopped down on the sofa in front of Od's desk. Luna walked in after me with her gloved hand over her mouth. To my horror, I saw that her previously pale-yellow glove was now wet and red. It was toasty in the hexagonal office. Maybe the gods were helping keep the place warm. Luna sat down next to me and kept the glove over her mouth.

I looked unhappily at her. "I didn't mean to. I'm so sorry."

"Issokay," Luna slurred. She tried to smile, but her face distorted in pain.

On my other side, the woman sat down. She stayed as far from me as possible without ending up on the floor. A makeshift bandage was wrapped around her neck, and she looked at me fearfully, her cloak pulled close around her. The blood in her nostrils had dried and turned brown.

I jerked back as a sheep's head was placed on the table before me with a wet sound. It was Elias who set it there with an irritated motion.

"I have to get the last of my supply," he mumbled to Od and disappeared through one of the many doors, wiping his hand on his pants.

The sheep in front of me had bulging eyes, and its tongue hung out of its mouth from behind narrow, pulled-back lips. I stared at it, mainly to avoid looking at the two people I had attacked. Od sat in the chair on the other side of the desk. There was still a spatter of blood on his neck, but I had come to understand that it was only sheep's blood. He reached into a drawer, pulled out glasses and a bottle of golden liquid, filled the glasses, and then pushed them toward us. I took one and held it out to the woman, who cowered at the other end of the sofa.

"I'm sorry about . . ." I made a slicing motion with my finger in front of my own throat. "I thought you were sacrificing Od."

"The sheep." She didn't move to take the glass I held out to her.

"I know *now* that you were only sacrificing a sheep." I had to blink because suddenly it was Od's decapitated head that sat on the table in front of me. The woman sat completely still and said nothing. "Come on, drink some mead of poetry." I sloshed the glass, a drop landing on the cowhide on the floor. "You'll feel better."

She twitched, and I looked down with concern; I knew what was hidden under the floor. Helheim. An underworld of death and suffering. I knew it because I had been there myself.

"It'll help your nerves." I tried a final time.

The woman went from mute to speed talking. "No one can kill a demigod. They can't die. And even if they could, I would never . . ." Finally, she accepted the mead but quickly scooted back to the farthest edge of the sofa.

"Demigods can't die," Od said pensively, and though that could have been anything from a confirmation to a complaint, it sounded mainly like he was contradicting her. His beautiful, blue-green eyes shifted to me, and we had a moment of mutual understanding. Then he cranked up the volume on his divine side, and I felt as though the sofa had vanished. It was like I dropped down slightly before regaining control.

"What did that sheep ever do to you?" I managed to say.

Od gave a bemused smile. "We made an offering to the gods to give them the strength to mitigate the weather. Jytte is here because she's a Norse Pagan."

"It's my first time," Jytte whispered.

Something told me it was probably also her last. Luna nodded. She seemed to know Jytte from Norse Pagan circles.

"The gods want more than a sheep that you yourselves get to eat afterward," I said. "Odin is always going on about hangatyr. Human sacrifices."

"Human sacrifices?" Jytte repeated.

Od looked sharply at her. "You didn't hear that." His eyes glimmered with a silvery light, and she slid sideways toward me in a comatose state. Her head hit the sofa's seat cushion with a thump.

"Seriously, how often do you do that?" The hypnotized woman's head grazed my leg. She was still clutching the glass, though half of its contents had spilled out.

Od laughed, and he looked more human than godlike. "Pretty often."

"I wonder if we'll have permanent damage?"

Od didn't respond, and just then, Elias came back with a little vial in his hand.

"Whoops." He leaned over and snatched the half-full glass about to fall from Jytte's hand. In a fluid motion, he drained it and rounded his full lips in satisfaction.

"Elias," Od said gently. "The women need to be treated."

Elias bowed in his uniquely old-fashioned way before turning toward Luna. He gestured to her, and she stuck her finger out obediently. A drop was placed on it, and she dabbed it on her busted lip. With eyes closed, she licked her lips as the effect set in. Elias unwrapped the bandage from the unconscious Jytte's neck. Then he rubbed laekna on the wound. The red line closed up, leaving the skin smooth and delicate. With a regretful expression, he turned the empty vial upside down.

"It takes a week to make new laekna, and I've already tapped a lot of Od's blood."

"But I gave you . . ." I stopped as Elias gave me a sharp look.

"I'm sure Mathias would be happy to donate his blood if it's to be used for medicine," said Luna, who hadn't noticed that I had almost said too much.

"Tell him he's welcome to." Then Elias turned from Luna toward Od. "Of course, if I tap his blood, I will keep a record of it. As I promised."

Od said nothing but studied Elias with mild indulgence. He knew his four-hundred-year-old adoptive son well.

Elias leaned against the desk. "And you, Anna, are unscathed."

"I already said I'm sorry I attacked them. I thought Od had been hurt."

Od ran a flat hand across the top of his desk. "My kind don't really get hurt."

I raised my eyebrows as a sign that I disagreed wholeheartedly.

Luna began to speak as soon as her lip was healed. "Jytte is dating Brenda from The Healing Tree. There are already rumors circulating about you in the alternative community, Anna. They probably won't be any better after . . ."

Od turned his head and looked at her with twinkling eyes. Luna's face immediately went blank, and she slid back into the sofa.

"Od! It's not okay to hypnotize people all the time."

"*Now* can you tell me what you're doing here?" Od folded his hands and leaned back.

"I uhh . . ." I looked at Elias. "Maybe we should talk alone."

"I keep no secrets from Elias."

"I simply don't believe that."

Od laughed hoarsely and sent Elias a get-out-of-here look. He traipsed off reluctantly, but I stopped him by placing my hand on his forearm. At first, he looked stunned, but then he elegantly laid his free hand on the back of mine.

"Yes?"

"I need to talk to you afterward. I may want to buy your services."

"Some of my services you don't need to pay for."

I glanced at Od. My cheeks burned.

"Elias!" Od admonished mildly.

"You know I'm always at your disposal." Elias bowed formally, let go of my hand, and walked out. Od watched him until he closed the door. Then he held out his hands, inviting me to speak.

My heart began to hammer again. "I keep seeing a vision of the future."

"The future can go many ways."

"This is pretty specific, and it doesn't seem to change."

Od stiffened.

"I see death and destruction. Natural disasters and giants. Odin was there last night, and I've also seen Loki and his children."

"What about me? Am I there?" Od raised his hand to his neck, but he didn't seem aware he was doing it.

I wasn't able to say it outright. Unfortunately, my gaze fell on the disembodied sheep's head. Od followed my eyes.

"If I allow myself to be sacrificed, I can stop Ragnarök," he said quietly. "I've told you, there is great power in a god's child who sacrifices himself. *He* did it, and his people have flourished ever since."

"That's a last resort, I'm assuming."

"When my father decided that Ragnarök would be part of the future, he designed it so that doomsday could be averted if his child allowed himself to be sacrificed."

"What do you mean by *designed?*"

"To create the world, he also had to plan its downfall. That's the trade-off for all living things. If you want to be born, you must accept inevitable death. Worlds are no exception."

"Did Odin really insert you as a clause? It's a good thing I have another plan since your dad's so cynical."

"My father isn't cynical. He will go to great lengths to make sure nothing happens to me."

"In the vision, Odin seemed pretty unbothered about sending you to your death." As soon as the words left my mouth, I wished I could take them back.

"Did you see how . . ." For a moment, Od lost his usual calm. He drank from his mead. The hand that held the glass shook.

"In the vision, someone says that I can stop it. I'm pretty sure it's Hejd."

Od set the glass down hard on the table.

"When did she die?" I asked.

"In the year 1000," Od said as casually as if he had said *the day before yesterday*.

"It's pretty wild that she can send me visions and talk to me."

Od's face was expressionless. "She was a powerful völva. Odin's völva."

"I'm a völva, but I'm not sure what it's all about. And I don't feel particularly powerful."

"Your powers are no match for Hejd's."

"What was she able to do?"

"See the future and the past. She would also help unborn babies come into the worlds of the living, and the dead leave them. On top of that, she was supposed to serve Odin. With a völva like Hejd, he's all-powerful—assuming the völva cooperates—but Hejd gave him a lot of opposition." Od looked me up and down. "Odin has a tendency to choose servants who work against him and even harm him. Loki, Mimir, Hejd, and you."

"What happened between you and Hejd?"

Od looked down at his desk. "I'm willing to do my part to help Odin, but she wouldn't accept it. She said she saw a different fate for me, and she refused to indulge the All-Father. Odin wanted to force her, and she feared ending up like Mimir. So, she disappeared."

"By dying?"

Od's mouth pulled back crookedly. "To the gods, there isn't a big difference between the living and the dead. Hejd did something much worse. She changed religion. My father was furious, and I was miserable. After the trouble with Hejd, Odin realized it was too dangerous for him to consolidate the völva powers. It took him almost a thousand years to get them back so he could create new ravens. He could only do it when Hejd's bones crashed into the sea. Then he placed them in Thora's womb, and they became you and your sister. Huginn and Muninn. Thought and memory."

"If Hejd is gone, why is she always babbling on in my subconscious?"

"I woke her when my father was at his weakest," Od whispered. "Perhaps I'm ready now."

"Ready to be sacrificed?"

Od didn't answer. I rubbed my forehead and tried to connect the dots.

"Does all this have something to do with the weather?" I asked. "All the snow? I think it's Fimbulwinter, and that Ragnarök is coming now. Did you start something when you woke Hejd?"

Od's face was expressionless. "I've already said too much."

"All your damned rules." I scowled.

"You're subject to them, too."

"Maybe." I smiled sweetly. "But I choose to break them." I stood and leaned over him. I was expecting Od to admonish me, but he merely looked up at me.

"How?"

"How what?"

"How will you break the rules?"

"To answer that, I need to know your past." I stretched my hands toward him. Tentatively, Od snaked his fingers forward, hooked his little finger in mine, and let me into this past.

I stood and watched the ceremony taking place in the churchyard. A monk was saying something I couldn't hear, but I had no doubt what it was about: there was a gurney, and on it lay a body that was clearly dead. There was no coffin or box. She just lay out in the open—but that was apparently normal in the year 1000.

Even at a distance, I could see Hejd's blue-white skin. Her hands were placed at her sides. Only a couple of women and a single man participated in the burial. The women's heads were bowed, and they folded their hands in prayer. The man at their side was tall and stood up straight. I knew him well. In fact, in another dimension, it was his hand that I held across the desk at The Boatman.

I looked around and recognized the cliff where The Boatman sat now, though it hardly resembled itself. There were scattered fields, grazing horses and sheep, and a few low wooden houses with log roofs. The sea could just barely be glimpsed in the distance, though I tasted the salty spray in the air. There were piles of sand here and there, but it was nothing like the sand drifts that characterized the place now. The cemetery was only half full of graves. They were all fresh, with small wooden crosses stuck into the earth, which was overturned in high, narrow stripes. The piles of dirt were black against the green grass, and crows flapped around them. Occasionally, a raven or jackdaw landed on a cross. One grave was open. It was just a hole in the ground.

In the present, the headstones and skeletons had long since tumbled down the sheer drop to the beach fifty yards below, and the final remnants of the church had been removed by museum workers several years earlier.

The stones of the church appeared freshly hewn, separated by bright-white stripes of lime. A wooden bell tower stood slightly apart from the church. On the grass slope next to me stood the woman who also lay dead on the gurney. She watched her own funeral with a slightly awed expression. I recognized Hejd, although she was paler and a bit more transparent than usual.

"Ahhh . . . there you are," Hejd said.

"You can see me?"

"I am a spirit, and we transcend above the rules of the flesh. I am so glad to finally meet you."

"But we've met before."

"You met me in the past, but I've only seen you in my prophecy."

"Have you also seen my sister?" I blurted.

"Lots of times."

"Is she dead?" The word *dead* came out hysterically.

Hejd furrowed her brows. "Well, yes."

"What?" Everything spun around me, and a chill went up the back of my neck.

Hejd raised her hands in a calming gesture. "You're dead, too. I mean . . ." She closed her eyes and tried to explain. "I don't know when you live. My prophecy wasn't that specific about you. I have seen both of you die, but I don't know when it happens. Everyone must die one day. She may still be alive in your present."

"I live in the year—"

Hejd waved a blurry hand. "Years mean nothing to me. Especially now." She looked first at her transparent fingers, then toward her grave.

I looked down there, too, and watched Od as he wrapped the burial shroud around Hejd's body, lifted her carefully, and laid her in the ground.

"He sent me here," I whispered.

"It can't be *that* Od." She pointed down to the churchyard. "He doesn't agree with me. You must have been sent by the Od you know."

"Are they not the same person?"

"No one remains the same."

Od turned from Hejd's grave and walked toward us.

"Can he see me, too?" I took a couple of steps back.

"*This* Od can't see you, but Od from the future wants you to hear what's coming. Listen, raven."

Od from the past reached me and Hejd's ghost.

"You can still avoid it," he said. "I can get your body and place it in Odinmont."

"I'm sure." Hejd jutted her jaw out slightly.

Od looked at her with desperation. When their eyes met, his expression softened, and he tried to stroke her cheek, but his hand went straight through her face. In the churchyard, the monk raised his arms, and Hejd's ghost fluttered.

"Can you remember it?" she asked quickly. "Can you remember my prophecy?"

"Of course. I remember everything."

"Get someone to write it down."

"No one can write here."

"Yet." Hejd raised a transparent hand and laid it on Od's cheek. "When the time comes, find the raven and protect her. Muninn. Memory. Now that you've opposed my plan, you can at least do that."

"It's too dangerous."

"You don't have to tell her yourself. I'm sure she'll figure it out when she hears my prophecy."

"How can she do that?"

Hejd grinned, and Od looked at her longingly. "Just wait until you meet her. She's something special. I wish I could be there to see it."

"I wouldn't believe anyone else, but if you're saying it, it must be true."

Hejd smiled secretively. "She's going to turn your world upside down. It's funny that someone as old as you can still be surprised."

"I'm only two hundred and fifty."

She grew serious again. "You'll be much older by the time you meet her. Make sure she hears the prophecy, and do whatever it takes to ensure she lives long enough to do her duty."

"Hejd."

"Promise me!"

"I've already promised many times."

The monk chanted something in Latin, and Hejd trembled.

"I'm going to miss you when you go to heaven," he said.

"I'm not going *up there*." Hejd snorted contemptuously. Then she held out her arms. "My body will decompose, and I will become everything here. The earth, the plants, the air, and the water. When the graveyard falls, my final remains will be swallowed by the sea."

"I will build my home in this place," Od said. "So that I'm always close."

Hejd's nearly transparent figure swayed as though someone had nudged her. "Did you place a coin in my shroud?" she asked sternly. "I told you not to."

"If you change your mind and want to cross Gjöll, you need to pay the boatman."

"Helheim is no longer my underworld." She held out her hand. It was almost invisible now. "Farewell, my love." Her outline was gone.

"Farewell," Od replied. He cried, and from his eyes dripped crystal-clear gemstones. "I will stay here on the edge of Denmark and watch over you, even if you are choosing against me and my faith."

"I have to," she whispered. It sounded like the whistling wind. The monk walked away from the grave as the women sang and covered the figure in the hole with black dirt.

And then she was gone. Od stood there, alone. His clear, crystallized tears surrounded him, glittering in the grass.

Back at The Boatman, Od let go of my hand. In the present, too—if there even was such a thing we could call the present—a pile of gemstones lay before him. They were just like the ones in my ring, except Mathias's tears were green.

I shook as the past filled my body; I was also reliving my own memories. It was as though Od's deep history had opened my own recollections.

I gave a startled jerk when I was back in the office. Luna was already talking, having picked up where she'd left off when Od hypnotized her. She hadn't noticed a thing. Giving Od a look of comprehension, I reached my arm back and grabbed Luna's hand.

"What does Hejd want me to do?" I asked Od.

He pressed his lips together.

"She must want me to reunite with Serén so we can avert Ragnarök together. Come on, Luna," I said. "Let's go home."

I had dropped Luna off and was heading into Odinmont when I saw something gleaming in Kraghede Forest. Confused, I stumbled down there to investigate.

I didn't immediately see anything unusual in the frozen forest, but I walked down to Kraghede Manor, where Varnar and Aella had lived when they were my bodyguards.

When Varnar and Aella were there, they had to protect me with their lives because my death by Ragnara's hand would've set off Fimbulwinter and, subsequently, Ragnarök. I stood in front of the manor, which, without trees for protection in the clearing, was nearly covered in snow on its west-facing side. Varnar and Aella could have saved themselves the trouble because Fimbul had come anyway, so now no one was worried about whether I lived or died.

I looked at the visible east-facing part of the facade. The once-grand manor was painted over with graffiti, the windows were smashed, and the roof had collapsed on one side. It had gotten worse since I'd last been there because the heavy blanket of snow had pressed down on the roof structure. In a vision of the past, I saw myself and Aella walking into the dilapidated manor house. When I saw Varnar following my past self, my heart threatened to burst out of my chest; I saw him watching me in a way I hadn't been aware of at the time. I considered going inside the house, but I was afraid I would collapse from sadness if I did.

I turned away from all the bittersweet memories and walked back into the trees. I noticed a spot a little farther on, where several trees had fallen.

It didn't normally look like that here. There had always been small mounds on the forest floor that simply looked like piles of earth, but the moss and topmost layers of dirt had been scraped away, and I could see that they were, in fact, boulders. They now stood upright and had been brushed clean. They were decorated with carvings and arranged in an oval. When I got closer, I saw a figure kneeling in the middle of them. I hid behind a tree.

"I saw and heard you a long time ago. You've been stomping around the forest for the past half hour." The voice had a deeper timbre than usual. He was still on his knees with his back to me in the center of the stones. His broad neck was bent down, and there was a pale-green shimmer around him. He was twice his normal size, and his giant green hands rested on the withered leaves on the ground.

"What are you doing here, Mathias?" I asked quietly. For some reason, I felt unsafe leaving my place behind the tree.

"I'm feeling the worship." Mathias straightened his neck and sniffed the air. I saw blue beams of light from his eyes hit tree trunks several yards away. "This is an old blót site."

Using my clairvoyance, I investigated the area. It was so natural for me to get glimpses of the past that I rarely dwelled on them, but when I concentrated, I saw the stones covered in flower garlands, the ground scattered with grain and berries, and bowls of steaming food and drink. The stones' carvings were painted in black and ocher, depicting fertility figures and images of animals and ships.

"That was back in ancient times. Can you really still feel it?"

Mathias still hadn't turned around. The green halo around him shone even more intensely, and his back muscles quivered under his thin T-shirt. "This was an important spot."

Something in the air vibrated electrically, and I was inclined to agree with him. The green glow looked like what I had seen among the trees from Odinmont.

Suddenly, I saw berserkers come stomping up, followed by

Ragnara and Eskild. They dissolved like smoke, as it was only a vision, but I had already fallen backward with a shriek.

Mathias leapt up and was standing over me in the same instant. "Anna. Are you okay?" He sounded like himself, but the sight of him bent over me, his face close to mine, nearly made me cry out again.

"I've never seen you so godlike," I croaked.

Mathias's head was the size of a bull's, and his eyes shone fluorescent blue. I had to squint to keep from being blinded. His usually golden skin was neon green, and an intense honey scent wafted off him.

"I'm still me," he whispered, but his voice was so powerful, it forced its way under my skin.

"I know you are." I swallowed. "But you're really fucking scary."

Mathias helped me up and shrank a little, probably from embarrassment. The green hue diminished. "What did you see?"

"When Ragnara attacked Odinmont, they came from here. It's a kind of portal between Hrafnheim and Ravensted. I had no idea it was here." I laid a hand on one of the stones and saw people appearing and vanishing between the erect runestones in zapping flashes of light. This had been a busy transit point in the past. I would have been spared a lot of problems if I had known before.

I was yanked back to the present when the electric sound grew louder. I realized that the noise was coming from right now—not the past. Flashes danced between the stones, and I pulled Mathias away, even though he was probably the one who should have been protecting me.

A huge crash made me cover my ears, followed by an iridescent glow resembling the northern lights. I heard something land heavily on the ground.

"Agghhh," groaned the blurry form, now standing in the middle of the stone oval, flashes dancing around them. I saw the outline of a human-shaped figure.

"We'll get help," another person frantically said, and a very particular scent hit my nostrils. Sun, forest, and fresh air. I fumbled my way forward but still couldn't see much.

"Anna," Varnar said. In that single word, I heard longing, forgiveness, and loss.

I had just been missing him, so I couldn't believe he was actually there. It was impossible to stop smiling, and I ran toward him.

"I'm sorry we parted on bad terms. The whole thing doesn't even mat—" The light finally subsided, and I froze.

Varnar was just as beautiful as ever, but in his arms, he held a woman who, at first glance, appeared to be dead. It was only because of my clairvoyance that I could see she was still alive. The woman's aura was familiar, as though it were a part of myself.

"Serén?" I gasped for air, but the waves of light were now completely gone, and it wasn't red hair that ruffled in Varnar's arms. It was black curls with small streaks of white, and I was neither sucked toward her nor pushed away, like I had been the few times I was in the presence of my sister. Her face was hard, resembling my own at my most stubborn. Her eyes were closed, she wore a pained expression, and her arm was wrapped around Varnar's shoulder. When she finally lost consciousness, her arm slid down and flopped backward.

Although I knew I should do something, I couldn't take my eyes off where her fingers had been on Varnar's neck. His nut-colored skin was marked with a red handprint, and something dark glinted on his leather jacket.

As though in slow motion, I looked back to her. Her entire front glistened, and the smell of iron spread through the air.

Blood dripped from her body as her aura quickly weakened.

The woman was Thora. My mother.

CHAPTER 6

Thora was in bad shape. Her coat was ripped to shreds, and a large wound was visible on her stomach.

My mother's eyes rolled back in her head. "Back," she whispered. "Eskild . . ."

"Shh . . ." I reached out with my clairvoyance.

In Thora's recent past, she stood with Eskild in a snow-covered clearing surrounded by berserkers. None carried a weapon. Neither did my mother.

"Thora," called a voice from the forest. "This is an ambush."

The voice grew louder with each word.

Eskild stared through the trees. "You!" he shouted.

At that moment, Varnar came into view at the edge of the forest. "Get away, Thora. It's a trap."

Thora bent down and pulled out a knife hidden in her boot.

The vision shifted, and now Varnar was running across open land with Thora in his arms. The surroundings jumped around, and I sensed a violent rage. My mother wasn't afraid of dying from her injuries, but she was absolutely furious over having gotten them. They reached a stone circle with a tree in the middle. I recognized the place, which was in Vindr Fen in Hrafnheim. It was a place I had once been with Sverre.

Thora growled. "I'm staying here."

"You'll die from that wound if you don't get help. You need to go to Midgard. The Brewmaster can heal you. If anyone can survive a trip between the worlds in this condition, it's you," Varnar pleaded.

"I almost had him."

"A dead leader is of no use to us," Varnar said. He leaned forward. "I don't want you to die." He laid a hand on a rock, and they whizzed off through a dark tunnel with white flashes of light. I was yanked back to the corresponding stone circle in Kraghede Forest, where my mother lay, ashen, in Varnar's arms. Oddly enough, I remembered my mother being much larger.

"Get Elias," I said.

Mathias was gone in a flash of green, and I was left standing there with Varnar and Thora. He laid her carefully on the frozen earth, and I slid down, too. Not knowing if this was my only chance to be with her while she was alive, I sat with her head in my lap, as if she were the child and I the mother.

"Elias is on his way," I said softly. "I'm sure he can save you."

Varnar knelt alongside us. He said nothing but placed a warm hand on the back of my neck. I leaned my head toward his shoulder.

"You're alive," Thora whispered, having regained a tiny bit of consciousness.

"Yes."

"You're the worst thing that ever happened to me. You, your sister, your father. Love—" She coughed. "Love is dangerous. Just look at me."

Varnar ran his hand across my back, and I was immeasurably happy that he was there with me. Thora looked up at us both.

"You're also the best thing that's ever happened to me." Her eyelids drooped again, as though they weighed a ton.

I stroked her black curls. "Hold on. Help is on the way."

Thora convulsed, and I ran my fingers uselessly over the grotesque wound on her stomach.

"Fimbul," she moaned. "Fimbulwinter..."

"Save your strength." I burrowed into her mind with my clairvoyance and saw her speaking to her people.

Ragnarök is coming. We have to be ready.

"I agree, Mom," I said, hoping she could hear me. "Mom? Mom!"

But Thora had passed out again, and though I shook her frantically, she was unreachable. I gasped desperately for air, and I felt Varnar's arms around me.

I asked him the question I most feared the answer to. "Do you know if Serén is alive?"

"Your sister is alive. Anna . . ." Varnar began, but he stopped as a green light flashed, and Mathias arrived with Elias on his back. His jacket was open, and his boots were unlaced. Before Mathias came to a complete stop, Elias jumped down. On his way over to us, he looked at Thora with equal parts horror and professionalism. His blue-gray eyes, which never missed a single detail, also trailed over Varnar, but he didn't comment on his presence.

"She needs laekna," I said. "You don't need to examine her."

But Elias unbuttoned Thora's coat, exposing her stomach. Her pale skin was caked in fresh red blood along with brown and black scabs. Beneath them was a deep cut from which blood continued to bubble up. It resembled boiling red liquid. Elias pressed his scarf over her stomach, but it wasn't enough to stop the bleeding. He shook his head and said something to himself.

"Give her the laekna," I ordered hysterically.

"I don't have any. I used the last of it earlier today at The Boatman." He didn't have to say who was responsible for the wounds he'd had to heal.

I looked up at Mathias. "What about him? He's full of demi-blood."

"You, of all people, know what happens if you take it undiluted, and I'm not done making laekna from the portion you gave me."

"Then do something else. If you can only heal people with supernatural assistance, then you're not much of a doctor."

"Even if we were in a hospital with access to all the remedies in the world, I wouldn't be able to do anything. Thora is mortally wounded."

I moaned in frustration, and from somewhere in the ground beneath me, I heard the goddess of death laugh. *I've taken so many of the people you care for, and I will take more.* I had no doubt she was waiting to grab my mother's spirit. *I've almost got her, raven.*

I looked up at Varnar, and his expression was desperate. "There's only one thing you can do, Anna."

"What in all the worlds can *I* do?"

There was pain in Varnar's eyes, but he clenched his jaw. "There's someone else you can ask for help. Only you can convince him."

It took me a moment to figure it out, but at the sight of Varnar's anguished face, it clicked. I eased my mother's head from my lap, nudged Varnar to get him to move, and lay down on my side. With one hand, I held tight to Thora. I placed my other hand on Elias's thigh.

"Have you lost your mind?" Elias balked.

"My sister is alive."

Elias looked at me, uncomprehending. "That's great news, but now's not the time . . ."

I interrupted him. "You need to fix my stress."

"Anna!" Elias sounded like a negotiator speaking to a deranged hostage taker. "You're upset. It's completely understandable. There are limits to what the mind can handle. But right now, this is not about you. It's about Thora."

I looked up at him. "You need to do a guided relaxation. Brenda held her hands here." I took his hand and placed it on my head.

"Brenda?"

"From The Healing Tree."

"The homeopath on Grønnegade?" Elias looked more than a little doubtful, so I grabbed the collar of his shirt and pulled him close to my face. His blue-gray eyes widened.

"You were right. I can't get through to my sister because I'm stressed. Just like you said. Brenda helped me, but I still need the last bit to get ahold of Serén. Together, we can open portals to other worlds. We did it last summer when I traveled back from Hrafnheim. You told me you're the best treatment provider in the country. Prove it."

Understanding finally reached Elias's face. Nevertheless, he looked uncertainly around the oval of stones. "This is a portal."

"I'm not going to Vindr Fen. I need Serén to send me somewhere else."

"Where?"

"Just do it!"

"I can't help you relax under these conditions, on the ground next to your dying mother."

"You have five minutes to de-stress me."

"What's in it for me?"

I was prepared for him to bargain, so I was completely calm. "I'll pay you with my trust."

"Will you trust me from now on?"

"I swear it."

"It's a deal."

Elias placed his hands on my head. His pinkie fingers pressed on my temples, his ring fingers on my brows, and the rest pressed into my scalp. Before I closed my eyes, I grabbed Varnar's hand. He widened his eyes when I looked directly at him.

"Thank you for bringing Thora. I owe you everything."

Varnar's expression grew tender. "You don't owe me anything. I would do anything for you. You know that, Anna." His eyes flitted over Elias briefly before looking back at me.

"I'll find you again," I promised Varnar. "Take care of yourself and the others." Then I closed my eyes and dug my fingers into Elias's leg. "De-stress me," I commanded.

Elias pressed my temples and said in a low voice, "You're standing at a high point in the landscape." I stood on the hill that rose at one end of Sømosen. It was a summer day, and bees hummed.

The bog emitted its characteristic sour smell of peat. I had been there in person with Elias, and in dreams with the little myling—the ghost boy who haunted the place.

"Fill your lungs. Hold in the air. And then breathe out. As hard as you can. Keep doing it. Do it nine times."

I obeyed until my head was spinning.

"Find the path. Step down. Exhale hard, step by step."

I looked down the green slope. An almost-hidden staircase of stones was embedded directly into the hill.

"Breathe in and out with each step. Keep it up."

I drank in large gulps of air, exhaled hard, and released my tension. Even though I felt the wind caressing my arms, a branch scratching my skin, and the earth yielding beneath the stones, at the same time, I felt Elias's fingers pressing against my skull. I think he hit some pressure points. I also felt my one side, the one turned toward Thora's body, growing wet and warm.

"You see water."

The bog was still and dark. A gigantic, shining eye that stank of stagnant water. I walked down to it. The ground squelched beneath me, but it was more of a feeling than a sound. I reached the water. There was a small height difference between the path and the bog's edge, and I stood as close as I could without falling into the water. Even though I knew this was imaginary, I was very aware of how dangerous the bog was. Those who fell in did not come out alive. With my toes jutting out into the air, I held tight to a small tree so I could lean out over the water's reflective surface.

"Look down," Elias said from somewhere above my head. "Look at yourself in the mirror."

I hesitated. What if Hel was there and dragged me down into the bog's depths?

"I'll take care of you," a voice piped up, and I flinched, nearly falling into the water. I looked up to see a figure standing there. It was small. A child.

Ohhh. It was the little myling. Oddly enough, it was reassuring to see him.

"You owe a debt to me, völva," he said.

"I will find your earthly remains and lay them to rest properly," I promised. "Just not right now. I need to get in touch with my sister."

"I'll help you." The boy laid a small brown hand on my shoulder.

"Time's running out." That was Elias again. He sounded as though he were the trees. I took one last deep breath, leaned as far forward as possible, and looked down into the bog.

At first, I saw nothing. Then, my own face undulated. I saw my messy red hair, my stern expression and dark brows—one with a scar running through it. The image rippled and changed.

"Look at yourself, Anna." Elias or the trees spoke. "It's only you."

I stared intensely down. Black hair appeared, and I was about to pull away when Hel came into view. She laughed her laugh of death and reached up with her skeletal hand. A white finger bone nearly pierced the surface from below.

"Yourself," the trees repeated.

"Me?"

Down in the water, Hel stopped. Her bony finger extended and poked the place where air met water. Rings spread across the surface from the spot she touched.

"You're in the way," I said. "Go away! Go!"

In the water, Hel fluttered away, and she resembled a squid spewing dark-blue liquid. At first, there was a blue cloud, but it dissolved. What remained was only my face. I smiled, even though I couldn't remember ever smiling at myself in a mirror. Suddenly, my reflection changed; it looked desperate. It shouted noiselessly and flailed its arms. I lay flat on my stomach so I could bring my head all the way down to the water. My hands ran over the surface but only managed to ripple the water even more.

". . . na" bubbled up from beneath. ". . . na."

I got so close, my nose touched the surface.

"Anna."

"Serén!"

My sister spoke quickly, and there were tears in her eyes. "Finally! I've tried and tried to reach you. Are you okay? I've been so worried."

"Stop, Serén," I cut her off. "We don't have a lot of time."

Serén held out her hand. I placed my palm over hers on the water's surface. At lightning speed, I explained what had happened. "When I was at Haraldsborg," I began, and Serén finished my sentence.

"We opened the portals between the worlds by combining our powers."

"We need to do that again."

Serén shook her head. Her red hair brushed the water's surface, creating small waves. A leaf cradled her face. "We're too far away from each other."

"We have to."

"You risk getting stuck between the worlds. That's not even death. It's nothingness."

"I'll take the chance."

Elias's voice shook the trees. "Thora doesn't have much time left."

"Now, Serén. Now!" I urged.

Serén pursed her lips in a determined expression. "Reach out to me."

"What do you mean? Mentally?"

She made a *tsk* sound so loud, a bubble burst on the surface. "This *is* mental."

I stretched my hands down into the water. It was cool and got colder the farther my fingertips reached. It was swampy and full of fibrous plants. Ice-cold fingers interlaced themselves with mine and pulled me down. I turned my head. My cheek was hovering less than an inch above the sloshing water. It forced its way into my ear, and everything became distorted. There were glugs and splashes inside my head, and Serén's voice grew louder.

"Where?"

"Sverresborg."

"Outside the castle?"

"As close to Sverre as I can get."

"Now!" Serén pulled, and at that moment, I opened my eyes on the forest floor, looking up at Midgard's gray sky. I made eye contact with Elias, whose head was close to mine, but then I rolled over and wrapped my whole body around Thora's nearly dead form. With a forceful suction, we were both ripped away. I curled in the fetal position around my unconscious mother, terrified of losing her. Just as I remembered from my other journeys between the worlds, I was pushed and pulled from all directions. Then, a small dot of light appeared. It grew larger and larger, and I saw the outline of Hrafnheim. I saw Svearike, Sverresborg, and in the sea beyond, the Midgard Serpent writhed. Its head plunged into the waves, and its long body arched behind it. Ice and snow covered the kingdom, just like in Midgard. Then we plummeted down through the castle's roof and several stories until I saw a long table. Quite a few people sat around it, all wrapped in skins and blankets. At the head of the table sat a long-haired figure hunched over his wooden bowl. His hair was so light, it was nearly white, and his hand, which held a spoon, was tattooed with a large eagle.

My mother and I landed with a crash on the table. Food flew and splattered in every direction, and cups of water were overturned. Most of the people stood and stumbled back, but the man at the end of the table sat completely still and stared at me with his dark brown eyes. The spoon was raised in front of his mouth. I was still rolling around, clutching my mother. There was porridge on my cheek, and my hair was wet with bog water and Thora's blood.

"Anna?" Sverre whispered.

"Help me," I pleaded.

For a moment, no one in the room spoke.

"Are you really here?"

"I am really here," I said. "And I really, really need your help." I lifted my mother slightly. "She has minutes, maybe only seconds, left to live."

The spoon in Sverre's hand clattered to the floor. Although we hadn't seen each other in almost a year, I embraced him. His body was as warm and strong as ever. He gently extracted himself from my grasp and turned toward Thora. He placed his hands on her stomach, the one with the eagle tattoo resting on the other. I felt a vibration from him, but he held his healing powers back, even though his face was contorted with longing.

"I will heal her," he said quietly.

"Do it, then."

"If you pay me for it."

"I . . . uh . . . what?" I looked at him with tear-swollen eyes. He looked different from how I remembered him. Thinner and with a grayish cast to his skin. The dark circles under his eyes made him look older. For a moment, I wondered whether more time had passed in Hrafnheim than at home, but I knew there was no time difference between our worlds.

"You have to pay for it," he said clearly.

"I have nothing."

"You have exactly what I want."

"What?"

He removed his hands from Thora's stomach, tilted his head back, and straightened to his full height of nearly six foot five. Tilarids hung at his side. The bloodthirsty sword, which he normally despised. It was hardly as aggressive as usual, and it seemed like it had fused to his leg. It had become part of him. Or he had become part of it. He didn't even seem to notice that he was rubbing his tattooed hand across the hilt.

"I want . . ." he said steadily, stressing each word so I didn't miss a single syllable. "I want a night with you."

CHAPTER 7

I don't know if the words only echoed inside my head, or if they actually rang out in the hall.

"Ah . . ." My exclamation hung in the air between us. I was so stunned I merely stared at Sverre.

"I thought you would do anything." There was no emotion on his face.

Something was very wrong with him, but there was no time to think about it now. I remembered a bit of advice Elias had given me: *In a situation where your life is in danger, accept any help you can get and consider the consequences later.* The rule must also apply when your loved one was about to die.

"Fine." My voice was much more confident than I felt. "Heal her, then. I'll keep my word."

For a long moment, he stared at me as though trying to work out if I was lying. I looked back at him defiantly, and he took half a step backward as if I had slapped him. Then he leaned over my mother and laid his hands on her stomach. The eagle on the back of his hand flapped its wings with the movement, and its beak closed as Sverre stretched his thumb along his index finger. A force shot out of him, and I watched as he filled Thora's lower torso with energy. Then Sverre reversed the current and pulled the energy out of her, along with the injury. I saw the wound get pulled along in the maelstrom and disappear into Sverre's hands. On Thora's stomach, the gash turned into a wide, bright-red, vertical scar, the end of which intersected the old horizontal scar just above her pubic bone. The color returned to her cheeks, so she no longer appeared dead. Her lips parted, and for a moment—relaxed, eyes closed—she looked vulnerable. But then she twisted her mouth into an animalistic grimace. Sverre stood with a blissful look on his face as my mother got onto all fours. She resembled a panther waiting for the right moment. Then she leapt.

Sverre fell backward with a surprised *umph* and landed on his back with Thora straddling him. Without me noticing, she had taken a fork from the table. Sverre fumbled for Tilarids and got the sword halfway out of its sheath, but Thora smacked his hand so hard that Tilarids tumbled a short distance away, where it lay trembling angrily. In the same movement, she brought the fork up to his neck. I looked at her, impressed, as she sat atop Sverre—streaks of dried blood everywhere, dark curls in a cloud around her head, and a fork pressed against his jugular.

Weapons clattered around us, and the soldiers stepped forward, but Sverre would be dead before they could come to his aid. They stood with horrified expressions, their hands on their swords' hilts.

"King . . ." one of the soldiers shouted, and I looked up.

Is Sverre the king now? I didn't have time to think about it.

Sverre didn't move, but he looked at the soldier who had called out. "Quiet."

"That's my daughter you just claimed," Thora hissed and pressed the sharp iron tines into Sverre's throat so hard, blood began to flow. He healed himself quickly, prompting a struggle between his healing powers and my mother's destructive ones.

"I just saved your life," Sverre said. He looked so taken aback and suddenly much more like himself.

"Thanks for that!" She smiled sweetly. "That makes it much easier for me to kill you."

I grabbed her shoulder, but she paid me no mind. Although her body was warm and alive, her muscles were as hard as stone.

"Thora," I tried, but there was still no reaction. "Let him go, Mom!" I shouted, and she finally turned her head.

We looked at one another. Before, I could only see how much Arthur looked like Serén; now I felt like I was looking into a mirror. Thora was an older version of me with white streaks in her hair, fine lines, and an even harder gaze. She breathed heavily as she studied me. Slowly, she pulled the fork away from Sverre's neck and rose to her feet.

Sverre was still lying on his back, but he got up with as much dignity as he could. He signaled to his people to drop their weapons. Without looking in Tilarids's direction, he extended his fingers. Tilarids glided back to Sverre on its own, as though he were a magnet. He slid the sword into its sheath, where it appeared to press itself against his leg. The troubled expression had returned to his handsome face. He ushered us out of the hall, where, under the circumstances, I wasn't too comfortable anyway.

Outside the door, I recognized the stone passage that Elias and I fled down after the Sverresborg soldiers had tried to assault me the previous year. The mere sight of it caused my muscles to twitch. My heart pounded, but I didn't have time to dwell on my fear. Sverre pushed open a heavy wooden door leading to a small chamber with a cot and a chair.

"You can stay in here," he told us. His voice was deeper than I remembered. "Someone will come get you when it's time to pay your debt."

We didn't manage to say anything before he slammed the door closed behind him. It was freezing cold in the room. There was an object on the table.

Whoa.

It was a crystal encased in an iron holder. It was dark right now, but I knew that it could glow and give off heat. I leaned over it and studied it. It was the crystal Rorik had had with him on our journey. I knew, of course, that *Rorik* wasn't his real name, but I simply couldn't stop calling him that in my head when I thought of the gentle, fair-haired young man I had spent all those weeks with. Back then, he had rarely let the crystal out of his sight, but now it was just packed away in this cold room. Carefully, I cupped the white crystal. It was slightly transparent but completely dull.

I thought of Luna, and the crystal flickered slightly but went out again when my thoughts turned to Mathias and his smug demigod attitude. I still loved him as a friend, but lately he had become difficult to be around. I tried Odinmont. Again, a little light flickered inside, but it was weak, and it went out like a burned-out bulb. *Monster!* I squeezed my eyes shut and thought of Monster and his broad snout. In my memory, he stood close to his daughter Rokkin. Then I remembered Varnar. I recalled the nights we had spent together, and his intense gaze. Warmth spread beneath my hands, and I continued. Arthur's kind eyes, Serén's slightly flustered and sweet smile. My stomach fluttered at the thought that she was alive. I also thought of Sverre. Not the cold king he was now, but as I remembered him, smiling in the sunset in Frón. With an *ow*, I jerked my fingers back, having burned them on the crystal that now shone so brightly I could see it through my closed eyelids. Heat radiated toward me.

Thora looked at the crystal. Then she stepped closer, held out her hands, and made a waving motion as though she could waft the heat up toward her body. She was one big mess, with her coat ripped down the front, revealing her stomach beneath. Splotches of blood and knots in her hair so large they resembled Ben's dreadlocks. I sat down on the cot.

"What a day."

Thora's forehead creased, but I wasn't sure if that was her usual expression or if it was just because she was looking at me.

"Yes," she agreed. "What a day." She sat on the chair, and for a while, we just sat there and let the warmth seep into us. Finally, Thora found the words she'd been looking for.

"I'm really bad at all this . . ." She made a face. ". . . feelings stuff."

"So am I," I said quickly and looked away. I had no idea what to say to my mother now that I actually had her in front of me.

"It's nice to meet you," she said formally.

"You, too." I focused on a slightly lighter stone in the wall as I tried to come up with the right thing to say to my mother, with whom I had never had a conversation. I failed completely when I blurted out an accusation.

"Why were you even meeting with Eskild?"

Thora's forehead crease deepened. "He has something I want. In return, I offered him safe passage."

"What does he have that's so important you would risk your life?"

"Augustin Odion."

"Who?"

"It doesn't matter. I didn't get him. Eskild didn't uphold our truce. I was lucky Varnar defied my order to stay away."

"Fortunately, I've taught him to be critical," I said with a sly expression. "Some orders shouldn't be followed."

"You taught him to put himself in danger to save an insignificant person? Well done, Anna!"

"You're not insignificant."

"You shouldn't have taken the risk of bringing me here, either. Children aren't supposed to save their parents." The crease in Thora's forehead was now so deep, it must have been causing her pain.

I turned my head, surprised. "Are you going to scold me for saving your ass?"

"You could have died."

"I *have* died. I took a trip to the realm of the dead to get Dad last year. He's alive again, too, thanks to me. Well, and Elias, who reanimated him."

"Elias." Thora said the name slowly and emphatically.

"He's not as bad as you all make him out to be."

"No. He's much worse." Thora pursed her lips pointedly.

"Maybe it's easier for you and Dad to project everything onto Elias so you don't have to deal with your own bad decisions."

"*Project*. Nice word. Someone must have spent a lot of time in therapy."

"And whose fault is that? If you hadn't left . . ."

"I was kidnapped by Ragnara, for God's sake."

"You wouldn't have been if you had stayed away from her and Eskild. I have no idea what you were up to before I was born, but I'm convinced you share part of the blame for all the shit I'm dealing with now."

This reunion wasn't going at all the way I'd expected.

Just as she was about to say something more, the door opened. I flinched at the sight of a soldier with snake scales tattooed on his cheeks. My mother moved in front of me protectively, assuming an attack position. The last time I was here in Sverresborg, similar men had attacked me, but Elias had killed them with poison. It didn't seem like this soldier wanted to attack me, though. In fact, he appeared to fear us.

"Make yourself ready for the king." The soldier bowed his head and held out a clean set of clothes just like the ones Gytha had sold me, which had accompanied me for most of my trip with Sverre. "I'll wait outside while you change." He stepped out, apparently more concerned for his own safety than for my honor.

Thora spun around toward me. "You don't owe Sverre anything."

I raised an eyebrow. "He just saved your life."

"So *I* owe him something."

I jutted out my jaw. "I haven't seen him since that day in the arena. It's high time we talk things out." I pulled the clothes on and banged on the door to indicate that I was ready. When I left, Thora let out a growl only Ben could surpass.

"Just don't let anything happen to you," she called after me. I walked down the stone passageway toward the king's chambers. In my hands, I carried the glowing crystal, which at least warmed my upper body. My red hair was loose. The soldier who accompanied me pounded on a heavy wooden door and eased it open when a voice inside responded.

Sverre stood in front of the fireplace. The fire behind him sharpened his silhouette. Tilarids hung at his side, and the sword's hilt caught the light of the flames, and it appeared to be ablaze. The room was warmer than the hallway. There was a long table, and against the wall was a large bed covered in blankets and skins, which I tried not to look at.

In front of Sverre, the table was full of food, the likes of which I hadn't seen since before the long winter. There were pies, bottles of mead, and platters of steaming vegetables. The smell was fantastic, and it took some effort not to run over and throw myself at the delicacies. When I came closer, I saw Sverre had also changed clothes. He had on the gray shirt and brown pants that he had worn for most of our trip together.

"This looks like a blót." I looked down at all the food.

"It is." His voice trembled.

"Who are you making an offering to?"

"You."

There was something different about Sverre's face. About his whole appearance. I searched for the person I knew. The man I had fallen in love with once and perhaps still loved, but his features were hard, and his posture was stiff. His eyes landed on the shining crystal in my hands.

"You got it to glow. It's been dark for more than a year."

"You don't usually have any trouble getting it going," I said, setting it on the table.

"I forgot where I'd put it." He smiled, though his eyes were still sad. He ran his hand over it. "But now it's glowing like it's supposed to."

"I don't believe that anything's *supposed* to be a certain way."

"I do." He looked me up and down in a way that sent chills down the back of my neck. I looked at his hip.

"Will you do something for me?" I asked.

"Anything."

"Take your sword off. Take Tilarids away."

Reluctance was clear on Sverre's face, and with a wistful expression, he laid the sword on a sideboard not far from the table. Tilarids writhed angrily at having been set aside.

"Why are you wearing it?"

Sverre looked at the sword. "It gives me powers I don't normally have. I'm a terrible warrior, but with Tilarids, I can be strong for my people. I'm the king now. I have a responsibility."

"You openly healed Thora. Is it no longer forbidden?"

"That was the first thing I changed when I came to power, after you had Ragnara . . ."

"After I had her killed?"

"Yes." Sverre bit his lip. "I don't think I would have become king if I didn't have Tilarids. It's very powerful."

"That sword is an asshole, and you know it!"

Sverre laughed. Relieved, I saw the man I knew and cared about. "Can a sword be an asshole?"

"Hey!" I said, a smile tugging at the corners of my mouth. "I can sense it with my clairvoyance. It has an unpleasant personality, even though it's an object."

I caught a glimpse of some shining fabric on the wall above the sideboard. At first, I hadn't noticed the green silk hanging like a macabre decoration. With tears in my eyes, I stepped closer. It felt like an eternity since Luna had given me the beautiful silk dress. I had worn it to the hálfa celebration in Ísafold, where Sverre and I were together for the first time. When we were overcome with love magic by the river Iving. Later that night, I had given the dress to Faida, and it had been her death sentence. It felt like so long ago—a whole lifetime. And I was a different person back then.

I reached up, and my fingers found a small tear in the front of the dress. It was black with old blood. The sword that Ragnara had plunged into Faida's back had gone all the way through her body and out her stomach.

"I'm sorry, Faida," I whispered. "I had no idea what I was doing. It's my fault you died."

"We laid Faida to rest in a burial mound, but I kept her dress in remembrance. It gets brought out for special occasions. The dress is holy."

"That sounds sick."

"No more so than any other ceremonial object. Where do you think myths come from?" Sverre laid a hand on my shoulder and led me to the middle of the room. I shoved his arm away incredulously when he touched me.

"That's really what you want?"

He waved his free hand. "Of course not! I just wanted to make sure you stayed here tonight so we could talk. You have a tendency to leave in the middle of a conversation." He pulled a chair out from the table and nudged me to the seat.

I sat in front of the fragrant dishes. "Do your subjects have enough food?" I didn't want to stuff myself while others were starving.

"It's a holiday for everyone because you came to Sverresborg. If my people go without food, I do, too. If I have enough, I share with them. If I'm happy, they should be happy, too."

I returned his smile. This was the Sverre I remembered. Always eager to help and do good. He filled my plate and placed it in front of me and poured mead into a green glass. I sipped cautiously and sighed with pleasure as the sweet alcohol warmed me up. Then I bit into a tart, the crunchy crust tasting of butter and flour. The filling was egg and mushroom.

"This is so good." I didn't even finish chewing before I praised the food. I looked at Sverre, expecting that he, too, would be caught up in the pleasure, but he had turned his chair and was studying me.

"Has it been a long time since you ate?"

"No." I swallowed the mouthful. "But we're rationing, so it's mostly canned food or unseasoned meat."

"We can send you food."

I had raised my glass to take another sip of mead but stopped. "You have enough? I thought you were starving here, too."

"There was a famine here. When it was at its worst, I called for a huge blót to the gods, and the next day we found a cache of food my mother had hidden in Danheim. Say what you will about Ragnara, but she was prepared. Every time we're running low, we sacrifice to the gods, and then we find food."

"I had no idea you had become a believer."

"I learned it from you."

"From me? I do nothing but argue with gods and demigods."

There was a smile in his dark brown eyes. "Nevertheless, they care about you."

I couldn't stop myself from taking another large mouthful of mead and more food. When I tasted a steamed leek, I couldn't help but express my enjoyment. "Mmmm."

Sverre laughed, and the sound was so familiar, I nearly hugged him again. I hadn't been treated this way by a man in over a year, and I had to admit to myself that I really missed being cared for. The way he looked at me made my whole body warm.

"It's not just the gods who care about you, Anna."

I slowed my chewing and looked down at the table. But after I swallowed the food, I no longer had an excuse to keep quiet. "I care about you, too. I really do. And I've missed you so damn much."

"And yet you went straight from my bed to that of another."

I had known that was coming. Sverre hadn't forgotten that I had been with both him and Varnar in less than twenty-four hours.

"Well, you married Ingeborg." It was a weak defense, and I was about to admit it, but Sverre spoke first.

"My wife is a good woman."

My throat felt scratchy when he said *wife*. "Isn't it an arranged marriage?"

"That doesn't make her a bad person."

"Of course not." I rubbed my forehead. "I didn't sleep with Varnar because you married someone else. I just couldn't help it."

Sverre stared at me, and because we were talking about Varnar, I noticed how the two men were opposites in both appearance and character. Sverre was sensitive behind his strong exterior of tattoos, long hair, and imposing height.

"Varnar and I are allies now, but I'm never going to like him," Sverre said. "He's so cynical."

"You just have to get to know him, just like . . ."

"Just like me?"

"Uhh . . . you did have a bad reputation before, but I think people like you now. If you're healing people and giving out food and stuff like that." When Sverre still looked wounded, I added, "Varnar was really pissed when he found out we had been together. He doesn't like you, either. Especially now."

Sverre sat up straighter in his chair. "He found out?"

"Yup. And I punched him in the stomach soon after."

"Did you really punch Varnar in the stomach?" Sverre laughed in surprise.

"It's not funny. I actually think it really hurt." But not as bad as finding out about me and Sverre.

Sverre was elated, but I couldn't tell if it was because Varnar was jealous of him or because I had punched him in the gut. I also started laughing; it was so freeing to be with the warm, pleasant Sverre again.

"It's really not funny." But I couldn't wipe the smile off my face. At that moment, it was so easy to forget doomsday was approaching—but there was no way around it. "What do you think is causing the winter?"

Sverre put his elbow on the table and rested his chin on his fist. "I think the gods are angry."

"How do you even know anything about the gods?"

"I found people who know the myths. Even though my mother killed many believers, there was still some knowledge hidden away. We neglected the gods for all those years, and now we have to make amends. When they forgive us, the warmth will return."

"You don't think it's Fimbulwinter?"

Sverre blanched, and suddenly, the dark rings under his eyes became stark. "That's what I fear."

My hand found his. "I have a solution. If my sister and I are united, we can change fate. I'm leaving to find her as soon as I've repaid you." I jokingly made an irritated face, but it suited me just fine to be hostage to the handsome king. Sverre would certainly let me go if I really wanted to. He leaned in toward me. His voice was low and had a hot edge that I remembered well. My heart skipped a beat.

"The world might be ending soon." Sverre squeezed my hand. "It's only for these few hours that I can allow myself to be your friend. In a while, I must go back to leading my people."

It might all be over soon. I looked at Sverre and laid my hand on his cheek. He closed his eyes and laid his own hand on mine. For a few seconds, he just sat there as I caressed his cheekbone and jaw. Then I moved my hand to his white hair and ran my fingers through it.

"Anna . . ." He sounded almost breathless.

"Let's make the most of our time, then, if the world is ending soon. I want you all to myself before I have to share you with your people again."

Sverre knelt in front of my chair, and I put my arms around his neck. He came closer to me. For a moment, he held his mouth in front of mine. Expectant. When I couldn't stand it anymore, I leaned the last few inches forward and kissed him.

The light from the fire flickered across his face, and the feeling of him was so familiar, I cuddled up to him. In a fluid motion, we were on our feet. I held him, and we made our way to the bed without even breaking the kiss.

I wouldn't have to wait until the next morning for him to become someone else—someone entirely different from the gentle king who was kissing me at that moment.

I woke up alone in the bed in the middle of the night. I had rolled up against the wall in my sleep, so one side of me was ice-cold.

"Sverre?" I called.

Something rattled at the other end of the room, but it was too dark to see what it was. It sounded like iron against iron. I fumbled for my clothes, which were scattered across the dark room. With the blanket wrapped around me, I stepped onto the floor. The fire in the fireplace had gone out, and I shivered when the bare soles of my feet hit the cold floor tiles.

"Sverre?" I tried again.

"She must see it. She must be it," said a voice that sounded both familiar and completely foreign. Again, I heard the sharp, metallic sound. I walked toward it, but because it was so dark, I walked straight into the edge of the table. A stabbing pain shot through my hip.

"Ow, shit." I put my hand on the table, and my fingers found Sverre's crystal, which was currently dark. I picked it up and thought about what I had just experienced. The feeling of Sverre above me. His fervent kisses and his hands on my body.

The crystal flared, and a pink glow bathed the room. I spotted Sverre over by the dresser. He was dressed—Tilarids once again hanging from his belt—and he was pulling the green silk dress down from the wall.

"What are you doing?" I went up to him and embraced him from behind, the crystal in one hand. "Aren't you coming back to me?"

Sverre stopped mid-movement when I touched him. One of his hands fingered my forearm, and I giggled, ticklish. I set the crystal on the dresser so I could hold him. With my arms still around him, he turned around with the ill-fated dress in his hand.

"Put it on." Sverre's voice was scratchy. I couldn't see his face because the crystal shone behind him, casting his front in shadow.

"Put what on?"

He held out the dress to me.

It took me a couple of tries to find the words. "The . . . what?"

"You need to put it on," he said slowly. "You have an assignment."

"Faida died in that dress. Her blood is still on it." I couldn't seem to remove my arms from their place around his waist, and our close contact allowed me to feel his aura, which was currently black as coal. The strongest vibe came from his side. I looked down at Tilarids, its runes glowing faintly.

"Take the sword off," I said quietly. "Sverre . . ."

"Sverre . . ." he repeated with his foreign, scratchy voice. "My name means *sword*. It has always been my destiny."

"I think Tilarids has possessed you."

He let out a low noise that I thought at first was a growl, but I then realized was laughter. "It hasn't possessed me. It is me. I *am* Tilarids."

It dawned on me that I was speaking with the murderous sword, not Sverre. Perhaps he was watching from somewhere in there.

"Put the dress on," the man commanded. He looked like my beloved, but it wasn't him at all.

I tried to catch his eye, but his face was in shadow. "Sverre. Resist. I know you can hear me."

Sverre bowed his head, causing his matted hair to glide down. Our night together had tousled it. "Why do you think we've survived?" he said quietly. "Why do you think my people have food?"

"Because you're a good king," I whispered. "Because—"

"They've survived because I'm sacrificing myself. Anna, I have to do this." Behind the layers of hardness, the Sverre I knew was speaking.

He laid a large hand on my neck and squeezed. Tilarids must have taken over again, as the real Sverre would never treat me so roughly. "Put. The. Dress. On." He ripped the blanket off me, and I stood naked before him. He pressed the dress forcefully into my hands. "If you don't do this, your mother will suffer the consequences. The Midgard Serpent is always hungry."

I had stood face-to-face with the Midgard Serpent, and the memory of the gigantic sulfur-smelling snake made me pull on the dress. My hands shook, but I managed to get it on. The silk fabric warmed me slightly, but the cold air hit my stomach and back where the dress was torn open. It was low-cut in the back, so my shoulder blades were freezing. Sverre looked me over as though I were an object. Then he nodded, satisfied, and took my arm. I wanted to jerk away, but he held me tight against him with an iron grip.

"This feels right," he said. "The two of us, side by side, as king and queen of Hrafnheim."

I resisted saying that this felt anything but right. In fact, it was very unsettling to stand there in a dead girl's dress with a man who looked like someone I loved but wasn't him.

"You already have a queen," I said.

"Ingeborg," he said absently. "I had to secure the line of succession, and I didn't know if you were coming back."

"I'm not *back*."

"Don't worry, Anna. Our children will be heirs to the throne. You are Odin's raven, after all. My son with Ingeborg is just a spare. It was my duty to produce him."

"You have a kid? That . . . You don't just *produce* a child."

Sverre shrugged, and I stole a glance down at his hip, where Tilarids hung. I thought I could hear the sword laughing in my head.

"Why are you doing this?" The question was directed downward.

"I have to be ready for Ragnarök," Sverre said, but it was Tilarids who was speaking. "Conflict and destruction strengthen me. Worship and fertility do, too."

"Sverre," I begged. "Rorik . . ."

Sverre yanked me into the stone hallway outside his room. My toes nearly lost all feeling from stepping on the ice-cold floor. Sverre held the shining crystal. He held it carefully, in a way that did not at all match up with his violent presence. The light came from under his chin, and the shadows made his face look like a skull.

"Your light," he mumbled, "will never be extinguished." He didn't ask if I was cold, even though there was a layer of frost over the stone wall, and I was dressed only in a thin silk dress. In fact, I was shaking so much from the cold, I wasn't sure if I'd be capable of fighting or fleeing if it came to that.

What are you? I asked inside my head.

Tilarids didn't respond, but I got the feeling it would have stuck its tongue out at me if it had had one.

We reached another passageway, and I was dragged along with my fingers in a vise grip. I recognized the staircase that I had been pulled down once before. That time, it was the sorcerer Gustaf who had dragged me down into the cellar beneath Sverresborg. I focused on a charred spot on the railing where he had thrown an energy ball at me. I knew very well what there was access to down here. Or, more precisely, *who*.

"What are we doing?" I asked meekly.

"I want to show you something," Sverre replied. With firm steps, he descended the stairs with me at his side. "Something amazing."

When we reached the foot of the stairs, my frozen feet touched dirt. I was now trembling so much from the cold that my legs swayed beneath me. Fortunately, the door out to the sea was closed. The Midgard Serpent was right out there, and before Sverre moved into Sverresborg, they had made offerings to it from here. I had no idea if Sverre had continued that practice, but the little pool that gurgled in front of the doorway had a raft frozen to the side. It didn't appear to have been out on the open water in a long time.

In the middle of the room was something that hadn't been there the last time I was down here. It was an oval arrangement of stones with a platform in the middle. Each stone was as tall as I was, and they were draped with jewelry, dyed fabric, garlands of onions, and sheaves of dried grain. In total, the offerings must have been worth a fortune.

On the platform in the middle lay a body—or what was left of one, as the bones stood out beneath dried skin and collapsed muscles. Small flickering lamps were on the ground all around the corpse.

Sverre let go of my hand, and I stepped forward, breathless, because I knew the dead body lying on the platform surrounded by light.

I knew him and loved him.

CHAPTER 8

Finn lay on his back with his claw-tipped fingers clasped over his chest. His leathery wings were unfolded beneath his shoulders. They were the only part of him that looked like they had when he was alive. His wings were thick and shiny, while the rest of him was more or less mummified. There was a thin, delicate sheet of ice over him. He must have been half decomposed when the winter came and halted the process.

"Finn," I whispered.

Sverre stepped forward with me. "It's our little Finn."

I felt like saying that Sverre was officially batshit crazy for placing my beloved fingalk where everyone could see his decay, but I couldn't speak. I had no words for what lay before me. I wanted to squeeze between two boulders and enter the oval, but Sverre stopped me with a hand on my shoulder.

"This is a holy stone circle."

"Why . . ." I stammered. "Why do you think Finn's grave is holy?"

"You don't know?"

"No. For gods' sakes, no!"

"Everything from our journey is holy. The objects from it—those I could get my hands on—are relics." He stroked his hand over my silk dress. "You and I created a legend together."

"Finn isn't a relic. He's a . . ." My voice broke. "He *was* a person." I looked down at myself in the green dress. "Faida was a person. They were real! There was sorrow and pain."

Sverre's tattooed hand found my cheek. "And love."

"You don't know what love is." I was speaking more to Tilarids than to Sverre.

"My people will worship you."

"I don't want to be worshipped."

"Odin chose you. He is the All-Father, and you are his völva. The sign is on your back. You must transmit our worship to the gods." He touched the ansuz scar on my exposed shoulder blade. I quickly jerked away.

"That scar is the proof that I died!" I shouted. "That Elias had to hurt me so I could go to Helheim."

"You died, and you came back to life." Sverre nodded, ignoring the fact that I had just yelled at him. "That sure sounds like a legend."

"I'm just me."

He raised his head and furrowed his brows, uncomprehending. I stretched out my arm to display the fehu rune that Gustaf had imprinted on it. "I also have this mark. It means *slave*."

Sverre let his fingers trace the fehu tattoo, and his touch made me nauseous. "That was my mother's mark," he said quietly. "It's beautiful that you've reclaimed it."

"I had Odin kill your mother. It was necessary, but there's nothing beautiful about it." I gestured to the offerings surrounding Finn's corpse. "And there's nothing beautiful about this, either. He has no use for all this now."

"We're honoring him."

"He's dead, Sverre. Finn is gone. Our fingalk is gone forever, and he's not coming back." My longing for Finn cut deep, and I hadn't even given myself permission to grieve properly.

"You agreed to give me one night." Sverre's voice was suddenly hard. "It's not over yet."

I gawked. "Do you really expect . . ."

He held out his tattooed hand. The eagle spread its wings. "My people will worship you, and you will give them Odin's blessing."

He nudged me toward the stairs, but I slipped around him and back to Finn's body.

"Goodbye," I whispered to the mummified fingalk, well aware he couldn't hear me. Then I walked back to the mad king, my eyes focused on the bloodthirsty sword at his side.

I will destroy you, I vowed. *You will not get away with using Sverre like this.*

No matter whose hands wield me, I'll get my way. Ragnarök is coming, and the gods will meet their fate, Tilarids replied.

Svidur, I said in my head. *Odin.* Then I sighed and called him by the name Od had taught me to use when summoning him—even though right now I wanted to call him something else entirely.

All-Father! Care to check in?

An invisible hand tickled up my back. *Yes, raven.*

What in Hel's name is going on?

I sat in the throne room at the end of the long table, which was laden with offerings. Candles shone, and food and drink covered the table's surface. I had snatched a blanket and a pair of socks, but it was still painfully cold. The giant crystal flickered on the tabletop.

Odin laughed hoarsely inside my head. *You're bound to me. What did you think that entailed? Having a nice little blót in private? Noooo . . .* The word was said lazily, as though Odin were reclining comfortably. *You serve me: lead the people in their worship of me.*

I clenched my teeth together. *Can't they just worship you directly?*

I want you to taste the worship yourself. The young king idolizes you. You should have a chance to try it. Odin laughed again.

Yeah, yeah . . . the first hit is free. But aren't you worried about Tilarids ruling through Sverre? That will start Ragnarök. I'm sure you don't want that, seeing as you'll die in the battle.

Pah! Odin scoffed inside my head. *Just let the sword have its way a little longer. Come on, raven. Send me their worship. Bless them for me.*

But—

I wanted to say something, but at that moment, Sverre appeared in the doorway.

This conversation isn't over, I vowed bitterly.

At Sverre's side, Ingeborg stepped forward timidly with a sleeping baby in her arms. A sharp twinge went through my stomach at the sight of Sverre with his little family, even though I didn't want to trade places with Ingeborg. Sverre nudged her toward me until she stood in front of the platform with me towering above her. She held the baby close.

"Let Anna hold him," Sverre ordered.

Ingeborg clutched the bundle even tighter. In his sleep, the baby nuzzled into her and smacked his lips.

"Surely, I can bless him from here," I said.

Sverre looked like he wanted to protest.

"I mean . . ." I hurried to add. "That's the kind of völva I am. I always give blessings from a distance. A niiice, big distance." I waved my hands.

Ingeborg backed up obediently. More people had gathered behind Sverre and Ingeborg. They shoved one another to see me properly. I saw Merit and several other children previously afflicted with leprosy, whom Sverre had healed in the Kyngja Swamp outside Sverresborg. It felt like a lifetime ago, but they looked lovingly at the king, so for them, it must have still been a recent memory. Ingeborg stood expectantly in front of me with the sleeping baby. I tried to remember how a priest would say it.

"What is the child's name?" I asked formally.

"Finn," Ingeborg answered with a shaky voice.

This threw me off, but Sverre nodded proudly at me. He must have thought I would be touched. Kneeling before me, he pulled his wife down with him. I looked at the sleeping baby. Too many children were forced from birth into roles their parents had chosen for them. Myself included. Far too many children were not in charge of their own fates. I cleared my throat and spoke with as clear a voice as I could manage:

"In Odin's name, I bless you, Finn, son of Ingeborg and Sverre. I wish you a long and happy life, and that you yourself choose how you spend it. Odin forbids forced marriages," I said, although I had no basis for saying this. "He forbids thralldom, and the sacrificing of food. You should eat it yourselves. It's sufficient to pray and offer weapons or jewelry. Both are useless anyway, and lead only to unrest."

Gods, I hoped Sverre would listen to this and throw Tilarids in the swamp, but a quick glance at him convinced me that that wouldn't happen. He squeezed the hilt tightly, and the sword seemed practically glued to his hip.

I stood and called out into the room. "Get rid of the weapons and unnecessary adornments, and you'll have the freedom to simply be humans." The blanket fell from my shoulders, and I was standing before Sverre's people in the thin, ripped green dress, my long red hair trailing down my back. The wool socks probably detracted from my dramatic völva look.

"Humans," everyone repeated. Now, even the people in the very back were kneeling. Some reached out toward the giant, glowing crystal. Or maybe they were reaching out to me. "The freedom to be humans."

"That's the most important thing," I bellowed. "You are humans."
Ha! Take that, Odin.

"Mannaz," Sverre said in a low voice.

"Mannaz," Ingeborg said. Soon, everyone in the room was singing.

"Mannaz, mannaz, mannaz . . ." Waves of worship washed over me.

I wasn't cold anymore, and I was growing. At first, I tried to shield myself from the adoration, but I had to give up, and an effect stronger than any drug Elias could create pounded through my veins. I groaned and felt the tidal wave crash over me.

You have the aptitude to be a god, Odin said. *Should I be worried?*

You're the one that pushed me into this. Isn't this what you want me to do?

Don't provoke me. Ragnara broke off, too. Look how that went for her. Give me their worship. Now!

I leaned my head back and yelled: "Odin. We worship you." A beam of light shot from my mouth toward the ceiling, and Odin moaned joyously. Lightheaded, I stood up straight again. Over the kneeling crowd, I spotted my mother on the other side of the room. She stood leaning against the back wall and observed me with a strange look in her eyes.

I collapsed, trembling, as people dispersed. I was exhausted by the intensity of the ceremony. On the platform in the large dining hall, I tried unsuccessfully to stand up. I kept falling forward. The iron sculpture hanging on the wall depicted a snake, and its open maw was pointed directly at me. In my hallucinations, it appeared alive, and for a moment, I feared it wanted to devour me.

Through the window streamed the anemic yellow morning light that also settled over Midgard. The sky was not blue, but a murky grayish tone. When I squeezed my eyes shut, I saw my sister in my mind. She said something, but it crackled and echoed in my skull. I held my temples with both hands.

"Serén," I said. "Slow down. Speak more clearly."

. . . your powers. Serén's voice rang out like a gong.

"I don't understand. What are you saying?" I tried.

. . . happened? Her voice cut like a knife. *. . . elt it all the way from here.*

Thora is okay, I managed to get out, but I had to stop speaking at the protestation of my stomach. Saliva gathered in my mouth, and nausea bubbled in my throat.

Serén kept talking. It sounded like she was ripping me a new one, but her voice was so distorted, I didn't understand the half of it.

. . . out of control.

I'm trying to harness it, I choked, before my stomach gave up and spewed its contents up into my throat. My connection to Serén was cut off when I threw up, fortunately into a bucket someone was holding under my head.

"Come on, let's get you up." Only now did I notice my mother sitting by my side, and she'd had the presence of mind to find something I could vomit into. I got to my knees, and everything around me swirled. Thora supported me as I struggled to my feet. There were no tender words or motherly hands stroking my forehead, which I was grateful for.

"You're high as a kite."

"It's the worship." I tried to put one foot in front of the other, but my body refused to obey, and Thora ended up practically carrying me. She propped me up against the table.

"I stole something for you."

Hands shaking, afraid any movement would make me throw up again, I took the clothes she handed me. They were a little too big, but it was better than wearing the green dress. I tossed it on the floor in disgust. The boots Thora had nabbed were heavy and warm.

"And your coat."

"Isn't it yours?"

Thora gave me a crooked smile. "Not anymore."

I pulled the ragged coat tight around me.

"Tilarids has possessed Sverre," I said.

"Eskild's old sword?"

"Sverre has gone completely nuts."

"He's always been like that," Thora said. "I knew him in Sént, back when I was under house arrest, and he was an unpleasant boy. Now he's become an unpleasant man."

I shook my head. "It used to be a role he played. Now that's who he is."

"Or maybe it's part of his personality that Tilarids is taking advantage of. We all have faults and weaknesses. Before, Tilarids belonged to Eskild. I should have figured it out."

"What?"

"Eskild was also a fanatic, but he only worshipped Ragnara. He mellowed out after he gave Tilarids to Sverre."

"You could say it was a Trojan horse." For a second, I thought I might throw up again, but I managed to control my stomach. "I don't understand what Tilarids is up to. Ragnara was against Odin, so back then the sword was fighting *against* the All-Father."

"Maybe Tilarids just wants their dedication, regardless of who it's aimed at," Thora mused. "Eskild—"

"Mom," I said. "Serén and I can prevent Ragnarök."

My mother turned her head and raised an eyebrow. "How will you manage that?"

"The sources say the ravens must meet to change the course of time. The past and future must come together. I need you to take me to my sister."

Thora looked at me for a long time. "I wish you had grown up together. You two could have given one another so much. I wish . . ."

"Wish-smish." It took me a few seconds to make my voice calm again. "Where is Serén?"

"In Haraldsborg, but you can't meet. It's too dange—"

I ignored her and closed my eyes. *Serén*, I called.

Yes, Anna.

Did you know Sverre would go insane? I couldn't keep the accusatory tone out of my thoughts.

I was aware of the possibility, Serén admitted.

Can I help him?

Yes . . . but it will have horrible consequences.

Not for the first time, I considered how many potential future scenarios she always had to keep track of. I suddenly thought of the very first time I had seen the Ragnarök vision. Sverre had been there, and he told me to let him be consumed. He must have meant consumed by Tilarids.

I hope you don't see me as his queen.

Not too often, she whispered.

I scratched my forehead. *Help me get to you. We need to be together so we can stop Ragnarök.*

Anna . . . Serén sounded sad.

Come on. Send me and Mom there.

I'm pretty sure we can't be together. I've seen countless versions of the future, but we never succeed. Most of the time, we die. We explode or get thrown far away from each other. Occasionally, we're lucky, and only one of us dies.

But does it work? Do we stop Ragnarök?

No idea. I can't see beyond my own death.

This comment made my blood run cold. *We have to try.*

I've heard you say that in my visions, and . . .

The past and future must be brought together. The myths say so, I insisted.

If you're the past, and I'm the future, then together we create the present. But maybe there is no present! Maybe that's why it won't work.

What do you mean?

There's the future, and there's the past. The present is always shifting, so you can never really be in it, because it doesn't even exist, Serén said.

We came from the same egg, and we were together in the womb for almost nine months. Hejd had the ability to see both the past and the future, and she didn't explode. It occurred to me that I didn't actually know how Hejd had died one thousand years ago. *Let's try.*

Serén sighed inside my head. *If it goes wrong, I'm sending you back home.*

Fair enough.

I heard Serén breathe heavily with concentration, then something pulled at me. With both hands, I grabbed my mother and held her tight. The whooshing drowned out my voice, and it pulled even more forcefully.

"What are you doing?" Thora protested.

My sister cried out with effort, and I reached out for her with my mind. Then I lifted off the floor, and with my mother in tow, we barreled forward with unbelievable speed. We flew down the dark tunnel surrounded by stripes of light. As with every journey between the worlds, I was smushed and yanked from all sides. Thora screamed as she struggled to keep her grip on me. We were pulled directly into a stone chamber and landed on the floor with a crash.

Thora got to her feet.

I had been there before. In fact, it was the exact room where I had spent a night with Varnar, but there was no need to reveal that. I sensed an intense pressure against me. Serén was nearby. I propped myself up on my elbow at the same time Thora bent down toward me. Just then, the door flew open.

In the doorway stood my sister, Aella behind her. They both had wide eyes and held their arms out protectively in front of them against the pressure being created between Serén and me. When I finally had Serén right in front of me, I smiled. She returned it, but her expression changed to one of surprise as she shot backward. It was only because Aella was there to catch her that she didn't end up back out in the hallway.

I, too, was pushed back toward the wall. Along the way, I felt the uneven paving stones dig into my back. Then I was rolled onto my stomach. It took all my strength to get onto all fours and crawl toward my sister. Serén also fought her way forward to me, and I dug my nails into the floor to hold on.

"That's enough, future!" Serén's voice sounded like whistling steam, and I think she was yelling at her precognition in the same way I yelled at my retrocognition. "I will change you."

She held out her hands, and I did the same. Our fingers nearly touched, but we kept getting shoved backward.

"Help us," I shouted at Thora.

She knelt and put her arms around Serén's chest. It looked like she was shielding my sister with her own body. Aella stood over me and pulled, trying to get me across the last few inches to Serén. It was painful to be struck by the insurmountable current, but we were so close to each other.

"Come on, come on..."

The warmth of her skin fluttered against mine, and it felt like pressing my hand into a lump of clay.

Aella pulled so hard I feared I would tear in two. Serén cried out in pain as a hot blast pushed us apart. Finally, the very ends of our fingertips brushed against each other.

There was a bang, and I thought the subsequent explosion would rip my hand off.

I was flung far, far away. I landed in a bush and lifted my head, confused, in the warm sunlight.

In front of me was a head the size of Ben and Rebecca's VW bus.

CHAPTER 9

For a second, I thought it was the Midgard Serpent, but on closer inspection, I saw that the head was slightly smaller. The scaly skin was grayish brown, and there was a hint of orange in its reptilian eyes. Black, bushy feathers stuck out around the back of its head. In all, it stood over twenty feet tall and had small arms in front with sharp claws. Its back legs were each the size of a sectional sofa, and behind it, a thick tail extended into the green foliage.

I sat among tall fernlike plants, while large flying insects with metallic wings flitted around me, but my attention was focused on the monster a few yards away.

The animal blinked and sniffed. When it exhaled, I was struck by breath that stank of meat. A deep rumble caused the ground to vibrate.

At first, I was frozen in shock. What had happened? Where was I? *Serén*, I called desperately. *Where are you?*

She answered inside my head. *I'm floating in nothingness. There are stars and space, but no Earth. Far in the distance, there's a glowing red sun. Where are you?*

I backed away cautiously. *A better question would be* when *am I*. I quickly threw myself sideways, and the large animal leapt after me. When it set off, the ground shook beneath me. I crouched behind a large tree.

I can't breathe, Serén croaked.

Reach out, I commanded frantically. *We both need to get out.*

Everything's spinning. There's no up or down. Serén's voice was slurred. Terrified, I reached out mentally on my own, my sister unable to act. I held out my hand, and the ring on my finger flickered. Mathias's tears flared, and just when the dinosaur peered around the corner, a beam of light shot out from the flower-shaped ring. The animal jumped back, frightened, and its stamping feet made the ground shake.

Using all my powers, both physically and psychologically, I got ahold of Serén and pulled her back from the distant future. I was the one controlling us now, but suddenly, I couldn't feel her mind. My heart pounded. She had just said she'd seen one or both of us die in every version of the future where we tried to meet. Still clinging to the minimal spark I could catch from her, I fought my way back to the moment we had left Haraldsborg, where I plopped her down in Aella's arms.

In a floating, semi-dissolved state, I looked at my mother. "Come with me to Odinmont. Come home to Dad."

Thora looked back at me, shockingly calm. "I can't." She pressed her lips together. "Tell him I said hi."

"Dad is waiting for you."

"I have to find Eskild first. He has Odion, and I fear he'll give it to the giants."

"What's Odion?" I asked.

"The little figurine Ben and Rebecca had. Ragnara and Eskild stole it."

Oh, right. "What's so special about it?"

"I can't tell you, but it contains something dreadful. We need to get it back before anyone else can set it loose. I don't even dare think of the harm it could cause."

"I could send Arthur here so you can be together?"

"He needs to be there for you. We all have a role to play. Mine is to confront Eskild. Your father's is to support you."

"Ben and Rebecca don't believe Fimbulwinter is here."

"Tell them I'm certain. Tell them not to listen to the authorities!"

I landed in my bed in Odinmont. Arthur shouted in fear. He had been standing and looking out my bedroom window, but he quickly left his place and leaned over me.

"Where were you?" He plucked a fresh green fern frond from my hair and rolled it between his fingers.

I laid my head on the pillow, exhausted. "I didn't get hurt. Everyone's alive."

"Praise the gods," he exclaimed.

"I would prefer not to talk about the gods right now," I replied, motionless. As always, it took a minute for my soul to catch up to me after the journey between the worlds.

Arthur moved around anxiously. He had likely heard from Mathias that Thora had been on the brink of death. I ran a hand across my forehead at the thought of everything that had happened since I left the stone circle in Kraghede Forest.

"When is Thora coming?" Arthur looked at the vacant side of the double bed as though he expected Thora to plop down next to me any minute.

"She couldn't come back with me, but she says hi."

Arthur sucked in air. "She says *hi*? I haven't seen her in eighteen years, then she shows up in Midgard, dying, jets back to Hrafnheim to be healed, and she SAYS HI?"

I struggled onto my elbows, feeling like I weighed a ton. Whether that was because of the journey or the current circumstances, I wasn't sure.

"If you really want to know, I tried to get her to come back with me."

Arthur rubbed his face. "If she stayed, she must have a good reason. I just hoped she would come with you."

"You're a very forgiving man," I said, rising to sit on the edge of the bed. Arthur took my elbow to support me. "I'm okay." I just had to breathe. "Is Varnar still here?"

"He went back to Hrafnheim to help your mother, but he

wanted me to . . ." Arthur paused. "He wanted me to tell you he says hi."

A bitter laugh escaped my lips. "We sure know how to pick 'em, huh?"

Arthur shook his head and let go of my arm. "Can I get you anything?"

"Elias."

"What?"

"You can get Elias for me."

For a moment, Arthur studied me. The yellowish light made him look almost transparent, like the ghost version of himself. "Elias is downstairs."

I gave my father a sharp look. "What's he doing here?"

"He waited all night to hear if you were alive."

Elias sat in the living room at the large dining table. When he saw me, he stood up. "Anna."

"Did you know?" I walked toward him. If I had had more energy, I would have accused him or at least shouted at him, but I was so exhausted and sad, I could only give him a reproachful look.

"Where did you go?" was his reply.

"Sverresborg."

"Oh . . ."

"Yeah . . . oh."

Elias sat back down.

"What happened?" Arthur asked.

"Sverre has gone insane, or he's been possessed by Tilarids. Maybe both. The thing is, Elias didn't mention that."

Elias kept his eyes trained on the large crack in the tabletop. "I wasn't sure." He glanced up at me. "I had only heard rumors."

I folded my arms. "What do the rumors say? It's so typical that you know so much when not even DSMA has been informed that it's also winter in Hrafnheim."

"The king is becoming more religious every day, and he talks about you as though you're a saint. After Ragnara's death, he started an Odin cult. Or a warped version of an Odin cult. Everyone in Sverresborg has to honor a dead fingalk and a bloody dress."

I rested my forehead in my palm. "Both are from my journey with him."

"He thinks you're Odin's messenger, that everything about you is holy. Because you're Odin's völva, he thinks you can rule in both worlds with the blessing of both the gods and the king."

"I can't rule over anything." In fact, I had appallingly little control over anything at all.

"Isn't it enticing?" Elias's face was neutral, but his aura flickered excitedly. "Sverre is ready to make you his queen. With Tilarids on your side, the two of you could be invincible."

"And turn into Ragnara and Eskild version 2.0? No, thanks!" I crossed my arms. "Why didn't you tell me Sverre had gone crazy?"

"To be completely honest, I don't think it matters. It's not the first time in history that a man lost his mind."

I wanted to protest, but he had a point. "I guess, relative to the end of the world, Sverre's insanity is nothing special."

"But the world isn't ending," Arthur objected. "Niels says . . ."

I looked at him, exasperated. "Mom said to tell you she also thinks this is Fimbul. Niels and the prime minister just don't see it."

"You shouldn't talk about them like that."

"It was Thora who said it."

Arthur laughed, despite the grim subject. "That sounds like her. We'll talk to Ben tomorrow. He's gone to Copenhagen to speak with the prime minister and Mardöll. They're considering hypnotizing the public again, but if you and Thora are right, the gods will need the people's devotion to fight. In that case, it would be best not to enchant the population. Existential angst is a great way to make people more god-fearing."

"If Odin's ravens meet, they can also change time, but I can't get close enough to Serén. Our clairvoyant abilities are connected. I don't know what's getting in our way."

Elias looked up. "So, it didn't work?"

"Apparently not." I gestured at the snowdrifts outside.

Elias cursed. "Maybe it's about time—"

"About time for what? And why didn't it work when I tried to meet my sister?"

"I think you're the one with something wrong. Not Serén."

I threw up my hands. "Of course there's something wrong with me. That's abundantly clear. But you and Brenda already treated my stress. Serén said something about the present always shifting, but it's not normal to get sent from the present back to the time of the dinosaurs."

"I think the spells Ben placed on you are pushing you away from one another." Elias looked down. "I've always thought so."

"What about the spells?"

"It's because of them that you can't get close to Serén. They keep you from coming together because it's repulsion magic. I thought stress treatment might help because Ben's magic is like a blockade in your mind."

"Elias! The whole thing about stress was a lie?"

Elias had enough grace to look a little ashamed. "I was certain your lack of contact had something to do with overexertion, and I hoped the repulsion magic could be treated in the same way. I took a chance, and if the treatment didn't work, no harm would come of it. With all your wild adventures, I figured you could use a little relaxation. That's how doctors always approach things. You start with the least dangerous course of treatment, even if it might not work. And you did get rid of Hel in your subconscious. That's a positive."

I wavered between rejoicing and yelling at Elias, and I ended up going with the former. "Finally, a problem with an easy solution."

The next day, Ben would return from Copenhagen, and he

would lift the spells so I could unite with my sister and stop this madness.

That night, I dreamed of Ragnarök again. I stood on the red field in the fog as the stench of burnt flesh billowed over me. I heard the heartbreaking sound of people and animals screaming along with squishing sounds of which I didn't even want to know the source.

I stumbled around in the mist. I kept tripping over bodies on the ground, and in my confused dream state, I turned them all over to see if they were my loved ones.

"Völva," Hejd's voice called out. "It's hard for me to reach you."

"Hey," I shouted. "Show yourself."

"I don't have a body anymore."

"Lucky you!"

The fog cleared slightly, and I saw Sverre in front of me. Thunder rumbled in the distance, and electric flashes flickered from the clouds. The sky was a leaden gray, with large spirals of cloud. Sverre looked like himself, albeit a more desperate version. He wasn't holding Tilarids.

"Anna." His brown eyes searched the scene. "This is your doing. This is your fault."

The mist enveloped him, and I spotted Arthur, who was fighting against flapping fingalks and a corpse-swallower. Just then, my foot slipped in something, and I teetered, close to falling. I looked down and leapt backward with a shriek. My mother was lying on the ground, her chest ripped open. This time, not even a hundred healers could have saved her.

Loki, half naked and enormous, approached with footsteps so forceful the ground shook. Behind him stood his children: Hel, the Midgard Serpent, and Fenrir, all gigantic and terrifying.

Loki's flaming sword was raised over his head. In front of him, Od stood expectantly. This time, I could hear what Loki was saying. His voice was sharp enough to cut through flesh.

"Apparently, the sons of gods are popular sacrifices."

Od said nothing. He simply dropped his weapons.

"Oooohh . . . you're sacrificing yourself. Even better." Loki snaked his way across the battlefield. In a strange way, I could see the family resemblance between him and the Midgard Serpent. When he howled at the sky, he also resembled the wolf Fenrir.

Od's face was blank. He knelt, exposing the back of his neck.

"You can rebel," Loki cajoled him. "Go against your father. You can reemerge as the new god."

Od kept his eyes trained on the slushy ground.

"All right." Loki shrugged. "You're following your father's unreasonable orders. Suit yourself." He raised the flaming sword.

Od sat completely still, like a sacrificial lamb that had accepted its fate. Loki held the sword over his head. Flames encircled it and made it smolder. I caught a glimpse of runes down the blade.

Shocked, I inhaled sharply, but the smoke made me cough. "What are you doing in my dream?"

The sword didn't reply; instead, it whizzed toward Od's neck, led by Loki's hands. Od's head was separated from his body and rolled toward me. I stared at Loki's hands. Even when Od's disembodied head hit my foot, I didn't look down at it.

The sword smoldered red and black.

"What are you doing with Loki, you horrible piece of iron?"

I had gotten the sword's attention, and it flared. Inside my head—or perhaps aloud, across the battlefield—there was a drawn-out howl. Loki's face turned upward, and he looked around. For a bone-chilling moment, his gray eyes caught me in their gaze. He bared his teeth and started to run toward me. He picked up more speed with every stride. I tried to move backward, but I fell over my mother's body.

"Völva," Loki hissed when he got closer. "Raven! You cannot destroy my . . ."

I didn't hear what it was that I couldn't destroy, because now

Loki was right in front of me. His head was the size of a church bell, and his voice was just as loud and hollow. He swung the flaming sword toward me, screaming wildly.

I woke with a start and sat up in bed. I instinctively rolled out onto the floor, and as though the dream were continuing, I heard a metallic *ziiiing* as heat flicked at my neck.

Then it was quiet in the room. It was ice-cold, with no sound but the incessant wind outside. But the image was burned into my retinas, and it wasn't Loki's furious eyes and giant head I saw.

"Tilarids," I whispered. My heart was pounding, and I sat down on the bed. Tilarids would become Loki's sword in the future. Maybe it had always been his. I rubbed my face.

Someone cleared their throat, and I yelped, startled. There was no light in the room, so I couldn't see who was there. Out of habit, I reached out with my clairvoyance but didn't detect anything. The sound came from a corner. Cautiously, I tiptoed toward it. On the way, I fumbled for Auka, even though I had a feeling the axe wouldn't be able to help me.

"Who's there?"

"If it's real, it will never be over," someone mumbled. The words were repeated. "If it's real, it will never be over, never be over, never be over."

I stiffened; these had been the final words spoken to me by someone now dead. Only he and I knew about that conversation.

"Hakim?"

"Anna!" His voice was cautious.

I knelt, and a profound feeling of joy filled my chest. It was enough to make the giant crystal begin to glow on my nightstand. I could now make out the cowering figure. Hakim's ghost looked up at me. His familiar green eyes sparkled.

"You're here," I said, exhaling. "Everyone says it's impossible for us to see each other because of our different faiths, but I knew we could make it happen."

Hakim flashed the smile that had always turned girls' heads, but he remained seated on the floor. The giant crystal flickered, but even in the unsteady light, I could see that his contours were blurry. "You made it happen. I've never met anyone who can break the rules like you."

This comment made me smile, too.

"I'm still weak," he whispered.

"But you're here." I sat on my knees and held out my hands. "And me seeing you will make you stronger, Hakim." I repeated his name deliberately, as I knew the dead benefited from being named.

"I can barely remember anything." He was trembling. "Apart from you. You're so clear." Carefully, he reached toward me but stopped just before his transparent hands met mine. "I'm not solid."

It was cold on the floor, but I sat and pulled my knees up to my chest. I placed my hands firmly in his, even though I couldn't feel them. "I can make you stronger."

His hands vibrated.

"I can already feel you a little more." I scooted closer. "You're here, Hakim. You were a good police officer, which means a lot coming from me because I really don't have a good relationship with the police."

The corners of Hakim's mouth pulled back, and again, I felt his palms a little more solidly. All I had to do was talk about who he was when he was alive, and he would get even stronger.

"You were my good friend: you're smart and you're loyal." I switched to the present tense because Hakim was still all those things, even though he was dead. With every word, I felt him a little more. Finally, his outline was almost fully defined.

"It's wonderful that you're here, but what are you doing here?"

"I came to help you. You live so dangerously."

I laid my cheek tentatively on the back of his hand. He reached out his hand and caressed my cheek, even though he was just as reticent as when he was alive.

"Get into bed," Hakim said sternly. "You'll catch a cold."

I couldn't help but laugh since, compared to Hakim, I was in very good health. "I won't be able to sleep more tonight." I stood up and walked toward the bed anyway.

"Why not?" Hakim's spirit looked at me without blinking until I was back under the covers. He sat at the foot of the bed.

"I have nightmares," I said lamely, quickly waving my hand. "It's nothing." I had an incredibly strong urge to ask Hakim about the night he died. Who had killed him? But it would send him back to his earthly remains if I brought up the subject of his death, especially now when he was still so weak.

"Close your eyes. I'm here." He laid a hand on my leg, and I felt a slight pressure through the duvet. I actually did relax quite a bit, and I breathed deeply.

"I don't dare close my eyes."

"You won't have any more bad dreams tonight."

"I'm afraid you'll disappear when I fall asleep."

"I'll stay here," Hakim promised.

I obeyed. The crystal warmed the room, Hakim was back, and tomorrow, I would have my much-despised spells lifted.

For the first time in a long time, I slept undisturbed the rest of the night with Hakim's ghost watching over me.

CHAPTER 10

The orange VW bus was parked in front of Rebecca and Ben's house when Arthur and I came tramping down from Odinmont. To be honest, I was surprised that the vintage car had made it to Copenhagen and back in one piece. Judging from the paint color and the interior's brown upholstery, it had been manufactured sometime in the 1970s.

The snowdrifts were so high, we brought a shovel to dig ourselves out when we got stuck. Luna came running from the front door and embraced us. Behind her stood Mathias. He looked normal again, although his eyes flickered a bit more intensely than usual.

"Thank you for helping my wife," Arthur said seriously. He held something out to my friend and knelt.

I looked closer. It was a handful of dried apricots. I cleared my throat, embarrassed to see my father crouched in front of Mathias, who started breathing faster as he took the apricots. He placed his free hand on Arthur's shoulder. It was so formal that I had to look away, even though no one else seemed embarrassed. Arthur got to his feet, and Mathias gave him the apricots back.

"You don't want them?" I whispered to him.

"Your father offered them to me, so I no longer need them."

Ben came up to us. His ankle-length reindeer pelt was decorated with beads and feathers, the skin pale gray. His Cossack hat was made of dark fur.

"Did you take care of your business with Niels and what's-her-name?"

"Mardöll." Ben breathed warm air into his fists, and when he flexed his fingers, I saw his tattoos. The blue symbols contrasted with the lighter skin of his palms.

"Do you know where I was?" I asked.

Ben glanced at Mathias. "I do."

"Could it be true that my spells are connected to Serén's clairvoyance, and that's what is keeping us from coming together?"

Ben furrowed his brows. "Those spells have kept you alive."

"Are there side effects?"

Ben looked down. "As long as you have them, you can't be united with your sister. But it's dangerous to remove them."

"Benedict," Arthur interjected. "You knew as well as the rest of us that this was coming sooner or later." He laid a hand on Ben's arm. "Fimbul is here, and Ragnarök will follow unless we do something."

"We don't know for sure that this is Fimbul."

"It's winter in Hrafnheim, too. There's no other explanation." Arthur patted Ben on the back.

Ben seemed to take a moment to process that information. "What do we do?"

"My daughters have a plan." Arthur struggled to conceal his pride. "They need to meet so they can change time."

"You put the spells on me to protect me against Ragnara, but she's dead, so they don't serve a purpose anymore," I said.

Ben looked desperate. "I advise you to leave them alone."

"You're probably right, but I'm an adult now. It's my choice."

"You should lift the magic, Benedict," Rebecca said gently. "If you and Mardöll stop hypnotizing people, panic will break out. People will react poorly to her spells under the influence of mass hysteria."

This convinced Ben. "This will be a new life for you, Anna. You haven't known anything different. Are you prepared for this?"

I smiled tentatively. "I doubt I ever will be. I don't know what to expect."

"You won't feel much. It's a minor procedure." He sounded like a surgeon.

I shivered, thinking of the time Védis tried to lift the spells. It had felt like she was trying to tear my ribs out of my body. "I hope you're a bit gentler with your approach than Védis was."

"I'm more concerned about your life afterward."

I thought it sounded nice to be free from being either ignored or outright hated.

"This is a big day. While Ben lifts the spells, I'll prepare a feast. I'll use the last of our rations." Rebecca stroked my hair.

"Let's go inside." Ben led me into the house with a firm grip on my shoulder. He really was strong. We walked up to the green bedroom in a ceremonial procession. The choice to walk in single file had more to do with the narrow stairs than the occasion, but that didn't stop a solemn atmosphere from settling over us.

Inside the room, I lay down on the mattress, and Ben positioned himself behind me, his hands under my head. Rebecca lit a stubby candle and sprinkled something into the flame. The smell of sandalwood and musk spread through the room.

"Anna and I need to be alone," Ben said.

Luna jumped and clapped. "Yaaay! I'm so excited. We can stand at the bar together. We can go out . . ." She composed herself and pressed her lips together, though this couldn't suppress her supercharged smile. With clenched fists, she skipped all the way to the door, which she closed behind her.

Alone in the room with Ben, my heart began to pound. The smoke pulsated around us, and Ben's large hands were warm. The symbols on his palms heated the back of my head. I felt like a patient on an operating table, half excited to get a years-long problem fixed but also wanting to run away screaming before someone could sink a scalpel into my flesh. Ben chanted and pressed his fingers into my head.

"We'll start now." Ben had a good grip on me.

"I'd like to say something first," I rasped.

"What?"

"These spells have saved my life several times. Many times, in fact."

"Should we leave them?"

"No," I said quickly. "It's time to remove them. It's just . . ."

"You're welcome," he said. There was a smile in his voice, and I was silent, glad to have been spared from saying thank you. The spells had created so many problems in my life that those little words were impossible to get across my lips.

"*Ti o bẹrẹ.*" At first, Ben's voice was so low, I couldn't hear the individual words, but as it grew louder, I realized I couldn't understand because he was chanting in an African language. Yoruba, probably. "*Isakoṣo latọna jijin. Ajẹ. Idaabobo ko.*" He dragged out the vowels so each word lasted several seconds.

I breathed in slowly and exhaled into the scented air, one hand clenched into a fist. To distract myself, I ran my fingertips across my large ring made from Mathias's tears. On the back of my head, Ben's hands grew warmer and warmer, and he sang himself deeper into the magic. Just like when Védis tried to remove the spells, I felt something pulling on me. My whole skeleton creaked, and though I fought to lie still, my body shook with involuntary jerks.

"*Awọn tu,*" Ben bellowed loudly. "*Awoooooooooon. Fréttatilkynning og losunar.*" His hands were blazing hot, and I could smell burnt hair. I might come out of this with a bald spot on the back of my head or my hair completely fried, but it would be worth it.

A crunching sound echoed inside my head, and I knew it must be coming from me. The spells must be really stuck inside me. Ben's hands had moved and now encircled my neck. The heat was so intense, I would surely come out of this with burn marks, but I forced myself to lie there.

Through our close contact, I was able to see Ben's past. It stretched far back in time, showing hot, dry savannas mixed with the fertile, chilly north. Chains rattled around Ben's wrists and ankles, and I sensed a weight around his neck, presumably from an iron collar. A young Rebecca flickered past, Luna as a baby, and Arthur arm in arm with Thora. The whole time, I felt Ben's chains around my neck. He must live with a constant remembrance that he had once been a slave. The collar tightened, and I realized it wasn't the chains of the past I was feeling. It was very much the present, and it was Ben's hands around my neck, squeezing. My airflow was being cut off. Panicked, I brought my fingers to his and tried to wrench them away, but he was far too strong. I felt a strange vibe coming from him. Aura-wise, he felt like a completely different person.

"Ben," I tried to say, but it came out as a little *pffff*. I rolled around, but with my neck held fast in Ben's powerful grip, I only managed a few awkward twists of my body. I was able to tilt my head back and saw Ben's face.

His eyes were half open, and red light shone from them. His lips were parted, but behind them, his white teeth were gritted as though he were in battle.

"Help," I hissed, but hardly any sound came out. My father, a demigod, and two powerful witches were sitting downstairs and chatting while I fought for my life. I knew I had no chance of twisting myself free, and several valuable seconds had already passed.

From my training with Varnar, I knew I had one, maybe two heartbeats left before I lost consciousness. Resolutely, I lifted my ring-adorned hand over my head and hammered it into Ben's chest. The stone glowed green. At first, Ben merely trembled, but his hands loosened their grip ever so slightly. Again and again, I pounded my fist into him. Eventually, the green crystal tears were covered in both Ben's blood and my own. He finally let go, and I turned over onto my stomach with my hand held out in front of me.

Ben's eyes were open, but the light that emanated from them was now pink. I could see that he was fighting an internal battle, but whether he was trying to hold back or throw himself at me, I wasn't sure.

"Landráð," he roared.

My ring shot out energy, and both it and I were surrounded by a flickering shield. In response, magic flowed from Ben's fingers. It shot directly toward me but bounced off.

"*Da awǫn,*" Ben hissed. "*Da awǫn. Landráð.*" He cast another spell, which my ring flung right back at him. The magic crackled and surrounded him. He shouted something, which turned into an animalistic scream. Ben turned his face to the ceiling, and there was a crash that made the walls shake.

His torso exploded open as though there were a bomb in his chest.

Fire shot out of him, and he crackled. It looked like a vase being dropped on the floor. Then he sank sideways and landed in a thundering heap. His body caught fire, and within a few seconds, he was engulfed in flames.

I knew that witches were flammable, but I had never imagined it would go so quickly. I tried to put out the blaze with a thick blanket, but in a violent torrent of flames, he was quickly turned to ash.

I lifted the blanket and saw that there was nothing left of Ben but a scorched spot and some cinders. Confused and horrified, I lowered my hands.

The door swung open, and the four others rushed in. Rebecca screamed when she saw what lay on the floor, Luna buried her face in Mathias's chest, and Arthur stared at me instead of the appalling sight.

PART II
THE HORN OF HEIMDALL

She knows of the horn of Heimdall
Under the high-reaching holy tree
On it there pours from Valfather's pledge
A mighty stream
Would you know yet more?

Völuspá, 10th century

CHAPTER 11

I sat on the bed, rocking back and forth. My dad had wrapped the duvet around me, but I was still freezing. Downstairs, I could hear Rebecca and Luna crying beneath Mathias's low voice, but it didn't fully sink in what was happening. Before me was a burnt spot in the shape of a human. Small piles of ash resembled miniature sand dunes. Ripples snaked across the fine dust, and it was unfathomable that, just a little while ago, that had been Ben.

At first, there had been chaos. The women chanted spells, and Arthur begged Odin and Týr for help. Those were the gods Ben worshipped. Finally, in desperation, Arthur called out to Freyja, but she didn't bother to respond to her ex-boyfriend's prayers.

I knew it was futile to ask the gods for help because I had felt the sharp pop of a soul leaving its body when Ben exploded. It wasn't the first time I had seen someone die, and I knew for certain he was gone.

"What?" I raised my head and interrupted Arthur, who was apparently in the middle of a sentence.

"Can you tell me what happened?" Arthur spoke clearly, trying to get through to me.

Before I could respond, another voice cut through the room. "Was it you?"

I hadn't noticed Rebecca in the doorway. She squeezed the doorframe and stared at me with a look I had not been on the receiving end of before. The otherwise gentle woman was capable of being very scary. Her eyes were bloodshot, and bewilderment had settled over her face like a dark shadow. I could physically feel her misery.

"I'm only going to ask you once, Anna Stella Sakarias," she said slowly. "Did you kill him?"

"I don't think so," I said cautiously. "I'm not in control of my völva powers, but I don't think they're strong enough to blow someone up. Especially not a powerful sorcerer like Ben."

Rebecca squeezed the doorframe even harder when I said his name.

"What happened?" It was Arthur who, despite it all, had enough presence of mind to ask again.

"In a way, Ben killed himself. The magic he threw at me bounced back onto him."

Rebecca gasped. "Did he cast harmful magic on you?"

"It sure wasn't friendly." At the thought of Ben's choke hold, I raised my hand to my throat. Something stung between my collarbones. Arthur leaned forward to study my neck.

"Your khamsa necklace is gone. It's been vaporized." He looked at Rebecca. "What she's saying is true. She's been burned."

Rebecca released her grip on the doorframe and came over to me.

"That was the last memento I had of Hakim," I whispered. It was stupid to get upset over a piece of jewelry when Ben had just died, but everything felt so hopeless.

Arthur stood and eased a mirror down from the wall. He held it in front of me, and I saw that the silver pendant symbol—a hand—was printed directly into the thin skin of my neck.

"Hakim's totem is with you forever."

For whatever reason, this statement punched a hole through my numbness, and my lower lip began to tremble. I closed my eyes and felt Rebecca's arms around me.

"I'm so sorry," I whispered into her ear. I couldn't bear knowing that another person was dead because of me.

She held me at arm's length with a sharp expression. "It wasn't your fault. I'm going to find out who did this."

"Is he still here?" Arthur asked.

"As a ghost?" I reached out mentally, but there were no spirits. Then I called out loud. "Benedict?" I cleared my throat. "As a völva, I command you to come here. In Týr's and Odin's names." I had to shake my head apologetically. "He's not here."

"And he's not coming back." It was Rebecca who spoke.

"You're a seid-woman, and I can see the past. Maybe together we can—"

"He never renounced his Yoruba religion, even though he started worshipping the Norse gods when he came to Denmark. The Yoruba believe in reincarnation. Death will send him to a new body. His soul is already looking for a life conceived at the same time as his death." She looked down. I got the sense that this had been a subject of discussion between them because it meant eternal separation after death.

Arthur took her hand. "I won't leave you."

Suddenly, Rebecca looked very tired. "You did leave me, actually. For eighteen years."

"Ben said something right before he . . ." I couldn't finish the sentence.

Arthur and Rebecca were still holding each other's hands.

"What did he say?"

"*Landráð*. But I don't know Yoruba."

"It's Old Norse," Rebecca said.

"What does it mean?"

Arthur's and Rebecca's eyes met. Some time passed before my father spoke.

"It means *traitor*," he said. "Ben's final message to us was that someone had betrayed us."

What should have been a feast to celebrate my spells being lifted had turned into a wake. There wasn't a whole lot of food, but in relation to the scarcity we were living with, it was a big meal. I was racked with guilt. I found it strange that we were just sitting here when the world was ending.

As if Rebecca had heard my thoughts, she gave me a stern look. "Since ancient times, people have taken the time to grieve for lost loved ones, even amid the worst crises."

Luna looked gray. She hung from Mathias like a limp rag. He kept his arm around her at all times. Od arrived and gave Rebecca a long embrace. She sobbed into his shoulder, and through my clairvoyance, I saw how he poured divinity into her.

Od disappeared upstairs and returned with a clay pot. It was decorated with runes and animals, and there was a lid on top. It evidently held Ben's earthly remains, of which there weren't a lot. Rebecca carried her large basket and held her seid staff in the other hand. As a group, we stumbled across the snow-covered field to my house. At the edge of the forest, I spotted a figure. He had big curls, and his sorrow reached me despite the distance. Elias didn't join us, but he said goodbye to Ben in his own way.

In Odinmont's living room, Arthur pushed the bench aside. We crawled into the mound beneath the house on our hands and knees. When we were finally inside the crypt, we filled the entire space. My father relaxed down there, surrounded by all the skeletons. He leaned against the stone table where he had spent eighteen years as a corpse. Atop it lay a blanket and a pillow. It did, in fact, feel very safe and homey. I understood his choice of hideout.

Rebecca laid a swan's wing on one of the shelves. She had brought it with her in her large basket. She smoothed all the snow-white feathers, then carefully placed the clay pot on top. She bent forward, kissed the side of the pot, and rested her forehead against it as she whispered. Then she stood back up.

"Benedict Kehinde Sekibo," she said, holding her staff. Her face was even paler than usual. An eerie calm surrounded her, though I sensed that just beneath the surface, her mind was in tumult. "You are my beloved. You are my best friend." She inhaled deeply. "You lived a long life, and you were a brave man, an indomitable fighter, a talented sorcerer, and a fantastic father."

When Rebecca said these last words, Luna sobbed. Mathias held her, and his eyes, too, were shiny. Two green gemstone tears fell from them and landed on the dusty floor.

Rebecca managed to continue. "We place you to rest on the wing of a bird so you can fly to the realm of the dead. But I know that you have already left. Obatala came to get you, and together you are looking for a new life you can inhabit as it forms in the womb. You did not complete your mission, and I know you well. You will find a way to come back to fulfill your duty. I only hope that you also find me again. Farewell, my love."

Od stepped forward. His voice hit me like a hot wind.

"Benedict Kehinde Sekibo." He closed his eyes. "Ben. You were a good friend and an impressive sorcerer. If you are wandering as a spirit, come find me."

Luna sprinkled dried flowers over the bird's wing. "My teacher, my source, and my rock in life."

When the others looked at me, I shook my head. I had no words suitable for this solemn funeral.

When there was nothing left to say, everyone crawled out except Arthur, who remained in the crypt, presumably to have a personal talk with Ben. Od took off running toward Kraghede Forest. Rebecca, Luna, and Mathias walked back, and I sat at the large dining table in Odinmont's living room. I felt deflated. It grew dark, and the temperature dropped, but I sat in the shadows and listened to the wind blowing. A green glow flickered in the kitchen. It was Mathias, and he was walking toward me.

"Shouldn't you be with Luna?" I asked.

"She's asleep." He reached the living room. He pulled out a chair and sat at the table. "Now I'm here for you." Heat shot toward me, and his mere presence warmed my stiff limbs.

I noticed Mathias's glowing, bare torso. "Why aren't you wearing a shirt? It's below freezing outside."

"I'm never cold."

"For my sake, then. It's a little . . ." I held my hand over my eyes to shield them from the sight of half-naked Mathias, who was becoming more and more godly to look at. I had also noticed from being around Od that demigods had a very laid-back approach to being undressed, but that didn't stop me from feeling a little embarrassed.

"Luna needed to be comforted," he explained. "As soon as she fell asleep, I rushed over here. I didn't take the time to put clothes on."

"Thanks."

"What do you think happened?"

"It was like . . ." I searched for the right word. "Ben was booby-trapped. The bomb went off when he reached for his magic."

Mathias leaned back in the dining chair. It creaked under his weight, but it held. "Is there a connection to the fact that he was trying to lift your spells?"

"It was triggered the second he tried to remove them."

"And he tried to kill you?"

My hand flew to my burned neck. "Basically, but I think he was fighting against it. It was like he was possessed, but he was trying not to hurt me."

"Who wanted Ben dead?"

"Ragnara, but she's dead. Maybe Eskild. He also tried to kill Thora."

"Is there anyone who would stand to benefit from your spells not being lifted?"

It had crossed my mind, though of course I hadn't said it aloud, that with Ben dead, no one could remove my spells.

"If Serén and I can't come together, then we can't stop Ragnarök. Not that way, at least."

"Maybe the real intent was to destroy your plan."

"You think someone wants to keep me and Serén from meeting?"

Dots of blue light danced on the table, and after a moment, I realized they came from Mathias's eyes, as if they were laser pointers. "If *someone* is willing to kill Ben to keep you and Serén from meeting, you must be close to stopping Ragnarök. You can't trust anyone."

Maybe there was one person I could trust.

"You know something." I stared at Elias without blinking.

"Of course I do! I'm over four hundred years old. I know a lot. In fact, I would say that, aside from the higher powers, I'm the one who knows the most."

I waved my hand dismissively. "You're overestimating yourself."

"I *never* overestimate myself." He winked.

We stood in his driveway. He turned back to the snow he had been clearing when I'd come careening up on my bike. He tossed a shovelful of snow onto a white pile. With trembling hands, I clutched the handlebars. The temperature had dropped overnight, and the ride to Store Vildmose had been freezing.

"When I came home from Hrafnheim, you said it was time to explore other avenues, and I'm not sure you meant my spells. The only other thing I can think of is that Odion figurine everyone keeps talking about."

Elias stiffened, holding the shovel midair.

"Why is the Odion figurine important?"

He shoveled snow onto the pile and plunged the shovel's blade into a snowdrift, leaned against the wooden handle, and brushed his unruly curls away with a leather-gloved hand. His hair had gotten longer, I noticed.

"Odion is important for several reasons." He drummed his fingers on the shovel's handle.

"What do you want in exchange for telling me what you know?" I sighed.

Elias ran his hand down the wooden handle as though to smooth it. "Are you keeping your last promise to trust me?"

"This is me trusting you," I said. "Can't you see that?" In fact, that was the reason I had come to see Elias at all.

He took a step away from the shovel. "Let's go inside."

"Say it here." I couldn't shake the feeling that I'd be walking into the lion's den if I went with him.

"Your lips are turning blue," Elias said.

"So?"

"It'd be impractical to get frostbite on your mouth. Then you couldn't whisper dirty secrets to me."

"Just tell me: What's your price?" I said impatiently.

"Your dirty secrets."

"Ughh . . . I don't have any," I said brusquely, earning another satisfied smile.

"Then I'll be content with your other secrets."

"Can you be a little more specific?" My lips were tingling, and I wondered if they could freeze together.

"Tell me what happened with Benedict." His typical flirty expression dissolved into bottomless sadness. Elias was more upset by Ben's death than he wanted to let on. I nodded, and Elias didn't say anything else. He stretched his hand toward his front door to indicate I should go in.

Elias's home was as I remembered it. The house had low ceilings, it was simply and cozily decorated, and the living room was stuffed with shelf after shelf of books. The spicy scent I associated with him was even stronger inside. It came from the production of his many concoctions. He pulled out a bottle of alcohol. The bottle and the liquid inside were transparent but filled with leaves and herbs.

"Last I checked, it was strictly prohibited to make your own spirits," I said, nevertheless accepting the glass he held out to me. I pulled off my hat and laid it on the table, along with my gloves and scarf. The first sip made me cough, and I sat down on a dining chair with a thump. The drink tasted like herb schnapps but much stronger. It warmed me all the way down to my toes, and a faint tickling sensation reminded me of consuming laekna, though not quite as strong.

Elias laughed. "Guðlega is left over when I make laekna, so it doesn't really count. Should I just throw it out? Then I'd risk the giants taking it and using it as liquid courage for Ragnarök."

"I'm surprised you believe in folklore." I took another sip, and this time, I could appreciate the bubbly sensation and the flavor of rosemary and thyme. "But it would undeniably be a shame to waste it."

He poured guðlega for himself. "Divine," he said, raising the glass in a toast. "I'm making more. A lot more."

"More alcohol?"

"More laekna. It was awful to see Thora in that state and not be able to help. As a doctor, it's heartrending to be unable to save a dying person."

I looked down at the table. "That's how the rest of us feel all the time."

"I'm working to produce large quantities of laekna so we won't go through that again. In fact, I took so much blood from Od that he's gone to Valhalla to regenerate."

"Why is Odion important?"

Elias swirled his glass, and the liquid lapped up the sides. He studied the streaks it left behind and looked thoughtfully out his living room window. The wind was blowing, and a new bout of snowfall swept in, undoing all his work clearing his driveway.

She knows of the horn of Heimdall
Under the high-reaching holy tree

> *On it there pours from Valfather's pledge*
> *A mighty stream*
> *Would you know yet more?*

It was Elias who spoke the words, but Hejd's voice rang in my head. Everything spun around me, and the ring on my hand glowed faintly.

"Who is 'she'?" I asked, once I was capable of speech again.

"I don't know. Maybe it's Hejd; maybe it's you."

I leaned back in my chair. "Me? I don't even know *what* Heimdall's horn is, so how would I know *where* it is?"

"Heimdall's horn is the Gjallarhorn. He has to blow it for the gods to come to Ragnarök." He continued when I gave him a blank look. "Most of the gods are asleep, but when Heimdall blows the Gjallarhorn, they wake up and come to the battle. The problem is that the horn is gone."

I ran a hand across my forehead. "But we don't want Ragnarök to happen. They should just keep sleeping. Luna says that if there aren't any gods, they can't meet their fate. It's actually a pretty good way to avoid doomsday."

Elias poured another glass and drank the whole thing in one gulp. It was so strong, he needed a second to recover. "Brrrrr," he said before he could speak again. "Odin created the Gjallarhorn to ensure that he has backup when Ragnarök one day occurs, but it's a double-edged sword. If the giants get ahold of the horn, they can force Heimdall to blow it, thereby starting Ragnarök."

"So, the giants can't get ahold of the horn." I furrowed my brow. "But what does that have to do with the Odion figurine?"

Elias cleared his throat uncomfortably. "They're already collecting it."

"Collecting?"

He looked down into his glass.

"Elias!"

"The Gjallarhorn was found by regular people, and they put it on display. It was safe, but then it got stolen, and some of it got melted down."

I opened my mouth. "Wait . . . Are you talking about the Golden Horns of Gallehus?" I remembered learning about the theft of the ancient horns in history class.

"Only one of them. The other is plain gold. Or it *was*, I should say, because it's gone. Melted down and sold as coins and jewelry. But it wasn't magical." His words sounded like a defense.

For a moment, I studied him. Then I smacked my hands on the table. "Were you the one who stole the horns?"

Elias writhed in his chair. "I could never do something like that. Not myself." This last bit was muttered toward the table.

My lips formed several words, but nothing came out at first. "You outsourced the theft of Denmark's national treasure."

"Both horns were sitting out in the open," he protested. "The giants could have just waltzed right into the Royal Art Museum. My plan was to destroy it so it could never be used to start Ragnarök. I thought it would change fate."

"When was this?"

"1802." Elias looked down, his soft curls concealing his face. "Unfortunately, the thief didn't keep his end of our agreement. I had promised him the other horn as payment, but he destroyed the Gjallarhorn, too, dividing it into four pieces."

"Were the gods involved?"

"Odin took a piece, Od nabbed one, and Benedict got ahold of a tiny flake of gold. With some help, I was able to secure the largest piece of the Gjallarhorn."

"Where is it?"

"It's hidden."

I pinched the bridge of my nose with my thumb and index finger. "What will it take for you to tell me where you hid the largest piece?"

Elias placed his hand under his chin and smiled deviously. "You finding the other three pieces."

I let go of my nose. "Can I keep them once I've found them?"

"They just need to be found. Then we'll take it from there."

"Great," I said reluctantly. I gestured with my hand for him to continue.

"Odin hid his piece in Valaskjálf."

"What's that?"

"Odin's private quarters."

"Seriously? In Valhalla?" Of course it would be in such a difficult place. Typical. "Where are the other two pieces?"

"When your father died, Freyja cried red gemstones. Od set them in his gold, and then gifted the piece of jewelry to your mother."

"Oh . . ."

"You wore it to the Equinox Ball two years ago. Do you still have it?" Elias asked hopefully.

"I took it to Hrafnheim."

Elias paled. "Did you lose it?"

"In a way. Védis has it."

Elias rubbed his forehead. "The witch? She's unpredictable."

"I know, but at least we have a general idea of where she is. Besides, she's mainly interested in Freyja's tears, and she can keep those for all I care."

Elias raised an eyebrow.

"The third piece?" I asked.

"Guess."

I set my elbows on the table and dug my fingers into my hair, letting my head fall heavily in my hands. "It's in the Odion figurine."

"Bingo."

"I could just destroy one of the pieces. That's a lot simpler than getting ahold of all four."

"No!" Elias's outburst was so loud, I jumped. "The pieces must be brought together. Only then can it be destroyed with a god's breath."

"What if, theoretically, I manage to get all four pieces? Do I just slap them together with superglue?"

"It's magical gold. Only an Ulfberht smith can weld it back together."

"I remember you mentioning Ulfberht before. Who is he?"

"It's not a specific person, it's a type of metalsmith. Tilarids is an Ulfberht sword. To my knowledge, there's only one Ulfberht smith left, but I don't know where he is."

"Oh, this'll be a piece of cake. We just have to get all the pieces, have an Ulfberht guy weld the horn together, and then destroy it again."

"I have no idea how to handle this," I admitted.

Hakim, who had regained a bit more strength, looked at me. The world outside my window was deep-frozen, and the wind shook the trees. He had listened to my story about the Golden Horns of Gallehus—one of which was actually a magical, mythological instrument. He let me finish, nodding slowly.

"Why you?" was all he asked when I was done. "Why do you, in particular, have to go through all this danger to save the world?"

My finger traced a seam on the duvet cover. "So many people have died." I looked up with concern, fearing this might have been too much for Hakim's ghost, but he didn't even waver.

"People are constantly dying."

"If I'd never existed, they would still be alive. Sometimes I think it would have been best for everyone if Ragnara had killed me when I was a baby." Without even noticing that I'd moved my finger, it was tracing the scar on my chest.

"It wouldn't have been best for everyone. I never would have met you."

"You also wouldn't have . . ." I stopped, but Hakim still didn't falter. Just to be safe, I didn't continue.

"It's a heavy burden for you to bear. Too heavy for one person."

"Then help me carry it," I said and squeezed his hand.

He nodded resolutely, and his face took the thoughtful expression that made him look like what he was: a detective. "You said there's Gjallarhorn gold in Hrafnheim and Valhalla?"

"Thora is already after Eskild, and I can easily get Freyja's tears back from Védis. The hard part will be getting the piece Odin has hidden in Valaskjálf."

"How will you get there?"

"I could die... again... Valhalla is a realm of the dead, after all, but to be honest, I'm not a big fan of that approach. And, anyway, I can't bring the gold back unless I get brought back to life, and as far as I know, there isn't any more gods' blood to do that with."

Hakim looked up sharply when I said the word *die*.

"Oh, sorry."

He held up a large yet slightly transparent hand. When he was ready, he smiled his typical smile. "What about Elias's piece?"

I sucked in air between my front teeth. "He won't tell me until I have the other three."

Hakim lay down with his head on my pillow, even though he had no need for rest. For a ghost, existence was one long sleep.

I rolled onto my side and stared into his green eyes. "What do you think I should do?" Teasingly, I added, "Do you have any *hunches*?"

Hakim looked warmly at me. "Valaskjálf."

"How will I get there?"

"Who do you know that can go to Valhalla?"

"Od, but he would never help me get there."

Hakim put on his sneakiest expression. "Can he be convinced?"

"Not right now—he's already there. Elias said so. And I've seen him right after a visit to Asgard before. He gets all hyped up from it."

"What do you mean, hyped up?"

"He becomes more godlike from visiting Valhalla."

"And how do you convince a god to help you?"

A wide grin tugged at the corners of my mouth. "Hakim! You're a genius."

CHAPTER 12

The Boatman was open when I walked in. The bike ride there had been freezing cold, and I rolled my shoulders to get my blood circulating again. People sat at the small, shabby wooden tables with their heads tucked down. They held steaming mugs, but their eyes were haunted. The authorities had decided that the country's witches shouldn't cast any more spells on the population, so the illusion of everything being okay was slowly evaporating. There was a creeping awareness that we were experiencing a harsh, inexplicable winter, food scarcity, and almost no electricity. A mysterious illness was running rampant, and no one seemed able to explain any of it. This sparked hostile vibes and muttering among the tables.

The small, black-haired bartender, Veronika, looked surprisingly happy. I remembered that dark elves thrived on discord and fear.

"Is Od back from Valhalla?" I asked her across the bar.

The piercing in her septum, which resembled a bull's ring, quivered. She licked her lips with a pink tongue. "You taste good." As always, her voice sounded like that of an adult man. "Let me taste you again, then I'll tell you."

I wrinkled my nose. The six months I had spent in an elf mound were not something I wanted to replicate. "Isn't it your job to pour drinks and take people to see Od?"

Veronika leaned toward me. "Let me sniff you. Just a little whiff. Then I'll let you in to see the boss." Her nostrils flared.

Reluctantly, I reached out my hand and laid it flat on the bar. Veronika lowered her nose to it and inhaled deeply. "Ahhhhh."

"Are you done?"

She straightened her back. "Come with me." She slipped out from behind the bar. The top of her head reached only to my armpit. She walked ahead of me toward Od's office. In the mirrored walls, I saw many duplicates of myself and the elf, looking slightly different in each image. With an ironic, gallant motion, she showed me into Od's office. He sat motionless behind his desk as I cautiously stepped toward him.

"Od?"

He didn't respond. I saw he was emitting a silvery glow. He was much larger than usual, and his gigantic hands were resting on the desktop. With measured movements, I walked up to the desk and sat on the sofa. Od didn't notice me—or he was ignoring me. He simply stared down at the desk with shining metallic eyes as his sharp fingernails dug into the wood.

"What do you want, Anna?" Od's words made my heart leap. His voice was so forceful, the sound waves made the sofa tremble.

Warily, I kept my voice low. "I have a request for you."

He looked up, and I was pressed backward into the sofa by his wild, gleaming eyes. He breathed heavily. "A request?"

Even though he spoke quietly this time, I gasped for air. With my hand in my coat pocket, I squeezed the crumpled tea bag I had found in the back of my kitchen cabinet at Odinmont.

"What do you want to *request* from me?"

I cleared my throat. "I need you to take me to Valhalla."

For a second, he resembled a wild animal. "No." Again, his voice made the sofa quake.

"I have to go there."

Od stood and walked around the desk. He stood in front of me, and an intense heat hit me. His feet were bare, and his shirt was unbuttoned, exposing his smooth chest. What I could see of his body resembled a marble statue. He lowered his head to my eye level and held it still, but there was immense power behind every little movement. I fought to stay calm. More than anything, I wanted to abort the mission and flee the scene.

"I was just there." Beams emanated from Od's eyes, and his gaze was incapacitating. If he wanted to, he could charm me so thoroughly that my brain would never function again. "I won't be able to control my divine side if I go back now."

My pulse pounded in my throat. "I'll keep an eye on you."

Od ran his hands up and down my arms, and I was acutely aware that, with a little squeeze, he could pulverize my bones. His eyes burned, and in them, I was consumed by his godliness. I forced myself to look into them anyway.

"I insist." My voice faltered, but I got the words out.

Od let out a loud, resounding laugh. I felt like a gong being whacked with a mallet.

"You're just a human, and I'm a demigod."

My mouth was dry, and his gaze so bewitching, I felt like I was in free fall before I gained control.

"This is a prayer. I'm begging you to help me."

Od knelt in front of me and cupped his scalding hot hands around my cheeks. "Humans are extraordinary. I love it when you pray to me."

"You gods and demigods wouldn't even exist if it weren't for our worship."

"Worship?"

My voice was unsteady. "That's what I said."

"My father is growing stronger and stronger. At one time, I, too, had worshippers. I could have become a god, but I left Asgard in favor of Hejd." Od took a long, deep breath. "She died and asked me to keep living. For over a thousand years, I've ensured that the equinoxes were celebrated and that offerings were made to the gods." He exposed his chalk-white teeth and came even closer to me as he made a sound that was far from human. I heard volcanoes rumbling, the sea crashing against the shore, and the wind howling deep in his chest. For a while, we just sat like that. Him kneeling, and me pressed into the sofa.

I reminded myself that I had a mission. Hakim's idea was good, but I was on the verge of forgetting my own name. The memory of Hakim's cool voice brought me back to my task, and I found my courage. "Do you want to be worshipped again?"

Od trembled. I gently pushed him away so I could get on my knees, too. I sat with my head bowed. Od stood and placed his hand on the back of my head.

"Betra er óbeðit en sé ofblótit, ey sér til gildis gjöf," I said. "Betra er ósent en sé ofsóit." That was the prayer Luna had said to Mathias.

Od breathed heavily but didn't move.

"Sér til gildis gjöf, betra er ósent en sé ofsóit." I looked down at Od's bare feet the size of tree roots.

"A sacrifice." Od's voice sounded like the wind rustling through a tree.

I dug in my pocket and presented Od with the crushed tea bag on my flattened palm, careful not to look directly at him.

"I don't have anything else," I apologized. "There's a little pocket lint on it, but—"

A strong hand the size of a dinner plate closed around mine. I didn't dare look to see how big he had gotten. The hand pulled me to my feet. Od clenched my fingers in his gigantic ones and raised my hand to his mouth. For a moment, I feared he would bite my whole arm off, but he simply closed his eyes and kissed my knuckles.

"Thank you for your sacrifice, völva. Thank you for your sacrifice, raven. I will reciprocate your gift and take you to the Hall of the Fallen."

I tried to pull my arm back, but Od didn't seem to even notice my movement.

"It's at your own risk. I can't protect you there. Not even from myself." Od suddenly sounded like the normal, caring person I knew.

"Try," I beseeched him quietly.

"We'll leave now." He quickly transferred me onto his back before I even knew what was happening.

Then he took off running, as fast as the wind. There was no ground beneath us, and above us were only the stars and moon.

We landed in a kind of courtyard, although the word *courtyard* was too mundane. It was a huge field surrounded by enormous buildings. People walked around in clothing I couldn't place. Luna could probably guess where and when they belonged, but I just saw them as clean, colorful, and fancy. There were leather cords, beads, metal buckles, and feathers. Some women wore pants, and others wore dresses. Some men dressed in jumpsuits resembling those of Hrafnheimish soldiers, but others wore tunics that looked almost Middle Eastern. Everyone was hurrying back and forth as if they had something important to do.

"Are they gods?"

Od made an amused puffing noise. "This is one of the realms of the dead. Look again."

There was a big difference between the dead here and those in Helheim, but their blank expressions were identical, even though the dead here looked healthy, well-fed, and nicely dressed. The buildings before me were as tall as skyscrapers. The sun shone so sharply that I had to put my hand over my eyes to shield from its rays. Upon closer inspection, I saw that the brightness was the roof reflecting the sunlight. The roof was made of thick plates of gold, layered like shingles.

Od followed my gaze. "Those are gold shields."

"The gods clearly aren't lacking anything." I tried to keep the sarcastic edge out of my voice but wasn't quite successful.

"There's plenty of everything here. It comes from all the offerings people have given over millennia."

I noticed a door as high as the tallest windmills back in Midgard. The door was also made of gold and covered in beautiful figures and ornamentation. There were serpent knots, eight-legged horses, oxen, and fish. Wolves leapt at the bottom of the door, and farther up were decorations depicting ravens. I stared with my mouth hanging open but tried to compose myself.

"There's no shame in being dazzled. Asgard is overwhelmingly beautiful. Look over there." Od pointed at the sky, which was so blue, it looked surreal. I knew perfectly well that the sky in Midgard had been blue, too, before Fimbulwinter, but having been deprived of the sight for so long, it occurred to me how strange it was to live under a blue dome. On the horizon, I could make out cliffs and a waterfall that looked like they came out of an animated kids' movie. Up in the sky, behind the falls, there was a rainbow. It appeared to have sprung directly from the spring itself.

"Bifrost." Od's head was close to mine. "That's Fólkvangr you can see over there. My wife lives there."

Birds flitted playfully in the air, the flowers were colorful firecrackers, and green leaves and grass lay like a blanket over everything. Luna would have loved it. I loved it. A tree trunk as big as a mountain was to the left of the waterfall and Bifrost. The trunk stretched up, up, up, only to disappear into a covering of clouds.

"Yggdrasil," Od said, tilting his head slightly. "The tree of life. It's the source of all existence."

"We're in Valhalla?"

Od strode across the courtyard toward the tall door. "This is the Hall of the Fallen." He pressed on the door, which glided open easily as though it didn't weigh thousands of tons.

The smell of food, fire, and fresh straw hit me when we walked into the hall. The space was bisected by a table so long, I couldn't see the other end. Sunk into the middle of the tabletop was a burning indentation.

"The eternal bonfire," Od whispered.

"I'm afraid to meet Odin," I admitted. "I'm not the best follower." Not to mention I had technically come here to steal something from the All-Father.

"The one thing he can't do is kill you. It's impossible to murder someone in the realm of the dead."

"Why?"

"In a way, while you're here, you're already dead." He patted my back. "Plus, my father has a strange view of those who speak against him. His enemies are the people he values most." Od seemed enormous as he walked next to me, and I had to jog to keep up. "In his own way, he's smitten with you, even when he's angry with you."

We walked along the table, which seemed miles long. Men and women sat around it, eating and drinking as they chatted cheerfully.

"Great training today," a woman said to the man next to her. "That dagger really got me good!" She pointed, chuckling, at her eye, which was a little red, but no more so than if she'd gotten a piece of dust in it.

The man laughed. "It's an honor to die with Odin's mark." He pulled a knife from his belt and juggled it between his fingers.

The woman pulled at the skin on her cheekbone and placed her face close to the dancing knife. The red mucous membrane beneath her eyeball was exposed. "Do it again."

He feinted at her a couple of times with the tip of the knife. She didn't pull back. In fact, she leaned even farther forward. Eventually, he put the knife away. "We can't fight in the hall. Imagine if the All-Father sends us to Helheim."

Disappointed, the woman let go of her cheek and turned back to her plate. "He won't find out. He's far too focused on his blood brother."

I looked sharply at Od. "His blood brother?"

Od walked just as quickly as before.

"Isn't that . . . Loki?" I tried to look down to the head of the table, where there was a two-person seat. I had only seen Loki in my visions. Never in real life—if you could call Valhalla *real life*.

There were two people on the seat, but they were so far away, I couldn't see them properly. The walls were lined with sleeping alcoves so tall, people had to climb to get into them. There were open-weave hangings in front of the beds, and behind them, figures moved in such a way that it wasn't hard to figure out what they were doing.

Od stopped in front of an empty seat. "Sit." He climbed over the bench, and, not knowing what else to do, I squeezed myself in.

"I kind of have something important . . ." I was distracted by an enticing smell and breathed it in. My stomach whined, and I realized it had been a long time since I last ate.

In front of me was a plate with meat, steaming beans, parsnips, and celery. It hadn't been there a moment before, but it was right in front of my face. Magically, an identical plate had appeared before Od. The meat had been topped with fresh berries and nuts along with green herbs, and the plate was delicately garnished with finely grated horseradish. The whole thing swam in a dark, fragrant gravy. I was no culinary expert, but the feast looked like it had been prepared by a celebrity chef. The smell was nothing short of fantastic, and I could have wept with the desire to sink my teeth into the meal.

"Eat, Anna," Od said hoarsely. "You're allowed."

"I'm here to—" But I couldn't hold myself back, and to be honest, I was having trouble remembering what was so much more important than the food in front of me. A dissonant murmur scratched my inner ear. Maybe it was guilt, in a way, but it was little more than a faint grumble.

Od put a green glass into my hand. It was encased in an iron spiral that reminded me of the metal holder of Sverre's giant crystal. The thought of Sverre evaporated when I brought my nose to the edge of the glass. It was filled with a golden liquid that smelled of honey and alcohol.

"That's the mead of poetry from Heidrun's udders."

The drink tingled on my tongue and warmed me all the way down to my knees. "It's the same as you have at home." My mouth was full of food, even though I didn't remember starting to eat. Once I got started, I couldn't stop. Each mouthful complemented the one before. There was the potency of the horseradish with the sweetness of the berries. The nuts were roasted, and the meat was so juicy that, with every bite, I could taste what the animal had eaten. Mushrooms, grass, bean sprouts, and pure water.

"I do have mead of poetry back in Midgard," Od confirmed and put a piece of meat in his mouth. He closed his eyes in enjoyment. "But everything tastes better here."

"Why would you want to leave here?" It seemed illogical that someone would leave their place in the Hall of the Fallen. It suddenly seemed pretty appealing to die in battle.

As though Od had read my thoughts, he smiled at me, and he looked as close to being a god as he could get. Beautiful, strong, and vital. His eyes sparkled silver, and he grew larger and broader. "When I ask myself that same question, that's when I know it's time to go home to Midgard."

I had the fleeting thought that he was warning me against something, but it fluttered away when I took another bite of delicious food. I mopped up the juices with a piece of flatbread that had also appeared out of the blue. The bread had dark lines from where it had sat on a grill, and I could taste the wheat rustling in the sun, the bees' joy at finding nectar, and the wood from the open fire in the crumbs. I consumed everything alongside large quantities of mead, so that in the end I was full and tipsy, but not in a nauseous or overstuffed way. A profound contentment spread through every atom of my body, and the feeling was so foreign to me that I stood up.

Od looked questioningly at me.

"Air," I said briefly. "I'll be back in a minute." As discreetly as I could, I slipped through the golden door, which looked like it weighed as much as a ferry. When I pushed it, though, it swung open more easily than a plastic patio door.

Outside, dusk was falling. The sky above was blue-black, fading to pale blue and then mint green toward the horizon. At the bottom edge, where the sun had sunk down, lay a delicate salmon-colored band. It smelled like grass and clean air, and the temperature was neither too cold nor too warm. A couple—dead, presumably—walked arm in arm toward a lower building, which was still taller than Ravensted's tallest apartment complex.

I sat on a carved bench with my back toward the Hall of the Fallen. For a moment, I allowed myself the pure enjoyment of simply existing. I wasn't hungry, I wasn't cold, and I had a hard time remembering my many problems.

"Welcome to my seat, raven."

I flailed my arms when I realized that Odin was standing next to me. "Wow, you startled me!"

He sat and wrapped his cape around his body. He leaned his head back with a contented exhalation.

"Are you mad at me?" I neither practiced blót nor prayed, and I talked back to him pretty often. Plus, I was there to steal something from him, but he hopefully hadn't caught on to that.

Odin sighed. "I like your antics. I like that you dare to oppose me. But if you betray me here in Valhalla, you risk a triple death." He said this with a crooked smile that did not at all match the words.

I didn't know what a triple death was, but I didn't dare say so.

Odin looked at the colorful sky. The side of his face that I could see was the one where he still had an eye. He was dark in both his skin and hair, and his facial features were exaggerated to the extent that he could have looked like a caricature if he hadn't been so attractive. He had a cloak wrapped around him, but I could see that the body beneath was young and strong. He didn't have a single wrinkle, and he opened his mouth slightly when he looked up at the moon.

"It's you, old friend. You are a wonder. All the worlds are wonders. Every celestial body. Every ant. Every human."

I looked at the moon, too, which was crystal clear. I saw craters, mountains, and the large white expanses on its surface.

"Do you like my home?" Odin's voice was soft.

I answered without reservations. "It's amazing here."

"You could make a home for yourself here with me. I saw you in Sverresborg. You have the flair to become a god."

"I'm happy just being a human."

"Mannaz." Odin dragged out the *z*, so it sounded like a buzzing insect. It was hard to figure out if he was angry or pleased by my statement.

"It's not that I don't like it," I hurried to add. "It's gorgeous here."

"Have you taken a good look around?"

I hesitated. Maybe he would be angry if I told him what I'd seen, but Odin was already mad at me, even though he was behaving civilly right now.

"Asgard is a copy of Helheim, but at the same time, it's Helheim's opposite. Everything that is disgusting there is beautiful here. Your hall, Valhalla, is light and warm; Hel's hall, Eljudnir, is gray and cold. Hel's table is empty. Her platter, Hunger, is an abyss, while your table is piled with the best food and drink and the eternal bonfire. Your beds are full of love; Hel's are full of death." I looked down at my hands. "I could go on."

"And the dead?"

I looked at two men who walked, smiling, toward a shadow. They didn't look particularly dead, but I knew in my heart that they were. "The dead are also the same," I whispered.

"There are so few who have been to both realms. So few can really compare them. And most only see the surface. Not the bones beneath."

"Have you been to both places?"

Odin turned his face, and I saw his empty eye socket. His face was, like Hel's, a contrast between beauty and decline.

Of the runes of the gods
And the giants' race
The truth indeed can I tell,
To nine worlds came I,
to Niflhel beneath,
where the dead go from Hel.

His words surrounded me like a pillar of smoke before disappearing.

Where the dead go from Hel.

I couldn't help but place my hand on his cheek under the empty eye socket. My thumb grazed the opening, and I felt an intense pull from the socket.

"They're the same place," I said. "Helheim and Asgard."

"I can't hide anything from you, little seer. That will be my downfall."

"So, all the dead end up in the same place, or what?"

Odin tilted his head. "Death is what you make of it."

"You can't really make too much of anything if you're dead," I scoffed.

Odin laughed. "That's how the world is, raven. Past and future, life and death, summer and winter, love and hate, pain and joy, sickness and health, memory and oblivion."

"Opposites," I said.

"You can also see them as scales."

"Ahhh..."

"The universe consists of processes. Circles."

We sat together as the night deepened. Dew fell on us, but we didn't move. Odin was a statue, and I leaned against him. Eventually, it got so dark that I saw only the stars and the moon.

These, too, flickered away, and I swam down into a warm pool.

I woke in one of the alcoves on a soft, long-haired animal pelt that bore an unsettling resemblance to the one in Hel's bed. The hanging around the alcove was also identical, but this one didn't have dead bodies dangling from it like a giant flypaper. This one was gauzy and billowed gently. Od slept alongside me with his arm around my waist. I quickly checked that we were both dressed.

His black hair had a glossy shine, and cool godliness slipped into me from his arm and filled me with strength and happiness. For a frightening moment, I thought it would be okay if someone had to be sacrificed for us to live so comfortably here. Fortunately, this thought lasted only a second.

I lay back on the pelt and rested my cheek against Od's chest.

CHAPTER 13

Think, Anna. Why are you here?

I was back at the banquet table in the large hall. We had already reached the day's third meal, consisting of juicy pieces of meat, fresh berries, and boiled vegetables. Ravenous, I threw myself over the food, and each mouthful filled me with energy and well-being. While I enjoyed the meal, a small voice kept chirping faintly in the back of my head.

Remember why you're in Valhalla.

For a moment, I stopped and considered why I was there, but with a sip of the mead of poetry, I shrugged. Whatever it was could wait.

I had had one of the most wonderful days of my life. First, I trained with the fallen. The Valkyries went around the battlefield and touched the dead, reanimating them. I took down a tall man and then a woman, but just when I had gotten into a good rhythm, I was impaled by a spear through my back. I saw its tip come out near my sternum. It didn't hurt, but I was pinned to the ground until a Valkyrie had time to fix me.

"That wasn't fair," I shouted to the man who had impaled me. "I didn't even see you coming."

"All's fair in love and war. We can see about love tonight." He sent me an impish air kiss before jumping back into the fighting with an eager cry.

When the victors were declared, the rest of us were allowed to get up and start over.

After training, I came running back, bathed in sunshine, and dressed only in leather pants and a little undershirt, with bare feet and arms and my hair tied up. Od stood leaning against a wooden pen in which gigantic horses bowed and played. He grinned when he saw me, and I laughed joyfully.

"I've never seen you so happy," he said.

"I don't think I've ever felt this carefree." That was true. My mood was so light, I felt like I was about to float up over the golden roofs. I was usually so burdened by the past, but in this place, I could barely remember what had happened the night before. It was like being cut loose from a heavy anchor. Od pulled me into a hug. Touch was natural for demigods, and I snuggled up to him.

"Did you have fun with the fighters?" Od nodded toward the battlefield.

"It was wild! It was game over for me pretty quick, but I managed to kill two before I died."

"They're beguiling you," he whispered in my ear when I got close enough. "Someone knows what you have in mind."

I tried to pull away, but Od's strength—which certainly hadn't diminished during our stay—kept me pressed against his body.

"But it's so nice here," I whispered back.

"Exactly. You'll never get out of here if you let them dazzle you. You'll be stuck in a beautiful spiderweb. It's drawing me in, too. I can barely resist it anymore."

I listened to what he said. I tried to cement the words in my head, but someone whistled for the horses, and my attention was diverted. Od, too, seemed to forget what he had been telling me.

"Is it just me, or does that horse have eight legs?" I asked.

"That's Odin's steed."

Eight legs. A spider also has eight legs. Od had said something about a spiderweb. I shook my head as my thoughts kept slipping away from me.

It was evening again, and the day's marvelous training was over.

We would eat an unforgettable meal, and tomorrow, it would all start again. And it would continue for an eternity.

Shouts and laughter echoed through the Hall of the Fallen along the endless banquet table, and I wrapped myself in my mother's coat. I sat closer to Odin's spot at the head of the table than I had the night before, but it was currently vacant. A woman juggled seven swords, each made of gleaming gold. They glinted, and once in a while, she made them strike one another, giving off the metallic sound of battle. Everyone, myself included, applauded.

After the woman's demonstration, there was dancing. Two men beat drums in a rhythm that, I had to admit, was a little exciting. Over the intense beat was the sound of plaintive wind instruments, and the music became a strange metaphor for the joys and sorrows of love. Male and female acrobats came slinking in from every entrance, and the people at the table clapped ecstatically. The dancers moved to the intoxicating music in provocative ways that turned into handsprings, human towers, and breakneck swings. They wore nothing but loincloths and small pieces of fabric over their breasts, and one of the women had a round bronze disk attached to her belt. When she rotated her hips, the disk reflected the light of the fire.

"Lovely maiden," one of the fallen shouted deliriously. "You've brought the sun inside."

In response, the woman danced around him, jutting her hips and shooting blinding beams of light at the audience. She slid her fingers over his face and shoulders but then removed them so quickly that he couldn't catch her, though he grasped out. The dancer did a backbend and kicked her legs over her body, bringing her back upright, and the beams from her disk hit us all. People snatched at the air for the flashes while the warrior at the center of the woman's dance sat as though paralyzed. When the dancers were done, the applause was deafening. I couldn't help but join in, slapping my hands together.

Two people came in, and the hall grew quiet. One of them was Odin, and he was as young and strong as the night before. I couldn't understand how he was the same ancient, frail man I had met before. Back then, his hair had been thin and white, his face wrinkled, and his back hunched with age. But now, he didn't look much older than I was; he was remarkably handsome and full of strength and power.

Another man walked at his side.

I recognized Loki from my vision, in which he had been half naked, large, and much closer to his wild nature than he was now, but it was definitely the same person. Instinctively, I pulled my coat tighter around me and hid my face in its high collar. Loki was bare-chested and wore leather pants; he looked like a rockstar bursting with self-confidence. His arms and chest were painted with blue spirals, and around his neck, he wore a wide, gold ring. He smiled, and I saw how beautiful he was. If it weren't for the calculating expression in his dark, painted eyes, I would have thought he was innocence itself. His smile appeared to conceal a thousand secrets, and I suspected his hands, which were folded behind his back, held knives ready to stick in the backs of all his friends.

"The All-Father has had mercy on his blood brother," a woman whispered from a little farther down the bench. "After all his betrayal, he is now welcome within the walls of Valhalla again."

"He served his time. A thousand years in the cave in Hrafnheim, bound by his son's intestines beneath the serpent's venom. Besides, you can never turn a blood brother away."

"Did you hear he killed his wife when he got free?"

There were grumbles and *hmphs* in reply.

"Odin can't live without him. Look at them. The god and the giant in unity."

The two men sat on a carved seat on a raised platform above the rest of us. Odin and Loki leaned toward one another, either in brotherhood or true flirtation. I couldn't figure it out. Each was more beautiful and terrifying than the other. Even though they were several yards away, their voices carried through the hall. They intended for everyone to hear their conversation.

"Help!" Loki shouted in a girlish voice, writhing in his seat. The air shimmered around him, and he changed shape.

I sputtered when he took on a form I didn't think I would ever see again. His hair was black, and he was as small as a child, only as tall as Odin's chest.

"Help me, Loki. We had a deal," Ragnara begged. Or rather, Loki, who had taken on the appearance of Ragnara as she had been on the night I ordered Odin to kill her. "Help me, Loki." Ragnara let out a high-pitched laugh, and Loki's deep voice was right behind it. "She thought we had a deal, but I simply didn't feel like coming to her aid."

Odin laughed, too, which made me nauseous. "I stabbed her three times with Gungnir." He patted the spear, which stood behind him. I sensed Gungnir's personality as it squirmed with pleasure. "That woman. That pathetic woman," he grunted. "It was a good thing my raven bade me kill that human."

Although Ragnara and I hadn't exactly been best friends, bile gathered in my mouth to hear those two words said in such a condescending tone. *Woman* and *human*. I also didn't particularly like being referred to as *his* raven.

"Your raven is lovely," Loki said. "Tough and vulnerable, gentle and brusque, frightened and brave. She is all of that, and beautiful to boot."

"Stay away from my raven," Odin warned jokingly.

Loki leaned back with a self-satisfied smile. "It may be too late."

"Men!" A woman's voice whispered right next to me. I jumped, startled. Moments before, my neighbor had been a long-haired Viking with a large scar across his cheek, but suddenly it was Freyja who sat there. She shook her head, and the movement caused some of her hair to brush across my hand. The touch made my whole arm tingle pleasantly.

She looked up at Loki through long eyelashes. "I hate him," she muttered.

"You do?" I whispered. "Everyone else seems so excited about him."

At the head of the table, Loki had gotten one of the musicians to start drumming again, and he danced in time with the music, showing off every muscle of his bare torso. Everyone stared. The Valkyries stopped and turned their heads in his direction, and even the burly warriors couldn't take their eyes off him. When he rolled his shoulders, arching his back slightly, the blue spirals on his forearms swirled, and I caught myself staring at him, hypnotized. Odin leaned back and observed his blood brother with open fascination. Loki's steel-gray, shoulder-length hair touched his shoulder blades as he curved his spine even farther back.

"He's caused so many problems for us." Freyja nodded her head in Loki's direction. "Did you know he promised me first to Thrymr, and then to the Sons of Ivaldi? Thrymr was supposed to get me in exchange for Mjolnir, and the dwarfs made Gungnir trade for me." She clicked her tongue. "As though I were just an object to be sold at market."

"That's not okay."

"There was also the time he cut Sif's hair off."

"Why did he cut Sif's hair off?"

"It was probably a bet, but most of all, he did it for fun. That's how he is. He does things for fun, or just because he can. He simply can't help himself, even if it costs him a thousand years tied up in a cave or a year as a pregnant horse. Did you know he's the mother of Odin's eight-legged steed? He turned himself into a mare and seduced a stallion." Freyja laughed gleefully.

I caught myself staring at her, open-mouthed, but I shook my head and snapped myself out of it.

"Loki also gave Idunn to the giant Tjasse because he owed him a debt."

"He obviously doesn't care much about women."

"Loki loves women. He also loves men. In fact, I've never met anyone so desirous of everything and everybody." Freyja shrugged, the neckline of her golden dress sliding down one soft shoulder, and I had an intense urge to kiss it. Or to sink my teeth into it as though she were a delicious piece of cake. "Loki seduces women, men, gods, and goddesses, and he's as unpredictable as early spring. It can get light, it can snow, you can die of cold, and you can make love in the freshly plowed dirt, all within the course of an hour."

"Loki was tied up in a cave for a thousand years." I remembered the dried snakeskin and the matted ropes.

Freyja didn't seem to think there was anything wrong with that. "Sigrun was an idiot to stay with him," she said. "Who knows where she ended up."

"Sigrun is dead." My nose tickled as the sweet smell of old corpse flitted, a bit too lifelike, through my memory.

"Hmmm." Freyja studied her nails.

A chill ran through my body. "Why was Loki in the cave?" I asked through narrow lips.

"He got Baldr killed. Odin's son."

I looked at the two men, who were now engrossed in a conversation I couldn't hear. But they were closely entwined, which gave me an idea of the subject matter.

"If he killed Odin's son, how can they be such good friends . . . or whatever they are?"

"It was a long time ago. And Odin did kill Loki's son afterward. It was his intestines Loki was tied up with."

I raised my eyebrows. That apparently meant they were even.

"Loki is useful," Freyja explained when she saw my skeptical face. "He's also . . ." She looked up at the half-naked, attractive man who resembled a force of nature. He shook his head so his thick gray locks moved away from his face. "Loki is funny. He's cunning and dangerous. Sometimes to us. Sometimes to our enemies. So, Odin set him free."

"What? No, Ragnara set Loki free." I was certain because I had seen it myself in the past.

Freyja took my face in both her hands, and I was incapable of moving. She looked straight into my eyes, and I swam away in her slanted amber gaze. Her already nearly transparent dress disappeared entirely, and she sat naked before me. She leaned into me, so her head was right in front of mine. I smelled honey, sunshine, and fresh grass.

"Human girl," she whispered. "Raven. Völva. Anna. Of course Odin was behind it. Odin is always behind it." She came closer to me and planted a long kiss on my lips. I was unable to escape it, but she broke the kiss herself after a while.

"Why are you telling me this?" I managed to stammer.

"Because," Freyja moved one hand to the back of my head, "we women have to stick together, otherwise the men will sell us. They'll use us. Can't you see that, völva? You. Are. Being. Used. We. Are. Being. Used. Ragnara. Was. Used." She said the words slowly and emphatically, nodding with each one. I found myself nodding along. Her divinely beautiful face was right up close to mine. A golden light blinded me, and I leaned forward again, hungry for more.

"What are you doing?" she asked.

I blinked.

"Not that I'm complaining, but you're really close."

I was leaning into the large, long-haired, scarred Viking. So close, my nose nearly touched his. He smelled of mead and roasted meat.

"Sorry!" I exclaimed and jerked backward.

The Viking laughed and leaned over his mug again. "Unlimited food and drink, and women who throw themselves at me after a whole day of harmless fighting. I love Valhalla."

I blushed deeply, confused, unsure if others had witnessed my conversation with Freyja.

"We have a new skald," Odin announced. He had stood at the head of the table. His long black hair framed his face, with its dark eyebrows and one empty eye socket. He raised one fist and extended the index and middle fingers. There was something slightly mocking about the gesture. "Up. Come on, up with you." Odin moved his hands and clapped slowly. The applause was echoed by the many soldiers along the table. Far away at the other end, I could hear footsteps. Heavy boots on the tabletop. At first, they were hesitant, but as they gradually got closer, they became steadier and louder.

"My skald," Odin said. "Come."

The boots came closer. The first thing I saw were black leather pants. He wore a sky-blue shirt with arabesque embroidery. His dark mustache was pointy and twisted up at the ends, and his shoulder-length, brown hair was tied up with small silver and gold rings braided into it. Although his attitude was confident, he kept clutching one hand in the other. When he passed me, he looked down, and our eyes met. Our eyes widened simultaneously.

"Tryggvi?" I had met him in Hrafnheim when he was alive. In fact, in a way, I had been responsible for his death—but in my defense, he had tried to kill me first. Monster's daughter bit his hand off, and afterward, the giant wolves had eaten him. He was nice and whole again, which I planned to point out if I were unlucky enough to bump into him later.

He looked at me in disbelief but continued on his way, still holding his right hand protectively. He stopped in front of Odin and Loki and bowed reverently and exaggeratedly, making a rolling motion with his arm. When he stood back up, he hurried to grab his hand again.

"Welcome to the Hall of the Fallen." Odin's voice rang out. "How will you entertain us? Remember, there's plenty of room in Helheim if we aren't pleased."

I could only see Tryggvi's back, which slumped slightly. "I . . ." He composed himself quickly. "I will recite Njál's Saga, a tale of outlaws, friends, and enemies. It was—"

Loki cut him off. His clever gray eyes sparkled wickedly. "I would rather hear the story of my son, Fenrir." For a moment, I felt his eyes fall on me, but they flitted away so quickly, I wasn't sure if I had been mistaken.

"The wolf?" Tryggvi said meekly.

"He bit off Týr's hand, so now he's tied up at Amsvartnir, but when Ragnarök comes, he'll be freed and eat most of you warriors." Loki pointed around lazily. "Oh, and you, too, Odin."

The warriors seated at the table paled, as did Odin himself.

"You're a skald, so you can tell the story much better than I can," Loki said innocently.

Tryggvi swayed, and Odin sat stiffly in his seat. "I would rather hear a love story. Brave heroes and beautiful maidens—"

"Boooriing." Loki's hand caressed the armrest of the carved wooden bench. Odin started to object, but Loki took Odin's hand in his. "And you aren't boring, are you, All-Father? Not as *I* know you."

Odin pursed his lips in bitter acceptance.

Loki clicked his tongue as though hurrying a draft horse along. "Go on, Tryggvi. We don't have forever." He turned his gray head lazily toward Odin. "Well, actually, we do, unless Ragnarök starts."

Tryggvi paced nervously. "Loki had three children with the giant woman Angerboda. The Midgard Serpent, Hel, and Fenrir."

"Who is a . . ." Loki cupped his hand behind his ear.

"A . . . wolf," Tryggvi stammered.

"Yes," Loki bellowed. "He's a wolf. A hand-munching, blood-drinking killer of a wolf." He pounded his fist on the table with each word, causing the plates and cups to dance.

I wasn't particularly enamored with Tryggvi, especially not after he beat me up and tried to deliver me to Ragnara, but the dead are very sensitive about being confronted with the way they met their end. Forcing Tryggvi to recount the story of a wolf who bit someone's hand off balanced right on the edge of reliving his own death. The uncomfortable feeling that had, until then, lurked like a dormant little seed in my stomach, grew into a tall stalk up my throat and made me nauseous.

Tryggvi continued, but there were tears in his voice. "The gods tricked Fenrir into being bound with dwarf-forged magic chains. He is now in a cave by the lake called Amsvartnir," Tryggvi concluded. I could see from his back that he exhaled with relief.

"How did they trick him? How did they trick my son?" Loki yelled. It was more of a *boom* than actual words.

Tryggvi's shoulders drooped. "Týr put his . . . hand in . . ." he whispered, but he was once again interrupted.

"The stupid god put his hand in the wolf's wet, warm maw." Loki thrust his own arm out and studied it. "No, it doesn't look like it." His hand was covered in blue tattoos and drawings. He stood and jumped onto the table as well, where he crouched down as though he were a wolf himself. "Let me see yours. Yes. That looks much more like it." He grabbed Tryggvi's hand and pulled it toward him. "Týr put his hand in Fenrir's mouth, and he felt the sharp teeth against his skin."

Before, Tryggvi had protected his right hand with his left, but now Loki squeezed it with all his might. Tryggvi tried to grab his hand and pull it back, but Loki held tight and pulled. He rose to his knees, opened his mouth, and tried to fit it around Tryggvi's hand, but he shook his head. "That won't work." He tried several times, his head tilted first one way, then the other.

The warriors laughed.

"What is Loki doing now?" my long-haired neighbor said. There was laughter in his voice. "There hasn't been a dull moment since he came back."

At the end of the table, the air around Loki shimmered as he shifted form. Where before he had been crouched comically, there now sat a large black wolf that looked unmistakably like Rokkin.

"No," Tryggvi wailed.

His fear tore at my heart.

Tryggvi jerked away violently, but the wolf already had its mouth around his hand, and no matter how hard Tryggvi pulled, he couldn't pry himself free.

Loki in wolf form looked up at him with a cheerful expression. "Stand still. We're trying to tell a story here." Rokkin's voice sounded muffled because she had Tryggvi's hand in her mouth.

People screamed with laughter as Tryggvi begged for mercy.

"Calm down," the wolf slurred. "Your hand'll grow back again afterward. You're an einheri now. We can repeat this scene a thousand times, and you'll get your hand back again, and again, and again." The wolf's snout pulled back into a nasty grin. "Recite, my good skald." The voice shifted from jovial to threatening. "Remember what the All-Father said. There's plenty of room in Helheim if you don't want to fulfill your destiny. I'll make sure my daughter gives you a warm welcome."

Tryggvi sobbed. "Týr was on good terms with Fenrir when he was a pup," he began. "But he grew bigger and bigger with every passing day. Eventually, he was the size of a house."

Rokkin grew until she towered several yards over the table. She had to bend over to keep Tryggvi's hand in her mouth.

Tryggvi breathed raggedly. "The gods decided to bind him, but he would only allow it if he could take Týr's right hand as collateral."

My nausea had now turned into a real threat of throwing up. Tryggvi had died because of me, so it was indirectly my fault that he was standing at the end of the table, reliving his biggest trauma in front of a whole hall of dead people. I climbed backward over the bench and snuck away. I couldn't stand it a second longer.

When I turned my back, I heard a crunch, a scream from Tryggvi, and then a peal of laughter from the audience. I ran from the hall as fast as I could.

The reason I was there was suddenly clear as day. I almost considered thanking Loki for waking me up from the sugary-sweet life in Valhalla, but I honestly had no desire to.

"Valaskjálf, Valaskjálf." I spun around in the enormous courtyard, which was now completely dark. I sensed its size more than I saw it. The emptiness pulled at me, and my footsteps echoed even though I tried to tiptoe. I felt like a tiny mouse between high walls I couldn't see. I knew they were there only because they blocked the starry sky above. I figured the dark holes must be palisades. What I could make out was a path as wide as a highway surrounded by hedges. I couldn't see the horses in the paddocks, but they snorted loudly and stomped at the ground.

"Where are you going?" The voice was harsh and sounded like a thunderstorm. The figure was only a silhouette.

I suppressed a scream and was ready to book it out of there until I realized who it was.

"Od! You scared the crap out of me."

"Where are you going?" Od repeated. He sounded different from usual. The voice came from higher up, and I could barely see him in the shadows.

"I'm looking for Odin's quarters. Valaskjálf."

"It's dangerous for you to wander around here alone." Od didn't sound human. His voice was more like crashing waves or a thunderclap. I grabbed his arm. Cool divine strength slipped into me, but I held tight and sent humanity back to him.

"I'm not alone. You're here." I smiled, turning my face up, but I couldn't see if he was smiling back. His head was too high up.

There was a rough laugh that sounded almost like Od's normal one. "Valaskjálf, you said? It's over here." He took my hand in his, and even though I couldn't see our fingers, his hand felt the size of a chair.

Od pulled me along, and we ended up in front of a door that I wouldn't have noticed without his help. It was made of fragrant carved wood. When Od got closer, his radiance illuminated the door's surface, and I saw falcons, wolves, ravens, and a large tree with branches spread over everything else. I pushed on the door with all my strength, but it didn't move an inch.

Od placed his large index finger on it and pressed gently. The door immediately swung open to reveal a corridor only faintly lit. Torches were stuck into rings along the wooden walls, but they were so spread out that there were several yards of complete darkness between them. We walked in beneath a torch, and I gasped.

I could see Od properly, and the orange light of the flames lapped at him. He was enormous. I came up only to his waist, and his eyes shone manically. He was completely high on divinity, and I could only hope he would keep enough of a grasp on reality to not go into full demi-mode.

"Are you in control of yourself? You look like a giant statue."

"No! I am not in control of myself."

"Can you try to be? Just a little?"

He nodded, and his hair fell around his face in gleaming waves. His teeth glowed neon blue as he clenched them together.

"Okay." I squeezed his huge hand. "Where is Odin's office?"

Od laughed, and I squinted against his blinding teeth. "Office? You mean his private room." Od pulled me along, and I had no choice but to go with him. After barreling down the long hall, he stopped before a narrow door that looked more like a hatch in the wall. I would have thought it was a broom closet if he hadn't given it a meaningful look.

"In there." His words sounded like an earthquake. "I'll keep watch. Hurry."

I stepped into the office—or whatever you were supposed to call the All-Father's lair. It smelled like burnt herbs. To be precise, I smelled a specific herb that my fellow residents at Nordreslev

Youth Center had enjoyed in large quantities when there were no staff members around. It also smelled of spoiled meat, straw, and wool. Disembodied birds' wings hung on the wall alongside carved animal skulls and strings of bones. A pointy hat, a cloak, and a pirate-like eye patch hung from a hook, and in the corner, a bed was covered in skins, blankets, and pillows. There was something enticing about it, and I quickly looked away.

There were piles of animal hides covered with drawings and writing. On a desk were scattered tiles that looked like those from Rebecca's bag of magic runes and a spherical form covered with a stained cloth. A black branching piece of bogwood was mounted on a board on the desk. Totem poles, drums, and a seid staff leaned against the walls, and flames in the fireplace illuminated the room.

"Yep. Odin is a slob."

A window looked out onto the courtyard below with the gigantic wall around it, which I could see better from this angle. The stars twinkled up above, but I didn't know enough about astronomy to tell if they were the same constellations we had back home. I stuck my head out the window and took a few deep breaths of the fresh night air. Then I turned back toward the room. To keep from being affected by the herbs, I pulled my scarf over my mouth and nose before starting to dig around the piles of hides covered in dense writing. I had no idea where the gold from the Gjallarhorn was. Elias had simply said it was in here somewhere.

"Where are you, where are you?" I whispered. I let my fingers glide aimlessly over bones and severed wings. I studied the rune tiles on the desk.

Ansuz, fehu, and mannaz lay in a row, set apart from the other runes. God, slave, and human. It gave me an uneasy feeling about the future, even though I had no idea what it held.

At the end of the table was a carved chair. Its high back and heavy armrests made it look like a throne. That must be Hlidskjalf. The throne from which Odin could see into all realms.

Is Serén okay? Is Varnar?

I quickly clambered onto it and felt the energy swirling beneath me. I sat there a moment and composed myself before placing my hands on the armrests and squeezing tight. My body arched, still holding the arms of the chair. I saw Odin's room but also a deep chasm beneath me, as though I were flying away. In my head, I heard screeching, which I recognized as the sound of ravens. I looked to the side along my arm, but I saw black wings instead. Then I swooped over a realm blanketed in ice. Even under the frost-covered trees in the dark of night, I could see the golden leaves of the Bronze Forest. I dove under the tree canopy; the light was muted but not so much that I couldn't see. Or maybe it was my raven eyes that took everything in.

Two figures walked on a path. One man, one woman. The man held a lantern, and it lit a small circle around them. He wore leather clothes and a thick knit hat, and dark, shoulder-length hair stuck out from beneath it. His face was just as lovely as it had always been, and it had those familiar, intently focused eyes. I longed desperately to see him smile, but he was serious. Varnar walked with firm strides, and Thora scurried at his side. I called out to them, but only a raven's shriek came from my beak. Varnar raised his head when he heard my cry, and Thora looked around.

I circled around them and headed back toward the deep-black sky. I flew onward and ended up at Haraldsborg, where I flew in through the gate and continued into a large room. My sister sat there with Aella. When I sat on the back of a chair and cawed, they looked at me. Serén smiled.

"You're on the right track," she said to me. "I've seen this before."

Everything rotated like a calving iceberg, and I was looking down at Midgard. Odinmont was right in front of me, and I flapped past the window. Arthur and Rebecca sat hunched over the cracked table in the living room. Rebecca was crying, and Arthur put his arm around her. I scratched at the window, but they didn't see me.

The world tilted again, and I flew over the realm of the dead, where Hel stood at the Beach of Corpses, looking out over the neon-green sea. She looked right at me and waved. Then she laughed with her beautiful, rotten mouth, and on one side, I saw every tooth in her skull.

"Raven. Welcome," she called.

I saw Alfheim and elf mounds with captive, comatose humans inside. With cries and screams, I tried to wake them so they could get away from the parasitic elves, but it was no use, so I flew on. Finally, I reached Jotunheim, with all the giants sharpening their axes for battle. The realm had smoking volcanoes, snow-covered mountain passes, and large, prehistoric animals grazing on a cold, yet snowless, plain. Mammoths and woolly rhinoceroses snorted in the cold. I cawed as a saber-toothed tiger galloped toward them. A forest bordered the grasslands, and I recognized its gray trees. I followed a river that flowed from the iron-colored forest and into the plain.

The stream grew wider when it flowed over a cliff, and the water foamed noisily. Fish leapt in the water, and I saw a giant catch one directly from the river. I wanted to fly away again, but I spotted a small group of figures. I circled above them.

Eskild strode forward in the snow-filled head wind along with a small group of five male and female berserkers. They were following the river, which twisted and turned off into the distance. I circled over it and saw where it stopped. It was a large manor that, in height, could almost be compared to Valhalla. Drumbeats sounded from the hall, and orange flames flickered through the windows from their great fireplace.

"Loki, Loki, Loki . . ." people chanted wildly from inside. The air around the manor was heavy with roasted meat and burnt wood. Hundreds of giants exited the manor, and they blew into the air. Their mouths emitted ice crystals and a wind so strong, it must have reached all the way to Midgard and Hrafnheim. I was blown backward and tumbled away from Jotunheim. Because time flowed like water around me, I didn't know if what I saw was present or past.

And then I was back on the chair in Odin's quarters.

I got to my feet and hurried away from Hlidskjalf. I would have liked to take it home to Odinmont to oversee all the worlds, but I knew it was impossible. Instead, I kept looking for the Gjallarhorn gold. I reached the cloth-covered spherical shape in the middle of the table. I lifted the stained fabric and jumped back with a cry that was, fortunately, muffled by the scarf over my mouth.

In the middle of the table sat a disembodied head. It was not . . . fresh, for lack of a better word. I'm not familiar with decapitation terminology. *Recently severed*, I suppose, which was absolutely not the case for this head. The skin was bluish green, and black around the eyes, which were rolled back so the whites faced outward. The mouth was open, exposing yellow-brown teeth frozen in a shocked grin. The hair was tousled, and the forehead bore runes carved with small, gaping incisions. My stomach turned as I recognized the symbols from Belinda. This man, however, had many, in row upon row of small, bluish-black, puffy lines. Shortly after I had removed the cloth, a swarm of blue bottle flies gathered and circled around the long-dead body part. The smell that wafted from it was sweet and decayed, like a rotten piece of bacon.

"Jesus," I gasped once I'd regained the ability to form words. "Odin, you are one sick son of a bitch." I held a hand over the scarf that covered my mouth, suppressing waves of nausea. I turned around and sniffed the smoldering cannabis from the fireplace—anything but the stench of corpse. The smoke made me lightheaded, but I welcomed its effects. Someone behind me cleared their throat, and I froze with fear.

"Well met, raven," a man's voice said.

Is that Odin? If so, all would be lost.

I slowly turned around. The room was just as empty as before. I stood completely still, but my eyes scanned from side to side.

"Good evening."

Again, I searched the room, which was empty apart from me.

"Are you invisible?" I managed to ask.

"Invisible? I'm right here."

But there was no one there. No one aside from the macabre, rotting old head.

"Look properly, raven."

I spun all the way around. "This isn't funny."

"Funny! No, it's not funny. There is no amusement in sitting around here for over a thousand years."

Finally, I focused and stepped back with a horrified intake of air, which nearly sent me to the floor with its combined stench of rotten meat and hash.

The head's eyes were no longer white; they had rolled into place. What had once been blue irises were now nothing more than watery circles with black pupils in the middle.

"Would you be so kind as to come over here," it said with a paper-thin voice as sharp as a knife. "My nose itches something awful, and as you can see, I can't reach it myself."

CHAPTER 14

I felt my jaw move as cold prickled the bridge of my nose. I may have tried to say something, but I had completely lost control of my mouth. Fortunately, the head didn't seem quite as stunned as I was.

"I know. I know. *Ewww, you're gross. Your eyes are half rotted, and your tongue is blue. You stink, and the flies lay eggs that turn into maggots in your skin.* Blah, blah, blah . . . I've heard it all before." He rolled his watery eyes, and one got stuck, making him momentarily walleyed. He grimaced so violently that the whole head teetered on its neck stump, which was caked in black dried blood. I was scared he would roll onto the floor, but the eye slid into place, and the head remained upright.

"Maggots?" I whispered and yanked the scarf away from my mouth.

"Why do you think my nose itches?"

"Are you Mimir?" My voice was shaking so much, I didn't recognize it.

"I am Mimir. I would bow, but as you can see . . ." He laughed dryly. "It is a great honor to meet Odin's raven and völva."

"I'm actually pretty new to this. I'm not really sure what this whole völva thing is about. You're Odin's friend?"

Mimir pursed his lips. "Adviser."

As I remembered from my history book, Mimir was a kind of oracle. I studied the stinking head. He didn't look particularly oracle-like.

You would think Mimir could read my thoughts. "Before you know it, you'll be entrusting me with your deepest, darkest secrets," he said.

"I don't think I will." I formed my lips into a little smile. "I'm not one for talking about myself."

"Are you sure?" Once again, the head laughed its brittle laugh, which rattled a little, and I wondered where he got the air to speak. I decided not to dwell too long on that thought. "Come over here and scratch my nose."

I hesitated. In fact, I backed up slightly.

"I will shout for help if you take so much as a single step away from me." He suddenly sounded threatening. "Come here and scratch me."

"Or what?"

"Or I'll shout for Odin. I bet he's promised you a triple death if you disobey. I wouldn't put it past the old grouch."

Anger gave me the strength to speak clearly. "Stop trying to psych me out. You're just a severed head."

Mimir laughed. There was indeed something rattling in his throat. "I should think I'm living proof of the opposite. Did you catch that? *Living* proof." He wiggled his thin brows, and a couple of hairs fell from his forehead. "Come on. Be a good raven and come over here and scratch me. I'll pay you well."

I took a deep breath and changed direction, walking toward the table. The half-rotted head smiled seductively.

"Come on. Come on. And don't peck at me. I know how you vultures can be."

I reached him and cautiously extended my finger. "I'm not a vulture, but if I survive this, there's a fair chance I'll become a vegetarian." When my fingertip met the bridge of his nose, the yellow skin was cold and stiff. It was a little like touching a raw pork chop. Something squirmed beneath my finger. It took everything in my power to keep my stomach from an upheaval.

The head had closed its eyes, and he let out a long *aaahhhh*. "Don't stop, don't stop, don't stop."

I quickly removed my hand. "Is the Gjallarhorn gold in here?" It was my turn to negotiate.

He looked up at me pleadingly. "If I tell you, will you scratch me again?"

I held my fingers so close to the tip of his nose that he must have been able to feel their warmth. He wrinkled his nose as though trying to reach me with it. "Yes," he said, when he saw that wouldn't work. "It's in here."

"Where?"

"You have to scratch me a little more," Mimir begged, nearly hysterical. "You have no idea how desperate you get after so many years."

I hastened to scratch him again, and his facial expression was almost funny beneath my hands. Aside from the dried blood and the bulging runes on his forehead, he resembled an excited dog.

"So, where is it?"

"Do you want me to shout for Odin?" he warned.

"Are you really going to call him? Odin won't scratch you, but I will."

Mimir uttered a curse so vulgar, even I balked. He bared his brown teeth in an expression of resignation. He let out a couple of rasping coughs. Then he pressed his eyes shut, and because the blue-black skin hung beneath them, it looked exceptionally disgusting. "What do you want the Gjallarhorn gold for?"

"I want to reassemble the horn."

Mimir looked shocked. "Do you want Heimdall to blow it? You'll start Ragnarök if you do that." He looked me in the eyes, and there was a blue flicker at the edge of my field of vision.

"I want it so the giants don't get their hands on it," I assured him. "No one is less interested in doomsday than I am. I want to destroy the Gjallarhorn. Wow! How did you get me to tell you that?"

Mimir's face took on a cunning expression. "I did say I can get everyone to talk about their secrets."

I opened my mouth in an outraged grimace. "You . . ."

"Do you mind just looking behind my ear while you yell at me?" Mimir interrupted. "There's something pressing there."

I studied him. "It must come in handy, being able to get people to talk like that."

"It's a rhetorical trick. And a little magic," Mimir added, but the word *magic* ended in a grating cough.

Pensively, I reached out and folded the top part of his ear down. "I just found out that Eskild, who has some of the gold, is on his way to Jotunheim. I'm sure he plans to sell it to the giants or something. Hey! You did it again. You diverted my attention." This time, I wasn't angry; I was more amazed. I really wanted to learn his trick. "I don't want to go to Jotunheim," I said.

"And you can't anyway. You'll need to train your völva powers much more before you're ready for that journey."

"Do you know about völva powers?" I asked.

"I know about *everything*! Come on, look behind my ear."

"I'm actually pretty busy. Odin could come at any moment . . ." Despite my protests, I looked behind his ear. "Ew! What the hell is that?" I studied a swollen, red bump just beneath his hairline.

"I don't know. I can't see it myself."

I pressed lightly on it, and a little yellow pus seeped out.

"Ow!"

I bent over and studied the boil. "Why hasn't anything been done about this? You also have sores on your scalp."

"The All-Father is too busy with his other dealings to look after me—or maybe he doesn't care. He just wants answers from me when—once every three hundred and twenty years—he isn't sure about something."

"That's cruel," I muttered. "Back in Midgard, they take away your children and animals if you don't take proper care of them.

It's absolutely not okay that Odin has neglected you this way. It's abuse."

"Head abuse." Mimir nodded. It looked strange at the end of his short neck stump.

Absentmindedly, I scratched his chin. He moaned with evident relief, his eyelids lowered. He stuck his bluish tongue out and sighed deeply. I looked critically at the boil behind his ear. It would require long-term treatment if it was going to heal. I pulled myself together. "Now tell me where the gold is!"

"Hmmmm." He leaned his head back slightly and got a distant look in his eyes.

"Hey . . . You sounded pretty wise there." If he'd had a body, I would have nudged his shoulder.

"I'm extraordinarily clever," he confided. "But no one can think clearly when their skin is crawling."

"Tell me." I tried with all my might to stay focused so Mimir couldn't distract me again.

Mimir looked at me with dignity—as much dignity as one can possess with a swarm of flies buzzing around one's head. "I have the gold," he said, and for the first time, he sounded like a real person.

"You have it?" I looked at the head from all angles. "Where? I mean . . ."

"I'm sitting on it."

"Ugh!" I covered my mouth but quickly removed my hand, which smelled suspiciously sweet. I swatted the flies away resolutely. "Okay. I'm going to pick you up. Ready?"

The head was heavy, and it made a squelching sound as it left the table. I looked beneath it, where a crusty brown ring marked where it had been sitting.

"There's no gold."

"It must have gone up into my throat. I thought I felt something scratchy."

For Christ's sake. I set him down carefully with the back of his head against the table. "Are you comfortable?"

"It's nice to see the ceiling for the first time in two hundred years. I haven't changed position since the time Odin got drunk and knocked me over."

I knelt and looked up into the disembodied piece of flesh. I steeled myself and stuck two fingers up into the windpipe.

"Hrrrr," Mimir said.

"Sorry." I pressed my fingers farther up and spread them. Finally, I felt something hard, nearly all the way up Mimir's throat. I gathered my fingers and grabbed the hard thing with a pincerlike grip. I pulled it toward me and felt Mimir's throat muscles spasming. "Sorry," I said again. "I'm really sorry about this. Sorry."

"Bwrrrr," Mimir said nauseously. He stared up at the ceiling with a pained expression but allowed me to continue the operation.

I managed to yank the hard object out. Mimir lay groaning and clearing his throat. As gently as possible, I shifted him upright. I wiped the slimy object on my coat. The gold shone dully.

"Are you okay?"

Mimir smacked his lips a couple of times and coughed again. The rattling sound was gone. "It actually feels great to get that out."

I studied the chunk of gold, which wasn't much bigger than my thumb. It was curved and ragged at the edges and looked like it had been cut off the end of a tube. A figure was printed into the metal. I turned the gold between my fingers. Life reverberated through it like a faint pulse, just as the pendant with Freyja's tears tended to do. The imprinted figure depicted a man with one body and three heads. Where there should have been nipples, the man had sun symbols instead.

"Who is that?" Something made me keep my voice down. "Is it Odin and his brothers?"

"The Gjallarhorn is much older than Odin, Vili, and Ve. It was made when Lúgh was the supreme god."

"Then why does he have three heads?"

Mimir cleared his throat again. "Lúgh is obsessed with the eternal cycle: birth, life, and death. He thinks it all works together."

"Lúgh as in Loki?"

"Everything and everyone overlap."

I stuck the gold in my pocket. "Thanks for the help." I scratched him one last time. "I have to go now."

Mimir didn't respond but merely looked back at me sadly. The maggots still squirmed beneath his skin, but he kept his face calm. With hesitant steps, I walked toward the door.

"I'm really sorry you're so neglected," I said. "Odin shouldn't even have you if he's not going to care for you."

"I know, but I can't leave," Mimir said. "I can't die, either."

At the exit, I looked over my shoulder, and Mimir was looking back at me. His yellow skin sagged and the flies buzzed over his head, some landing to lay more eggs in him. Mimir could look forward to hundreds of more years under these conditions. Death wasn't even an option to free him.

I carefully closed the door to Odin's office. My bag, one strap hanging over my shoulder, would just barely close. Od was leaning against the wooden wall with his eyes closed and his head tilted back. He had placed himself directly under a torch, the light reflected in his shiny hair. For a moment, it appeared to be on fire. He was unbearably beautiful, and the divinity in him seemed ready to overflow.

"We need to go," I said cautiously.

He nodded, eyes still squeezed shut, and straightened to his full height. My head reached only as high as his hip.

"Did you find what you were looking for?"

"Yep."

He exhaled, and a warm breeze hit me.

We left Valaskjálf and ran across the square. It was a short trip, and we would soon be out of Asgard. The shadows looked threatening and reached out after me. Even though I wanted to grab Od's hand, I didn't—he was trembling like an electric fence during a power surge. I could tell he was clinging to his last shreds of humanity.

"Soon," I whispered. "As soon as we get back, I'll get ahold of Elias so he can discharge some of the divinity from you."

Od didn't respond. His gleaming silver hand reached out to the door that led out of Asgard. The cool light hit the wooden palisade, making its splinters and knots stand out. Although the handle was several yards above our heads, I didn't doubt for a second that Od could reach it.

"Raven. Nephew," a voice said in the darkness. Loki stepped out from a shadow as though from thin air.

It was my first time seeing him close up. His presence nearly brought me to my knees, even though I was used to being around gods and demigods. Loki was different. He was breathtaking in the way only nature can be, right before it kills you with a tornado or a volcanic eruption. Impressive and deadly.

"Uncle." Od bowed and wrapped his arm around himself.

"What are you doing here at this late hour?" Loki slunk around us as smoothly as a cat. First, he was on one side, then the other. "I thought my little performance with the skald had scared you away." He looked directly at me, and I got the sense that he had bitten Tryggvi's hand off just for me.

"We came out for some fresh air." Od was still looking down at the ground. The back of his neck was exposed, and Loki bent over him. I had the urge to go between the two men, but I forced myself to stay back. Loki breathed in my ear, and I jumped; I hadn't even noticed he was so close.

"What will your wife have to say about that, Od?" He laughed, and it sounded like a cackling bird. "She's probably too busy sleeping with your father or the four dwarfs." Although the words were directed at Od, he looked at me. "And what about your friend? Or should I say *friends*? What will they say about you sneaking around late at night with Odin's son?"

I had no idea who he was talking about, so I didn't respond, but I thought I saw jealousy in Loki's eyes. My instinct was to get as far away as possible, but at the same time, he drew me to him like a magnet. Loki glided back in front of Od.

"We just came out for some fresh air," Od repeated. He was apparently unable to formulate a new sentence.

"I don't believe you. I. Think. You're. Plotting. Something." With each word, which he pronounced slowly and clearly, he tilted his head, first one way, then the other, as he got closer to Od. He got down on his knees and looked up into Od's manic, shining eyes. The next thing he said sounded like a machine gun firing. "I know all about plotting. I can smell it when someone's up to something."

Od trembled, but he kept his head bowed and his voice monotone. "We just came out for—"

"Lies," Loki hissed.

"Don't call a god's son a liar." Od raised his head. His eyes glinted with anger, and I took a sideways step away from him. Divine fury was nothing to mess with.

But at the same time, Loki moved in a fluid motion. A wide smile split his mouth. This was precisely the reaction he was looking for. "Or else . . . ?"

Od stepped forward, and in my memory, I saw Loki cut Od's throat with Tilarids. I quickly took Od's hand. A tidal wave of divinity flowed into me.

"He wants you to attack. That would give him an excuse to kill you," I said. It was pointless to speak softly as I knew Loki would hear me.

Od squeezed my hand so hard it hurt, but I didn't move. "He won't be able to kill me."

That's what I'm afraid of.

"Go," I said to Loki. "Go back to the feast. Don't you have more hands to bite off?"

Loki looked at me. "I'll gladly bite any hand. Even the hand that feeds me, my raven."

"I'm not *your* raven."

He came so close, it felt like he was permeating my skin. His gray eyes were right in front of mine, and ice crackled in my ears. Everything spun around, and it took all my strength to stay on my feet.

"That's where you're wrong," he purred. One more step, and he would disappear into me. "I see you as my own terrifying black raven. You and I know each other well, and we're going to get to know each other even better."

I couldn't breathe. Even though Loki wasn't touching me, I felt a strong hand squeeze my neck. I brought my fingers to my throat and struggled for air. Od put his arms around me.

"She's mine."

Immediately, I once again felt cool divinity gliding into me. My airways grew stronger. I felt my tissues toughen through Od's strength. Loki's invisible hand vanished, and I inhaled loudly.

"She's mine," Od said again, and it sounded like a thunderclap.

It felt like we'd become one person, his arm melting into my body where it lay. I didn't want to belong to anyone, but if the choice was between Loki and Od, I knew very well who I would rather belong to. I leaned into Od's chest, which swelled beneath his shirt. His anger was very close to setting the god in him loose. For a moment so brief that I would have missed it had I blinked, Loki actually looked scared. Then, his expression returned to nonchalance and suppressed amusement.

"Yours?" He chuckled. "We can share." His long fingers snaked toward me, and I jerked backward into Od's arms. "We could have a great time, the three of us. A god, a giant, and a delicate little human." This last part was said as though I were no more significant than a pillow.

Oh no!

I turned my head, but in my peripheral vision I saw a white flash from Od's aura. I felt him growing above me. Fabric ripped, and he suddenly looked like his true form. A mythical warrior. He was usually good at hiding it, but it was beyond his control. Both his enormous arms were wrapped around me, and a chilly current of pure divinity shimmered around him. He was extremely beautiful, brutal, and frightening. Almost as frightening as Loki himself.

"The raven is mine," he bellowed, and his breath looked like it could separate Loki's flesh from his bones in an instant. It sputtered like boiling water, and a scalding hot cloud flew forth.

Loki managed to duck just in time, and in the same movement, he leaned over in an agile bow.

"If a woman is spoken for, I can't take her—no matter how much I would like to." He walked backward into the shadows.

"Thank you," I panted. "Now, let's—"

My words were cut off by Od's mouth, which he placed on mine. It was hot, but fortunately not scalding, and he kissed me in a way that made my knees buckle. The human was gone, and the god in him had taken over. Pure power and wildness flowed into me from his lips, hands, and torso, which were pressed against me. He broke off the kiss just as I was about to swoon.

"Focus, Od! We have to g—" He kissed me again, and I couldn't help but kiss him back. Pure, mercurial divinity glided down my throat and dispersed throughout my body. Od's hands slipped into my hair, and I melted in his strong grip. He released my mouth and moved his lips down my neck.

"Od. Stop," I gasped.

He stopped and placed his shining metallic face in front of mine, his hands forming a crown around my head. He unleashed his powers of persuasion, and I was incapable of doing anything other than putting my arms around him.

"I love you." I couldn't tell if his voice was inside my head or if he spoke out loud, but I felt the words deep in my bones.

"But you love all humans," I managed to whisper.

"Yes," he sighed, and it sounded like crashing waves. I smelled sand and seaweed, and I was rocked gently by the waves. "You are a human." Coming from him, the word sounded like the greatest praise. Nothing like the dismissive way Odin and Loki had said it. "I love your humanity. All your vulnerability and all your faults. All your strength and your unstoppable will."

"Od." I didn't know if I was asking him to let go of me or to kiss me again.

"Human." He said it again, and I felt the sun on my skin, the wind in my hair, and the water splashing around me.

The next morning, I woke up in my bed at Odinmont. I had no idea how we had gotten there. Next to me in bed, Od was sleeping. He once again looked like a normal man—albeit an exceedingly handsome one. His skin had a healthy, human color; his hair was soft but totally normal, and his muscles were no longer swollen like those of a mythical hero. When I lifted my own hand, it shone slightly, and my nails were so hard and sharp they resembled claws.

My ratty backpack was tossed in a corner of my bedroom. It had a brown spot on the side, and inside it was something that looked like a ball. It was so big, the zipper could barely close.

CHAPTER 15

"You stole Mimir's head?"

Elias stood in front of the dining table at Odinmont. His hands were buried in his soft curls, and he looked horrified. On the table, atop a white handkerchief that was already turning brown from old blood and pus, sat Mimir. He looked back and forth between us like a child watching his parents fight. He kept his blue lips pressed together, but his face quivered with emotion. And with maggots.

"I rehomed him," I said calmly when Elias had to interrupt his hysterical tirade to inhale.

Elias breathed faster. "You rehomed him?"

Mimir's eyes moved to Elias, but he still said nothing.

"Just look at him," I said.

"He's a severed, embalmed head that's over a thousand years old. How did you expect him to look?" He turned toward Mimir. "No offense."

"None taken," Mimir replied. The bridge of his nose squirmed with larvae.

I reached out and carefully scratched Mimir's stiff yellow skin, and he sighed with contentment. "Odin has neglected him, and I didn't have any medicine to treat his wounds. And besides, I was there to steal something anyway. Mimir is just an extra theft."

"The Gjallarhorn gold is different."

"No matter which way we look at it, it's theft." I parted Mimir's hair down the center. "There are sores on his scalp, but I don't know where they came from. He's infected with parasites, and there's a boil behind his ear."

Curiosity won out over Elias's anger, and he looked where I was pointing. "You'll invoke the All-Father's wrath when he finds out," he said, but he already sounded less mad.

"I think it was invoked a long time ago. Besides, he only checks in with Mimir once every three hundred years. By the time he notices, I'll be long gone."

"It's one thing to refuse to carry out Odin's orders," Elias mumbled distractedly. "Stealing his property is something else entirely. You risk a triple death."

"I know." I still had no idea what a triple death was, but it didn't sound pleasant. The Gjallarhorn gold burned in my pocket.

Elias studied Mimir, moving about the head, his mouth slightly open. Pensively, he jutted his jaw sideways, sat on a chair, and pulled it up to the table. "May I examine you?" he asked Mimir, who nodded to the extent that he could. Elias said nothing, nor did he show outward signs of what he was thinking, but his aura flared with anger.

"That's what I'm saying. It's neglect." I looked over Elias's shoulder. "That's why I reached out to you."

"I was hoping you needed me for something else." Elias felt along Mimir's jawline, the back of his head, and across his maggot-infested cheekbones.

"Is it bad, doctor?" Mimir's water-colored eyes looked up pleadingly.

"I need to finish my examination, then I can give you my final verdict," Elias said jovially. "Go get some water and a clean rag, Anna," he said to me over his shoulder.

"I can't heat it up. There's no electricity during the day."

"Cold is fine."

I realized that horror had been plastered all over my face as I looked at Mimir's wounds. I quickly wiped the expression from my face and followed Elias's orders. I set a bowl next to him on the table and handed him a piece of fabric Luna had left behind.

Elias dug around in the leather pouch that always hung around his neck. It wasn't as full as usual, but there were nevertheless some bottles in it. He found a little ampoule and a needle, and he carefully injected various places on Mimir's face. "I'm sedating you," he said kindly to the severed head, and I felt a jolt of warmth. There were sides of Elias that I really did like. "I know you aren't in pain, per se, but this will take a while. I think it's best if you sleep through it. When you wake up, you'll already feel a lot better." Elias was so comforting, I would have gladly placed my life in his hands.

Mimir looked gratefully at Elias before his eyes rolled back in their sockets. Soon after, he was asleep. Elias checked to make sure Mimir was fully unconscious by pulling at the skin below his eyes and snapping a few times in front of his face. Then he shouted indignantly.

"I've never seen anything like this. I have no idea how to treat someone who's both embalmed and alive."

I looked at him, startled. "You seemed like you knew what you were doing."

"Of course I'd want to give that impression right before the drugs kick in. The patient shouldn't feel uneasy before an operation."

"Are you going to operate on him?"

Elias raked his hand through his unruly curls, which were starting to get quite long. "I'll have to make some incisions. They're small, but there's a lot of them." He moved his fingers back and forth over Mimir's skin. "It's been decades since I've had such a challenge." He suddenly broke into a grin. "Thank you, Anna. Thank you." He stood up, embraced me, and kissed me on the cheek. It was chaste and friendly, but nevertheless, I stiffened in his arms. "There is a lot to be learned from doing something for the first time. You did the right thing, both for him and for me."

Elias bent over again and pinched something on Mimir's chin between his thumb and index finger. Whatever it was wiggled under Mimir's skin.

"Great!" I said, nausea bubbling in my throat.

"Get my bag. It's in the hall."

"Can you cool it with the commands?"

Elias looked up with equal parts enthusiasm and determination. "You asked for my help, and I'm giving it, but I'm the one who calls the shots. You do as I say. This is about Mimir's welfare. Not you."

I grimaced but tromped into the hall.

"Do you have tweezers?" Elias called from the other room.

"I think Mathias left some here." I was already on my way to the bathroom, where I rummaged around before returning with the supplies.

"And a small bowl?" With his free hand, Elias pulled out a white lab coat, a mask, rubber gloves, and scalpels. The fingers of the other hand still pinched Mimir's skin.

I gave him one of Luna's ceramic cups. "Can you use this?" I cried out in horror as Elias made a small incision and used the tweezers to fish something white and alive out of Mimir's chin. My stomach rose up threateningly as the sweet smell intensified.

"Hand it to me."

I obeyed, eyes wide, and Elias plopped the maggot into the cup. It wriggled around, and I breathed through my nose.

"I need an assistant," Elias said. He was still staring at the sedated Mimir and struggling to fish the next living creature out of the head. "If you can't hack it, you can call Ulla."

I'd be damned if Elias's old flame was going to surpass me.

"If I could smuggle him out of Asgard, I can handle this."

"Great." His tone was completely neutral, but I thought I could detect approval in Elias's voice. "There are masks, gloves, and an apron in my bag. I'll walk you through it."

It took several hours to fix Mimir. During that time, Elias uttered several *tsks* and *arghs*. Everything he hadn't said while Mimir was awake, he got out during the operation.

"Mange!" Elias shook his head when we were almost done. "Do you realize how itchy this must be?"

"He was really miserable when I found him."

"The gods can be cruel at times." Elias pulled his mask down and let it hang around his neck. Darkness fell, but we didn't need to turn on a light. My teeth glowed bright white after my night with Od, even though I tried to keep my mouth closed as much as possible.

The demigod had left in the morning after kissing my hands and holding me close. I felt a strong love but nothing romantic. I asked him to let Elias know I needed his medical assistance, and Od had simply said *yes* before disappearing like a bolt of silver lightning across the field toward Kraghede Forest. Soon after, Elias arrived.

Elias rolled his shoulders and glanced at me. Mimir mumbled weakly but was still too sedated to pick up on our conversation.

"It'll take a couple of days. Then it won't be visible anymore." Elias nodded his head toward my mouth.

I closed my lips in front of my telltale teeth.

"It makes me jealous, seeing what happened between you two." Elias kept his eyes focused on the boil behind Mimir's ear, which he was smearing with salve. The rest of the head was covered with small Band-Aids and one thicker bandage.

I chose to play dumb. "Od has enough divinity for the both of us. You won't be deprived."

"That's not what I meant. I'm starting to feel like you're throwing your love at everyone but me."

"You're one to talk, with your whole harem. You might be able to hide it from others, but not from me."

Elias's face was devoid of the devious expression I usually associated with him. "Of course, you have every right to spend your nights with whomever you please. I'm just hurt."

Because we sat so close over the severed head, it felt very intimate. "I didn't think an operating room was a place for hurt feelings." I looked at Mimir and would have preferred to closely search for a particularly stubborn maggot than look into Elias's eyes. Even though Elias was sitting down, he did his typical half bow.

"Or niceties," I added quietly. "There's something else I'd like to ask you about."

Elias raised his eyebrows to signal for me to continue.

"Do all religions end with an apocalypse?"

"All the religions I've studied have a built-in doomsday prophecy. It's pretty consistent how people think it all ends and how to fight against it."

"How do you avoid the apocalypse? I mean, what do sources from other religions say?"

Elias wrapped the scalpel in the rag I had donated for the operation. "Doomsday can be delayed with offerings, an ascetic lifestyle, or prayer."

"I don't buy it."

"It doesn't really matter what you buy."

I clenched my fists indignantly. "What about science? Surely that's more rational."

"Science says the exact same thing. We try to delay the inevitable with sustainability initiatives or puritanical behavior, but in the end, doomsday will come. It doesn't matter who you ask. The only questions are *when* and *how*. I've been around everything. Even astrology." He made a face. "And I hate astrology."

"I thought your stargazing was a way to decompress."

"If I need to relax, I'll choose something more effective."

"So, what does astrology say?"

"That the world will end."

I got a vague feeling but pushed it away. "I'm done with prophecies and warnings. I want to change fate!"

"What makes you think you can? So far, everything has been true. Down to the most minor verses of Hejd's predictions."

"If Hejd's clairvoyance is like Serén's, then *Völuspá* is just one of many possible outcomes."

This made Elias drum his fingers pensively against the table. "That's a good point, but she saw the events and made sure Od wrote them down, so Ragnarök must be the most likely outcome. And if Ragnarök comes, we must soften the blow. We can prepare for doomsday, so the catastrophe is as small as possible."

"Is it possible for the destruction of everything to be modified?"

"I can't believe you don't know the mythology better. It's so important for you." Elias inhaled as though to tell me something, but he stopped himself when Mimir's eyes flew open. He noted that it was dark, that we were wearing operation gear, and that Elias's lab coat was covered in brown splatters and yellow streaks. He looked over at the bowl, which was half full of larvae.

"Did all those come from me?"

Elias moved the bowl out of Mimir's line of sight and reached out with gentle fingers to ensure that the large bandage was properly secured. "How do you feel?"

"Better than I have in the past several hundred years," Mimir replied and grimaced gingerly.

"You'll just need to heal before the last of the pain goes away." Elias had dark circles under his eyes. "We removed the bugs. Some of the maggots had buried themselves deep under your skin. There was swelling in the runes on your forehead, but now they're just scars."

I shuddered, aware that I had an identical scar on my back, only bigger. The ones on my upper arm closely resembled Mimir's.

"You had several abscesses, but they've been drained and treated. I'll give Anna the salve because it needs to be applied twice a day for a week. Then you'll need another lice treatment in nine days. I'd also like to fix your teeth, but now's not the time. I'll do that later."

We exchanged a look. Seeing as how we didn't know if the

human world would even exist much longer, there might be no point. Elias pulled off his lab coat and packed his instruments into his bag.

"You can keep the tweezers. I'll never be able to pluck my eyebrows with them again."

"I have somewhere I need to be." Elias lifted his old doctor's bag and tucked the leather pouch back under his shirt.

I wanted to beg him to stay or at least ask where he was going. I had the unpleasant thought that he was meeting a woman, which was unfair of me, to put it mildly, considering how and with whom I had spent the night. So, I just took my dirty apron off and handed it to Elias. I didn't walk him out, and I heard his car door slam in the driveway, after which he took off down the dirt road. Mimir looked from me to the door that Elias had just left through.

"Is he a good man?" His voice was deeper, and without the bugs, Mimir really did look like an oracle. His color was much better, and his hair was full and wavy.

"Elias is complicated." I sat down heavily on a chair. "He rarely does anything unless it's for his own gain, but I think deep down he has a good heart, however deep down it may be."

"He just helped me because you asked him to, knowing full well that you had spent the night with someone else."

"You don't know what you're talking about."

"I was sitting in the bag and witnessed what happened between you and Odin's son, so I know exactly what I'm talking about."

I laid my head on the table in despair. Mimir looked down at me, and despite all his bandages, he managed to look soft. "What is Elias Eriksen to you?"

"I don't know anymore."

"But he's there for you. Always."

"He is. Despite all his faults, he's always there. He's never left me at any point, which isn't something I can say about many other people. And he accepts all my weird and irrational sides."

I thought of Varnar, Sverre, Hakim's ghost, and the night with Od. "Who would have ever thought there would be so many men in my life."

"Mighty whoredom!"

I lifted my head. "Hey, that's not fair."

Mimir spoke slowly, and his deep voice sounded like a skald's, but inside my head, it was Hejd's voice I heard.

Brothers shall fight and fell each other
And sisters' sons shall kinship stain
Hard is it on earth
With mighty whoredom
Axe-time, sword time, shields are sundered
Wind-time, wolf time, ere the world falls
Nor ever shall men each other spare

"There will be mighty whoredom before the world ends."

"What does it even mean for whoredom to be mighty?" I was still a little insulted.

"It's intense. Or there's a lot of it."

I bit my lip.

Mimir looked down at me with a crooked smile. "In our faith, there is nothing wrong with being a little loose."

"What if my loose lifestyle causes the end of the world?"

"Anna," Mimir said seriously. "You aren't causing anything. Open your eyes and look at me. You are not at fault for this. You have to believe that. What Hejd saw is in the future. If anything, it's the future's fault that you're getting dragged though everything."

"I just don't want to keep killing everyone."

Mimir laughed. "You might be giving yourself too much credit. Many other people over the past thousand years have played a part in the road toward the end."

"But if I hadn't survived as a baby, a lot of people wouldn't be dead." My voice was now paper-thin. "All the red-haired girls, Finn, Faida, and Benedict. The people I killed myself. Even Ragnara's death—I wish I weren't responsible for that. I ruin everything."

"If Hejd is to be believed, you're going to make everything right again."

"Did you know her?"

Mimir swallowed, although I don't know what he swallowed or where it ended up. "I knew her. She was beautiful, and Od loved her. But they saw things differently, and therefore, they had to part ways."

"How did they see things differently?"

"Od thinks he must sacrifice himself to postpone Ragnarök." There was a small, sad flicker of Mimir's mouth.

The image of Loki cutting Od's head off hit my retinas. "But Hejd never went to Valhalla when she died?"

"She converted to keep that from happening. Odin searched all the worlds for her with no luck." Mimir's voice sounded like a gentle song.

Of the runes of the gods
And the giants' race
The truth indeed can I tell,
To nine worlds came I,
to Niflhel beneath,
where the dead go from Hel.

"Then he put the völva powers in a new place."

"In Thora's womb. The völva powers were given to Serén."

"But they were split."

A chill ran down my spine. Now that Ben was dead, my repulsions spells would never be lifted, and Serén and I would be separated for all time. I cleared my throat and changed the subject. "What did Hejd think?"

Mimir sighed deeply. "She thought Heimdall should blow the Gjallarhorn so that the world ends. Ragnarök must come so the fields can grow again."

"But the gods die?" My head was still lying on the table.

"Most of them. But Hejd had a plan for who would then reign."

I didn't dare say it aloud, so I whispered it instead. "Od?"

Mimir nodded. "The problem was that Od wasn't on board with that plan. It's very hard for the children of gods to betray their parents."

"I think that's hard for all children."

Smile lines appeared around Mimir's eyes. "You're probably right."

"What's my role?"

Mimir looked down at me stoically. "You have to figure that out for yourself. But I will advise you to gain better control over your völva powers."

"How do I do that?"

"You need a staff, for starters. Luckily, you know some witches."

"What do witches have to do with it?"

"The völva staff must be cut from a birch tree during the night following the autumn festival, uppskeru."

I looked at the dark square that was my window. At the bottom of the glass were layers of ice.

"Kind of impractical that we're living through an eternal winter, then, if we need an autumn festival."

Mimir made a *tsk* sound. "Uppskeru doesn't go away just because there's an unusual winter. We've celebrated that day for as long as I can remember, and I can remember very far back."

"I've completely lost my sense of time."

"It's tomorrow night, Anna. I imagine the celebration will be reinstated now that the sun is gone."

"So, I'll have a völva staff if I can get ahold of a birch tree harvested by Luna tomorrow night?"

"It has to be consecrated with alms."

"What kind of alms?"

"A gift from your monarch. Royal powers have always been magical."

"Our royal family doesn't give out alms anymore. Unless I can consecrate the staff with moral support, they aren't much use to me."

Mimir looked thoughtful. "A lot has happened in Midgard during the thousand years I've been gone. I should think your leader would count as a monarch."

"The authorities are handing out packages of food. Could that work?"

"The monarch is called *the authorities* now?" Mimir tutted. "Things really have changed."

I sighed and rested my cheek against the table's surface. And we sat. Two heads side by side in the darkness, illuminated only by the divinity that still streamed from my mouth and eyes.

"Ahh!" There came a voice from the door. "What happened?"

I rose from my awkward position half lying on the table. From where Arthur stood, I could imagine that Mimir and I had looked like two severed heads instead of just one. Arthur ran up to me and held me close. He was shaking and wouldn't let me go. "I thought you'd been executed."

"I'm totally fine."

Arthur turned toward Mimir. "What are you doing with a severed head?" My father was very matter-of-fact when it came to body parts since he had spent eighteen years as a corpse in a crypt surrounded by skeletons.

"Good evening," Mimir said. His voice was deep and clear.

Arthur jumped back and pulled me with him. With a force that must have come from the fatherly urge to protect, he pushed me behind him.

"Arthur, this is Mimir. Mimir, this is my father, Arthur," I said from behind him.

Arthur looked down at Mimir with horror, but it apparently wasn't the talking head that frightened him. "*The* Mimir?"

"The one and only," I said.

"You're Freyja's little boyfriend." Mimir furrowed his brows, which were still a little thin, but at least they weren't falling out anymore.

Arthur glanced sideways at me. "It's been many years since I was Freyja's boyfriend."

Understanding reached Mimir's face when he looked between the two of us. "Anna is your daughter with Thora Baneblood."

"Mimir is also mad at the gods." I explained how I had taken him away from the mistreatment he had been subjected to.

"He looks pretty good, aside from the bandages."

"You should have seen him this morning. He had mange and scabies and who knows what else, but Elias fixed him up."

"And what are we going to do with him? The All-Father will take revenge for your thievery."

I crossed my arms and walked forward, and this time my father couldn't hold me back. A night with Od had boosted my strength. "Odin can fight me! If he's not capable of looking after Mimir, then he doesn't deserve to have him in his care."

Arthur patted me on the back. "That's right, Anna. I'm proud of you." He carefully picked Mimir up. "I think my daughter needs some rest. Would you like to come down to the crypt?"

Mimir lit up. "I've been hearing about Odinmont for a thousand years. Since before Odin lost his eye. But I didn't think I would ever visit the mound myself."

"It's my home," Arthur said. "I think it's an old passage grave, but I'd love to get your opinion." Cautiously, he eased Mimir into his arms.

"I knew the woman who constructed the mound," Mimir said. "But I didn't get to see it before . . ."

Their voices grew fainter as they made their way down the stairs to the mass grave under my house, as the severed head and my re-animated father chatted merrily.

I really liked Mimir. He fit in perfectly with the rest of us.

CHAPTER 16

We stood in line in what used to be the supermarket's parking lot. I looked up at the new sign that had been hung over the store's old name.

Food and Consumer Goods Center, it said now. The center itself was closed, but a trailer open on one side was parked in front. People poked their heads through a small window in the trailer and held out boxes and bags they had brought with them.

The line moved slowly, and my feet tingled from standing on the frozen asphalt. A man in front of us let out a deep, rattling cough.

"You should go home if you're sick." Arthur looked at him with concern.

The man tightened his grip on his son's hand. "I need medicine. My wife has a fever." He sounded a bit distant, and his cheeks flamed.

Arthur left his place at my side and walked up to the counter, where he spoke to someone. He returned with a man who normally worked at Ravensted Public Library.

"Come with me," the librarian said, gesturing for the sick man to follow him.

While my father helped the sick man, I walked in place to get blood circulating to my feet. Finally, it was my turn to go up to the window and receive my alms.

"Greta," I said.

She looked up from her place behind the counter. A heater was running at full blast behind her, but she still seemed freezing in her layers of sweaters topped with a thick coat and a knit hat.

"Anna." The skin around her nostrils was red, and she was thinner than usual, if that was even possible. I felt a rare tenderness at the sight of the person who, aside from Arthur, had been the only consistent adult presence throughout my entire childhood. I must have gotten soft recently, because without thinking, I leaned over the counter and embraced my old case worker. At first, she let out a little cry of surprise, but she quickly hugged me back.

"How are you?"

Greta looked stunned. In all the years she had had me as a client, we had never talked about her. Now I was embarrassed that I'd never asked. She looked at me warmly. "I'm good, Anna. How about you?"

I gestured toward the snow-covered parking lot behind us. "Aside from the weather, everything's the same." That was a flat-out lie, but I couldn't very well let Greta in on my travels to other worlds and new relationships with various supernatural beings. "I'm going to school and working at Frank's."

Greta nodded approvingly. She leaned forward slightly. "Are you still dating that janitor?"

I had to rack my brain to realize she was talking about Varnar. So much had happened in the meantime, it was hard to remember the days when everything was normal. When there were only two measly murderers after me, and I had two private bodyguards, one of whom was Varnar. Compared with the impending apocalypse and the fact that I now had to defend myself, that had been a simpler time.

"Varnar had to leave town," I mumbled.

Arthur came back and stood at my side. His red hair stuck out from beneath his cap.

"Who's your *new* friend?" Greta pursed her narrow lips in the disapproving way I had become very familiar with growing up.

"My da—" I realized that, in Greta's eyes, Arthur was a regular guy in his mid-twenties. "My roommate," I corrected myself.

"Hmmm." Greta quickly looked down, probably to keep from admonishing me. She shuffled through her papers. "It's a good thing I still know your ID number by heart," she said. "Anna Stella Sakarias, Anna Stella Sakarias . . ." Her gloved finger ran down a list. "There you are. Give me your bag."

Obediently, I held out the pink tote that Luna had sewn for me. Greta disappeared through the back and returned with the bag bulging with goods. Then she looked at Arthur.

"What's your date of birth?"

"I'm just here with Anna." He pointed at himself. "Pack mule." He quickly grabbed the fabric bag, put his arm around me, and turned me away from Greta, who watched me from her place behind the counter. I looked over my shoulder. All I could see were her hat and her eyes, which followed me with a combination of pride and melancholy.

There were already five people gathered on the other side of the supermarket. Arthur hurried over to them.

"We got a dishcloth and some headache pills that we won't use," he said. "Who wants to trade for food?"

A man waved. "I have a can of beans and a bag of bulgur."

"For the dishcloth?" Arthur knew very well that the pills were in highest demand.

A woman coughed.

Arthur continued talking to the bulgur man. While they negotiated, I looked in my tote bag. There was hand cream, a large bag of oats, a tin of cod roe, dried lentils, and some nuts. The hand cream could probably be used for a little völva staff consecration.

"Are we done?"

Arthur looked at me, a little irritated. "Why are you in such a rush, Anna?"

"I have to do something, but I can just go ahead."

"We're coming! Just a second." Arthur leaned back toward the group. "What else did you see in Kraghede Forest?" he asked the woman who had coughed.

"Big stones. They must have been there all along, but when the trees fell, you could see them. I take walks in there with my dog." Then she coughed again. She hacked and gasped. It took a minute for her to catch her breath. When she did, she continued. "I always thought they were little mounds, but they're stones with runic inscriptions. If the museums were open, I would have called an archaeologist."

These were the same stones I had used to travel to Vindr Fen. The stone circle that was really an old blót site and a portal to Hrafnheim.

"Where are they?" Arthur pulled his scarf in front of his mouth and took a step back.

"Not far from Kraghede Manor." The woman coughed again. This time, the attack lasted longer. Arthur got a strange look on his face. He put his arm protectively around me and pulled me back.

A man pounded the coughing woman on the back. "That's quite a frog you've got in your throat." Someone else in the crowd started to cough, too.

Arthur pulled me away from the group. "Put your scarf over your mouth," he said quietly.

"What?"

"Just do it!"

I obeyed and pulled my scarf up over the lower half of my face. Then I looked back at the growing crowd of people. Several of them were coughing, and one was crouched in the snow.

"What's wrong with you guys? You're coug—" The bulgur man stopped mid-sentence and gasped for air. Arthur ran away from the people, pulling me behind him.

"This is how it always starts. I've seen it before." Arthur had pulled me over to our bikes and ordered me to head for Rebecca's without any explanation. Our bag of food and hand cream sat in the basket at the front of Arthur's antique delivery bike. He didn't even bring the bag in, leaving it all in Rebecca's driveway.

"Has she been infected?" Arthur turned my shoulders so I stood right in front of Rebecca in her living room.

She studied me. Then she closed her eyes and slowly inhaled through flared nostrils. There were rapid movements beneath her eyelids. "It's small but dangerous."

"There's something small and dangerous in me?" I had the urge to jump into the shower, even though I was sure it wouldn't remove whatever I was infected with.

"Hey, Anna and Arthur!" Luna bounded into the living room. "What are y—"

"Stay over there," Rebecca warned, holding her hand out toward Luna in the doorway.

Luna stopped. "What's going on?"

Rebecca was right in front of me, and she sniffed my neck. I stood still as Arthur paced around us with a distraught expression. Rebecca found a few dried herbs and crumbled them into a bowl, where she inserted a burning stick. The herbs flared, but the fire went out immediately. The dried leaves smoldered and created a strong, spicy smell. She murmured spells.

"It's here." Her hands followed my contours without touching me. "It's crawling in you." With a shout so loud the windowpanes vibrated, she flailed her arms around me and grabbed something from the air behind my head. In the same motion, she reached for Arthur with her other hand and pulled him to her. She caught something near Arthur's ear, then leaned back with her cornflower-blue eyes wide, her nearly white hair swinging around her. Her hands were clenched into fists, and she made a crushing motion. When she opened them, brown dust sprinkled to the floor.

Up against the wall leaned an old-fashioned broom, and she swept the dust away with a forceful swish. In that moment, she looked like a witch from a fairy tale.

"You were both infected. Come over here, Luna."

She obeyed, and soon, all four of us stood close together. Rebecca drew a circle around us with chalk and chanted something in Old Norse. Luna joined in the obscure rhyme with enthusiasm. She swung her arms and bobbed her head. I wasn't sure if she was supposed to be included in the magic's effect or help to strengthen it. Apparently, she didn't know, either. There was a loud bang, and we were surrounded by green smoke. I gasped for air and fanned the smoke away from me.

"You are protected," Rebecca proclaimed, her head bowed and arms outstretched.

"Do you mind explaining what's going on?" I wiggled out of what felt like a claustrophobic group hug.

"An epidemic has come to Ravensted." Arthur's red hair stuck out in all directions, as it always did when he was worried.

"I put a protection spell on us all. No one in this house will be infected," Rebecca promised.

"Was that a magic vaccine you just made? That's pretty cool." My grin froze. "All those people in line?"

Arthur put his hands on my shoulders. "We're going into the city now. Those we reach in time, we can help." I walked quickly toward the door, but Arthur grabbed a fistful of my coat, bringing me to a halt. "You and Luna are staying here!"

"Aren't we vaccinated?"

"We're not taking any chances," Rebecca said.

The gravity of the situation began to sink in. My heart pounded. "Will you find Greta first?"

Arthur nodded.

"What do you think it is?" Rebecca asked as she rummaged in a cabinet and pulled out bags of herbs.

"Fever and cough. Four or five started showing symptoms while we were there. Maybe an aggressive form of meningitis, based on how quickly it progresses. It's also reminiscent of tuberculosis or the Spanish flu, but even faster. I don't know how soon death occurs; I rushed out here with Anna."

Arthur looked at Rebecca somberly, and suddenly, a memory flashed from him. I was so overwhelmed that I stumbled backward.

"Anna!" Arthur's voice was hysterical. "Did the spell not work?"

I regained my composure. "It's not that. I saw the past." Squinting, I looked at my father. "You had white clothes on. There were rows of beds in a big hall. People were lying in them who didn't seem to be doing well. Ben and Elias were there, too. When was that?"

Arthur cleared his throat awkwardly, and Rebecca was suddenly very busy looking in the cabinet again.

"1918," Arthur said cautiously.

I had thought I was done getting shocking news. "How old are you, Dad?"

"About one hundred and fifty."

"What?"

Arthur searched for the words, but Rebecca interjected. "We don't have time for this conversation right now. You'll have to tell her later."

"I'll explain everything," Arthur promised, though he didn't seem eager to tell me anything at all.

Rebecca had filled her basket with remedies and wrapped herself in layer upon layer of scarves and hats. "Come on!"

They left, and I stood with Luna.

"So, my dad is old," I said dully. "Is anyone actually who they say they are?"

Luna was still mourning her own father's death, but she had begun to smile a little again. Her cheeks had a glow the rest of us had to go without. "I'm just myself."

"I know." I put an arm around her, and we sat on the sofa.

"An epidemic? As if the lack of food and severe frost in August isn't bad enough." Luna sighed.

An uneasy feeling crept up on me. "I think the prophecy is coming true. You yourself said that part of Fimbulwinter is disease."

Luna leaned back. "That's true."

"Did your parents tell the DSMA that it's also winter in Hrafnheim?" I covered my mouth with my hand. "Oh, shit. I meant your mom. I'm sorry I mentioned Ben."

Luna furrowed her brows in anguish, but she didn't reproach me. "You're right, things are ramping up."

"It's like we're running a race against *Völuspá*."

"How can we go faster?" Luna asked.

"I need to gain better control of my völva powers. Which reminds me, I need your help."

"I'll do anything for you."

I wanted to hug Luna. She never asked what she would have to do before agreeing to help. "I need you to cut down a tree. It's a small tree, and it's already been chopped most of the way down. You just need to cut the last few fibers. I need a völva staff, and it has to be made from birch harvested by a witch during uppskeru. The harvest festival."

"A völva staff? Are you planning to practice? I can get owl pellets." She pondered briefly. "And henbane seeds. I'm sure my mom still has some around here. You get super high when you burn them."

"It'll be great if you just harvest the birch."

"How long do you think the Fimbulwinter is?" Luna leaned even farther back into the sofa.

"The signs are almost all there. Natural disasters, check. Winter, check," I listed. "Loki has been freed, and the Midgard Serpent let go of its tail."

"What's it like, Jörmungandr?"

"It's huge." I reflected. "And scary—but the scariest part is that it's not biting its tail anymore. That means there's direct access to Hrafnheim from the giants' world. Even though it wasn't great that it was keeping people from leaving Hrafnheim, it was also protecting them."

Luna shivered. "There's supposed to be famine, disease, broken family ties, murder among close friends, and whoredom."

"We don't have a whole lot of food." I lifted a finger.

"But we're not starving, and as far as I know, no family ties have been broken."

"Ragnara and Sverre," I reminded her. "They had a falling out." I held up another finger. "That's two things."

"Sverre became king after Ragnara died, so that tie isn't totally broken."

"Okay, then," I mumbled.

But Luna was on a roll. "And what kind of whoredom are we talking about here?"

"Uh, well, I've been with both Varnar and Sverre."

"Two different guys in two years isn't exactly *whoredom*." Luna snorted. Then her eyes landed on my teeth, which were still glowing neon blue. She pointed at me, her eyes wild. "Oh my god! Or should I say DEMIGOD!"

I snapped my mouth closed and bit my lips to hide my teeth.

"You can hide it from everyone else, but I have a demigod boyfriend. You...You..."

"Yes, I did," I brushed her off and crossed my arms. I had absolutely no desire to talk about this.

"Is it Od? It has to be Od. He's SO hot."

"Luna," I tried, but my friend clapped her hands.

"Yay! Now we both have demigod boyfriends!"

"Od isn't my boyfriend. And he isn't going to be."

Luna gave me a sympathetic look.

"It's totally fine. I'm not crazy about him. It was just that one night." I couldn't help but giggle. "But it was a *really* nice night."

Luna smiled knowingly. She had often praised Mathias's abilities to an extent that made me extremely embarrassed.

"I don't want to talk more about it, aside from it being a possible sign that Ragnarök is coming."

Luna smirked. "I still don't think three men in two years makes you a whore, but I don't know how people viewed that kind of thing in the olden days."

"I think it's a lot. Too many."

Luna laughed. "You prude."

"I'm just looking at it from a logical perspective. Does it fit the prophecy?"

"I think you're twisting it to make it fit. People always overinterpret the myths, and it's just so facile. You can always make a horoscope or tarot reading fit if you contort it enough." Luna suddenly sounded more fierce than usual. I sat and stared into space, a little insulted, while Luna stroked her arm, deep in thought. I was not happy to be stuck inside, so I stood up and wandered around the room. Luna didn't move. She sat completely still and mumbled something inaudibly. Her eyes shone darker than usual. Outside, the frost began to crackle, and I looked out the window, worried.

It was a frost storm. They didn't usually strike during the day. Getting caught in one could be deadly. After an hour had passed, the front door opened, and Arthur and Rebecca walked in with dark circles under their eyes and dough-colored skin. Arthur was shaking with cold in his snowsuit, and Rebecca set her basket on the table.

"I almost miss being dead," Arthur said through chattering teeth. "At least I was never cold. We just made it before the frost storm hit with full force."

Luna rushed to the window, which was quickly getting covered in ice. "The frost is spreading over the fields. I hope no one's out there. They would die on the spot."

I laid a hand on my giant crystal, which was already glowing faintly, and turned it up with a bunch of loving thoughts for Monster and his family. Soon, waves of heat flowed into the living room, and my dad and Rebecca stood close to it, rubbing their hands together.

"So?" I asked anxiously. I couldn't shake the thought that I was to blame for the epidemic.

"There was disease in Ravensted," Arthur said. "It originated with those who had been in Kraghede Forest by the old stone circle. The authorities are working to pinpoint the infection, and Rebecca vaccinated them and everyone else she could get to. The disease is contained."

"If only Ben were still alive." Rebecca sat on a chair. She looked haggard and tired. "He would have had the strength to do so much more. A lot of people will succumb to the disease just because my magic is limited."

Arthur went to the window to look out at the frost storm. His face was distraught.

"Dad was a lot older than you. You're just as strong of a witch, only younger." Luna put her arm around her mother's shoulders. "But it's sad for all those people."

"Are they totally freaked out?" I asked.

"They're scared. Ben's hypnosis is wearing off, and it's all become clear to them. The winter, the disease, the lack of contact with the rest of the world." Arthur placed his hand on the windowpane. It was getting dark out, and his face was reflected in the glass.

Rebecca must have been completely exhausted, and she rested her cheek on the dining table. I caught a memory from her: Residents of Ravensted looked at her suspiciously. A woman spat and called her a witch.

"That woman—" Arthur said into the window.

Rebecca stopped him from speaking with a sharp look. "That woman was sick and afraid. People have intense reactions in this kind of situation."

Arthur didn't press the matter.

"How many?" I looked questioningly at my father.

"There are only ten dead, but that's ten too many. I have to tell you something."

Without realizing it, I had raised my hands to my mouth. Arthur turned away from the window and laid his hands on my shoulders.

"No." I shook my head forcefully.

"I know she was important to you."

I took in big gulps of air but still couldn't get enough oxygen. Dizzy, I staggered over to the bench and sat down.

"Did she suffer?"

"Not for very long."

"Greta . . ." I squeaked, as a flood of childhood memories washed over me. Sure, it wasn't exactly sunshine and rainbows to remember all my visits to Ravensted Social Center, but Greta had always treated me with respect and even a little warmth in a time when no one else gave a crap about me. "Were you with her when she died? She doesn't have any family." I almost added *other than me*.

"I was there, and I told her everything. She'd already suspected there was something supernatural about you, and I confirmed it. She cared for you very much. I will always be grateful to her for being there during your childhood." Arthur squeezed my hand.

"Me, too." My hands were shaking. "Was she infected by that man in line?"

"There has to be physical contact. A kiss or a hug."

I raised my head with a jerk. "I hugged her, and I've been down by the stone circle. Oh God. I killed Greta."

"It wasn't on purpose." Arthur's eyes were miserable.

"On purpose or not. I did it." I looked at Luna, and she looked back, horrified. "Disease, check," I said. "Murder between friends, check."

"Now we just need Fenrir to get free from his cave," Luna said.

CHAPTER 17

"Where's the witch?" a child in front of me asked. Practically all of Ravensted had gathered on the field between Odinmont, Ostergaard, and Rebecca's house. We stood in a trembling huddle in front of a giant pile of branches and wood that looked like twisted arms and legs with claws. The light, as always, was grayish, and if I hadn't known it was around four o'clock in the afternoon, I wouldn't have been able to tell. Nor would I have ever guessed it was late August.

"There won't be any witches at this bonfire," the child's mother said.

"Last year, on the beach in Løkken, we had a fire with a witch on top."

The mother didn't respond but instead spoke to the man next to her.

"I heard it was Od Dinesen who insisted on the bonfire and celebrating the harvest. He organized the whole thing. It's his gift to us, to provide comfort during the cold plague. A memorial for the dead. Od Dinesen will soon be the only person we can count on."

The mysterious epidemic had colloquially been dubbed the *cold plague*.

Several people gave me hostile looks, and I could feel with my clairvoyance that they were reacting to me with anger, but for now, they were behaving themselves.

"But why isn't there a witch? Isn't that the tradition for this kind of bonfire?"

"Od didn't want one. He's paying, so he gets to decide." The woman's voice faded away as a horn blasted. I didn't know where the sound came from, but the music—if you could call it that—was slow and melancholy. A dot of light approached rapidly from the other side of Ostergaard. As the light got closer, I saw it was a well-built man holding a burning torch over his head with a muscular arm. His torso and feet were bare, despite the snowdrifts surrounding him.

"He runs fast."

Od no longer bothered to hide the fact that he wasn't a normal human. With long, elegant strides, he ran toward us dressed only in thin pants and rolled-up shirtsleeves. He moved so quickly, it looked supernatural—which it was.

Even though I had spent the night with him the last time we saw each other, I felt neither nervous nor ashamed. What had happened between us was love. A god's love for a human. It wasn't romantic love, and I knew it would never happen again.

"Isn't he cold?"

"He must be blessed."

"Wow, he's attractive." The woman in front of me sighed.

Od arrived, tall and handsome. The orange light of the torch flickered across his face and made him look like a statue. He also lacked the pallid hue the rest of us, apart from Mathias and our classmate Mads, had acquired. He stood for a moment with the torch raised above his head and looked at us all, and for a split second, I felt him staring directly at me. A little smile reached my lips, and suddenly, I felt significantly warmer. The woman in front of me gasped, and there were small outbursts from several places in the crowd.

Mathias stood right behind Od, and his eyes shone like sapphires. I realized now that he was the one blowing the horn, the plaintive tones flowing over us. He lowered the instrument and also looked at everyone in the crowd. It was clear that he and Od were of the same kind.

Slowly, Od lowered the torch and held it to a corner of the heap of wood, where the flames caught immediately. He walked around the pile and let the torch touch the stacked kindling, which instantly burst into flame. He eventually ended up where he had started. The flames had taken hold of all the wood, and they lapped at the sky.

"If the sun can't reach us, then perhaps we can reach it," he said, and the words carried clearly over the sound of the roaring fire. Od turned his face toward the gray sky. His dark, shiny hair caressed his back and reflected the flames. People stepped back from the fire, and reverence billowed toward him.

Od stepped onto the podium. "We are here to celebrate uppskeru," he whispered into my ear, even though he was far away. I think everyone present felt like he was standing close to them. "Although these are tough times, we gather and light a bonfire, just as our ancestors did for millennia. In olden times, the fires were lit on the tops of burial mounds."

As though connected by a string, people's heads moved in unison. They all stared at Odinmont and my little house perched at the top of the hill. A man gave me a prickly look.

"What are you staring at?" he hissed, but before I managed to reply, he disappeared in the crowd.

People stared at the fire again. The flames reflected in their eyes, and for a moment, I feared they would throw themselves into the crackling branches.

Demihypnosis. From now on, no one would remember what happened. Od could pull a ton of worship out of them and send it directly to Odin. I wondered how I was still conscious. Maybe I had gotten strong enough to withstand his divinity, or maybe Od had excluded me. It could also be my burgeoning völva powers that strengthened me.

"Óðinn," Od shouted, and it sent a pleasant tingle down my spine. "Freyja. Heimdallr."

The crowd repeated the Old Norse gods' names. Odin's voice tickled inside my head.

Little seer. See the crowd. Feel their worship.

"We looooove our country," someone sang the opening bars of the traditional midsummer song. It sounded shrill and distorted on the snow-covered field with the bonfire burning in front of us.

Several others joined in. ". . . but at midsummer most of all." They were singing, but it sounded more like sobbing. "When every cloud sends blessings across the field . . ."

A deeper voice took over. It was Od, his voice piercing and clear.

I dreamt a dream this night
of prosperity and justice
Wore a robe so light and smooth
in the light of the sunset
now the clear morning is waking

Mathias joined in on the horn, and we sang the same ancient verse over and over again until I felt euphoric and part of the greater whole. Even though Od wasn't hypnotizing me, I bellowed along in the shared ecstasy. I was just a little flake in one big snowdrift. It was an endlessly spinning wheel. We sang and sang, and people danced rhythmically. Od wove through the crowd and laid his hands on the people in turns. When he reached me, I saw him as though through a foggy lens. Instead of asking me for worship, he placed something in my hand. I looked down, and the ground beneath me undulated threateningly. It was a large tooth. So large, it filled my whole hand. It may have come from a horse.

"Hejd used this when she needed to access her völva powers. You'll need it," Od said. Before I had a chance to thank him, he had moved on.

Much later, when the bonfire was only glowing embers, people woke from their trance. Their cheeks were redder than they had been in a long time, and the mood was high. They headed for the city, not remembering that they had sung and worshipped.

Od disappeared along with Mathias, and Arthur and Rebecca staggered toward their respective houses as though drunk. Luna was heading after her mother, but I ran to catch up with her. She swayed, and I grabbed her arm.

"Luna," I said. "It's time."

"For Hel's sake, it's cold," Luna panted. We trudged through Kraghede Forest. It was pitch black. The ring on my finger lit our way. Maybe it was my simmering fear that made it shine. The green light flickered over Luna's shoulders and gave the trees around us an even more sinister appearance.

"Where's the tree?" Luna's voice trembled from the cold.

"We're here now."

We reached the spot where the little birch tree stood, half broken. Elias had done it after he killed me. As though time had stood still, the little tree formed a weird bridge with naked branches sticking out on all sides. It was encapsulated in a membrane of ice, but otherwise, it looked exactly as it had that fateful night eight months ago. Through the transparent layer of ice, I saw the birch tree's white bark with its dark markings. It had neither grown nor decayed in the frost.

I shook the tree. The ice crackled, fell from the trunk, and hit the forest floor with little *clicks*. I handed Luna my axe, Auka. She accepted it with some trepidation and raised it dramatically. Then she swung the blade into the splintered tree trunk.

It hurt me to see the indomitable birch tree fall to the ground in a pathetic *whoosh*. Luna had a strange look on her face.

"Are you okay?"

She didn't respond. In fact, she was completely frozen.

"Luna! What is it?"

"That was amazing," she whispered breathlessly. "The earth's energy flowed through me." She let out a scream. "Woooohooo!" She sounded wilder than usual, and her voice was deeper. "It was like something inside me was set free."

I dragged the tree away. Including the tiny branches at the top, it was as long as I was tall. Luna slipped under a branch on the other side of the trunk, and we must have looked like oxen pulling a cart. We made our way through the trees back toward the field.

"Anna, I'm shaking right now. But in a good way. So much power. There's still life in everything. Despite the winter, it's not all dead. Yaaaay!" she cheered.

"Where can we put this?"

"We can put it in our barn." Luna turned toward her parents' house. Together, we maneuvered the mutilated tree into the dark barn.

"Ow, shit." I hit my foot on something, and when I turned my ring toward it, I saw a six-foot-tall African-looking drum.

I stared at the platform where Monster's body had lain. There were dark spots, but fortunately, nothing wolflike remained, just the cloth he had been wrapped in. We pushed the tree onto the platform. There were dried flowers and colored beads around it, and suddenly, it seemed like the tree was lying in state.

Luna brushed her hands off. "What now?"

"I need to train my völva powers. Mimir says I can't travel to Jotunheim until I'm in control of them, and that's where Eskild went with the Gjallarhorn gold. If we get rid of the worst of the branches, I can get to work." I started hacking at the tree. It splintered and chipped under Auka's blade.

Luna's shoulders went up. "Ahh. No! Stop, Anna. Stop it!"

I stopped mid-swing, Auka raised. "What?"

"You'd think that tree hurt you or something. You can't treat nature that way." She took the axe from me and carefully cut the largest side branches away. "There, there," she murmured softly to the birch tree. "I'll make you pretty again."

"The tree is dead, Luna. It can't feel anything."

She looked up. "And what if Odin said the same thing about Mimir's head before he massacred it?"

I put my hands on my hips as Luna lovingly removed the worst of the splinters. "That's good enough, Luna. I don't have time for all this babying." I grabbed the trunk, which still had a bunch of long, skinny branches at the top. They kept smacking into my head, but I brushed them away.

Luna looked at me critically.

"I'm sorry I snapped. I'm really glad you helped me." I got the tree upright and held it with a firm grip. "What do you think I should do now?"

"A völva sees the past."

"I can already see the past. I don't need a tree to do that." In fact, sometimes I wished I could get rid of my clairvoyance.

"A völva can also cleanse a space. You can start with this barn."

"Good idea." I closed my eyes and tried to cast my power around me. A lot had happened in here, but it was primarily Ben doing witchcraft and Rebecca drying plants and brewing decoctions. I coughed in the smoke that rose from the past.

"What do you see?"

"Your mom and dad."

"What's my dad doing?" Luna sounded sad.

I focused on Ben, who sat cross-legged on the podium, chanting intensely. Before him lay an unconscious little girl who looked around four years old. She had red hair and a long scar on her chest. My stomach dropped when past-Ben laid his hands on child-me and shot magic into my little body. My body jerked as though someone were pushing it, and my red hair rose in a little cloud. Mentally, I tried to wipe the memory away. I managed to smudge it, but I couldn't remove the vision entirely. When it looked like I was viewing the scene through a windowpane smeared with Vaseline, I saw someone walk up to the platform.

The figure shouted and tried to grab Ben to stop him, but Ben didn't react. I squinted but couldn't make out who it was.

I walked forward but stopped when something tickly fell over me. I was pulled back into the present and realized it was the top of the tree that had once again flopped onto my head. Irritated, I swatted the small, flexible branches away.

Luna still had her arms crossed and looked skeptical.

"I definitely get more power with the staff," I panted. "But it's not enough."

"If you let me fix it, I'm sure it'll help."

I looked at the birch tree in my hand. Its bark hung in strips, there were bare spots where the branches had been chopped off, and the top looked like a bundle of twigs. "But it's a staff now."

"It's a denuded tree," Luna said patiently. "It'll take me a couple of days at most to carve it."

"A couple of days! The world is about to end, and you want to start a woodworking project," I said incredulously. "We don't have time for that."

"Do we have time for your failed attempts? If you want to go to Jotunheim, you have to let me carve your staff. In the meantime, you can try to find out why my dad thought you needed spells that separate you from your sister. Maybe it would also help to find out why your dad is so old."

"Ahhhhh . . ." A man's scream sliced through the nocturnal silence at Odinmont.

I woke from a vivid dream with burning swords, flying fingalks, and Od's head sailing through the air toward me. At first, I thought the shouts had been part of my dream, but they continued after I opened my eyes. I immediately rolled out of bed. Someone was screaming downstairs, and the next thing I knew, I was rushing down the stairs. In one hand, I held Auka; in the other, the giant crystal, which glowed intensely.

Mimir sat on the dining table. He looked bewildered and continued to scream. A groggy Arthur came up from the crypt.

"What's going on?" he mumbled.

I held the axe aloft and spun around. The room was completely empty apart from us.

"Loki," Mimir panted. "Loki was here."

I squeezed Auka's shaft and looked around. All was calm, and there wasn't so much as a trace of the past hanging in the air. As far as I could tell, there hadn't been any strangers in the house in a long time.

"Were you dreaming?"

Mimir scoffed contemptuously. "I think I can tell the difference, having existed for over a thousand years."

Arthur looked out the window, then walked to the glass door and jiggled the handle to check that it was locked. "You've been through a lot."

"I know Loki when I see him. He was creeping around in here."

I reached out with my clairvoyance again, this time with more concentration. *Nothing.* "I can't see him, and I know what he looks like." I shuddered involuntarily when I remembered the frightening, paint-covered giant I had met in Valhalla.

"He was only a shadow, but it was him. He was looking for you."

"Me? And what do you mean, *he was a shadow?*"

"Loki is a shape-shifter. He can take on any form."

Arthur finished examining the doors and windows. "But Odinmont is protected by magic. No one who isn't welcome can come in."

"It must have been a dream," I said.

Mimir blinked a couple of times. "He was right here. It was so real."

I set Auka and the giant crystal on the table. Now that the shock was starting to subside, its glow turned down to a minimum. Mimir studied it.

"Where did you get that?"

"My friend Mads gave it to me. He's a half giant."

"That's a very nice gift."

I leaned my head forward to catch a little of the crystal's heat. "I'm pretty happy with it."

"It reacts when a giant is nearby."

I stopped. "But it's glowing now." My fingers found their way back toward Auka.

"I'm a giant. It's probably because of me."

"You're a giant?"

"Bestla is my sister."

I looked at him blankly.

"Odin's mother. You really should know the mythology better now that your life depends on it."

"You're not the first person to point that out." I rubbed my forehead. "Aren't you on Loki's side if you belong to the same clan?"

"Don't you know it's impossible to take sides right now?"

"That's becoming clearer and clearer." I yawned. "If Odinmont is Loki-free, can we go back to bed?"

"There's no way I'll be able to sleep if Loki is creeping around in here." Mimir glanced around the living room.

For the third time, I cast my clairvoyance around. "There's no one unwelcome here."

Mimir's eyes were still wide, but he seemed to accept this. "Tomorrow, we should cast runes for protection. Loki can crawl in through the tiniest of cracks."

Arthur walked up to him. "Do you want to come down to the crypt with me? I would love to hear more about the people laid to rest down there."

Mimir cast one last worried look toward the window. "I'm happy to tell you about them. Many of them were my friends or foes. Some of them both."

Arthur gave me a quick glance before picking Mimir up and

walking down the stone stairs toward the mass grave with the frightened head. Arthur left the hatch open and the light on down below.

I gathered my things and went back to my bedroom. I stopped in the doorway when my eye caught a figure on the edge of my bed. A big smile pulled at the corners of my mouth.

"Hakim!"

"I heard screaming and shouting."

I walked up to him. "It was just a terrified severed head's nightmare."

Hakim's ghost lifted the blanket so I could slip back into bed. I closed my eyes immediately. "I'm so tired."

"I'm here with you."

"I bought Odinmont in 1890."

"Mhmm." In the morning, I forced Arthur to sit at the dining table to give me an explanation for his advanced age, as Luna had suggested. Mimir had been set on the table as a mediator, while I looked at my father with lowered brows. "But why are you so old?"

"Anna..."

"And why did it have to be a secret? I feel like you've been lying to me for years."

"I would have told you."

"You would have told me that you're more than one hundred and fifty years old?"

My father winced. "Of course I would have. At . . . at some point."

"You're neither a witch nor a demigod. Were you in an elf mound or something?"

Arthur looked uncomfortably down at the cracked tabletop. "Remember, I was dead for eighteen years."

"One hundred and fifty minus eighteen doesn't equal the present."

"Why do we have to discuss this? My past is my own."

"I'm trying to prevent Ragnarök, but that's pretty difficult when I don't know how everything fits together."

Arthur cleared his throat. "You do know that people age slower when they're around gods and demigods, right?"

"And? I don't suppose you've been spooning with Od." I put a hand in front of my mouth. "Or have you?" I said into my palm.

"With his wife." It was almost impossible to hear what Arthur said.

"Freyja?" I closed my eyes. Elias had once said that the goddess had had a thing for my dad, whatever *had a thing for* meant.

"My crops were failing, and there was a pagan practice that was supposed to help. I didn't believe in it, but I was desperate. You had to go out into a freshly plowed field in the spring and lie down in a furrow. Freyja would come and . . ." My dad didn't finish his sentence. "It was Ben who told me that." He sounded a bit defensive. "My crops thrived as long as I performed the ritual, and after ten years, I realized I wasn't aging." Arthur didn't seem to want to share too many details, which was fine by me. "If you really want to know, Elias was against it. He said you should never involve the gods if you could avoid it."

"Elias. You knew him back then?"

"Ben was already friends with him. They met in the 1700s."

"You're an old trio? You, Ben, and Elias?"

"We were friends, but that ended when he betrayed me."

"Are you sure Elias betrayed you? Wasn't it Eskild who stabbed you?"

"Elias made sure we were at The Boatman that night and that Od wasn't there. Elias, Ragnara, and Eskild set a trap."

"Elias's life must have been in danger."

"What do you mean?"

"He once told me that if your life is in danger, you have to save it no matter the cost and think of the consequences later."

Arthur gaped. "I died. You would've been dead, too, if Ragnara hadn't been pregnant with Sverre."

My chest tightened when my dad mentioned Sverre. "Elias reanimated you, and I didn't die. Maybe he knew Ragnara could heal wounds temporarily because she was pregnant with a healer."

"You're defending Elias!"

"I'm trying to find a reasonable explanation. Some things about him don't add up." I thought about how he had helped Mimir free of charge, and he had told me about the Gjallarhorn.

"You're right about that. He's an egotistical liar."

This was not a conversation I wanted to be having. "Elias isn't what I wanted to talk to you about."

Mimir said nothing, but he followed our argument like a tennis match. Arthur looked like he was just getting started, but he let me change the subject. "What is it, then?"

"Fimbulwinter. What can you tell me about it?"

"This isn't the first time Fimbul has come," Arthur said slowly. "Mimir, you're much older than I am, and you agree, right?"

Mimir made his oracle face. "I can list twenty periods of disease, war, decadent lifestyles, or harsh winters. They've always ended."

"But have there ever been so many signs present at once?"

Both Arthur and Mimir shook their heads.

"How do people usually stop it?"

Arthur's face took on a desperate expression. "I've only experienced it once, but that was plenty. That was in 1918."

"What was it like?"

Arthur stood and looked out the window toward Kraghede Forest. It was barely visible through the falling snow. Since he didn't say anything, I reached out mentally and let myself into his past.

I was in the large hall full of sick people I had already seen in Arthur's past once before. A woman in a dark high-waisted skirt and a light-colored shirt with gauze over her mouth rolled a hospital bed behind a curtain. Ben, Arthur, and Elias sat there. Elias wore his hair in a side part, and Arthur had a small pointed goatee. The space was full of microscopes, large glass bottles, and rubber hoses connected to metal devices I didn't recognize.

The man in the bed was pale and sweaty, and he coughed continually. At the sight of Ben's dark skin, he tried to get away, but he lacked the strength to climb over the bed's metal sides. Ben clenched his fists in the same way as when Rebecca healed me. He gave up with a frustrated growl. "The disease is in deep. It's too late to remove it."

The man whimpered and writhed up toward the head of the bed, but the woman with the gauze mask leaned forward. Only her eyes were visible. "Opus ad relaxat—oportet somnum."

The man's eyelids dropped, and he breathed slowly. She pulled her mask down.

In another scene, in the living room in Odinmont, I sputtered in surprise. It was the prime minister's wife, Mardöll, though the prime minister himself couldn't possibly have been born yet.

She looked at Arthur. "I agree."

"Stop reading my thoughts, Mardöll. I've told you a hundred times."

She put her hand on her hip. "You're practically shouting them. This one won't survive, either." She looked at Elias, who wore a white open lab coat with a gray vest and bow tie beneath. "Is there any help from the gods?" Mardöll leaned against a metal table. "Od Dinesen?"

Elias shook his head. "I haven't finished my experiments with demiblood."

"This one's certainly going to die, too." Mardöll crossed her arms. "Only the gods can help us now." Ben looked up with a wild look in his eyes, but Mardöll cut him off before he could speak. "There are already ten thousand dead in Denmark." She gestured toward the hall. "Hundreds of sick people are just out there. They might as well be of use, and we only need nine. I promise to hypnotize them first."

"Not again," Elias pleaded. Ben shook his head.

"What do you want to do?" Arthur asked.

Mardöll stuck her nose in the air, defiant. "I'm in contact with Odin, and he wants hangatyr. Otherwise, he doesn't have enough strength to stop the disease. There's been so much focus on science lately, he and the other gods are completely depleted. It's a good thing they're still worshipped in Hrafnheim."

"But—" Elias began.

"It's the only way," Mardöll said. "That's an order."

Elias and Ben quickly turned their backs, and together, they studied something on the table with great concentration.

The vision shifted, and I saw Mardöll and Arthur standing at the base of a large tree. Heavy, sun-ripened apples hung from its branches. Something else was strung up alongside the fruit. The sacrifices still wore their hospital clothes, and their bare feet were blue.

I fled from my father's past. Small beads of sweat dotted my forehead. He turned from where he stood at the window and looked nervously at me. Mimir, too, glanced at me without saying anything.

"You sacrificed people," I said. "Dad?"

Arthur looked unhappily at me. "The Spanish flu disappeared within a few months, even though it had been on its way to wiping out the whole population."

"But . . . human sacrifices?"

Arthur said nothing, but his furrowed brows were pronounced on his pale face.

I hadn't been to Ravensted High School in a long time. The single-story 1970s brick building looked the same, only darker and colder. The halls were still a bizarre color palette, and the carpets were made of worn-down acrylic fibers that, in combination with the below-freezing temperatures, charged us all with static electricity.

Students and teachers exchanged worried glances, having realized we were in the midst of a crisis. Even though I hadn't attended school in several months, mostly everyone inside had continued their daily lives. They now looked perplexed, but they had shown up because the DSMA had ordered us to go to school. Since neither TV nor the internet was working, the DSMA had driven around in electric cars with megaphones on top, proclaiming that everyone was to report to their place of work or school, or to Ravensted Social Center, if one wasn't associated with either. Anyone who failed to appear would have their food ration revoked. This got everyone to leave their homes in a hurry.

I hadn't spoken with my father since the earth-shattering revelation that he had participated in human sacrifices.

I walked toward Blue Hall, shaking in the cold under all my clothes. A voice called out: "Anna."

I stopped and looked around. Someone bumped into me from behind. It was Kamilla from my class, who, because of Ben's magic, never would have noticed me otherwise. In any case, she had a mild temperament, and I had never had any problems with her.

"Move." She glared at me from beneath her knit hat.

It was evidently no lie that the spells Ben had cast on me as a child had a negative association with collective fear.

"Anna!" the voice called again. It came from Brown Hall, which had no students in it.

I traipsed down the hall, breath steaming from my mouth as I walked. It got darker as I went because the skylights were covered in snow, and the lights had been turned off to save electricity. At the end was a door leading to the school's basement. I had once gone down there with Varnar to speak to Janitor Preben. The iron door stood ajar.

"Anna," the voice called from below.

The voice was familiar. I walked up to the door and pushed it open. Stairs led down to the extensive system of hallways beneath the school. My studded boots created an echo on the long metal staircase, and I couldn't see the bottom.

Janitor Preben had apparently not turned the motion sensor off, and when I stepped onto the cement floor, neon lights flickered on as far down the hall as I could see. They hummed, and the ceiling was so low, I only had to reach my hand up to touch them. While it was freezing cold aboveground, down here it was quite stuffy. Maybe parts of the old district heating system were still working.

"Come here, Anna."

I walked forward, and like the last time I was here, I got the sense that dramatic events had taken place in this basement—though they were either faded by time or erased on purpose. When I passed Preben's office, an arm reached out and grabbed my wrist. I screamed as I was pulled into the room. Fear and training caused me to lash out with lightning speed, but I was caught in a strong embrace.

"Hakim, for gods' sakes. It's just you? You scared the crap out of me." I took a step back. "You've gotten strong. Are you a poltergeist now?"

Hakim shook his head regretfully. "I have more strength down here. This is where I am when we're not together."

My father had also stayed underground when he was dead, so this seemed highly plausible. I looked around. Preben's chair was pushed back from the desk as though he had just stood up and left the room. Nevertheless, something told me he hadn't been down here in a long time.

"I can feel that this is a special place. Maybe Ravensted's entire underground is supernatural."

Hakim smiled. "Everywhere's underground is supernatural."

I dug around in my pants pocket and pulled out the small, curved piece of Gjallarhorn gold I had found in Mimir's throat. "Look what I've got. I forgot to show you last time."

Hakim's ghost looked approvingly at me. "Only you could manage that." He held out a large hand, and I placed the gold there; even though the gold couldn't weigh more than a couple of ounces, it dropped straight through Hakim's palm and onto Preben's desk. Fascinated, he lowered his face all the way down to it.

"It wasn't without cost."

Hakim was still looking at the gold. "I hope you didn't suffer too much."

I thought of Od's divine kisses and the night we had spent together. Pensively, I held my hand in front of my face. It still glowed slightly, and my nails looked like ivory. "I'll survive."

Hakim didn't say anything, and I studied the bulletin board, where there hung small notes written in neat handwriting and a yellowed photograph of Janitor Preben's son, Thorsten, standing with Arthur and Ben. The picture had been taken on a summer day, and three tall windmills towered behind them. All three men had since died, although my father was the only one who had come back to life.

"Did you find out anything else?" Hakim asked.

"I sat in Hlidskjalf."

Hakim stood up straighter. "What did you see?"

"Eskild was on his way to Jotunheim. He must be there already. He might give his piece of Gjallarhorn gold to the giants. It's becoming clear to me that I have to go after him. I need to hone my völva powers before I take that trip, but I'm working on it."

Hakim's green eyes were intense. "Jotunheim."

"I flew over it as a raven. It was a lot more beautiful than I expected."

"Why wouldn't Jotunheim be beautiful?"

"I thought it was a creepy place, kind of like Helheim, but I would actually describe it more as primal. There were extinct animals and enormous plants. Maybe the giants aren't bad at all."

"I heard the giants came before the gods," Hakim said. "In a way, they're like nature. It's neither good nor bad, even though it can be both dangerous and nurturing."

"What about the gods?"

Hakim looked down at the little piece of Gjallarhorn gold again. "You forget I don't belong to the Norse faith."

"The same must be true for your god."

"Gods need people. A temple isn't maintained by a god himself."

"So, if we just stop believing in them, it's all good?"

Hakim shook his head. "People need to believe in something. If you take that away—whether it's money, companies, or gods—there's no humanity left. But the gods aren't real."

"Then what is?"

"Nature, or the giants, if you will. Does a river disappear because no humans look at it? Does an apple become inedible because there's no human to eat it?" Hakim closed his eyes. "In the old days, people worshipped nature. The sun, the moon, the stars. None of them disappear, even when we turn our backs. In my faith, there's an old poem that says:

> *Who knows and who can say*
> *Whence everything came and how was made*
> *The gods are newer than creation*
> *So who in truth knows how they came to be*

"The gods are newer than creation," I repeated. "They came after the beginning."

"The giants, or nature, came first. Then came humans, and then the gods. Or at least that's what I believe. You have to decide for yourself what you believe in."

I reached out to stroke Hakim's cheek. He felt completely solid today. Hakim brought his hand up to mine.

"I'm so glad you're here," I whispered. "Everyone says it's impossible for me to see you, but here you are."

"Deep down, it's a question of what you believe in." Hakim leaned his forehead against mine. "Maybe your faith in me is so strong, it brings me into being. Like how the gods become real by being worshipped. But I can't stay forever. I have to go back to my own realm."

My throat constricted. "You can't leave me." *No more.* I couldn't stand it if more people left me.

But my pleas were futile, and even as I stood with my arms around him, he became more and more transparent until finally he was gone. I stood for a moment with my heart pounding and the feeling that he would soon be gone forever. Then I pulled myself together and walked back to the metal staircase. The whole way, the feeling of energy and violence pressed down on me until, eventually, I started running.

I emerged from the basement, panting. Only a few minutes had passed, though I felt like I had been in another world. Classes hadn't started yet, and I hurried toward Blue Hall.

I met Luna and the others on the way. She was wrapped in a lime-green shawl so large and thick, only her head stuck out. She wore a pair of dark-green platform boots, which made her tower above me. Maybe she wanted to be as tall as Mathias and Mads, who walked right behind her, but she hadn't considered how small I would look among them. To top it all off, she wore a pair of fake plastic glasses. Altogether, she looked like an enormous grasshopper. Mathias put his arm around her and didn't seem to notice her strange outfit.

"Hey, Anna." He continued his conversation with Mads, but Luna tilted her head and studied me.

"Where did you just come from?" she asked suspiciously.

"Uh . . . I was just . . ." I gestured vaguely in the direction of Brown Hall.

Luna looked craftier than usual. "Who were you talking to?"

"Hakim," I whispered.

"Hakim?" she mouthed.

I nodded conspiratorially.

"But that's impossible. You don't belong to the same faith."

"I just saw him, so yes, it is possible." I scratched my cheek. Today I was wearing a pair of fingerless gloves. "Will my staff be ready soon? Mimir wants to help me train."

Luna made a starstruck *ahhhhh* sound. "I'm so excited to meet him. We can do it tomorrow. I'm almost done."

"Can't you just cut off the little branches at the top so it doesn't get stuck in everything, so we can move forward? Time's running out."

We reached the classroom.

Luna rolled her eyes. "You'll just have to wait for the staff. You can be so impatient sometimes!"

"Wow, you've gotten so bombastic lately," I said.

She simply shrugged her shoulders high above me. "Are you going to Frank's tonight?"

"Probably. You'll be busy working on my völva staff anyway."

Mathias looked at me critically. "How will you get from Frank's out to Odinmont?"

"I'll just run," I replied.

"I'll be at Frank's at five o'clock, and I'll take you home after." A little more gently, he added: "I want to see the news, too."

"Shouldn't you put some more clothes on?" I eyed his thin T-shirt.

He suddenly looked a little self-conscious. "I haven't been cold since the winter began. Especially after uppskeru." He stopped, well aware of my attitude toward worship.

I was going to say something critical, but I came to a halt. It was not our French teacher standing at the front of the room.

It was Od.

CHAPTER 18

Everyone stared in disbelief at the demigod, who stood in a short-sleeved shirt in front of the shabby blackboard. He looked completely out of place. He smiled his most charming—but fortunately not hypnotic—smile. That alone was enough to bring several students to the brink of passing out.

"What are you doing here?" I asked when no one else dared speak to him.

Od looked directly at me, and I felt like I was standing on a trampoline. "I want to practice something with you."

"Something?"

Just then, we were joined by Mr. Nielsen, our homeroom teacher. He shot a flustered look at Od, who put his hands behind his back.

"We have been lucky," Mr. Nielsen panted, even though he hadn't been running. It must have been the proximity to Od that made him so out of sorts. "The country's leadership has decided it's important that all citizens learn Old Norse."

"The country's leadership?"

Mr. Nielsen was suddenly very focused on brushing something off his sweater. "There has been a shake-up, so the state is now in charge of all schools in the country. Of everything, actually. Od is their representative."

"When did that happen?" I was still the only one who dared to say anything.

"During uppskeru," Mr. Nielsen replied stiffly. "But I've only just now been informed."

When everyone was under collective hypnosis. The authorities had sneaked the changes in without anyone noticing.

"Did you know that?" I asked Mathias, but he shook his head. Luna held up her hands to the extent her green cocoon shawl allowed.

Mr. Nielsen looked nervously at Od. "Not many people can speak Old Norse anymore, but Od Dinesen is taking time out of his busy schedule to teach you some basic skills. He can only teach you the chants today. You'll need to repeat them at home every evening."

"Why is it suddenly important to practice rhymes and chants?"

"You're extremely lucky that—" Mr. Nielsen began.

"I'm not asking you. I'm asking Od Dinesen," I interjected.

Mr. Nielsen stopped, his mouth hanging open. He looked at Od with wide eyes. "She's always causing problems."

"She asked a question," Od said mildly. "It's not against the rules to ask questions." He looked out over the classroom. "If you choose to pray to the gods, they'll hear you better if you speak in the old language."

I glanced around to see if my classmates were reacting to the mention of gods, but no one aside from Mads seemed to mind. He, though, seemed to mind very much. I took a step toward him to indicate that I was on the same team.

"Do we have a choice of whether we want to pray or not?" I stepped even closer to Mads.

Od's face was so friendly, it must have been false. I thought I could see danger lurking just beneath his smile. "Of course you have a choice."

Mr. Nielsen hurriedly handed out sheets of paper along the horseshoe shape the desks were arranged in. The handouts were full of Old Norse words beneath a Danish translation. Before he had even finished passing them out, people's mouths were moving in prayer.

Od didn't need to read it. He knew the prayer by heart.

Auk nær aftni
skaltu, Óðinn, koma,
ef þú vilt þér mæla man;
allt eru ósköp,
nema einir viti
slíkan löst saman

People joined in, and the more they repeated the words, the glassier their eyes became and the more their skin flushed.

I pressed my lips firmly closed, and Od looked me in the eyes. Then he unleashed his divinity, and I realized I was chanting along.

A pleasant heat spread through the room. I saw my classmates either sit down on chairs or simply drop to the floor.

"You must know the past so you can survive what the future has in store."

I think people were too hypnotized to hear what he was saying, but it was probably stored in their subconscious. I, too, sailed off on a pink cloud.

That was the last thing I remembered before I came to several hours later at Frank's.

I blinked. In my hand, I held a bottle that I was about to pour from, and I stood behind the bar in the café. Od sat on a barstool, looking at me. There was an empty glass in front of him, and my hand and the bottle hovered over it. I was still wearing the black fingerless gloves.

"Are you going to test us?" I asked, thankful for the training I had when my dad was a ghost. I was used to acting naturally when someone showed up unannounced, or when I found myself in an unexpected situation. With pride, I filled Od's glass with steady hands. The smell of alcohol wafted up toward me.

"Thanks," Od said, accepting the glass with a ceremonial nod.

"It'll be a little weird for the two of us. You know . . ." I gestured back and forth between us with a snarky grimace. I actually didn't feel much of anything, being close to Od.

"It was the only way."

"Forcing us to go to school when the end of the world is imminent is just weird."

"I came to tell you I was forced to do it." Od took a sip of his forbidden booze. No one else was allowed to consume alcohol anymore.

"You were forced?" I didn't think anyone could force Od to do anything. "You were forced to fire our teacher and hypnotize my class?"

He leaned over the bar. "A god's child cannot disobey their divine progenitor's orders. Well, we could, but then we'd be plunged into the underworld."

I raised both eyebrows. "Maybe it's time to plunge."

"What do you mean?"

I remembered how Odin had been ready to sacrifice his son in the yard outside Odinmont. Od only survived because I, with all the völvas at my back, ordered Odin to save his son and the others. In a flash, I saw Od's head being cut off by Loki and Tilarids. Was that the ultimate sacrifice Od would end up making? "Odin wouldn't give a shit if it were the other way around. If you needed his help."

"Anna. Language," Od scolded me, smiling instead of asking me to explain.

"I mean it. I advise you to rebel."

His eyes grew dark. "I'm going to pretend I didn't hear you say that. I'm very old, but I've never gone against my father."

Suddenly, I was incredibly sad on his behalf. There were so many worries resting on Od's shoulders.

"I came to warn you," he said.

"What now?" I asked, resigned.

"Some people think you're difficult." He folded his hands around his glass. "I'm inclined to agree." His laugh was entirely human. "But that doesn't mean I want you to get hurt."

"The fact that I'm difficult has been well established."

"You're still carrying around Benedict's magic. People are getting more and more scared. Everyone is starting to realize that something unusual is afoot. Mass hysteria combined with your spells can be a dangerous cocktail. You need to be careful." Od stood. No one at the bar turned their head. They sat completely frozen. Frank was bent over the old TV on the platform at the back of the café. He had stiffened in the middle of fumbling with the buttons.

"Hey . . ." I didn't manage to say any more before Od was out the door. The patrons started moving as though they were in a movie and someone had pressed *play*. Od's empty glass remained on the counter as the only proof he had even been there.

A man shoved his way up to the bar. He looked directly at me and wrinkled his nose. Fortunately, he spotted the bottle in my hand. "Give me that."

My quick reflexes came in handy, and I pulled the bottle out of his reach.

"Give me that, or else . . ." he said. A frantic redness spread across his cheeks.

"This?" I looked at the bottle, acting confused. "It's melted ice flavored with pine needles. It still has chunks of ice in it."

The man shivered. "I want something warm."

"We don't have anything else."

The man muttered something bitterly in my direction but threw up his hands and went away.

It got quiet at the bar, and everyone sat expectantly, ready to watch the evening's broadcast. I noticed that Mathias stood at the other end of the bar. While everyone else was bundled up in layers of down coats and sweaters, Mathias wore only a hoodie. Everyone looked expectantly at the silver plastic box with its large screen, and a festive mood spread as the image changed from the screensaver to the news studio. The jingle played, and a couple of bar patrons moved their lips in time with the Muzak.

"Welcome to the news," said the anchor, a woman with horn-rimmed glasses. She had been an anchor before the harsh winter, but all I recognized were the glasses—gone were her usual pastel-colored clothes and shiny brown hair. Now, she was dressed in skins and furs and a thick woven scarf. Her hair was tied up in a new style, with a wide braid across her forehead. She squinted her eyes nervously, and I got the sense that she was sitting on terrible news. The program cut to an official-looking hallway. Niels Villadsen was being interviewed.

"Here at Christiansborg, the head of resources is talking about the food that's being distributed."

Head of Resources. New title.

Niels looked into the camera. "Fortunately, there is something the citizens can do themselves. You are all encouraged to pray to the gods using the verses you received today. Unfortunately, the bad news is that we need to cut back on provisions. Citizens are encouraged to ration what they have."

An angry outburst billowed through Frank's.

"This is appalling. Why didn't they do anything to prevent this?"

"Who is responsible?"

"We barely have anything left."

"They forced us to show up today with the threat of cutting off our food, and now they're doing it anyway. It's all a con!"

People shouted at the television as Niels continued speaking. They cut to the studio again. Next to the anchor's head hovered footage of the west coast. This made people shush one another.

"Yesterday, the ice cap could be seen from Skagen."

First, the camera panned across some dunes with frost-covered houses and stiff, white lyme grass. A sprinkling of snow lay on the sand, but the harsh wind ensured that it didn't cover everything. The camera turned, so the beach came into view. There was a black mark on the pale sand where a bonfire had been set during the harvest festival.

The camera shifted to the water. At first, there was just a sloshing blur, but then it came into focus, and the guests at Frank's gasped when they saw the ice wall.

"It's huge," one said. "It must be miles high."

I stared, frozen, at the screen showing the glacier. Even though it could only just be glimpsed on the horizon from the coast, everyone could see how high it was. The camera turned to a researcher who, dressed in a snowsuit, hats, and gloves, looked fearfully at the wall of ice.

"It's a bit like watching a car crash in slow motion," she said. "We can see that it's slowly coming closer, but we can't do anything or predict whether it's going to stop. As far as we can tell, the ice cap is moving nine yards a day."

It was dead silent at Frank's, probably because people were furiously trying to calculate the distance from the ice to Ravensted, and how fast nine yards a day actually was.

A glass was flung at the TV with a crash, and the combination of ice water, pine needles, and glass shards slid down the screen, which had cracked in a spiderweb pattern. The news anchor's face was distorted as everyone in the café held their breath.

"Researchers have ruled out an ice age," she said. "During an ice age, sea levels drop, and there's no snow . . ."

"We don't want to hear any more about the useless researchers," shouted the woman who had thrown the glass.

"Quiet."

The woman stood up. "They aren't doing anything. They're hoarding the food, and they're not making good use of their time. We need to blót and pray."

"No—"

"Yes—"

Now several people were standing up. People had given up on

following the broadcast. I left my place behind the bar and went closer to the TV so I could at least hear what the anchor was saying.

"... enough electricity," she said.

Ravensted's citizens continued to argue.

"I don't want to blót."

"Everyone has to pray so the gods can help us. We got the Old Norse prayers today; there's no other way."

"We need to stay calm."

"We've stayed calm for six months. We're starving."

A man threw a punch and hit the woman on the side of the head. She fell to the floor, and others grabbed the man who had hit her. The TV was knocked over in the heat of the moment. The sound was projected in a totally different direction, and I had to get closer to hear what was being said.

"... not the first time in world history," the journalist said to the ceiling. "... can be survived." Someone kicked the device, and the journalist's voice became a long string of deep sounds. *Suuurrviiiiiiivedddd* was drawn out for an eternity and ended in a continuous howl. The screen was smashed to pieces, exposing the cords and wires behind it.

I tried to grab ahold of some of the combatants, but they turned against me instead. Seconds ago, they had been fighting each other, but now they looked at me with hateful eyes.

Ohh! I had forgotten the whole thing about the spells combined with mass hysteria.

"This is all your fault!" A man walked aggressively toward me, and I was repeating my self-defense lessons with Varnar in my head. "You burned your foster family's house down. Maybe it's your turn to burn."

I tried not to argue because I knew how that would end. Maybe I could go to the storage room at the back of the bar. I ran toward it, but several people had seen me. They circled me, and my escape route was cut off.

"I heard you were rude to Od Dinesen today. The man came here to help us find our way back to the gods, and you had an attitude with him."

"Hey," Frank shouted, but he couldn't break the circle that was forming around me. "Leave her alone."

These were normal people from Ravensted who, until six months ago, had had plenty of food, safe, warm homes, and a secure future. But now they had dead eyes and bared teeth.

"Anna," Frank yelled. He smashed two bottles and held one in each hand as a weapon. He looked ready to stab people to get to me. I knew what a good fighter he was, but no one, not even him, could handle a bloodthirsty mob.

"STOP," someone shouted. The sound made the floor shake, and warmth shot over us.

No one moved. Mathias shoved people aside and came to the middle of the circle, where I stood pathetically with my hands around the back of a chair, ready to use it as a shield. Mathias's eyes shone blue, and he let them scan the crowd. Everyone who was struck by his angry gaze flinched.

"Go home. Now!"

The grown adults obeyed the nineteen-year-old boy. Everyone took off into the winter night without saying anything, though several gave me hateful glares. Mathias was currently more god than human, and he wasn't trying to hide it. He towered several heads over everyone.

Finally, he, Frank, and I were alone. My hands were still on the back of the chair since I hadn't thought to move them. Frank ran his fingers through his hair and looked around the bar. There were shattered glass and toppled tables everywhere, and the TV lay broken on the floor. I let go of the chair and exhaled. Mathias shrunk to his normal size.

"Are you okay?" His voice was still somewhat in god mode.

I ran my gloved hands over my hair. "I'm totally fine."

"Anna..."

"I said I'm totally fine!" I went up to the bar to get a broom and dustpan. I fumbled for a long time with the supplies in the cabinet to grab a bucket and rags. Behind me, Frank and Mathias spoke quietly. Eventually, I just stood there with my head pressed against the shelf.

Frank stood behind me. "It was a matter of time before they got the pitchforks out."

"Have you seen anything like that before?"

"In Hrafnheim."

I thought of the time Ragnara had sent my friends into the arena against a bunch of fingalks and berserkers. I, too, had seen a crowd turn into a mob.

"Mathias will escort you home."

"I just need to step outside and get some air. I'll be fine."

"Should I go with you?"

"I need to be alone. Just for a minute." Dressed only in a sweater and jeans, I shivered immediately in the cold.

"Anna," I heard faintly.

I put my hands over my ears. I wasn't ready to talk to Mathias or Frank yet.

Anna...

I ignored it again.

Anna! Duck! It was Serén's voice inside my head.

CHAPTER 19

Without thinking, I dropped to my knees just in time to feel something swish over the top of my head. The brick wall shattered behind me, and a cloud of red dust floated down.

A man who had been the local baker before the winter walked toward me with a gun. He stopped and aimed directly at me. "You must die!"

What I could see of his face was twisted and so angry he almost didn't look like a human anymore.

Turn! Serén shouted inside my head—then her voice dropped off. Still crouched, I spun around on one leg. It must have looked like a clumsy yoga pose, but the movement got me out of the way of something that whizzed past my ear. I felt a searing heat, and something dark appeared on my sweater. Facing the entrance to Frank's, I pressed the door open with both hands and crawled on all fours into what I thought was safety.

It had been maybe five seconds since the first blast hit the wall. Frank stood with his back to me, sweeping shards of glass and unaware of my problems outside. Mathias, though, had already turned around, a terrified expression on his face.

Frank began to speak. "Mathias will accompany you—"

The door slammed shut behind me, and I held my hands over my ears, trying to make myself as small as possible, pressing my back against the glass door. There was yet another swish followed by a loud crash that jolted my body as the pane of glass in the door shattered.

Mathias was already at my side. He gathered me in his arms and rotated us both so that his back was to the smashed door.

Some *pop-pop-pop* sounds followed, and Mathias's body shook with each blast.

"Huggh," he grunted, but he didn't budge. His arms were tight around me, and I curled up in his embrace. Without knowing how we got there, the three of us were suddenly sitting behind the bar. Frank had a knife in his hand, and a cold wind blew into the café. Mathias jumped over the bar and ran outside. His metallic voice blared, and a blue flash reflected off the countertop.

"I command you to go home. Pray to the gods tonight and stay away from Anna from now on."

The man said something inaudible.

"Home!" Mathias bellowed, and I heard footsteps rapidly fading away.

Frank peeked over the counter. "Who was that?"

"It was—"

Frank cut him off with a shout. "Are you okay?!" Without taking his eyes off me, he fumbled around for a dishcloth.

"I wasn't hit."

Frank pressed the cloth against my right ear.

"Ow, shit!" It burned, and when I looked down, I saw my sweater was red with blood and brick dust.

"You got cut."

"By what?"

"A bullet. Someone shot at you." He took the rag away and let out a sympathetic noise.

"What?"

"The top part of your ear is split."

I raised my hand to my ear. It felt more like a ragged lump than a normal ear.

Mathias returned in an elegant hop and landed in a squat in front of us. Then he rolled his shoulders. Little metallic *clink*s rang out behind him. We looked at his back. His hoodie was perforated like a bloody sieve. The bullets were gradually pushed out of his rapidly healing body, and what I could see of his skin through the tattered, wet fabric was once again golden and lovely. He straightened his shoulders.

"Holy shit." Frank stuck his finger out to touch the blood.

"I wouldn't come into contact with that if I were you," I warned, and Frank pulled his hand back. "Wipe it up and save the rag. Elias can use it to make laekna."

Mathias pulled me into his arms. "I'll get help. Will you be okay?"

Frank, who still held the knife in his hand, flipped it around in a practiced motion. Just then, he looked like more than just a peaceful bartender in North Jutland. He was also a cold-blooded assassin with many lives on his conscience.

Mathias ran, and I felt like we were flying. He had gotten faster, and in no time, we arrived at Rebecca's house. Luna screamed when she saw us, and Mathias had to shout over her agitated chatter to explain that no one was seriously hurt. Most of the mess was red brick dust and demiblood, and only a little bit came from my split ear. The voices around me rang as though I were underwater.

The gray, dead-eyed crowd gathering around me kept appearing in my memory, along with the rapid swish of bullets. By now, the entire side of my head had begun to hurt. The wound throbbed, and flames lapped at my cheek and neck.

"Do you want me to hypnotize the pain away? I can totally do it now." Luna moved right in front of my head. Her dark brown eyes bore into mine, and she said something I didn't understand. Flickers of gold appeared in the corners of my vision, and I swam in Luna's gaze.

"Engin sársauki," she said. "Slaka."

I felt pleasantly relaxed and sank into the pillows on the bed in the green room, where Mathias had carried me. I heard them talking, but I didn't really care what they were saying.

"It was her spells," Mathias said. "People became totally zombielike."

Luna's magic overpowered me, and I melted into a thick, comforting porridge.

"Anna," a high voice called. "Anna."

I looked around. Because I was floating in water or air, I spun around and let out a scream of terror when I found myself staring straight into a brown face. His dark curls were dripping water, and he smelled sour. I recognized the myling—the little ghost boy from Sømosen.

"What are you doing here?"

"I want to show you something." He took my hand and pulled me along. "Come."

We glided away and landed in the middle of some tall grass. The sun shone from a cloudless sky. I immediately knew I was in the myling's past.

I looked out over Sømosen, which was calm and surrounded by tall spruce trees. It was an early spring day, and even though the sky was blue, the air was cool. I looked back over the lake, which was actually a bog. It was larger than I remembered, but it must have been bigger at some point, and I had no idea what time I was in. Here and there, birch trees stuck up directly from the water, and tufts of grass gave the illusion that it was safe to step out into the bog, but beneath the still water, it was deep, dark, and deadly.

The little myling stood at my side. He looked up at me with his big brown eyes. Dirt caked his cheeks and ears, and his feet were bare on the sandy ground. His clothes were tattered and dirty. A chill ran down my spine, but I steeled myself. He was the one who was dead, after all.

"What year is it?"

The myling looked out over the water. "1816." He took my hand when he saw that I was moving around nervously. "I'll take care of you."

I looked down. The boy couldn't have been much more than seven or eight years old.

"You have to see this." He pulled me away, and we walked together among the green stalks. The smell of grass was so wonderful that I drank it in large gulps. The myling stopped at a knotty tree. I heard faint singing. It sounded suspiciously like Ragnara's herders and Jytte sacrificing the sheep in The Boatman's parking lot. I spotted something moving in the forest. A little procession emerged from the trees. They walked toward the water. There were three people dressed in capes. They chanted melodically and beautifully, and the song contrasted sharply with the somber parade. The person at the front was quite a bit taller than the others. The myling pointed to a figure being dragged along. It was so small, I hadn't seen it at first.

I threw myself forward. "Let him go," I shouted. "He's just a kid."

But they could neither see nor hear me. The boy, whose hands were tied behind his back, couldn't hear me, either, but his ghost at my side looked up at me mournfully.

"I was so scared," he said.

I put an arm around his shoulder to comfort him. "That's not okay. That's absolutely not okay."

He cuddled up to me. "You don't have to be sad about it. Everything's fine now. It only lasted a second."

The procession reached a little raft, and they pushed the boy up onto it. "Mama," he shouted.

His cry was so pleading and fearful, I squeezed the rough grass tightly in my hand. "Can you handle seeing this? I mean . . ." I didn't quite know how to formulate the question.

He understood. "I've lived out here for more than two hundred years, so I've gotten used to it. Or at least, I'm not sent back to my corpse anymore."

I looked out over the water again, even though I could barely stand it. No one came to the boy's aid as the raft was pushed out onto the still lake. The shortest person raised a club. I closed my eyes and turned my head away. The dull crunching sound was unavoidable.

The myling standing next to me stroked my cheek. "It's over. You have to look again. Now!"

I forced my eyes open just in time to see the boy being tossed into the water with a big splash. Large bubbles burst on the surface.

"Gjǫf. Myrkr dauði." The voice belonged to a woman, and she sang in Old Norse. The two shortest figures knelt in front of the tall one. The raft rocked slightly as they looked down at the wooden surface and raised their hands in submission to the standing person.

"Is your body still out there?"

"Shh! More happens." He pulled me down in the tall grass.

"But they can't see us."

"The people can't," the myling replied. "But . . ."

The standing person pulled their hood back, and I let out a little cry from my hiding place among the reeds. His hair was black, his features beautiful, but he looked older than when I saw him in Valhalla. One eye socket was a dark hole, and the skin around it hung loosely. For a moment, his gaze rested on where we were crouched, but then he closed his remaining eye and inhaled.

"A good sacrifice." His muscles swelled, and his wrinkles smoothed out. "Ragnarök will not come now. You have given me the strength to resist it." He held his hands out, and the kneeling figures took them meekly. "You will live long lives."

We ducked as they pushed the raft to the shore and headed down the small path. Their prolonged singing and prayers would have sounded comical if I hadn't known what lay out in the bog beneath the ever-expanding rings on the water's surface.

"Odin, you asshole! A child. A—"

"Look." The myling sat up straight in the grass. When the cloaked figures were gone, someone appeared from behind a bush and crept toward the bog.

I craned my neck. Though the clothes were old-fashioned, the hair shorter, and the sideburns longer, it was unmistakably Elias.

He had a bundle in his arms. He stepped onto the raft and quickly pushed it onto the water.

"What's he doing here?" But then I shushed myself. Elias from the past couldn't hear me. The myling laughed as I hit myself on the forehead. "There's nothing to laugh about! You were just killed in a human sacrifice."

"I've had lots of time to get used to it." The boy flashed me a grin and pointed to Elias, who had reached the middle of the lake. There were still bubbles coming up from the deep. Elias loosened his narrow tie, unbuttoned his vest, and pulled his shirt off. When his torso was bare, I saw he was already wearing the little leather pouch around his neck. He kicked his boots off and dove headfirst into the bog.

I anxiously watched the ripples moving away from where Elias had disappeared. It was taking far too long. Then I pulled myself together. Elias was alive and well more than two hundred years after this moment.

He bobbed to the surface and coughed. Brown water ran down his face, and his hair clung to his cheeks. In his arms, he held the boy's body, and he shoved it up onto the raft.

"No. No." Elias's desperate shouts carried all the way to where we crouched. He carefully touched the boy's head, one side of which was a bloody smudge. He found an ampoule in his leather pouch, and he dripped the liquid onto the boy's temple, rubbed it in, and held his hand pressed flat against the wound.

Nothing happened.

"Come on. Work, damn it. Work!"

But the boy simply lay still, bleeding. Elias's hair dripped water onto his bare chest, where the pouch hung open, revealing a wealth of colored vials. He clenched his fists and pounded them against the raft. Then he buried his face in his hands. He sat like that for some time before he squared his shoulders.

Elias sniffled loudly, but his face was now hardened. He wrapped the body in a large piece of blue fabric that had been in his bundle. It looked as though he were putting the boy to bed. He stroked the child's one intact cheek softly before rolling him back into the bog. Once again, the rings spread across the water over the spot where the boy sank to his final resting place. Elias pushed the raft ashore, clutched his clothes and boots to his chest, and disappeared.

"Your body is still in Sømosen?" I measured the distance from the end of the path to the spot that still marked the center of the diminishing ripples. "I'm going to find you and give you a proper burial. Where do you want to be laid to rest?"

"Just somewhere nice," the boy said with a smile. "Do you know one?"

"I know a grave that's good to rest in. According to my dad, anyway."

"Thanks." He started to flicker, and my surroundings and I rushed upward.

I opened my eyes expecting to see the ceiling of the green room, but blue sky was above me. I heard trickling water, and sunbeams reached me through green leaves. I felt around with my hands and found I was lying on soft moss. I sat up.

I had been here before, several years ago, the time I drank Mathias's demiblood and sent myself on a really bad trip. A woman sat cross-legged in front of me, motionless. She had shiny hair and a makeup-free face. Behind her lay a staff with a carved bird's head.

"Hejd?" I looked around at the lush surroundings. "Where are we?"

Hejd squinted as though straining to understand what I said. Then she began to speak. At first, it was an unintelligible stream of speech that I couldn't make heads or tails of it. Then the words aligned themselves, and I understood.

She knows of the horn of Heimdall
Under the high-reaching holy tree
On it there pours from Valfather's pledge
A mighty stream
Would you know yet more?

She gesticulated wildly at me, as though it were difficult to get the message across.

"The high-reaching holy tree? Isn't that Yggdrasil?"

Hejd shook her head slowly and leaned forward, and we were nose to nose. For a moment, I swam in her eyes. Then everything swirled, and she was simultaneously in front of me and inside my mouth, forcing the words out.

"Valfather's pledge," we said together. "A mighty stream. The holy tree is death, and the pledge is the sacrifice. The mighty stream is the bog. Would you know yet more?"

Hejd disconnected herself from me and returned to her place, looking satisfied with herself. In fact, there was amusement in her eyes, and I wondered whether I resembled her a bit with that sarcastic expression.

"While I have you here," I said hurriedly; I didn't know how long I would be able to sit in this place I suspected was beyond time. "What is it that you and Od disagree on?"

Hejd looked down at the grass. "He wants to save the humans."

"But the rest of us do, too."

"Od also wants to save the gods."

"Of course he does. Odin is his father."

> *Hither there comes the son of Hlothyn*
> *Odin's son*
> *The warder of Midgard*
> *The snake in anger smites*
> *He falters, wounded*
> *The race of men is gone from the earth*

Along with Hejd's poem, I saw images of Od being decapitated. "You don't want him to sacrifice himself?"

Hejd shook her head slowly, and the tips of her smooth, dark hair brushed across her forearms.

"You want Odin to die and for Od to become the new god."

She nodded silently.

"Your poem says this, too." I closed my eyes and reached back in time.

> *In wondrous beauty once again*
> *Shall the golden tables stand mid the grass*
> *Which the gods had owned in the days of old*
> *Then fields unsown bear ripened fruit*
> *All ills grow better*
> *Baldr and Hoth dwell in Hropt's battle-hall*
> *And the mighty gods*
> *Would you know yet more?*

Hejd said the last words along with me, and she held her hand to her chest as though it was nice to hear the prophecy again.

"It's a bit more upbeat than the rest of the poem."

"Upbeat?"

"It's more positive," I tried. "What does it mean?"

"All that is bad will get better." Hejd looked like she doubted her own prediction.

"So, it'll get warm again? Fimbul will end?"

"In wondrous beauty once again." She smiled.

Oh . . . "As I understand it, there is a time after Ragnarök, and it will be good."

Hejd nodded, but her brows were lowered in a skeptical expression. She abruptly looked to the side as though she'd heard something.

"Now she must sink." Slowly, her body sank into the green bog. I crawled forward and stopped in front of her upper body, which was still free from the quagmire.

"So, I can lead us into this wonderful time?"

Hejd waved her arms wildly from where she sat with her lower body buried. She reached up and tapped a finger against my chest.

"*She* knows of the horn of Heimdall," Hejd said before she pushed me, sending me flying backward.

I awoke in the green guest bedroom to find Luna squatting in front of me, talking in a continuous stream. Her words sounded fuzzy. I realized my good ear was against the pillow. The other was covered in a thick layer of bandages.

"What?"

Luna smiled her winningest smile. "Are you awake?"

I sat up, dazed. "Well, now I am."

"Come." She took my hand and heaved me out of the bed. "I can't wait any longer."

"For what?"

"Just come." She wrapped me in a thick pink cardigan and pulled me out of the room and down the stairs. In the hall, she pushed my boots toward me. Drowsily, I put them on.

Luna flung the door open. It was snowing, and she pulled her green shawl over her head to shield it from the stiff, ice-cold wind.

"Ugh," I said as I tried to pull the cardigan's hood over the thick bandages. I finally managed after several tries. We walked out into snowfall, and Luna laid an arm around me and ushered me forward.

"I was up all night working."

"On what?"

"It's a surpriiiise."

I caught a glimpse of my reflection in a window. Dressed in a pink sweater, with the white bandage under my hood, I looked completely different from my usual ratty, black-clad self. I leaned toward Luna, and arm in arm, we ran for the barn.

Luna pushed the door to the side, and the hinges complied with a metallic whine. A pile of snow had accumulated against the peeling outer wall, and she had to struggle a bit to open the door wide enough to squeeze through. Inside the barn, I had to get accustomed to the dark. At first, it was pitch black around me, but gradually, I was able to discern shapes. The scent of fresh wood was all around like a wonderful perfume, and I inhaled deeply through my nose to take it in.

My ring began to glow, but it was no longer on my hand. The green light came from beneath a piece of white fabric—Luna must have removed my ring when I slept.

The barn was full of drums and African masks, and from the ceiling beams hung bones and dried herbs. The platform where Monster's corpse and, later, where the birch tree had lain was once again covered by the white cloth. Though it wasn't exactly white anymore—splatters and stains made it look like a macabre batik. Beneath the sheet lay an oblong form, shining green.

"Take it off." Luna pointed at the cloth and shimmied ecstatically.

I tentatively grabbed the corner and lifted the cloth, full of fearful foreboding. Luna didn't always grasp what would and wouldn't excite people—the sheet could conceal anything from a corpse to large quantities of narcotics or owl pellets. It finally slid off, and I stared at the object that lay on the platform.

"Ta-daaaaa," Luna whispered and bit her lip with a squeal.

Luna had carved the birch tree into a staff. A völva staff, I knew immediately, but it was far nicer than I had dared hope. I knelt and carefully grasped the smooth wood. In the middle, Luna had embedded my ring with Mathias's tears and her magic iron. It looked as though the ring had always been there. When I touched the wood, a certain . . . I wouldn't call it a *power*, more like a *memory*, slipped into me. As though the staff *were* me and all the other völvas before me. At the very bottom, holding hands in a spiral around the staff's base, were a myriad of female forms. Each one was no larger than my fingernail, and they danced in a band a couple of hand-widths wide up the staff.

I could see facial features and different costumes on the figures, and I was impressed that Luna had carved them with such detail. The final völva held the hand of a girl. The girl wore a hoodie and ripped pants. Because she was carved on a knot, she was dark, while all the others were light. My fingers ran across the figure in recognition. She was so small and fragile, but she had a stubborn expression.

My whole story continued up the staff. I raised it into a vertical position as I studied it. I was marked by the knot, but I was also in other places. I was there alone, though an unclear figure billowed just behind me: Arthur. Luna had polished a discoloration in the wood so it resembled a person. Monster, Luna, and Mathias appeared in clear carvings. Varnar was there, too. It was just his face, and he was kissing a slightly older me. It continued with Frank, Elias, and Hakim, and what happened in the woods. My journey through Hrafnheim with Rorik and Finn, and Monster's reanimation.

Luna stood behind me. The wood grew lighter in color toward the top, and Luna had depicted ice crystals on the uppermost section. The staff was a head taller than me, and it ended with two ravens. They sat slightly apart from one another, but their beaks were connected. Between them and the winter was a raw piece of wood the length of my forearm where Luna hadn't carved anything. She hadn't even sanded it, and it still had splinters and knots.

"Your story isn't over, so I left the top part blank, but it's consecrated with hand cream and everything. You know, the alms."

I spun around and buried my face in her neck.

She held me tight. "It's you. I knew it as soon as I held the wood in my hands. You have a shared history, you and this birch tree. It knew you so well, it told me everything." She held me slightly away from her. "Look. I made a place for your giant crystal between the ravens." She fished the dull stone out of my pocket and, sure enough, it fit perfectly in the space between the birds. As soon as it was in place, a glow flickered deep within the crystal.

"This staff has the powers of witches, the strength of gods, the might of giants, and the history of völvas. It's perfect."

"I know," Luna said. "It's amazing."

"I had no idea you knew how to carve wood."

"Neither did I." She giggled.

Suddenly, everything seemed funny, and we laughed uncontrollably. Maybe it was a response to the heinous events of the day before. With the völva staff in my hand, I felt stronger than I had in a long time. The power of the other völvas reverberated through it.

"It needs a name," Luna said and wiped her eyes, though her tears had come from laughter.

"How do you say *friend* in Old Norse?"

"Vinr," Luna replied.

"Then that's what I'll call it. Vinr. I've only made it this far because of my friends." I suddenly remembered Od's words from one of the first times I met him.

Cherish your friends. You can't get through this alone.

I swam around, and there were *plop*s and sloshing sounds around me. Something red floated in the waves. At first, I thought it was afternoon sunlight filtering through the water, but then my sister swam toward me. It was her red hair, swaying over her head.

"Anna." There was longing and desperation in her voice. We met in a big, floating embrace and held each other tight. I felt sucked back in time to a place that was just . . . right. Here, in Serén's arms, everything was as it should be.

Up in Luna's room, I had been eager to test Vinr, and as soon as I closed my eyes and called to my sister, she appeared. Vinr worked as a satellite that strengthened my signal to Serén.

"I was so worried." Serén sniffled. "It happened so suddenly, and I had no idea what he was throwing at you." Her hair floated over her head like a mermaid's.

I held her at arm's length. "Throwing?"

"He must be a powerful magician to make nails fly so fast. I didn't see them until they hit."

"It was a gun. We have those here in Midgard. It's not magic."

Her hands kept running over my neck as though to inspect it.

"You actually saw the bullet hit me." I placed her hand on the spot just behind my jaw. "Here."

Serén avoided my gaze. "It went so fast, like he made up his mind at the last second. I saw it a few seconds before it happened."

"I survived. Really! You don't need to worry. There's something else. You need to tell Mom that Eskild is no longer in Hrafnheim. He's in Jotunheim, and as soon as I'm ready, I'm going after him. I have a piece of the Gjallarhorn, but we can't let the giants get ahold of the remaining pieces. You need to find Védis. The pendant she has, Freyja's tears, is also made from that gold."

Serén stared at me. "Gold? Eskild? Freyja's tears?"

Oh, right! Serén clearly hadn't been updated. I explained the Gjallarhorn to her.

"Jotunheim. Why haven't I seen—" Just then, she was hit with a cascade of invisible waves. There was movement beneath her closed eyelids. "Now I've seen it. It'll be a dangerous quest, and you will need help."

"I'm getting help. Luna and I will start völva training tomorrow. Mimir is also on board."

Serén held me against her, and we swayed in the wind or the water—whatever it was we found ourselves in. "I'll send assistance. You'll be glad. I promise."

She slipped away from me, and I searched for her in the warm substance, but she was gone. I swam upward in the thick soup. Then I opened my eyes in the little green room, where Luna stared intensely at me.

"So?"

"This völva gear is strong," I panted, both exhausted and fueled from using Vinr. "Come. It's time." I stood up and banged the end of the staff against the floor. It felt like it had always been in my hand. Outside Rebecca's house, I stuck it into a snowdrift, and the snow melted immediately. The staff's power vibrated beneath my fingers. Luna grabbed a bongo drum, and together we walked across the field toward Odinmont. With every step I took, I thumped the staff against the ground.

Inside Odinmont, I found Mimir on the dining table. He looked much better now that the bandages were off.

"Your father has gone into Ravensted," Mimir said. He shifted slightly and looked at Luna, who stood timidly behind me.

"Mimir, this is my friend Luna," I said. "Luna, stop standing over there. Just come here."

Red-cheeked and wide-eyed, she walked toward the severed head on the table. Mimir looked at her with dignity—without the maggots, he actually looked pretty oracle-like. "A mighty witch," he said and studied her with a crooked smile. "I would say you have enough powers for two."

Luna giggled, stunned. "I'm totally starstruck. I mean . . . you're legendary. I can't believe I'm meeting Mimir himself." She bowed formally.

With a strange feeling in my stomach that I couldn't explain, I leaned against Vinr.

The rune-shaped scar on Mimir's forehead creased as he raised his brows. "Did you make that völva staff? It's magnificent. Not since Hejd's day have I seen such a beautiful staff."

Luna clapped her hands to her cheeks. "I don't know what to say. Praise from Mimir. That really means a lot."

"We're going to train, and it would be great to have a coach," I said. "Do you have time?"

Mimir sniffed. "Time? I have more time than I know what to do with."

We went out into my little garden. The ground was still covered with a layer of compacted ice. I didn't think of it, of course, but Luna made sure Mimir sat on a pillow on the patio table and was given a knit hat against the cold. I stood, a bit lost, in the middle of the frozen lawn with the staff in my hand.

"What do I do?" I asked.

"You can unscrew the top," Luna said. "There's a compartment under the ravens. There's henbane in there, the horse tooth you got from Hejd, some ritual paint, and a few bones."

"Uh, thanks, I think."

She played a few hollow beats on her bongo drum, then continued in a rhythm that sounded like a heartbeat. Mimir's voice grew deep.

"The völva can cleanse places, she can dispel evil spirits; the völva is a cult leader, and she can summon dead to her."

I inhaled deeply and tightened my grip on Vinr.

"Use your power."

I fumbled around and tried to pull energy from my surroundings.

"Wooshh." Luna laughed. "That tickles."

"No," Mimir said. "*Your* power. It's inside you."

I squeezed my eyes shut and turned my gaze inward. I searched inside myself but found it empty. My clairvoyance interrupted and kept sending annoying images from the past.

"I can't. My clairvoyance is in the way."

"Maybe you should try some henbane," Luna suggested.

I mentally searched myself again for völva power, but the past became more and more insistent. I tried the tricks Elias had taught me of listening, feeling, and smelling, but this had the opposite effect. I rubbed my forehead. "What do you guys think is wrong?"

"You're trying everything at once. It's best to practice things one at a time."

"Well, I don't have a cult on hand, and I think there are already plenty of dead people running around all the time."

"Can you summon them?"

"Not in the same way Ulla can. You know, the medium Elias knows. She's a spirit magnet. I would say it's more like ghosts just haunt me, and I don't have a whole lot of control over it. There was one time I managed to make one appear, but that was just Belinda, and she was already breathing down my neck."

"What about oskoreia?" Mimir said. "You could practice cleansing on them."

"What?"

Luna bounced excitedly. "That's a really good idea. I think there are a lot more of them after the epidemic outbreak."

"Does anyone care to tell me what oskoreia are?"

"I've told you before," Luna said, but I gave her a pointed look. "Oskoreia are known as *the wild dead* or *Odin's wild dead*. Those who die in a violent or unexpected way risk joining them. They're restless spirits who wreak a lot of havoc. They have a negative effect on the living. If there's a bad vibe somewhere, you can be almost certain that there are oskoreia nearby. It was my dad's job to keep them at bay. My mom and I still do the rituals, but I think there have been more oskoreia lately. The frost storms catch a lot of people off guard, and the disease was also brutal."

"Where do they hang out?"

"They come over the fields as part of the wild hunt, but I think they're everywhere. We try to stop them at the edge of the forest."

I peered out across the field. The clouds were so black, it was completely dark out, even though it was not yet noon. I didn't particularly want to leave Odinmont, but both Luna and Mimir looked so determined, I didn't seem to have a choice.

"Okay, then," I said reluctantly.

Luna closed her eyes and mumbled something in Yoruba. When she opened them again, they were black and didn't look like her own. She grabbed the bongo drum and marched into the shadows.

CHAPTER 20

We trudged across the field between Odinmont and Kraghede Forest. The temperature had dropped again, and I squeezed Vinr in my hand. The giant crystal at its top shone and cast a warm circle around us, a little like a heat lamp at an outdoor café, but the frost crackled ominously around us. Behind me, Luna beat her drum, and from under my arm, Mimir sang a song in a language I didn't recognize as Old Norse. Maybe it was the original giant language from ancient times. I banged Vinr against the ground with every step I took. The light moved with me, and the others made sure to stay inside its radius.

In the middle of the field, Luna stopped. She continued to beat the drum, and her voice, somewhat deeper than usual, blended with Mimir's. I raised Vinr.

There they were. Oskoreia. At first, I saw them only as an outline, swaying slightly, but the more I looked, the more they resembled humans. There were four of them, and they had matted hair and tattered clothes, but I couldn't tell if they were men or women. Their eyes were pleading and confused. I thought I could see the bones under their transparent skin. It didn't seem like the afterlife was treating them particularly well. They neither came toward us nor went away. They simply stood there, staring with faintly fluorescent eyes that reflected my giant crystal, like how a cat's or owl's eyes would reflect artificial light.

"What now?" I asked out of the corner of my mouth.

"Can you see anything?" Luna sounded like herself again.

"They're right there."

"I can't see them."

"Lucky you." I was used to ghosts, embalmed heads, and man-eating giant wolves, but the oskoreia were some of the scariest creatures I had ever encountered. Maybe it was the frustration that emanated from them even as they stood still. It crept into me and made me angry and despondent at the same time.

"They're restless spirits," Mimir whispered. "They affect the living."

"Can you guys feel them, too?" The despondency was now replaced by the stage immediately preceding panic. The distance between me and the dead was all that kept me from hightailing it out of there.

"I can't detect them at all." Luna turned her head from side to side.

"Technically, I'm dead myself," Mimir said. "So, they don't affect me, but I do see them."

"Why do they make me so scared?" It was hard to speak, and my tongue felt dry in my mouth.

"They're Odin's servants. He thrives when people are afraid because fearful people make more offerings. He sets the oskoreia loose to frighten the living. As a völva, you should be able to send them to one of the realms of the dead."

"Won't that make Odin mad? That definitely wasn't what he had in mind when he appointed me as a völva." Not that I was planning to let that stop me from sending the oskoreia away.

"He doesn't think you have the nerve. I would bet he didn't think you had the nerve to steal me, either."

I looked at the dead, who stood and swayed, their eyes empty. "How do I do it?"

"Hejd always spoke gently to them. She tried to find out where they had died so they could be sent to the right place. Pick one of them. You shouldn't address them all at once. It's too much of a mouthful."

"Ulla taught me that you can't ask a spirit about their death directly. They get all jammed up."

"You have to skirt around it." Mimir was now speaking so quietly, he was nearly inaudible. I inhaled and tried to brace myself, but my hands wouldn't stop shaking. Then, I focused on the smallest of the figures and walked toward it.

"Hey, you," I tried. I pointed Vinr toward it, and I could see its features better in the light from the giant crystal. It looked like a living corpse. It had desperate, deep-set eyes, black bloodstains across its neck and down its clothes, rotten skin, and exposed teeth.

"They look like death."

The oskoreia limped toward me. It stretched its arms forward like a real-life horror-movie monster.

"They're different from normal ghosts," Mimir said. "Send it away."

"You . . . y-you . . . should—" Suddenly, my words were gone. I couldn't think clearly, and the oskoreia was coming closer. Now I saw it was a woman. I tried as hard as I could to calm myself. "What's the last thing you can remember?" I put on a soft voice. In truth, I wanted to shout at her to go away.

"Cold, cold . . ." the dead woman stammered. She was almost right in front of me now.

"Frost storm?"

She stopped and swayed her head as though trying to remember something. "Ice. Freezing." Her teeth chattered loudly. Her bluish teeth were already visible because her lips had rotted away. "My daughter. Warmth."

"Okay . . ." I couldn't see her past so I had to guess. "Your daughter. Where is she?"

The oskoreia folded her hands and placed them under her cheek. She closed her eyes and hummed a lullaby. I snapped my fingers and felt like I was playing a macabre version of charades.

"She died in her sleep?"

The woman shook her head and continued to sing softly and rock back and forth.

"Oh! You warmed her up. She survived. You saved her, but it cost you your life." Arthur had been sent to Freyja's hall because he died protecting his family. "Fólkvangr!" I shouted triumphantly. "I'm sending you to Fólkvangr."

It was a huge relief to figure it out, and I pounded Vinr against the ground. The oskoreia's deep-set eyes opened and were filled with gratitude. Then she evaporated.

"That was pretty easy. I can totally—hey . . . Why are the others coming toward me?" I backed up as the three remaining restless dead staggered toward me.

"They want help, too, but you're not ready." Mimir's voice faded as panic washed over me. The oskoreias' negativity surged into me, and soon, I was unable to form a coherent thought.

"How did you die?" I blurted.

This was far too direct, and the zombielike figures hissed. A man who looked more like a skeleton started running toward me.

"No . . . no . . . you need to move on," I said feverishly. When he came closer, I smelled sour dirt and decayed flesh. "Valhalla. Fólkvangr. Helheim." He didn't evaporate, and he was getting closer. The others were right behind him. "Help."

But Luna couldn't help me because she couldn't even see the oskoreia, and Mimir had neither the ability nor a body to fight them. Luna tried to get between us, flailing her arms in the air, but she was hindered by the fact that she was still holding the drum. The dead simply whooshed right through her. Now entirely incapable of thought, I dropped both Vinr and Mimir, and I ran away. Mimir cried out in pain as he rolled on the frozen field. I gave no thought to my friends, nor to the fact that I was heading straight toward Kraghede Forest.

"Anna!" Luna called from somewhere far behind me.

Only when I reached the tree line did the panic let up, and I slowed my pace. Among the tall spruce trees, I stood for a moment and panted, my heart pounding.

Without Vinr, it was so dark I could barely see. My pulse thumped loudly in my ears, and I felt nothing but the cold against my skin. My mouth was dry and tasted like dust.

Nevertheless, I inhaled deeply through my nose and stiffened when a very specific scent drifted into my nostrils. At the same time, a familiar sensation came at me hard and fast.

"Anna . . ." Luna shouted from the field. Because Vinr was near Mimir, it glowed faintly, but I couldn't make out more than a little dot of light. Between the trees, something glimmered like the northern lights, and the ground vibrated.

I tried to orient myself in the dark.

"Hello . . ." My voice was still shaking. The scent was now so overwhelming that I was about to collapse under the weight of bittersweet memories. I started running again but was heading straight into the middle of the forest. I used my clairvoyance to recall the route, which I had taken so many times that I raced through as fast as I could, even though I couldn't see.

I inhaled. It was unbearable, and tears pressed at the corners of my eyes. At first, I thought the past had overcome me in the oskoreia's wake and that I had started to hallucinate. I reached the stone circle, blinked, and stared at the person standing right in front of me among the shimmering boulders. Fresh air, sun, and forest hit my nostrils.

He smiled that smile that made my legs give out beneath me.

"Your sister said you needed help. This is for you." He opened his hand, and in it lay the jewel, Freyja's tears.

"Varnar," I whispered.

PART III
THE WRATH OF GODS

Ere thou take off the saddle,
or farest forward a step
What hast thou done in the giants' dwelling
to make glad thee or me?
Odin grows angry, angered is the best of the gods
Freyr shall be thy foe, most evil maid
Who the magic wrath of gods hast got for thyself

Skírnismál,
9th century

CHAPTER 21

Varnar rested his cheek on my shoulder. The weight of his body was not unpleasant. Quite the opposite. I wanted to feel every inch of him, and I ran my hands over his silky-soft back. The smell of fresh air and sunlight that I had missed all the way down to my marrow was now abundant around me, and I drank it in greedily.

Snow covered my slanted window, cutting us off from the last little bit of daylight. Vinr lay on the floor, glowing, and the unnatural light made me feel like I was in a dream. A very nice dream.

Varnar shifted, and his dark hair brushed over my chest. It tickled, and I couldn't help but giggle. He lifted himself up over me, his arms straight, so he could see into my eyes. I reached up and caressed his face. My hand slid down across his neck and upper arm. The small scars were uneven bumps on his skin.

"I've missed you so much. The last time we saw each other, it went all wrong. I wish we hadn't parted like that."

"I didn't think you wanted to see me. Serén said you were hurt by my words." Varnar furrowed his brows only slightly, but I knew this little grimace covered several months of self-reproach.

"Maybe Serén should hold back from giving relationship advice. Just because she can see I'm sad doesn't make her an expert in what you should or shouldn't do." I wanted to punctuate this with a *hmph*, but then I remembered she had sent him to me now, which I was very grateful for.

Varnar smiled cautiously. "I can think for myself, you know, and I thought it was best if I stayed away. What I said to you at Haraldsborg was unfair."

I shrugged. "We were both under a lot of pressure. That makes people say things they regret."

Varnar bent his arms, bringing his body close to mine. I could feel his warmth, smell him, and feel the rhythmic beating of his heart just behind his ribs. I happily wrapped my arms around his torso and pulled him against me. His kisses banished all thoughts. Gentle electricity crackled across my skin, sparks flew between us, and I melted like caramel between his hands. He broke off the kiss, and my dignity was the only thing that kept me from complaining about it.

"What did you do to your ear? Serén just said not to be scared when I saw you."

I brought my hand to the side of my head. The bandage was starting to slide off, and Luna's hypnosis had long since faded, so it hurt when I prodded my wound. How must I have looked just then with the white bandage and my hair a mess? I had forgotten all about the fact that Rebecca had patched me up.

"I just got shot. It's no big deal."

Varnar got me to sit up and pulled off the long strip of gauze. I gritted my teeth against the pain as he carefully peeled the innermost layers away. The gauze was stuck in the wound, and it stung when Varnar removed it completely. I practiced slow, controlled breathing.

"You always get hurt," he said. "Every time I turn my back, someone does you harm."

"Maybe you should stop turning your back on me." The words came out sounding more pointed than I had intended, and I hurried to lay my hand on his arm.

Either Varnar didn't hear it, or he chose to ignore my wounded comment. He studied the top of my ear from various angles with a professional expression. "Was it treated with magic?"

"Rebecca fixed it."

"It's not too bad. Just let it air out, and it should heal. You'll have a scar, but I'm sure you knew that already." He placed the bandage on my nightstand.

"I don't care about scars."

"I know." He squeezed my shoulder. "I have some læknir, but I would rather save it for serious injuries."

Varnar apparently thought worse things than a mangled ear awaited us.

Right now, I didn't want to think about that. I just wanted to enjoy the fact that Varnar was back with me, and I wrapped my arms around his body. With his elegant strength, he turned me around and lay me on my back. He lowered his face toward mine and kissed me until I lost all sense of time, place, and my own name. Tonight, I would allow myself not to think about Fimbulwinter, Ragnarök, or the tsunami of other calamities heading toward us.

"You've gotten slow."

"Hey!"

Varnar furrowed his brows in the familiar way I had replayed in my head again and again over the past year. Yet now that I finally had him in front of me, he didn't quite match my memory. The night I'd just spent with him made my body vibrate, and it was hard for me to concentrate.

"It's been months since I was in a real fight. I'm totally out of pra—"

Varnar kicked my legs out from under me, and before I knew what was happening, I was lying on my back on the frozen ground. My völva staff rolled away with a *clunk*, and Varnar was upon me with a feline leap. His face was right in front of me, and his brown eyes with small flecks of green stared into mine.

"I don't want to hear any excuses. You can never stop training, even if the fields turn green again." He didn't smile, but warmth nevertheless flowed through me. Each of his hands was planted on the snow-covered ground, and he held himself up on straightened arms above me. My heart pounded. I had to remind myself to breathe because Varnar was far more beautiful than I had been able to remember.

"If you're going to survive, you have to be as good as you were. Serén saw—" He stopped.

"What did she see?"

"That this is going to be tough," he concluded. He moved away from me in a fluid motion. "You need all your strength and all the help we can give you."

I got to my feet, grabbing Vinr on the way. I pounded Vinr against the ground to signal I was ready to try again. I exhaled slowly and composed myself. I'd be damned if I was going to let the sight of him and that entrancing smell ruin my ability to fight. I pointed Vinr forward. Varnar attacked, but I remembered all his moves so well I could predict exactly what he was going to do. I swung Vinr low, and he jumped over it, which I was counting on. I decided to experiment with Vinr's power. As Varnar landed, I touched the giant crystal, which sat between the carved ravens, to the ground. It released a surge of energy, causing the snow-covered earth beneath Varnar's feet to ripple.

Yes!

He lost his footing, and at the same time, I shot my free hand out and hit him in the chest, sending him toppling backward. Now I was the one who leapt over him. I pointed my staff directly at his face so the ravens and the giant crystal were right over his head. Arms shaking, I held the position, ready to strike. I stood straddling him with one foot on either side of his body. Varnar turned his head so he could see me, but he didn't lift it. There were snowflakes in his dark hair, and he smiled broadly. I had to work hard to stay in my steely warrior position.

"Your völva powers have grown stronger, and you're combining them with your fighting skills."

I stepped back and spun Vinr around in the air. The speed at which it moved through the wind produced whistling. The staff was not only my source of power but also an excellent weapon.

Varnar got to his feet. "We just need to polish your technique."

I leaned against the staff. "I think what I just did was pretty damn good."

Varnar brushed the snow from his hair. "I could have taken you down in a myriad of ways, and I don't even have a weapon." He patted my shoulder. I wanted to protest, but he gathered his fingers around my upper arm. He leaned in close, and my heart did a backflip. He whispered: "But you're right. What you did was pretty damn good."

My mouth moved toward his, but I happened to look at the glass door leading into Odinmont. Luna stood there with her nose practically pressed against the glass. She held Mimir's head under her arm, and next to her stood Mathias. With a smile, I waved for them to come out.

She opened the door cautiously. "Are you done?"

"With what?"

"With . . ." She looked from me to Varnar.

In her armpit, Mimir mirrored the expression. Because Luna had wrapped her green shawl around him, it looked as though she had grown an extra head from her ribs. They walked out toward us. Varnar and Mimir looked at one another.

"You're the warrior. I think Hejd saw you," Mimir said. "Way back in ancient times, she saw you with the raven."

"We don't know the myths very well where I come from," Varnar said. "But I'm old enough to remember a few from my childhood, so I'm pretty sure I know who you are. I'm just uncertain about what you're doing here with Anna."

"The raven is the defender of the weak."

"You don't look particularly weak." Aside from the blue rune scars on his forehead, Mimir looked healthier than most.

"I was powerless when she helped me. You should always judge people based on how they treat the powerless. That's when you see their true selves." Mimir turned his head with a dignified look. "Hejd did not predict that Anna would take me with her, so the prophecy is now moving in a different direction."

Mathias's lips formed a narrow line. "You stole Mimir from the All-Father."

I raised an eyebrow. "If Mimir had legs, he would have run away from there as fast as he could."

"Are you ready to test your völva powers again?" Luna interjected, probably to avoid a fight between me and Mathias. I sighed, not particularly proud of how it had gone the last time.

"You might as well get started. Time isn't exactly moving backward."

"Not oskoreia again," I begged.

"Mimir and I were talking about maybe trying a cult ritual."

"Oh, were you?" Mimir and Luna were apparently becoming good friends. "And who would be my cult members?"

"We will." Luna beamed. "Mimir said he sensed Loki here in Odinmont. I've cast a protective spell, but as a shaman, you can journey into the dream world and fill all the gaps and cracks."

"Am I supposed to be a shaman now, too?"

"A völva *is* a shaman. Gods, Anna, I have to tell you everything." Luna ushered us upstairs. Inside my guest bedroom, I saw that she had pushed the furniture aside and drawn a bunch of runes on the wooden floor with chalk. Mimir looked in wonder at the mural, which depicted a beautiful valley. In the middle of the valley was a lake the exact same color as the bright blue sky. At the end of the valley sat a dark forest, its trees the gray hue of iron. Horses grazed around the lake.

"The border of the giants' realm." Mimir kept his eyes trained on the wall as Luna carefully placed him on the floor. Thoughtful as always, she had laid out a soft piece of velour for him to sit on.

"Have you been there?"

"I was born there and lived there many years ago.

The giantess old in the Iron Forest sat,
In the east, and bore the brood of Fenrir;
Among these one in monster's guise
Was soon to swallow the moon from the sky

As Mimir recited the poem, the völvas on my staff joined in, and a chorus of women's voices rang out in my head. I heard Hejd shouting the poem, the loudest of all. A vision came with force.

In the vision, I saw Monster leap toward Luna with teeth bared. He hit her in the chest with his front paws. She fell backward with him on top of her. His white teeth sunk into her neck. This had to be the future, but I didn't know if Serén or Hejd had sent it.

No, that can't happen. I had to blink a couple of times as my enhanced powers tore through me. Breathing heavily, I leaned against Vinr for support. Everyone looked expectantly at me, but I didn't want to tell them about the deadly vision. To redirect their attention, I pointed at the wall. "Is that in Hrafnheim?"

"Jotunheim starts there. The giant forests belong to both realms." Mimir still looked at me with suspicion, but he didn't pry into what I had seen.

"Who is *the giantess old*?"

"Angerboda is the giantess," Mimir said.

"Isn't Angerboda Loki's lover?"

"She is the mother of three of Loki's children." Luna sat crosslegged and folded her long legs up under her. "The Midgard Serpent, Hel, and Fenrir."

Mathias and Varnar sat down, too, but they both looked skeptical. Luna unscrewed the top of the völva staff and shook some things out into the middle of our circle. There was a small, round box with a lid decorated to look like a sun; a little pile of bones; the big tooth Od had given me; and a bag containing five large bell-shaped seedpods. I picked up the tooth. It was worn smooth and filled my whole palm, and the side was carved with a crooked H.

"It's from a horse," Mimir said.

"A mythical one?" Maybe there were several eight-legged steeds in Valhalla.

"It was a normal horse from near Thisted. Our friend owned it. A splendid but entirely normal animal. We offered it to the gods."

My finger traced the dark rune on the side of the tooth.

"Hagal," Mimir said softly. "It was Hejd's favorite rune."

I got the feeling that Od was not alone in missing the völva who had been dead for over a thousand years.

"*Hagal* means *hail*." I remembered that the rune had also been part of Gytha's hnetafl game in Hrafnheim. I looked out the window, where the snow was once again pummeling down. "Hail is just one step worse than snow."

"Hejd always said that hagal is a destructive rune, but that it's also life-giving. After the hail has covered the earth and killed the weakest ones, the ice melts, and the water creates new life. It symbolizes the removal of obstacles, and problems being turned into something good."

"A bit of a harsh view to take."

"Hejd lived in a harsh time. Hagal is associated with Heimdall because he represents the laws of nature, which cannot be changed."

When Mimir said *Heimdall*, Mathias sat up a bit straighter. I was pretty sure he was trying to figure out who his father was. I no longer had any doubt. I absentmindedly closed my hand around the tooth. It fit perfectly in my grip.

I got a vision of a ritual from it. Hejd herself danced with it in her fist. Her upper body was naked and covered in a layer of chalky white paste. Painted on her in red were serpent knots, sun symbols, and stylized ravens. Her eyes were closed as if in a trance, and her long black hair hung in big, messy tufts around her head. I felt an affinity for the woman who had died so many years before. *Raven,* she said. *I know that you're watching from the future.*

I blinked the vision away and picked up the round box. "What is this?"

Luna took it from my hands and removed the lid. "Pigment." The box was divided into two chambers containing red and white pigment, respectively. Luna began painting my face and neck white. She dipped her fingers into the red pigment and dragged her fingertips across my forehead, cheeks, and shoulders. When she was done, she put all the supplies, aside from the horse's tooth, back into Vinr's top, keeping a seedpod in her hand. She went to screw the top on, but right before she closed it, I laid a hand on her arm.

"Wait." I pulled the two pieces of Gjallarhorn gold from my pocket and tucked them into the cavity inside Vinr alongside the other objects.

Luna crumbled the dried henbane seed into the flame of a candle.

"You've waited so long to get to do that, Luna." I smiled.

In response, she moved a flat hand over the smoke that rose from the candle, dispersing it into the room. There was a smell somewhat like licorice, and I stood up in the middle of the circle. In one hand, I held Hejd's horse tooth; in the other, I held Vinr. The henbane smoke made me relax, and I heard Hejd chanting in my head. I think I was channeling the past from the tooth. In the circle, Luna hit the drum, and Mimir sang. The others joined in, and I moved in time with the rhythms.

Close your eyes and reach out, Hejd said from the past. Over a thousand years ago, when she performed the séance, she had known I would be watching from the future. Maybe she had held the ceremony for me to learn from it. Even though she spoke in Old Norse, I understood her words. I also knew what she meant. My mind was stretched like a rubber band, and I hopped around.

My spirit became lighter, and with each hop, it took slightly longer to return to the ground. It took a little getting used to, but after a few attempts, I was hovering over us. I saw the room from above, with myself dancing in the middle, painted red and white. The others sat on the ground with their arms stretched out, with red cheeks and giant pupils. Above each of them, I saw their essence—if I could call it that. They weren't dead, of course, so they didn't look like real ghosts. Only Mimir looked like an actual ghost, though he was in better condition in ghost form. He had a body, arms, and legs. Amazed, he raised a hand and looked at it.

Mathias was a beautiful, gleaming green god; Varnar a perfect warrior with bulging muscles and weapons in each hand; and Luna was a wild witch with magic sputtering around her. I let my soul fly around Odinmont, which also looked different from normal. I saw the mound with all its skeletons as though with X-ray vision. The house was small and rickety, but around it lay a bubble of magic. Just as I was about to declare Odinmont fully secured, I spotted something slithering around at the edge of the magic bubble. Angrily, I dove toward the little creature. My spirit was like the raven, and I screeched furiously.

The little worm tried to squeeze itself into a minuscule crack in the bubble. It was pasty white but had a tiny human face. I landed in front of it and pecked at it with my beak. The little maggot writhed.

"You aren't coming in here, Loki," I cackled. "This is my home."

The little worm didn't reply but burrowed into the ground to escape my attack. I moved around the dome. I filled and patched the weak points around Odinmont until the house was completely impenetrable. I flew back to the room where my cult's song and drumbeat gave me strength for my shamanistic journey.

Spirit-Varnar saw me arrive. He radiated, dark and dangerous, in his warrior attire. He wore a black leather harness with weapons hanging from leather straps. He looked stronger in this version, and the look he gave me made my stomach flutter. In this version, he was more direct, and he looked intensely at me as I hovered in front of him.

"I threw Loki out," I said to Witch-Luna.

"He can be as tiny as a flea," she warned. "Are you sure you closed all the holes?"

"I saw him as a disgusting maggot, and I sent him back into the dirt where he belongs."

"Then he can only come in if you invite him."

"That will never happen."

Mimir stood before me. He was a pretty handsome guy when he had a body and no scars on his forehead. "You have strong völva powers," he said. "You were even able to conjure me. But you should stop now before you wear yourself out."

I spread my arms, and they felt like wings. Power vibrated through me. It came from the other völvas in my staff, from Hejd's horse tooth, and from the air itself. I was nowhere near exhausted.

"Anna... You need to return to your body now. Your powers are untrained, and you need to recover your strength," Mimir insisted.

I tried to make myself heavy so I could return to my body. My feet drifted toward the ground. When I was almost back in my body, I heard a faint voice.

"Anna..."

I looked around. The voice wasn't coming from the others in the room.

"Anna! It's time. Eskild has long since reached Skrymir's manor." The voice was breathless.

I tried to trace where the words were coming from. I squinted. The voice was coming from inside the mural. I let go of my body again and floated toward the painting. Maybe because I was in spirit form, or maybe because of the henbane, but now the trees were swaying, the grass was fragrant, and the lake in the middle was lapping at the shore.

"The giants' realm is right there," said the man's voice, which had now gained some strength.

"Hakim? Are you inside the wall?"

"Just outside. You have to leave now if you're going to get the Gjallarhorn gold. It's your last chance."

"Come, Hakim," I called, and the ghost appeared. I could see him through Odinmont's slightly transparent walls. He pushed against the bubble that surrounded the house like a membrane. Maybe I had patched it a little too effectively.

Hakim looked first at my body, painted white and in a trance in the middle of the floor. Then, he looked at my spirit self. An impressed look slid across his familiar face. "You are so strong," he said. His voice was muffled by the membrane between us. "The first time you have an out-of-body experience, you're able to travel to other worlds. You have access to Jotunheim now, but only now. The passage will close soon."

I cautiously brushed my knuckle over the mural, which rippled like jelly. "I'm going to Jotunheim," I whispered.

Mimir, who couldn't see Hakim, looked at me, frightened. "You're not ready. You can't—" But I had already reached out toward the mural. My fingers penetrated the wall, which pitched and crackled as I stuck my hand all the way into the image.

"No, Anna. No!" I heard Mimir say, but I was already halfway through to the other world. "It's too dangerous. It's—"

The rest of his words stopped abruptly as I stuck my head through the wall. Before I fully disappeared into Jotunheim, someone who was still on the Midgard side grabbed one of my hands.

I popped through and landed on the carpet of grass in front of the forest. I looked to see who had grabbed me and come through to the land of the giants. It was Varnar, and we were both back in physical form.

"You can't go on this journey by yourself. I'll never let you fight alone again."

CHAPTER 22

I looked down at the lake, where my face was reflected: white with a bunch of red drawings. Luna had drawn a snake on my forehead and suns the color of my hair on my cheeks. I carefully splashed water onto my face and washed the paint away. "Ooh." Even though the sky here was blue with scattered clouds, and the grass was free of snow, the lake was ice-cold. I tasted it. The water was pure and tasted wonderful. A river ran from the lake into the forest. "It's not snowy here like at home." I looked around. The wind was still brisk, but the winter air didn't bite like it did in Hrafnheim and Midgard. The horses galloped away when we stood up. Their manes were long and uncut, and their tails were raised as they thundered away.

We followed the river into the forest, and the trees shifted quickly from dark brown to iron gray. Our surroundings were dark, but I could still see easily, as the trees weren't as close together as they were in Kraghede Forest.

"Do you know where to go?"

"We have to follow the water." I pointed to the river. "That's the river Iving, and the lake up there is its source. It also has an offshoot in Hrafnheim, near Frón. Even during Fimbulwinter it never freezes over.

> *Iving is the river that 'twixt the realms*
> *Of the gods and the giants goes*
> *For all time ever open it flows*
> *No ice on the river there is*

I was starting to know the poems so well, they just flowed out of me without effort. Varnar scanned our surroundings with a watchful eye. His hand never left the knife in his belt, and his body was constantly ready to fight, but there was nothing here apart from some brown birds that occasionally dove down from the treetops.

We walked through the forest along the Iving, which lapped and splashed. It was crisp and fresh in Jotunheim, not at all bone-chilling and damp like in Midgard and Hrafnheim.

We heard a whining sound. From the undergrowth ran an animal that I, at first, thought was a giant wolf. It was dark gray, with lighter gray flecks on its long fur, which was caked with dried mud underneath. The wild pig was the length of a grown man and the same height as me. Curved teeth shot out from her jaw, and she had eight small piglets running after her. They were brown with yellow stripes down their backs and sides. The pigs took no notice of us, and we pressed ourselves against a tree trunk as they passed. Varnar's hand was in front of my chest. Protection was so natural for him that he hadn't even noticed he was touching me. When we were about to move on, a new animal came barreling out of the forest, and again we leaned back against the trunk.

The bull was so large, it looked like a trick photo. It must have weighed a ton, and its pointed horns were spaced more than a yard apart. The bull snorted, and steam rose from its nostrils. It stopped near us and stamped on the ground. Chunks of moss flew up from the forest floor, and the bull inhaled. It gradually came closer to us. The muscles beneath its shiny fur were tense, but it was moving in a way that seemed aloof. The pointed horns ended on either side of us, and its narrow eyes studied Varnar and me with more wonder than hostility. It snorted again, and small droplets hit my face.

I stood completely still, my heart in my throat. Suddenly, the bull turned around and tromped away.

"Why didn't it hurt us?" Varnar whispered when the aurochs was gone.

"I don't think it knows what a human is."

"Is this the giants' land?"

I wiped the bull spit off my face. "Jotunheim is the source. Our origin. Many of the animals here are extinct in the human world now, but apparently, they live on in this time warp."

Varnar was still holding on to me. I placed my fingers on his upper arm and tightened my grip. He cautiously turned his head, and we were so close that his face was right in front of mine. His leather jacket creaked, and his brown hair brushed his shoulders. He gathered his lips in a little smile. "Why do I always end up in such impossible situations with you?"

"That's just how I am."

He turned, and his body was pressed against mine. I could smell and feel him, and he lowered his head toward mine. The birds sang in the treetops, animals rustled in the undergrowth, and the brisk wind lifted my hair slightly. Varnar caught a red lock and turned it between his fingers. I wanted to kiss him, but he stepped back.

"Your . . . *acquaintance* with Sverre hurt me."

"It's over between—" I began.

"It's none of my business," Varnar said. "I left you, and that's the biggest mistake I've ever made. You absolutely did the right thing by going to Hrafnheim alone. I was a coward for not staying by your side."

This was a totally new Varnar. Normally, he could barely even manage to say goodbye, but now he was pouring his heart out. I chose to repay his sincerity.

"When you left me, it hurt so bad. I've been abandoned my whole life, so you fulfilled my worst fear."

"I was trying to protect you."

"How is it protection when the world's most talented fighter leaves?"

"I didn't earn your love, but you gave it so willingly. I feared that you would die to protect me. I had already caused one innocent girl's death."

"Am I an innocent girl?"

Varnar stroked my cheek. "You were back then. That's why I left." He bit his lip. "But that's no excuse. I did the wrong thing."

"But you're here now."

"I can't stay away from you. I want to have you for as long as I can. Alone, my life has no meaning." He leaned into me and kissed me just as intensely as the very first time.

When we reached the plain, it had gotten colder. The air was dry, and small flakes swirled around but didn't stick, and it didn't turn into a heavy snowfall. We walked along the Iving, which wound through the heath. I sensed that Eskild and his people had walked here not too long ago. I let my eyes wander across the flat landscape. In the distance, I saw the silhouettes of animals that belonged to the past. A flock of elephant-like mammoths loomed large, even though they were far away. Their outlines resembled the ones from cave paintings.

After we crossed the plain, we went uphill. The Iving flowed in a ravine far beneath us, but we were forced to follow the rocks up. The snowfall became heavier, and the ground more slippery. Varnar turned around and gave me his hand so I wouldn't fall. Buzzards circled in the sky, and I couldn't help but think they were waiting for one of us to fall into the abyss. Darkness fell, and the stars and moon appeared. Because it had been so long since I'd seen the celestial bodies in Midgard, I stopped and looked up. A strange happiness flowed through me at the sight of the dark blue sky, the luminous specks and the full moon shining like white porcelain. When we reached the top of the pass, a cloud moved before the moon, and it became completely dark.

"We need to seek shelter," Varnar said. Vinr, our only source of light, illuminated just a circle around us. Varnar's face was hidden in shadows by the hair hanging along his high cheekbones.

"Let's keep going."

"If we fall into the ravine, we can't complete the mission."

He used his hands to feel along the rock face, found a crack, and led us inside. Vinr and the green ring Luna had embedded in the wood glowed. The giant crystal gave off intense heat, but I wasn't sure whether that was because it was home in its own realm or because sparks were flying between me and Varnar.

We found a small chamber where a clear spring bubbled up in the center. We drank some of the water, and it tasted amazing. I detected notes of iron and salt from the earth's interior, and my thoughts became sharper.

"You don't need food when you have this spring water." Varnar looked at me, sending my stomach into a backflip.

"I could live off this water and love alone," I mumbled. On a whim, I fished an empty ampoule from my coat pocket from when Elias had given me klinte, even though the drug was long gone. I carefully filled it with water. Then I sat down and held Vinr upright. The carved ravens were above me. Varnar sat across from me. The giant crystal sent heat and light out over us.

"Do you know anything about Jotunheim?" I asked.

Varnar pushed his dark hair back. "I heard stories when I was a kid. That was before Ragnara banned the gods."

"Can you remember any of the stories?"

"I was really young, but I remember the old people talking about the giants' realm. It's a dangerous place. The gods can't help us here. The human world is protected by the Midgard Serpent. Jörmungandr, which lies between us and Jotunheim. As long as it's wrapped around us with its tail in its mouth, the giants can't get in."

"The Midgard Serpent let go of its tail," I said quietly.

Varnar said nothing, but he studied me.

"It's a good thing you weren't there." I knew he had heard about my encounter with the Midgard Serpent. "You couldn't have done anything, and I survived."

Varnar changed the subject, probably because he felt guilty. "Do you know anything about this place?"

I shook my head. "Maybe the völvas know something." I screwed the top off Vinr and took out Hejd's horse tooth. I slowly stroked my thumb over an indentation in it.

"Are you sure? Mimir said you risk wearing yourself out by using your völva powers."

"I don't feel tired at all. Especially not after drinking from that spring." I closed my eyes and reached out to my predecessors. There wasn't a concrete response, but I felt the presence of the many völvas.

What can you tell me about Jotunheim?

The völvas whispered inside my head, and I had to concentrate to hear them. At first, it was a jumble of Old Norse, but the ice-cold water flowed through my system and made me remarkably clearheaded. The words became comprehensible, and I parsed them out.

I beheld go forth a maiden dear to me;
Her arms glittered, and from their gleam shone all the sea and sky
To me more dear than in days of old was ever maiden to man;
But no one of gods or elves will grant
that we both together should be

Then give me the horse that goes through the dark
And magic flickering flames
And the sword as well that fights of itself
against the giants grim

> The horse will I give thee that goes through the dark
> And magic flickering flames
> And the sword as well that will fight of itself,
> If a worthy hero wields it

I conveyed the völvas' words when I sensed Varnar sit down at my side.

"I think the first stanza is about me," he said quietly. He interlaced his fingers with those of my free hand, stroking the back of my hand in a way that produced a pleasant shiver. I didn't mention my suspicion that the second and third stanzas referred to Sverre. I squeezed Vinr, and the völvas continued:

> Dark is it without, and I deem it time
> To fare through the wild fells and through the giants' fastness
> We shall both come back, or us both together
> The terrible giant will take
> Art thou marked by Hel or already dead?
> Barred from speech shalt thou ever be
> With the maiden fair

Neither I nor Varnar commented on the poem, as we didn't want to guess which of us was marked by Hel. Which of us was going to die? The völvas were trying to tell me something. They were insistent, now shouting so loudly that I had to let go of Varnar's hand and press my fingers to my temples. Vinr fell to the ground, but the women's voices continued:

> Ere thou take off the saddle, or farest forward a step
> What hast thou done in the giants' dwelling to make glad thee or me?
> Odin grows angry, angered is the best of the gods
> Freyr shall be thy foe, most evil maid
> Who the magic wrath of gods hast got for thyself

My head hurt like crazy, and I shielded myself instinctively from external blows, even though the words were inside me. They cut like knives. I screamed and fell backward, but fortunately, Varnar managed to catch me.

"But I'm trying to help the gods," I said, my eyes still closed.

Varnar held me. "I don't understand the poem."

"I don't either, just that the völvas are trying to warn me or prepare me for something."

"What do they want to warn you about?"

"The wrath of the gods." My eyes slid closed. I couldn't hold them open anymore. Maybe there was some truth to Mimir's warnings that I risked draining myself of energy. I sank deeper into my subconscious.

Varnar wrapped his arms around me. Later that night, I awoke, and we made love in front of the spring by the light of the giant crystal before falling back asleep. In my dream, I got the sense that I was on the cusp of Ragnarök. I could neither see the ground nor my surroundings. Odin emerged from the chlorine-smelling haze with an orange flash behind him. He looked like he had the first few times I met him. His hair was long and gray, he had wrinkles on his face, and the skin around his empty eye socket hung slack. Under his arm was Mimir's head.

"You're getting stronger, völva."

I held out my arms and saw that I was semitransparent. Black feathers sprung from my wrists, and I knew that I could fly like the raven if I wished.

"Am I dream walking right now?"

"You're doing it without a cult."

"Why are you here, Odin?"

"I'm warning you, raven. You should be careful."

I put my feathered hands on my hips. "You're the one that made me like this. I'm actually trying to help."

"By stealing from me?"

"It was for your own good that I took the Gjallarhorn gold."

"That's not the only thing you stole." Odin held Mimir's head out at arm's length. His large fingers squeezed Mimir's hair, and Mimir cried out in pain.

"If you can't take good care of him, you can't have him," I said. "Mimir is staying with me as long as you're such a terrible owner."

Odin furrowed his brows. The hairs were long and gray. The brow over his empty eye socket resembled a caveman's. "You're not obeying me anymore, raven."

"I'm actually trying to work for the good of everyone, and I'm trying to think for myself."

"This is a warning. You're being manipulated."

"By you?"

Odin lowered his large head. "By Loki."

I took a step back. "I secured my house against Loki. He can't get near me. I threw him out."

Odin laughed harshly. "I know my blood brother well. He has insinuated himself. He's sweet-talking you."

"I've hardly even spoken to him, and when I did, he was about to fight your son."

Odin smiled grimly. "Loki is a shape-shifter. He can be anyone. And if you've invited him in yourself, he can roam freely. Have you invited anyone in recently? Someone you trust?"

"Yes," I whispered. "I welcomed Varnar."

"Loki tells me you're beautiful. That you're a lovely girl. He praises your wit, your strength, and your beauty. He says that your bed is so soft."

"Loki said that to you?"

Odin lowered his bushy old-man brows. "You're supposed to serve me, not steal from me." He shook Mimir's head.

"I told you. Mimir wasn't doing well, he—"

Odin raised his large hand toward me. "Who among us is doing well?"

I thought of myself, lying under my mother's coat in the cave, spooning with Varnar. "I'm doing great, actually."

"You also stole from Mimir."

"I most certainly did not. He's my friend."

"You drank from his well. It's hidden deep in Jotunheim. My eye saw you because it's still down there." He stuck his finger all the way into his empty eye socket. Then he pulled it out and held his flat hand out toward me. It looked like he was trying to feed an animal, but flames shot up from his palm. They grew higher and higher until Odin formed them into a ball. "Let's see how well you humans are doing now." He threw the fire, and it split into five parts. I soared away as the raven and followed the flaming miniature comets, but they got away from me.

I was silent the next day as we trudged along the Iving. With my clairvoyance, I searched our surroundings for Eskild and his people, but they had passed through this place long ago. I was pretty sure they had already reached their destination. Maybe they had sold the Odion figurine to the giants.

The last bit went steeply downhill, and near the bottom, the river splashed up over the rocks. Because it was freezing here, a treacherous layer of ice covered the ground; I slipped several times, but I stayed upright by clinging to Vinr.

For the umpteenth time, I nearly fell. Varnar reached his hand out to steady me, but I pulled away.

He looked at me, uncomprehending.

I couldn't shake the sneaking suspicion, and I walked quickly ahead of him to avoid looking into his eyes.

When we turned a corner, I saw the manor that the giants had come out of when I spied on them from Hlidskjalf. The manor where Hakim said Eskild now were. I crouched behind a rock and looked up. Varnar followed me, and we were pressed up against the boulder together. He reached out, but I pulled back slightly.

"You're looking at me weird," he whispered.

I tried to brush it off. "No, I'm not."

"Yes, you are. Is something wrong?"

"I'm just focused on our mission." I glanced at him, and he looked at me with his typical intense expression. His brown eyes bore into mine, and it was hard not to melt under his loving gaze, so I quickly looked away.

"Last night, you were someone else. When we lay in bed, I was certain of your love. In the forest, you kissed me so earnestly. Last night in the cave, you said you loved me."

"Later," I said. *Loki had praised my soft bed.* My heart was beating hard.

"Now, Anna! I don't know how much time I have."

I looked at him suspiciously. "Are you planning to leave again?"

He looked down. "I don't think I can stay with you forever."

I inhaled, about to speak, but someone behind us cleared their throat. It was a discreet cough with quite a lot of amusement in it, and the sound echoed strangely. Fearfully, I turned around and instinctively crawled backward but was caged in by the large rock that moments before had been my shield.

The giant before us had knelt down to bring his face close to us. His nose was the size of my entire body, and black hair stuck out of it. The giant's hair was long and straggly, and his eyes were just like normal human eyes, except they were the size of a blue whale's.

"My name is Skrymir," he said. I think he was making an effort to whisper, but nevertheless, the stone behind us shook. "Welcome to Utgard."

CHAPTER 23

"You stink of human. I've known you were here since you entered the Iron Forest." Skrymir ushered us along, each of his footsteps shaking the ground. He was jovial, but I didn't doubt for a second that we were his captives.

The manor, which was called Utgard, drew nearer. It was built of thick posts, with a turf-covered slanted roof. I supposed the giants didn't care for the nonsense of golden shields or layered shingles.

"It's been a long time since we've seen humans in these parts, and now we've gotten two parties in just a few days. What's going on in the human world right now? You're running around like confused ants."

I looked up at Skrymir. My head came up to his knee, and I could see that, to him, we must have seemed tiny. Varnar looked at the giant, too, but it was impossible to know what he was thinking. Several times, Skrymir looked at him knowingly, setting off all my alarm bells. I was realizing more and more that I was alone on this journey.

We had almost reached the manor, its doors as tall as a three-story house, matching Skrymir's size. Other giants walked across the yard, and they smiled down at us in a somewhat indulgent way. I could practically hear them thinking, *aw, humans*. A pack of giant wolves stood panting and smacking their lips at the edge of the yard. They must have been a slightly different breed from Monster and Rokkin because they had longer legs and shorter fur. Their expressions, however, were very similar to those of my giant wolf friends. Always on the verge of attack, with slightly raised lips revealing sharp teeth. Their eyes glimmered dangerously, and their ears lay back against their heads. The giant wolves would bite first and ask questions later.

"In you go, little guys," Skrymir said, placing his hand behind our backs just as I decided to try to run in the opposite direction. He carefully pushed us into Utgard. His palm formed a semicircle around us, as tall as the walls of Nordreslev Youth Center. His hand smelled of smoke and sweat, and its deep lines were full of excrement. I took a closer look—it wasn't excrement. It was rich soil with earthworms, moss, and clumps of grass. I had no choice but to go inside. Skrymir nudged us in as though herding a flock of confused geese.

"Don't go out. No. Come here. The wolves will just eat you."

I gasped for air when we entered Utgard. The river Iving ran straight through the room, which actually couldn't be called a room at all. Above us, roots hung down from the ceiling. There were both thick tree roots and small, thin roots from bushes and grass. The bottom halves of onion bulbs were visible, along with wedge-shaped parsnips and carrots. What I had thought was a roof was a living piece of nature sitting on top of the manor. I could see worms and bugs crawling above, and birds swooped around and slipped into holes under bats that hung sleeping upside down. I saw a squirrel dart up a branch, and sunlight fell in slanted beams over us, though I couldn't tell where it came from.

The blue, splashing ribbon of water flowed in a straight line through the hall. Far in the distance—so far I could barely make it out—fire flickered as though directly from a volcano. There was no banquet table. The giants sat on the ground while animals ran around among them. Some of the giants were incredibly beautiful, others were overgrown with plants, and a few had crystals sticking out of their heads like punk hairstyles. I tried to look for similarities to Valhalla and Helheim.

"Is this a realm of the dead, too?"

Skrymir looked down as though he had completely forgotten we were there. He crouched down. "What did you say, little friend?"

"Is this a realm of the dead?" I said it so loudly that everyone in Utgard went silent. Even the animals stopped their activities and looked at me.

Skrymir laughed explosively. Dirt sprinkled down from the ceiling, and he clutched his big, round stomach.

"Jotunheim is not a realm of the dead. It's a realm of the living." He gestured around him with his giant hand. "Have you ever seen so much life gathered in one place?"

I shook my head because I hadn't. Animals and giants returned to whatever they had been doing. It smelled lush and potent, and it occurred to me that nature really didn't care about us small humans and our crises, even if it meant the end of the world. I was pretty sure Ragnarök only meant the end of *our* worlds.

"Come over here," Skrymir said. "It will only be a moment." He was still crouched down, and he held open the door to an enclosure that resembled a dog kennel.

"Wait! I need to talk to you about something."

Skrymir positioned his index finger and thumb as though to pinch me. If he did, I would be crushed to smithereens. Varnar pulled on my sleeve, and I recognized it was too dangerous to refuse him, so I reluctantly entered the fenced area. Skrymir closed the gate after us with a bang and slid a lock into place. He didn't bother to take our weapons away; he probably feared my axe and staff about as much as he did a mosquito's proboscis. He looked over the fence. I could see straight up his nose, where an entire bush was growing.

"It's for your own safety, little friends. I'll be back soon." He stomped away with thundering footsteps.

"That's what he said to us several days ago," someone said behind us. Fear shot through me as I recognized the voice, but Varnar's reaction was even stronger. He spun around, wide-eyed, and looked at the man who sat leaning against the fence. He had gray hair and a shabby leather jumpsuit with cords and straps full of weapons. One eye was light blue, the other black. One shoulder of the jumpsuit was printed with the rune that had been Ragnara's symbol. The crooked F, its normally horizontal lines tilting upward. *Fehu*, which meant *slave*.

"Long time no see, Varnar," he drawled. "For a long time, we thought you were dead. Ragnara grieved as if her own son had fallen in battle."

Varnar's jaw jutted to one side, then the other.

"Eskild," he whispered.

CHAPTER 24

Eskild was surrounded by five berserkers, one painted the same way I had been when I took on the role of shaman. When they saw us, they stood, but with a small hand gesture, Eskild held them back. He sat completely still as he looked at me.

"My old sword is mad at you."

"Tilarids?" I couldn't help but pull my lips back in a grin. "That sword is destroying Sverre, and you know it."

Eskild inhaled through his front teeth with a sucking sound. "I thought Tilarids could make him into a real warrior. It would make him strong. He would be more—"

"Like you?" I finished. "Sverre is a much better man than you've ever been. Sverre can heal; you can only destroy."

Hearing these words, Varnar looked down at the ground.

But I was just getting started. "You murdered my father and nearly killed my mother."

"Your father came back to life, and Thora survived. No harm was done," Eskild drawled and shifted his heterochromatic eyes to Varnar. "I should have given Tilarids to you instead."

That was a horrifying thought. If it were up to me, Tilarids would have been reforged into something peaceful and useful a long time ago, but Eskild didn't seem to share that opinion.

"You two could have made a wonderful pair. You still can." His voice was as rough and gravelly.

"Tilarids and I could have made a wonderful pair?" Varnar asked.

"You and Anna."

My head shot up. Eskild slowly got to his feet until, at last, he towered above me.

"Anna, Anna, Anna . . . I saw you as an infant, when Ragnara held you in her hands. You were so little and fragile, but you refused to die."

"It wasn't *me* who refused to die. It was Sverre, in Ragnara's stomach, who ensured I survived."

Eskild appeared to have an *aha moment* nineteen years in the making. "Of course! Although I resent his curse, it was good that Sverre saved your life. Tilarids has big plans for you." He looked me up and down, which made me shiver. "Now I understand why. You have ruler potential."

"People have made decisions for me my whole life. I'll be damned if I'm going to be the one tyrannizing others."

Eskild smiled deviously. "I know someone else who said the same thing. She ended up being a good ruler."

"You think Ragnara was good? She killed people and dictated what they could and couldn't believe in."

"And you removed her. Doesn't that make you responsible for putting something else in her place? The human worlds are about to collapse into chaos."

Varnar interjected. "Do you want to kill us?" It was direct, but Eskild knew him well, and he didn't seem surprised.

Eskild shook his head slowly. "I hope we can work together to get out of here. It won't be long before we all die of starvation. We haven't eaten anything since Skrymir locked us in here four days ago. My guess is he won't come back until we're desiccated skeletons."

"But he said he'd be back soon."

Eskild looked up at the high plank wall. "The giants' idea of *soon* appears to be different from ours."

"Do you have the Odion figurine?" I could be just as direct as Varnar if I needed to be.

"I do."

"Why in the worlds did you bring it here? The Gjallarhorn gold can't fall into the giants' hands. Are you crazy?"

Eskild blew air out his nose in a mocking snort. "I see the giants as the inheritors of power since no one else can seem to get their act together."

"I'm sure you see yourself on the side of those in power. It makes no difference to you if it's Ragnara or the giants."

To my surprise, Eskild laughed. "It's like talking to Ragnara from years ago." He bore his peculiar eyes into Varnar's. "I can understand why you love her."

This made Varnar take a step back. "I . . ."

Eskild followed. "So, let's work together . . . again. You and me and the girl." He pointed to the painted berserker. "Dádýr Kvärker."

She came up to us and fished a small cloth bundle from her pocket. Dádýr must have been some kind of witch or necromancer, but no magic crackled around her. Her hair hung in matted locks, as mine had back at Odinmont. She was painted white, with red symbols on her cheeks and forehead. The symbols were painted with blood—not pigment—and it had dried a crusty black.

She unwrapped a small figure from the layers of fabric. While she mumbled spells, it trembled, and I could feel its anger from where I stood. She placed the piece of cloth with Odion in its center on the ground. The inside of the black fabric was painted with a vertical yellow stripe with an X through it, so it resembled a star.

I sensed determination and aggression from the figurine, and I heard a laugh, much like Ben's, ring out like an echo. I knelt down and stared at Odion. He didn't look particularly dangerous because he was so little. He had long dreadlocks, but where Ben's had been broken up with colored wraps, Odion's were all dark brown. He was frozen in a surprised position with his hands facing out as though ready to cast a spell. His small palms were tattooed exactly like Ben's.

Iwó, said the rough voice in my head, and I jerked back as though I'd been electrocuted. Varnar managed to grab me, and I slid down, my head resting in his lap.

Awon free, Odion said. I understood the words. *Free me*. His voice was so hoarse that he sounded like a hissing cat. Varnar held my face as I fought to maintain consciousness.

"Not a chance," I said to Odion, and the little figure quivered in response. I stood up from Varnar's arms and walked a few paces away. Odion's power dimmed.

"Take him," Eskild said. "Then you'll have all of it."

I neglected to mention that I just needed Elias to tell me where the last piece was. When Eskild saw that my expression hadn't changed, he stupidly appealed to Varnar, believing he could use our romantic relationship to convince me. "Tell her it's the right way. The only way."

I looked first at one of them, then the other.

"Anna," Varnar said slowly. "It's our only chance. We have to collaborate with Eskild."

I looked at the man who had killed my father and almost killed my mother, and who had hunted me and my sister. The berserkers moved, and they looked like more-focused versions of Naut Kafnar. These were my enemies, but I nodded anyway. Dádýr wrapped the Odion figurine back up and held the small bundle out to me, but Eskild stepped between us.

"Swear you'll find someone else for people to worship if the old gods fall. Now that it can't be Ragnara, it has to be someone else."

"Okay."

"Say it."

"I swear to find someone else for people to worship if it comes to that." I crossed my fingers behind my back.

"You must also swear not to betray us."

"I swear not to betray you."

Eskild nodded, and Dádýr gave me the bundle containing Odion. I could feel his anger even through the layers of fabric. I screwed the top off Vinr and only just managed to squeeze him in with the other items. The chamber under the carved ravens was now completely full.

"It's a difficult decision," Varnar said and placed his hand on my shoulder. "But it's the right one. We have to make sure there's something to replace those we remove."

I heard Odin in my mind. *You're being manipulated, raven.*

Varnar seemed strangely optimistic. I looked at him sadly. At that moment, I knew he wasn't the man I loved. He couldn't be Varnar, who always expected the worst.

I was standing next to Loki in disguise. He was there to trick me out of all the Gjallarhorn gold so he could take the place of supreme god himself.

We waited for the hall to grow quiet. Through wide cracks, I glimpsed a little of what was going on out there.

The giants danced and sang, beat drums, and occasionally screamed wildly toward the ceiling. An intense atmosphere was building up among the progressively ecstatic creatures, and the one with the pointy crystals on his head jumped around and headbanged noisily. It grew cold, even though the fire at the end of the hall blazed. We were hit with small gusts of frost and snow.

"Loki, Loki, Loki," the giants shouted, and I couldn't help but glance at Varnar, who was watching through the crack alongside me. I couldn't read his face, but he squeezed the rough board so hard he must have gotten splinters in his fingers. I looked back at the wild creatures. Several of them were blue in the face, and they puffed out their cheeks as though they were full of water.

Skrymir hopped around in an erratic dance, and each time his large feet landed on the ground, the dusty floor shook beneath us, and dirt came down from the ceiling. Now I understand why people in the old days thought earthquakes came from dancing giants. The ecstatic giants reached a climax, and their faces were now deep blue.

"Out, out, out." Skrymir laughed and pushed the bluish giants with bulging cheeks through the door to the yard. "If you're gonna throw up, do it outside."

But it wasn't vomit that came out of their mouths. We heard bangs and crackling noises, after which a burst of cold reached us. The giants had sent a frost storm toward the human world. While they blew frost over the worlds, Skrymir danced as though in a trance. He spun and hopped and rolled his broad neck. Eventually, he was about to burst, and he, too, ran toward the exit, but he didn't make it.

Frost poured out of his mouth, and it was heading right toward us. The fence we were clutching was covered in ice, and I quickly let go. Varnar held fast until he realized he was about to be stuck to the wood. He let go with a shout and ran backward. The corral turned glacier blue right in front of him, and it seemed to smoke as though it were cooled down with dry ice.

Dry ice! I remembered a physics experiment from my school days.

"Stand back," I said to the others and hiked up my mother's coat so my legs could move freely. I raised my foot and did the best ninja kick I could muster.

The wood cracked like glass, and shards flew around us. I closed my eyes to avoid getting splinters in them, and when I opened them, there was a hole in the fence big enough for us to get out.

It was hard to run in the dark. The frost storm the giants had created made the rocks even slicker, and far beneath us, the river Iving churned. I couldn't see the ravine, but it pulled at me and echoed every time a pebble fell over the edge into the abyss. My foot slipped several times, and my heart flew into my throat with fear, but Varnar managed to grab my hand every time. Loki, for mysterious reasons, must have wanted me to survive.

"Do you want me to take your staff?"

I clutched Vinr, which contained the Gjallarhorn gold. "Absolutely not."

Fortunately, the full moon cast enough light for us to see where we were going, and we fought our way up the steep mountain. When we reached the top, we heard thunderclaps—except it wasn't thunder, but Skrymir's voice.

"The humans ran away. They're gone."

The ground shook beneath us as loud footsteps came closer. Icicles and piles of snow landed on the path, blocking us from going farther. The giants were right behind us. We tried to climb over the avalanche amassing in front of us, but in my hurry, I slipped and slid down it. I was about to fall over the edge into the ravine. For a terrifying moment, I hung right on the edge while gravity decided whether I would fall. Then, I plummeted down.

A strong hand grabbed mine, and I found myself hanging with one arm stretched above my head, Vinr dangling in the other hand. The staff weighted me downward, and my shoulder made a little *click* as my body weight was concentrated on the joint. A sharp pain shot up in my throat, and I couldn't hold my screams in. When I looked up, Eskild's face looked back at me. His arm was extended, and his rough hand was locked in mine.

"Up you go," he said hoarsely.

"Ow!" I swung my legs and tried to get a foothold on the rocks.

Eskild hoisted me up. "You're going to have to help some."

I gritted my teeth and fought to get out of the chasm. I pressed my boots against the frozen rock face and used my muscles to pull myself up. Vinr seemed to weigh as much as one of the mammoths I'd seen on the plain, but I held on to it for dear life.

I finally got up over the edge, and although I would have liked to preserve my dignity, I sobbed from the pain. Eskild looked coldly at my arm, which hung limply, while I pushed Vinr against the ground to get to my feet. Before I could react, he grabbed me and pressed on my shoulder. I howled desperately but wasn't able to defend myself before he let go of me. My shoulder still hurt, but I could move my fingers again. I stood, panting, as Eskild gave me a little shove and a harsh smile.

"That's how you survive. With pain and the humiliation of receiving help from your enemy."

"Thanks."

"Onward," he commanded. We crossed the pile of snow, but I suddenly heard something crackle. This was punctuated by small bangs. I knew those explosions. It was a frost storm, splintering trees and rocks in its path. The sounds were coming closer.

Varnar had appeared at my side. He took my hand and started to run.

"Let go of me."

"Come. Quickly." I tried to pull my hand away, but he held tight.

Eskild and his people were right behind us. We ran as fast as we could, but the frost was faster. I allowed myself to look back up the hill, and though it was dark, the moonlight reflected against the avalanche of snow that was heading toward us. Large quantities of white powder had collected at the top of the mountain. It went against the laws of nature, seeming to slide uphill, and when it reached the highest point, it careened down again, straight toward us. There was no way we could escape it on the narrow path, but Varnar pulled me into the side tunnel we had slept in on the way toward Utgard. Eskild was right on our heels, but Varnar turned around at the opening. With superhuman strength, he grabbed a large rock and rolled it in front of the entrance.

Eskild's light blue eye hovered in front of a little gap on the other side.

"She swore not to betray us."

"Anna isn't betraying you. I am."

"Varn—" Just then, there was a tremendous crash, and someone screamed. Snow filled the little gap, and a clump no larger than my fist fell on our side. Then it was as silent as the grave. We stood in the cave, and Vinr glowed, but now it looked like a merciless fluorescent light. Varnar's face was so white, it was verging on green. He turned around to face me, and I raised Vinr toward him.

"Now will you tell me what's wrong?"

"You're not who you claim to be." I still held Vinr pointed forward.

"I love you, and I want to spend the rest of my life with you. I don't know how long I have left." He took a step forward.

"Don't come any closer."

"Anna . . . ?"

"I said, don't come any closer to me."

"What's going on with you?"

I walked closer to the spring in the center of the cave.

"I want to protect you, I want to help you, I want to love . . ."

He looked so much like Varnar. The brown hair, the intense eyes, the strong body—but he wasn't fooling me. Not anymore.

"You're sweet-talking me. I won't let you manipulate me anymore, Loki!" I shouted.

"Loki?" He opened his mouth. Oh, he was good at mimicking Varnar. It broke my heart, but I steeled myself and walked farther back.

Anna! A voice rang out inside my head. *Anna . . . I can feel that you're scared. What's wrong?*

It took me a second to place the voice. *Hakim? Oh, I'm so glad you're here. I'm trapped in a cave with Loki. He turned himself into Varnar. I don't know if he's going to attack soon.*

I felt loving hands pulling me backward, even though no one was behind me. *Come.*

There's nowhere to go.

Yes, there is. Jump.

I stood at the edge of the spring, which, according to Odin, was Mimir's well. My heels stuck out over the edge.

Varnar—or Loki—widened his eyes when he saw what I was about to do.

"You have to believe me. I want to help you."

"You just killed Eskild."

Varnar's hands hung limply at his sides. "That was for your sake. Eskild was evil. He once ordered me to murder an innocent girl."

I looked coldly at him. "You are a murderer."

And then I jumped.

At first, the water was so cold, I thought I would pass out. Air bubbles burst around me, and a strong current pulled me. When I looked around, I saw a large eye watching me. The eye was the same sea-green color as the one in Odin's eye socket. Hakim's ghost was there, and I swam over to him. I was about to run out of oxygen, and my pulse was pounding in my ears.

When I reached him, Hakim put his mouth against mine and breathed air into it. I had no idea a ghost could do something like that, but I didn't have time to think about it. Hakim also seemed more solid than usual, maybe because we were hovering between worlds in Mimir's well. He embraced me and pulled me through the water. He blew air into my mouth several times, and miraculously, we made it through the spring. It was connected to the Iving, and I came up at its source. With a big cough, I broke through the surface and was back in the grassy valley in front of the Iron Forest. Hakim was nowhere to be seen, and I hoisted myself from the water, shaking and soaking wet.

I looked around. As far as the eye could see, there was forest and green heaths, but I knew the mural was just ahead. Maybe if someone looked at it right now, they would see me standing next to the lake with Vinr in my hand and my red hair dripping over me.

I thumped the völva staff against the ground. Mentally, I reached out and drew from the völvas' powers.

"All the worlds," I said aloud. "I travel in all the worlds."

Reality flickered around me, and I could see the thin membrane between the worlds. I saw my guest bedroom from the other side, and separating me from it was only a hazy film that looked like softened gelatin. I placed my hand against the membrane, which billowed. I dug my fingers into it, and it parted willingly for me. Then I pressed myself into the tear I had made, and I felt like I was in a narrow, transparent, rubber tunnel. Even though it was claustrophobic, I forced myself through the rest of the way until I finally plopped down on the futon in the empty, cold guest bedroom.

CHAPTER 25

"What happened to your arm?" Rebecca looked critically at my upper body, which had turned yellow and blue due to my shoulder being dislocated.

"I fell."

"You fell." Rebecca raised an eyebrow but didn't probe any further, which was fine by me.

"I would normally give you a poultice and a sling, but of course, there's no more oats, so I'll hypnotize the pain away. You'll need to keep your arm still for a few days." She stood in front of me and looked into my eyes. There was a golden flicker in my field of vision, and suddenly, I felt no pain. I pulled my shirt on.

"Aah!" Rebecca scolded. "You're putting too much strain on it already. That's why you have to be careful with pain hypnosis."

"Have you been gorging yourselves on oatmeal or something?"

Rebecca looked up questioningly.

"You said you don't have enough for a poultice? There were four pounds in the last ration."

Rebecca furrowed her brows at first, but comprehension reached her eyes. "You were in Jotunheim when it happened."

"Oh no, what's happened now?"

Rebecca was suddenly very focused on the fabric she was folding into a sling. Carefully, she placed my arm in it and tied it in a knot behind my head. For a moment, she let her hand rest on my neck, and through her, I saw it.

She was in an office with Niels Villadsen. He stood leaning over a desk with a map of Denmark, his hands fumbling over points on the map. Around him stood officials from the DSMA, along with the prime minister, his wife, and Rebecca. Niels's clothes were disheveled, and his wire-rimmed glasses sat slightly askew. At first, I couldn't hear what he was saying, but he moved frantically and agitatedly. I sniffed. He smelled a bit like smoke, like a Boy Scout's clothes after a campfire.

"What happened, Niels?" Rebecca spoke slowly and pronounced every word clearly.

Nevertheless, he looked at her as though he couldn't decode her words. His face was black, except for white stripes around his eyes, as though he had squeezed his eyes shut just before being covered in soot. Niels coughed a couple of times, straightened his back, and placed his finger on Copenhagen. Then he circled four other places on the map.

"The supply warehouses have burned down," he said. His voice was eerily calm.

"How will we inform the citizens?" the prime minister mumbled.

Rebecca and Mardöll exchanged a glance.

"We'll have to ration more. The people will get through it. It'll be tough, but they'll . . ." The prime minister looked around.

"Everything is gone. A ration of nothing is still nothing. There's no medicine, fuel, or food left." Niels sat down heavily on the desk chair; his legs didn't seem capable of supporting him any longer. At his side, Rebecca searched for comforting words but said nothing. Instead, she laid her hand on his back. The prime minister leaned against the table, and an official held his hand in front of his mouth.

"How are we going to survive?"

I was hurtled out of the vision.

"The fires hit five places simultaneously. All the supplies were lost."

My throat went dry as I recalled seeing Odin send the five balls of fire. He had done it because he was mad at me. This was my fault, too. Rebecca went to the dining table and shuffled through a stack of papers. She came back and placed a flyer in my hand.

Information for the Danish public, it read. The paper warned against going out at night because frost storms were more frequent and severe. I had seen the source of those storms in Jotunheim.

"There was also an earthquake yesterday. That's highly unusual in this area. Mathias caused one a couple of years ago, but the last big giant-induced earthquake was in Lønstrup in the 1800s," Rebecca said.

"Oh, come on—not you, too?"

Rebecca cocked her head, confused. "What? Ohhh . . . Ben told me. I am actually the age I look, but I hope to live just as long as Ben did, if I can survive that long."

I quickly looked down at the paper again.

There have been several outbreaks of the cold plague. If you suspect you may have been infected, hang a white sheet on your front door and isolate yourself from others to avoid spreading the disease.

"No treatment?"

"People are saying the authorities might as well just tell them to die quietly. Read the part at the bottom. That's the most important part."

The index finger of my non-bandaged arm followed the lines.

The authorities will no longer distribute food. From now on, citizens must make do with what they have. Theft will be severely punished.

The paper, formatted as a letter, ended with the prime minister promising to do everything in his power to help the people. His signature was inserted beneath the typed words. I didn't understand what he thought he could do since he couldn't conjure up more food or stop the natural disasters.

"People are angry and afraid," Rebecca said. "You can bet the hunting rifles are coming out. From here on out, it's anarchy."

Mathias, Luna, and I were in my bedroom, and I had just told them about my trip to Jotunheim. "I have all the pieces now. The only one I'm missing is the one Elias has hidden. I'm sure he'll tell me where it is when I get ahold of him." I leaned my back against the wall at the end of my bed.

"You can talk to him at the ball. I'm sure he'll be there."

"What ball?"

"Od is hosting the Equinox Ball at The Boatman early this year. I think he wants to try to pull some worship out of people. The gods and demigods are in a deficit." Luna looked out the window. Today, heavy, wet sleet was falling, and the semi-frozen water ran down my tilted window.

"Jotunheim wasn't a scary place at all," I told them. "It was actually amazing and beautiful in its own rugged way."

"I don't get it," Luna said. "You left Varnar in a cave? That was pretty harsh."

"He *looked* like Varnar, but it was Loki. I should have known because he wasn't acting how Varnar normally does." The stoic, self-flagellating, emotionally inaccessible Varnar I knew so well.

"People should be allowed to change, though."

I looked forward coldly. "Varnar left me, just like everyone else. Loki manipulated me, and he manipulated you, too. He rushed to follow me when I crossed over to Jotunheim, and the whole time, he was trying to get his hands on the gold. He kept offering to carry it or hold it. Loki wants to get that gold and start Ragnarök by blowing the Gjallarhorn so he can have a chance of becoming the supreme god. I figured out his plan."

"Why would Ragnarök give him that chance?"

"Odin is predicted to die, so there will be a power vacuum. I'm sure that's his plan."

"Should we work on training your völva powers again? Mimir and I planned—" Luna began.

"There's no time to plan anything," I interrupted.

Luna looked a little hurt, so I quickly specified:

"What you did for me was awesome. It got me to Jotunheim, and that was the whole point of training."

"But shamanism, cleansing of spirits, journeys between worlds... You'll need all those skills in your continuing work as a völva."

"If humanity survives, I'm taking a long break from anything supernatural, thank you very much!"

As we spoke, Mathias was wandering around the room.

"Come sit down, babe," Luna said.

Mathias sat down and took her hand, but then he jumped back up and started pacing again.

"Seriously!" I exclaimed.

"Something is churning inside me. I'm so angry." Mathias breathed heavily, and a puff of steam came out when he exhaled. "Don't look at me." He held up a hand so we couldn't see his steaming mouth.

I laid a hand protectively across Luna's chest, even though I had no idea what I would do if Mathias started shooting steam uncontrollably.

"Did your anger start before or after the warehouses burned?" I asked cautiously.

"After," Mathias panted. He had grown by several inches. "It started during it. I felt the god in me protesting as if something horrible were happening."

I didn't dare say that it was Odin himself who had burned it all.

"Something horrible did happen," Luna said. "We have barely any food left."

"It's not horrible for the gods," I whispered. "They can live off our worship," I added when Mathias looked reproachfully at me.

"But no one is worshipping!" he roared and turned around. "The humans are busy putting out small fires and thinking of themselves."

We pulled back when we saw his brilliant blue eyes.

"The destruction of your supplies was a punishment because no one was worshipping!" The windowpanes rattled. "And now you're all worried about the stupid food. You've learned nothing. What about us?"

"We can't worship you if we're dead from starvation."

"You don't worship at all."

"That's my own business." I stood up.

"It's *my* business."

"Mathias," Luna interjected. "Religion should be voluntary."

"It makes me mad that Anna doesn't worship. She should be punished!" Mathias's jaw clenched, but at the sight of Luna staring angrily at him, his face turned unhappy. "Sorry."

"Don't say it to me," Luna said pointedly.

Mathias turned his head. "Sorry, Anna." He wrapped his arms around himself.

I was encumbered by my arm in the sling, but with my other hand, I grabbed on to him. His cool, divine strength slipped into me. "I don't know what's going on with me sometimes." He shook in his own embrace.

"You're going through withdrawal," I said. "I saw it with some of my fellow inmates at Nordreslev. Come here." I held out my free arm.

Mathias crawled onto the bed and lay between us, teeth chattering. He rested his cheek on my shoulder. Luna snuggled up to us, and we lay in a big clump.

"What helps?" Mathias's voice was frayed.

"In the short term, it helps to get the thing you're addicted to. In the long term, you should think about getting clean."

"Or make sure you always have access to your drug," Luna added. Annoyed, I leaned forward and gave her a sharp look. She shrugged. "It's true, though."

I pulled my mouth into a crooked grin. "Okay, fine."

Mathias trembled in our arms. "Would you guys worship me?"

he said with his head lowered. "Just for right now. I'm sure I'll find a way to fight my addiction later."

I'd heard that before. People were always enthusiastic about going cold turkey when their systems were still full of drugs or alcohol.

"Of course, honey." Luna kissed his palm. "Betra er óbeðit en sé ofblótit, ey sér til gildis gjöf, betra er ósent en sé ofsóit."

Mathias took a deep breath and exhaled slowly. His breath was hot but not scalding. His body quivered slightly. He tried to suppress it but wasn't quite successful. I held him close, my bandaged arm sticking out at an awkward angle.

"Better to pray than to sacrifice too much. A gift will always be reciprocated," I whispered.

"Thanks." His voice was calmer and deeper. The heat emanating from him was amazing, and he let it seep into us. Mathias lay on his back with an arm around each of us, and Luna and I were in the fetal position at his sides, holding on to his body.

I relaxed completely, safe and warm with my best friends, and we all dozed off. The last thing I thought before falling asleep was that during the ball at The Boatman, I would ask Elias where the final piece of the Gjallarhorn was.

Shouting and the sound of metal against metal made me jump, the world tipped, and I found myself standing up again. People and animals ran around me, and the stench of blood and sulfur made me cough. The vision of Ragnarök had once again snuck into my dreams.

I still hadn't managed to avert it. Not yet.

I looked around to see if anyone I knew was there. My stomach clenched.

"Luna!"

She was staggering around, confused and frightened in the chaos, casting spells in all directions, but she was so frazzled they didn't hit anyone.

"Luna!" I screamed. But I knew she couldn't hear me.

Luna was immediately attacked by creatures with sharp teeth and claws.

Fortunately, Mads from our class—who, at his full height, towered over six foot five—came to Luna's rescue. He swatted the fingalks out of the air like they were flies. His hair was as long as Skrymir's, and his eyes sparkled wildly. I could easily picture him dancing with his giant relatives and blowing frost over the worlds. I exhaled with relief when he reached Luna.

He grabbed her in his enormous fists, and she whimpered with pain.

What the hell?

Mads picked Luna up. She whined and kicked as his hands squeezed her shoulders.

"What are you doing? Let go of her!" I ran toward them.

Mads obviously didn't react—if this was a vision, it hadn't even happened yet. He roared in my best friend's face. Mads's giant powers had grown considerably. A cascade of ice hit Luna, and the damage to her skin was horrifying.

Other creatures came into view. A large gray wolf fought side by side with a slightly smaller black wolf. A network of pale scars was visible through the gray wolf's fur. I got to my feet.

"Monster!"

Luna appeared again. I had no idea how she had escaped Mads, but she was in bad shape. She stumbled around blindly and tripped over a dead fingalk. On the ground, she felt her way forward, calling out pitifully.

"Anna. Help me."

Monster bared his teeth and leapt.

"No, no, no!"

Monster's sharp teeth sank into Luna's neck. She managed to send a ball of energy into Monster's side, which threw him several feet away from her. Luna sank, lifeless, to the ground. Monster stood for a moment, but his front legs collapsed. I stood indecisively between them, not knowing who to run to. Smoke engulfed Luna and the pitiful remains of Monster, and when I ran over to see what had happened, I couldn't find them.

Suddenly, something red flashed through the smoke. At first, I thought it was blood or fabric, but then my sister's face appeared. She looked more angular and exhausted, but I didn't know if dream versions of people reflected how they looked in reality. I ran to her and held her in a tight embrace. She clung to me, and I felt how thin she was. I held her at arm's length to get a look at her.

"Are you starving?"

"This is nothing. People are dying from hunger and the cold. Sverre says he'll do something soon to turn our luck around, but I can't see what it is." She pursed her lips. "Where's Varnar?"

"You mean Loki?"

"No, I mean Varnar. He traveled to Midgard, and I saw you together." Her cheeks turned red, and she looked down.

"You were tricked. Loki is a shape-shifter, and he appeared to me as Varnar. Someone I trust. He's smart, but I'm smarter. Some things just didn't match the person I knew."

Serén's red eyebrows sank so low she nearly closed her eyes. "Varnar has changed a lot over the past year. Longing and soul-searching can work wonders. Besides, I see people as they are in the future. You do the same with the past. That's how clairvoyance works. Maybe magic and shape-shifters can trick you while you're awake, but they can't fool our gift. I'm certain I saw the real Varnar."

My mouth hung open. "So, you're saying . . . Shit! I left Varnar in a cave in Jotunheim." My legs were shaking beneath me. "He's going to freeze to death, he'll die of hunger, he . . ."

Serén closed her eyes, and they moved under her eyelids. "He'll make it out and find his way home. I see it as a very certain part of the future. Tomorrow, or in a couple of days at the latest."

"Tell him I said I'm sorry. Sorry, sorry, sorry."

Serén furrowed her brows like she was concentrating. "Let me try." She gritted her teeth. "No . . . It's not a good idea for me to do that. I can . . . ooh. No, that's not good."

"What do you see?" I asked impatiently.

"He needs time. It's just that he doesn't have a whole lot."

"A whole lot of what?"

"Nothing." Serén opened her eyes. The smell of sulfur grew stronger, and I coughed.

"What are you even doing in my vision?" Nearby, someone was being slaughtered. I heard a splat and a scream as a poor human or giant was impaled. My mouth formed a nauseous grimace beyond my control. My sister didn't react to the repulsive noises.

She looked around. "I was going to ask you the same thing."

"Ragnarök is terrifying!"

Serén smiled with an *are you crazy?* expression. "It's so nice here."

"Uhhh . . . you seem to have a slightly warped idea of what *nice* is."

"You don't think the two of us at the hálfa festivities in Frón is nice?" Serén asked.

"We're surrounded by death and destruction."

"Vitality and warmth. We're together. In this version of the future, everything ends well."

"Do you think everything can end well?" A seed of hope sprouted in my stomach.

"Of course! Everything is possible in the future. Nothing is definite until the time has passed."

"That's a nice thought, Serén." I wasn't entirely sure I dared believe in it, but it sounded good. Another fingalk screeched desperately, and I flinched. "I just don't understand why we aren't seeing the same thing," I said. Then I reached out. With my strengthened powers, I could wipe the vision away like an eraser on a chalkboard. Here was the green grove with the little pond in the middle.

The ground undulated beneath the grass, and the treetops swayed gently in the breeze above me.

"Oohh," Serén exclaimed. "How did you do that?"

"I learned how to cleanse using my völva powers. This is Hejd's place. I've been here before." I turned around. "Hejd?" I called. "Hejd." When I had completed a full rotation around myself, I stopped with a cry of surprise, as there she sat, cross-legged, calm and smiling.

Serén saw her, too, and she raised her bony fingers to her mouth. "The mother of all völvas."

"Hrafn . . . Ravens . . ." she said. "I'm so happy to see you together."

We sat down in front of her. The ground was muddy, and water soaked into my pants, but it was warm and pleasant sitting there. Without thinking, I reached out and grabbed my sister's hand. She felt real and solid, even though I knew it was a dream replica.

"Ragnarök is coming," Hejd said, and we both protested, but she held up a hand. "Ragnarök is coming. The question is, *when*."

"Not for a long time if I have my way," I said. Serén said nothing, but she looked down at the green surface and prodded it thoughtfully, making it ripple like a waterbed.

"Oh, raven." From Hejd, this sounded loving. "Did you get my letter?"

It sounded like the long-dead, thousand-year-old völva had sent me something in the mail. "Uh, your letter?"

"I asked Od to remember it and write it down."

"*Völuspá?* That was for me?"

Hejd laughed heartily. "It's your guide." She snapped her fingers. "How do they say it in your language? Your manual."

"*Völuspá* is my manual?" I said doubtfully. "Couldn't you have maybe expressed yourself a little more clearly? I mean, I've read the whole poem. Many times, in fact, and a lot of it is totally obscure." I recited:

> *Eikinskaldi, Fjalar, and Frosti,*
> *Finn and Ginnar*
> *For all time shall the tale be known*
> *The forbears of Lofar*

"That makes no sense."

"You've met them. Maybe they have different names in your time, but they're the same people. Eikinskaldi is a skald who looks like a red rooster—I think he's called Tryggvi in your time. Fjalar is the dark-skinned sorcerer, and Frosti is the frost giant Skrymir. Ginnar is the friendly giant."

"That must be Mads."

"And Finn . . ." Hejd gave me a mischievous look.

"And Finn!" My beloved fingalk, Finn. He had been heralded for over a thousand years, and even though his life was far too short, I was incredibly happy to know that Hejd had known about him from so long ago.

"Finn will always be remembered."

Hejd nodded excitedly, like she was relieved that I finally got it. Then she thought of something:

> *O'er Midgard Huginn and Muninn both*
> *Each day set forth to fly;*
> *For Huginn I fear*
> *Lest he come not home*
> *But for Muninn my fear is more.*

"Muninn. Memory. The past. That's me?"

Hejd looked sadly at me. "I fear for Muninn. I fear for your fate."

CHAPTER 26

The only thing we had was electricity. The windmills were running due to the constant wind, so we could at least keep the heat on. Those with electric cars could drive around, but otherwise, society was about to disintegrate. The phones worked, but the internet was out, so I couldn't call Elias, and considering the speed at which the frost storms hit, it was too dangerous to run to his place. I would have to wait patiently for the ball at The Boatman.

People were scared and frustrated, and I felt their aggression when they saw me. My repulsion magic went head-to-head with their fear. There was a medical clinic in the old town hall, but because the doctors had run out of medicine, they couldn't do much but send people home with comforting words.

"The doctor couldn't help at all," Mina told me the afternoon she came over with a couple of turnips Paul had found in their old barn. Their pigs were long gone, but he had scraped together the last of their feed, and now they were sharing what little they had with us.

"What was wrong with you?" I scanned her with my eyes and my clairvoyance.

"I had a fever. My dad was scared it was the cold plague, but it went away after I went to see Brenda."

My mouth formed an *ohh*.

"Brenda told me to pray to the gods and scatter a few grains on the ground. It was okay to pick them up and eat them afterward."

"So, you did it?"

Mina shrugged. "It was better than sitting around twiddling my thumbs, and it couldn't have hurt. And my fever did go away."

The day after I returned from Jotunheim, a little red car was parked in my driveway. A short woman leaned against it, dressed in faux fur and a shiny fur hat. She was in the middle of a conversation, although I didn't immediately see anyone else around, apart from a faint flicker in the air. I pulled on my coat, grabbed Vinr, and walked outside, half prepared to attack her with the staff if it came down to it.

When I got closer, I recognized her. I had met the woman two years prior at The Boatman. Ulla. She was Elias's ex-girlfriend and one of Denmark's most powerful mediums. Upon closer inspection, I saw a bunch of nearly transparent ghosts in a circle around her.

"Cross over," she said. "You shouldn't be here anymore. No . . . no . . . Stop talking over each other." There was a pause as one of the ghosts said something, but I heard only a faint *bbbbbzzz*.

"They do?" Ulla asked. There was an angry edge to her voice. "Okay. But stop interrupting me. And each other." She raised an admonishing finger. "I'll look into it." She spotted me. "Anna, my dear. How good that you're here. I need to speak with you—just give me two seconds." She listened to the ghosts again, nodding. They must have been very weak because I could barely detect them.

Finally, Ulla finished the conversation, which I could only hear her side of. She smiled at me with a bright-red mouth. Ulla had no intention of cutting back on lipstick—Fimbul be damned. I wrapped my coat around me. It was even colder than usual today.

"What are you doing here?"

"I need to show you something, dear." She pursed her red lips.

"Does it have to do with Elias? It's really important that I get ahold of him."

Ulla furrowed her pencil-thin brows. "Elias? I don't see him."

"Right . . ." I kicked the snow-caked gravel in my driveway.

"Come with me."

"Can't you just say it here?"

Ulla shook her head. "There's someone who wants to talk to you. A spirit. I can't transport him, so you'll have to come to my place."

I looked suspiciously at her. "What did you say to me the first time we met?"

"Why do you ask?"

I thumped Vinr against the ground. "I just need to check something."

"Uh . . ." Ulla racked her brain. "I told you that you had a clingy spirit." She moved her head and studied me from several angles. "You don't have it anymore. Did you send him to the realm of the dead?"

I exhaled discreetly. "You could say that. Okay, I'll go with you." I got into the passenger seat and struggled to fit Vinr in the small vehicle.

Ulla sat in the driver's seat and turned on the silent electric car. "Good thing I was environmentally conscious before the winter came," she said. "Electric cars are impossible to get these days."

I leaned back in my seat and enjoyed being transported. All movement took place on bikes or foot, which, in the biting cold, meant people always had frozen toes. I looked through the windshield. Even though I knew the landscape inside and out, I had trouble orienting myself. We drove past farms and fields, but everything was blanketed in piles of snow, so I couldn't make out the usual landmarks. The only recognizable things were a couple of burial mounds and the tall windmills that could now be credited for keeping us alive, delivering electricity to radiators and stoves. The sun was gone, but there was plenty of wind. In North Jutland, wind would never be in short supply. I looked out the window as we passed the slim, white giants. The clouds were so low that the tops of the blades were swallowed by the gray mist when they reached their peak. Despite the resistance, they turned steadily, and I was struck by how, in many ways, we were back at our starting point in the deepest past. We were dependent on high places and the forces of nature. You could call it divine power, renewable energy, or whatever you wanted. At its core, it was about survival.

We drove in silence, and it was nice to be with someone without being forced to make conversation. Many people need to constantly talk, talk, talk, but Ulla let me relax in peace while I looked out at the white landscape.

After about twenty minutes, we turned into a driveway resembling hundreds of other driveways in northern Denmark. The former farmhouse was surrounded by snow-covered fields. The house's walls were covered in peeling paint, the barn door sagged a little on its hinges, and the surface of the driveway was a combination of compacted snow and gravel.

I got out of the car, and Ulla did the same. She unlocked the front door and walked ahead of me into the narrow hall.

"It's warmest in the living room."

We passed her husband. He stood leaning against the floral-papered wall, dressed only in a shirt and jeans. Ulla smiled up at him. The look he gave her was so loving that I felt deeply jealous.

"Hi," I mumbled, and he returned my greeting with a wide grin beneath his handlebar mustache.

"Keep the Brewmaster away from my wife," he said.

"I'll try," I said as I passed, even though it was beyond my power to keep Elias away from anything at all. In fact, I would be happy if he showed up.

We neared the living room, and I stopped in the doorway when I saw the room was full of people. I didn't know what to do with myself. They looked curiously at me. Ulla turned around.

"Come on. Don't just stand there, child."

I studied the translucent spirits. They weren't oskoreia; they had deep-set eyes and desperate expressions but weren't half decayed or aggressive.

Ulla waved me in. "Just sit down, Anna." She shooed a little boy from the largest and softest armchair in the room and sat in it herself as though it were her throne. The boy's contours were hazy, and he looked frightened, but he smiled cautiously at me. When Ulla was situated, the child placed himself on her lap. "Sit down," she repeated to me.

"Uh, where?"

She snapped her fingers at a woman in the other armchair. "We have company," she said to the ghost. "Where are your manners?"

The woman stood reluctantly.

"You have a lot of . . . guests." I didn't know what else to say.

Ulla's eyes traveled around the room. "I had to take them in."

"Had to?"

"They were about to join the oskoreia." Ulla closed her eyes and rubbed her forehead. She looked older and more tired than I remembered her, but the winter had had that effect on us all. I looked around at the many spirits. The thought of them all becoming oskoreia was unfathomable.

"Can't you just send them to the realms of the dead?"

"For a long time, I didn't understand why they kept coming back when I sent them over, but I've since found out they're being kept out of the realms of the dead. Odin won't let them into Valhalla. If they wander around here in Midgard long enough, they become oskoreia."

"I've met some of them. They're so scary!"

"Odin's wild dead haven't been a problem in a long time. As long as they got offerings, they stayed away from people. They might possess some weak souls on rare occasions, but Benedict kept them at bay for many years. It got even better when he met his wife."

"Ben and Rebecca? So that's why they put the sheaves of grain in the fields during jól."

"Their number is growing," Ulla said solemnly. "More people are dying than usual because of the cold and disease, and the unrest is making the spirits roam around Midgard rather than cross over to the realms of the dead. Those who stick around Midgard without a connection to the living gather in unruly, dangerous groups. Now that they're being kept out altogether, the situation could become chaotic. In the worst case, it could lead to mass hysteria. Together, the oskoreia can galvanize hordes of the living."

I shuddered. "But they won't become oskoreia if you take care of them. Are you able to handle them all?"

"I'm doing what I can." Ulla didn't look convinced. "But I heard you're a völva now. I would appreciate it if you could help some of them cross. Even Odin can't stand in the way of a völva sending spirits to the realms of the dead."

"What in the worlds does Odin stand to gain from keeping them out?"

Ulla shrugged. "He's a god of death, so he likes having a court of ghosts in Midgard—now that he's here more frequently than before. Plus, it's a way for him to demand more offerings."

"The disease outbreak in Kraghede Forest?" I asked.

Ulla ran her hand over her armrest. "I would hesitate to accuse the gods, but I don't know who else could have caused it."

"Him and his fetish for offerings. What should we do? We barely have enough food for ourselves."

"Odin doesn't want food anymore."

A chill ran over my body, making me colder than winter was capable of. "Human sacrifices?" I asked quietly. "Is that why you wanted to talk to me? I can't do anything about that. Odin can't be controlled on that point."

"I asked you to come because there's someone who wants to talk to you. He didn't have the strength to go to you himself, but I'm like a magnet for the dead, so he was able to reach me. He's been trying to find you because he wants to warn you about something, but he's fragile. Be careful with him."

Ulla closed her eyes and mumbled something unintelligible.

The deceased appeared. He was a nearly invisible figure pressed against the door. His features were blurred beyond recognition, but he had yellowish hair and a strange tinge to his skin.

I couldn't help but sigh with disappointment. "I thought . . . I was sure it was Hakim."

Ulla's thin eyebrows lowered. "Hakim from the DSMA? Hakim Murr? You can't reach him. He followed a different faith, and you're bound to Odin. You know these things already."

"I've spoken with him a bunch of times, but recently, he's gotten a little . . . fuzzy."

"I don't understand how that could be. Anyway, that's not what this is about. If you're going to talk to this guy, then you'd better do it now. He says he has an important message." She looked toward the ghost. "Come back. You're safe with us. We won't hurt you."

He returned slowly like a blinking hologram.

I concentrated on the ghost, who flickered in and out of focus. "Lars?" I asked. "Lars Guldager?"

The ghost immediately became clearer. I could make out his facial features, even though he was still transparent and fluttered nervously. "That's my name," he whispered. "I had forgotten it."

"Is that what he's called?" Ulla asked. "I couldn't even get his name out of him. He just kept saying *Anna Sakarias*."

"Aaaannnaaa." It sounded exactly how I imagined a ghost would call my name in a horror movie. "Aaannaaaa Saaakaaariiiiiasssss."

"Yes, Lars. I'm here." When I repeated his name, he became a little more visible. "Your name was Lars Guldager. You were a police officer in Aalborg, and your partner was called Hakim Murr." Lars became sharper and sharper with every word.

"I'm sorry." His wandering eyes were set deep in his skull beneath dark shadows. His lips were bluish, and his skin was white, bordering on pale green.

"Why are you sorry?"

"Hakim was on the trail of the redheaded girls' murderer, but I stopped him." He laughed. "Or I tried to stop him from figuring it out."

"Why did you want to stop Hakim from finding my murderer?"

"To protect him. It didn't work, and Hakim had to die."

"Did you kill him?" I blurted.

Ulla inhaled sharply. "You can't ask a ghost that!"

"I don't care what you can and can't do. Who made these rules?"

Lars's ghost let out a high-pitched whine and floated up under the ceiling like a loose balloon. He stayed there, huddled in the corner farthest from me.

"No," he sniffed. "I did everything else he said, but I refused to kill my friend, so he got the other servant to do it."

"Who ordered it? Was it Loki?"

"The All-Father."

The bridge of my nose prickled. Odin had ordered Hakim's murder. He would pay for that. I lowered my chin to my chest. "Who was the servant?"

"I can't remember the name. It was . . . It's all so jumbled. All I know is that you submitted to the All-Father."

"Me?"

"You died by Ragnara's hand, and therefore Fimbul began."

"I'm not dead."

"But it was you."

"It wasn't Ragnara who killed me. It was Eli—" I stopped. "Was Elias working for Ragnara?"

Ulla looked up sharply. "You didn't know that? Elias works for everyone."

I didn't even have the wherewithal to close my mouth. When I realized I was gaping, I brought my teeth together with a snap. "Elias made me think it was my idea for him to kill me."

"It was Odin's idea," Lars said.

"That was when we were together." Ulla blushed. "Odin gave Ragnara the idea, but she developed it further, although I never found out what it was all about. But Odin indeed wanted you to die by Ragnara's hand as a baby. Elias, on the other hand, was against it."

"Odin? Why would he want me to be killed by Ragnara?"

"It would start Fimbulwinter. Odin was pushing us toward it."

"Why did Odin want to start Fimbul? Hejd's prophecy says that he'll die during Ragnarök."

Ulla shrugged, and I looked to Lars, who floated with his head down in the corner of the ceiling.

"I had decided to tell you what I knew that night, but then, Odin's servant came. There was no struggle. I died . . ." The word cracked in a deep rasp. "I died . . . I died . . ."

"Who is Odin's servant? Is it Elias?" I tried to hold him with a steady gaze.

But Lars continued to regurgitate. "I died . . . I died . . . I died . . ." He sounded like a broken record.

"He's going to end up returning to his corpse," I said frantically.

Ulla stood. "Your name is Lars Guldager. You were a police officer. A good officer. A well-liked officer." Lars grew a little more solid and stopped babbling. He eventually drifted to the floor, where he crouched. "I don't want to be here anymore." Suddenly, Lars sounded like a child. "I don't want to become an oskoreia."

"He needs to cross soon. It's cruel to keep him here."

"Wait. Wait. Can you just give me a hint about who . . . *unalived* you and Hakim?" I had no idea whether my workaround for the don't-ask-about-a-ghost's-death rule would work.

"I trusted h—"

"Send him across," Ulla commanded.

Even though I desperately wanted to ask him more, I didn't have the heart. "Cross over," I said with authority. "You died without a fight, so you will go to Helheim." The many völvas spoke through me.

Hel was suddenly standing in the middle of the living room, but she smiled at Lars in a way that made me like her a little more. She opened her arms, and Lars leaned into her. Hel's arms—both the good one and the one that was all bones—wrapped gently around Lars. She looked at me and nodded respectfully.

Thank you, she mouthed before they both disappeared.

I collapsed into Ulla's plush chair. The many curious ghosts came closer, but they didn't scare me. The thought of them becoming oskoreia was far worse. Ulla and I made eye contact. She looked questioningly at me.

"It's going to take a long time. I can't ask them directly how they you-know-what, but I need to know so I can send them to the right place."

"I have loads of time."

The ghosts gathered around us. I stood heavily and thumped Vinr against the floor. "You." I pointed to a man. "Do you know how to play charades?"

CHAPTER 27

"It's not too much?" Luna pushed her dark curls back.

"No," Mathias and I said in unison.

Mathias took a moon-shaped hair clip and fastened half of her hair back. "You're stunning."

Luna looked at herself in the mirror and turned her head from side to side. "You did a good job on my makeup, Mathias. I've totally gotten used to not wearing any, but isn't this a little too much blush?"

Mathias appraised her with a professional look. "That's just you. You have the prettiest natural glow."

Luna fanned her face with her hand. "It's really warm in here."

I looked at the slanted window. Hail pummeled it with aggressive little *plock-plock-plock* sounds. "What? It's not warm in here. You don't have a fever, do you?"

Mathias quickly laid his hand on Luna's forehead and exhaled with a smile. "She doesn't feel warm."

"I feel fine," Luna said. "Great, actually. Let me see your dress, Anna."

We were getting ready for the party at The Boatman. Luna had ransacked her stash and found scraps of fur, beads, and wool, and in no time, she had created two incredible dresses. A bottle-green dress for herself and a burgundy dress for me. Mine had a high collar of black rabbit fur and a large rune symbol embroidered on the back. When I looked at myself over my shoulder in her large mirror, I saw that it was mannaz.

"You always talk about that rune," Luna said. "And it follows the shape of your body really nicely." She trailed her finger along the symbol.

She had sewn the sleeves so they reached halfway down my fingers, which looked elegant while keeping my hands warm. The neckline was low enough to frame the khamsa-shaped scar that Ben had left on my neck. I held Vinr in my hand, and it occurred to me how eccentric I must look with two ravens and a giant crystal hovering over my head. Mathias had given us both very subtle makeup looks, but they went a long way toward livening us up. My red hair was pinned up in a simple style. Mathias wore a suit that the rest of us would have frozen to death in.

"I'm so excited to talk to Elias," I said. "I'm sure he didn't think I could get all three pieces of gold. I also have a bone to pick with him about my little trip to Helheim."

Mathias smiled but doubt lurked in his eyes.

"How are we getting to The Boatman?"

"My mom and Arthur went ahead," Luna said. "They had to do some kind of prep. Something crazy is happening tonight." She wiggled her eyebrows. "They were very secretive."

Mathias pushed his makeup kit aside. "Ladies." He spread his arms.

Luna jumped into his embrace, and he held her with one arm. The other was extended toward me.

"What do you want in exchange for being our taxi?"

"It's on the house."

I laughed and clung to him, and in a leap so fast I barely even noticed it, we were down the stairs and out the door. The snow-covered fields flicked past, and both Luna and I squealed like we were on an extreme roller coaster. In no time, Mathias stopped in front of The Boatman. I hopped out of his arms and stared up at the sky, which was almost dark. Mist crept up from the shore, and I sensed something large in the water. It creaked and groaned, and once in a while, there was a huge splash when something hit the water's surface. Luna crawled down from Mathias's embrace, and like me, her smile stiffened.

"The ice wall is here," she whispered.

Several of the other guests were looking out at the dark sea. I was glad we couldn't actually see the ice cap. They had shown it on TV, but to see it in person would be a different thing entirely.

"Out of sight, out of mind," I heard someone mumble to their companion before hurrying inside The Boatman.

Veronika stood in the doorway. Today she wore towering leather boots with sharply pointed heels, fishnet tights, and a red miniskirt. Her fur top appeared, unsettlingly, to have been made from a skinned giant wolf. She held her hand out for guests' invitations and made rude comments in her deep voice, which sounded like she smoked forty cigarettes and drank a bottle of whiskey a day.

"That long beard suits you. I can barely see your face," she said to one man. "And you shaved yours!" That was directed at his wife.

She seemed to be the only one in a good mood during this collectively depressing time.

"Come into the mound with me," she whispered when Luna and Mathias handed her their invitation. "It'll only take a second." She looked impertinently at Luna's lower body.

I gave Veronika an impatient glare. "Can you not try to lure my friend into an elf mound?"

Veronika licked her lips. "You don't know how delicious she is to us."

Luna and Mathias walked ahead of me into The Boatman.

"No escort?" she asked me.

"No one wanted to come with me." I had tried to coax Mads into being my date, but he had declined. The corners of Veronika's mouth turned up ever so slightly, but given how surly her face usually was, this was equivalent to howling with laughter. She seemed to be searching for a suitably rude comment, but she couldn't even choose one. I walked past her, shaking my head.

"I would have come with you," she said after me. Her voice dripped with sultriness. "I would have brought you down to the home of the elves."

When I entered the bar, the smell of food hit my nostrils, and my stomach growled. People were already gathered around a banquet table. Luna, Mathias, and I squeezed our way through the crowd and saw the table, which was covered in bread, boiled grains, and meat.

"We have to wait until later to eat," a woman said longingly. "The gods must be worshipped first."

The man at her side tightened his grip around her arm. "I haven't seen such a spread since Christmas."

His wife elbowed him in the side. "Jól."

Luna and I stared at the dishes, and my mouth watered, but Mathias turned around and looked contentedly at the many people leaning over the food. As always, the guests were dressed in gowns and glitter, and a famous band was playing like their lives depended on it. They literally may have, in fact—while the singer let his soft voice flow over the crowd, he didn't take his eyes off the fragrant bowls. The women's makeup looked overdone, even though it was identical to what they had worn last year. Their haunted eyes and pale, angular faces looked distorted. The men had full beards and long hair, which looked odd when paired with their suits. We made our way to the side of the room, as the smell of food threatened to bring Luna and me to our knees. The whole time, I kept an eye out for Elias, but he was nowhere to be seen.

"Drinks are served!" someone announced, and everyone ran to the bar. Mathias disappeared as well and, of course, was first in line. He returned quickly with fancy glasses with wires around the stems.

"Pine needle water," Luna said, disappointed.

Mathias looked down dispiritedly at the transparent liquid with the dark green needles. "It's warm, at least."

We accepted it, and I took a sip. "Ohhh!" I exclaimed. "It's sugar water." I took another, larger mouthful. "And there's alcohol in it."

Luna drank greedily, too. Finally, she crunched some of the pine needles. My glass was soon empty, and I wished I had more. The alcohol tingled pleasantly in my blood, and everything took on a hazy glow. We found ourselves standing next to a small group by the wall.

"Od Dinesen must have answers," one woman said. I recognized her from back when everything was normal. She had been on TV all the time and was full of self-confidence, with bleached blond hair and colorful clothes. Now, she had brown roots and a look of uncertainty in her eyes. She tipped her glass upside down and caught the last pine needle with the tip of her tongue.

"He's our last chance," a politician said. I had to look closely before I recognized him behind his beard. Before, he had always been clean-shaven, with short hair and unwavering opinions, but now he emanated fickleness. "Everything else has been tried."

"What's been tried?" The woman leaned forward.

"The scientists didn't have a solution." The politician raked his fingers through his hair. "Now everything depends on the gods."

Pessimism washed over me, and the individual memories I glimpsed were horrible. In this deep crisis, people clung to superstition and vigilantism, and the alcohol in my malnourished body made it hard to shield myself.

As we walked through the room, everyone looked at us with reverence. Or that's how they looked at Luna and Mathias, at least. Even I was impressed with the power couple. Mathias didn't bother to conceal his divine side, so he was tall, beautiful, and golden, with a faint green shimmer around him. Luna looked gorgeous, her springy brown curls around her face. I, on the other hand, received hostile glares, but because I was accompanied by

Luna and Mathias, no one dared try anything. I tightened my grip around Vinr.

Nice to see you again, seer, I heard close to my ear, though no one was standing near me. My eyes searched, and finally, I spotted Mardöll by the bar. She gave me a little wave from several yards away as she laughed inside my head. Remembering the vision where she had sacrificed nine sick people in the early 1900s made my mouth pucker.

Oh, stop it, she said, detecting my thoughts about her crime. *Think of all the people I saved.*

I didn't feel like discussing human sacrifices with her. *Where's your husband, Mardöll?*

She pointed, and I saw the prime minister deep in conversation with Od.

Come over here, I thought. *I don't like having you inside my head.*

I'm pretty comfortable in here. She gave a bubbly laugh that echoed in my skull. Mardöll moved with long, graceful strides through the crowd and ended up in front of us. She wore a bold yellow dress that evoked springtime and optimism. I tapped Luna and Mathias on the shoulders, and they turned around. Mathias smiled warmly and grasped Mardöll's hand, but Luna looked nauseous.

"It's nice to see you again," Mathias said.

Mardöll held her hand out to Luna. "My condolences. Your father was a remarkable sorcerer."

Hesitantly, Luna took her hand as the color drained from her face. "Thanks," she said dully, then she looked at the first lady and paled further. "Excuse me." She held a hand over her mouth and ran toward the exit.

Mathias followed her. "What's wrong?" he called.

Mardöll and I were left standing there alone.

"You were there when Benedict passed?" It was impossible to figure out what she thought about Ben's death.

"I was there."

"What a horrible way to die," Mardöll said. "A trap inside of you, set off by your own magic. And then to burn up." She raised a penciled eyebrow. "Though that is the fate of most witches."

"Being magically booby-trapped?"

"Catching fire. It happens to pretty much all of us, sooner or later." She shook her head elegantly. Then she studied Vinr. "I heard you're a völva now. Congratulations." She said it as though I had won an award or gotten a new job. Then she walked back to the bar.

Luna and Mathias reappeared. Luna's curls were slightly damp, as though she had splashed water on her face. "Whew," she said.

I looked at her, surprised. "I don't think you've ever been so repulsed by another person before. The first time you met Mardöll, you didn't feel anything?"

Luna looked at Mardöll by the bar but quickly turned her back. "I can't stand her. Just the sight of her. Ew."

"Wow." I looked at Mathias, and he shrugged. I didn't have the most faith in the first lady, but Luna's reaction surprised me. Mathias also looked puzzled. He started to say something but was interrupted by someone tapping their glass. Od took the stage, and a ceremonial atmosphere descended over The Boatman.

Niels Villadsen, the prime minister, and Mardöll stood behind Od, Rebecca, and Arthur. They were all looking down at the floor like they were at a church service.

Where the hell is Elias? He usually stood close by when Od gave his speeches.

Two people suddenly appeared on one side of the stage. They were very tall, but no one in the audience seemed to see them. Od nodded imperceptibly at both Odin and Freyja. Odin looked well-fed and toned. He was young and broad-chested and wore only leather pants and a sleeveless shirt that revealed large, muscular arms. His hair was sparkling black, and his eye socket was deep and dark. He breathed heavily and expectantly. I glared at him. He was behind Hakim's murder, and he had also wanted me dead. I stared him down angrily, and he blew me a kiss. Freyja wore a nearly transparent gold dress, and her long, flaxen hair flowed over her shoulders.

Mathias placed a scalding hot hand on my arm. I don't know if this was to protect me or to calm himself down. Freyja looked at her husband, and Od looked back. He looked sad, but there was determination in his eyes. The guests looked imploringly at the stage as though Od were an oracle.

"The winter is severe," he began. "If we're going to survive this cold time, we must act now." His voice was so powerful, he didn't need a microphone. "The gods need our help to gain the strength to save us."

There was a murmur of approval, and a chill ran down my spine.

"We have enjoyed abundance for a long time, and we have squandered it. The time has come for us to pay it back." He stopped. "Sacrifices are necessary."

"We'll give anything," someone shouted from somewhere behind me. "Whatever it takes."

"You don't know what I'm about to say; I must share the truth with you all."

I suddenly remembered the time Od told me I wasn't ready for the truth. Maybe *being ready* meant being pushed beyond all understanding to accept even the most unbelievable things.

"There are multiple worlds." Od said only this one sentence and let it roll through the crowd. He was quiet for a long time as he scanned the room.

"He looked right at me," a man behind me said. He sounded blissful.

"Me too," a woman said. "My body feels so warm." She held out her arms.

"There is a place where the old traditions were preserved. The gods were worshipped, and the population ensured that the balance was maintained. We owe them a debt of gratitude. The place is called Hrafnheim. The ravens' home." Od paused dramatically.

I turned around to see who would first protest this outrageous claim, but everyone swallowed it whole. Demihypnosis? No. The guests seemed to be so desperate that they were willing to believe anything.

"Ravensted was the bastion of this world for many years, but you chose the wrong god, and then you lived without any gods at all. You were blinded by greed and gave no thought to the common good."

Od, what are you doing? I didn't say this aloud, but nevertheless, his eyes flitted briefly to me. He looked uncertain.

"Are the gods mad at us?" came an anxious voice from the crowd.

"The gods are very angry," Od said. His voice deepened. "And when the other world scorned them, they nearly disappeared. This has left us defenseless in the face of chaos."

"What should we do?"

"Hrafnheim is once again god-fearing, and they have offered to help us by making the ultimate sacrifice."

"What?" I whispered.

Od looked toward the rear wall, and the door scraped open. People moved through the crowd, which parted subtly.

"Who is it?" Luna asked, craning her neck.

Mathias gaped when he caught sight of them. He was quite a bit taller than us and had keen eyesight, so he could easily see the back of The Boatman. His expression was a combination of anticipation and fear.

"What's going on?" I asked, but Mathias didn't have a chance to reply before a small group of people stepped onto the stage.

The air was sucked from my lungs. On stage next to Od stood Sverre and Ingeborg, who held their son, Finn, in her arms. Sverre's beard had grown even longer, and his white hair was gathered in a thick knot. He looked more like a Viking than ever. His face had become more angular, and in the sharp light of the stage, I saw deep wrinkles between his brows. He wore thick furs, and his brown eyes gleamed coldly. Tilarids hung at his side and vibrated contentedly. I had difficulty recognizing the man I had once loved. He stroked his beard, and the tattooed eagle flapped its wings on the back of his hand.

Ingeborg's face was even whiter than the last time I had seen her. Her lips were thin, and her breathing was shallow as she held her child tightly to her chest.

"This is King Sverre of Hrafnheim and his queen, Ingeborg." Od bowed to them.

Sverre's eyes searched for mine, but he kept his face neutral. There was a hint of bewilderment in his gaze, but then he remembered himself and reciprocated Od's gesture.

"To protect us against the forces of chaos, the king is offering a communal sacrifice," Od said. "A sacrifice that will protect both our worlds."

Sverre cleared his throat. "I want peace between our people. We must ensure our joint success."

"Damn, he's hot," a woman behind me whispered.

"We will give the greatest sacrifice to the All-Father, and all I want in return is an alliance."

"You have our allegiance," Od said. "What do you want in return?"

"I want our people to commit themselves to the gods. I want the human race to survive."

I opened my mouth, but no words came out. To keep my legs from buckling beneath me, I clung to Vinr.

"But we must make offerings," Sverre said. His voice was entirely devoid of emotion. "For Odin to regain his strength, he requires a hangadrott. A royal sacrifice. That is the only thing that can fully restore his power so he can stop the winter."

Odin stood up straighter at the side of the stage. He rubbed a hand over his own bare bicep and breathed so heavily, I could feel the heat of it from where I stood. The other guests couldn't see him, but they nevertheless closed their eyes, enjoying the warmth.

Finn fussed in Ingeborg's arms.

A *royal sacrifice? He can't mean* . . . *No!* I looked up at the stage in horror, but then Sverre continued speaking.

"Ingeborg is the queen."

Ingeborg?

Odin moaned so loudly that I had no doubt what this was doing for him. I stared at Ingeborg, who looked back resolutely as the audience began to murmur. Some looked appalled.

"Hangadrott," one woman said, and her husband joined in.

"No!" I shouted. "This is insane."

But another continued: "Hangadrott."

"Oskoreia," Odin said quietly. "Come tell the living what they must do."

A host of flickering figures appeared among the living, and each of them placed a hand on a guest's back. The oskoreia had half-rotten faces, messy hair, and hunched postures. The wild dead nudged the will of the audience, and the living raised their arms.

"Hangadrott, hangadrott, hangadrott."

Ingeborg looked at her son for a long time. She kissed his forehead tenderly, and he whimpered as she laid him in Od's arms with a miserable expression on her face.

"So you can live," she said to the baby, who reached his small hands out for his mother. She quickly turned away from him with a heart-wrenching sob. The child wailed, which made Ingeborg double over in agony.

Od looked Finn in the eyes with a gleaming, silvery gaze, and the child immediately grew quiet. Ingeborg removed her blue wool cape and stood on the stage facing the crowd. Her dress was low-cut, and her exposed neck made her look vulnerable.

"Stop it." I walked toward the stage. "Od!" I yelled, but he ignored me. He simply looked down at the baby with so much love that it seemed to be directed at all of humanity. Luna pushed through the crowd after me.

"Come up here, Anna," Sverre said and spread his arms.

I squeezed past the last few people to reach the stage. "You're all crazy."

Sverre reached down to me. "Come, my love."

"I'm not your love. Not anymore."

Sverre crouched down, and Tilarids clanged as the tip hit the floor. "I love you, and you will learn to love me again." The fanatic madness shone in his eyes.

I looked at the sword on his hip. *You got what you wanted. You consumed him.*

Tilarids laughed in response. *His love for you helped me achieve my goal.*

Strong arms lifted me onto the stage. Although I writhed, I couldn't withstand the large mob. Still on one knee, Sverre was now beneath me with his head bowed.

"Hangadrott, hangadrott..."

"Take Tilarids off," I begged Sverre desperately.

Slowly, Sverre rose to his full height, a head taller than me. His brown eyes never left my face. In a calm, fluid motion, he pulled the sword. It made a metallic sound as it slid from its sheath. But Sverre held the sword in his hand, and it retained its power over him. Resolutely, I took Tilarids from him. When I grasped the hilt with both hands, Vinr fell noisily to the floor.

"You're doing the right thing, Anna," Sverre said appreciatively.

Yes! The sword sighed in my head. Odin was suddenly right next to me, and he whispered in my ear:

"It's your turn now. If you give me hangadrott, raven, Ragnarök will not come." He was breathless with desire. "All your loved ones will live."

Ingeborg trembled, but she stood still in front of me, and I looked around, perplexed, with the evil sword in my hands.

Sverre smiled at me. "I want to give this sacrifice."

"It's not your sacrifice to give. It's a human life."

"Hangadrott, hangadrott, hangadrott," everyone in The Boatman chanted, and suddenly, it was like we were in a large vessel heading toward the realm of the dead. People were depleted, and among them stood all the dead oskoreia.

Kill her, kill her, Tilarids said.

"Anna!" Luna shouted. "What should I do?"

I looked around desperately. Elias still wasn't there, and Mathias was frozen. He simply stared at Ingeborg's neck. Rebecca had closed her eyes and was huddled against Arthur's chest. My dad looked in horror at the whole tableau but did nothing to stop the sacrifice.

Ingeborg knelt and leaned her head back, exposing her neck. She put her fingertips on the floor behind her back so her body formed a backward arch in front of me as she moaned in fear.

Confused, I looked down at the young woman who sat leaning back with her neck stretched out. Her eyes were half closed, but her gaze was directed toward Finn in Od's arms. Tilarids vibrated in my grasp.

Save the people. Stop the apocalypse. Come on, raven. It's just one little human, and Ingeborg will die anyway, along with the rest of you during Ragnarök if you don't.

Frustrated, I laid a hand on Tilarids's blade to make it shut up. The edge cut into my palm, causing blood to stream from it. It stung, but I didn't register any pain. All I saw was Ingeborg's neck in front of me. The blood ran from my hand and soaked my sleeve. At the sight of it, the audience let out a collective sigh.

Sverre gently took my hand and traced a finger over the wound. At his touch, it healed immediately, and the warmth his healing produced trickled into me.

"See? I'm good for you. You're good for me. We belong together." An intense love flowed toward me. He was magically immune, so my repulsion spells had no effect on him.

Wait a second!

I looked more closely at Sverre. The fire of madness burned inside him. The insanity of the possessed.

Why isn't the king immune to you, Tilarids?

Tilarids scoffed mockingly. *My magic isn't new. It's ancient sorcery, unaffected by the weak spells of some talentless witch. I only stop working if I'm split apart.*

I appealed to Sverre again: "Can't you see that this is all wrong?"

"This is the right thing to do. It's the only way we can stop the apocalypse. Think of all the people we can save. Children and the weak. Loving families." Then his voice changed. "Anna . . . When my wife is dead, we can get married. I'm also doing this for our sake. For your sake."

I grasped Tilarids's hilt with both hands. *For my sake.* Once again, someone was going to lose their life because of me. If I hadn't asked Elias to kill me, Fimbulwinter wouldn't even have started.

The starving people in the crowd held their breath and waited.

I looked down. Ingeborg's jugular throbbed rapidly under her skin, and with a glance at Luna, who looked back at me, I raised Tilarids. The vision Hejd had shown me flew through my memory. I remembered Sverre fighting during Ragnarök and the words he had said to me from the future:

Let me be consumed. We can be happy together.

I knew what I had to do.

CHAPTER 28

With the sword raised, my eyes found Luna's. "Use your magic," I whispered.

"How?" She pushed up her sleeves, and blue energy was already crackling from her palms. Her witchcraft had become significantly stronger, and she looked like she was ready to bomb everyone in the room.

"Remove Sverre's magical immunity," I said. "Take it off of him entirely."

"What about the other part?"

"What other part?"

"He's connected to you with magic. It comes from a different witch than Védis. He's willing to do whatever it takes for you to be together."

I spun around, Tilarids still in my hand. Now, I pointed the sword at Sverre. It screeched furiously in my hands: *I must kill.*

"Shut up, you miserable piece of iron," I said. In a fluid motion, I knelt and grabbed ahold of Vinr so that I had Tilarids in one hand and my völva staff in the other. Vinr's power clashed against Tilarids's. "Take all the magic off him, and I'll take away the sword."

Sverre looked first at me and then at Luna with all-destroying desire flaming in his eyes. Luna raised her hands, spread her fingers, and mumbled spells.

When the king realized my plan, he looked pleadingly at me. His brown eyes caught mine, and I felt a love so great and terrifying that it felt like a physical blow threatening to topple me backward. He took a step toward me.

"Stop her. Don't do it. Don't—"

Blue lightning flew from Luna's fingers and struck him. Sverre raised his arms, but it was too late. The magic filled him, then sucked something out. A puff of purple smoke rose around us as Luna burned the spells away. Sverre sank to his knees.

In my hands, Tilarids jerked toward him, and Sverre tumbled back in horror when he focused on the weapon. Instinctively, he pulled Ingeborg close to protect her.

Odin shouted angrily, Od looked aghast at Luna, and Ingeborg opened her eyes in confusion as her husband toppled her over.

It was completely still for a moment as Sverre sat with his wife in his arms, both shrouded in the cloud of purple smoke. He raised his face toward me and twisted his upper lip in disgust. He stood and staggered backward as if to get far away from me.

"But you're hideous, and you're holding the sword to my wife's neck." He looked at me as though he were finally seeing me clearly, although the opposite was true. Ben's repulsion spells were working on him, and the extremes he was willing to go to to have me were gone. He saw me as everyone else did. In fact, he saw me with even more revulsion.

In front of the stage, the oskoreia squeezed around the guests, and they began to shout at me. The crowd became more and more agitated.

"And the agreement?" Od asked. He suddenly looked threatening with Finn in his arms.

I pointed at him with both the sword and the staff. "Give Ingeborg her son."

Ingeborg ran to him and held out her arms.

Though Ingeborg tried to take her baby back, Od was a brick wall, and her efforts were in vain. Od stared at me in disbelief.

"You didn't do it. You refused to follow the order." He composed himself. "Kill Ingeborg." His eyes shot flashes of silver toward me, but the green ring embedded in Vinr created a bubble that surrounded me protectively. It blocked the blast of demihypnosis that whistled like a bullet as it bounced off Vinr's shield.

I raised Tilarids toward Od.

Then let me have the god's son instead, it whistled inside my head. *I've always wanted to kill a god's child.*

"You're not getting anyone," I told the sword. "Stay away from the people I love." I held Od's gaze. "Give the child back to Ingeborg. What you're doing is wrong."

Od's voice was uncertain. "Hejd is speaking through you. This is her doing."

"I'm capable of deciding not to sacrifice an innocent woman myself, thank you very much."

"Anna. You're condemning yourself to death."

"Pfft!"

"You're condemning everyone if you don't sacrifice the queen. Many more will suffer because of you."

My eyes flitted to Rebecca and Arthur, then to Mathias and Luna. "I'm sorry," I whispered. "But I can't."

Od slackened his grip, and Ingeborg was finally able to take hold of Finn. Sverre looked like he had just awoken from a deep sleep. When he saw his wife and son near the demigod, he spread his arms protectively.

"What were you about to make me do?" He looked at me with horror, standing with the sword and staff in my hands. I was actually pointing them at Od, just behind Ingeborg and Finn, but Sverre didn't catch that particular detail. He only saw me threatening his family.

"*I* wasn't trying to make you—" I began, but Sverre placed himself between me and Ingeborg.

"Stay away from us."

I felt a wounded twinge in my chest. "I will."

Sverre looked at me, bewildered. "What did I ever see in you?" He stepped back and grabbed Ingeborg's hand.

Odin paced back and forth like an agitated lion at the side of the stage.

"This is the second time you've robbed me of a hangadrott, seer." He stamped his foot. Everything trembled, and people whined in fear. The walls shook and glass cracked.

"The gods are angry!" someone screamed. "It's another earthquake."

Sverre's contemptuous gaze was almost unbearable. I had known for a long time that it was over between us, but now I had lost him forever. Some people cried, and others stared angrily in my direction.

Odin said something in Old Norse to the oskoreia who stood among the living. The wild dead pushed the guests, and everyone in The Boatman moved forward. Their hollow eyes were aimed at me, and they staggered in my direction.

"What a bitch!" a woman shouted.

"Ugly!"

"Evil!"

In a fluid motion, I turned around and sped toward the back door. I ran, my eyes stinging, to get away from the crowd.

When Sverre realized it, he shouted: "She's running off with my sword!"

I raced onward, jumped onto a chair and then up onto the table. With Tilarids in my hand, I hopped over platters and bowls of food. The end of the banquet table pointed to the mirrored hallway leading to Od's office. The horde followed me as I fled.

"Die, witch!"

"We're gonna catch you."

In the many reflections, I saw them all distorted. I managed to fling the door open, slam it behind me, and lock it before the people threw themselves against it.

"She should burn."

"It's all her fault."

I was inclined to agree with them, but burning me wouldn't help anyone.

Frantic, I pulled the sofa in front of the door that threatened to give out as furious fists and heels pounded against it. Then, a flash of silver was visible beneath the door, and I heard a metallic shout.

"Stop!"

A hypnotic stillness descended over the bar. Only a couple of sniffs and the scraping of shoes could be heard.

"Nothing happened here tonight. You saw nothing."

I only had time to breathe a sigh of relief before I heard Odin's raging roar followed by heavy footsteps. The ground shook, and the crashes grew louder. The floor moved so much that my legs seemed to disappear beneath me, and I fell. I plunged Tilarids's tip into the floorboards and pushed myself up. Desperate, I looked around at each of the many doors. I considered whether I should seek refuge in one of the other worlds, but under no circumstances would I return to Helheim, and Hrafnheim would also be a bad choice. Tilarids needed to be kept away from Sverre; it was far too dangerous to leave in human hands. I had no idea where the other doors led, so I ran out the exit to the private parking lot behind The Boatman. Tilarids smoldered in my hand. The runes down its shaft glowed red against the dark gray metal.

You can kill them all with me, the sword tempted. *Together, we can do great things. You can become a goddess. You can marry a god. Kill your enemies.*

The enticing words crept into my head, but Vinr, still in my other hand, cleared my mind enough to withstand Tilarids's mind control.

"Be quiet."

You can live forever with me by your side.

"I don't want to live forever."

You have it in you, and we'll be an incredible team. We'll get ahold of Varnar. The three of us. We'll have the worlds at our feet.

"I don't want to."

You don't want Varnar? Your greatest love? I can give him to you, and he'll never leave your side.

I gasped for air, tempted beyond all belief, but again, Vinr's stable energy made me see reason. "Varnar and I don't want to be tyrants."

I can remove your guilt. You'll rise above that kind of petty concern.

I saw colorful flashes at the edge of my field of vision. Tilarids was starting to overpower my will. I tightened my hand around Vinr.

"Help me, völvas," I begged, and they responded with calm strength, giving me the power to speak firmly to the sword. "I'm not interested in you like that. You should be melted down and made into a plow or something useful."

I was a plow. Freyja's plow. But the giant Surt set me free. He asked Ulfberht to reforge me.

"So, you can be both? You can both create life and take it?"

We're all double-edged. Tilarids trembled in my hand. *I'm just double-edged in a more literal sense.*

I ran as far as I could toward the cliff behind The Boatman, stopping right at the edge. My feet peeked over the abyss, and the mile-high ice wall towered above me. It creaked and groaned deeply like a machine that needed oil.

Someone growled behind me, and I turned with Tilarids in one hand and Vinr in the other. It was Odin, and his one eye shone with begrudging admiration. I must have been quite a sight in my red dress with black fur, völva staff, and burning sword in front of the gigantic ice wall.

"Little seer." Odin stood in front of me and reached his giant hands toward my neck. Each was enormous, and I knew he could crush me like an ant if he wanted to. But I held my head up and looked into his eye.

"I'm not just a *little seer*. I'm your raven, your völva—I warned you when I bound myself to you. I said it would be worse for you."

One of his large fingers trailed down my cheek, and I thought he would snap and crush my skull, but he caressed me instead. "I admire your strength. Let's make peace."

"You almost had a woman killed tonight. You had Hakim and Lars killed. I hate you."

"Hmm," he said, as though it were totally irrelevant. "The little humans will die anyway. I'm only shifting the timing slightly."

"I am one of those little humans. You tried to clear me out of the way, too."

Odin raised his index finger. "That was when you were little. Just a baby in Thora's womb. Now I've discovered that I can use you in another way. You can become a war goddess. I'm offering you the universe. You just have to give yourself to me fully and completely."

"I want to get away from war and unrest."

Odin raised an eyebrow. "But you have such a talent for it."

Do it, Tilarids whispered. *Say yes. The three of us together as a trinity.*

I tightened my grip on the objects in my hands. Tilarids sang bloodthirstily in my head, and Odin reached for the sword. Vinr sent cool calm into me. I breathed heavily, but Vinr functioned as a lightning rod. It sent all thoughts of murder and despotism directly into the ground beneath my feet.

"Give me Tilarids." Odin's burning eye was now very close to me.

"Can't you just take it from me?"

"Tilarids must be given away."

"That's useful information." I bowed my head and inhaled. Then I found strength from the other völvas, leaned against Vinr, and let the staff's power build in me. I raised my head again.

"Raven . . ." Odin said warningly. "Loki cannot get his hands on the sword."

Loki had the sword in my Ragnarök vision. Sverre was himself because he didn't have it. Odin wasn't there. I thought frantically. The ice is chaos. Chaos belongs to the giants.

"Give it to me," Odin commanded. "Give—"

I whipped around and flung Tilarids toward the glacier. The sword spun in the air and flew high above us. Vinr must have given me strength as Tilarids hurtled toward the top of the ice wall, where it embedded itself with a hollow *thunk*.

"I give Tilarids back to chaos," I shouted.

Odin tilted his head back and bellowed toward the sky. A cone of fire came out of his mouth and rose like a column toward the clouds, and I tumbled backward from the force of it. I lay on my back with my head hanging over the cliff and Vinr across me.

For a moment, Odin's fire removed the clouds, and I saw the moon and stars above us. Pure joy flowed through me when I saw that the celestial bodies were still there. I could happily die now, with a view of the stars.

"Raven," Odin said dully when he was done. "You'll be the death of me."

In a scalding gust of air, he was gone.

CHAPTER 29

I ran through the woods in my long dress with Vinr in my hand, glad I had insisted on wearing my biker boots despite my elegant outfit. The wind had grown in intensity in the ten minutes I had been running, and the staff gave me the strength to continue.

Around me, frost spread up the trees. A dead trunk shattered, covered in ice crystals. There was a loud bang, and flakes of ice and black sawdust drifted down onto me. It happened quickly as the temperature fell.

Crap! A frost storm had hit, and I was in the middle of it. Even Vinr's power shooting through my arm wasn't enough to keep me warm.

"Hey," I grumbled. "I just gave you Tilarids, Loki. Is this frost storm the thanks I get?" But I knew that the giants—much like nature—did not answer gifts with gifts. Whether you were rewarded or punished was totally random.

Letting out a scream to find my strength, I pushed on. Fortunately, I was able to orient myself using my extrasensory perception as a torch. I fought my way through the dark on feet numbed by cold. I was getting closer, but the cold was becoming crippling. At first, the pain in my skin and lungs was bearable, but it had been replaced by a frightening numbness in my limbs and face—a total lack of sensation.

My teeth chattered as I neared Elias's yard. With uncoordinated movements, I somehow made my way up his stone steps. I slipped several times, but I couldn't even feel it when my knees pounded against the granite stairs. I flung the door open and tumbled into the small foyer. Unable to keep my grasp on Vinr, it clattered to the floor. With the very last of my strength, I slammed the door behind me. The wind whined outside, and I sank, gasping, onto my stomach. My windpipe prickled, but I couldn't feel my cheeks, fingers, or toes. An all-encompassing exhaustion came over me now that I was inside in the warmth, and I was ready to fall asleep right there on the tile floor. Something prodded at my consciousness, but I couldn't bring myself to address it. Again, it pushed—enough that I physically felt the pressure.

Anna! It was Serén's voice inside my head. *Anna. Anna!* It got louder and more desperate. *Stay awake!* She was shouting now, and I opened my eyes wide as the words rang out. I got onto my knees. A faint aura flickered in the living room, and unable to stand, I crawled toward it.

"Elias," I moaned as I approached the figure, which lay in the fetal position on the floor. "You murderer, you sneaky asshole." My anger gave me the fuel to drag myself toward him. I slowly came closer, but I saw him as though through smudged glass. His eyes were closed. His curls stuck to his forehead, and his lips moved drowsily. I nearly collapsed on top of him. With hands that didn't work quite right, I finally rolled him onto his back. "Where have you been? I have all the Gjallarhorn gold. You have to tell me where the big piece is." I looked at his pale face. "Have you been attacked?" I whispered and tried to hold him, but my fingers were still numb and looked like cramped, blue-tinged claws. I steered my hand toward his cheek but couldn't feel it touching him. But his eyes flew open with a startled gasp since I must have been ice-cold.

"Is it over?" Elias's pupils were almost as wide as his irises, and he blinked to focus. He couldn't even lift his head, and he looked at me through narrow slits.

I rested my forearms on his chest. "Did you know what Od had planned for the party?"

Elias's forehead beaded with sweat. "I couldn't watch." He squeezed his eyes shut. "I couldn't."

Only now did I notice the empty ampoule and syringe that lay on the floor.

"God damn it." I pounded at his chest, but since my hands weren't working, I produced only a floppy slap.

He briefly opened his eyes but slipped back into semiconsciousness and whispered: "You're a hallucination. A nice one, yes, but a mirage nonetheless."

"I'm not a hallucination." The room spun, and I looked at my nails, which were now blue-black. Small needles prickled at my wrists, but from my knuckles down, it was like I didn't exist. "I think I'm losing my hands." I shook him helplessly.

He opened an eye, but it was hard for him to control it, and it rolled around. "You're still here, you beautiful delusion. Or is that you, Loki, torturing me? Have you taken on her form?"

"I'm not . . ." The prickling sensation had reached my lips, and it felt like my whole mouth was a big hole. I thought of Védis's exposed teeth, where her skin was burned away. "Elias," I begged. "Wake up."

Elias squinted at me and furrowed his brows in what felt like slow motion. I wasn't sure if it was because he was high or because I was about to pass out.

Frantically, I searched for the leather pouch around his neck. My fingers were stiff and useless as I struggled to open the pouch. When I finally succeeded, I discovered that it was empty. *Shit!* Maybe he still wasn't done making the laekna.

"Elias," I pleaded, and he opened his eyes again.

"Your nose is blue." His voice trailed off in a slurred sigh.

Fortunately, Elias's sharp logic was still functioning through his drug-induced haze. I raised my black fingers toward him. The skin that wasn't ink-colored resembled sallow wax. Elias studied my hands. Carefully, he brushed his fingers over them. The furrow between his brows grew deeper, and he lifted his upper body minimally off the floor.

"You're cold."

"Frost storm," I stammered.

His head drooped, but he forced himself not to doze off again. "Shit!" he exclaimed, slowly rising to his feet.

As he moved, I rolled onto my stomach on the floor, from where I could see only Elias's bare feet. He lurched over to the cabinet in the corner of the room and opened it. Bottles, powders, and dried herbs hit the floor, and shards flew everywhere. He stepped on them, and soon, the floor was covered in a paste of blood and medicine. He cursed as he rummaged around inside. Finally, he found what he was looking for and stumbled back to me. He dropped to his knees on the tile floor, but either he was totally numb, or he just ignored the pain of the impact. With difficulty, I turned my head toward him as he squeezed my arm and held two fingers to it.

"Your blood is too cold." He bent over and breathed on my arm. "It's not circulating." Then he nipped at my skin with his teeth. "Finally."

With one hand, he removed the cork from a small bottle. Then he reached for the used syringe. Even though the syringe still contained a little of his blood, he filled it with the transparent potion and carefully placed the needle along my forearm. His hands shook, and he was struggling not to fall over. With great concentration, he pushed the tip into my arm and managed to hit the small vein. I couldn't even feel the prick, but an intense wave shot into my body. I had never had such a large dose of laekna before, and I convulsed. My heart was pounding so hard I could feel my pulse in my mouth. The feeling returned to my lips, and they burned intensely as what felt like a wave of lava poured over and through my body. Elias held me up so I wouldn't hit my head on the floor. Then he unwrapped my layers of clothing and rubbed me.

"I'm still freezing," I said through chattering teeth.

Elias held my hands in his and blew hot air on them. Finally, he pulled his shirt off and embraced me.

"What were you doing out at night? It's dangerous." He grabbed a blanket, which he wrapped around the both of us. I clung to him and took in his body heat. He stroked my back with rhythmic motions. His body and touch felt heavenly, and I snuggled up to him.

"Away from the heart, away from the heart," he repeated, moving his hands methodically. My arms wrapped around him, and I looked at my fingers behind his back. The black was receding, leaving them red and swollen. They tingled and throbbed. Gradually, my pulse slowed, and I pressed myself closer to him. Close to sleep, I drooped forward. The only thing holding me up was the blanket Elias had wrapped tightly around us.

"What are you doing here?" His voice sounded like it came through several layers of glass, and I felt like I was sinking deeper and deeper into a warm, pleasant mud puddle.

I didn't have the wherewithal to answer him and sank even further down.

"Did something happen?"

My cheek slid across his burning hot skin.

"Anna?"

But I couldn't respond, and like this, with my face resting against Elias's bare chest, I fell asleep.

CHAPTER 30

Screeching animals, shouting people, and the sound of sharp weapons cutting through flesh and bone reached me before the vision did. At first, it was completely dark, but I could hear everything.

Luna called: "Anna, help me."

Monster growled and tore into a body. Ice crackled, water splashed, the Midgard Serpent hissed loudly, and the people around me let out heartrending wails. Fenrir barked and gnawed on bones.

I opened my eyes, but I was in the middle of a cloud, so the fighting was still concealed. I stumbled around in the fog, unable to find any familiar faces. I tripped over someone on the ground but spared myself from looking to see who it was.

"Ragnarök is becoming more real," sang the disembodied woman's voice around me. "Look, völva."

"Hejd?"

Hejd didn't answer, and suddenly, I was gripped with doubt. All strength left me, and I stood with my arms at my sides.

"I did something yesterday," I said. "Or I stopped something from happening. I'm scared that I've condemned a bunch of people to death."

"I know," the disembodied voice sighed. "I was almost certain you would prevent the only sacrifice that could have delayed Ragnarök. The future showed your possible sacrifice of the queen, but I wasn't sure you would do it."

"You knew all along? Why didn't you tell me?"

An airy laughter crept around me, along with the fog and the myriad screams from the battlefield. "Only now do I see everything clearly. Only now do I understand the big picture."

"Is there even a big picture?" I looked around in the inferno. "It all feels so chaotic."

"There can be context in chaos."

Apologies and regrets sat on the tip of my tongue, but I clenched my fists. "I refuse to be sorry. I'm not going to say Ingeborg should have been sacrificed. It's wrong to kill an innocent person, even if it could save everyone."

In the burnt-smelling fog, someone screamed in fear.

"You may have condemned your loved ones with your actions." Hejd's voice was like a hand stroking my cheek.

"I know." My legs gave out beneath me, and I sat in a gust of acrid smoke. The ground below me was cold and wet, soaking through my clothes. A body lay next to me, but I didn't turn my head to see who it was. "I hope there's another way."

The smog let up slightly, and Loki, in half-naked and enormous form, came into view, his footsteps so violent that the ground shook. He held the burning Tilarids raised over his head. Before him, Od stood expectantly. I felt the unseen woman, presumably Hejd in some form, flutter away.

Od knelt and exposed his neck. Loki raised Tilarids. I closed my eyes and covered my ears as he let it fall. The head hit the ground with a loud thump and rolled in my direction. The rolling sound came closer, and I felt a bump as it hit my leg. I sat cross-legged with my arms over my own head.

Footsteps gradually came closer. The moist earth gave in beneath me. The rumblings carried up through my body. I felt the heat of fire and bodies, and I smelled sulfur and burnt hair.

I didn't lower my hands. "Tilarids?"

The sword laughed in response. *Thank you for putting me in giants' hands again.*

"Völva," said another voice, whom I could easily identify. Loki said only that one word, but it sent shivers through me. His voice was deep and beguiling with a hint of humor.

"Yes," I replied meekly.

A large hand stroked my hair and neck and followed the curve of my back. I sat nailed to the ground in fear, while at the same time, it calmed my tense body. I lowered my arms but kept my eyes closed.

"Is now when the world ends?" I asked. "Is this the apocalypse?"

"You humans." Loki laughed in his strangely alluring way. "You think of everything as having a start and a finish. Birth and death. Beginning and end. Creation and destruction."

"Everything is created and then dies. That's the only thing we can be sure of," I argued. "It's part of the contract. If you want to live, you have to accept that you will also die someday."

Now the fingers moved to my face, and they gently caressed my eyelids, my cheekbones, and the bridge of my nose. "I understand that gods and humans see it that way. You're limited by your one life. But you're wrong."

"How so?" I asked.

In a fleeting movement, Loki planted his scalding hot lips on my mouth. The kiss was unexpectedly soft and tasted of fresh spring water and salt of the earth. I heard raindrops falling, wind blowing, waves crashing. Birds sang and a cat purred incessantly. Loki took his lips away. "Everything goes in circles," he whispered.

I woke with a start, like I had fallen from a great height. It was light out, or at least, as light as it would get beneath the gray clouds. I lay in a soft bed, weighed down by a duvet that smelled like lavender and clean cotton. I was warm and relaxed, and when I checked, my hands thankfully looked normal. Someone had their arm around my waist. I rolled over.

Elias slept next to me. With his wild curls in a crown around his young face, he looked like an angel. His spicy scent enveloped me.

He mumbled something in his sleep and pulled me closer. In a natural motion, he kissed my neck, and though a pleasant shiver ran through my body, I pushed him gently away. He was half awake, but his eyes were closed, and his voice was soft, as though he still had one foot in the dream world.

"Stay in my arms." He opened his blue-gray eyes and looked at me with a hazy tenderness. "You're so lovely."

"Elias," I said quietly and pulled away slightly. "I think you're dreaming."

Clarity seeped into Elias's eyes. He loosened his grip but kept his arm around me as he blinked a couple of times. "Anna?"

"It's me."

"I was centuries away." He ran a hand over his face and let go of me in the same motion.

"I figured."

Elias was more awake, and he begrudgingly moved away from me.

"I'm assuming we're both naked because you had to warm me up with your body?" I raised one eyebrow.

"Of course that's why." Elias smiled smoothly. He grew serious when I still looked at him uncomfortably. "I would never take advantage of you in a defenseless state. Besides, that wouldn't be very fun for either of us. Let me see your fingers." With a professional look on his face, he took my hands and turned them this way and that. "You won't have any lasting damage."

"Thank you for helping me."

"Dare I ask why you showed up at my home all dolled up, albeit a little blue around the nose?"

"I'm pissed at you!"

He yawned. "Again?"

"You knew what you were doing when you killed me." I stared at him.

His yawn turned into a resigned sigh. "I had no choice."

"You could have refused."

"Then I would have been killed. In a situation where your life is in danger—"

"Accept any help you can get and consider the consequences later. I know that's your motto." I had practiced it myself, but there was no reason to admit that.

"Everyone wanted you dead. You would have been killed sooner or later anyway. I was the only one capable of bringing you back to life. If you look at it that way, I did you a favor."

"And started Fimbulwinter with the same blow! Do you realize how many people are suffering and dying because of you?"

"People are suffering and dying because of the gods, Anna. Not because of me."

I struggled to come up with a counterargument, so I simply furrowed my brows. "Aside from the fact that I'm mad at you for killing me and setting off an extreme winter, I actually have good news."

Smiling, he leaned forward slightly, but I placed my hand flat on his bare chest.

"Not that kind of good news."

The smile faded from his lips. Then he got out of bed and found his clothes. He pulled his shirt over his head. "Meet me in the living room when you're ready. I'm eager to hear what you have to say." He disappeared through the door, and the room suddenly felt much colder.

I had no choice but to put my party dress back on, and I padded downstairs in my socks. In the living room, I found Elias bent over the mess on the floor. He was almost done sweeping glass and powder into a dustpan. When he saw me, he leaned against the broom.

"Are you hungry?"

"Starving. Do you have food?"

Elias shook his head. "I only have the medicines I managed to steal. A little laekna and klinte, although I used a large dose of it on you last night."

I couldn't help but think of the delicacies on the banquet table at The Boatman, which I never had a chance to taste. I hoped the other guests had gotten to eat, despite everything that happened.

"What happened at the party?"

I told him, but I couldn't meet his gaze as I spoke. "I may have condemned all of humanity," I concluded. "Leave it to me to wipe everyone out."

To my surprise, Elias smiled.

"I thought you would totally freak out. You're so intent on surviving, you know," I said.

"I am very much opposed to human sacrifices."

"But Ingeborg's death could have saved us."

"The survival of humankind isn't worth sacrificing an innocent person." A memory shot out of Elias that was so powerful he couldn't hide it. There were flames, and a woman on top of a large bonfire. She screamed in terror. I took a deep breath and tasted the smoke from Elias's past. Elias opened his eyes wide when he realized I was having a vision, but he didn't ask what I saw.

"Humans have always done that, haven't they?" I asked quietly.

He turned his face toward the final shards of glass, probably to avoid my gaze. He swept them into the dustpan. "What's done is done." He picked the syringe up off the floor. It was the only thing he hadn't swept up yet. At the bottom of it was a reddish-brown residue.

"Your blood mixed with mine last night."

"Not that it matters if we're all gonna die from starvation or during Ragnarök anyway."

"We're bound together from now on." It was impossible to tell if he was joking. "Mixing blood is an old ritual, and there's a lot of power in it. Loki and Odin are blood brothers; it's brought them both big problems but also many victories over time."

"I thought they were enemies."

Elias bobbed his head and tossed the syringe and needle into the dustpan. "They're both. Loki is always welcome in Valhalla, regardless of how angry Odin is at him. I hope it can be like that for the two of us." He stood for a moment and looked at me, and I looked back at him.

"I have all of it now. All the Gjallarhorn gold."

At first, Elias simply stared at me, uncomprehending, then his eyes grew wide. "You did it. Anna! You did it!" In one long stride, he came over and embraced me warmly. "Can I see it?"

I picked Vinr up from the floor, where I had dropped it the night before.

Elias studied it with reverence. "Luna?"

"She didn't have to be so thorough. But it's just so beautiful. I've named it Vinr."

On the staff, Elias had found a carved figure in conversation with a wooden version of me. It was a man with unruly curls and a cheeky smile, and his hand was on my shoulder. It wasn't entirely clear if the man was grinning at me or the viewer. Elias's fingertips found the spot where we were joined together. "Vinr is a magnificent völva staff." He spotted a detail at the bottom. It was one of the things I liked best about the staff. "Luna carved a little gripping beast down here."

I nodded, and warmth flowed into my chest at the thought that Luna knew me so well. Elias traced a finger over the goofy, apelike creature.

"You have an affinity for gripping beasts?"

I looked at it, too.

"It was something Rebecca said once. They symbolize the complex human."

Elias's large curls stood out in a cloud around his face, and he brushed them away from his forehead. "What do you like about the complex human?"

"I don't know if I like it, necessarily. Everything would be a lot simpler if we were more black and white. But that's how it is with humans. We're both good and evil, and sometimes we do horrific things."

He looked softly at me. "Sometimes we also do beautiful things."

I unscrewed the top of the staff and fished out the pendant, the curved piece from Mimir's throat, and the little Odion figurine. I set them all on Elias's table. When Elias saw Odion, he took a step back. The figurine trembled slightly, and I felt the anger rising from it.

"I don't know where it's hiding the gold," I said, pointing to Odion. "I've thought about smashing it."

"No!" Elias protested quickly and loudly. He went into the kitchen and fetched a pot holder and a knife. He carefully grabbed Odion and poked him in the chest, where a tiny gold amulet was painted on the porcelain.

Even more rage pulsated from the figurine, but after some effort, Elias pried the little piece of gold free. It wasn't much bigger than the head of a pin.

He hurried to rewrap Odion in the fabric and handed him to me. "What should I do with it?"

"It's up to you. If it were me, I'd burn it. He's horrible. But . . . Eskild stole him from Ben and Rebecca. You should probably give it back."

I stuck the bundle into the top of Vinr and looked at the three unequal pieces of gold that apparently came from the same magic horn.

"So, where's the big piece?"

Elias hesitated. "Can I tell you something else first? I want you to know what to do if I'm not here myself."

This comment sent a chill through my heart, but I nodded.

In wondrous beauty once again
Shall the golden tables stand mid the grass
Which the gods had owned in the days of old

> *Then fields unsown bear ripened fruit*
> *All ills grow better*
> *Baldr and Hoth dwell in Hropt's battle-hall*
> *And the mighty gods*
> *Would you know yet more?*

Elias looked at me as he recited the final verse. I had to take a second to recover as the prophecy echoed. As always, it was Hejd's voice that shouted *Would you know yet more?* Almost as if to say: *Don't you get it by now?*

"I've asked Hejd about that verse," I said. "She thinks it's good for the world to end."

Elias turned the curved piece of gold between his fingers. "It's not really my place to decide what's good for the world. I just want to make sure there's a plan in case . . ."

I smiled warmly. "Oh, Elias."

He had never before been on the receiving end of such a smile from me, and his cheeks took on a subtle glow. "What?"

"The rest of us are all running around thinking about the end of the world. You're the only one who's considered what will happen afterward."

"I want to show you something," Elias said. "Put your boots on."

"Are we going outside?"

"No."

Puzzled, I stood up, and Elias led me into the back room. His was an old house designed with many small rooms. I had never been in this one, but something told me it was the formal sitting room. A sofa with fine silk upholstery sat along one side, portraits and landscape paintings hung on the walls, and a thick carpet lay on the floor. It was like stepping into a different era, but that was often the case with Elias, who floated between centuries with equal parts effortlessness and melancholy. He pulled the sofa to one side and kicked the carpet away.

"Oh, what a surprise. I've *never* seen a trapdoor hidden in a floor before." I rolled my eyes demonstratively. "It's not like my dad is constantly stomping up and down the stairs to the crypt under my bench."

Elias looked at me over his shoulder. "Who do you think gave him the idea?" He grabbed an oil lamp from a nearby table and lit it. Cautiously, he let the ornamented grille and glass tube slide into place over the flame. He took a couple of steps down an unseen ramp and held his hand out behind him. I took it.

An unexpectedly wide passageway extended downward. There were no stairs, but the ramp formed a spiral shaped like a snail shell, like the one in his observatory. The difference was that this one led underground while the other rose toward the stars.

"Okay, I didn't see this coming," I mumbled.

"I have a lot more beneath the surface than above it," Elias replied, squeezing my hand.

"You're a real iceberg."

He pulled me down the passageway, and the door clicked into place above us. We followed the corridor down for some time before it stopped in front of a heavy metal door.

Is the Gjallarhorn down here? Did he really hide it in such a predictable place? Sometimes, the most obvious hiding places were the best.

Elias placed the oil lamp in a niche in the wall. On the door, there were deep furrows with transparent wires that were not illuminated for the time being. I looked up at the passageway's ceiling, a layer of daubed clay pierced in several places by what appeared to be brown cables.

"What are those?"

Elias looked up. "Tree roots. They're encroaching on my territory. I'm in an eternal battle with them for the right to the underground." He pressed some symbols on a luminous panel in the metal door. With each selection, a low beep was emitted. I looked closely at the device, which stood in sharp contrast to the rustic corridor. When Elias finished putting in the code, the wires lit up to reveal a meticulous glowing design of serpent knots and runes.

"Is it magic?" I took a step backward, half expecting the whole thing to explode in a ball of blue energy.

"It's just for decoration."

"It looks like a spaceship."

The door swung open with a groan. We were immediately met with humidity. The echo of our footsteps gave me the sense that we were in a great hall, though I couldn't see it. Elias flicked a switch, and row after row of fluorescent lights turned on with a hum that grew deeper as it moved through the room. They cast a cold, white light over us.

We appeared to be in a high-tech nursery with no windows or plants. The grow boxes stood open, full of black soil. I noticed a carving on a plaque high up on the wall. It depicted an atom or a solar system, perhaps. A spotlight shone directly on the carving and gave it a supernatural appearance.

"Is this some kind of church?" I asked and walked tentatively through the hall.

"One might call it my cathedral. You should see the inner sanctum." He walked ahead of me with long strides.

We reached another decorated metal door, from which cold wafted toward us. The door was covered in frost, but beneath the rime were dots of light that looked like constellations. Elias pulled on a glove and entered another code, after which the door made a deep *pop*. Vapor seeped out along the edges. He took a couple of jackets from a hook and wrapped one around me. The thick acrylic fabric crackled, and bewildered, I zipped up the heavy-duty zipper.

"You'd better put the hood up." Elias had also pulled a jacket on and looked like an Arctic researcher in the field. I didn't want to think about how I must look in my ball gown, combat boots, and down jacket.

I pulled the hood up and stuffed my red hair inside. Elias gave me some thick gloves, which I put on. Then he grabbed my hand again and pulled me into the frigid room.

At first, I couldn't see anything because of the fog, but the room was completely white and freezing cold. There were crackling and creaking noises around me, and I could make out tall, dark silhouettes in the mist. Something about it reminded me of my recurring vision of Ragnarök.

"What is this place?" I whispered.

"It's a bank. Or a vault, I should say. It's pressure- and water-tight and fireproof. On top of the aluminum, which protects against radiation, a thick layer of concrete is kept at a constant temperature of -0.4 degrees."

My lungs froze every time I inhaled. The feeling was the same as when I'd died. I looked at the row after row of shelves that stretched several yards above my head. I walked up to a shelf covered in ice crystals. With my gloved hand, I brushed the frost off a Styrofoam box.

"What's in here?"

"The future."

I wiped more frost away and leaned closer to read the label on the side of the box. My lips silently formed the words. "What is *hordeum vulgare?*" My thoughts flitted between everything from animals in suspended animation to artificial intelligence that would take over the world when we were gone.

"Six-row barley."

"What?"

"It's one of the oldest varieties of grain in Denmark. It dates back to the Iron Age."

I turned toward him. Because the jacket was so big and heavy, my movements were clumsy. The cold robbed my fingers of feeling. Inhibited by the hood, I leaned my head back and looked up. The shelves were packed with Styrofoam boxes.

"Is it all grain?"

"It's taken me hundreds of years to collect them. They remain in a state of stasis as long as it's cold enough. You have no idea how hard it was to keep the temperature down before electricity." He opened a box, pulled out a small brown grain, and laid it in his gloved palm. "It's sleeping now." He whispered as if not to wake the seed. "If I take it outside, it'll sprout. Well, it won't now because it's so cold, but that's because of the temperature fluctuations. I've tried everything, but we need sun, water, and heat for it to grow."

The box creaked as Elias pushed the lid aside. It was full of grains. I eyed them hungrily.

"Does the DSMA know you have all this hidden down here?"

Elias raised his head. "You can't tell anyone. If word gets out that I have a stash of grain, people will eat it all. Humans are notoriously bad at long-term planning."

"On top of that, I think the punishment for hiding food is very harsh."

He carefully replaced the seed. "They'll sprout when the temperature rises again, and I'm becoming more and more certain that that won't happen until after Ragnarök."

We resurfaced in the sitting room, which felt warm after our trip to the basement.

"We'll get the Gjallarhorn now. It'll be exciting if we can get it up."

I pulled my boots up. "Up from what?"

Elias looked mysteriously at me. "Wait and see."

My stomach leapt. Soon, I would have all the gold for Heimdall's horn. Then it would just be a matter of finding Ulfberht so the horn could be forged.

"I'm going out to start the car," Elias called from the hallway.

"I'll be there in two seconds." I gathered the gold from the table and tucked it back into Vinr's cavity.

Elias walked outside, and I heard a car door slam.

Optimistic and excited, I wrapped my scarf an extra time around my neck.

Elias shouted something from the driveway.

"What did you say?" I picked up my mother's coat. The lining was now so worn that there was a rip in the armpit, and I accidentally stuck my arm in the wrong hole and got stuck between the layers of fabric.

Elias shouted again.

"I can't hear you." I laughed. "And I've actually gotten myself in a bit of a situation in here. Can you come help me?"

There was no reply.

"Elias!" I kept fighting with the coat and finally managed to get it on properly. With Vinr in hand, I walked to the front door and opened it.

The wind was blowing, and the driveway was devoid of people and cars.

"Elias?" I stepped cautiously down the stairs I had slipped on the day before.

Tire marks led away from me through the snow and out of Elias's driveway. Elias himself was nowhere to be seen. I spun around.

"Hey. Where—" I stopped as my extrasensory perception confirmed no one was there but me.

Elias was gone, and he was the only one who knew where the last piece of the Gjallarhorn was.

PART IV

Remember, Odin, in olden days
That we both our blood have mixed;
Then didst thou promise no ale to pour,
Unless it were brought for us both

Lokasenna,
10th century

CHAPTER 31

My dress was torn, and I was gasping for breath when I arrived at Odinmont. I had a stitch in my side from running the many miles from Elias's house, but I had pushed myself onward with a combination of the strength of the völvas in Vinr and pure willpower. Arthur came running out the front door.

"Anna!" His voice was hysterical. "I searched for you all night. You disappeared from The Boatman, and then a frost storm hit." He touched my arm, but I knocked his hand away, my anger almost uncontrollable at this point.

"Don't come near me."

Rebecca showed up behind him. Neither she nor Arthur appeared to have slept the night before. "I'm so relieved to see you, you—" She stopped when she saw the look on my face. I aimed an accusatory finger toward them.

"You were ready to sacrifice an innocent person."

Rebecca took a step back, but Arthur frowned angrily. "It's better if one person dies so the majority can survive."

"It's wrong to kill someone that way."

Arthur raised an eyebrow. "So, you think there's a right way? You're Odin's völva. You're his raven. What did you expect?"

"I don't want to perform hangadrott."

"Then you're a coward." My father continued mercilessly. "Now everyone's going to die because you were squeamish. It's awful to be the executioner—I know that better than anyone—but someone has to take that responsibility."

"We were trying to save the people," Rebecca explained. "Ingeborg consented. If I were a royal, I would have done it, too."

Arthur arranged his face into a softer expression. "I actually did that when I died. I gave my life for my family. You did it last year when you asked Elias to kill you. It's hardwired into people, this willingness to sacrifice themselves for others."

"Why should it be that way? In nature, there's no connection between self-sacrifice and reward." I knew from the giants that they couldn't care less about this kind of thing. The sun could shine on the worst criminal while the rain beat down on a saint.

"Those are the rules," Rebecca said. "A gift will always be reciprocated. The injustice of the giants was done away with. The greater the sacrifice, the bigger the gift."

"Who made these rules?"

Rebecca furrowed her brows. "The gods, of course."

I was still out of breath. "If that's how the gods have made the rules, I don't want to play."

Arthur's red hair stuck out in all directions as he raked his fingers through it. "What do you want to do?"

I looked coldly at him. "I'm going to change the game."

"Anna is right."

We all looked up. For a moment, hearing the deep and firm voice, I thought Ben was standing with us. But then I realized Luna had joined our conversation. Her eyes shone darkly.

"The rules of the game must be changed." She reached out her arm and pointed at Odinmont. "Go inside, all of you. There's no time to fight among ourselves."

We trudged inside like chastened children as Luna stood authoritatively in the doorway.

"Get Mimir," she ordered. Arthur, stunned by her sudden authority, obeyed. Soon, we all sat around the table at Odinmont. Luna and Rebecca on one side, Arthur and me on the other, while Mimir's head sat at one end. He had become quite handsome over the past few days, now that his maggot-infested wounds had healed and the boils were finally gone.

"Speak!" Luna commanded and looked at me. I looked at her, dismayed.

"Elias hid the fourth piece of Gjallarhorn gold. I thought he was going to give it to me yesterday."

Arthur's eyes grew wide. "The Gjallarhorn? What have you gone and done now?"

I pursed my lips. "While you were busy appeasing the gods with human sacrifices, I was trying to find a loophole in their rules."

"Tell me what you did." My father was still staring at me.

I rubbed my eyes. "I'm assuming you know the Gjallarhorn was divided in the 1800s."

Rebecca nodded sadly, and Arthur continued to stare at me in disbelief. Luna stood up from the table and paced around the room.

"I've collected three of the pieces. Freyja's tears, Odion's amulet, and the piece in Mimir's throat."

Mimir cleared his throat as Arthur, Rebecca, and Luna looked at him.

"It was really nice to get that out of there," he said timidly.

"YOU STOLE FROM ODIN?" Luna shouted. "It's bad enough that you took Mimir, but the Gjallarhorn gold, too?"

"You know that I did." I was disappointed she didn't have my back. It felt like she was teaming up with Arthur and Rebecca. "Elias was going to find the last piece, but he's gone."

Luna was hopping mad and Arthur still sat frozen, but Rebecca was shockingly calm. "How typical of Elias not to give you the gold. Even if it could save humanity."

"Elias did want to help. He's been preparing for this for centuries. If I don't succeed, he has a plan. Or at least . . ." I looked down at the table. "He did."

"Where is Elias Eriksen now?" Mimir wrinkled his nose, and I scratched it. It felt like the severed head was the only one on my side. I scooted my chair demonstratively closer to him.

"Elias went out to his driveway this morning, and when I got there, he was gone."

Arthur's look turned sharp, but he didn't comment on the fact that I had spent the night at Elias's place. *Fine!* Let him believe the worst.

"He fled," Luna growled. "When we need him most, he runs off to seek shelter."

"I don't think he disappeared on purpose," I said. "There was an impression in the past out there. Someone had tried to conceal it, but I sensed a struggle. I think he was kidnapped, or worst case . . ." It was impossible to finish the sentence, and I couldn't shake the feeling that Elias had feared this might happen. That was why he had shown me the grain stored in his basement. I pushed my concerns aside. "There's no time to look for him. We have to find the last piece of gold and reassemble the Gjallarhorn so it can be destroyed. That's the only way we can prevent Ragnarök."

"How do we destroy the Gjallarhorn? It's magical gold—it's not like we can just smash it." Luna rested her elbow heavily on the table as though she had suddenly been struck by a wave of tiredness.

"We have to find an Ulfberht smith, but I haven't gotten that far yet. I think we need to secure the gold first so no one else can get ahold of it."

When I said *Ulfberht smith*, Rebecca raised her head.

"How much time do we really have? I know that Ragnarök is coming soon, but over time, I've learned that *soon* is a broad concept." I studied her suspiciously.

"Margit said she's looking into it," Rebecca said.

"Our history teacher? You know her?"

"She's also active in Norse Pagan circles. She's Jytte's sister, friends with Brenda. The three of them are a tight-knit group. The last time I saw her, she said she was working with the historical sources and was on the brink of discovering something big."

I had already managed to assault both Brenda and Jytte, so Margit probably didn't have a great opinion of me.

"Could you come with me to ask her?" I couldn't meet Rebecca's gaze. "She probably won't listen to me."

Rebecca looked out through the glass door over the flat, white landscape. "Margit won't listen to anyone. After she made some discovery, she barricaded herself inside her apartment. She won't let anyone in. Not even Jytte."

I cursed quietly.

"Do you have even a vague idea of where the Gjallarhorn gold is hidden?" Arthur asked.

"I'm pretty sure the answer is in here." I tapped my temple. "Hejd said so, too."

> *She knows of the horn of Heimdall*
> *Under the high-reaching holy tree*
> *On it there pours from Valfather's pledge*
> *A mighty stream*
> *Would you know yet more?*

"Elias said we would have to get it up from somewhere."

"Up from the ground or a cellar?" Rebecca wondered.

"A mighty stream," Arthur said. "It's a wet place."

"The sea?" Luna asked.

I wrinkled my nose. "Maybe." Seagulls shrieked in the vision I had seen of Hejd's burial on the coast. But her grave didn't even exist after the churchyard had fallen into the water. If Elias hid it in the sea, I was screwed because the wall of ice had come all the way up to the coast. I had no way to get under the tons of ice.

"Elias must have hidden the piece after 1802 because, until then, the golden horns were intact." I looked at Arthur. "You knew him back then."

Arthur rolled his eyes at me. "I'm not *that* old. I was born in 1840."

"That means no one here knew Elias when he hid the gold."

Luna had closed her eyes and leaned over the table. In front of her, a glass trembled on a plate. She rocked gently.

"Luna," I said. "Are you okay?"

"Elias said," she mumbled in a deep voice, as though in a trance, "that only a single sacrifice had been useful. Just one during his long life."

Rebecca stood and grabbed Luna's shoulders. "What's wrong with you?"

Luna opened her eyes and blinked a couple of times. "Oh," she said in her normal voice. "I guess I dozed off for a second. Why . . . why are you all looking at me like that?"

"When did you talk to Elias?" I asked.

Luna pulled gently on her upper lip. "I've never been alone with him."

"You just said—"

"Hey, babe," Luna interrupted.

We looked to the doorway, where Mathias had appeared. Even though snow was once again drifting down, he wore only a yellow T-shirt. Luna got up and ran over to him. Unconcerned with the rest of us, she kissed him passionately and clutched his shirt. With a sigh of pleasure, she laid her cheek against his chest. Suddenly, she made a strange noise that sounded like a guttural, rumbling belch.

"Are you okay?" Mathias stroked her hair.

She made the sound again and moved away from him.

"What's wrong?" Mathias took a step forward, but she held a hand in front of her eyes and made another retching noise.

"Luna," I said desperately. "What is it? You're acting really strange."

She turned her back to us and inhaled deeply. "Mathias," she said in a controlled voice, as if to keep her stomach contents down. "Please put a different shirt on."

"A different shirt?" he said, confused, and brushed his palm across his chest.

"Arthur's shirt is hanging in the hall."

"Why?" Mathias began, but I made an irritated, flapping hand motion in his direction.

"Just do as she says."

When Mathias left the room, Luna blew out a long exhalation of air.

"Is it his divinity?" I asked.

"I don't know. Suddenly he just gave me the worst nausea. I couldn't stand to look at him." She looked nervously at us. "Is that a bad sign?"

"You shouldn't ask me for relationship advice," I said, glad for once to have been unlucky in the love department. It couldn't possibly be good to react that way to the guy who was supposed to be the man in your life, but I didn't want to be the one to point that out. Mathias came back in, dressed in Arthur's white button-down shirt.

Luna beamed. "You don't make me nauseous anymore." She pinched a couple of flecks of dust off the shirt, then gave him a friendly pat on the shoulder.

He stared at her. "Seriously?"

"Can you make me invisible?"

Luna pulled her green shawl tight around herself. "What?"

"I need to sneak into someone's place," I admitted.

Mathias, Rebecca, Mimir, and my dad sat at the table talking while I caught Luna in the kitchen pouring herself a third glass of water.

"Isn't it easier to wait until the people aren't home?"

"Aren't you going to scold me for wanting to do something illegal?"

"I'm assuming you have a good reason," she said with a sensible expression.

"Your mom said Margit hasn't left her apartment in several days."

"You want to break into Margit's apartment?" Luna set her water glass on the kitchen table with a bang.

"Shhh. We have to find out what she's discovered. Maybe it could jog my memory. Don't you have a spell or a potion or something?"

Luna held her hand out toward me. "Come."

"What?"

"I have an easier solution." She wrapped the green shawl around her head and nudged me out the front door.

"What are you guys doing?" Mathias shouted from the living room.

"We're just going . . . into town . . ." Luna mumbled the last bit.

"Do you want me to carry you?"

"No!" Luna and I said over one another.

"I want to get some fresh air," Luna said clearly. "Anna has Vinr, and I'll cast heat magic if a frost storm hits. We won't be long."

We hurried out before Mathias could protest. In the driveway, we hopped onto our bikes. Luna was out of breath before we even reached the main road.

"There must be something wrong with the chain," she complained. "Or maybe the tires need air."

"There is a strong head wind." I had to stand up on the pedals as we swung onto Kraghede Road, but I could thank my physical fitness for the fact that I wasn't panting as hard as Luna.

We reached the town and rode down Algade toward Ravensted's largest housing complex. The light was on in Margit's window when we parked our bikes. Luna pushed the building's door open, and even in the stairwell, I could already feel Margit's agitated aura fluttering. I stared at my friend as she walked determinedly up the stairs.

"Are you going to attack her?" I asked. Although Luna had become somewhat more brusque since her father's death, the thought of her being violent clashed with every image I had of her.

Luna looked over her shoulder in a cloud of brown curls. It was so unfair that her hair still looked healthy while everyone else's had gone limp.

"There are other ways of getting in, Anna." She knocked on Margit's door.

No one opened it, but we heard persistent, desperate meowing from inside.

"The giants are coming, the giants are coming . . ." Margit's voice was muffled by the door, but the words were unmistakable.

Luna knocked again.

"No, noooo! Spare me. I don't want to be sacrificed."

Meeoooww. Meooowww.

"Cat food." Luna had knelt down and opened the mail slot. "I have cat food."

We heard footsteps and a jangling noise. The door opened a crack, and our former history teacher stuck her nose out. Through the sliver, I saw she held an orange cat in her arms. When the creature saw Luna, it hissed. Luna held up her empty hands and looked into Margit's eyes through the little crack.

"Look what I have."

She had nothing, but judging from Margit's expression, Luna had hypnotized her to see something.

"Bast is so hungry."

"And here's a whole bag of kitty kibble. If you open the door, your sweet cat can have it all."

Bast put his ears back. A deep, threatening sound came from deep in his stomach. Luna might be able to enchant Margit, but Bast didn't buy it for a second. Margit still looked hesitant.

"Opna dyrnar. Ég segi opna dyrnar." A golden flash came from Luna's eyes.

The door swung shut, and we heard a metallic rattling on the other side.

"Open sesame," Luna said with a devious grin.

Margit opened the door with a blank expression. When it stood wide open, Bast leapt out of her arms and ran into the living room with a shrill whine. When Margit saw me there, she held her hand up. It looked strenuous, as though Margit were moving through water.

"She can't eat Bast." Her gray hair escaped from her limp bun.

"No one is going to eat your cat." Luna flashed Margit a beaming white smile. She rummaged around in her pocket and pulled out an empty cotton pouch. "If you have hot water, I have some apple leaves. We can have a cup of tea and talk for a while. I have sugar, too." Luna put her arm around Margit's shoulder and turned her around. She led them both to Margit's living room, from which we once again heard a desperate caterwauling.

"Luna." I stuck my head into the living room. "Isn't this a little . . ."

"I'm making her a cup of tea with sugar. And you wanted in."

Margit now sat like a statue on the sofa. She didn't even hear us. I glanced at Luna's empty pouch.

The cat cowered in a corner and looked pleadingly at me. When Luna focused on the creature, it spat and hissed and disappeared under a chest of drawers. It stuck its head out, eyes wild.

"I won't hurt you," I promised, but it still looked skeptically at me.

Luna went into the kitchen, where she clattered cups and chatted loudly with Margit. I crept into the office, but I didn't know what I was looking for. The shelves were overflowing with books. *Saxo Grammaticus*, *The Little Book of Bog Bodies*, and *Historic Battlefields*. I moved to the desk and leafed through the piles of paper. Fortunately, Margit didn't seem to have joined the digital age, but at the same time, it was an overwhelming task to look for an unknown needle in a haystack.

A sheet of paper was folded up and tucked into an edition of the *Prose Edda*. I would have left it alone, but an agitated energy hit my fingers when I touched it. Margit had been excited about something when she last handled it, so I stuck it in my pocket.

I returned to the living room, where Luna sat on the sofa talking to Margit, who was leaning back against the cushions with a blank expression. On the table sat two empty cups. I made a face to let Luna know I was done.

When I reached the front door, I heard a snap behind me. "Thank you so much for the chat," Luna said. "I'm relieved that you're in good spirits."

"I'm in good spirits?" Margit mumbled.

"You're very happy that everything will be fine. You're going to stop isolating yourself. In no time, you'll be back at the high school."

"I am glad, actually." Margit already sounded more upbeat.

"There's a bag of apple leaves in the kitchen." Luna's voice came closer, and I hurried out the door. "And some sugar." Luna slipped out and closed the door behind her. "Did you get what you were looking for?" Luna asked me.

I stared at my friend, who, until ten minutes ago, I couldn't imagine forcing her way into a private home with the help of magic. "I think so."

Back at the dining table in Odinmont, I unfolded Margit's paper. It took a few strokes of my hand to smooth it out enough to even see Margit's notes. Then it took even more time to decipher her handwriting.

536 – Volcanic eruption sent ash up into the atmosphere, blocking the sun. It was cold that summer, which resulted in famine.

That was so long ago, I couldn't see what it had to do with anything. Not even Od had been born yet. I kept reading.

Middle of 9th century – Total lunar eclipse. People thought the moon was being swallowed. They threw spears at the sky to chase the monster away.

1816 – Less sunlight, colder weather, and lower harvest yields.

I paused to think. That was the year the myling was sacrificed in the bog.

The sheet was full of dates and lists of floods, volcanic eruptions, and epidemics, the last one quite recent.

1997 – Warnings that a comet was headed directly toward earth. New converts killed and . . .

And then there was nothing more on the paper. I turned it over a couple of times to see if I had missed something on the back, but the graph paper was blank. It seemed that Margit had quickly scribbled it down. The line with the volcanic eruption in 536 was circled in red, but there was no explanation for why that event was emphasized over the others.

I sat for a moment and stared into space. Then I put my hands on the table and stood up. The bench had been pushed over the hatch in the floor since my dad was at Rebecca's. I pulled it aside.

"Mimir. Are you down there?"

"On the altar."

I headed down the stairs and nearly had to get down on my stomach to crawl into the burial mound. Inside were all the skeletons and the clay pot holding Ben's ashes. Elias's table sat in the corner with the old-fashioned defibrillator, books, and piles of paper on it, and on the stone table in the middle, Mimir rested with the back of his head on my dad's pillow. The blanket hung limply where there should have been a body, but for a moment, I could trick myself into thinking Mimir was a whole person. He looked at me.

"Who would have thought one could enjoy a nap after so many hundreds of years?"

"I didn't know this was an altar." I brushed the stone surface with the palm of my hand.

Mimir leaned to the side, and again, he looked like a real human. "It's older than the gods."

I sat on the table as though sitting at the foot of someone's bed. "Speaking of. I have to ask you something. You're a giant, right? And the giants are older than the gods. When were you born?"

Mimir's eyes looked up at the crypt's stone ceiling. "We didn't keep track of the years back then, but around the year 500."

I waved Margit's paper. "So, you know what happened in 536."

Mimir got a strange look on his face. "What do you know about that year?"

"Not a whole lot." My finger traced Margit's notes. "But it says here it was a cold summer."

Mimir closed his eyes.

"Hey! You look like you don't want to talk." I laughed. My smile faded. "You *really* look like you don't want to talk. What relevant things could have happened over fifteen hundred years ago?"

Mimir cleared his throat. "I was alive back then. I had a body, and Odin was still a human, albeit a very ambitious one. He wanted to become a god."

"Why did the natural disasters start? Were the gods involved?"

"Only the giants have that kind of power. They rule over nature's forces of chaos. Frost and cold are their specialties." Mimir spoke slowly, as if each word caused him pain.

"Were the giants trying to annihilate Odin before he became the supreme god?"

Mimir searched for words. "The opposite. We helped him."

I rubbed my forehead. "You helped Odin by starting a natural disaster?"

"I gave him the idea. Or . . . I gave them both the idea."

"What idea?"

"Odin wanted to be supreme god. Loki had only just come onto the scene. He was called Lúgh back then, but he was weak because all his followers were dead."

"So, Odin and Lúgh teamed up?"

"They swore a blood oath over it. That kind of bond can never be broken, and even though they've been at odds over the years, they are blood brothers. I was their adviser."

"What did you advise them to do, Mimir?"

"Keep in mind that I am a giant. We see things differently." He sighed. "At least, I did back then."

"Mimir!"

"The humans didn't believe in Odin enough. They worshipped Freyja with her life-giving plow, and her brother with the big—"

"Okay!" I held up a hand. "You can skip over the details." I had seen stone carvings of Freyr.

"I suggested that if they frightened the humans enough, they would worship the strongest god. If the gods made them nervous, the humans would make offerings. Odin terrified them with a deadly war against the Vanir, and Loki created a harsh winter."

A chill ran down the back of my neck. "Ohhh . . . ohhh!"

"Loki can start the winter. Odin can stop it when he's strong enough." Suddenly, Mimir wept silently. "I paid for it with my body. The Vanir decapitated me during the war as punishment for my role in it. Odin thought I was so smart that he wanted to keep me. Maybe his plan all along was for me to become helpless so he could keep me forever."

I stroked Mimir's cheek. "It's okay."

"It's *not* okay." Given his short neck stump, Mimir twisted his head away as much as he could. "I had no idea how many hundreds of years of suffering I was setting off. Both my own and the suffering of others. My idea worked perfectly, and Loki and Odin use it whenever Odin is in need."

"So Fimbulwinter has happened several times?"

"Tons. And it will happen again."

"That's why Odin is propelling us toward Ragnarök."

"Odin doesn't want Ragnarök. Not at all. But he can delay the apocalypse when he regains all his strength."

"And how does he regain his strength?"

"Sacrifices. Especially hangatyr, or even better, hangadrott. As an absolute last resort, the child of a god can sacrifice themself."

I closed my eyes. I had seen Od willingly allow Loki to chop his head off. Now it made sense.

"You've played Odin's game perfectly."

My eyes widened. "Me?"

"You started Fimbulwinter with your death and then made sure to cause the death of the only person close to taking him down."

My heart went cold. "Ragnara." That was what she had been trying to do. She wanted to starve Odin and start Ragnarök so he wouldn't have the strength to survive the battle. But she lost focus and became addicted to being worshipped herself, and Eskild was possessed by Tilarids.

"Tilarids is Loki's sword," Mimir said.

"It was smart of him to plant it, so Eskild and Ragnara were led astray." I wanted to yell at Mimir, but I knew I was just as much to blame as he was. Neither of us had known what we were starting. "What happened in 536?" I finally asked.

Mimir was still sniffling, and a book on Elias's table caught my eye. It was a reference book about world history. I stood up and flipped back in time. I found the obscure year that was apparently critical to my own survival.

In 536, an event occurred that has been termed a "climate shock." It was cold in the summer, with a dark, constant cloud cover, weak sunlight, and flooding in normally dry areas. The crops failed, and famine struck. Both in Denmark and elsewhere, large quantities of jewelry, weapons, and even humans were sacrificed during the climate shock of 536. These offerings were intended to bring the sun back. Some believe that the event may have been the inspiration for Norse mythology.

Odin was practically unheard of before the 6th century, but afterward, he became the supreme god. Some historians claim the climate shock of 536 is the origin of the Ragnarök myth, in which the sun and moon are swallowed up, and Fimbulwinter indicates the coming of doomsday. In that case, Fimbulwinter is thought to last for three consecutive winters without a summer in between. Its culmination with Ragnarök comes in mid-September on the autumnal equinox.

Three winters in a row? The autumnal equinox?

Fimbul didn't last three years. Only one year. I thought frantically about what day it actually was. It was September seventeenth.

If this was true, Ragnarök was just around the corner. Unless Odin could stop it, we had only five days before the world ended.

CHAPTER 32

"The giants are coming!" I had run upstairs to get something very important, but I couldn't recall what it was. Amid it all, I collapsed on the edge of my bed. My ears were ringing, and my legs trembled.

"That's what Margit said, too." The voice came from right next to my ear.

"Hakim? Oh! Hakim. I thought you had disappeared into the spirit world." I turned my head. He sat right behind me on the bed. With a sob, I snuggled up to him. At first, he sat stiffly, but then he stroked my back comfortingly.

"There, there. I can't stay away. Especially when you're about to give up. It's going to be okay."

I pulled away from his grasp, which felt strong and almost alive. "How can you say it's going to be okay? The world is about to end. Odin doesn't have enough strength to prevent Ragnarök. I stopped the hangadrott that could have saved us. I can't meet Serén because of my spells, which only Ben could have removed, and he's dead and gone. If I don't get ahold of the Gjallarhorn and destroy it, Od's self-sacrifice is the only option."

Hakim looked sympathetically at me. "Not all the worlds will end during Ragnarök."

"No?"

"What exactly do you think happens?"

"Uhh . . . I actually don't know. In my dreams, there's just a lot of fighting and crazy weather. The giants swoop down on us."

"What are giants?"

"In a way, they're nature. Giants are neither good nor evil. They just *are*. Odin said that once about the Midgard Serpent. Their lineage is so old, good and evil didn't exist when they came into being."

"Good and evil didn't exist when chaos came into being," Hakim said slowly. "Could that mean that gods and humans simply can't understand chaos?"

"I can't speak for other humans, but I understand chaos. I'm drawn to it, in a way."

Hakim lowered his face toward mine. "I don't doubt for a second that the feeling is mutual."

"I have no idea what to do. I don't know where Elias hid the Gjallarhorn gold. Only by destroying it can Ragnarök be averted for good."

Hakim gently pushed me down against the bed. "Right now, you should gather your strength. You can put the time to good use."

"No, no . . ." I tried to fight my way up. "Not now. The end of the world is coming! There's no time to rest."

Hakim pressed me down again. "The end of the world can wait." He looked into my eyes and stroked my cheek, and I relaxed completely. It occurred to me that ghosts could possess people. Maybe that was what Hakim was doing: my arms moved mechanically on their own and wrapped themselves around him.

"Sleep, Anna. Sleep. There's something you should see." In a surreal flicker, I felt him embrace me with his strong arms.

"No!" I mumbled, but my voice lacked force.

The last thing I heard Hakim say was "You need to see something. Then you can make your decision."

I drifted down through a pleasant, warm pool. I saw myself and Hakim from below, but then I was too far away to make out what was happening in my bedroom at Odinmont. I was falling through water, but I could breathe just fine. My hair floated around my head in a red cloud. I saw blue and green, and large black bodies slipped past me, but the water was so murky, I couldn't see them properly. I could hear a prolonged whale song through the waves.

I swam a few strokes. *Serén. Are you here?*

Anna. It was hard to hear if it was my sister as the words flowed through the water.

I just found out that Ragnarök is coming soon. I couldn't stop my voice from shaking. *But I can't—*

To my great surprise, the other person laughed.

I really don't think this is something to laugh at.

You should see this.

What are you talking about? I asked.

Come! The water around me was too cloudy for me to see her, but I felt a hand slip into mine. The person pulled me along. We glided through the water until I was pulled through a small duct and fell.

I landed in my own body, but it felt different from before. Strong and healthy with a fundamental sense of contentedness and joy. I sat at a long table in the sun. The table was covered with delicious foods. Hard-boiled eggs sprinkled with fresh herbs, butter with small pieces of ham, freshly baked bread, small, crunchy carrots, and light-green asparagus. A wrinkled apple was going around, and people bit into it, smiling. What stood out the most was the bright blue sky and the gentle sunbeams shining down on us.

I was at the hálfa celebration in Frón, but neither Faida nor Sverre was there, so it wasn't a replay of the one I had already attended. Tíw sat directly across from me, and one of his sleeves hung limply. He had lost his arm in the arena in Sént, so this must've been the future. He had developed smile lines around his eyes and white streaks in his hair, but he laughed cheerfully, and people looked at him with admiration. I guessed he was still the leader of Ísafold. I leaned forward and saw my sister a little farther down the table next to Aella, who had her arm around her. My sister turned her head and gave me a knowing look.

I spun around and found myself standing in the kitchen at Odinmont. The window was open, letting in a warm breeze. I could hear birds chirping outside. At my side, Luna was babbling in an incoherent stream as she chopped vegetables. She was apparently in the middle of a very funny anecdote, and she had to stop and laugh at every fifth word. A few times, she stood on her tiptoes and looked out the window as though checking for something in the yard.

I felt a thump from my stomach and looked down. With a small gasp, I discovered a bulge where my waist normally was. Was I fat and happy in the future? I cautiously placed a hand on my round stomach, and I could feel something moving inside. Like a little fish darting around.

"Has it started to kick?" Luna stopped in the middle of her amusing story.

"What?" Again, I felt the little poke. It wasn't uncomfortable. In fact, it was quite pleasant. I ran my fingers over my camisole, which was stretched to its limit.

"You can borrow some of my clothes. Most of it is pretty colorful, but you'll just have to deal with that. I have a really cute oversized orange dress you can . . ."

Once again, the vision changed, and I stood in a forest. The leaves on the trees were golden, and it smelled like Varnar.

Am I in the Bronze Forest?

Sunbeams broke through the golden foliage. Panicked, I touched my stomach, which was now flat. Fear and an all-encompassing sadness made my legs sway. I had felt the round stomach for only a few seconds, but I felt an enormous sense of loss that it was now gone.

The smell of the copper trees permeated everything. It must have been sunset, because I had been told they always smelled that way at dusk.

"Anna?"

The voice made me stiffen, and I turned my head. The smell

wasn't coming from the trees at all. It was Varnar, who stood right next to me.

"You were miles away." He smiled. "Who knows what's going on in there?" He gently drummed his fingers on my temple.

In a rapid motion, I took his hand and pressed it against my face, while my other hand clutched my flat stomach. My heart was pounding.

Varnar looked at me inquisitively. "You look scared."

"Where is . . . ?" I pressed my palm harder against my stomach.

Comprehension reached Varnar's face. "I don't even want to think about what Ast is up to." He turned his face toward the most distant trees, where they turned into a bronze-colored mass.

"Ast?" I pressed slightly less hard.

"She's with Etunaz. Only you would dare let our daughter be alone with a pack of man-eating wolves."

I exhaled. "If she's with Monster, she's safe."

"It's not Ast I'm worried about." Varnar chuckled. His voice grew a little deeper, and he came closer. His soft hair tickled my cheek as he leaned over and kissed my neck. "Maybe we should take advantage of the fact that someone else is watching her. We're finally alone. I don't think Ast should be an only child." He whispered this last part.

My heart was still pounding, but now it wasn't from panic. I put my arms around Varnar's strong body and pulled him close as I leaned back against a thick tree trunk.

The smell was everywhere, his body pressed against mine, and his lips were as soft as ever.

The light of the setting sun slid over my closed eyelids, and everything turned red and blurry. I was back in the water with the slow whale song.

Do you see the future? the disembodied voice asked.

That future is so beautiful. I had no other words for it.

It can be yours. The All-Father is ready to make it happen.

Who are you?

Who do you think I am?

Serén? If it's you, why aren't you showing yourself?

The All-Father asked me to show you how you'll be rewarded . . . if . . .

If what?

Nothing. Just bask in the wonderful time that awaits you. Goodbyyye. The voice grew quieter, as though moving away.

I tried to swim after it. *Hey . . . Stop!*

You've seen enough. Odin doesn't want you to see more. The words became fainter and fainter. Then they grew louder again. *I can't help it! I just can't help it.*

I felt a jerk as someone took my hand and pulled me forward. I dropped down onto a field between Odinmont and Kraghede Forest.

There were snowflakes in the air as I walked toward the forest.

The light was blue-gray, even though it was daytime, and the clouds hung heavily, almost touching the ground. The tall trees cast no shadows, and my surroundings looked like a black-and-white photo, the contours of objects hard to make out. The snow lay in drifts over the fields and trees, and the air was ice-cold.

It was quiet in the forest. No birds rustled, no wind moved through the trees, and when I looked out over the North Jutland landscape toward Odinmont, the hill looked empty.

I smiled to myself, my hand still on my stomach. It would all work out. The future I had just seen made me happy and lighthearted.

The frozen leaves crunched under my feet, but above me, it was completely silent. It became darker as I made my way deeper into the forest, and without thinking, I headed toward the stone circle. I had to squint to see in the increasing darkness. A bird suddenly cawed, and I jumped. The sound came from above me, but when I looked up, the thick tree trunks disappeared into the mist. The raven—or were there two?—cackled far above me in the fog.

I reached the stone circle, which looked tidier than the last time I'd been there. The stones had been scrubbed clean, covered with runes and figures painted in ocher and red.

I walked into the center.

The trees seemed somehow fuller, but it was so foggy I couldn't see their tops. I got the feeling that their crowns reached all the way to the middle of the stone circle and gathered over my head, but I couldn't see them. Something dripped onto the back of my hand. I carefully dragged my index finger through the drop. It was viscous, smelled like iron, and was bright red. There was no doubt what it was. The ravens cackled again. I looked up.

"What is this?"

"The price for the sweet life. It's only fair for you to know," a voice said from everywhere around me at once.

The mist had receded in a small circle above me, and I could see what hung from the trees' branches. I stood frozen.

"There's always a price, raven. That's how the gods made your world. And considering that humans created the gods, you could say it's your own fault that this is how things are."

Hanging feet rotated slowly over my head. When I realized what was up there, I leapt back so I wouldn't be right beneath the dead.

"A gift will always be reciprocated. Caaaaw!"

Is the voice coming from the raven?

"See how Odin is swimming in offerings in the future. Your offerings. Caaaaw."

There were nine people. They hung from the trees with ropes around their necks. Their faces were distorted and swollen.

"This is the price. Are you willing to pay it? If you want a gift, you have to give a gift." The statement ended with prolonged raven laughter.

"No!"

The raven cawed from the mist. The blood poured down, the ravens screeched, the ropes creaked, and someone sighed deeply, making the treetops sway and the leaves rustle. It sounded like Odin moaning with pleasure.

Me and Varnar in the Bronze Forest. Our daughter. My sister with Aella. It was all within reach. I tried to get a handle on my thoughts. "The threat of Ragnarök will return—just not in my lifetime or those of my loved ones. Odin will keep setting it off so he can draw worship from people."

"Fimbulwinter is necessary from time to time. You need to be reminded of who ultimately has the power."

"The gods?"

"Nature. Caaaw."

I bit my lip to keep the tears back.

"You've done enough, Anna. You've fought so hard. You deserve it."

Od had sacrificed, Elias had sacrificed, even my own father had sacrificed, and now Odin wanted me to repeat their actions. I sniffed. "I don't want to give human sacrifices. It's so incredibly old-fashioned. The prayer says so, too. Better to pray than to sacrifice too much."

"Will you pray to Odin?"

"I will," I said. "If he behaves nicely so I actually want to worship him."

"Nicely?"

"Sympathetically. It's more popular these days than putting people in their place through fear."

An enormous fist slammed down right in front of me, toppling several of the stones. It was a god's fist. "I want sacrifices!" The word *sacrifices* was screamed so loudly, several trees splintered and fell over with a crash.

My heart was in my throat, and I took off running out of Kraghede Forest. I fell to my knees as the ground tilted, and I slid back to the offering site. On the way, I hit stones and tree trunks. I was sore and beaten when I found myself lying in the middle of the stone circle, looking up at the soles of someone's shoes. The ground leveled out, and I struggled to my feet again.

"I want to wake up!" I demanded.

A roar came in reply, and the earth once again rippled under me like a choppy sea. My legs disappeared from beneath me, and I landed back on the forest floor.

"I want out," I gasped. I tried visualizing Vinr, hoping the staff could help me, but it failed. I gathered all my strength and called on the dead völvas. The women stood behind me, with Hejd at the front. She laid an invisible hand on my shoulder.

I slowly got to my knees and placed my fingertips on the ground. With insistent words, I began to speak, and again, everything swung, but this time the force was coming from me.

"Let me go!" I commanded. "Free me from this vision." Again, the whole forest wobbled.

"Fine. Caaaw. I'm just trying to help."

The ground tilted in the opposite direction, and everything dissolved around me. I slid down the now-smooth surface, which resembled a ramp. I tried to grab on to something, but I shot over the edge, and then there was only air around me. I landed on the frozen ground exactly where I had started on the field between Odinmont and Kraghede Forest. But now I could see Rebecca's house and Ravensted in the distance.

"Ragnarök is near," Hejd shouted from the clouds.

"I'm trying to stop it. I'm trying. I just don't want to do it on Odin's terms." Frustrated, I pounded my fist against the frozen ground. "Give me a hint. Tell me where Elias is, where the Gjallarhorn is, or what you think I should do."

"Galdramaður. The sorcerer."

Two people were running toward Kraghede Forest. I stared.

"Ben?"

He didn't respond, of course, because he couldn't see me. Instead, he looked around with nostrils flaring. Rebecca was right behind him. He held her hand, but she stopped with a jerk when he pulled hard on her arm. She whimpered in pain.

Ben shouted something to her in Yoruba. I didn't understand it, but it didn't sound friendly. In response, she spat in his face. He simply looked at her. He wiped his forehead lazily.

"Ti o ba wa okú," he said. "You are dead."

CHAPTER 33

"Ben was there, so it must be something that happened in the past," I said to Mathias. "Or maybe Ben's going to come back. I don't know. In any case, Ben and Rebecca were fighting. Should I tell Luna?"

"I don't think you should say anything. Luna's been through enough. Her dad died suddenly, and now we're living in total anarchy."

Mathias and I were walking down Grønnegade, where I had gone to ask Frank if he had seen Elias—he hadn't. I had no clue where the last piece of Gjallarhorn gold could be.

"Odin has to be stopped. He's becoming more and more insane."

Mathias said nothing, and I spoke out loud to bolster my courage. Even armed with Vinr, I didn't dare walk alone into town—people gave me angry looks, and more oskoreia had started to appear. The incident where the man shot at me was still fresh in my mind. People looked desperate and hollow-cheeked, and the windows of the corner store and the little cheese shop on the main street had been smashed. There was a crunching sound when someone walked on the carpet of broken glass to check if a single scrap of cheese crust might remain. The wild dead didn't bother to hide in the shadows but walked around openly. They pushed Ravensted's citizens, making them stumble.

A woman turned to her husband right after an oskoreia had given her a good shove in the back. "Stop it," she said.

The oskoreia behind them punched the man in the shoulder.

"Don't hit me!" The man reached out and smacked his wife on the face. The couple started to fight, and two more oskoreia gathered around them, whooping and cheering.

"Hey!" I didn't address the couple, who were now rolling around on the ground. I spoke to the oskoreia. "Cut it out!"

The dead stopped their cheers and turned toward me. The skin hung from their bony faces. Heads cocked, they began to stagger toward us.

"They're so gross," Mathias said.

I tightened my grip on Vinr. The frustration of the dead seeped into me, making me feel discouraged, but I gathered my courage and strength and pounded Vinr against the ground. The green ring shot its protective bubble out and around me. The oskoreia stopped when they saw it.

"You have to go to the realms of the dead," I said to them.

One—a man, I think, though it was hard to see—gnashed his teeth. I couldn't ask him how he had died directly, but I saw he started clutching his stomach. Something told me he had starved to death.

"You're going to Helheim," I said. "Sorry."

He looked at me for a moment before disintegrating. I turned toward the two others. They were probably women, maybe even sisters or partners, because they were holding on to each other. There was something protective about their grasp.

"Fólkvangr," I said. "You died protecting one another." The two women fluttered away, and the man and woman on the ground stood up, dazed. When they saw me standing there holding Vinr, they hurried away.

"Witch," the man hissed before running off.

I sighed.

Mathias patted me on the shoulder. "No good deed goes unpunished."

I wrapped my coat around my shoulders and kept walking. A

group of girls passed us. They had braided their hair to resemble old Norse styles, with wide braids across their foreheads. I didn't have the heart to point out that the style came from bog bodies much older than the Viking Age, and that Odin hadn't even been worshipped back then. But it did look cool. When Mathias looked at them, they nodded reverently. I couldn't help but roll my eyes. Mathias grew slightly and shone green. The girls continued on their way.

"I feel like I should tell Luna."

"Why do you have to interfere in everything, Anna?" I hadn't noticed the anger spreading across Mathias's face.

If he had yelled, I would have known how to handle it, but he spoke very softly and coolly. I stared at him, stunned.

"Maybe it's time you dropped your ambitions. The gods think you've gotten too difficult."

"But I've always been difficult," I whispered. "You knew that before you even met me."

"I've lost my patience."

"Mathias, are you having withdrawals?" I asked cautiously. "I can worship you a little if that's the case."

"You didn't sacrifice Ingeborg—in fact, you don't sacrifice at all—you don't pray, and you publicly speak badly of Odin, even though you're supposed to be bound to him. You blame the gods for being insane."

Hey, wait a second! "Is this about me not being pious enough?"

"What do you have against the gods?" Mathias jutted out his jaw.

"I have nothing against the gods."

"You seem pretty busy opposing everyone else's beliefs." He pointed down at the street. "You just sent oskoreia away, even though they're Odin's wild dead here in Midgard."

I suddenly wished I hadn't told him I wanted to get Odin out of the way.

"You can believe in aliens or pink unicorns, for all I care. The Norse religion is perfectly fine, just like the other religions. I don't give a shit about *who* you worship. It's the *way*—"

Mathias cut me off. "You don't care about the gods?"

I heard a gasp and realized a group of people had gathered to observe our discussion. It was the girl who had bowed to Mathias earlier, who now held her hand in front of her mouth.

"That's not what I said. You're twisting my words."

"It sure sounded like you said you don't care." Mathias folded his arms across his now-bulging chest. His skin glowed neon green, but he did nothing to hide it.

"Mathias," I said out of the corner of my mouth. "You're green. Let's get out of here."

Mathias took a step forward and towered over me. I raised both eyebrows. A torrent of oaths and curses was on its way out of my mouth when someone grabbed my arm and led me away. I tried to escape the firm grip until I realized who it was.

"Come on, Anna."

"Mads." I jogged at my classmate's side. I hadn't seen him since the last time I'd been to school.

"You two belong together," Mathias shouted after us. "A giant and a nonbeliever."

Mads didn't turn around, instead pulling me through the alley from Grønnegade to Algade, where Alice was murdered. Mads's long hair cascaded down his back, and I had to tilt my head back to see his face.

I snorted with rage. "He shouldn't be allowed to talk to you like that, Mads. Or me, for that matter."

"He didn't mean it," Mads said. "He's not himself."

"You're damn right about that. He used to be our friend."

"He still is," Mads said. He acted like nothing was amiss as people gave us a wide berth. My repulsion spells and his giant presence made them nervous.

"Where are we going?"

"You'll see." Mads was still pulling me along. Like Mathias, Mads was dressed only in a T-shirt.

"Why was Mathias so agitated?"

"There was a big sacrifice last night. It affects them." Mads said *them* with a knowing hand gesture. "It'll wear off."

I couldn't help but think of the dream I had had last night. The feet dangling from the trees in Kraghede Forest were hard to erase from my retinas. I put both hands over my face.

"Thanks." I knew Mads had done me a favor by pulling me away. My anger had been about to get away from me, which wouldn't have been good standing in front of a worked-up demigod.

"Have you seen Elias? It's really important that I find him."

Mads turned his head from side to side. The movement was so forceful, his hair swirled like a hurricane. "I haven't seen Elias in a while."

"I have to go. Maybe Od knows where he is." I was already heading in the other direction, but Mads held me back.

"I was actually looking for you. I didn't expect to find you in a fight with a demi." Mads grinned, and I saw the warm, kind friend I was so fond of. "I mean, I wouldn't have been surprised to find you in a fight with *someone*, but a demigod is something else."

I couldn't help but smile. There was something comforting about being around people who had known me since childhood.

"Why were you looking for me?"

We had reached the edge of town, and he dropped my hand in front of a little house with an apologetic look. The back of the house faced Kraghede Forest, but not the part adjacent to Odinmont. Because the forest circled Ravensted, it curved like a crescent moon around the town. One point reached all the way to the houses.

"There's someone who wants to talk to you."

"Someone?"

He walked up to the front door, and I had to run to keep up with his long strides.

"Do you live here?"

"With my mom, yeah."

"Who wants to talk to me?"

"Someone who's been looking for you." Mads didn't unlock the door. It was already unlocked. Before the winter, people had always joked that the doors in Ravensted were never locked because criminals couldn't be bothered to travel this far north. Now, locks didn't matter because no one had anything useful to steal.

In the foyer, I looked at the brown floral wallpaper. School pictures sat on the sideboard, depicting Mads at various ages. In all the pictures, he looked uncomfortable and out of place. I cast a glance at the real-life Mads, and it struck me how much he had changed. His features had grown sharper, and his eyes glittered with self-confidence and intelligence. He was comfortable in his body, and he no longer looked uncertain.

The door slammed shut behind me. Mads took my wrist and led me into the living room with a strength I had no way of matching. Maybe this wasn't such a good idea.

I tensed every muscle in my body to prepare for whatever I was about to walk into.

I stopped in the living room and let out a cry when I saw who awaited me.

CHAPTER 34

The two man-eating giant wolves filled the whole room. There was an extreme contrast in seeing the creatures in the middle of Mads's mother's living room. Next to the sofa, I could see how big Monster really was. I always managed to forget because, in my head, he was just a cuddly friend, but now that he was in front of me, I saw that his shoulders came up to just under my armpit. I saw his sharp teeth, his thick fur, and his blood-red tongue. His daughter, Rokkin, stood at his side. She was pitch black and a little leaner, but still an impressive being.

I threw myself at them, flinging an arm around each of their necks.

"How . . . When . . . I've missed you so much." I couldn't figure out which word to put first, so my speech came out in an incoherent babble.

Monster leaned against me, exhaling into my hair in the way I had missed so much. Rokkin, for her part, stood completely stiff, but she didn't move away, which was probably the most exuberance I could expect from her. I leaned back but kept my hands on both their flanks. Beneath my fingers on Monster's side, there were noticeable skin-colored branching lines. They were scars from when Eskild had tortured him so brutally that he died. Suddenly, it felt pretty fair that Eskild had been swept away by the avalanche.

Though there's wasn't a lot I wanted to thank Odin for at the moment, I was deeply grateful that he had made me a völva, enabling me to bring Monster back to life with the mead of poetry.

When I thought about what it had been like to be without my best friend, with the firm knowledge that he was gone forever, I had to move my hand from Rokkin's side and once again bury my face in his fur.

"There, there," he mumbled into my ear.

"God, I'm glad to see you, but what are you doing here?" I sat down on the sofa, and Mads placed himself in a large armchair next to it.

"We're here to tell you how things are in Hrafnheim," Rokkin said. Her voice resembled Monster's, but it was a little lighter. "The divide between humans and giants is deepening."

My thoughts flitted to the vision in which Monster killed Luna.

"How?" I asked weakly.

"We're trying to keep the peace," Monster said, "but everyone's scared. People have realized we're going through Fimbulwinter. King Sverre has become a devoted Odin-worshipper, and he thinks he can keep Ragnarök at bay if he sacrifices and prays enough. But the outbreaks of disease are becoming more frequent, and the food is running out. I think Odin is desperate."

"I'm sure you're right." In the previous night's vision, Odin had seemed ready to fight tooth and nail to maintain power.

"Have you spoken to Varnar?" I blurted.

Monster quickly looked down, but Rokkin laughed. "You left him in Jotunheim."

"He told you?"

Rokkin breathed heavily. Her blood-red tongue hung out of her mouth. "I've become good friends with Varnar. I like him. If he weren't an ally, I would enjoy eating him."

"Hey, come on!"

Rokkin continued, unfazed. "And I must say, you're behaving more and more like a giant yourself. Just think, you abandoned him at Mimir's well the day after you mated with him in that very same place." She laughed hoarsely. "Impressive!"

"Rokkin!" Monster scolded.

There was something else they wanted to tell me, but they were holding back.

"Say it!"

Monster revealed every chalk-white, razor-sharp tooth in his mouth. "What?"

"There's something wrong, but you're having a hard time coming out with it."

Monster closed his mouth. Then he grudgingly inhaled through his large snout. "Now that the Midgard Serpent has let go of its tail, there's free access to Jotunheim."

"I know. I've been there myself."

Monster was searching for a suitable way to say something. I could clearly see him choosing each word. Rokkin rolled her eyes.

"Ragnarök is approaching, and Ragnarök is a showdown between us giants and the gods. Because humans worship the gods, you've chosen your side. Loki oversees the giants, and he can order us to fight. Our giant blood makes it impossible to resist. If Loki sends us into battle, we'll eat you all. Even you and your sister."

She might as well have said *and that's that*, and if Monster had had hands, he would have buried his face in them. As it was, he just let out one more exclamation: "Rokkin!"

"That was what we came to say, Dad." Rokkin sniffed in a very wolflike manner. "I don't understand why you insist on treating humans like they're made of glass."

"It's fine," I said. "I would rather know how things really are." Suddenly, my dream of Monster attacking Luna made sense. The wolves and the other giants would simply be unable to refuse Loki's orders if he commanded them to fight us. "Why can't we just live together in harmony?" I sighed.

Rokkin flashed me a look that seemed to say she would like to ask humans the same question.

"I would really like to avoid being eaten by you."

"And we would like to avoid eating you," Monster said earnestly, but behind him, Rokkin's grin ruined his statement. She brought her jaws together with a big chomp.

"Rokkin!" Monster growled. He turned back toward me. "This isn't the first time Fimbulwinter has heralded the coming of Ragnarök. The other times, it was stopped with offerings and prayers, but if Ragnarök happens this time, I want you to hide yourselves. Seek refuge in one of the other worlds. We can't stop the other giants or ourselves."

I had seen Monster maul berserkers and Rokkin bite Tryggvi's hand off. I had absolutely no desire to go to battle against the giant wolves.

"Back, back," Luna shouted and flailed her hands, which were encased in dark-green knit gloves. We stood outside Mads's mom's house and were guiding Rebecca, who was parking her orange VW bus.

I had gone to get the witches because I had no idea how else to transport two giant wolves out to Odinmont. They had suggested sneaking through Kraghede Forest and meeting me there, but I was afraid they would be discovered and shot before they made it through. The inhabitants of Ravensted had gotten more and more jumpy due to Fimbul and the many oskoreia.

"Mathias feels so bad." Luna held her hand up to signal to Rebecca that she was in place. "He wanted me to tell you he's sorry."

"He can tell me himself."

"He's at home, mortified."

I imagined Mathias lying in bed under his colorful duvet in his teenage bedroom with the rainbow poster. When I remembered his red cheeks, and the fact that we had seen his dirty boxer shorts, I softened a little but nevertheless pursed my lips.

"He was under the influence of greater forces. He knows that he was wrong." Luna waved the wolves and Mads into the VW bus.

I glanced at the others. "It's amazing how everyone is influenced by others these days."

We climbed after the rest of the group into the orange vehicle.

Monster had ridden in a car before, so he remained calm, but Rokkin couldn't sit still and moved around in the backseat.

"Hey. Watch out. *Mfff*," I complained when, for the third time, she crawled over me to look out the window. If she was at one window, she wanted to see out the other, and vice versa.

"It's just so exciting." She sniffed at the corner, and a wet, foggy spot appeared on the window. "The speed, the smells, all of it."

"Rokkin! You're wagging your tail," Monster said from the other side, where he looked stoically at the landscape between Ravensted and Odinmont.

"Oh, stop." I laughed. "I remember the first couple of times you rode in a car. As I recall, it led to your tongue flapping in the wind and your whole head out the window."

From where she sat in the passenger seat, Luna turned her head. "You guys okay back there?"

"Hunky-dory," I said and formed my thumb and index finger into an *okay* sign. My assurance was ruined by Rokkin, who wriggled her way back across my lap.

"Ow," I said. "Your claws are sharp."

"Can we open the window? Can we?" she asked without concern for the fact that her claws were digging into my thighs.

"If you hang your head out the window, this whole venture loses its secrecy." I sighed. "You're pretty noticeable."

Rokkin gave me her best puppy-dog eyes. I felt it all the way in my diaphragm as she stared into my eyes without blinking. When she cocked her head, I gave in.

"Just a crack," I said. I struggled with the handle to roll the window down slightly. An icy chill immediately spread through the car, along with the sound of Rokkin sniffing. Monster looked embarrassed. I couldn't help but place a hand on each of them. Rokkin didn't notice, as her instincts had completely taken over, but Monster leaned toward me.

In the driveway, we all hopped out of the orange bus. I stretched my back. Though the VW was plenty big, the ride with the restless giant wolf had been a little tight. Rokkin was still in the grip of her senses, and she ran around along the walls, investigating the territory.

"I can smell all kinds of things here," she said when she briefly lifted her head. "Berserkers, demigods, witches, humans. Your home is a meeting place for different times and types of beings."

I had to admit she was right. I remembered when I moved to Odinmont. My plan had been to live out in the country, isolated and as far as possible from disturbing elements. Instead, I had ended up inhabiting a supernatural train station, where an array of living and dead beings came and went.

"There's been a fight. I smell blood." Rokkin's red tongue ran over her sharp teeth. "Varnar's, too." She licked the gravel vigorously. "Goat," she said abruptly.

We all looked at her, uncomprehending.

"What kind of goat?" Even though this was a crossroads, as far as I knew, there hadn't been any goats at Odinmont in recent years, especially since domesticated animals had become so rare.

"It's coming from the woods." Rokkin stuck her snout in the air. "Take a sniff, Dad."

Monster inhaled loudly through his nostrils. "It's true." He aimed his snout toward Kraghede Forest.

We walked down there as an ominous feeling spread through my system. It was almost as dark as night when we entered the forest. We reached the spot where the birch stump stuck up into the air. The splintered tree came up to my stomach. Monster went over and sniffed it, after which his eyes flicked from me to Luna and then

Vinr, but he said nothing. Then we reached the stone circle, which I had just visited in my dream. Someone had been there recently, and they had used it for religious acts. Now I, too, could smell the heavy animal stench of wool and urine. We cautiously stepped into the middle and studied the bloody corpse that lay there.

The goat lay in the middle of the circle, its horizontal pupils staring out into nothingness, with a thick rope tied around its hairy neck. From its neck down, it had been sliced open and the flesh removed. In the recent past, I saw the town's butcher making the cut, so only the head, intestines, and skeleton remained. I couldn't help but wonder if the bones could be cooked into a soup, even though they'd been lying on the ground.

Rebecca's face was calm, and Luna mirrored her expression. The only thing they were upset about was that they themselves hadn't participated in eating the meat following the sacrifice. The giant wolves, too, looked at the dead animal, unfazed. Rokkin licked the frozen ribs and tasted the dried blood, which had a nice bouquet.

"It happened last night" was her assessment. "It must have been right after we arrived."

"That fits with how Mathias was hopped up on divinity this morning."

I could sense the crowd. The voices from the past started up. They hummed and spoke inside my head. Luna said something.

"I can't hear you," I tried.

"Why are you shouting?"

I held my ears—there was now a cacophony of frightened and frustrated people. They screamed and tried to tell me something. I crouched down, and Vinr fell from my grip. This was starting to remind me of the dream Odin had sent me last night.

"What is it, Anna? Your face looks really wei—" Luna froze as she looked up at the trees that stood around the stones in the circle. The fog had let up a bit, and whatever it revealed was terrifying, judging from the look on her face.

I looked straight ahead because around us there now stood semi-transparent people, speaking confusedly—not to one another, but into the air.

"Why me?" A woman I recognized as a cashier from the local supermarket pointed at nothing. "Why not her instead?"

"Stay away from Bast." Margit's ghost clutched something in her arms protectively. "Leave the cat alone."

"Take me, I'm old anyway." A man with deep wrinkles stepped forward.

The majority of the nine people were begging or arguing for their lives.

I lifted my gaze and saw the feet dangling from the trees.

CHAPTER 35

We spent the afternoon taking the sacrifice victims down from the trees. Fortunately, the witches could use magic, so we didn't have to climb up the trees ourselves. We placed them in the burial chamber under Odinmont.

Mimir, who had settled permanently in Odinmont's crypt with Arthur as his roommate, observed the transportation of the corpses. Even though the burial mound was filling up with skeletons and ashes, there was still room for several more.

"They'll be content here," he said. "Odinmont is a good place to rest."

"What about their families?" Luna asked. "Should we say something to them?"

"Their families chose them to be sacrificed." I had perceived the past clearly from the bodies. Jytte, pointing at her own sister and her cat, made the strongest impression.

Luna looked more and more nauseous, especially when she and her mother placed Margit in one of the crypt's alcoves. She tenderly wrapped the yellow scarf around Margit's neck, then clapped a hand over her mouth and ran upstairs. When she came back, she was pale and tired.

"We're done," I said. "You can go home."

"What about the ghosts in the forest? We run the risk of them becoming oskoreia."

"What ghosts?" I tried to play dumb.

Luna rolled her eyes toward the stone ceiling of the crypt.

"You're such a bad liar. I saw you looking at them. As soon as we're gone, you're gonna go down there to help them cross over."

"You don't have to come."

Luna placed her elegant brown hand on my shoulder. "It's a heavy task, and you shouldn't have to do it alone."

"I'm a völva. It's my job to help spirits to the realms of the dead."

"I'm coming with you." Mimir cleared his throat. "That is, if you'll carry me, Anna?"

I nodded.

"Remember to put a hat on Mimir." Luna yawned and stood up. She leaned against Rebecca for support, and it seemed like her feet were made of lead.

I made my way toward the blót site in Kraghede Forest along with the two man-eating giant wolves and the severed head. I was glad to have all three of them with me since ghosts could be really scary when there were a lot of them.

In the circle, I bade farewell to Monster and Rokkin. I was exhausted and sad, and to make matters worse, I had to say goodbye to my best friend. With my bottom lip quivering, I held Monster.

"Just don't let anything happen to you," I said.

"I'm supposed to be the one who says that kind of thing." He snorted a couple of times, and when I pulled my head back, I saw that his large eyes were glassy.

Rokkin also received a hug, and in return, she gave me a big lick on the cheek, which I chose to interpret as friendly and not as an I-would-really-like-to-eat-you gesture.

"Please intercede on my behalf," I told her. "Tell Varnar I love him. It was wrong of me to be unwilling to accept that he's changed." I had gotten so mad when he complained that I had moved on, and then I turned out to be no better than him.

The wolves vanished through the portal, and I walked back to the stump where I had placed Mimir. He was bundled up in Ben's hand-me-down fur hat. I picked Vinr up off the ground.

"Let's get started."

I called out to the ghosts, and they came creeping toward me.

"Don't push. You'll all get your turn."

The woman from the supermarket kept furrowing her brows. "Why not her?" She raised her arm. "Why not her?" This repeated on a loop like a clip from a movie. The others spoke in a muddle. Margit kept begging for mercy for her cat.

"You were sacrificed," I told them, and they all fell silent, even the loop lady. They listened to what I had to say. "It's a great honor." The saliva pooled in my throat, but I pushed on for the sake of the dead. "You're all going to Valhalla as reward for your sacrifice. Do not be afraid. Valhalla is a wonderful place. I've been there myself. You'll get plenty of food and drink." I pounded Vinr against the ground, and a circular forcefield shot from it. Like rings in water, it rippled out into the forest.

"What about our friends and families?" The man who had sacrificed himself willingly had enough strength to ask.

"Maybe they'll join you in Valhalla, maybe they'll go to other realms of the dead or stay in Midgard. In that case, you can visit them on All Hallows' Eve. On that day, all rules are suspended, and the dead can move freely." I had no idea how accurate this was, but seeing as I didn't even know if the worlds would exist by next Halloween, I figured it couldn't hurt. I now had the ghosts' full attention, and they looked at me trustingly. It gave me a strange warming sensation to know that someone finally trusted me, while at the same time, I felt the weight of my responsibility. "Now go. Cross."

The spirits bowed their heads and flickered. Then they dissolved and vanished into the surroundings.

"I killed nine people," I cried as I sat with my head in my hands on the forest floor. Though the cold seeped into me, I didn't care. Mimir watched from his place on the stump.

"If I had accepted the responsibility and sacrificed Ingeborg, it wouldn't have happened. I might as well have strung those people up myself."

"Anna. Listen. You—"

I ignored Mimir. "No matter what I do, I'm an executioner."

"Anna! RAVEN!" He shouted so loudly, I looked up. "You didn't do this. People did it. They were desperate."

I sniffed.

"You cleaned up afterward, and that's what a true raven does. In the old days, people knew that once the ravens had been to a battlefield, the corpses were gone, and the living could move on."

"That's because ravens are scavengers," I said, wiping my nose. "I'm not sure how flattering that is."

"You make sure that life goes on, even after the worst things have happened."

My tears subsided. "I can't figure out where Elias hid the Gjallarhorn. I keep thinking and thinking, but I'm coming up blank. The answer is inside my head, but it won't reveal itself to me."

"Do you have a way of getting wiser?" Mimir's expression was neutral.

I looked at Vinr. "Oh . . . oh . . . of course!" I unscrewed the top of the staff. "Did you know I snagged some water from your spring in Jotunheim?" I pulled the little ampoule from the cavity.

"Of course, I knew it the second you stole it."

I had taken the lid off the vial and let it hover in front of my mouth. "It is actually yours," I said. "Do you want it back?"

Mimir grinned. He still had brown teeth because Elias hadn't had a chance to remove the tartar from them, but apart from that, I could see that he was a handsome giant. "I drank from the spring every day for half a millennium. I can't get any wiser. But you have to give me something in return."

"What do you want?" I was well aware that Mimir had no arms, so he couldn't do anything if I just drank it without giving him anything for it.

"Let me see. Odin gave his eye as a pledge for drinking from the spring," Mimir mused. "And both you and Varnar have already drunk from it."

I placed my hand protectively on my cheekbone. "I didn't know then that it was your well."

"That's true. So, you only have to pay for that one." He nodded toward the ampoule.

"What do you want?" I went through my body parts to decide which I would miss the least. The ear that got shot was all scarred, so maybe—

"What about you, what do you think? I'm a giant, so I only know what a giant would do." Mimir smiled.

I let out a little *heh*. "A giant would drink it without thinking she should pay anything for it. The whole thing of returning a gift with a gift was invented by humans and gods."

Mimir raised an eyebrow, and I knocked back the vial.

The water was ice-cold and fresh, and it tingled on my tongue. Although there hadn't been more than a few drops in the ampoule, the spring water rolled around my system. I rose above my body. Someone called out to me, and I looked down at the stump where Mimir's head still waited in its Cossack hat. Behind the stump, his spirit version stood tall.

"Wow . . ." I said. "You look good, Mimir."

He turned from side to side and flexed his arms. He hopped a couple of times, his thick hair billowing behind him.

I held out my hand. "Come."

He took it, smiling, and we soared away. It was getting easier to travel across the worlds using my völva powers, but the place we were going was beyond the cosmos. We were going to where Hejd was.

Finally, I saw a little green bubble hiding between Midgard and Helheim. It was wedged between the worlds like a little mussel. I pulled Mimir inside, and we landed in the green space. The ground rolled under our feet. There must have been water just beneath the layer of moss. I looked to my side, and Mimir looked neither dead nor decapitated. He was solid, strong, and tall.

Hand in hand, we walked forward, and I felt as though we were moving across a large, bouncy inflatable. We reached a little pond where a dark-haired figure waited for us. Hejd tried to maintain her mask, but when she saw us, she raised both hands to her mouth. "Vinr minn."

I looked at my völva staff, but then I realized she was talking about Mimir. He had been her friend back when they were both alive, back when he was . . . in one piece. Hejd stood, and without any of the dignity she normally possessed, she embraced the giant.

Mimir held her and kissed her hair. "You were the rain," he whispered. "You were the wind. You were gone."

Hejd pulled back slightly. Her eyes were shiny, and she ran a hand over Mimir's collarbone. Her finger traced the line where his body had been separated from his head.

"You stole from Odin, raven." She grabbed Mimir's neck. "You stole his oracle."

I shrugged. "Odin couldn't take proper care of Mimir."

"You'll have a triple death as punishment." Mimir shook out his mane with a couple of *tsk-tsk* sounds.

"What actually is a triple death? Is it three people getting killed at the same time?"

Mimir kept studying his hands. "It's a murder that happens threefold. You strangle a person, then you crush their head, then you slit their throat."

I already knew Odin was pissed that I'd stolen Mimir's head, and that he still hadn't taken his revenge for it. I swallowed and waved a hand. "I'll worry about the triple death later. Right now, I need your help, Hejd. We've collected almost all the Gjallarhorn."

She sat cross-legged on the ground, and we followed suit, even though I felt water rising from the ground. We had limited time here in this green orb beyond the worlds because we were rapidly sinking. Under the thin, green membrane, long serpents moved around. Hejd was back in her role of ceremonious seeress.

She knows of the horn of Heimdall
Under the high-reaching . . .

I held my index finger up. "I know that I know it, but I just can't figure it out, and we don't have time for these long, convoluted poems. Can't you just tell me?"

Stunned, Hejd blinked, and Mimir bit his lip with a smile at my side.

"I know the gold is somewhere wet. It's connected to a sacrifice that Elias alone thought was useful."

Hejd shook her head regretfully.

"Shit! You don't know, either." I slammed my fist against the ground, breaking the surface, and water sprayed up. The sinking was happening faster now that there was a hole. I put my hand over the tear to stop the splashing water. "Then help me figure it out."

Hejd buried her fingers in her hair.

In wondrous beauty once again
Shall the golden tables stand mid the grass
Which the gods had owned in the days of old

"Days of old?" Another piece. "There's something to do with an offering made in the old days, but it must have happened after 1802 because that's when the golden horns were melted down." Just then, it dawned on me. "I've got it, I've got it, I . . ." *Bluuuurrrrp.* My body weight won out over the thin layer of moss. I sank through it like a cannonball. Mimir plummeted with me, and we tumbled in a green primordial soup, not knowing which way was up.

We whirled around, and I saw Kraghede Forest from above and myself sitting in a trance with my elbow on my knee and my cheek resting on my fist. Mimir's head sat on the stump, his eyes rolled back in his head. With a roar, I slammed into my own body and felt my spine compress with the impact. Mimir made a frightened noise as his head rolled off the stump and onto the forest floor.

I fell to the ground and noticed how cold and stiff my body was. Lying on my back, I looked up into the gray clouds. It had begun to snow again, and the flakes floated down toward me.

"I've got it," I said. "I know where the gold is hidden."

"I'm so sorry," Mathias was quick to say when Mads and I appeared at his small two-bedroom apartment in the middle of Ravensted. I had gone to get Mads first, and he had come with me to Mathias's with no questions asked. Mathias lay under the covers with a shameful look on his face. He peered over the edge of the colorful duvet. "I also want to apologize to you," Mathias said to Mads. "I have nothing against the fact that you're a giant. Heimdall is half giant. I'm pretty sure he's my father. If I'm right, then I'm actually a quarter giant." He was going to keep rambling, but I stopped him.

"Apologies received and accepted," I said quickly, brushing him off. "I need you and Mads to help me."

"With what?"

"I need to get something from Sømosen, and I can't balance myself, Vinr, and a corpse all on my bike, even if it is a very small corpse."

"Uhh . . ." Mathias emerged from his duvet nest and pulled on his shoes, but he looked like one big question mark.

I explained the task at hand. Mathias took on a light-green tinge and looked slightly uneasy. He pulled himself together, gathered me in his arms, and ran toward the eastern part of North Jutland.

Sømosen was colder than ever, and the lake in the middle had frozen into a white disk. In my vision with Elias and the myling's murder, the lake had been calm, and in my head, I had imagined just jumping into it. Now I stomped critically on the icy surface and considered how I would get down there.

Even beneath several layers of knitwear and leather, I was frozen stiff. I was bundled up from head to toe, but Mathias wore only thin pants and a shirt. Mads was dressed in shorts and a tank top.

Show-offs.

Mathias looked around at the deep-frozen forest.

"He's down here." Carefully, and without lifting my feet, I shuffled out onto the middle of the lake as I tried to recall where Elias had thrown the boy into the water. I slipped several times, but using Vinr for support, I was able to stay upright. Mathias glowed more intensely as I knelt down and tapped on the ice.

"Good. I need some light." Although it was only early afternoon, a heavy deep-gray cloud cover had formed, and it was almost dark. The crystal at the top of my staff cast white light over the frozen lake, so I actually didn't need Mathias's light, but it was probably a good idea to encourage him. Mathias followed me, his legs also skidding out from under him a few times. Mads walked across without so much as wavering, and I got the feeling he was demonstrating how well his giant powers suited the ice.

I bit my frozen lips. "How the hell do we get down there?"

"Stand back," Mathias said.

Obediently, I moved backward without lifting my feet. Mathias took a few deep breaths, and with each inhalation, he seemed to inflate. He shone neon green and held the last breath for a moment. Then he released it, and the air that streamed from his mouth was scalding hot. The ice sputtered and seethed, until finally, there was a hole the size of a manhole cover. Mathias groaned as he shrunk to normal human size.

"Great job." I wasn't quite sure how to praise someone for using their divine powers. I leaned forward and looked into the dark hole, where a thin film of ice had already formed on the surface. "There's a bog body down there, and we need to get our hands on him."

Mads had stood up straighter when he heard me compliment Mathias. Then he put his hands together in a way that, at first, made me think he was praying, but then he dove headfirst into the water. I shuddered with fear to see my friend disappear into the icy depths.

Mathias and I stood there for several nerve-racking moments, looking down into the dark hole, the surface still sloshing a little after Mads had jumped through it. When the seconds turned into minutes, I started to wonder if I would survive diving in after Mads, but then the surface broke. Mads stuck his head up with a roar and gasped for air. He pushed a long bundle up onto the ice and rolled it toward me. Then he crawled up and flung himself onto his back. The water froze immediately, covering his clothes and eyelashes with frost.

"Are you okay?" I crouched at his side and laid my hand on his massive shoulder. It was rock-hard and as cold as ice. My feet slipped out from under me, and I landed on my knee, but my grip on Mads stabilized me.

"Of course I am." Mads got to his feet. At the sight of him with tiny icicles in his hair, I realized once and for all that a large part of him was not human. "I almost couldn't get it free." He pointed at the bundle. "It was held down by vines."

Still crouching, I spun around toward the pile of fabric. The movement must have made me look like a clumsy figure skater, but I was almost certain to fall again if I stood up. Carefully, I unwrapped the cloth. It was dark brown with black marks from the aquatic plants, but after so many years submerged in bog water, I couldn't expect it to still be blue.

The boy lay in the bundle. It was hard to recognize him, as his skin was brown, his hair reddish, and his squeezed-shut eyelids had collapsed as though there weren't eyeballs behind them. His nose was crooked, and his ears were completely gone. I gently stroked his leathery cheek.

"I found you," I whispered. "You can be at peace now."

The myling suddenly stood behind me and placed a little hand on my shoulder. "Thank you, Anna. You're a nice grown-up."

I reached back, grasped his fingers, and held them. Both Mads and Mathias stared at us, Mathias probably because he could see the ghost, and Mads because, to him, I was reaching out to nothing at all.

I let go of the myling's hand and unfolded the bottom part of the fabric. My fingers searched the boy and hit something hard. It didn't match the rest of the body, which was parchment-like. I fumbled briefly with his bony arms, which held something. I pulled it out. The tube was made of some kind of metal that had turned almost black after spending many years in the bog. I rubbed it on my sleeve, and it immediately shone gold. It throbbed just like the pendant with Freyja's tears, the piece of gold in Mimir's throat, and the little piece of gold leaf from Odion's amulet. It felt like a beating heart.

"The Gjallarhorn!" Mathias's voice had taken on a strange quality. There was longing mixed with recognition.

"It's still in pieces," I said, rubbing more grime away and removing a half-decayed leaf. The golden metal was imprinted with an archer and snakes and fish, and the large piece was the length of my forearm. At the bottom part of the horn, something had been cut off. Mathias reached his shining green fingers toward it.

"It looks like the one in the museum. Mardöll is traveling around the country with the ancient objects now, so people can worship them."

"This is the original."

When Mathias touched the horn, he jumped as though he'd gotten an electric shock. "It's calling to me."

A deep sense of relief coursed through me. I had been right, and Elias had been smart to hide it here. He was always so damn smart, and right now, I missed him terribly. Mathias carefully picked up the golden horn, and his eyes flashed sapphire blue. "This is my inheritance."

I looked up at my friend as he stood with the horn in his arms. "It was your father's, but he's asleep. Which means it's yours now, and you can call the gods to Ragnarök if you blow on it. You shouldn't, though," I hurried to add. "We have to destroy the Gjallarhorn so that Ragnarök can be taken off the table entirely. I'm thinking that if we remove the possibility of calling the gods to battle, we stop Ragnarök altogether. If the gods can't go to battle, they can't meet their fate."

"But it is a shame to destroy the Gjallarhorn." Mathias sounded sad.

"Until a few minutes ago, you didn't even know it existed, so maybe tone down the melancholy." I fingered Vinr, where I kept the other gold pieces.

"Can I at least hold it?"

"It's too dangerous for you to be near it as long as you're unstable."

Mathias carried the mummified boy to Odinmont, while Mads carried me. The Gjallarhorn was tucked in my backpack to keep it away from Mathias. We walked silently down to the crypt, where Mathias carefully eased the lightweight bundle onto the shelf next to the clay pot containing Ben's earthly remains. It didn't appear to weigh much at all, although nothing weighed much to Mathias.

The boy's remains had withered to nearly nothing. The myling appeared in front of me and snuggled against my hip. Mathias smiled at him.

"Thank you," the boy said to him in his characteristic high-pitched voice. "Tell your friend I said thanks, too. You wouldn't have found me without each other."

"He says thanks to you, too," Mathias told Mads, and at that moment, I knew the two of them were friends, regardless of the hostility between their lineages.

The boy's spirit stood close to me. "It's nice here."

"You're not the first to say so." Then I squatted down in front of the myling. "Mimir is kind. You'll be happy here."

The myling nodded. "Will you come visit me, Anna?"

"Of course. I live right upstairs."

I walked up to the living room and looked into my backpack at the horn, which shone dully as though it had an internal light source. Then I ran my hand over Vinr, where Luna had made the compartment. I had all the gold from the Gjallarhorn. It just needed to be put together and then destroyed to remove the threat of Ragnarök forever. I just needed a god to blow on it.

"We need to visit Luna and Rebecca," I told Mads and Mathias, who had lumbered up after me. "I'm sure Rebecca knows where we can find an Ulfberht."

"They're not home," Mathias said. "They went to see Brenda at The Healing Tree. I don't know why, but it has something to do with Luna's problems." He looked anxious, and I realized he had been hiding his concern for my sake. Sometimes, I wasn't very attentive to my friends. The end of the world wasn't really a good excuse.

"We're supposed to meet at their house early tomorrow morning," Mathias said, and I could see that fear caused a twinge in his stomach. "Luna said you should come, too. Then we'll find out what's wrong with her."

CHAPTER 36

The rope groaned as it slowly twisted around. The weight at its end caused it to move lazily, making a creaking sound.

The man's neck was only partly visible, but where the skin could be seen, a wide strap peeked out and revealed that his neck was bound tightly. So tightly it had squeezed the life from him. Beneath the strap was a small incision where he had been drained of blood. His whole front side glinted and steamed, so it hadn't been long since it happened. There was a dark blue indentation in his temple where someone had smashed his skull.

I studied his face. It was white and swollen, almost beyond recognition, but I could tell who it was. The nation's prime minister hung from a tree on a hill in North Jutland beneath three enormous windmills.

I shoved my clairvoyance into him, which revealed he'd stood calmly when they strangled him. He had sacrificed himself willingly. I couldn't see his executioners' faces because they were dressed in white, hooded cloaks. The one who killed him was tall; another was smaller with more delicate contours. A few more stood behind them, but it was like they were smudged, although I got a familiar vibe from them. I looked back to the hanged prime minister.

He had been killed in an exaggerated manner. He was already dead from the strangulation when they slit his throat and smashed his head. This was a triple death. My heart skipped a beat when I realized this was revenge for me stealing Mimir. When Odin threatened me with a triple death, I never considered that he was talking about someone else's death. I had assumed it would be my own.

When the body had swung all the way around, its clear eyes stared momentarily at the massive tree. The roots grasped toward the gray sky; the crown was buried in the ground, giving the tree an even more surreal appearance. It shone, wet and reflective, and there was no difference between it and Ragnara's fehu trees in Hrafnheim. None of this would have happened if I hadn't challenged her. Everyone would have been better off with Ragnara on the throne. Everyone except the people she persecuted and punished. Maybe a few needed to suffer so that the majority could thrive. I quickly pushed that thought away. That wasn't what I believed.

The frost glittered on the tree's bark, and the hill behind the scene was dusted with a light snowfall; someone had cleared the largest snowdrifts away when they buried the tree's crown. Tire marks were still visible, but the falling snowflakes were quickly filling them in. The tracks led to the main road, blending with tracks left behind by other vehicles, so I couldn't have followed them to their owner anyway.

"I know it's brutal," Niels Villadsen said. He was the one who had brought me here. We stood alone beneath the ghastly sight. "I just had to find out if you can see who did it."

The early-morning light crept over the hill. "I've gotten used to brutality." This was a lie. This was the kind of thing you never got used to. In my mind, I called on the prime minister's ghost. *Who hanged you?* I walked right up to the hanged man's feet, which dripped red onto the snow. A puddle had formed on the ground, and it had already developed a thin layer of frost on the surface. The blood looked almost orange against the white background.

Were Rebecca and my dad involved in this? Was Od? I asked silently. Predictably, the dead man did not answer my questions, and after a moment, he spun around again.

"What can you see?" Niels stood right behind me.

"I think he did this himself. Or . . . He let someone do it to him." I was whispering, even though there was no reason to. The moment just called for me to speak quietly.

"How did the tree get into the frozen earth? It would take divine strength to dig that hole."

"Have you seen the megaliths in Hrafnheim? They weigh several tons."

"Do you think a god did this?"

I suspected it was none other than Odin himself who had placed the tree. With all the offerings he'd received in the past few days, he must have grown strong. But evidently not strong enough to stop Fimbulwinter. I crouched down and placed a hand flat against the ground, using Vinr to support my weight.

"Excavator."

"What?"

"It was dug using an excavator. Odin didn't put the tree here. Humans did it in his honor. Whoever they are, they used heavy machinery and fuel to do it." The recent past buzzed through me, and I heard a metallic roar from the large vehicle. The hollow thumps of the grabber pounding against the frozen earth made the soles of my feet tingle.

"Who has those kinds of resources?" Niels asked.

"I'm sure you already know that." I struggled back up to a standing position and leaned heavily against my völva staff.

Niels looked thoughtful, but he was silent.

"Where are we, actually?" I looked out over the white landscape. It was hard to make out any landmarks because everything was covered in snow.

"Three miles south of Ravensted." Niels pointed at the three white giants. "Those are Paul Ostergaard's windmills."

"Are they the ones from the Windmill Murders?"

"Yes."

"And this was also where Lars Guldager died?"

"Yes."

I turned around. I didn't feel anything from my surroundings. People had died or had accidents pretty much everywhere. I felt it constantly. Growing up, I had often been frightened by the awful glimpses of the past, but I had gotten used to it. This place didn't immediately seem different from any other, even though I got a few emotionally charged images from the past.

"He didn't get up there on his own," I said to Niels.

"It's a hangadrott because he was the country's leader." Niels had to take a moment to compose himself before he could continue. "This killing was not sanctioned by the DSMA."

I raised an eyebrow. "But other killings were?"

Niels looked down, but I managed to catch the pain on his face. "People are desperate. All other solutions and explanations have failed, and the ice wall is coming closer every minute. Doomsday is approaching."

"Did it help anything at all that those people died in Kraghede Forest? No! It was a total waste of li—"

"A large cache of food was found right after that." Niels brushed snow off his jacket. "It wasn't documented in our archives, but it must have been left over from the Cold War. The canned goods are still edible. There's enough food for another week."

I wanted to tell him I thought the end of the world would come in a few days, but there was no reason to shock Niels any further. "What about when that week is over?"

Niels looked out across the white field. "We have to take it week by week. Day by day. What else can we do to survive?"

I bit my lip, breathing in. "Survive," I emphasized, looking at the dead prime minister.

"Can you see what happened?" This was the third time Niels had asked me about the event.

"I know you think I'm like a clairvoyant security camera, but I can't actually see everything, and the people who killed him had their faces covered. I can see that it was voluntary and that they were thorough." I glanced at the smashed head. I didn't need my clairvoyance to see that much.

"Well, the fact that it was voluntary is something," Niels said.

I turned around. "There are many reasons why someone would do this voluntarily. Maybe he was promised his children would receive food, heat, or medicine. Maybe he was hypnotized. Maybe, maybe, maybe . . ."

Niels placed his hand on my shoulder. "I'm upset about this, too. He was my friend."

I pushed his hand away and rubbed my face. "Wasn't *I* the one who was supposed to do this? As Odin presented it, I was supposed to give him a hangadrott so he would have enough strength to delay Ragnarök. The prime minister gave his life for nothing."

"Look," Niels said.

"Look at what?"

He placed his hand on my arm again, this time with a pincerlike grip. He pulled me to a bush covered in a layer of ice crystals, just like everything else.

"Look at it," he said.

With a frown, I bent over the bush. I had to look at the uppermost branches for a moment before my eyes focused on something I hadn't seen outdoors in almost a year.

It was a droplet.

It was thawing.

CHAPTER 37

I stared distractedly inside Frank's while people celebrated around me. Niels had dropped me off because there was going to be a nationwide message for the people, so all the citizens of Ravensted had been ordered to meet there. Electric cars had driven through the streets, with officials hanging out the windows and instructing through megaphones to go to Frank's.

Luna ran up and hugged me, but my arms hung limply. The whole thing had been a waste. My efforts to collect the Gjallarhorn gold, Ben's death trying to lift my spells so I could meet Serén. It was all pointless. I knew I should be happy, but my chest felt empty. The price for our joy had been too high. Nevertheless, a tiny voice piped up in the back of my head and sent me images of Varnar and me in the future in the Bronze Forest.

A woman bumped into me. I raised my hands, ready to defend myself, but the sight of me prompted only a slight furrowing of her brows before she continued on her way. After experiencing so much outright hatred because of my spells, it felt strange to be ignored like I used to be. What kind of feeling was this? I was embarrassed to realize it was relief.

"This is so great." Luna did a little dance in front of me. She grabbed me and twirled me around joyfully, but I did only a half-hearted pirouette.

"Mhhmmm . . ."

She put her hands on my shoulders. "I have to tell you something." I caught sight of Mathias, Rebecca, and Arthur, all grinning ecstatically behind her. They climbed onto barstools and sat in a line in front of us, looking at me expectantly.

"I know." I had, in fact, been the first to know that Fimbulwinter had released its grip. "It's really wonderful." I smiled, but I could feel it was an artificial grimace. In my mind's eye, I saw the prime minister's distorted face.

Luna furrowed her brows. "How could you know? You weren't there for it."

"There?"

"You never showed up so we did the ritual without you. Mathias and I stayed in the background, so Mom and Arthur really did most of it."

Feelings began to tumble in my chest. Mathias looked so blissful, I thought he would levitate from his stool. Of course he did.

Suddenly, I couldn't control my frustration. "You really did it?"

Luna looked perplexed. "Should we have waited for you?"

"You shouldn't have done it at all!"

Their smiles faded in front of me.

"But it was good that we did it," Arthur said.

I stared at my father with so much hatred in my eyes that he retreated on the barstool. "Your idea of what is good is apparently very different from mine. It's one thing to watch passively or clean up after others, but it's another thing entirely to do it yourself."

"I don't see the problem," Mathias said.

"Of course you don't. You're on the gods' side." I looked at Luna, ready to cry. "And you." Everyone had let me down. "I know we've lost if even you can do something so horrible. Yes, I'm relieved it's over, too, but this is a day of mourning. Not of joy."

Luna looked taken aback. "I was just so happy."

"It's great to survive, but not at the expense of others. What good is it to the dead that we're alive?"

"But new life is always good," Luna said timidly.

"New... what?"

"I figured out why I've been throwing up when I see the color yellow."

Arthur elbowed Rebecca in the side. "Wasn't it purple for you?"

"Violet. I still can't stand it."

I was one big question mark. Luna took my hand and placed it on her stomach. "I'm pregnant. We had it confirmed today in a seid. What did you think I was talking about?"

I looked down at my hand, which rested on the lower part of Luna's stomach. Something was moving around in there. All of Luna's strange outbursts and erratic behavior had come from the growing baby, not Luna herself.

"Oh my god. Or *gods*! Even though I have a tenuous relationship with them. But congratulations. Congrats. Congrats." I flung my arms around her, and she sniffled tears of joy in my ear. She pulled back and looked around at the crowd of happy people.

"What's going on? We were doing the seid all morning. I only just found out we'd been summoned here."

"Shhh . . . It's time," Frank shouted and struggled with the television, which had been repaired crudely with duct tape and a new piece of glass. He pushed a button on the remote, and an image appeared. It wasn't the test image we had been seeing for months. It was a still image of a blooming yellow dandelion in a field of green grass. I had never thought a photo could be so beautiful, even though it must have been a stock photo from before the long winter. Everyone went silent as the news anchor appeared in the studio. She was smiling so big she could barely speak.

"Temperatures have been above freezing since this morning. There are reports of buds on the trees and a much thinner cloud cover. In addition, a large cache of food has been found, which will feed us for a long time. Meteorologists were able to send drones up today, and there is widespread agreement that winter is now releasing its grip."

At this, a fervent round of applause and cheering broke out in the bar. One man dabbed at his eyes, and people held each other, even if they weren't friends. The image switched to the prime minister's office, though he wasn't sitting in the heavy dark-red armchair. It was his wife, Mardöll, along with Niels Villadsen. Only an hour had passed since I'd stood with Niels in front of the murdered man, so he must have been transported using magic—or at least a private plane—to be sitting in Christiansborg Palace already.

"We are pleased to announce that brighter times are ahead," Mardöll said. Niels nodded and only just managed to hide his anguished expression.

"Where's the prime minister?" a woman behind me whispered.

"This has been a difficult time and has cost us all dearly. My husband." Mardöll's voice quavered. "My husband is dead."

A murmur went through Frank's.

"He gave his life so the rest of us could live," Mardöll whispered.

There were scattered murmurs. No one had heard anything about the death, but it seemed that the collective ecstasy far surpassed the shock of losing the country's leader.

Niels cleared his throat. "The government needs to fill several important positions; we have unfortunately lost many key politicians during the harsh winter."

"We will, of course, elect a new prime minister democratically, but for now, Niels Villadsen and I constitute Denmark's heads of state." Mardöll looked into the camera, and her eyes flashed so quickly that it was almost impossible to catch. I felt it was entirely reasonable for them to rule the nation—until Rebecca mumbled something in Old Norse and snapped her fingers in front of my face.

I woke from Mardöll's hypnosis. *Hey!* Why should the deceased prime minister's wife be in charge?

"They have done a good job," a man remarked.

"Despite the tremendous crisis, they managed to feed the nation, even when we had nothing."

Yep! Mardöll had enchanted the population remotely, but she probably did it to keep the peace while they got everything under control.

The screen showed a montage of chirping birds, melting icicles, and a full-on waterfall flowing down over the gigantic glacier that had nearly buried The Boatman. The bar looked like an island on a little rock formation with the water splashing around it. For the final shot, it zoomed in on a tiny patch of blue sky. The cloud cover was starting to dissipate.

Everyone whooped and clapped again. People hugged and kissed each other, and even Frank couldn't help but cheer. He gave me a big squeeze. "Everything's going to be okay. We're going to live normally again."

I didn't know what a normal life was.

People began to sing, and they swayed back and forth, arm in arm. When the song reached its climax, someone's voice broke, then another's. Someone else started coughing. Several people bent over, crying out, their cheeks flushed with fever. It happened so quickly, some hadn't even managed to sit down before falling to the ground. Mathias leapt up and held Luna protectively.

"Anna." Rebecca pulled me to her.

"Cold plague," Frank said, standing right next to me. He ran over to Halfdan, took him in his arms, and backed toward the kitchen, grabbing me on his way. "Get Od Dinesen." Then he disappeared with his grandson. I turned to Mathias in appeal.

He held Luna close. "We have to get the others home first."

"They're magically vaccinated."

He looked at me stubbornly and tightened his grip on Luna. "We don't know if the vaccine will also protect our child. I can carry all of you."

We climbed onto his back, and he took off with all four of us. I raised Vinr, and it formed its protective bubble around us. With my clairvoyance, I sensed the contagion flying around and sliding off Vinr's shield. Above our heads, the clouds regathered in huge vortices. Tornadoes raged over land, ripping up houses and trees and flinging them through the air. We arrived at Rebecca's house and dropped the others off in no time. Mathias kept me in his arms, and I held Vinr up high like a lantern.

"Stay here." Mathias didn't wait for a response from Luna, Arthur, or Rebecca before we took off again.

It grew dark around us as black clouds covered the sky and spewed snow and hail onto us. The giants in Jotunheim must have been sending out massive quantities of frost. The temperature fell drastically. The cold attacked me, and my lips, fingers, and toes tingled. Vinr's warmth helped, and Mathias had turned up his divine power until he was glowing intensely green, but still my teeth chattered, and I could barely hold on to my völva staff. Although Mathias was strong, he eventually had to wade through enormous snowdrifts toward The Boatman, which sat like a frozen black pearl in the middle of a sea of ice. The gushing river had frozen, and by the time we reached it, Mathias had built up so much momentum that he simply jumped onto the ice and slid the rest of the way to the front door. We flung the door open to a strange scene before us.

There were several patrons in The Boatman, and they had also been struck suddenly by the cold plague. Dead and dying people lay scattered on the floor, and Od stood at the bar. The ghosts drifted in front of him. Many of them hadn't realized they were dead, and they wailed in fear. A large flacon of laekna sat on the bar, and Veronika dripped a green droplet onto Od's index finger as people stood in a line before him. He had a horrified but highly focused expression on his face.

"My blood," he said and held his finger in front of a woman's tongue. She licked it off. The next person in line came forward, coughing. "My blood," Od said again.

The man sucked up the droplet and stopped coughing.

Od continued mechanically. "My blood, my blood, my blood."

As soon as people received the laekna, they stopped gasping for air, and the redness in their cheeks diminished. They tottered off to the side, where they sank, healed, to the floor. Od worked methodically.

We ran past the line. "People are also dying at Frank's."

Od didn't even look up. He continued distributing the laekna. "I'm busy." He shone intensely silver, and he was much bigger than usual. With each drop he gave out, the person looked at him with gratitude, and he grew even larger.

"But . . ."

"You have the son of a god at your side, and you're the raven. Mathias can heal people using laekna, and you can help the dead. Send as many to the realms of the dead as you can. Otherwise, they'll turn into oskoreia."

I spotted Ulla. With a steady voice, she was trying to calm the dead before sending them away. Veronika poured laekna into an empty gin bottle and handed me a pipette. Then she continued her task of dripping green, healing laekna onto Od's finger.

"One drop each. Say 'gods' blood' when you give it to them." She directed this instruction at Mathias.

We didn't have time to do anything but take off again. Outside, the temperature had fallen even more, and tree trunks shattered into clouds of dust along the side of the road. I closed my eyes to protect them from splinters. Mathias groaned with the effort of moving through the frost storm, despite his demigod strength.

"Stop them, Skrymir!" I shouted. "Can't you stop the giants?" But I knew the giant probably couldn't hear my pleas, and even if he could, he wouldn't listen.

At Frank's, we were met with a horrible sight. A ton of people were already lying on the ground, and only with my clairvoyance was I able to see which ones still had a spark of life. Those who had tried to go home lay frozen to death outside. They hadn't made it more than a few steps from the door.

Shivering, I leapt from Mathias's arms and ran inside. The spirits of the newly dead stumbled around. A desperate, transparent man threw himself at me, but his clenched fists went right through my face. Then he tried to grasp my coat.

"Help me."

At first, I leaned away, but when I realized the man couldn't touch me, I stood up straight again. I pounded Vinr against the floor. "To Helheim," I said, but he didn't listen. I reached out to the other völvas, and my staff vibrated in my hand. "I said, go to Helheim. You died of illness and cold, so you belong to Hel."

The man stopped. Then he whizzed backward and disappeared. *One down.* I looked around at the many ghosts, which were constantly growing in number. *Several hundred to go.*

"The cure!" Mathias shouted to the living, and they gathered around him. With shaky hands, he sucked laekna into the pipette and placed a drop on his finger. "Gods' blood," he said, and a man knelt and opened his mouth.

As soon as the man had taken the laekna, he rolled onto his back with relief. Mathias continued. As people realized he could help, they crawled over to us and surrounded him with arms outstretched. It wasn't as organized as Od's orderly line, but it worked.

Meanwhile, I worked on moving the spirits to the realms of the dead. They were all going to Helheim because that was where people went when they died of disease. With the help of the völvas, not too many of them got away. Every departure cost me energy, and after a while, I was exhausted to my core.

I saw two people huddled in a corner. They resembled one another, although one of the women was thirty years older than the other. It was the local florist. Although she was coughing, she rocked her adult daughter in her arms. The daughter was as white as a corpse apart from the dark red splotches on her cheeks. With my clairvoyance, I saw that her aura was nearly extinguished. The mother was stronger, but it was only a matter of time. Her aura sputtered unsteadily. I pulled her arm to bring her to Mathias. Maybe we could make it.

The mother held her daughter. "Help Janne. Help—" She was overcome by a coughing fit so violent that she couldn't say anything more.

I looked down at the young woman. Her spirit was already starting to leave her body. I stood on tiptoe and spotted Mathias among the sick. "Get over here, quick."

He took off, and it looked like he was flying toward us. In a rapid motion, he placed a green drop on his finger. The mother coughed and held out her now-limp daughter, but her ghost stood next to her body, and her aura had gone out like a light bulb.

I shook my head at Mathias, and he instead pressed his finger to the mother's lips. "Gods' blood." The words rang out like a bell. Then he was gone again, and the woman collapsed over her dead daughter's body. The cough subsided, and she moaned weakly. I made eye contact with the spirit and thumped Vinr against the floor.

"Helheim."

I left the woman where she was because so many others needed help. Mathias worked hard to give everyone laekna, but for each person we managed to save, another succumbed. Finally, everyone was either dead or healed. The living lay panting on the floor among the bodies.

"You can't go out in the frost storm," I said to them again and again.

"My husband is at home," one woman rasped. "My kids."

I looked at Mathias, and he nodded. With a leap, I was in his arms, and we ran out into the cold yet again. I had to force myself to think loving thoughts to keep the giant crystal aglow. I allowed myself to replay Serén's vision with Varnar and my unborn daughter. The more love I called up, the more I had in me, and eventually, Vinr shone like the North Star.

Mathias and I went from house to house and found the dead and the sick. Mathias healed everyone he could, and I closed the eyes of the corpses and sent their spirits on. Finally, we had been to every home. I was so exhausted that I hung over Mathias's shoulder. He ran to Odinmont and gently placed me in bed.

In the fog of sleep, I heard him talking to someone.

"Is she okay? Is she alive? I came as fast as I could."

"She's tired, but she's all right."

A very particular scent grew stronger, and someone leaned over me. How could I have ever believed that Loki had disguised himself as Varnar? No matter how talented a shape-shifter Loki was, he could never replicate Varnar's scent. It could come only from Varnar himself.

With my eyes still closed, I reached up and hugged his neck. I pulled him toward me, and the fragrance grew even stronger and more intoxicating.

A finger carefully brushed a wisp of hair from my forehead. I forced my eyes open but was so exhausted that they quickly fell shut. I managed to catch a glimpse of Varnar's smiling face in front of mine. He closed the small gap between us by placing his lips against mine and kissing me softly. Then, he cautiously broke the kiss.

"I'm here," he whispered. "I'm going to stay with you. Even if you run to the ends of the earth, I'm coming with you."

CHAPTER 38

The end of the world. Ragnarök. What did it have to do with me? Right now, in Varnar's arms, I couldn't care less. Varnar was my entire world, and his body was my atlas. First, my fingers followed his spine, then I moved my palm over the many scars on his right arm. New ones had been added. So many that they spread down to his forearm.

Varnar let his fingers slip into my hair and held my face. His brown eyes, with their flecks of green, were right in front of mine. Then he kissed me, and comets exploded everywhere. His mouth moved down over my collarbone, and his dark hair brushed my neck and shoulders. The weight of his body was not unpleasant—quite the opposite. I wanted to feel every inch of him.

Although it was amazing to wake up with Varnar and, together, do our best to forget all our problems, there came a point when we couldn't ignore reality anymore. It was dark in my room, but it wasn't clear whether it was still night or the clouds were so black and stormy that they blocked all daylight. Varnar lay behind me with his arm around my waist. He absentmindedly stroked the skin of my stomach. It tickled in an agonizingly pleasurable way.

"Did the plague hit Hrafnheim the same way?" I really didn't want to know.

"A lot of people died either from disease or from the cold. Our best healers and magicians saved some people, but not enough."

"Why did you come here?" I turned to face him. "Not that I'm complaining."

"Serén saw the plague would return to Midgard and that it would strike without mercy. At first, she thought Fimbul was over and everything would go back to how it was before, but that changed. It happened very suddenly."

Nothing would ever be how it was before. Maybe it would be a lot better, but I didn't dare tell him what Serén had shown me as our possible future.

"Serén saw that Fimbulwinter loosened its hold because Odin had regained his strength, but the giants must have struck back. They're still stronger because the disease suddenly came back to Midgard along with a frost storm worse than any before it. Serén is upset because she wasn't able to react in time. As soon as I knew you were in danger, I left. Even though, unlike some people, I can't do anything to stop the disease."

I knew very well who he was referring to. "But you came."

"Of course I came. I didn't even hesitate. You are my life. Together, we create something bigger than ourselves. Ast."

I felt a jolt as he said our unborn daughter's name. "Ast?"

"It means *love* in Old Norse. Together, we create love."

This information tore at my insides, but I formed my lips into a smile and laid my hand on his cheek. Serén hadn't told him that, in a version of the future, we had a child together. I leaned forward and kissed him. I pulled back, and he carefully brushed away a strand of hair that had fallen over my eye.

"I've spoken with Rokkin a lot," Varnar said.

"Yeah, she told me."

"The giants like you. Both the wolves and . . . the others. Rumor has it that Loki himself has been praising you left and right."

"I've heard. It's strange because I barely know him." I thought that he had taken the form of someone close to me.

Varnar shrugged. "Well, he likes you anyway."

"Yeah, but I think he's awful. He insists on killing all my loved ones and destroying my world."

"For giants, the two aren't necessarily related. Loki actually helped us," Varnar said.

"When has Loki ever helped me?" To my knowledge, he was busy biting people's hands off and taunting gods and demigods.

"If you think about it, it was really easy to get into Utgard. We got locked up in the same place as Eskild, who had Odion, and we got out because Skrymir blew ice onto our holding cell. Do you think that was a coincidence?"

"I did, actually, but I can tell by looking at you that you think otherwise."

Varnar didn't say anything. Smiling, he rested his head on my pillow, and his hair framed his face in the way that made me lean forward instinctively. Before my mouth reached his, I paused.

"Of course! Skrymir is Loki. It's one of his forms." I smacked myself on the forehead. "We met him! That's how he knows me."

"And he helped us."

"Why did he do that?"

"Giants are capricious. He could have just as easily blown us over the cliff with a gust of wind. They're impulsive. I also think that was why Serén didn't see the cold plague until it was too late."

I remembered how Freyja had said the giants were like early spring, bathing you in warm sunbeams one minute, then freezing you in a snowstorm the next.

"So, there's no point in appealing to Loki?" I was so mad at Odin, I was considering switching divinities.

"It wouldn't work. It's not like with the gods, who actually get something out of humans' worship and offerings."

I rolled onto my back and looked up at the ceiling, which was barely visible. Only my giant crystal, which flickered faintly at the top of Vinr, cast a bit of light around us. When Varnar ran his hand over my shoulder, the crystal flared, thanks to all the love in the room.

"Monster and Rokkin are loyal. So are my friends Mads and

Mimir. I know they're different from us, but I trust they won't suddenly turn against us." I ignored the vision Serén had sent me where Loki had ordered all the giants to battle. I knew they wouldn't hurt us.

A prolonged honking sound came closer. It sounded like a car being pushed to its limit.

"Rokkin and Etunaz are half giants." Varnar smiled. "Maybe their wolf side softens them up a little."

The honking was now very close, and someone leaned on the horn in a continuous, shrill, insistent screech.

"Anna. Annaaaaa . . ." It was Luna's voice outside. I heard the car coming at full speed. Was she hanging her head out the window or something?

I propped myself up on my elbow. Varnar was already out of bed and had opened my tilted window. Snow and ice slid down the roof, and the freezing cold hit my naked body. I quickly grabbed a camisole and a pair of pants, but I froze when I saw Varnar's expression. His face was painted with pure terror. It wasn't very often that I saw him paralyzed with fear, but now he stood like a stone pillar. Then he found his clothes at lightning speed. Meanwhile, Luna screamed for us to come.

I didn't have time to get my socks on before Varnar pulled me down the stairs. The only things I managed to grab were Vinr and my backpack, which contained my coat.

The orange VW bus was idling in the driveway. Rebecca sat behind the wheel, and Luna opened the door. Arthur sat in the back with a desperate look on his face. My feet seized up when my bare soles hit the frozen driveway, but Varnar pushed me onward.

We heard shouts and the rumbling of a crowd, but because I stood on the other side of Odinmont, I couldn't see down to the road. As always, Kraghede Forest lay calmly at the foot of the hill like a gray ribbon, and the sky was pitch black with a few light-gray, rotating spirals. I was struck by ominous gusts of wind. I took a step, made difficult by my cramping feet, and looked down to the bottom of the driveway. There was screaming and shouting coming from down there, and I saw what Varnar had seen from my bedroom window.

Torches, glinting metal, bared teeth.

"Go!" Luna shouted breathlessly. Her big curls formed a messy cloud around her head.

Varnar's hand closed around mine, and with his free hand, he pushed me toward the car. I still stared, paralyzed, at the driveway and the growing spectacle.

"Come on!"

The crowd walked toward Odinmont, the people shouting at the tops of their lungs, eyes wild. I saw baseball bats, flaming branches, and hunting rifles, and among them were the distinctive dark shadows of oskoreia, egging the humans on. These were no longer my fellow citizens of Ravensted. They were a bloodthirsty mob. I recognized cashiers from the former supermarket, civil servants, and workmen I had seen at the high school. There were several hundred of them, and they were heading straight toward us.

"Get in, get in, get in . . ." Varnar pulled me toward the car.

Crap! I twisted out of Varnar's grasp and ran back into Odinmont. Meanwhile, the wild screams of the crowd drew nearer.

"No, Anna!" Varnar's voice was desperate.

Fortunately, Mimir sat on the dining table and wasn't down in the crypt. Through the window, he could see the throng approaching. His eyes were wide, and he was rocking helplessly on his neck stump. I grabbed him by the hair and ran back to the front door.

"Owww," Mimir howled, dangling from my hand.

"Sorry."

Varnar was back inside Odinmont, and he held the door open for me as I came running. I leapt out into the driveway and got in the car. Varnar followed me, and Rebecca started driving away before I'd even gotten the door closed.

"There she is!" A bank manager raised his torch. "Get her."

"What did I do?" I struggled to get the side door shut, but it was stuck.

"This is all Anna Sakarias's fault." The local florist snipped in the air with a large pruning lopper.

Luna shouted a spell, and the door whirled shut. "Láss," she screamed, and all the locks in the car slid down just as the angry florist reached my side and tried to open the door. She pounded the lopper against my window.

"My daughter is dead. It's your fault," the woman yelled.

I recognized her from the previous evening. "I'm sorry about your daughter. Mathias saved you, and I wish he had gotten to your girl in time, too."

But the woman evidently didn't hear me through the car door, and even if she could, she wouldn't have reacted. Outside, people continued to shout. They threw stones and clumps of ice at the car.

"Damned ignorant horde," Rebecca hissed. "They won't get you. Over my dead body."

Although her words were meant to reassure me, they only scared me. I realized that the people with their torches and improvised weapons would indeed kill me if they got ahold of me. Rebecca steered us directly toward the agitated mob. I saw crowbars and hammers. The people's eyes shone with hatred, and their sallow skin hung from their bones. Mimir actually had a better complexion than most of these people.

"They really hate me." I sighed.

"It's your spells," Luna said in a low voice. For a moment, she didn't sound like herself. "The people have gone nuts after living through last night, and you shine like a lantern amid the misery. The oskoreia see your magic and push the living out here to find an outlet. The worst thing for a group of people is to taste salvation only to have it snatched away again."

"Isn't Odinmont protected by magic? How can they even get out here?" I pulled back from the window as a teenage boy pounded on it with the palms of his hands.

"Oskoreia are stronger. Nothing can stop a bloodthirsty mob."

"This mound is for reaching the gods," a woman raged so loudly, I had no trouble hearing her through the window. "It is reserved for Odin. You have no right to live on this sacred ground, you demon." Her face was so close, she left spittle on the car window. "This is a signal mound. Let's have a bonfire."

We rolled through them, and they hammered against the car's windows and doors. Rebecca steered with great concentration as Luna closed her eyes and mumbled something in Old Norse, surrounding us with protective magic.

After a tough blow to the window with a bat, Rebecca cursed and picked up speed. People jumped out of the way, but one man refused to move, and he swung a golf club at the front of the car. He leaned forward and spit on the windshield. In response, Rebecca hit the gas and drove into him. At first, he hung on to the front, but when she slammed on the brakes, he lost his grip and fell. Rebecca started again, and the car bumped unsettlingly as the wheels moved over the man's body. Mimir slid off the seat and landed on the floor, where he cried out in pain with every bump. A window smashed at Odinmont, and I saw through the rear window that the people had already descended on my home.

"Better the house than you," Rebecca growled.

The crowd continued their fury, and the house caught fire when someone tossed a torch into the living room. The front door had already been kicked down, and people poured into my home. There were shouts, thumps, and the sound of breaking glass.

As we raced away, clouds of smoke were already rising from my bedroom window, where Varnar and I had been floating on a pink cloud just a few minutes before.

Red flames licked toward the overcast sky. I didn't need to see the future to know I would never see the house again.

It was the only real home I had ever known.

CHAPTER 39

I looked out Rebecca's kitchen window and saw Odinmont in flames. The orange tongues flicked toward the gray sky. I memorized every person who participated in destroying the house.

"There's no use watching it," Varnar said quietly. He was the only person I allowed to stay with me as I followed the destruction. Everyone else had been left in the living room. I didn't even blink because I wanted to take it all in—every last one of the vandals.

"Revenge doesn't do any good." Varnar's hand squeezed the kitchen table, and I wasn't sure if he was talking to me or himself.

"If they survive this, my retribution awaits them." Each word felt hot and painful in my mouth.

"Their animalistic sides have taken over. It's mass hysteria."

"Why are they doing this?"

Varnar looked down. "I've seen the same thing in gladiator battles when I lived in Sént. I'm not certain, but people can get into a state where they can't get enough blood and mayhem. I've decided that people aren't individually to blame for it."

Someone at Odinmont shouted so loudly I could hear it through the thick glass window. I instinctively took a step back.

"They can't see Rebecca's house. There's strong magic surrounding the place, concealing us." Varnar put his arm around me, and I rested my cheek on his shoulder.

Both Rebecca and Luna had chanted spells over me when we reached Rebecca's house, and now I was all wrapped up in a thick layer of concealment magic, although no one knew how well it worked if I was in a crowd.

"It's best if you stay away from people." Rebecca had patted me on the shoulder apologetically.

"Odinmont is gone." My voice sounded cold and emotionless.

"But you're alive."

I leaned forward and sniffed. The smell of burnt wood hit my nostrils.

"It was just a thing." Varnar tried to turn me around, but he wasn't able to tear me away from the sight of the flaming house. "You don't usually care about things and places."

"The one exception being my home."

It was now impossible to tell that a house had once been there. The blaze was so intense that people retreated to the field, where they could watch the burning from a safe distance. They stood paralyzed and stared at the fire. I looked back at the burning house. For a long time, Varnar and I stood in silence until Odinmont was burnt down.

There was no one alive inside, and the skeletons in the crypt below suffered no harm. When the fire died out, the people standing around the mound began to wrap their arms around themselves. Some beat their arms against their bodies for warmth. Soon, they trudged back toward the town.

"It's over." I could feel my face go hard, and I walked into the living room where Luna, Rebecca, Arthur, and Mimir waited. They looked at me sadly. Expectantly.

"Are you . . ."

"I've said my goodbyes." My voice was monotone. "Now we must act."

"We've done everything," Rebecca said. "We've sacrificed, we've lost our loved ones and our prized possessions."

Luna suddenly sobbed and clutched her stomach. "Mathias is gone. He kept healing people after you fell asleep, and he got so much divine power from people's gratitude that he just ran off. I have no idea where he is."

"I'll find him. And I know what we need to do." I tossed the largest piece of the Gjallarhorn on the table. An archaeologist would have been horrified by my rough handling of the ancient national treasure, but I simply dumped my bag out. Then I unscrewed the top of Vinr and did the same with the other pieces of gold, and they all lay in the middle of the table and glowed. The Odion figurine vibrated furiously in their midst.

"Ulfberht." I looked at Rebecca.

She turned her head away.

"What do you know?"

She swallowed.

"Rebecca," I said in a warning tone. "You know where the last Ulfberht smith is."

Her cornflower-blue eyes shone. "I am Ulfberht's protector and guardian."

I gaped. "Is he here? In Ravensted?"

Rebecca smiled harshly. "You're asking the wrong question."

I planted my hands on the tabletop and leaned in close to her. "Is Ulfberht in Ravensted?"

"Under it."

I knelt, placed the palm of my hand against the tile floor, and reached out with my extrasensory perception. There was a very faint clanking somewhere underground. I closed my eyes and called to the other völvas so they could help me follow the sound; I saw in my mind's eye how roots formed a network beneath us. Not just under Ravensted but under all of Midgard. It looked like an organic circuit board. I caught the sound of iron being hammered.

Ahhh . . . of course!

I slowly got to my feet. "Rebecca, would you drive me to Ravensted High School?"

She inhaled. "It's best if Mimir goes with us."

We reached the red entrance, where thick glass doors had once protected the school against thieves. Now they were shattered and hung from their hinges; people had undoubtedly broken in to look for anything that could be eaten or burned for warmth. An alarm whined continuously, but no one had made an attempt to turn it off.

"I'm going in with you," Varnar said, investigating the broken windows, which had cracked in a spiderweb pattern.

Rebecca stepped forward. Her nearly white hair was matted, and her blue eyes flared wildly. "You wait here. It's hard enough to lift the magic for Anna."

Varnar looked at the school in awe. "There's magic here? I worked in the basement for six months and never saw anything supernatural."

"This is the most enchanted place in Ravensted. Especially the basement." Rebecca gathered her long fingers around her staff, which resembled Vinr but had a bronze bird on top.

Grudgingly, Varnar waited outside the vandalized school.

I pulled the door open, the damaged hinges screeching. With Rebecca in front of me and Mimir under my arm, I walked down the school's empty halls, thumping Vinr against the acrylic carpet with every step. Shards of glass crunched beneath the pink boots I had borrowed from Luna. Books and papers had been tossed in disorganized piles, and the vending machine had been overturned and broken open from the back.

We passed the color-coordinated halls. Yellow Hall, Blue Hall, Orange Hall, and Red Hall, where the principal's office had once been.

Mimir exclaimed: "Watch out!"

I stopped, frightened, even though there didn't seem to be any immediate danger in the middle of the solid brick corridor.

"You really let kids come here?" Mimir's voice was laced with anger.

Rebecca walked with her back hunched. "It's safe enough."

"Safe! It's the brink of chaos."

I saw nothing that revealed anything but my old provincial high school, if in a somewhat damaged state.

"I patched the holes and cast spells on the entrances. Good color magic is the strongest," Rebecca muttered.

"You made the colored halls?" I took long strides to reach her side.

"Many years ago. I was a young witch, but even then, I already knew that color magic is the only magic strong enough to cover the entrance to Muspelheim."

"There's an entrance to Muspelheim under Ravensted High School?" I had been down there several times and sensed that a lot had happened there, but I wasn't able to see it.

"Where else would Ulfberht be? You can't have a blacksmith like that in any other world."

I drummed my fingers impatiently on Vinr. My nails were dirty and torn, and with the addition of my matted hair, torn coat, and visible scars—not to mention the covered ones—I knew I must look like a barbarian.

"WATCH OUT, ANNA!" Mimir screamed so loudly that I nearly dropped him in fear. I stood on the green acrylic carpet and looked around, confused.

"Ohhhh," Mimir whimpered. "One more step, and we would have fallen in."

"In what?"

"Look down."

I stared at my pink boots.

"Witch! Give Anna magical immunity before we both fall into the flames."

I stepped back. "What flames?"

Rebecca had finally stopped. She turned around and rolled her eyes. "As long as she can't see the abyss, she won't fall. Kids and teachers walked around here for twenty years, and no one ever fell in."

"I don't dare take the chance." Mimir's voice shook.

Rebecca sighed. "It'll be more dangerous, but of course, she will need to see the entrance." She pounded her staff against the floor, and the bronze bird glinted. Rebecca's head turned back and forth. She swung her hand in front of me and mumbled something in Old Norse. Then, there was a bang and a puff of purple smoke.

The smell of sulfur clawed at my nose, and suddenly, it was hard to breathe. My surroundings didn't look at all like themselves. Gone was the 1970s brick building. I couldn't even see there was a school at all. Instead, we stood on the edge of a volcano.

"Aahh!" I jumped to the side so I could step out onto the bridge Rebecca was standing on. All the time I'd attended this school, we'd been walking around on a bubbling pit of lava. The fear of heights and the general fear of standing over a sulfurous volcano made my legs sway, but I fought to compose myself.

We continued toward Brown Hall, and I walked carefully to avoid dropping Mimir or falling into the abyss. When we reached the brown environs, I saw it was actually the entrance to a cave. That must have been why Rebecca chose that color.

She tugged at my sleeve and pointed down the slope toward a small crevice. "Are you coming?"

I followed her. A couple of times, I sank so far into the loose lava rocks that I nearly fell.

"Do you think Ulfberht will help us?"

Rebecca mumbled something to herself that I couldn't make out. She used her bronze bird staff for support.

When I took another step down the steep side of the crater, my knees buckled, and I tumbled down in a cascade of ash and pebbles. Mimir came loose from my grasp, and I heard him shouting farther up. The stones were rough and sharp, and my hands and face were scratched bloody. I landed on my stomach as Vinr rolled away.

Rebecca followed me at a jog and picked Mimir up along the way. Banged up, I got to my feet and collected Vinr, but it was nice to no longer be right over the volcano. Now I was just in the middle of it. We entered the earth's interior.

The air grew thicker with gas and sulfur the farther we went. Foul-smelling columns of smoke seeped out of small vents in the earthen walls. Apart from the heat, this place reminded me more and more of Helheim. Rebecca pulled us down an even narrower side hall, from which we heard the hollow sound of iron hitting iron. The cave's ceiling was made of dirt. Like in the many caves I had seen in Hrafnheim, roots stuck out everywhere. They were rotten, and mice darted around and gnawed on them.

Rebecca pointed at them with her staff. "Yggdrasil's roots are being devoured. That's because Ragnarök is close."

Embedded into the sides of the passageway were skulls carved with delicate patterns. There were human heads along with snakes, horses, and wolves. Their eye sockets held painted spheres that made it look like they were all watching us.

"I feel like I always end up underground." I raised my hand toward a carved giant wolf skull with painted eyes.

Rebecca cackled ahead of me.

"Now what are you laughing at?"

"Don't you know that, in Norse mythology, caves symbolize death? I've never known anyone who's always balancing on the edge like you are. The very first thing you did after you were born was die."

We continued farther in, and I had the thought that we were also walking inside a root. A long, forked, pointing finger, though I didn't know what it was pointing at.

Finally, we reached an oval stone chamber. The air was thick with sparks, and a gigantic person stood with their back turned to us, their black silhouette difficult to distinguish from the shadows. I clutched the Gjallarhorn fragments to my chest. The figure was hourglass-shaped and had grayish-white hair gathered at their nape. The strands that had slipped from the leather cord were frizzy. The person hammered tirelessly at a piece of red-hot iron they held with their bare hand. Then they stuck it into a hole in the ground, which appeared to be the earth's interior. It hissed and burned, and orange flames rose from it. Lava bubbled, and around the edges were piles of sand that had melted into glass where they faced the flames.

"What do you want?" Ulfberht didn't turn around but tinkered with the scalding hot material as if it were cool mud.

"Did you make Tilarids?"

The large body stiffened. "I forged the flaming sword. I liked it better when it was Freyja's plow, and I said as much. As punishment, Loki cursed me to stay down here until Ragnarök and forge swords from the smiths' scraps. I get all the leftover pieces and make weapons for the final giant army."

"I need you to fix something for me." I coughed as I inhaled the sulfurous air.

"I'm not just a random blacksmith."

"I think you're the only one who can fix it. And this will remove the possibility of Ragnarök, so you can be free."

It sounded a little like someone banging a large gong when laughter flowed from Ulfberht.

"It'll save many lives," I tried.

Ulfberht let the metal rest for a second and hunched their shoulders. "Lives. Why should I care about human lives?"

"Gods' lives, too," I said. "Although some of them will die."

Ulfberht turned around, and I gasped for air. I was dumbstruck by beauty in the same way as when Od or Mathias looked at me, but the woman in front of me was wilder. The last Ulfberht smith in all the worlds was a woman.

Rebecca sank to her knees. Mimir was under Rebecca's arm, but he also looked reverently down at the ground.

"You are of my kin." Ulfberht's cheeks were red from the work and the heat of the volcano, but she didn't seem to be suffering from the heat. Her hair was ash gray, bordering on silver, and her eyes were black beneath thick, dark, nicely shaped brows. She trailed her finger along the bottom edge of Mimir's neck. "Where's the rest of you?"

"In Hel's hall." Mimir bowed his head in a reverent gesture.

"What are you?" I stammered.

"A demigod. But not the good kind."

"Are you not half human, half god?"

Ulfberht shook her head, and the mere movement resembled a storm. "I'm giant and god. Neither fish nor fowl. I don't belong anywhere." She bit her shapely lower lip. "So, why should I help a human?"

"Because, because . . ." I actually couldn't come up with a good argument.

Ulfberht came closer. "You're hesitating, raven."

"I can only pray you'll help me."

"Pray?" She perked up.

Oh, right. Ulfberht was also half god. I knelt with Vinr still in my hand, unwrapped the pieces of the Gjallarhorn, and held them out to her. "Will you put them together? Afterward, a god has to blow on the horn to destroy it."

"What god would do that?"

"A new one." I said no more.

"I accept, but I want more than your prayers."

"I have nothing else to give."

Her black eyes sparkled as she pointed at Mimir. "Yes, you do."

Under Rebecca's arm, Mimir blinked his eyes.

"He's not mine to give. He's my friend."

Ulfberht turned her head slightly. "That only makes him a better sacrifice."

"But—"

"Anna." Mimir sounded like the sage he was. "It's time for me to pay for my mistakes. I came up with Fimbul. Now I can atone."

Tears gathered in my eyes. "You suffered enough in Odin's chambers. I wanted to give you a good retirement."

"You've already given me a time of warmth and love. I accept." This last statement was shouted to Ulfberht.

Ulfberht nodded with dignity and began to forge. The gold must have been very strong, as she hammered and pounded on it. Meanwhile, I waited with Rebecca and Mimir. I kept petting the ancient oracle's hair.

When Ulfberht was finished, she handed me the reforged Gjallarhorn. Even though it had come directly from the lava of the earth's interior, it was cool to the touch.

"Put Mimir with the others in the hallway," she said.

When we left the cave, I placed Mimir beside the carved wolf skull. He actually fit right in with the other heads. I kissed him tenderly on the cheek.

"Goodbye, my friend."

I walked across the field between Rebecca's house and Odinmont. Under my arm, I held the repaired Gjallarhorn, and Varnar walked at my side. It was a little easier, having him with me, but my stomach was still in knots. Mimir's eyes, following me from the little niche in the earthen wall beneath Ravensted High School, would haunt me for the rest of my life. Maybe in the afterlife, too.

"Mathias. Mathiaaas." I knew he could hear me, wherever he was. A glimmer of green flashed by. It went so quickly that I couldn't make out a human form. The ball of light stopped in Odinmont's charred ruins. Reluctantly, I walked up the hill toward what was left of my first home. There was a pale-green glow in the living room. The black clouds with lighter gray spirals still swept across the sky, and cold gusts of wind came down. Every so often, lightning shot through the clouds, sending blue, electric light over the landscape. One bolt struck the forest, resulting in splintered wood and flames. Everything still smelled like smoke. I composed myself and climbed up the hill, as I had done hundreds of times before. Everything was different now.

"Mathias?" The driveway looked like it always had, though it bore traces of what had happened in the form of deep footprints and tire tracks from Rebecca's car. The barn had burned to the ground, and my bike was smashed beyond recognition. *Things. They were only things.* "Mathias?"

Through the window, I saw another flicker of green light. We reached the door, which had burned away. Only a blackened doorframe remained. The air was thick with charcoal dust, and I pulled my scarf over my mouth. Stepping over the threshold felt like climbing a mountain, but I entered Odinmont.

The stairs were completely gone, and one whole side of the house had collapsed, but in several places, I recognized my home based on where doorways and walls were located. I walked into the living room. The giant crystal on top of Vinr shone intensely, probably because of all I was feeling.

"Mathias, I need you to do something. You have to . . ."

I spotted him, crouched in a corner with his knees pressed to his chest and his arms wrapped around them. More accurately, he was *trying* to fit in a corner, although he was so big. He filled half the room. His head poked up into the second story, so it was actually fortunate the ceiling had fallen through. His skin glowed neon green, and his chin resting on his knees looked like verdigris, with a hint of copper beneath the green. He was frightening, alien, and incredibly beautiful.

We stood in front of him, and he looked down at us. Fear and simmering power were in his eyes.

"Mathias," I whispered.

He cocked his head as though he didn't quite recognize the name.

"You're my friend." I laid my hand on his leg, and Vinr was aligned with his large shin bone. I would have laid my hand on his shoulder if he weren't so big, but I couldn't reach that high. I worried I would burn my fingers, but he wasn't hot. He didn't react when I touched him. I held the Gjallarhorn out to him with my other hand, and he looked at it with both longing and horror.

"My inheritance," he said. The voice didn't sound like his.

"You're Heimdall's son. I've been sure of that for a long time. That means the Gjallarhorn is yours."

Mathias didn't move to take the golden horn. He looked like he didn't dare to.

"You have to destroy it. Otherwise, we won't be able to prevent Ragnarök from ever happening."

"NO!"

Both Varnar and I toppled backward and held our hands over our ears. The golden horn made a metallic sound as it rolled over the burnt tile floor, and Vinr scraped across some blackened rubble. Ash fell from the exposed ceiling beams, which creaked ominously. I looked up and tried to figure out where the charred rafters would land if they fell. Varnar immediately put his arms around me, though I had no idea how he would protect me from a raging god and a collapsing ceiling. I was almost certain that Mathias was no longer merely a demigod.

When the vibrations had abated, and we were relatively sure the roof wouldn't come crashing down on us, I reached my fingers out for the Gjallarhorn. I held it up toward Mathias like an offering. "It's yours. You can decide what to do with it, but I hope you'll smash it with your god breath. For the sake of your girlfriend and your unborn baby."

Mathias opened his large eyes wide and reached out with one of his enormous hands. As soon as I placed the Gjallarhorn in his palm, it grew to match his size. He looked greedily at it and nearly put it to his mouth.

"Think about it before you do it," I warned. "You'll start the apocalypse if you blow it. You'll remove the threat of Ragnarök forever if you destroy it."

"But then I wouldn't be a god anymore," Mathias said in his loud voice. I actually thought he was whispering, but I still had to force myself not to put my fingers in my ears.

"Luna will die in the battle," I said calmly. "My sister and Hejd saw it in the future. Listen:

The giantess old in the Iron Forest sat,
In the east, and bore the brood of Fenrir;
Among these one in monster's guise
Was soon to swallow the moon from the sky

You have to concentrate on protecting her. I think smashing that horn is the best way to do that."

He looked at me for a long moment, and his eyes bore into mine. If he wanted to, he could have cooked my brain into mush, but he didn't. Then he stood and leapt out of the house through the open roof. He turned around and leaned down so his head was hovering just over the rafters.

"Tell Luna I don't dare see her. She would be disgusted to see me like this. Tell her I'm always there and looking after her and our child."

"Luna can handle it. She's very—"

But Mathias was already gone, and with him, the Gjallarhorn. I stood there, feeling like it hadn't been so smart to give it to him when he was so unstable.

"Anna." I heard a faint voice. I turned around. It hadn't come from Varnar, and he didn't react to the fact that someone had said my name.

"Völva . . ." The voice had no body.

"Can you hear that?" I asked, but Varnar shook his head.

"I only hear the wind."

We went outside, mostly because we didn't want the house—or the sad remains of it—to fall down around us.

"Ragnarök—Ragnarök. The fate of the gods."

I spun around. "Who's there?"

Varnar went into attack mode, knees slightly bent. He looked around. "There's no one here, Anna. What do you see?"

"Come," the voice sang. "I can give you answers."

I walked over to where the hill sloped downward. A person was standing there whose face I couldn't see. The figure waited patiently.

I held Vinr firmly and stood with my feet planted solidly on the ground. The person moved up the hill but appeared to be floating rather than walking.

Varnar was still looking around. He couldn't see anyone.

The figure came closer, but I still couldn't see who it was. A hood was pulled over their face. Their silhouette was small, so it could only be a child or a small woman. The hair that flowed over one shoulder was black. Tentatively, I stepped closer.

"Who are you?" I held Vinr tightly. If it was Hel, I was ready to knock her down, not that a birch staff was much of a match for the goddess of death.

"I can tell you what to do," the person said with the same airy voice as before.

Suspicious, I paused. "Tell me who you are."

"I can tell you what the plan was."

The voice was that of a girl, and it was familiar, but I couldn't place it. Strangely enough, I thought of the first time Serén had met me in a vision. Her voice was also a distorted version of one I knew, and that was because it was identical to my own.

With an even tighter grip on my völva staff, I raised it, ready to thrust, even though it wouldn't help much against the woman.

She was my size and moved with the same determined strides

as I did. Something about her reminded me of Varnar, and I wondered if it could be me, appearing from the past or the future.

She threw her hood back and stepped into the beam of light radiating from Vinr. I screamed.

It was Ragnara.

CHAPTER 40

Ragnara came straight toward me. She looked at me stubbornly, and I was struck by how much her expression resembled mine. I raised Vinr toward her. Because the giant crystal sat in the carved ravens' beaks, she was bathed in a white light that revealed how translucent she was.

"Lower your staff; I'm not a poltergeist," she said, raising her translucent hands. "I can't hurt you."

"What are you doing here? Why aren't you in one of the realms of the dead?"

She laughed, but the laughter didn't sound like any I'd heard from her before. It sounded like she genuinely found something funny.

"I wasn't making a joke."

"There's no place for me," she explained. "I strove to become a goddess but didn't succeed, and I didn't get far enough to create a realm of the dead. A handful of people still worship me, so I have to wander around restlessly until I'm forgotten and disappear."

"Are you here to haunt me?" I asked, exasperated. On top of the destruction of everything I held dear, the hard winter, and all my other problems, it would be so typical to have an ex-dictator's ghost following me around.

Again, she laughed gruffly, without the least trace of the phony, genteel attitude she had had when she was alive. "It was good for me to die. I found my way back."

"To what?"

"Melkorka."

"What was that?"

"That was my name before I took the name Ragnara."

I lowered the staff slightly. "Why did you take the name Ragnara?"

"It means *ruler*. It seemed . . ." She closed her eyes. ". . . fitting."

"Fitting how?"

She came even closer, until Vinr's end poked her stomach. With a crooked smile, she looked down at the illuminated ravens. She took another step, and my staff bore through her torso. "You can't hurt me. There's no realm of the dead you can send me to."

I raised Vinr again, and it sliced up to her chest. She made a nauseous sound.

"What do you want from me?"

"I wanted the gods to die. They didn't seem to do any good for anyone but themselves and their chosen ones. And, I might add, loyalty and devotion are not synonymous with being chosen. Back when I was Melkorka, I prayed to Odin daily. When I broke free from my shackles, I thanked the All-Father, even though I had done all the work. He didn't lift a finger to help me. The first time I came to Midgard, I made an offering to him, but Odin never appeared. The first time I saw him was when he killed me. Everything I achieved, I did myself."

"That's very impressive, but what about all the people who suffered because of you? You oppressed, exploited, and sacrificed others."

Ragnara's brows flew upward as though I had slapped her. "We got on the wrong track, Eskild and I. Tilarids deceived us. It was never meant to happen that way."

"What was the right track?"

Ragnara's face was clever, and I thought that if you put Hejd, Ragnara, and me in a lineup, we would actually look pretty similar.

"We deciphered the prophecy, which said that if either you or your sister died, Fimbulwinter would start, leading to Ragnarök. It would end with the gods meeting their fates." She gathered her hands in front of her. "I did one good thing while I was alive."

"What?"

"I made sure you died." Ragnara smiled wide, and for a moment, she looked like Sverre when he was relaxed and in a good mood.

"I figured that out. Elias tricked me into thinking it was my idea for him to kill me."

"Elias." Ragnara made a sad face. "He knew what he was doing. He was reluctant, but he agreed with me. His only condition was that he wanted to bring you back to life. And look." She laughed. "You're very much alive."

"I don't think it's funny."

"But you did everything I wanted." The corners of her mouth twitched slightly. "Not *everything*. You put up a lot of resistance. I recognize a lot of myself in you."

"You were somewhat more murderous than I am."

She smiled teasingly. "Are you sure about that?" Then she became serious again. "I'm grateful. You saved my son from the fate of spending life with you. You two could have so easily become like me and Eskild. I condemned my son to that without knowing it. Fortunately, with your help, he was able to break free. I even named him *Sverre*. It means *sword*, for gods' sakes." She waved a translucent hand as if it were insignificant now. Then she looked behind me, where Varnar appeared.

"Who are you talking to, Anna?" He went silent when he sensed I was talking to a spirit.

Ragnara's expression changed from playful to compassionate. "He's alive." She reached up and caressed his cheek, but he didn't feel it.

When I saw how much love she had for Varnar, it was hard to keep hating her. After all, we had so much in common.

"Another thing I'm grateful to you for." Ragnara was still impaled on my staff, which was pointed straight ahead, and my arms had started to shake from holding it up.

"Could you maybe get to the point?"

She rested both hands on Vinr, and I felt a slight weight in my already trembling arms. Ragnara's ghost was more solid than she wanted to show.

"Do you know what *Ragnarök* means?" Ragnara tilted her translucent face.

"Everyone knows that it means *the fate of the gods*. It's when the gods get killed in the final battle, whenever and wherever it may be. I think it's imminent."

"Who says Ragnarök is a moment in time?"

I reflected. "No one actually says it, but I'm certain Ragnarök will happen on the autumnal equinox."

"Everyone thinks Ragnarök is a moment in time and a concrete event. They even fabricated the myth that Fimbulwinter lasts three years." She smiled again with one side of her mouth, and her face was charmingly pulled askew. "When I was alive, I believed in moments, too. It's very human."

"Where are you going with this?"

"I thought it was me."

"What was you?"

"I thought I was the fate of the gods. That it was my purpose to ensure that they met their fates. I was wrong, but I played a role in their path to doomsday."

I couldn't hold Vinr horizontally anymore. It was also pointless, as Ragnara didn't seem affected by the staff going through her. I moved it sideways to get it out of her body, but when she saw my motion, she spread her arms in a Jesus-on-the-cross pose, and the raven-topped end punctured her palm.

"Who am I now?" Ragnara hung her head at an angle.

"Cut it out with the references. And tell me what you want from me."

"You need to do something. You have a purpose."

I suddenly felt exhausted. "I've done nothing but run around and serve purposes for the past two years, and still, the world is about to end."

"Tsk, tsk, tsk . . . You are one with time. Maybe the events can be shifted. They can be delayed or pushed up, but time always gets its way, raven."

"Stop calling me that."

"I don't think you'll be Odin's raven forever, either, as Odin's time will soon be over."

"Then what will I be?"

"When Fimbul is over, you'll become Ragnarök. And Fimbul is almost over."

"*I* will become Ragnarök? What do you mean?"

Ragnara got very close to me.

"I'm certain that *you* are the fate of the gods."

PART V

ALL IN FIGHT SHALL MEET

Vigrid is the plain,
Where all in fight shall meet
Surt and the cherished gods
A hundred leagues it has on each side
Unto them that field is fated.

Gylfaginning,
11th century

CHAPTER 41

Luna stared at me as I sat, completely deflated, at the dining room table.

Outside the living room window, tornadoes swept across the fields. They tore houses down and picked up a tractor. Flames razed the edge of Kraghede Forest and steadily ate their way through the trees, but I noticed it only as a faint background noise. Arthur and Rebecca were out in the barn, performing a ceremony that would protect the little house against hurricanes and fires.

"Anna." Luna enunciated my name clearly, as though I were hard of hearing. "What happened?"

"I have to start Ragnarök because I am the fate of the gods," I said in a monotone. "It's my decision whether or not the world ends. My decision. Mine, mine, mine . . ." My thoughts kept slipping away from me.

"Anna, be honest! Have you taken henbane?"

My throat was dry. "No."

Luna held both hands on her stomach and looked at me as though she could stare the thoughts out of my head.

Ragnara's ghost walked around the living room. She trailed her translucent hand over the shelf with its many trinkets. When she came to the little Odion figurine, she laughed. "Odion, you little bully. You should have been mine."

The figurine trembled in response.

Ragnara shrugged. "I liked Ben better. Only a slave can understand a slave."

Varnar was sitting at the table. He had turned his chair around, so he faced me. "Shouldn't we talk to Thora, or at least Arthur or Rebecca? They've been around longer, they . . ."

The rest of his words blurred together. I tried to compose myself. "What?" Without knowing why, I was out of breath.

"Let's ask your parents." Varnar spoke slowly and clearly.

"No!"

We both looked up; it was Luna who had spoken. Her voice was deep.

"We're talking about the fate of humankind." I got a bit more of a grip on myself.

"It's gone on long enough." Luna squared her shoulders. Her words sounded almost guttural, and her stomach quivered. "Fimbulwinter and sacrifices are supplanted by a new Fimbul and more sacrifices. I've seen it too many times, and it won't stop unless we do something."

Ragnara stepped closer to Luna and looked down at her stomach with eyes wide.

This woke me up. "Hey! Don't even think about it." I knew better than anyone what Ragnara could do to a pregnant belly. Out of habit, I ran my finger down the scar on my chest.

"There are two people across from you," Ragnara said.

"I know. Luna is pregnant."

Luna raised her head, her face still bearing an unfamiliar intense expression. "Melkorka?"

I looked from one to the other. "You can see Ragnara?"

Varnar sat up straighter. "Is Ragnara here?"

Luna reached her hands out. She looked at her own fingers in surprise as she raised them. Ragnara's ghost placed her hands on Luna's palms. "I'm glad you've found a new home, Benedict."

Luna shook her head, her brown curls bouncing. Then she pulled her hands back and placed them on her stomach again. "Dad? He's in there. I believe he is."

"Wait a second." I rubbed my forehead. "You're pregnant with your own father?"

Luna looked both happy and horrified. "I think so. I got pregnant the night my dad died, and in the Yoruba religion, you can be reincarnated if you quickly find a new life to inhabit. He's still in his spirit form in my stomach." She grinned. "I'm so happy." Then her expression changed, and her voice sounded deep and resonant. "So am I."

"Congrats, I think." I realized that I was digging my nails into my forearm.

Varnar looked around and flexed his fingers a few times. "Ragnara thinks I am Ragnarök. It's not an event or a time. It's a person. Me, apparently! I'm supposed to ensure that the gods meet their fate."

"We've spent so long trying to prevent doomsday from happening," Varnar said.

"I don't like it, either." I held my head as the room spun again.

"I have long pursued Ragnarök." Luna's voice was deep again. "It's the right thing to do. I respect the Norse gods and follow them, but their time is over."

"I hate to admit it, but I agree. The human sacrifices are awf—" I stopped. "Oh no! I asked Mathias to destroy the Gjallarhorn. We can't let him do it. That horn is the only thing that can force the gods to battle."

"You sent my boyfriend off with the one thing that can kill all the gods?" Luna growled in the same way Ben used to, but I was certain this was all her.

"Mathias can destroy the horn by breathing on it because he became a full god from all the worship he got from healing people. But he shouldn't destroy it. He should blow it so the gods can meet their fate."

Luna brought a hand to her mouth.

Ragnara's ghost nodded. "*Finally*, you understand me!"

"I'm not sure I agree with your methods," I said dryly.

"The ends justify the means." Her eyes sparkled like a cat's right before sinking its sharp teeth into a mouse, and I remembered she had been a murderous dictator for many years. She had once been the slave Melkorka, but the brutal ruler had been hiding inside her the whole time.

"Is Mathias supposed to kill the gods now?" Luna held her stomach.

"It sounds so harsh when you say it like that."

Luna's eyes flashed. "The gods will fight to the bitter end to stay alive."

"Mathias is a god himself now," I said timidly. It wasn't often that Luna directed her fury at me, but when she did, she was pretty scary.

"So, in other words, he's a competitor, and you've given him the one object that can kill them. Damn it, Anna!"

"I didn't really think about that." I cowered in my chair. "How can we get ahold of him?"

"Mardöll is probably the only one who can. She can send him a message telepathically."

"Contact her now," I said.

Luna walked over to the window and looked out at the tornadoes and the burning Kraghede Forest. Lightning flashed beneath the dark gray clouds. She closed her eyes and mumbled quietly. It seemed like she was having some kind of conversation. Then, she opened her eyes. "Mardöll promises to get in touch with Mathias."

I exhaled, relieved. "That's one less thing to worry about."

Luna gave me a warning look that made me shut my mouth. She stood still and looked out the window. "I've believed in the gods for most of my life, and now we're supposed to kill them?" She raised her shoulders and said in a completely different voice: "It's time, my child. No one lives forever. Not even the gods."

Luna seemed to make a decision. "My dad is right. It's time to invoke Ragnarök. But what will become of you, Anna?"

"I don't know. It's not even clear if Serén plays a role."

"Maybe we should talk to her. Maybe we should—" Luna stopped when I held up a hand.

"Serén shouldn't know about it. Not yet."

"But you can't just keep her out. She's part of all this," Luna said.

"She won't understand. I'm afraid that she'll work against us."

Ragnara's ghost interjected. "Serén definitely won't understand it. I know her better than you do."

Regretfully, I had to agree with her. I stood and walked over to Luna. "Will you help me?"

The look she gave me was so trusting, I wanted to tell her to hide out somewhere until the crisis was over, but she squeezed my hand.

"You can forget about sending me away. My dad will take care of me."

I held her hand. "What signs are we still missing before Ragnarök can happen?"

"Pretty much everything has happened," Luna said. "The Midgard Serpent has let go of its tail; Loki is free; Fimbulwinter has raged for a winter, a summer, and a winter; and families and friends have killed one another. There's mighty whoredom." She winked at me, and I glanced at Varnar, blushing. "In fact, there's only one sign left."

"What's that?"

"Fenrir must be released from his bonds."

I exhaled. "Of course. An enormous, mythological wolf must be set loose. Typical."

"But where is he?" Luna asked.

I moved my head back and forth as I looked at her. "Ben? Are you still in there?"

"Yes," Luna said in a much deeper voice.

"Do *you* know where Fenrir is?"

"I've been seeking the answer ever since I joined the Norse faith, but I still don't know."

Ragnara's ghost and Varnar both shook their heads.

I walked into the kitchen and rested my hands on the kitchen table. A few moments passed before the others started talking in the living room again.

"Hakim?" I called quietly.

There was movement behind me. "I'm here."

I turned around, and there he stood. With longing in his eyes, he stroked my cheek, and his hand felt warm and strong.

"You're becoming more and more solid," I said.

"Your presence has strengthened me." He smiled warmly and came closer. "What's wrong? You seem upset."

I stared at him for a long time. His green eyes, his spiky black hair, his dark skin. His large hand was still caressing my cheek. I took it and wrapped my own fingers around it. Deep in thought, I turned it over and followed the lines in his palm with my index finger. Hakim's ghost quivered in response.

"Is it time for new gods? Or are you more of an advocate for the old ones?"

He opened his eyes wide. "I can't answer that."

I leaned my head back. "No, I guess you can't."

He furrowed his brows in confusion.

"I need your help."

"Of course!"

"Do you know where Fenrir is?"

He opened his mouth but remained silent at first. Then he composed himself. "How would I know? I come from a completely different religion."

I squinted. "Your religion is old. Very old. There could be overlaps."

"Tell me first. What do you want with Fenrir?"

"The wolf has a role to play." I got closer to Hakim. "You swore you would help me."

Hakim smiled his typical warm smile. "You live so intensely, Anna. That's one of the things I like best about you."

I nodded imperceptibly. "I really need your logic. You're usually able to solve even the thorniest riddles."

Hakim reflected. "What do you know about Fenrir?"

"There's something in *Völuspá*, but it doesn't really help much." I recited the poem:

Now Garm howls loud
Before Gnipahellir
The fetters will burst
And the wolf run free
Much does she know
And more can see
Of the fate of the gods,
The mighty in fight

"Where is Gnipahellir?" Hakim's green eyes sparkled.

"No idea." I stared intently at him.

"*Gnipa* means *apples* in one of the oldest languages," he said quietly.

The pieces fell into place, and I sighed with relief. "Thank you, Hakim." I patted his hand jovially. Then I walked back to the living room and grabbed Vinr. With a firm grip on the staff, I closed my eyes.

Serén, I called inwardly. *You need to get ahold of someone for me. Tell them to meet us at Vindr Fen.*

 # CHAPTER 42

"Burt eldí." Luna held her hands up in front of her. The burning trees surrounding the stone circle extinguished as a spell shot from her fingers. As soon as the magic evaporated, the forest burst into flames again. Luna looked down at her hands in frustration. "I need more power, Dad." She inhaled and looked like she was puffing herself up. Then she spoke with a somewhat deeper voice. "Burt eldí. Ina ina. Burt eldí. Ina Ina." She repeated the combination of Old Norse and Yoruba phrases, and magic once again flickered around her.

The fire went out, and Varnar and I ran hand in hand toward the blackened stones, coughing in the air thick with coal dust and sparks. Luna was right behind us, and she continued chanting phrases in Ben's voice. When we reached the carved stones, we placed our hands on them and were immediately sucked into the long, dark tunnel with its bands of light. The journey stretched and squeezed us, but Varnar grabbed me and wrapped his arms tightly around me and Vinr. Under pressure from all sides, it felt like we were one. Varnar must have felt the same, because he used the opportunity to place his mouth against mine and kiss me.

I could feel him everywhere, smell him and taste him. Even though we had slept together and kissed many times before, this was different. As if we had dissolved and were reassembled as one being.

All too quickly, the journey between the worlds was over, and we plopped down on a plain that was so blindingly white, it hurt my eyes. I had to hold my hand in front of my face and squint to distinguish any shapes. Although the sky was just as dark as it was back home in Midgard, the snow shone like a full-frontal assault on my eyes. The biggest difference from Midgard was that it didn't smell like burnt wood here. I could breathe freely again, and I drank in the fresh air. Vinr had fallen from my hand when we landed on the ground. I got to my feet and brushed the snow off myself before picking up the staff. Luna lay a few yards away, and I gave her my hand.

The wind was freezing cold, despite the many layers of clothes I wore under my mother's coat and Ben's black Cossack hat. Like at home, a large storm was swirling in the sky, but it seemed we were in the eye of the hurricane.

Luna, Varnar, and I were on the plain between Jorvik and Vindr Fen.

The stone circle was right in front of me, but it wasn't in disarray like the last time I'd seen it. Just like in Kraghede Forest, the stones had been scrubbed clean and straightened, and they resembled human silhouettes with equal distance between them. They were painted and wrapped with ribbons and chains. Around the circle, the snow had been trampled down into a hard, grayish-brown mass. Unlike the boat-shaped arrangement in Kraghede Forest, this one was a perfect circle. The tree still stood in the middle of the circle, but it was now free of leaves. The last time I was here, with Sverre, I had found a dying man on the ground and a corpse hanging from the tree, both beaten beyond recognition by Ragnara's soldiers. The experience would stay with me forever.

Bodies hung from the branches once again. There were nine people, and they were already frozen solid. Black birds circled them and pecked at their flesh. There were ravens, crows, and magpies, and they all cackled excitedly. I felt like I should shoo them away, but it wouldn't make a difference at this point; the birds might as well have something to eat. I reached out with my clairvoyance, and the past flickered by. A mob under the influence of mass hysteria had dragged the human sacrifices to the tree. This was a continuous cycle that would never end unless someone put a definitive stop to it. The ghosts of the dead stood in a circle around the tree.

I walked up to a woman. She wore a light-colored scarf, and I glimpsed dark hair at her temples. She wore a wool jumpsuit, but her feet and hands were bare. Of course, her clothing didn't matter now that she was dead.

"Hi," I said cautiously, but she didn't react. "Can you hear me?"

She slowly turned her head toward me and didn't seem surprised that I was talking to her.

"When Ragnara ruled, people were sacrificed if they worshipped the old gods. I myself helped to punish those who weren't faithful to her," she said. "Now I'm the one who refused to renounce my beliefs. Ragnara was a good queen."

I looked up at her dead body in the tree. Ragnara's ghost suddenly stood at my side. She had evidently come along with us from Midgard. She placed her transparent hand on the woman's equally transparent shoulder. When the woman saw her, she gasped and sank to her knees. "My queen. My goddess."

"Don't call me that," Ragnara said softly. "You can't find peace with me. I don't want you to wander restlessly like me."

This was the real Ragnara. Not the worship-addicted, Tilarids-possessed version. I saw the ruler that Ragnara—or Melkorka, as she was originally named—could have been.

"You were sacrificed, so you'll go to Valhalla," Ragnara said.

The woman's eyes flickered. "But I disavowed the gods to follow you."

"It is my wish." I couldn't quite tell if Ragnara was stating a desire or a real order. "Tell Odin I sent your soul."

Hah! She was still a little devious.

She looked to me in appeal, and I stepped forward. "You were sacrificed. That gives you access to Valhalla."

The woman bowed her head. "Then send me there."

Ragnara's ghost placed a hand on the back of her head in a gesture of blessing. Luna and Varnar watched on reverently. Even though Luna could see only a little of the spirit world, and Varnar was completely outside it, they understood that this was a solemn moment.

I pounded Vinr against the ground, and some of the black birds took flight. "Fly on the wings of death. The birds will accompany you on your way." I pointed to a couple of disheveled magpies. They turned the sides of their heads toward me and looked at me with black, beady eyes. "Obey my orders and escort her to the realm of the dead." The birds and the spirit fluttered away.

Ragnara watched the spirit longingly. "If only I could have that peace."

"I wish I could give it to you," I replied sincerely.

"Odin won't let me in."

I bit my lip. "Go to Sverre and Ingeborg. Try to protect them. Maybe you can get upgraded to poltergeist or something. I'm worried for Little Finn."

Ragnara leaned back slightly. "You're good enough, raven."

I raised an eyebrow.

"You're bad enough for me to like you," Ragnara corrected herself with a grin. Then she grew serious and looked at Varnar. "Tell him I said goodbye. Tell him I love him."

"He knows that you were behind the deaths of his parents. He hates you." I hoped Varnar didn't hear my words.

"That doesn't change my feelings for him." Then she flickered and disappeared.

I made my way around the circle, sending the ghosts away unless they chose to stay near their loved ones. "I don't know how long this world will last. Maybe you should make use of your time,"

I said to a boy who had been far too young to die. Finally, I reached an old man. He had gray hair and wrinkles but stood straight and strong. A slightly translucent Thor's hammer hung from a chain around his neck. "They've been really thorough. I'm shaken by how many human lives people have been willing to take to save their own. Even you, one of the faithful."

The man's ghost craned his neck. "Hangatyr has its benefits. Humans have become the cheapest sacrifice. My death meant one less mouth to feed, and we've run out of other offerings."

"You gave yourself willingly?"

He shrugged. "It was either me or my daughter."

I let my hand hover over his shoulder and was careful not to let it fall through him. "You made the greatest sacrifice for your family. Your life wasn't meaningless, I promise you."

I looked up in the tree and made eye contact with a large, dark bird. It let out an extended shriek.

"Take him to Fólkvangr," I told the raven. "Tell Freyja he deserves the best seat and the finest food."

The raven flapped its wings and circled around us. It dove down, but the man placed a transparent hand on my arm. I could see him touching me, but I couldn't feel it.

"Send me to Helheim," he pleaded.

I furrowed my brows. "Why in the worlds would you want to go there?"

"Many of my friends are in Helheim. I'm not afraid of that realm of the dead."

Will you take him, Hel? He did die to protect his daughter, after all.

Hel sighed agreeably inside my head. *All are welcome here. I'll take him.*

Let Modgud know. She's pretty strict about who she lets in.

Hel laughed. *You're sounding more and more like a ruler. All right, raven! I'll give my gatekeeper the message that this man is permitted to pass through Helheim's gate.*

"You are accepted in Helheim. Hel is expecting you." I pounded Vinr against the ground and called silently to the goddess of the realm of the dead. I stood with my head bowed and caught my breath. It was still strenuous work to send the dead away, but it was getting easier and easier.

Varnar and Luna stood back while I helped the spirits, but when my shoulders sank and I let out a long sigh, they were at my side immediately. Both laid their hands on my shoulders, and their mere presence gave me strength. When I had recovered, I looked up, and my heart skipped a beat when I saw three figures emerging from the whirling snow that surrounded the stone circle. They were galloping toward us, surrounded by sparkling ice crystals against the gloomy background of the dark gray sky. Thunder and lightning above us, I could easily see what they were. The giant wolves' long legs were powerful, their red tongues hung from their mouths, and their white teeth glinted brightly and sharply.

I ran toward them, reaching Monster first. I fell to my knees and threw my arms around his big neck. His fur was soft under my fingers, and I felt his scar when I ran my hands along his sides. Rokkin and Boda joined us, and they, too, received hugs—even Boda, whom I basically didn't know. Rokkin licked my cheek and nipped playfully at the Cossack hat's ear flaps, while Boda stiffened in the same way Rokkin used to.

A woman walked behind the wolves. With slow movements, she drove her staff into the snow. Védis approached, and like me, she supported herself against a staff. Mine was more beautifully carved, but hers had a raw power I hadn't noticed the first time we met. Védis's face was smooth and pretty, but I knew magic made me see her that way. Like an almost-invisible film, I perceived her true appearance, in which half her jaw was missing on one side of her face, and on the other side, her face was disfigured by burns. She carried a pack on her back, and knowing her, it was probably full of magical herbs, bones, and totems. We nodded at one another. Her eyes lingered over the hat I had inherited from Ben.

"I know you cared about him," I said.

"He was my teacher and my best friend. You were there when it happened." She didn't phrase it as a question. She was asking me if I had caused Ben's death.

"The attack was meant for me. He was removing the spells he had cast on me."

Védis nodded briskly. "He wouldn't see it as your fault."

"Thank you," I whispered. "And thank you for answering my call."

Luna stepped forward, brought her hands to Védis's face, and held it. She looked very authoritative, standing in front of the witch. Luna didn't seem much younger than her at all. Védis's lower lip trembled, and she looked intently at Luna's stomach.

"You've done well," Luna said in her deep Ben voice.

Védis smiled, and I could faintly see her skull beneath her skin. "I want to do my part."

Meanwhile, I unscrewed the top of Vinr, fished out the red stones—Freyja's tears—and held them out to Védis. "The gold is gone, but here are the crystals."

Védis's eyes grew wide.

"You weren't expecting to get them back?"

With an awestruck expression, Védis's hands closed around the dried tears. "It's rare for people not to be greedy. My long life has taught me that." She tucked the tears into her pocket. "Freyja was the first witch. She is my foremother."

"There's something else you should see," I said, pulling the little figurine from my pocket. When Védis saw mini-Ben, she took a step back. "Odion," she whispered.

"You know him?"

Védis brought her hand to her jaw. "I knew him."

I shook the figurine. "I had a feeling—"

"I wouldn't do that if I were you." Védis stepped back slightly.

I shook it a little more. A hot-tempered surge zapped through my hand. "Ow!"

Védis raised an eyebrow in an I-told-you-so expression.

I held Odion out. "Do you want to hold him?"

Védis took the statuette in her shaking hands. Very carefully, she turned it around. "I can try to look at him."

We stood there, a small, eccentric group in Vindr Fen with the wind whipping around us and swirling over our heads. Three giant wolves, two witches, a warrior, and a völva.

"What do we have to do? Why did you call us here?" Monster's large eyes swept across the dramatic landscape.

I looked at each one of them. "I'm very grateful you came. We need to go to Dyflin."

Hrafnheim was no warmer than Midgard. In fact, the land seemed even colder, but that might have been the lack of electricity and light. Monster and I walked side by side. I peered out across the white terrain. There were houses here and there, but they were dark, and no smoke rose from their chimneys.

"How many have died?"

"Many." Monster sniffed the wind.

"Any of yours?"

"We giant wolves are growing stronger by the day." He didn't meet my gaze. "If the gods don't step in, we'll go to battle against the humans."

We continued for a while. With every step, I pressed my staff to the ground. The many völvas vibrated in my hand and gave me strength to go on. Luna and Védis were deep in conversation ahead of us; Boda and Rokkin walked just behind us; and Varnar pulled up the rear. His vigilant eyes constantly roamed over the landscape. I walked with my hand resting on Monster's back.

"Do you plan to tell me why we're going to Dyflin?" he asked.

"We have something to do in Hibernia."

Monster gave me the side-eye. "Hibernia is uninhabitable."

"Then it's a good thing we aren't going to live there."

Monster snorted like he always did when I was a wiseass.

"We're just going to Lake Meare," I said to soften the mood. "You know what's in the middle of the lake?"

"The island Afallon."

"Odin once told me that delicious apples grow on that island. *Afallon* means *apples* in one of the old languages." I said nothing more but looked expectantly at Monster.

He looked straight ahead, occasionally glancing at me. "And?"

"*Gnipa* also means *apples*."

Monster didn't respond.

"Fenrir is bound in Gnipahellir." I said this very quietly, but Monster had no trouble hearing me.

"The son of the giantess. My forefather."

"I'm betting everything that he's out there," I whispered.

"He's ruthless and as close to the mercilessness of nature as you can get, maybe even more than the Midgard Serpent."

"You're from the lineage of Fenrir. I was hoping you could convince him not to eat us."

"Fenrir can't be convinced of anything, Anna!"

We grew silent again. I thumped Vinr against the ground, perforating the snow on my path. A gust of wind even colder than before reached me, and I realized that the sky had shifted from dark gray to completely black. Like before, the clouds formed a spiral, but they spun more quickly toward us. The wolves and the witches hadn't seen it yet, but I instinctively turned to check on Varnar. He shivered as the freezing wind hit him. Lightning shot from the tornado, and a rumble made the ground vibrate. In the distance, I saw a wave of frost coming closer.

"Frost storm!" I shouted, panicked. Previous frost storms had nearly killed me, and in those instances, I had had laekna or

Mathias's divine warmth to draw from. Now I had nothing but Vinr, and I wasn't sure it could protect us all. I looked around and spotted a small house on the horizon. It was so dark, the structure nearly blended with its surroundings.

Varnar was already by my side, and he took my hand. Together, we ran toward the little farmhouse. Behind us, the frost crackled, and I heard the loud cracks of trees being crushed. Védis and Luna ran, and Monster's family sprinted, too, although I didn't doubt their giant powers would help them withstand the frost. Védis mumbled spells, and from her staff shot a hot, orange bubble that provided a little warmth, but not enough.

We reached the house and flung ourselves inside. There was no door, but Luna shouted something in Old Norse, and the doorframe was covered in a stretchy, balloon-like membrane. With a crash, the frost storm struck the magical barricade. Both Varnar and I were thrown back as the cold hit the film with a violent force, and it bulged inward. We crawled backward in the dark, cold house, and I stared at Luna's barrier as the interior surface was covered with blue ice. She held both hands out as she mumbled spells with deep concentration.

Varnar put his arms protectively around my shoulders, and Védis crouched with her staff aimed toward the vibrating membrane, which looked ominously fragile. Unstable, orange energy bubbled from Védis's staff, just barely enough to cover us with warmth. The wolves squeezed themselves protectively between us and the trembling blockade, which I feared would burst soon. I put the tip of Vinr on the floor and asked for help with all my heart. The völvas answered me, and a protective bubble formed around the giant crystal, covering all four of us along with Védis's orange magic. Just in time to shield us from the doorframe, which shattered in the frost. Splinters of wood flew in all directions, but they slid off our shields. The wall started to crack, and I thought it wouldn't make much difference if we were inside because through the small peepholes in the stone wall, I saw the tornado coming straight toward us. Luna's elastic wall exploded like a dam behind a tidal wave. I turned my head and buried it in Varnar's chest, and he ducked his head and held up his arm as sharp pieces of ice flew in.

When the storm was so close that I saw trees being ripped up with their roots, a cart lifting into the vortex, and snow being flung around, I thought that the whole house, with us in it, would be pulled into the storm. But Monster opened his giant maw and inhaled. His chest expanded, and I heard suction in his throat. When he exhaled, a cold cascade of air struck the cyclone outside. The collision caused lighting and loud crashing sounds, but Monster's breath diverted the tornado's path around the house by a hair's breadth. In an inferno of stone shards, splintered wood, and thunder, the frost storm passed us, continuing its path of destruction across the land. Even though I wasn't too happy with the gods, I asked them to spare the few living people out there.

It became deathly silent after the storm had passed. We sat in a heap with my and Védis's staffs aimed toward the opening where the doorframe had been. It was almost dark and ominously quiet outside.

Varnar was the first to speak. "We're not getting any farther today. We'll have to spend the night here."

I looked around the empty room. There was a resounding absence of life. Monster went out to the barn and returned with a disappointed expression. "There's only frozen meat, and I don't think you'll want to eat it."

We had retreated into the farthest corner of the house. I rummaged through cabinets and drawers for something edible, but there was nothing. Even the fireplace contained only ashes, and the remaining furnishings were metal. The house's inhabitants must have burned the cupboards and tables, and I understood why there was no front door.

"Were there animals in the barn?" I asked. Maybe we could thaw them somehow.

Monster's expression was dark. "Not animals. Someone gathered all the dead. I think the last one dragged themself out there." He licked his lips, but I didn't want to know why.

My chest tightened. If I had sacrificed Ingeborg, this wouldn't have happened. I reached out with my clairvoyance to see if any spirits needed help going to the realms of the dead, but there weren't any. Maybe they had found their own way, or maybe they had become oskoreia. I sat down heavily on the floor.

"There's nothing here. No food, no fuel." I looked over at the empty doorway. "Not even a door to shield us from the cold." Varnar sat right up against me, and the giant crystal on top of Vinr immediately began to glow. We were caressed by beams of warmth, and I leaned my cheek against his shoulder.

A deep sense of calm spread throughout my entire body. Neither tiredness nor the thought of food bothered me. Varnar slid his fingers between mine, and a completely different need took over.

"The membrane burst. I've never seen it do that before." Luna's expression looked much more like Ben's than her own. She growled in annoyance. "I can't access my magic. I'm not strong enough."

Védis took Luna's hands and turned her bare palms upward. "Could it be because . . . ?"

Understanding reached Luna's face. "Do you want to do it again?"

Again?

Luna also seemed confused, which looked odd, since her face was constantly shifting from her mild expression to Ben's confident one.

Védis patted her shoulder. "I'll explain everything." She pulled Luna away, and with a look between themselves and the barn, the wolves lumbered off, too. I didn't want to think about what they would do out there.

Vinr warmed us up, and Varnar held his arms around me. Even though Fimbul had almost killed us and everything seemed impossible, for a brief moment, I didn't care. Especially when I turned my head and looked into his eyes. Judging by how close he held me, he felt the same way. I had missed him ever since he had disappeared from Midgard and left me behind, alone.

Vinr shone intensely, and it got very warm in the room. I took the Cossack hat off, and Varnar smoothed my hair while smiling one of his rare smiles. "How long has it been since you combed your hair?"

My hair stood in an unruly red cloud around my head. I ruffled his matted brown locks. "I could ask you the same question."

In one fluid motion that I barely noticed, and which was typical of him, he got me onto my back. He leaned over me. Now I was really warm. His look gave me butterflies in my stomach. I reached up and placed my hands behind his head.

"I can't even function without you. I've tried—"

"Shhhh . . ." He lowered his face to meet mine.

I flew over the realms. Maybe I was dreaming that I sat in Odin's seat, or maybe I had finally become a real raven. Time waved past, and I saw the living and the dead all mixed together.

"Anna. Anna . . ." It was Serén's voice. I flapped, and where my arms should have been there were black wings. Another black bird flew by my side.

"Serén?" My voice scratched.

"Odin came to me and also made me a völva." She shrieked hoarsely and swooped through the air.

"What?"

"We're both völvas. Maybe now we can meet. Then we can stop Ragnarök."

"No, Serén. We can't meet. Ragnarök shouldn't be stopped." I realized that maybe it hadn't been smart to keep Serén in the dark about my new plan. I mentally hit myself on the head.

"Caaw!" Serén shrieked, uncomprehending.

I spoke quickly. "This is our chance to get rid of the gods. Odin must be desperate. He knows I'm close to doing it."

"I don't understand."

"We have to stay away from one another."

"What about our future? I saw us at the hálfa festivities in Fron. I'm almost completely certain it'll happen that way."

"Did you see what we would have to pay for it?"

"No."

"I'm sorry, Serén. The price is too high." She started to protest again, but I cut her off. "I'm sorry, but they must be stopped. No more Fimbul. Odin and Loki have caused too much suffering, and they'll keep at it for the next thousand years if we don't step in."

Everything looked distorted through my raven eyes. As though the whole world were in a big dome. Serén flew faster, pulling away from me slightly. She half yelled, half sobbed.

"I thought—"

"Odin tricked you. He's fighting for his life."

"It's just . . ." Serén sniffed. "I love being a völva."

I didn't feel the same. It was a heavy burden to always be sending people to the realms of the dead.

"I help the unborn come into this world. I can always sense life being created. After all that death, it's amazing."

"Clearly you don't have the same duties as me." I flapped my wings extra hard.

"I'm the future," Serén bellowed. "My field concerns everything that hasn't happened yet. Possibilities. Potential." She snapped her beak a few times.

We flapped to a branch and sat. In bird form, it felt even more like we were together. It was more lifelike than our many previous dream visits. Our black bodies were squeezed against each other, and Serén tidied my feathers. She moved on to my wing, and I sharpened my beak against the branch.

Suddenly, Serén cawed and alighted from the branch. "Caaaw. Caaaaw. My future in Frón with Aella is dissolving, and the old one is coming back."

"What?" I flew upward, too.

Serén composed herself enough to drift back down to the branch, but she was hopping around nervously. I sat next to her.

"There's something I have to tell you," Serén cawed.

I don't know why, but my bird heart turned to ice. "What have you seen?"

She shook her black head and let out an unhappy wail. "He knew. He knew. He was aware of the risk. Even before he went to Midgard. He hadn't even met you yet."

"What risk?"

Serén snapped her beak, the sound of horn hitting horn. "He made me swear not to tell you. And then it went away. Now it's back. What did you decide, Anna? What have you done?"

"What do you see?"

She let out a long, high-pitched sound.

"Tell me!" With all my strength, I tore at my sister's head with my claws and pecked hard at the back of her neck. She hopped away on one leg, her feathers sticking out in all directions. "Tell me now." I spread my wings like a big, dark cape.

"I see that he'll die if he helps you. If he answered your call."

My whole bird body tingled. "Who will die?"

Serén murmured sadly. She curved her back, placing her raven head beneath mine. "I told him he wouldn't survive helping you. He replied that he'd already been dead for many years. The little bit of life he had experienced was thanks to you."

"Who will die, Serén?" I screeched. The sound cut through my ears, and I knew perfectly well who she meant. Nevertheless, she said it out loud.

"Varnar," Serén cawed. "Varnar will die."

CHAPTER 43

I woke up on the floor. Vinr lay at my side, the giant crystal was completely dark, and Varnar was nowhere to be seen. I leapt to my feet and ran into the main room. All I could think was *no, no, no*. On shaking legs, I rushed outside holding Vinr in front of me, ready to fight if needed.

No one was in the yard. The debris from yesterday's frost storm and a smudged, red track on the ground were the only evidence that anything had happened in this place since its inhabitants succumbed to cold and hunger.

I sprinted around the house, my heart pounding. On the other side, I crashed into Varnar, who stood right in front of the open door to the barn. He let out an *ummmph* when I ran into him.

"Are you okay?" I was breathless with fear, so my words sounded hoarse.

He immediately went into full-on protector mode and looked around, his eyes wild. Monster stood a short distance away, but he came running when he saw my dramatic arrival.

"Are you?" Varnar asked.

I spun around, swinging my staff in an arc, before turning back toward Varnar, who had assumed an attack position, his knees bent. We stood back to back with Monster in front of us. Boda and Rokkin came sprinting toward us. Their sharp claws sent snow and pebbles flying.

"Where's the danger?" Varnar whispered.

"I was going to ask you the same thing."

"There's no one here but the witches and the wolves."

Just then, Luna came around the corner. She held her hands out as if they caused her pain.

"Something *did* happen." I gasped. With my sudden burst of emotion, a bubble sprang from Vinr's top.

"Ow," she whimpered.

With my staff still raised, I ran over to her, and she showed me her swollen palms, which were lined with blue pigment.

"What happened?"

"Magical symbols," she moaned.

I looked closer. Luna had had her palms tattooed with markings identical to Ben's. The intricate symbols looked painful and bulged slightly, but they were unmistakably the same ones.

I couldn't help but grimace in sympathy. "Isn't that a little drastic?"

"Not if I'm going to help you properly." She pursed her lips in the stubborn expression I knew so well. In the time I had known Luna, she had dyed her hair red at a time when a serial killer with a preference for redheads was on the loose, after which she—a devout Norse Pagan—followed me to a land ruled by a fundamentalist, atheistic regime. She believed wholeheartedly in our cause.

I slowly lowered Vinr. "We weren't attacked?"

Varnar returned to a normal position. "Not at all."

I took a step to the side to see around the corner. There, I spotted Védis, who knelt in front of a snowdrift into which she had stuck the little Odion figurine. The drift had melted a bit, and the statuette had sunk crookedly into the snow. Around the snowdrift, Védis had sprinkled some crushed red powder in the shape of a circle with a star inside. At each point of the star, she had placed a bone or a little skull from a mouse or a bird.

"So, there's no danger here?" I turned toward Varnar. My eyes traced over him again to check that he was unharmed, and I realized I had grabbed him by the shirt.

"Everyone's safe," Varnar assured me.

"You're coming with me. Now!" With Varnar in tow, I returned to the house. I dragged the greatest warrior in the worlds away with a firm grip on his collar.

"What's going on?" He twisted himself free but came with me. Monster and Luna exchanged a nervous glance. In the main room, I spun around to face him.

"Why am I only finding out now?"

Varnar's face displayed a variety of emotions, but he said nothing.

"You could die from this mission." I hit him in the chest with clenched fists. With a frustrated whine, I let my hands rest on his torso. He laid his hands over mine and furrowed his brows in his familiar way.

"We could all die from this mission," he said quietly.

"But you more than the rest. Serén saw it in your future, and you know it, too." I stepped close to him, and his scent of fresh air and forest was intoxicating. "Serén just told me that you'll die because you answered my call." I fought to hold back tears.

Energy vibrated around Varnar, but he kept completely still, his hands still on mine.

"Serén tried to talk you out of coming, but you insisted. Why in the worlds did you have to be so stupid?" I sobbed.

He furrowed his brows again—confirmation enough that my sister had warned him, and that he had chosen to ignore it. His thumb brushed the back of my hand.

"I thought it had already happened," I whispered. "I thought you were gone." My fingers moved to his face. I wanted to touch him. I wanted to be close to him.

Finally, he spoke, but his voice was gentle. "I was so scared I would never see you again. When I left Midgard, the sorrow nearly killed me. I would rather die by your side than live without you."

"But," I cried, unable to hold my desperation back. "I just want you alive, even if it's not with me."

Varnar carefully wiped my tears away. "Don't you get it?"

I shook my head.

"I died many years ago. When I went to Midgard, before I even met you, I knew the mission would cost me my life. All the time I've lived since we met has been thanks to you."

"You can't leave me. Everything else doesn't matter. Ragnarök, all the others, future and past. I need you here with me."

He leaned forward. "I'm right here, and I'm with you. I'll never leave you."

We leaned our foreheads together, and for a moment, we just stood like that, joined like a bridge. He moved his face slightly so his lips brushed against mine, and he held his mouth there. I imprinted the feeling of Varnar's warm breath against my lips into my memory so I would never forget it. Then he kissed me. The warmth spread through my body, but not in the way that made me want him to carry me to the closest bed. This was even deeper, and I felt something break and flow into me. My lifelong fear that no one liked me disappeared. With Varnar, I had no doubts. He loved me, and I accepted that thought, even though it was hard. I moved my mouth slightly.

"I love you," I whispered. "And that's so dangerous because it makes me vulnerable as hell. I'm scared all the time. Scared of losing the people I care about."

"But if you don't have anyone to care about, life is meaningless."

I rested my forehead against his chest, and he kissed my hair. "Are you sure you don't want to go back to Haraldsborg?"

"And leave you to carry out your mission alone?" He let out a low laugh. "Not a chance."

"How did I know you would say that?"

I had to hold a hand over my eyes, but Monster's thick eyebrows shielded his. It was dark gray like at home, but behind the thick cloud cover with somewhat lighter spirals, lightning flashed, making our frosty surroundings shine. Ice crystals glinted everywhere, reflecting the sparse light. Monster sniffed the clear air and sneezed. My own airways hurt with every inhalation. Varnar blinked at the white expanse, and Védis pulled her coat tightly around her. We had reached the place that, by my calculations, should be the border of Hibernia, but oddly enough, nothing changed. We were walking through a landscape so flat, it gave northern Denmark a run for its money. It was eerily quiet, aside from the occasional thunderclaps, earthquakes, and ice cracking not too far from us. There was no wind, animals, or plants—no life at all. I looked around at the lifeless landscape in the dusk.

"This is the coldest place in Hrafnheim because it's right at the border of Utgard. Everyone in Dyflin and the surrounding area died when the first frost storm came. They were hit hardest by the forces of chaos." Védis used her staff as a walking stick just like I did with Vinr.

Our surroundings remained identical through the last several miles. I looked over my shoulder but saw only the same, snow-white world. I usually had a good sense of direction, but right now it was failing me.

Monster must have felt the same. "Where are we? I can't recognize anything with my eyes or my nose."

I reached out with my clairvoyance. I sensed that I had been here before with Sverre. With my eyes squeezed shut, I concentrated.

Black sand, trees, and steaming hummocks. My eyes shot open. "Wow!" I exclaimed.

"What?"

"We're only half an hour from Lake Meare." I pointed down. "We're standing above the treetops."

Monster hopped a few nervous paces.

We walked quickly to keep warm and to get there before nightfall. In one place, the ice was pushed up in a curve, as though someone had been using a gigantic ice-cream scoop. It took a while to get around it, and on the other side, I stopped. Although I didn't think I could get any colder, a chill ran down my spine. The glacier at the end of Lake Meare had grown to tremendous heights since I was last here. Only the lake with the little island in the middle and a bit of the town lay in a crater. Everything else was packed in ice and snow, and even though we stood on a glacier, it was much higher at the end of Lake Meare. It was just like the one swallowing Midgard.

The lake was frozen solid, and the wall of ice stretched several miles up in the air, completely immovable and damn scary. In the distance, I glimpsed half of Dyflin. The green lindworm bones glowed, and I saw some of the buildings' crystal-covered wood. The other part of the town was buried under the glacier.

I turned toward Varnar, Luna, and Védis. "You wait here." Varnar wanted to protest, but I cut him off. "You'll secure our retreat. The wolves and I will be back soon. We need you to be ready to help us." I crossed my fingers behind my back.

Varnar studied my face. He was looking for signs that I was trying to pull one over on him, but he saw no hesitation. With a nod, he agreed.

"Védis and Luna: Can you make a heat bubble around all three of you if a frost storm comes?"

Luna displayed her freshly tattooed hands. They were still a little swollen and red, but they were already starting to heal. "Now we can."

Védis thumped her worn staff against the ground brusquely, and the bird at the top gave off an electric flicker. "What kind of witch would I be if I couldn't?"

A *sensible self-taught witch*. I kept this last thought to myself as I turned away and walked toward the lake with Monster and the other two wolves.

"You're good," he said out of the corner of his mouth.

"At what?"

"Lying. You're protecting them."

"Hrmm . . ." I refused to look at him.

"Maybe you'll succeed in deceiving Varnar of the Bronze Forest and the witches. You can lie to all the others but not to us." The muscles in Rokkin's back tensed as she leapt over a treetop that stuck up from the ground.

"You're friends with Varnar, too?"

Rokkin looked back. "That's why I want him to die for something he believes in."

Giant-wolf logic!

"How do we get down?" Monster asked when we reached the edge. The snow had frozen into a kind of ice ramp.

"There's only one way," I said and gathered my coat around me. I held Vinr tightly against my body, then slid down on my back. The snow was smooth and hard, so there was no problem going down. Next to me, Monster slid down on his stomach. Rokkin and Boda followed after him.

"We're in a pit. How will we get back out?" Monster asked when, soon after, we reached the bottom.

"We'll cross that bridge when we get to it." I walked toward the lake in the last dregs of daylight, which could barely be called light. I walked ahead of Monster and reached the edge of the frozen lake first. Cautiously, I stepped out onto the ice. It took less than a second for me to slip and fall on my back. Monster walked out after me. His thick claws had a much better grip on the ice, and he reached me quickly. I pulled myself up by grabbing his long fur. Boda came to my other side so I could also use her for support. Monster's mate didn't talk much, but now she opened her large mouth. The teeth inside were just as white and sharp as Monster's.

"I know what's out there—or should I say *who* is out there. It's Gnipahellir, and Fenrir is bound inside. The question is whether we're going there to kill my forefather." Boda thrust her snout toward the charcoal sky and howled so wildly, I had no doubts about her wolf origins. Her large eyes were fluorescent, and wildness lay just beneath the surface. I trusted Monster, but in his wife and daughter, their giant side was more dominant.

Rokkin stood in front of me, and she placed her head in front of mine. "Fenrir will eat you whole."

"Maybe that will be my last duty before I become Ragnarök." Hejd spoke through my mouth:

> *Now Garm howls loud*
> *Before Gnipahellir*
> *The fetters will burst*
> *And the wolf run free*
> *Much does she know*
> *And more can see*
> *Of the fate of the gods,*
> *The mighty in fight*

Monster gaped as much as a wolf could gape. "That wasn't your voice."

"It was Hejd. She's following what's going on. She's been following me from the beginning, a thousand years ago. Even then, she saw me. This is my fate."

"The last sign before Ragnarök can start is that Fenrir is loosened from his bondage," Monster said.

I nodded toward the ice. Now it was completely dark, but neither the moon nor stars lit our way. Only Vinr and Monster's predator eyes shone faintly.

"The humans are defenseless against the giants. We can't help but kill you if Loki calls us to battle. It would be somewhat easier to kill Fenrir. If we kill him, Ragnarök can't start." Rokkin surprised me with her direct statement. "Bound in the cave, he's an easy victim. He's a wild animal, and he has no mercy, even for those who help him. He bit Týr's hand off, even though he was his only friend among the gods."

"I'm well aware of that. Concepts of good and evil or right and wrong don't exist for him." I glanced at Boda, who leaned toward me so I wouldn't fall. "I can't believe you're related."

Monster laughed, but it sounded like sandpaper on a board. "Fenrir is a full giant, even though he's in wolf form. We're interbred with real wolves, so we're only half giants, which has probably made us giant wolves a little soft."

We walked toward Afallon. A strong smell of predatory animals grew stronger with each step across the ice.

CHAPTER 44

The island was small enough that I could see the other end when we stepped up onto the shore. Monster sniffed.

"There haven't been humans here in over a thousand years."

I raised Vinr and illuminated the space around me. There were collapsed buildings that most closely resembled an old monastery. The place had once been inhabited and active, but now it was a ruin. I sensed activity from my surroundings, but it was so old, it was only a faint echo.

"Can you smell anything else?" The snow-covered ground creaked under my feet as I walked. We were walking through what had once been an alley, but the path was now covered with rubble and chunks of ice.

"Giants and gods," Monster said. "And something else."

"What?"

"Apples. There are apple trees here."

We had reached a clearing surrounded by bare trees that did indeed smell like apples, even though there were no fruits in the vicinity. Monster had obviously detected the scent long before I did. We walked under the black, naked branches, and he snorted in the cold air. Behind us, Boda and Rokkin breathed in short inhalations. A crumbling opening came into view. Broken stone steps led underground, and light flickered from below.

Monster stopped. "You and Rokkin wait here. Let me and Boda go down. Tell me what needs to be done, and we'll do it."

"What if I asked you to kill Fenrir?"

Monster's large eyes shone in Vinr's light. "I trust you, Anna. Whatever you decide, I'm sure there's a reason."

I sank to my knees and embraced him.

Monster laid his head against mine and breathed into my hair. The two other giant wolves came up behind us. Rokkin's jaw rested on my shoulder. Sitting there between them, I felt more part of a family than I did with any humans.

"I've tried to evade and circumvent fate for a long time, but I *am* fate. I can't evade myself. If I want to help people, I have to do this."

"You'll be the death of us," Monster mumbled.

"I hope to be your salvation."

"I fear for your life," Monster said sincerely.

I didn't respond, even though I, too, had the feeling I might have come to the end of my journey. Hejd's words rang in my head:

For Huginn I fear
Lest he come not home
But for Muninn my fear is more.

That was me. I was Muninn.

The wolves followed me to the opening. My giant crystal shone over the frozen ruins. The fine ice crystals looked like diamonds, and I saw the beauty in the winter and the unchanging, dormant landscape. We carefully descended the stairs underground. At the top, they were covered in a sprinkling of snow, but the air quickly became stagnant and musty. Farther down was a sharp stench of animal, ammonia, fur, and raw meat. Monster sniffed the air, too, although I didn't know if the smell was as disgusting to him as it was to me. I held Vinr in front of me, half as a flashlight, half as a weapon.

We reached a chamber. At first, I could see only the small path we were walking on, but when I lifted Vinr over my head, I saw that the walls were lined with what looked like shelving or alcoves. They looked like the ones in the crypt beneath Odinmont. I walked closer and cautiously illuminated one of the shelves. There were bodies inside. I didn't move, even though the hairs on the back of my neck stood up.

A woman lay on the shelf. I thought she was a statue at first, but I saw that her skin was firm and healthy. There was a basket at her side, and in it were golden apples. I could smell their sweetness from where I stood.

"Idun's apples." I didn't dare touch them.

I stood on tiptoe and shined the light into another alcove. There lay a one-armed man. In a third alcove lay a warrior with bushy red hair and a beard. He had a wide belt around his waist, and in one hand lay a mighty hammer.

I waved Vinr's light around and revealed a host of people, each with their own attributes and distinctive features. One man looked like Mathias, but he was bigger. That had to be Heimdall. I nudged Mathias, but he didn't react. In fact, it was like poking a foam mattress.

"Smart of Odin to park Heimdall down here," I remarked. "He can't blow the Gjallarhorn as long as he's lying here. Odin gave himself an extra layer of insurance. Only he hadn't known that Heimdall had already met Mathias's mom."

Rokkin stuck her head into a shelf where a woman with golden hair lay. She pulled back quickly and sneezed several times. "Ugh. Gods. I hate that smell."

All I could smell were sweet apples and honey. We left the gods, and I followed my nose toward the stench of wild animals. The hall turned, and a light flickered at the end. Shadows danced, and we heard a deep rumble. The ground shook beneath our feet.

Earthquake?

When we turned the corner, I saw it hadn't been an earthquake. The wolf looked like Monster but much bigger. His head alone was the size of a car, his body snaking behind it, and I could easily see that he was related to the Midgard Serpent. The three siblings—Hel, Fenrir, and the Midgard Serpent—formed a spectrum, where Hel was the most civilized and the Midgard Serpent the most savage. Fenrir was in the middle, but all three of Loki's children were wild and dangerous. As always, when confronted with giant powers, I had to admit they were overwhelmingly beautiful, in the same way a storm is the second before it capsizes your boat and drowns you. Monster gasped when he saw the impressive creature lying on the floor with his head resting on his front paws. Fenrir followed us with his eyes, which were as big as manhole covers. High-pitched noise came from his closed mouth. Even though it was only a restrained whine, I nearly lost my footing as the sound sent tremors through the floor.

Monster, Rokkin, and Boda sank down to their front paws.

"Forefather," Monster said.

Fenrir lifted his head and studied us. His enormous eyes focused on me, he opened his mouth, and a scent of blood and flesh wafted toward me. "Raven," he said in a voice so deep and raspy that the ground shook again. With a concerted effort and a firm grip on Vinr, I stayed upright, even though the smell of cadaver was enough to knock me out.

"I am Odin's raven, and I'm here to release you from your bonds."

Fenrir stood to his full height. Each of his sinewy legs was twice as tall as I was. His head brushed against the ceiling. "Is this a trick?" he asked Monster. "A trick is what got me here."

Monster was still in a deep bow. "The raven is not plotting anything. You have my word."

Boda glanced at him, but kept her mouth shut. I was pretty sure she didn't trust me as far as she could throw me.

I took a step forward to explain myself so it didn't rest on Monster alone, but my movement was quick and triggered Fenrir's wolf instincts. With a roar that nearly burst my eardrums, he flung his large body toward me and snapped his teeth. Each tooth was the length of a man's arm, and if Monster hadn't locked his jaws on my coat to pull me back, I would have been bitten in two. Fenrir was stopped midair by the tether around his neck, and he made an anguished, guttural sound as he fell backward and hit the ground with a crash. The other two wolves howled and jumped out of the way of their forefather, who seemingly had no qualms about killing us all. I flew through the air, catapulted by Monster's giant powers, and my coat made a tearing noise as his teeth ripped its back. Fenrir crawled forward again, snapping and frothing, and I pulled my legs back just in time. There was a ringing in my ears.

Boda backed away with teeth bared, while Rokkin barked angrily.

"Is that how you thank the person who wants to set you free?" I wrapped my arms around my legs as though to pull myself farther back, so I was a little ball. Little in comparison to Fenrir, in any case.

"I don't thank anyone," Fenrir growled. "I am nature. I am power. I *am*." His words sent clouds of dust swirling toward me. I sat there, whimpering, with Fenrir's snout no more than half a yard from my feet. Every time he took a breath, a wave of dust blew over me. The chain around his neck was thinner than one of Luna's threads of yarn, and I prayed it would hold.

"He'll kill you if you release him," Monster warned.

"He can't help it."

"That won't make you any less dead."

I slowly got to my feet. I held out my hands—one flat, the other holding Vinr—toward Fenrir's head. The wolf lay still again, and even though he was motionless, he was buzzing with energy. His wide eyes followed my every move, but when I stepped closer, he didn't lunge at me.

"Anna," Monster whispered, but I ignored him.

When the light of the giant crystal hit Fenrir's furry head, he relaxed a little more.

Maybe I could . . .

I carefully eased Vinr's raven-bedecked tip between Fenrir's neck and the thin chain. Even though I was now within range for him to eat me, he didn't move. When the giant crystal touched the chain, it loosened slightly. Still a captive to the chain, he lay still.

"Can you carry me?" I asked Monster.

"Pfft," he scoffed. "You weigh no more than a feather to me."

"When I say go, start running." I gestured discreetly toward Rokkin and Boda. "You, too."

In response, Monster tensed his muscles, and the female wolves moved toward the exit.

I jiggled the chain a little more. The clasp mechanism resembled a choke collar, so I would have to loosen it to get it off. A thousand years in the cave had knotted the thin chain into Fenrir's long fur, so I struggled to get it loose. It wasn't working, and my attempt to keep a staff's length between us failed. I leaned Vinr against the stone wall, pulled Auka from my belt, and walked up to the wolf.

"No," Monster snapped, but I was already right in front of the beast.

With cautious movements, I cut through the thick fur. Each hair was covered in animal fat, and my fingers were smeared with brown grease. Fenrir didn't move, but his large eyes followed even my slightest moves. His ribs expanded and contracted like giant bellows.

When I was done cutting through the wolf's fur, I slid Auka back into my belt, took Vinr, and once again stuck the giant crystal between Fenrir's neck and the chain. I got as far away as I could while still reaching Fenrir's neck with the staff. With effort, I fought again with the thin chain; it was somewhat easier now with the fur out of the way. Suddenly, it released its grip on Fenrir's neck. He pulled his head back, and the tether slid over his neck. In the same moment, I leapt onto Monster's back.

"Run."

Monster took off as I clung to him. His daughter and wife were just ahead of us. I had ridden on a giant wolf before, but Monster was faster and stronger than Vale—a good thing since Fenrir was right on our heels. Fenrir snapped at Monster's hamstrings several times, but Monster managed to jump out of the way. When he barked, scalding hot breath struck my back and dust sprinkled down from the brick passageway's ceiling from the force of it. Fenrir galloped through the narrow halls, and it was only because we were smaller that we managed to reach the alcoves where the gods slept.

Monster took a gigantic leap, and we were suddenly out on the island above. The other two giant wolves landed in a spray of ice and snow, followed by Fenrir. When he landed on Afallon with a boom, Monster nearly lost his footing, and I tensed my arms to hold on. I looked over my shoulder. Our split-second hesitation gave Fenrir the opportunity to get closer. His arm-length white teeth drew nearer, along with the stench of flesh and blood on his breath.

I'm going to die now were the words that ran through my head, clear as day. My mission was accomplished: Fenrir was free. All the omens had been fulfilled. Now Mathias just needed to blow on the Gjallarhorn so the gods would be called to battle and meet their fate. I was no longer needed. *I'm going to die now.*

Fenrir's large mouth came closer. It snapped in the air just inches from my face in a cloud of dog breath and rotten meat. A big lick drenched both Monster and me with slobber.

"What?"

Fenrir hopped and bucked lightheartedly, then stopped. He looked more like a playful, oversized German shepherd than a mythical giant wolf.

Beneath me, Monster took deep, shaky breaths. Fenrir did a

few more carefree leaps, his ears pointing up in the air. Finally, he chased his own tail in a wild romp that made our surroundings tremble.

Soaked in wolf saliva, Monster composed himself enough to keep running after his wife and daughter.

I clung to his back as we ran over the lake to create distance between us and Afallon. Behind us on the ice, Fenrir jumped and played, celebrating his newfound freedom. Finally, he took off running as though to get as far as possible from the cursed cave.

We ran away from the ice cap. It had come even farther over land and now engulfed the inn where Sverre and I had once spent the night. With a crunch, the roof collapsed beneath the mass of ice.

"Go," I whispered, scared to raise my voice and start an avalanche. We ran up to the snow wall we had slid down before. I hoped Monster's sharp claws would get enough traction to pull us up—without sending the snow crashing down. I buried my face in his soft fur, and the wolves ran as fast as they could while also trying to be quiet.

Suddenly, Serén screamed in my head. *The other way! The other way!*

"But—"

Just do it!

"Turn around," I shouted. My voice alone made the wall of snow crackle.

"Straight into the ice cap?" Monster asked.

"Apparently."

The wolves screeched to a halt so they could turn around. I looked back.

Behind us, Fenrir had stopped in his tracks. He turned his large head toward us. Then he tilted his head back and let out a long howl. The sound made everything quiver, and that was the last straw.

We watched as the snow wall collapsed, and an avalanche rushed toward us.

CHAPTER 45

If Serén hadn't gotten us to stop, we would have been buried under several tons of snow. Monster just barely had time to bark an order before a cascade tumbled forward. He ran backward and swung his body around so we were galloping away from the avalanche with Boda and Rokkin right behind us.

"Varnar!" He stood with Luna and Védis on top of the snow. *No more of my loved ones can get hurt!* I wanted to go back and save them, but Monster kept running, the wave of snow at his heels. He managed to stay on his feet even though the ground shook. When we passed the lake, I saw Fenrir running parallel to us out on the ice. Like Monster, he had no problem gripping the surface with his sharp claws. I could smell his hot, bloody breath even from this distance. We drew closer to the unstable ice cap.

Varnar and Luna, I thought desperately. *Serén? Serén? Is Varnar okay?*

Serén's voice crackled as if through a phone with poor reception . . . *can't see . . . Va . . .*

What? "What?" Although I shouted as loudly as I could, it was drowned out by the sound of the avalanche. Of course Serén couldn't hear me, either. In a fluid motion, we galloped onward, pursued by the masses of snow drawing ever closer.

"Boda," Monster called. "Rokkin."

"Where do we go?" I looked back and watched as the place we had just run through was buried in snow and ice. I turned my head forward. In front of us was nothing but the mile-high ice cap.

Blocks of ice dropped from it, and if we got much closer, we would be crushed.

Just as we were about to be swallowed by the waves of ice coming at us from both sides like a cold pincer, Monster ran to the side. "The ice caves are down here," he panted.

"The ice what?"

"The outermost part of Utgard."

We reached the entrance, which I never would have found on my own. It was nothing more than a narrow crack in the glacier. Boda and Rokkin ran ahead of us, then Monster squeezed through. I had to pull my legs up so they wouldn't get caught between his body and the massive walls.

We made our way farther into the crack, and at the end I could make out a chamber. Oddly enough, it was lighter inside than out. The avalanche outside fell against the opening, and we were hit in the back with a gust of icy air. The crash was overwhelming, and I hid my face in Monster's thick fur. This continued for several minutes, and the passageway we had come through was filled with snow. We wouldn't be able to get out that way. Monster pressed ahead the last few steps into the cave, and we threw ourselves on the ground. I lay with my arms over my head, and Monster held his paws protectively over his snout as our surroundings shook and something clattered. Finally, the spectacle stopped, and I cautiously raised my head.

"Wow!" was all I could say.

We were in a cathedral. A natural cathedral—this place was definitely not man-made, but the arches rose high above us, glittering with frost in every color of the rainbow. Light must have been coming in from somewhere, but I had no idea whether it was the sun or the stars that illuminated this magical space. Regardless of the circumstances, seeing true light after so much time in a gray, unreal glow was a balm for my soul. The shapes were organic, rounded, and soft, and even though there were physical boundaries in the form of ice, it was so pure that I could see through it for several yards.

If there was ever a time to become religious, it was now. I realized that Elias's grain store and the big museums had the same function as religion. Some people found that feeling in nature, and others found it in temples and churches. I reached out with my clairvoyance and investigated the feeling. It was comfort. I felt the presence of something greater. Not gods or powerful people, but existence, in all its wonderful relentlessness. Forms solidified in exquisite beauty, as though the universe had created this place millions of years ago just so that we could come and see it now. For some inexplicable reason, I wished Elias were here to experience it.

Monster had raised his snout, and the otherwise stoic giant wolf appeared to be moved. His large eyes glistened as he looked at the glowing vaulted ceiling high above our heads. Three-foot-long icicles pointed down toward us. Each of them was the length of Tilarids, and if they fell, they would impale us.

"I've only heard stories about this place." Monster's deep voice echoed. "This is Hrímhof. The sanctuary of chaos."

I kept looking around to take it all in, and every time I turned my gaze, something else caught my eye. "It doesn't seem particularly chaotic."

Monster suddenly laughed. "You still don't get it? Chaos—my origin—reigns over existence in its most neutral sense. Something that simply *is*. Destruction and the unfruitful stand still."

"This is the only thing I've ever wanted to worship."

Boda sat in front of me. She, too, seemed unusually reverent. "You're welcome to worship the giants and Hrímhof, but they really don't care. You won't get anything out of it."

"You don't have to get something out of everything you do." I placed my hand on an ice bubble. It was such a deep blue that it looked like my hand was over a wave paused mid-crash.

"Humans and gods never do anything unless they get something in return," Boda said.

I suddenly felt despondent. "Humans and gods aren't geared toward worshipping or being worshipped. It leads to suffering and petty, meaningless fights. Witch burnings, wars, human sacrifices . . ." My voice faded out.

"And yet faith is deeply ingrained in your nature."

"Not in mine."

Monster sniffed. "Sometimes I've actually wondered if you didn't have a little giant blood in you."

"Do giants not want to be worshipped?"

"Nah," Monster drawled. "Giants, or nature, which is what we are most of all, just wants to be. We want to be wild and gentle and destructive and creative. The wind keeps blowing even though no one sees it. The snow still falls even if no one worships it. We don't need it. We just want you to acknowledge our existence."

I furrowed my brows. "Someone else told me that before. Chaos and cosmos, destruction and creation, past and future, life and death," I began, the words appearing as though I were digging them up from ancient sand. "It all goes together."

"My foremother, Hel, comes closest to depicting it."

"How so?"

"She's both life and death. Life is ugly, and death is beautiful, and death is ugly while life is beautiful."

I inhaled slowly. The air was clear and cold, and it struck me that I was the first person in millennia to breathe this oxygen.

Serén . . . Serén . . .

The wolves and I had been walking all night and were now reaching the mouth of the ice cave. I had been trying to make contact with my sister for hours.

Anna!

"Yes!" I shouted out loud, and because we had been in silence for so long, Monster jumped, startled. I stopped and laid my hand on his back while I held a finger in the air to show I was on the line with someone. With eyes closed, I inhaled deeply.

We're all okay.

Varnar, Luna, and Védis are alive.

We spoke over one another, and we both stopped. Serén breathed in. *Rokkin?*

Rokkin is fine. I looked at the large, black giant wolf, who had sat down, scratching behind her ear.

A few moments passed before my sister responded. *I saw the future change. I saw . . .*

You saw Rokkin die! She's alive and well, I assured her. *Where are the others?*

Serén still sounded shocked. *I can't see them now, but I see you together at the stone circle in Vindr Fen in the future. There's a cave right next to it. You will need it. Go there. Varnar is afraid that you're dead, and I can't send him a message.*

I almost didn't dare ask. *What you said last night . . . about how Varnar would . . . has that been averted?*

I've seen him die many times, which then didn't happen. By his own hand jumping from the castle wall in Sént, fighting Naut Kafnar in Midgard, from the cold plague in Haraldsborg, and now in the avalanche near Dyflin, but it didn't happen, because he's still in the future, so he must be alive.

I tried frantically to think of every way around Serén's statement. I was sure she was leaving something unsaid. *You always see many versions of the future. Have you seen him die in other places?*

Serén cursed quietly.

What have you seen?

Serén sighed so deeply, I could hear it through our mental connection. *I've seen everything, Anna. I've seen us all die in countless ways. It's like constantly saying goodbye.*

I wished I could say something comforting, but I of all people knew how heavy a burden time could be. *Ragnarök could start at any time. I'm going to find Mathias and convince him to blow the Gjallarhorn. Try to warn people to seek shelter. I think there will be natural disasters and attacking giants. I'll try to get Mardöll to send a mass message to everyone in Hrafnheim and Midgard.*

Right as I said this, Serén whimpered.

What's going on?

I see . . . Oh no . . . I see . . .

What do you see?

It was quiet for a moment, as though Serén were composing herself. *Nothing.*

Hey . . .

Find Varnar. Hurry!

The connection was broken. "Serén," I called out loud and pounded Vinr against the ground, but there was no response. I opened my eyes, my forehead ached from creasing in frustration and strain.

Monster looked at me inquisitively. "What did your sister say?"

I rubbed my temples. "I'm not sure."

CHAPTER 46

The snow drifted so thickly over Vindr that I could barely see the stone circle ahead. I definitely couldn't make out the bodies hanging from the treetop. I strode ahead persistently, even though I didn't have much strength left.

"Varnar. Vaaaarnar." The howling wind swallowed up my voice.

We got closer to the stone circle, and, shaking, I sensed the many violent things that had happened here.

Monster and Rokkin stayed close on either side of me, and Boda walked right behind me. They were likely scared I would collapse into a snowdrift.

"There's no one here," Rokkin shouted over the whistling wind. "Oh, wait—I smell something. Mmm. He smells so good."

I held my hand over my eyes as sharp snowflakes flew into them. I looked intently at the stones and saw movement in front of them. The most humanlike of the forms shifted. I waded forward all too slowly, encumbered by the deep snowdrifts. The person moved. When he saw me, he ran forward, too.

We met halfway between the stone circle and the wolves in a fervent embrace. Varnar's hands were cold against my cheeks, but his lips were warm as ever. We kissed amid the snowstorm, and even though the wind whipped at us, we remained standing, joined together. For all I cared, we could have frozen in place and turned into one of the stones in the circle. But Varnar broke the kiss.

"There's a cave over here." He took my hand and pulled me away. The wolves followed.

I held on tight and never wanted to let go. The ice crystals were cracking wildly, and I knew a frost storm was about to hit. Varnar had waited for me, even though he didn't know if I had survived.

Down in the cave, Védis and Luna waited for us. They sat cross-legged, holding each other's hands and looking deeply into each other's eyes. It looked like electric currents would shoot between them at any moment, and they didn't even look up when we arrived. The cave was warm. I realized they had kept the frost storm at bay using their combined powers. When we were finally inside, they cast magic toward the entrance, sealing it with heat. They fell to the side, exhausted, and outside the cave, the frost crashed as the wind picked up. Inside, we were safe.

Varnar looked over my shoulder at the wolves, who collapsed with their bright red tongues hanging from their mouths. Though their giant powers were impressive, they were much more exhausted than I had thought.

"Were you successful?"

"My forefather is free. I thought he was going to eat us," Monster groaned. "I don't understand why he spared us."

"He's a giant, Dad! We change our minds all the time." Rokkin rolled her eyes, and I suspected that wolf teenagers were like human ones when it came to relationships with their parents.

I looked at Monster and Boda. Monster had laid his big head on Boda's side, and she licked his ear with long, slow strokes.

"I thought I had lost you." Varnar held me with a desperation I sensed both in his grip and with my clairvoyance.

"I made it. We all did, incredibly. I was sure Fenrir was going to kill us, but he didn't." I clutched Varnar's coat. "I thought you had died in the avalanche. I meant to protect you, but I put you in mortal danger instead. I'm sorry."

Varnar furrowed his brows in a way that said I was being extremely annoying. "You don't have to protect me. I've told you hundreds of times."

"That's for me to decide." I said the words lovingly, and he held me closer, kissing my forehead.

The fear of losing him overwhelmed me, and I clung to him. He moved his mouth to meet mine.

Still kissing him, I pulled him into a side room in the cave.

"There's something I want to say to you," Varnar said.

I looked up at the roots in the ceiling. He lay behind me, his strong arms around me. Vinr gave off enough heat that I could almost make believe we were lying on a bed and not the pitiful remains of my coat in a cave with a frost storm raging outside. I absentmindedly stroked his bare forearm. He traced a finger along the ansuz-shaped scar on my back. It didn't hurt anymore, but the skin there was a little more sensitive.

"I heard that you had the chance to become queen." The words were whispered into my back. "You and Sverre could have reigned together." I jerked my head up, but Varnar kissed the back of my neck. "I want you to be safe and happy, even if it's not with me."

I laid my head back on his arm. "I don't want Sverre. Not anymore. And the worship at Sverresborg was one of the most unpleasant things I've ever experienced."

"And you've experienced a lot." Varnar caressed the scar on my bare back. "So that's saying something. Jealousy made me say those things to you at Haraldsborg last year. I've regretted it ever since. You're free to do whatever you want."

I turned over so I was facing him. "I'm only happy when I'm with you," I said, stroking his brown hair.

He held my gaze. "And I'm only happy when I'm with you."

I put my hand around his upper arm, where the many rune-shaped scars stood side by side. In the middle of his bicep was the slightly larger, more prominent mannaz. The rune that meant *human*. He had earned that scar after he killed an innocent girl before we had met. We both looked down at it.

"I want you to hide. If you follow me, you'll die. Serén saw it in the future."

"Hide?" Varnar sounded incredulous.

"For my sake. You have to survive so we can be together after Ragnarök."

"I'm not leaving your side."

"If you just give up, she will have died in vain." I pointed to his scar.

"Is it giving up to follow you? To protect you? I was put in this world to protect."

"I want . . . no, I *order* you to go back to Haraldsborg. You need to help Serén protect the people. I'm just one person, but at Haraldsborg you can find an outlet for your need to protect."

"Anna!"

I looked at him pleadingly. "You have to stay safe until Ragnarök is over. Please?"

His smile faltered. "But Ragnarök is the final battle. I'm a warrior. I should be there."

"I don't think Ragnarök is *final*. I think Ragnarök is a new beginning. It's hard to explain, but there will be a time after the apocalypse." I suddenly felt a little self-conscious. "And if I'm still alive, I'd really like to share that time with you."

Varnar ran his hand over my red hair, which I'm sure was sticking out in every direction. "I'm yours forever. I have been since the first time I saw you."

"Swear it!" I demanded. "You can't fight in Ragnarök."

He nodded. "I swear I won't fight in Ragnarök."

We made our way back to the large chamber, my cheeks blazing, but neither the wolves nor the witches seemed to notice that we had been gone or why. Varnar was natural as he stood with his arms around me. Monster looked up with one bushy eyebrow raised.

With an embarrassed cough, I focused on Védis. I could see her ruined face, but it was only a faint trace beneath the beautiful surface. I wasn't immune to her magic, but I saw the past, and it contained her wounds.

"Your powers are getting stronger, raven," she said. "I can sense them." She turned her gaze back to the little Odion figurine, which stood in a black pentagram that she and Luna had drawn on the ground. I squatted down and studied it. It really did resemble Ben.

"Did your dad make this?" I asked Luna. "I assume it's supposed to look like him."

"It's his brother." Luna said this offhandedly, like she was talking to someone at a cocktail party.

"His . . . Wait, what?"

"Augustin Odion. They're twins. Augustin and Benedict. A and B. He's my uncle."

"I'd thought the figurine was all of Ben's negative attributes bound up with magic."

Luna laughed deeply, and I sensed Ben himself had taken over. "You're right about the negative attributes, but Odion is very much his own person. My brother is malevolent. The missionaries called him a demon and a devil."

"Odion is Ben's evil twin?" A stunned laugh escaped my lips. "Are we in some crazy, supernatural soap opera?"

"There are a lot more twins in the supernatural world than in the normal one. You are a twin yourself, after all."

"But still . . ."

Luna stuck her nose in the air with the commonsensical expression she always had when she came up with an explanation for the extraordinary. "Freyja and Freyr are twins, Huginn and Muninn, Dagr and Nótt, and Sköll and Hati. And not just in Norse mythology. There's Apollo and Artemis and Isis and Nephthys."

"I got it."

"Romulus and Remus," she continued.

"Okay, okay—"

"Oh, oh!" She clapped her hands excitedly. "Maybe Augustin Odion can lift your spells."

"Do you think he can?"

"They're identical twins, so his magic and my dad's are the same. Actually, I would think Odion is the only person in all the worlds who could lift them." Suddenly, she was shaking.

"Luna!" I grabbed her shoulders.

"Never set him free." Ben's voice came from Luna's mouth. "Odion can destroy you."

I felt a jag of dismay. "My spells shouldn't be lifted. As much as I would like to meet my sister, if we're suddenly able to be together, we risk accidentally preventing Ragnarök. If the giants had gotten their hands on Odion, they surely would have set him free. They love chaos and destruction."

"Good thing Eskild was killed," Varnar added.

I turned around. "It's not good. He was like a father to you. Even though he ended up being brutal . . . more than brutal. He killed Arthur. But . . . I . . . I think Eskild was possessed. Tilarids, the sword Sverre had, takes control of its owner. Once it's corrupted one host, it moves on to another. In a way, it wasn't Eskild's fault."

"It's a magic sword," Védis said. "It's Loki's sword, and it can possess a host. But there must be a spark in the owner that it can nurture. In that way, Tilarids functions as a bellows, coaxing an ember into a flame until it burns out." Her eyes were still directed toward Odion in the middle of the pentagram.

I looked at Odion. He didn't look particularly dangerous. He looked like a porcelain figurine from the colonial era, depicting a caricatured idea of an African "savage" with a loincloth and bare torso. His hands faced outward as though he were ready to cast a spell.

Ariran! he hissed inside my head, and I fell backward. This was the second time he had pulled this stunt on me. I lay on the ground, writhing in pain from the blow. It felt like I had been hit with a taser.

Védis shot a barrage of spells in the figurine's direction, but her magic was highly unstable, and several balls of blue energy flew past him. One of them landed near Monster, and he had to jump to the side.

"Stöðva," Luna hissed. "Galdrakonu. Pack it up, sorcerer." She aimed her tattooed hands toward Odion, and it was clear that Ben had taken over. Her palms bore the same markings as the figurine's miniature hands.

Odion laughed, but he released his hold on me. Védis drew another circle around him and tossed a handful of herbs on the fire, creating a thick smoke.

"He's getting stronger," Luna groaned. "He's not usually this unruly."

"He's reacting to our witch powers," Védis said. "There's a reason why Benedict had him standing by himself and didn't touch him."

"I'm okay," I moaned before anyone asked. I slowly got to my feet. At first, Varnar helped me, but he knew me well enough to let go quickly.

"Can you keep him in check for the journey back to Midgard?"

Védis had beads of sweat on her forehead. "I think so."

"Then let's go to the stone circle. It sounds like the frost storm is letting up."

"We're coming, too," Varnar said, and Monster nodded.

"You're going back to Haraldsborg." I pointed to Varnar. "You swore." Before Varnar could protest, I turned toward the wolves. "And you need to find your kin and keep them away from Ragnarök."

"I don't fear the apocalypse," Monster rumbled. "I'm not afraid to meet death for what I believe in."

I knelt in front of him. "It's been foreseen that you will kill Luna."

Monster looked stunned, and Luna jerked away slightly, looking insulted. "Seriously, Monster?"

"He can't help it. Loki will force him," I said.

Luna came back and patted Monster's large head.

I looked from one to the other. "I want you away from the battle for several reasons, okay?"

Monster reluctantly agreed with a stately nod. "Can we at least walk you to the stone circle?"

I sniffed. "Yeah, that's okay, but only because it's on the way."

Monster rolled his eyes. "And so, a little girl sent the leader of the Varangian Guard and the crown prince of the giant wolves to safety while she put herself in the middle of the danger."

The walk to the stone circle was quiet. Snow fell in the bitter cold, but the wind had died down. Over our heads, the sky was still gray and in constant motion with lighter cloud formations. Constant lighting streaked across the clouds.

Our crunching steps were the only sound.

Védis had wrapped the Odion figurine in several layers of fabric painted with five-pointed stars and runes. The layers were surrounded by dried herbs and, finally, a black bag. The whole thing had been stuffed inside one of the skulls she liked to use in her shows. On the skull's forehead, she had drawn yet another pentagram.

"My powers aren't that strong," she explained. "I have to use all the skills Benedict taught me."

Luna patted Védis on the back. "You're doing great!"

"It's impressive you can do so much without proper training," I said.

Varnar held my hand. I had never tried to hold a man's hand with people watching before, and even though our audience consisted of witches and giant wolves, it was an entirely new feeling.

"Are you doing okay?" he asked and smiled at me.

I looked up at him, taking in his brown hair, high cheekbones, and dark eyes with their little green flecks. "I'm doing great." Even though the apocalypse was looming, I had my best friends and the man I loved within reach.

Varnar put his arm around me, and I rested my cheek against his shoulder. "I'm happy, too, Anna. Despite everything, I'm really happy."

All too quickly, we arrived at the circle. Varnar embraced me, and I didn't doubt for a second that sending him away was the right decision. If I made it out of this alive, I would find him and live with him until the end of our days. For the first time in a long time, I allowed myself to think optimistically. To see the future in a positive light. Our future. I thought of the vision in which we had a daughter. Ast. The future was my sister's territory, and for the most part, I barely got as far as contemplating the next day, but now I was imagining myself together with Varnar and our child on the other side of Ragnarök.

I was already looking forward to that day when we would walk together in the Bronze Forest. I smiled at the thought of Monster as our daughter's babysitter. When the day came, I would reflect on this moment with warmth in my heart.

"Because of you, I got my life back," Varnar whispered.

I looked at his face. His dark hair framed his severe features, which were currently soft. Without thinking, I repeated the end of Hejd's prophecy.

Then fields unsown bear ripened fruit
All ills grow better
Baldr and Hoth dwell in Hropt's battle-hall
And the mighty gods
Would you know yet more?

"I think you're Hoth or Baldr," I whispered. "I've figured out that everyone in the poem represents someone else."

"I think I'm Hönir," Varnar said.

"Hönir?"

Hönir himself can choose his fate
In Vindheim vast
Would you know yet more?

A breeze ruffled through the snow around us.

I furrowed my brows. "What do you mean, you can choose your fate?"

A film of tears settled over Varnar's eyes. He leaned forward and kissed my forehead. "I love you, Anna," he said. Then, he let go and turned around just as something roared behind us.

"What?" I looked in confusion at Fenrir, who was galloping toward us. His large tongue hung from his mouth, his white teeth gleaming. Monster took my coat in his teeth and pulled me to the portal.

"Varnar!" I yelled, but he didn't look back. Instead, he slowly walked toward the enormous beast.

Monster dragged me backward, and Védis followed, her staff raised. Luna shouted spells and sent blue energy balls toward Fenrir. In front of us, Varnar went into attack position. I knew his movements well, and I knew not a single one was random. Varnar prepared for the fight of his life.

"He lied," I whispered. "Varnar lied. He knew it."

"Come on." Védis took my elbow and pulled me toward the stone circle where the dead were still hanging, surrounded by black birds. When we entered the circle, the birds flapped away. I screamed and kicked and tried to go to Varnar, who stood in front of Fenrir, but Monster and Védis were too strong. Fenrir lunged, and Varnar slipped around him. He had a long knife in each hand.

"But you let us go," I protested.

"I changed my mind. I want to taste völva meat," Fenrir growled.

Fenrir's wild eyes shone. He let out a bark so deep and resounding that a couple of trees released their blankets of snow in big puffs.

"If it's me you want, let Varnar go."

Neither Fenrir nor Varnar took any notice of me. They circled one another, Varnar with knives raised and Fenrir with his head lowered, teeth bared, and hackles up. I cried because I knew—just as Varnar knew—he couldn't defeat Fenrir. He could only delay him. Monster was still pulling me toward the portal.

"Don't let Varnar of the Bronze Forest sacrifice himself in vain," he said out of the corner of his mouth.

Boda and Rokkin placed themselves on either side of Varnar. This jolted Monster, but he continued to drag me toward the stones.

Fenrir looked down at Boda, who snarled, her raised upper lip revealing a row of razor-sharp teeth.

"You are my blood," Fenrir said to her.

She moved closer to Varnar. "Whoever says giant wolves aren't loyal to their friends is lying."

"I order you to fight the human." Fenrir stomped his paw on the ground, setting off tremors.

Boda laughed hoarsely. "You can't order me to do anything, old man. I decide for myself. I'm only half giant! We wolves have a sense of honor, after all."

I flailed, trying to get to them. "Boda! Rokkin! Varnar! You can't—" But before I could finish my sentence, Monster jerked his head and flung me toward the largest stone in the circle. He remained on the Hrafnheim side and threw himself into the fight against Fenrir. I only just managed to make eye contact with Varnar as he watched me go safely through the portal. He smiled at me, still holding my gaze, and I screamed as I was pulled backward to Midgard.

The last thing I saw was Fenrir opening his maw full of long, white teeth and his bright red tongue. Then I was gone. I hadn't seen if Varnar had managed to jump aside.

 # CHAPTER 47

We landed in the middle of the stone circle in Kraghede Forest. I screamed and tried to go back to the portal, but Luna held me. Maybe Ben's strength was flowing through her veins, because I couldn't move. Védis aimed her staff toward a stone and sent off a blue energy bomb, and the painted boulder toppled backward. I twisted myself free and ran up to another stone, placing my hands on it to go through the portal, but the connection was broken.

"Varnar, Varnar . . ."

Serén, I called inside my head. *You have to come right now.*

There was a long pause, and then a timid *I promised him I'd get you away.*

And I order you to send me back. I pounded Vinr against the ground. *Send me back.*

I'm sorry. She said nothing more, even though I called and called and finally collapsed in front of the stone, pounding it with clenched fists. Védis held me and rocked me in her arms as though I were a little kid. Luna knelt and slung her arms around me.

I twisted away from them and aimed Vinr toward Védis. "Did you know?"

The skull with Odion inside had rolled away, and she reached backward to grab it. Maybe she wanted to protect herself with Ben's brother in case I attacked.

"Varnar made me swear to keep you safe if it came to this," she said. "And Fenrir couldn't be allowed to follow us to Midgard. The giant wolves will try to lure him to the Iron Forest so he doesn't cause chaos in Hrafnheim."

"Serén had told Varnar that he would fight Fenrir at Vindr Fen." I was breathless with desperation. "That was why he waited up by the stones. So that we didn't run into Fenrir alone. Now he's fighting him on his own."

"Etunaz is there, too, along with the other wolves."

"If Loki orders Monster and Boda into battle, they'll eat Varnar." At that thought, my throat tightened even more. "Or Fenrir will just kill them all."

I leaned on Vinr as we crossed the field toward Rebecca's house. My stomach was in knots. I had set Fenrir free. I tried not to look at the hill and the charred remains of Odinmont.

Luna followed my gaze. "Do you want to go up there?"

"No, of course I don't."

"Arthur is still living there."

"What?"

Luna punched me in the arm. "He's living inside Odinmont."

"But the house is destroyed."

Luna clicked her tongue. "The house was never Odinmont. The hill is Odinmont, and it's doing just fine. Nothing happened to the crypt." She peered across the white landscape. The sky was almost black with cloud spirals. Thunder rumbled and lightning flashed.

"Are you looking for Mathias?"

Luna nodded. There was a worried twitch at the corner of her mouth.

"Have you heard from Mardöll?"

Luna shook her head.

"I'm sure he's okay." Even I could tell my reassurance was hollow.

Luna said nothing, and her failure to assure me of Varnar's survival, in turn, made me even more nervous.

Rebecca was standing in the kitchen and lifted her head. Her eyes flared azure blue, and she had already raised her arms toward Védis. In one palm was electric energy, in the other a sharp knife. Rebecca's cheekbones were sharp, and her cheeks were more sunken than they'd been just two days ago.

Védis cowered, holding the skull with the pentagram on its forehead toward the knife-bearing Rebecca. I didn't know if Védis and Ben had had something going on, and maybe Rebecca was angry at her, but when Rebecca looked more closely at the witch, she lowered her hands again. She didn't seem the slightest bit frightened by Védis's macabre appearance, which was certainly visible to her.

"You're..." Rebecca gasped. "You..." She tossed the knife onto the kitchen table and embraced Védis, who stood there, confused, holding the skull. It was squeezed between the two women. "My husband told me so much about you," Rebecca said, still clinging to the surprised witch. She held Védis at arm's length. "I'm so happy to finally meet you."

"Me, too," Védis stammered, standing stiffly in Rebecca's grasp.

Rebecca looked down at the skull. "Who are you?" she asked sweetly.

Sinister laughter emitted from the skull's mouth.

Rebecca put a hand on her hip. "Augustin Odion! I can sense you. It's a good thing you're back where I can keep an eye on you." She fished the package out of the skull's mouth and unwrapped the figurine from the pieces of fabric. Dried herbs sprinkled onto the floor. Meanwhile, she mumbled incantations. "No!" she said. "You can forget about it."

The Odion figurine protested.

Rebecca shook her head. "Absolutely not. No. No." He kept interrupting her. "NO!" she said firmly and held the figure away from her, pinched between her thumb and index finger. She walked determinedly into the living room and set him on the shelf. She looked at us over her shoulder. "This is where we let him stay. It would be horrible if he got out. It took Ben several hundred years to contain him."

"Mom, you're not gonna believe this," Luna said when she could finally get a word in edgewise. "Dad is in my stomach." Luna pressed her little bump against her mother. "Say something to him."

Rebecca didn't so much as raise an eyebrow in disbelief, but tears of joy sprang to her eyes. She gently put her hands around Luna's middle and placed her mouth against her stomach. "My love?"

"Vinkona," Luna rumbled in her deep voice. Then Luna laughed in her own voice again. "See? He's in there."

Rebecca didn't say anything more to Luna's stomach. To put it mildly, the scene was bizarre and a little gross, and I couldn't help but think *ew*. But it was nice to see the Sekibo family happy finally. Their joy clashed harshly with my own misery. I should've been celebrating with them, but I didn't feel a reason to be there.

"Have you seen Mathias?" I asked Rebecca.

Still holding Luna's waist, she turned her head toward me. "You don't know where he is?"

Luna shook her head sadly.

A sound or feeling reached me from upstairs. The witches were too distracted by Luna's stomach to notice as I placed Vinr in Rebecca's umbrella stand, then turned and went up to the green guest bedroom Luna had set up for me. I pushed the door open and let out a little cry of surprise.

Varnar sat on the mattress. He stood up when he saw me.

"You survived." Breathless with relief, I ran to him. "How did you get here so fast? We just got here from the stone circle. Where are the wolves? Did they make it?" I flung my arms around him, but they went through his body, even though he was standing right in front of me. I ended up hugging myself.

He looked at me lovingly. "Etunaz is fine. He tried to help me. Boda and Rokkin survived, too."

I could smell Varnar, I could see him, but I couldn't touch him. He was as ephemeral as the air.

"You . . ." I inhaled shakily and couldn't continue.

He spread his arms, but when I leaned into him, I fell straight through.

Does he not know?

Varnar answered my question without me having to ask out loud. "I know."

Very carefully, I placed my head as if it were resting on his translucent chest.

"I can feel you," he whispered. I didn't have the heart to say I couldn't feel him at all.

"You knew it was going to happen. Even before you left Haraldsborg. When we were in the cave, you knew it was coming." I gnashed my teeth. "You lied! You promised to take care of yourself."

He kissed my hair. I could hear him doing it but couldn't feel it at all. "I swore not to fight in Ragnarök. I will keep that promise."

"Damn it!" I exclaimed. "Stupid fate. Why did you sacrifice yourself?"

He placed both of his transparent hands on my cheeks. "Serén saw that if we reached as far as Vindr Fen, I would have to fight Fenrir. Otherwise, you wouldn't fulfill your mission. And if you don't, a lot of people will die. Serén saw it was unchangeable."

"You really are the greatest protector in all the worlds."

He nodded.

"But what about our other future? I saw it myself. I experienced it." My voice broke, and I involuntarily laid a hand on my flat stomach.

Varnar's eyes became shiny, too. "I know, but that future comes at a huge cost. Serén was honest with me about it, but I made the decision myself."

I sniffled. "That was a horrific choice to have to make, and she knew it."

"Serén deals with that stuff every second."

I pursed my lips, but I couldn't stop the protracted, plaintive sound that came from my throat.

"I won't leave you," Varnar said. "I'll never leave you. I'll watch over you for the rest of your life. I'll find a way to become a poltergeist like your dad was. That way I can touch you and protect you."

I pulled my head back slightly and looked at him. He was just as handsome as ever, but he flickered restlessly. I thought of the many years Arthur had lived a semi-existence in between worlds.

"Come with me," I whispered and went over to the bed, where I lay on my side.

He lay down with his beautiful eyes aimed directly at me. His hand hovered right over my temple. His scent was so pervasive, I allowed myself a couple of deep breaths. I inhaled deeply just to get a little more of his fresh air and forest scent. My head rested on the pillow, and I stared at him, taking everything in.

"I'm sending you to Valhalla."

Varnar's eyes became infinitely sad. "You're impossible."

I smiled, but the corners of my mouth kept tilting downward. "You've always known that."

"From the very first time I saw you, you've opposed my plans."

"You can't flutter around like a restless spirit. You should find peace."

"Anna—"

"You've done more than enough. It's time for you to feast in the halls of eternity. There's combat training every day. You'll love it," I whispered, trying again to smile. "I'll join you later. I'll go to Valhalla, I promise."

"You can't—"

With my most authoritative völva voice, I said: "You will cross to Valhalla. You will find the peace you never had in life. No sin follows you, all love endures." I kissed his crystal clear mouth. This time, I could almost feel him. "Goodbye, my love."

I watched him as he flickered until he was nothing but an outline. The last thing I saw was his brown eyes, looking at me.

And then he was gone. In the air hung a faint echo of his voice and a hint of his scent.

The house was quiet when I came downstairs. The living room was cold and abandoned. I rummaged in the hallway, and to my horror, Vinr was no longer in the umbrella stand.

I sensed an aura flickering from the barn. With my heart in my throat, I hurried outside. The cold attacked my limbs, and lightning flashes and rumbling crashes illuminated the sky. The wind lifted my hair, whirling it around my head. I saw light and a moving shadow through the barn windows. A persistent scraping noise was followed by a low, deep chant. Purple smoke seeped under the door, and I smelled burnt herbs. I sensed Luna's aura, which prompted me to brandish Auka and fling the door open.

"Whatever you're doing with my friend, I—" I stopped in the doorway. Luna stood at the workbench, Vinr clamped in a vise, and she held a knife over it. When I came storming in, she spun around toward me. Her eyes were wild, and her curls were matted into thick dreads.

"Akoko ti de," she said in a voice so deep, I had no doubt who was controlling her.

"Benedict?"

She nodded. The little knife was still in her raised hand, and because she was now facing me, it was aimed straight in my direction. I glanced at it, and she tightened her grip around the handle.

Finally, I could confront Ben with what he had done. It was the first time we'd been alone since he died.

"Did you know your spells would keep me away from Serén?" I stared into Luna's eyes.

Luna leaned her head back authoritatively, but kept her eyes focused on me. "You can stop Ragnarök if you come together, but it shouldn't be stopped. The time has come. Akoko ti de . . ." She stretched out the last word in a hiss. "Akoko ti deeeee. We agreed, Ragnara and I."

My jaw dropped. "You're on Ragnara's team. You have been all along."

Luna squeezed her eyes shut. "I thought Ragnara was Ragnarök. She thought so herself, but she and Eskild were deceived by Tilarids, and I had to part ways with them. She enjoyed the worship too much. But we agreed that it's high time the gods meet their fate."

"That was why you refused to lift the spells. Not because you were looking out for me."

Luna approached me with an authority and power she could never have mustered on her own. She was still holding the knife, and I reflexively laid my hand on Auka.

"I love you like my own daughter, Anna. The spells were also there to protect you."

I removed my fingers from the axe hanging from my belt. "But you were willing to lift them, in the end. You were in the middle of it when you died."

"The magic was complex. I was trying to remove everything hindering you, but I wanted to retain the magic that kept you from Serén. I needed help from Mardöll to reach the powerful spells and disentangle them from one another. She boosted me with extra . . ." Luna stopped.

"Mardöll boosted you?"

Luna nodded grimly, and Ben was just beneath the surface. "Landráð. Traitor."

I smacked my forehead. "Mardöll is the traitor."

"I thought Mardöll agreed with me, but she serves Odin."

A realization dawned on me. "Mardöll killed Hakim."

"I think she did."

I clenched my fists. "Did she also sacrifice her own husband?" I thought of the triple-dead prime minister hanging from the tree beneath the windmills.

"She had help."

I felt very tired. "Couldn't you have just told me all this? I would have stayed away from Serén if you had only said so. I could have—"

"You're a child."

"I'm nineteen years old."

"You weren't ready."

"I am now!"

"You're Odin's raven," Luna thundered. "Where would I think your loyalties lay? If I had told you that I agreed with Ragnara deep down, you would have seen *me* as the traitor."

He was right. If I had heard these things just one week ago, I wouldn't have agreed with him.

"Hey, Anna." Luna's voice was high again. She blinked and looked around. "How did I get over here?" She looked at the knife in her hand. "I'm almost done."

"With what?"

She took my hand and led me over to the workbench, where Vinr was clamped in what looked like a torture device. "I carved more of your story." She showed me the top of my völva staff, which now featured the trip to Hrafnheim. Monster and Védis were there, along with Rokkin and Fenrir. At the very top, I embraced Varnar.

As I carefully traced the carvings with my finger, Luna put her arm around me. "I'm really sorry." She stroked her stomach. "Maybe both of us will end up alone."

I turned around in her arms, and she hugged me. Ben was gone, or at least hidden away, and my friend was once again with me.

"We'll find Mathias. I'm sure of it."

Are you sure about that, little seer, or is that a platitude to comfort your sensitive friend?

I fell to my knees—the words were accompanied by a sharp pain in my head.

Mardöll?

Luna followed me down, still holding me. "What's wrong, Anna?"

I have him.

Who? Mathias?

The new god is a rival to my gods, and he has the horn that can spark their downfall. You, though, have the thing that can stop it. I want Odion.

I whimpered as pain sliced through my brain again. Luna held me even closer.

"She has Mathias. Mardöll has Mathias," I forced out.

Let's make a deal, Mardöll sang.

CHAPTER 48

The DSMA had set up an emergency office in one of the nicest hotels in Aalborg. Luna and I stood in the foyer. I had to slap my arms a few times to get the blood flowing after being out in the cold. I had bundled my pregnant friend into the cargo box on the front of her bike and ridden all the way from Ravensted. We must have been quite a sight, riding the delivery bike with my völva staff raised, the giant crystal lighting our way. Not that anyone saw us—the streets were empty. I suddenly missed using demigods as transportation or having Elias as my chauffeur.

Under her arm, Luna carried Védis's skull with the pentagram on its forehead. "Are you sure this is where we're supposed to meet?"

"That's what Mardöll said."

The entrance to the hotel, which now served as the ministry's northernmost outpost, consisted mainly of black marble with gold trim. A glass door leading to the hotel's interior declared—in white letters and with the logo of the Danish state—that we were on government property. An armed woman stood in front of the door, only letting people pass with an approved ID card. People with blank stares walked in and out through the glass door, holding up their access cards monotonously. There were more people here than we had seen on the whole bike trip. Four people sat behind a counter. They wrote and stamped papers without pause. With the computers out of service, people had evidently gone back to doing everything by hand.

I walked up to the counter. Behind it was a long desk. The man closest to me was meticulously groomed and wore horn-rimmed glasses, but his skin was a little red where the frames touched his nose, and his jawline and cheekbones were sharply delineated. It had been a long time since I'd seen a clean-shaven man. His cheeks were tinged with blue from the cold. His tidy appearance was marred by his worn-out puffer jacket and fingerless gloves.

"Excuse me," I tried, but he kept writing. The paper was covered in numbers and diagrams.

"The end of the world is equivalent to zero growth forever." He sucked air regretfully through his front teeth. Then he lit up. "But if we project the nonexistent public spending, the account balance will still be in the green for thousands of years." The man mumbled something more to himself as he did some frantic calculations on another sheet of paper.

"I need to speak with Mardöll," I said, a little louder.

The man leaned forward and shouted to his colleague farther down the desk. "Pick up the pace. We have a deadline that can't be pushed back."

"There are many layers of hypnosis on them." Luna looked appraisingly at the people. "This is what happens when you let civil servants run amok."

"Lift the hypnosis."

She leaned forward and studied the speed-writing man. "It's too dangerous. His brain is ablaze with models and spreadsheets. The magic has to wear off on its own."

"HEY!" I yelled. The civil servant finally spotted us. He moved backward on his desk chair at the sight of us and wrinkled his nose.

"You look really scary."

"I know," I said, tired. "We need to speak with Mardöll."

The man composed himself. "We can't let just anyone in. There are state secrets in there."

"What good are state secrets when the world is ending?"

"You can't—"

Luna leaned over the counter. "You're letting us in." She aimed her tattooed hands at them. "Allr gleyma. Allr sjá."

The faces of the four civil servants became even more blank. The armed woman was walking toward us. She raised her rifle. "Hey! What are you—"

Luna's head swayed in a serpentine motion that looked more like Ben's than her own. "Sitjá drauma."

The woman's legs seemed to turn into cooked spaghetti beneath her. She only managed to open her mouth before plopping to the floor. The rifle turned toward the ceiling, and a couple of shots went off. Luna stood still while I instinctively ducked. Brick dust sprinkled down, landing like white powdered sugar on our heads. I brushed it off my hair while Luna simply walked up to the glass door and kicked it down with a crash.

"Luna!"

"You wanted in," she said with a shrug as she stepped over the comatose guard and shards of glass. "And if Mathias is in there, I plan to find him. My daughter is miserable without her boyfriend."

"Oh, it's you, Ben." I looked over my shoulder at the civil servants, who had collapsed at their desk. "Can these people handle any more hypnosis?"

"We'll have to hope so. At least now they'll have a chance to rest and excrete the superfluous magic." Luna walked, and the shards crunched under her boots. I followed her. She shook her head and dry, white plaster sprinkled down. "Hey. There's dust in my hair."

"Luna?" I asked tentatively. "Is it you now?" The constant shifting between Luna and Ben was starting to get on my nerves.

"My dad is taking over more and more," she said.

It didn't sound fun at all to be taken over by another person, even if it was your beloved father.

"Do you think your child will be Ben? Like one hundred percent?"

"The child will also be themself. It is half Mathias's, after all." She suddenly looked sad.

"We're going to find him," I promised.

The hotel bar was empty. There were neither people nor bottles, although the Muzak was still playing. It was nice to think that people had gone home and had maybe even taken some booze with them. The elevator made a *pling*, and a young woman came out. She had perfect makeup, hollow cheeks, and snow-white skin. She wore a beanie, a fur coat, and stilettos. The woman's gaze was strangely absent, but when she saw us, she smiled placidly.

"We're supposed to m—"

"I'm Karolina. Student intern with the DSMA." She smiled politely. "Welcome. Follow me." She held the elevator door open with one hand. A lamp blinked inside, and a persistent *bzzzz* came from an exposed wire hanging in the middle of the little metal box. Karolina didn't seem bothered in the least to be riding in the rickety contraption.

"I hope your trip was uneventful," she said calmly.

"Can't we take the stairs?" I backed away from the elevator.

"It's a long way up to the seventh floor. In this heat wave, we'd better save our energy."

Luna glanced at the large window, which was covered in frost. "We would rather walk up."

Karolina dipped her chin toward her chest and looked at us over fashionable glasses. "Just come." There was suddenly more consciousness in her eyes.

Mardöll?

Come, little seer, she replied in my head. *We're waiting for you.*

It's really bad form to hypnotize people like this.

Mardöll laughed, and it took immense self-control to keep myself from clutching my head and moaning because her laughter came with a splitting headache. *Just come, raven.*

Without further discussion, I walked into the elevator. Luna and the hypnotized intern followed me, though Luna shot repeated glances at the bit of wire that was now shooting sparks from its end. Lurching, the elevator rose. The little metal box jerked several times. Vinr shone faintly, and the elevator music slowed way down. I couldn't help but imagine metal wires breaking and then us plummeting toward a painful and bloody death in the elevator shaft.

"This heat wave is unbelievable," Karolina said dully as the elevator suddenly stopped, dangling between floors. There was a slight drop, and Luna let out an *ohh*. Karolina was lost in her this-is-a-nice-normal-summer-daydream, which I actually envied her for.

The elevator started jerking upward. Finally, it pinged, and Karolina showed us into a dark hotel hallway with a peacock-blue runner on the floor. The walls were papered in an optimistic pattern of pale-purple flowers, accented by eggshell-white panels and doors. Karolina led the way. She kept talking, even though she got no response.

"I'm almost done with school. I just have to finish my thesis. Then I can graduate and get a real job. I'm writing my thesis on Anna Stella Sakarias's relationships with Varnar of the Bronze Forest and King Sverre, and what they mean for diplomatic relations between our worlds."

My stomach did a painful somersault when she mentioned the two men I had lost, each in their own way.

"She knows giants, gods, witches, rulers, and warriors. I'm concentrating on her trip to Freiheim . . . or Hrafnheim." She furrowed her brows. "They haven't agreed on the name. A working group has been formed, but they're delayed every time our colleagues freeze to death or are sacrificed." She breathed faster and looked around. Maybe Mardöll's hypnosis was starting to let up. "You're going in there." She pointed to a door.

"Sit down," Luna said softly, pressing her against the floral wall. Karolina slid down the wall and sat with a thud. Luna looked into her eyes. "It's safe here. You're in a totally secure environment. Relax."

Karolina smiled gratefully.

"You're no better than Mardöll," I said.

Luna's eyes had gone dark. "Who do you think taught Mardöll what she knows?"

I shivered. Then, I pushed open the door Karolina had pointed out. Two people stood before us.

Mardöll smiled sweetly. Next to Mardöll stood a clean-cut, well-dressed man. Unlike the rest of us, pale with dark circles under our eyes, dirty clothes, and matted hair, he looked like what he was. A god. Even though he wasn't the least bit green or out of control. His honey-colored hair was combed back, and his blowtorch-blue eyes focused on us. In his hand, he held the Gjallarhorn.

"Babe?" Luna held her stomach.

"Mathias," I said.

CHAPTER 49

Mathias looked like himself but somewhat more glamorous. A transformed Mathias who was more muscular and godlike.

On the desk was a large bowl of nuts and dried fruit that, in this time of scarcity, amounted to a fortune. Mardöll kept her distance from us, but her eyes remained locked on Luna, who walked toward Mathias.

She was still clutching the skull under her arm, and its bony face grinned upward. Mathias raised his head, seemingly struggling to recognize his girlfriend. He walked up to Luna, and I could see how big he was compared to her. With measured movements, like a wild animal, he sniffed her neck and held his arms forward. Greedily, he ran a hand over her stomach. At first, she lifted her arms so he could reach, but that changed when he tightened his grip.

"Ow!"

"Mine!" The word rang out metallically.

"Let go of her, Mathias."

Mathias took his hand away and looked at me. His crystal-blue gaze hit me like a laser beam. "The raven!" His words sounded more like two pot lids being clanged together than anything a human could produce. "My rival's raven."

"What's wrong with him?" Luna sniffled.

"He's high on divinity," I said. "He was already being worshipped when he healed people, but it's different now."

Mardöll took a nut from the bowl and held it out in the palm of her hand toward Mathias. "Colere deum." She bowed her head.

Mathias's biceps swelled a little more. He let out a sigh that was a mix of pain and enjoyment. When he looked at us again, his eyes were brighter blue.

"Leave him alone," I said to Mardöll. "I know whose side you're really on."

Mathias looked down at Mardöll with a crease between his brows. "Are you not faithful to me?"

"Of course I am." Mardöll rolled her eyes in my direction. "Brand-new gods are so sensitive. You would think he was the new messiah." She raised her voice. "Karolina!"

The door opened, and in came the hypnotized intern.

"Kneel before the god."

Karolina lay on the floor with her arms outstretched. "You are my only god."

Mathias breathed heavily and grew even bigger.

"That doesn't count. Karolina is hypnotized."

Mardöll shrugged. "That's how it's always been. If we were in a bind, we pulled the worship out of the people."

"I worship you," Karolina continued.

Luna's cheeks turned red with anger. "Make her stop."

"You know what it'll take for me to stop it."

I looked to my side. "Luna."

She tried to hand the skull to Mardöll, but Ben wouldn't let her, and it became a strange back-and-forth dance. Finally, I wrestled it from her, but a great fury flowed from the skull like an electric current, burning my fingers.

"No," Luna bellowed. "Do not give my brother to her. Not for anything in the worlds."

My hands were wrapped around the top of the skull, but it was too late. It zapped my fingers with what felt like many volts. I cried out in pain and dropped the skull. It fell to the floor and rolled toward Mardöll. The jaw fell off, and a little fabric bundle came out.

"Finally." Mardöll carefully lifted the bundle. It trembled in her hand, and when she unwrapped Ben's brother, she had to work to keep a firm grip on him.

Luna growled at the sight, and Odion rocked back and forth in Mardöll's palm.

"Thanks." Mardöll smiled sweetly.

"Now, let Mathias go!" I said.

"Of course." Mardöll raised her hand to command Karolina to stop, then paused. "Just one more thing."

I didn't have a chance to react. My legs shot out from under me, Vinr rolled away, and I landed on the floor.

"Clausa," Mardöll said, and suddenly, I couldn't move. Luna tried to come to my aid, but Mardöll moved closer to Mathias. "I *pray* that you'll help me. Hold the witch."

Mathias grabbed Luna from behind. She writhed and protested, but Mathias didn't let go. He kept his blue laser eyes aimed at Mardöll.

On the floor, I tried to wriggle free. Mardöll grabbed a Sharpie and drew a black pentagram directly on the floor around me. My head, arms, and legs each fit into one of the star's points. At each point, she drew a rune.

"Ansuz, fehu, mannaz." Carefully, Mardöll picked up the Odion figurine and placed it at one of the points.

The runes for *god* and *slave* were beside my hands, and *human*—mannaz—was above my head. By one of my legs, I felt Odion's aggressive energy. Mardöll placed herself at my other foot and raised her arms.

"Free. Awon."

The Odion figurine quivered near my foot.

"If I set you free, you will lift the raven's spells. You must not hurt her."

I couldn't understand what Odion hissed, but it sounded like a reluctant agreement.

"I'll kill you if you try anything, Odion," Luna swore from Mathias's grip. She didn't sound very Luna-like. Balls of energy sputtered from her hands, but Mathias held her too tightly for her to throw them.

My leg was getting very hot, and the figurine was shaking uncontrollably. There was a flash and a bang, and suddenly, a large figure stood over me. He looked like Ben but had none of Ben's warmth in his eyes. He stared at me without blinking. The whites of his eyes were very white, his irises very brown, and his tattooed hands moved around my head as though it were a crystal ball in which he was trying to see the future. There was a long rant I didn't understand, and then, simply, he reached into me. His hand disappeared into my skull.

I screamed, and Luna shouted, as Odion spat out spells. I convulsed, and if it hadn't been for Odion's heavy body holding me down, my back would have broken as it rose in an arc. Odion turned his head one way, then the other, his gaze piercing.

"Tu jagbe idan," he said, his eyes wide. "Tu jagbe idaaaaaan."

My head felt like it was about to explode as Odion's hands rummaged around in there. He moved his arms down through me. His fingers passed my throat and continued into my chest. Something was flopping around, and Odion snatched at it as though it were a slippery eel. I felt an uncontrollable urge to retch, but it had been so long since I'd eaten that nothing came up. Finally, Odion caught the spell and ripped it out of me with his bare hands. He held something that resembled a gigantic live leech. It writhed and dripped something black and foul-smelling. Frantically, I felt for the path he had carved through me, but my skin was intact and unblemished.

Odion was still staring at me, now with a triumphant look that was so frightening, I would have nightmares about it for the rest of my days—however few might remain. He opened his wide mouth, and his white teeth gleamed. He stuffed the leech in and swallowed it in one bite. When he bared his teeth again, they were covered in black blood. He slowly got to his feet and shifted his gaze to Luna's stomach.

"Kehinde," Odion said.

"Odion," Luna replied with Benedict's deep voice.

For a moment, the two brothers looked at one another. Odion's still-bloody hands hovered over Luna's stomach, and she whimpered desperately, knowing he could sink his hands through her skin.

Mardöll followed Odion so intently that she didn't notice I was free from the paralysis spell. I rolled to the side and grabbed Vinr. I got up on one knee and aimed Vinr toward Odion, who was now almost touching Luna.

"Get away from her," I commanded.

"Are you giving orders to a powerful sorcerer?" Mardöll asked. "It's two sorcerers and a god against you."

"I have the power of the völvas on my side." The giant crystal glowed alongside Luna and Mathias's ring, and I saw the carvings of Varnar, Sverre, Hakim, and Elias. I summoned all the völvas, and they sent me calm strength. A bubble shot out of Vinr's top, surroundeding us just as Mardöll cast her spell. Her spell slid off the bubble with a *kachiing*.

Odion sniffed the air. "We aren't done, brother." He laughed wildly before turning around. His movements were like a predator's. In a panther-like leap, he was out the door.

"So, that was my uncle," Luna said. She sounded like herself again.

"He fulfilled his purpose." Mardöll looked at me. "Now, you need to fulfill yours. Together with your sister, you can stop doomsday. Odin can reign again, and everything can go back to normal."

"Normal! You sacrifice human beings. That's not normal at all."

"Shall I ask the god to break your friend's back? Come willingly, and that won't be necessary."

"Mathias." I was still holding Vinr toward Mardöll, but I reached out to my side and grabbed his arm. His divine strength felt cool and powerful. I pressed humanity into him. "You're my friend. I love you—not as a god, but as a human. Luna loves you. You're sweet and silly, and we don't want to lose you."

I felt Mathias's divine strength flowing into me. Luna, whose whole body was pressed against Mathias's, did too. Like two pieces of paper towel, we sucked Mathias's divinity into ourselves. He was quiet for a while.

"Anna? Luna?" Mathias's voice sounded completely different. "What's going on? Oh, no." He let go of Luna immediately. "Luna!"

"Pull yourself together, Mathias! We have to get out of here."

Mardöll came closer, her arms raised, ready to cast a spell. Mathias picked us up and backed toward the door.

"Give me the Gjallarhorn, god," Mardöll urged. "I worship you, Mathias. I submi—"

"She's lying. She's a devotee of Odin. If she gets the horn, Odin will annihilate you."

Mathias held us both and the golden horn tightly against his body. Mardöll screamed in a high-pitched voice inside my head, bringing a throbbing pain behind my eyes.

"Go," I managed to say. I could barely hold on to Vinr. I summoned all the völvas' power once again, and they gathered around me and gave me strength; thanks to them, I was able to keep Vinr raised as Mathias ran from the room.

Mardöll screamed relentlessly inside my head like a Fury, and eventually, I hung limply in Mathias's arms. But we got out of there—one god status and a few stubborn spells lighter.

CHAPTER 50

"Fjarlægð! Óendanlega! Fjarlægð! Óendanlega!" Luna repeated the Old Norse spell while Mardöll screamed persistently in my head. Luna's spells were only marginally successful in muffling the howling witch. White flashes of pain flew across my retinas.

Mathias carried me and Vinr, while Luna ran alongside us with a hand on my forehead. I looked up at my two friends. There was light, but whether it came from an artificial source or Mathias, who had developed a halo, I didn't know. Hospitals were no longer running, so I had no idea where they were taking me. They probably didn't know, either. The pain in my head grew in intensity.

"Oowwww!"

"My mom says that Mardöll is half siren. If she were full-blooded, Anna's brain would have exploded by now. Fjarlægð! Óendanlega!"

"Where do we go now?" Mathias tightened his grip on me.

"I love my wife, but I don't dare go to her house," Luna said in a deeper voice. "Rebecca follows Odin, just like I did. I don't know if she's ready to destroy him. Að hætta að."

The pain lessened a little when Ben took over. I opened my eyes a crack and saw the tattooed symbols on Luna's palms glowing.

"Benedict?" Mathias asked tentatively.

"I'm in your child."

"Uh . . ." Mathias didn't seem to know how to react.

Because Ben was more successful keeping Mardöll's siren screams at bay, I was able to speak. "The museum."

"Get on my back, Luna. Or Ben. Or both of you."

Luna obeyed, and Mathias took off. In no time, we were at the white-painted museum.

"Where is Prehistoric Denmark?" Mathias asked a museum guard I could barely stand to look at. She was white as a sheet, and the circles under her eyes were so dark, they looked like bruises. *Yikes.* She was a ghost, but she didn't seem to know she was dead. She pointed us down a glass-lined hallway.

"The ceremony is over."

"What ceremony?"

"They make offerings to the sun every morning in hopes it'll come back."

"This isn't a museum anymore. It's a temple," Luna whispered.

Moving at high speed, we passed aurochs skeletons, arrowheads, and decorated pots. In the room where a golden sun disk was displayed, dried flowers lay on the floor.

Mathias set me down. "What should we do? What are you doing, Luna?"

Luna had bitten herself on the hand, and blood dripped from her fingers. She dragged her hand over the floor, creating a circle around us and the sun disk. When it was almost done, she hopped inside it with us and smeared the last bit of blood to complete the circle.

"Protection of the sun, protection of loved ones, protection of time." When Luna closed the ring of blood, there was a bang inside my head but then it went quiet. Luna chanted intently. "You are protected. From now on, Mardöll can't reach your mind."

I still wasn't able to speak, but I held up a finger to signal I felt better.

"Mardöll will do whatever it takes to indulge Odin." Then Luna coughed her voice into place. "Wow, my dad's strength is increasing. Maybe he's drawing from the baby's one-quarter-god part."

"Is that you, Luna? Or Ben?" Mathias asked.

"It's me."

I heard a kissing sound.

"I'm so sorry I held you like that, Luna. I can barely remember anything. After the healings, Mardöll came and got me; it felt so right when she made offerings to me and worshipped me. It really sucks to be a god. I don't have control over myself." Mathias was talking at high speed.

"Shh." Luna kissed him again. "I'm just so glad you're back and yourself again."

There was a flash of green. "I'm not myself. The god in me is strong, and it wants out."

I was finally able to sit up. My eyes felt raw and sore. When Luna saw I was upright, she hugged me, and Mathias put his arms around us so we formed a big ball. Luna held me away from her to get a look at me. She ran her hands over my cheeks and neck. Because her fingers still dripped with blood, I was smeared with it.

"Your spells are gone," Luna said. "Wow. That black streak disappeared, too. I thought that was just how you looked."

"What streak?"

Luna's finger touched my forehead. "You usually have a black streak here. I thought it was a birthmark."

"Why didn't you ever say anything?"

"It didn't occur to me."

"What should we do?" Mathias asked.

"Luna, is there any way you could send a mass message to people like Mardöll did? We need to tell everyone to hide. The forces of chaos are becoming more intense." As though to emphasize my words, the ground shook slightly. Bronze figurines rattled in the glass display cases around us. I placed my hand flat against the floor. "This is going to get worse. There must be bomb shelters and sturdy grain silos somewhere. In a way, it's lucky all the stockpiles have been eaten or burned."

Luna inhaled deeply. "Maybe with the baby's quarter-god powers, my dad's spirit, and my magic combined, it could work. But

Mardöll is undoubtedly sending out subliminal messages. She might order people into battle against the giants."

"All the more reason to work against her. Who will people believe?"

"Maybe Niels Villadsen." Luna snapped her fingers. "I'll get ahold of him, and we'll craft a message I can send out. Maybe that'll work." She stood up.

Mathias got up to go with her.

"I need to talk to you, Mathias," I said.

Luna stood on her tiptoes and kissed Mathias. "I can handle it. Seriously. I can." Her gaze grew darker, and she pulled her mouth back. With a deep voice, she said: "I will protect Luna and your child."

Mathias reluctantly let go of Luna, and she ran off. He looked longingly after her until she disappeared behind a case of potsherds.

I feared that Mardöll would start screaming in my head again, but the magic held. I laid my hand on the Gjallarhorn, and the gold throbbed like it had a pulse. "How much do you know about this?"

Mathias's eyes grew distant. "I remember a lot, but they're not my own memories. I can hear the grass grow, but right now, it's stopped; I can hear the birds breathe, but most are dead now; and I can see to the ends of the earth. There's usually a clear view, but now, there's a horde of giants standing there, waiting to overrun us."

"You inherited those memories from Heimdall."

Mathias lifted the horn. "If I breathe on it, it'll melt beyond recognition, and then Ragnarök can't start. If I blow into it, it'll call the gods to their fate, but I'm not sure what that fate is."

"Not even Hejd was completely sure, but Ragnarök will change everything. We're standing on the precipice of a kind of collective death. The gods are decadent, the humans lived extravagantly, but they got their punishment in the Fimbulwinter. Ragnarök is rebirth. That was why Hejd loved this rune." I fished the horse tooth with the hagal rune from the cavity in Vinr's top.

"You think I should blow into the Gjallarhorn?"

"That's what I think, but it's not my decision."

Mathias walked away. I stood up with the help of Vinr and went after him.

We stopped in front of a glass box the length of a person. Inside a hollowed-out tree trunk lay a dark corpse. The woman had a big gold ring in her ear and a complicated braided hairstyle that I recognized as being all the rage among the female inhabitants of Ravensted. She was much, much older, but she reminded me of the myling, lying there with protruding teeth and her skull visible under her brown skin. If I hadn't put the myling in Odinmont, this would have been a good place for him to rest.

I suddenly saw myself in the reflection of her glass grave. With Vinr in my hand, dark with Luna's blood, and my red hair sticking out under my hat, I saw my own image over the bog body. I saw how thin I was. My face also looked like a skull, with a prominent jaw and cheekbones, my teeth visible under my taut skin. I focused again on the girl in the coffin.

There was something comforting about seeing her lying there, and the strong pull of the past made me relax. The world had been through so many things, and it was still spinning. She had been eighteen years old when she died, and that was over three thousand years ago. A deep calm came over me knowing we'd all be dead much longer than we were alive. We were one and the same, the young woman in the case and me. The only thing separating us was time.

Mathias tore me out of my thoughts. "I'm not my father. I'm not Heimdall. We've never even met."

I looked down at the bog body. "We *are* our ancestors. I've seen that Luna dies in the version of the future where the gods don't take part in the battle. Just like we have to learn from the past, we also have to secure our future." I felt a jab in my heart at the thought of my own child from the future. Ast. I would never have her because Varnar was gone.

For a while, Mathias studied the Gjallarhorn. "When does the battle start?"

"The giants are on their way. The Midgard Serpent opened the passage for them, and they were all let out. Monster said that Loki can order the giants to do battle with us, but if you blow the Gjallarhorn, the gods will step in, and the humans will be spared."

Mathias's blue eyes looked like gas flames, and his skin pulsated green.

"You have to swear you'll take care of Luna and my baby."

"I swear it."

"Tell her I'm happy that Benedict is with them."

I wanted to reassure him that he would come back, but I had no idea whether he would survive Ragnarök.

There was one more god's fate I had doubts about.

CHAPTER 51

The wind tore at me, and the waves crashed not far below. Until recently, there had been a forty-yard drop to the beach, but now the salty tide splashed right beneath my feet.

I wrapped my mom's tattered coat tightly around me, but the wind blew through the fabric and chilled me to the bone. My hair swirled around my head in a little red cyclone. I felt more like a spirit than a human of flesh and blood.

The water was the color of lead. In some places, it was completely black, but whether that was because it was deep or because large creatures lurked beneath the surface, I couldn't tell. Maybe it was just the reflection of the dark thunderclouds. Although the waves didn't break, the entirety of the gray silk sheet folded itself in large swells. Only a short distance away, the mile-high ice wall creaked and groaned.

My boots moved closer to the cliff until their tips stuck over it. A bit of sand fell over the edge and headed toward the water, but the grains were caught in a gust of wind and swirled into the air like a translucent snake. I raised one foot and stuck it all the way over the precipice.

"You're standing on the knife's edge." Od's voice was close by.

"Just one more step," I said, as though he had been standing there the whole time. My hair was now blowing horizontally behind me. "If I step straight out, maybe I'll be carried away by the wind."

Od placed his foot across the toes of my boots and pushed my feet back. "Maybe you would be carried away. But it's more likely you'd plunge into the abyss."

I turned and looked at Od, who was looking out at the sea. In profile, he was heartrendingly gorgeous and not all that human. The night of healing had also put him on the cusp of becoming a god. His dark hair billowed around him, his eyebrows raised in an expression that was at once sad and hopeful, and his mouth was open, but I couldn't see whether he was smiling or simply searching for something to say. Every time I had him in focus, my hair flew into my eyes. Because he had placed his leg in front of me, he was standing so close I only had to lean to the side to prop myself against his strong body. I did so and immediately felt the divinity flowing from him and into me.

Od put his arms around me, and for a while, we simply stood on the edge of the cliff, intertwined in an embrace that wasn't the slightest bit romantic, but which was full of love. If someone had seen us, they might have thought we were a statue. Maybe we were pillars frozen in time.

I felt Hejd in the wind and the salty spray around us. She had rested here, before the bluff swallowed up the churchyard where her grave had been, but now she was free. Tears collected in my eyelashes. I blinked, and tears ran down my cheeks in hot streaks.

"Do you know where Elias is?"

"Yes."

"Tell me."

"What if he doesn't want to be found?" Od kissed my hair briefly.

"Too bad."

Od laughed hoarsely. "What if *I* don't want him to be found?"

I didn't have the energy to tell him off, so I blew a little air through my nose in a bitter laugh. "You kidnapped him."

"He's my son. Parents will do anything to protect their children."

I looked at the ice wall. "It's coming. Ragnarök. It's happening soon." I couldn't hear my voice over the howling wind, but I knew Od had no trouble hearing me. "I've been talking to Hejd."

Od stiffened. "Hejd and I don't agree about what should happen."

"I agree with her. It's time the gods met their fate. But people need something new to believe in, and there's a whole realm of the dead that's going to be left leaderless. Valhalla will need a new ruler."

Od tilted his head slightly, as he always did when something was upsetting to him. Others wouldn't see it, but I knew how affected he was. "Odin is my father."

"It may well be that you're a good adoptive father to Elias, but Odin is neither a good parent nor a good god for humanity. You know that, too."

"Would you follow me?" Od held his breath—the words themselves were so forbidden that simply uttering them was high treason.

I was completely calm when I replied because I was sure in my heart. "I will follow you, Od Dinesen. And it will be out of love and trust, not fear."

"Aren't you against gods and worship?"

"I was against it, but I've learned that people need to believe in something. I'm no exception. We need to know we'll see our loved ones again, and that we go somewhere nice when we die."

The wind lifted Od's shiny hair, and he emitted a silver glow. "Aren't we just switching out one god for another? What if I become just as bad as my father? Or worse?"

I reached up and caressed his cheek. It felt hard like marble under my fingers. The North Jutland wind blustered around me and stole the air from my lungs, but I held Od's gaze, even though it threatened to pull me down. "I promise to worship you."

Od raised his eyebrows in surprise. "You're only one person."

"Don't underestimate humans."

"But how?"

"All of Odin's fail-safes have been removed, apart from one." I inhaled sharply because I knew what was coming. I had seen it again and again in my vision from Hejd.

"Doomsday can also be averted if the child of a god sacrifices themself," Od said. "Other children of gods have done it before me." He swallowed. "Will I also be crucified?"

I exhaled slowly because I didn't want to say it. "You get decapitated by Loki, but you do nothing to stop it."

"At least it goes fast." Od closed his eyes. "I've never gone against my father's orders."

I grabbed his shirt in both hands and looked urgently at him. "You cannot sacrifice yourself for your father. He doesn't give a shit about you."

"Anna. Language." Sadness lay just beneath the surface of his smile. "It may well be that Odin doesn't give a shit about me, but I don't want to let humans die in the battle."

"The humans won't die. They hide, and the gods take the heat."

Od carefully brushed my hair out of my eyes, which stung with sand, salt water, and tears. "I've made my decision."

I pressed myself to him, suddenly aware that this was probably my last chance to hug him. He put his arms around me, and we stood there awhile, intertwined, on the edge of the cliff. The wind kept pushing us toward the abyss, but we stood firm.

"You should go inside now, Anna," he whispered in my ear. "The sea doesn't look kindly on the reckless."

"Are you calling me reckless?"

Od laughed hoarsely, and I leaned in toward the sound. "You are the foolhardiest person I've ever met, but that's part of your charm."

As Od spoke, I reached out with my clairvoyance and found what I was looking for in The Boatman. Elias was inside. Od was keeping him captive, and he was absolutely livid over being held against his will. I examined his past more thoroughly than before. I mentally pushed past the many images of women and intoxicants until I reached his core. I finally understood what the past contained.

My eyes met Od's. "Elias is inside. We have to let hi—"

Od cranked up his hypnosis, and I fainted on the spot. The last thing I felt was Od's strong arms gripping me.

I was a raven again. I hovered over the clouds, and I couldn't immediately see which world was below me. The ground was red, but I didn't know if it was clay or blood. I got closer to the ground and saw Sént's towers in the distance. The red plain beneath me was Vigrid. *Of course!* If I had had a hand, I would have smacked myself on the forehead, but as it was, I just flapped my wings a couple of times with irritation over my own stupidity.

Vigrid is the plain,
Where all in fight shall meet
Surt and the cherished gods
A hundred leagues it has on each side
Unto them that field is fated.

I should have figured out long ago that Ragnarök would unfold here. At the tip of my wing, I spotted Serén in raven form.

Serén screeched a bird's cry. "The future has changed."

"Mathias is sending the gods to battle," I replied, although my voice came out as a *caaaaw*.

"Look," Serén cawed. "Looooook." The word turned into a high-pitched wail. She dove toward the ground like a black lightning bolt, and I followed. We landed on the horrible plain. It looked different from how it did in other visions. The giants fought, and piles of human bodies were everywhere. The difference from earlier visions was that the gods were here.

"Why are dead humans here? Luna sent a message for humans to seek refuge." I recognized Odin and Freyja. Odin was young, strong, and divinely handsome, despite his empty eye socket. Pitch-black hair swung around him, and his bare chest was muscular and smooth. The spear Gungnir was in his hand and shouted with murderous glee every time it killed a giant. Whistling and sputtering, it impaled several of the painted giants. Freyja was as terrifying as she was beautiful in her nearly transparent dress. You would expect her to look vulnerable, nearly naked among all the weapons, but she looked like what she was: A goddess of war. A goddess of death. A goddess of revenge. Her wheaten hair billowed around her like a thousand cracking whips, and she held a mighty sword in one hand that seemed to swing itself. In the other hand, she had a large antler, which she used as a shield and to stab her opponents.

I saw figures come running. One was a one-armed god. Loki sauntered lazily toward him, and the two men crossed swords. A red-haired god with a large hammer threw himself into the fray. I had seen both him and the one-armed god in Fenrir's cave on Afallon. The Midgard Serpent rushed in from above and lunged at the red-haired god, who must have been Thor. Beast and god fought one another.

"It's awful to watch, but it's part of my plan." I flapped my wings, and Serén did the same. I shot up into the air and circled around the horrific scene.

"This isn't Ragnarök," Serén cawed.

"What else could it be? Gods and giants are fighting. Look at them!"

"Gods and giants have always fought. It's chaos and cosmos in conflict. It's been that way since the dawn of time. This isn't the fate of the gods. It's just a regular battle."

"Come, humans. Come and protect your god. All those who worship me, I order you to the battle," Odin shouted. "Oskoreia. Get them all."

Luna came running as though pulled by an invisible thread. She was followed by Frank, Mina, Arthur, and a ton of other people I knew. I cawed miserably as Monster sprang on Luna.

No! Caaaaaaww . . .

Rebecca was being dragged by Odion. I recognized this from a vision I had of them in Kraghede Forest. Back then, I had mistakenly believed Odion was Ben. He raised his tattooed hands and shot magic at Rebecca, and she collapsed in flames.

The people walked toward the plain and the many gods. At the very back, two young women walked hand in hand. Their red hair reached their waists, and they were identical. It was Serén and me, and we were following the others toward the battle.

"What . . . No!"

I spotted Mathias at the edge of the red plain. He clutched the Gjallarhorn, bewildered.

"Blow," I yelled. "Blow the Gjallarhorn."

Odin shouted again. "Good. Good. You are my followers. You are my einherjar." This made the gathering humans throw themselves even more eagerly into the fight. Serén and I squeezed each other's hands, and the mere sight of us together gave me a bittersweet pang.

The raven that was Serén flapped her wings at my side. "Caaaaw." She, too, was looking at us with longing.

We looked strong and happy, walking hand in hand. It felt so right. We had both lost so many people, but a future where we still had each other was within reach.

"Look at us. We're together." Serén let out a little peep, and I flew close to her and stroked her neck feathers with my beak. "We're together, so we must have averted Ragnarök. It's happening soon."

It was so unbearably tempting.

"Why," Serén cawed. "Why?"

CHAPTER 52

I awoke standing up. Maybe Od had placed me like that. Confused, I looked around in the drifting snow and found I was on the field between the charred Odinmont and Kraghede Forest.

The ground beneath me was shaking, and I had to fight to stay upright. Fortunately, I had Vinr in my hand and could hold myself up with its help. Lightning flashed and thunder roared. I tried to see through the snowflakes.

A horde was headed toward me from Ravensted. I remained still, even though the thousands of people were headed directly toward me. Several of them I recognized from when they wrecked Odinmont. Oskoreia walked among them and egged them on. The people's eyes were just as empty as they'd been when they wanted to kill me, and once again, they bore golf clubs, burning torches, and iron chains.

I tensed all my muscles, mainly to keep myself from running in the opposite direction. They were headed toward the stone circle. It wouldn't take them long to repair it so it could once again be used as a portal. If they went through it, they would almost certainly head for Vigrid and the battle that would kill most of them. I was the only thing standing between them and this certain death. Truthfully, I didn't have much sympathy for the people who had destroyed my childhood home and had tried on several occasions to kill me. I was *this close* to letting them pass. With a sinking heart, I spotted Luna and Frank among the zombielike people. Behind them, Odion pulled Rebecca by the arm.

See what I can do, my raven. Odin was speaking inside my head. *Even your tough witch friend, her mother, and the murderer you so mercifully spared are in my power. You fought well, but you lost.*

I looked angrily toward the sky. *I haven't lost yet.*

But Odin didn't hear me. *Ah! It'll feel good to spill some giant blood. It's been so long.*

I watched the staggering mob. *At least spare the humans. Spare Luna, Frank, and Rebecca.*

Those who survive will remember my courage and my fighting prowess. I'll be even more powerful than before.

The people were now so close to me that I had to decide if I wanted to sprint in the opposite direction. Last time, they would have ripped me to pieces if they'd gotten ahold of me.

I pounded Vinr against the ground. "Stop!"

A woman at the front focused on my face with a creepy skeletal grin. There were several thousand of them, and they continued moving forward like a human wave. The people at the back pushed ahead.

I pounded Vinr on the ground again, and the giant crystal flickered. I raised my voice.

"Stooooooop!"

The light shone on the entire horde. I was just about to kiss my life goodbye when they stopped. Some even smiled when they saw me. My newly lifted spells must have allowed them to no longer see me as horrible.

At the front of the mob stood a cashier and a teacher from Ravensted. Behind them, they dragged a person, bound and hooded.

"You can't go there," I shouted, pointing at the stone circle. The völvas gave me strength, and my voice carried to the farthest row. The crowd must have stretched all the way to Luna's house.

"What should we do?" The teacher spoke in a monotone. I realized he was listening to me instead of the oskoreia.

"Go home. Stay away from the battles."

The cashier pulled the hood off the prisoner. "What about her?"

It was Mardöll. Her hands were tied behind her back and a rag was fastened around her mouth, but her eyes gleamed.

"Where did you get her?"

"Odin delivered her to us," the teacher replied. "He said that everything's her fault. Fortunately, he's going to fix it. He will save us."

How typical of Odin to sacrifice his most loyal follower. It would only make him look better if Mardöll got the blame and he came along to rescue everyone.

I looked at Mardöll. "You sacrificed the myling in the bog, the prime minister, and the nine people in Kraghede Forest. You killed Hakim."

Mardöll locked her eyes on mine, and I saw a desperate plea in them. She couldn't say anything because of the rag in her mouth so she tried to get through to me mentally, but the words slammed against the spell Luna had cast earlier in the day.

"Burn the witch, burn her, burn her . . ." the crowd repeated again and again.

Mardöll had killed children and adults. She thought she was saving people by doing so, but that didn't make her actions forgivable. I didn't believe in the death penalty, but she deserved to be removed from the face of the earth. But . . .

"Don't burn her," I shouted, and again my words rang through the trees. "She should have a fair trial."

For a moment, the people stared at me. The oskoreia looked at one another in confusion until I raised Vinr. The giant crystal at its top gleamed. Now I spoke directly to the dead. "I know you. I rule over you in the world of the living because I am a völva. There may be gods in the realms of the dead, but as long as you're here, I decide, and I order you to help all these people to safety."

The oskoreia looked at me questioningly.

I closed my eyes and sent all the völvas to the oskoreia. *Tell them to find refuge for the living*, I asked.

I immediately got a response. The völvas stroked my soul lovingly, and I felt the warmth all the way to my toes. Then they raced off toward the wild dead. Each of the dead völvas put her arm around an oskoreia and whispered in their ear. Finally, the oskoreia turned around. As though on command, the humans turned, too. They walked in the opposite direction, dragging Mardöll with them.

Luna, Rebecca, and Odion didn't move. Odion's eyes were wide, and he tightened his grip on Rebecca. "Ti o ba wa okú," he said. "You are dead."

This interaction was identical to the one in my vision, although I had seen it from a different angle.

"Ben . . ." I said to Luna, and she threw herself sideways toward her uncle, while I aimed my völva staff at Odion. "Völvas," I called, and now the many women came sweeping back and surrounded Odion.

He bellowed and screamed, but Luna's, Ben's, and Rebecca's magic along with the many völvas overpowered him. Luna's voice burst forth in a very Benedict-like way. "Tengdur. Iwe adehun." Blue magic shot from her fingers.

Odion was encapsulated in the magic. Rebecca joined in with incantations, and Odion stiffened and shrank. Eventually, he was once again a little porcelain figurine, rotating slowly until he stood still.

"Go home, hurry," I said. "You need to get to safety."

"We're not leaving you alone." Luna's voice was a combination of her own and Ben's.

"You have a role to play after Ragnarök. You're needed, and I order you to seek refuge."

The Sekibo family obeyed. Before they left, Luna nodded appreciatively at me. Her eyes were completely black.

"Thanks for the help, Ben," I said. This time, it wasn't hard to thank him.

I watched as Luna, Rebecca, and the horde of people went off to safety. Hakim's ghost suddenly stood at my side. He pointed at Mardöll. "She's my murderer."

I looked up at him. "Mardöll killed a lot of people. She'll get a fair punishment."

"She's clever. If you let her live, she could cause a lot of damage. Right now, you have the chance to get rid of her forever."

I watched as the bound figure grew smaller.

"I met her when I was working for the DSMA," Hakim said urgently. "I had a hunch that she was bad news."

"Your hunches . . ."

"Burn her now!" Hakim said.

I furrowed my brows. "Are you sure?"

Hakim looked upset. "I'm just as opposed to it as you are, but you risk many lives if you let her live. She's just one person, but her death means everyone survives."

"Do you really think I should burn her?"

Hakim nodded. His green eyes glinted with distress. "It's in everyone's best interest."

I watched the little person flailing in her captors' grasp. With the völvas' help, I could make sure she wouldn't cause any more harm.

"The All-Father will reward you if you do. A new warrior has come to his halls, but as a god of death, he can bring Varnar back to life. You can raise your daughter together."

My brows shot up in a silent question.

Hakim's sincere green eyes looked at me in disbelief. "You don't know?"

"What are you talking about?"

"A new little life is growing inside you. I can see her spirit already. She's just as strong as her parents."

The air was sucked out of me, and I clasped my hands in front of my stomach. "Am I pregnant?"

"Yes." Hakim smiled. "And you can have Varnar back. All Odin wants you to do is get Mardöll out of the way."

So tempting. Tears collected in my eyes. Varnar and me in the Bronze Forest, while Monster babysat our daughter. I breathed in.

"I know who you are, Hakim," I said quietly. "Or should I say *Loki?*"

CHAPTER 53

"How long have you known?" Loki still looked like Hakim.

"I was sure when you showed me my future." My fingers rested on my stomach. "But I should have known all along: everyone told me it'd be impossible to see Hakim because of our different faiths."

"You think you're so different from other people, but denial runs deep in all humans. Even you, Anna. You believe what you want to believe."

"This stops now!" I held my head high.

Hakim looked kindly at me. "The future I showed you can come to pass. You just have to take it."

"Can you please stop taking the form of Hakim? You were never him. Not even when you showed up at my house and kissed me right after Mardöll had killed him."

"If it's real, it will never be over." Hakim, who was Loki, smiled. He leaned in toward me. "You're a good kisser."

"Stop it." I raised my voice.

Hakim's hair grew out into thick dark-gray locks. His eyes changed color from green to metallic iron, and he grew taller. His torso was bare but painted with blue spirals and symbols.

I forced myself not to take a step back. "What do you get out of this?"

Loki shrugged. "I just think it's funny to see you all running around like chickens with their heads cut off."

"You got Ragnara to pursue me, but when she asked for your help, you betrayed her."

Loki studied his fingernails. "I changed my mind." He suddenly looked young and vulnerable, like early spring. "Ragnara did well, but she got too close. Odin is my blood brother, after all."

"I'm guessing you think I did well, too."

Loki still looked fragile. "I really like you, Anna. But . . ."

"But . . .?"

His expression became savage, and he bared his teeth. "You're dangerous!" He wrapped his large fingers around my upper arms.

I flailed as I was lifted up and carried off. Bands of light flickered around me, and we flew between the worlds. When we were above Vigrid, I looked down.

Large giants fought against the gods. The giants wore only loincloths and were otherwise naked and barefoot. They were painted with blue circles and patterns. There was thunder and lightning above them, and tornadoes plowed through the soil. The gods were wild and beautiful, and they fought with raised hammers, burning antlers, and spears. I saw Freyja, her golden hair whipping in the wind, and Thor, with bulging muscles and a tightened belt. Neither Odin nor Loki was there, and I got the sense that the gods could leave if they wanted to. Mathias stood at the edge of the battlefield and looked at the Gjallarhorn with ambivalence.

"Blow the Gjallarhorn, Mathias," I shouted. I have no idea if he heard me, but he raised his head as Loki soared past with me in tow, my red hair flying around us. I heard the rustle of wings and saw that I was hanging in the talons of a falcon. The bird was enormous, and each flap of its wings threatened to rip the skin off my face. We flew over the abandoned city of Sént. I hadn't seen it since Ragnara was in power.

I tried to focus on the bird above me. "Why are you a falcon?"

"I stole this skin from Freyja," the falcon replied. "Come with me." It took a death-defying nosedive, and I was yanked down toward the middle of Sént, where I fell like a cannonball.

The falcon laughed. "Nice, raven. Very graceful."

I didn't feel particularly graceful, and I didn't care how I looked. I hit the ground and rolled inelegantly. Vinr lay in my hand, and I squeezed the staff. The giant crystal was blinding, and I lifted it to illuminate the space around me.

I was in the arena in Sént. The last time I was there, it had been filled with cheering people and a violent gladiator battle. Now, the round arena with rows of sloping stands was completely empty and covered in a thick layer of snow. In the center stood Ragnara's fehu tree, its roots in the air. It was leaning to one side, and the frost made the branches look upholstered with white velvet. The falcon hopped back and forth in front of me. It was now the size of a normal bird. It left tracks in the snow, absurdly flapping its wings to get free when it sank into the snowdrifts. It disappeared behind a smashed column. Suddenly, Loki stood where the falcon had been. A deflated bird suit lay on the ground, and he ran his hand lazily through his gray hair. He looked at me with a playful boldness that made my cheeks flush.

"Shouldn't you be out killing all your former friends?" I gestured toward Vigrid.

"Thanks for all your work. You do precisely everything we want you to do."

"I'm starting doomsday," I replied through stiff lips. "They're all done for."

Loki gave a little bow that was reminiscent of Elias. "We'll stop Fimbul now, as we've done hundreds of times. Although, we've probably never gotten this far before." He turned his head and looked like a wolf sniffing the air. "But we'll quit while we're ahead." He smiled with the grin of a wild animal. "Even though it is a good game we're playing, raven."

I walked toward him threateningly, and he looked at me with sheer amusement. To him, I was about as frightening as an ant. "Do you realize how many people were killed and hurt by your little game?"

Loki rolled his eyes. "Yes! And it was amaaaazing."

"Why do you even involve yourself with humans? You shouldn't care what happens with us."

"Humans had gotten too powerful. You were . . . self-sufficient." He spoke the word with a wrinkled nose. "The gods were almost gone. No one believed in them anymore because you simply had no use for them, ridiculously believing you knew everything. Humankind had devolved into whining, thinking you could prevent natural disasters, hunger, and disease. You would have believed you could stop the sun from exploding if it came to that. Imagine thinking you can stop chaos."

"Maybe you shouldn't throw stones when you live in a megalomaniacal glass house."

"I am chaos. Me!" Loki pounded his chest with a clenched fist; if it had been any other chest, it would have shattered. As it was, he unleashed a powerful earthquake, and the ground shook so forcefully that I fell to my knees. Cracks developed in the columns around the arena, and one toppled with a crash. The large fehu tree gave up and fell on its side. "Am I crazy for saying what I am?" A couple of more columns collapsed. "You should fear and love us."

"So, if we start respecting nature, would you stop killing us?"

"You're negotiating with chaos itself." Loki's voice turned soft, and he once again looked fragile and innocent.

"What is it you want? Do you want to be worshipped?" I asked.

"For now, you believing I exist is plenty for me. I'll leave the worship to the vain gods."

A low rumble made the ground shake. I realized it was laughter and that it didn't come from Loki. It came from the other end of the ruined arena.

"Odin?"

The supreme god walked toward us and stood side by side with Loki. He was young and fit with bare, muscular arms and long raven-black hair. He was so tall that I had to lean my head back to see the two men's faces. The only thing that marred his perfect appearance was the empty eye socket. They looked at one another, and Loki laid a hand on Odin's shoulder.

"You're playing a dangerous game." I looked directly at Odin. "It's been foreseen that you will die soon."

Odin stood up straighter. "Ragnarök hasn't started because Heimdall's son hasn't blown the Gjallarhorn. I promised him I would spare your witch friend and their unborn baby if he doesn't do it."

"You can't be certain of what will happen. Not even the future itself is certain. Isn't that right, Loki?"

"I'm enough of a creature of chaos to know that it's hard to predict what the future holds." Loki twirled a lock of Odin's hair with his free hand, and his fingertips found their way to Odin's neck, which they trailed up slowly. "But I would never destroy my blood brother."

"Can't you die, too?"

Loki raised his eyebrows and looked away as though he were really in doubt. "Nature doesn't die."

"No, but you're only one of many giants. Nature would carry on even if you were gone, I would imagine."

Loki shook his head, sending his gray hair flying around his face. "Well, now I don't want doomsday to happen at all."

One of Odin's shoulders sank slightly, but he kept his eye on me. "There's room for one more over here. With your worship, we can stop Ragnarök and live on as rulers. Loki can become a god again." He reached a large hand out to me. "You can become a goddess. You want to stop Ragnarök, don't you? All you have to do is believe in us, and we'll give you power, riches, and eternal life."

"I'm not interested in any of that."

"But you can save all the little insignificant mice . . . or humans . . . or whatever you call them. Join us and save your loved ones. Loki won't sic his creatures of chaos on Luna, your parents, or the other humans. Your sister will live, and without Benedict's nasty spells, you can be together. That's what you want most of all." His eye glinted.

Loki elbowed Odin in the stomach. "Say the part about Varnar. Say it." He giggled. "She didn't even know that she's pregnant."

"I will bring Varnar back to life," Odin promised.

Against my will, I took a step forward, and Loki's lips parted in a satisfied smile. I moved my feet once more toward them. Odin had his arm around Loki's shoulder. The god and the giant reached their free arms out to me, as if they were one creature with four legs. With my head in the middle, we would look like the three-headed creature on the Gjallarhorn.

"You need to believe in something. Everyone does." Odin stretched his broad arm out to me. "Remember, you bound yourself to me."

"That knot can be untied."

"You're just like all the others. You're no different from those who hang people from the trees and offer them to the gods. Let's stop this nonsense so we can get back to our normal lives."

Loki burst into a mirthful little laugh that made me jump in fear. "It's so cute how you think you have a say in this, Odin."

Odin rolled his eye. "Shut up, Loki."

"I can't help it. You're so fun to tease! The worst thing anyone can say to you is that you're powerless in the face of fate."

Odin clicked his tongue in annoyance. "She was juuuust about to fall for it."

"Anna?"

My head jerked up. "Arthur?"

My father was approaching from the other side of the arena. With him was Serén. For the first time, we weren't pushed away from one another. "Odin is right. Take your sister's hand and stop Ragnarök."

My breathing quickened.

"I don't care about everything else, as long as you and your sister survive. Now that Ben's spells are gone, it'll be easy. You won't feel a thing."

"No," someone said from the other end of the circular arena. "This ends now, Arthur. We've never agreed on this. I love you, but you were on the wrong path. That's why I left you."

My mother came striding steadily toward us.

CHAPTER 54

Both my father and Odin stared at Thora, who looked confident and wild with her big dark curls streaked with white. She wore leather pants and a leather jacket, and she walked with her legs slightly spread. Although our parents and Odin were looking at one another, my eyes were locked on Serén's.

Loki hopped ecstatically up and down in imitation of a gigantic frog. "What a lovely reunion. How beautiful." He croaked a couple of times.

"Anna."

"Serén," I whispered.

Serén's eyes widened as Arthur pushed her toward me.

"I'm so happy you're my sister," I whispered. "You're amazing, and I love you, but it's not going to work." I walked backward toward Thora.

Serén also tried to back up. "Dad. Leave me alone. Arthur!"

"Arthur allowed himself to be captured by Eskild and Ragnara," I told Serén. "I *saw* it." At The Boatman, when I saw Elias's past, I finally saw what he had been keeping from me for the past two years.

I was half hoping that Thora would contradict me, but she nodded. "Elias tried to stop it, but he ended up taking the blame."

"I was trying to save you," Arthur said with tears in his eyes. "It wasn't my plan that Ragnara would try to kill you and Thora. Thora, please believe me."

Thora touched the horizontal scar on her stomach where Ragnara had cut her open and pulled me out. "I believe you,

Arthur, but your plan went wrong. It's fortunate that Benedict was there to protect Anna from your foolishness."

"Let's just worship Odin now. I guess one deity is just as good as any other." My dad raised his hand in irritation. This was apparently a fight they had had many times before.

"No, Arthur. These gods sacrifice humans. They rule through fear."

Odin had been silent during my parents' conversation, but he looked at Thora with a strange longing. "I put the völva's power in you. You were the holy vessel. Let us become one."

Thora looked at Odin. "Your time has passed. Now you must die."

Odin grew to the size of a giant. "Die? DIE?! You're the ones who will die. Die of old age, like the puny humans you are, while I will live forever. Ravens, I order you to stop Ragnarök." Even though he was standing some distance away, his arms were long enough to grab both me and Serén and push us together.

As we were pressed up against one another, the world made a loud sucking noise around us. Then everything turned golden.

It was quiet, and we held each other. I heard splashing and gulping sounds, and through my closed eyes, I perceived an orange light. I almost didn't dare look because I feared we had been thrown back millions of years in time. A wave rocked us gently, but we didn't go very far because there was a membrane close around us. I tightened my arms around my sister. We just rocked in each other's arms for a while, and I was nearly lulled to sleep. Everything other than my sister was unreal and inconsequential.

"Where are we?"

Serén's words helped clear my head, and I opened my eyes. We were in a tiny pouch-like space, and the walls were made of a soft, organic material. It wrapped itself around us. Over the gentle sound of waves, I heard a rhythmic *thump, thump . . . thump, thump . . . thump, thump . . .*

"I don't know where we are. Could it be . . .? We're not back at the beginning, are we?" I ran my hand along the matte tissue that enclosed us. My arm was clothed in a sleeve, and when I looked down, I saw that it belonged to my mom's tattered coat. Serén was also dressed, and she was still the same age as the last time I checked. We hadn't gone back to Thora's womb.

I cupped both hands around her face. Then I held her close to me, and she squeezed her arms around me, too. My clairvoyance went back in time while I simultaneously felt her vision of the future.

"I think we're in some kind of limbo. A place between the worlds."

Her arms around me felt so right. I sighed. "Can't we just stay here?"

"And let Odin have his way? He's seizing power as we speak."

I saw the vision through her. The near future. Odin watched as Loki decapitated Od.

"So, what should we do?"

"There's another option." Serén smiled.

Yesss . . . The voice rang in my head. *Ravens . . . You're listening to me.*

"Hejd?" I turned my head, searching for the sound, but it came from all directions.

Then comes Sigfather's mighty son
To fight with the foaming wolf
In the giant's son does he thrust his sword
Full to the heart,
His father is avenged

"What's the other option?"

"You know full well what it is." Serén sounded calm. A rather different scene flowed from her.

Mathias held the Gjallarhorn to his lips and blew. He must have heard my plea as I flew past him. I saw our parents, Loki, and Odin from above the arena in Sént, and when Mathias made the metallic tones blare over Vigrid, Odin was pulled backward to the battle.

"No!" he screamed. "No!" But he found himself amid the savage giants with Gungnir in his hand. More gods came running from several directions.

The Midgard Serpent slithered over the plain and opened its mouth so wide that its lower jaw hit the ground, its upper jaw disappearing in the clouds. Thor appeared with his hammer raised. He threw the weapon at the snake. The hammer hit the Midgard Serpent's eye, and it fell to the ground, causing an earthquake that shook everything. The fighters were knocked off their feet. Thor stumbled, failing to get out of the way before one of the Midgard Serpent's venomous teeth pierced his leg. With a roar, he got up and staggered nine steps before collapsing. The death goddess Hel was felled by Freyja, and her head—half beautiful, half skeletal—rolled through the dirt.

Fenrir bit Odin in two and ate him, even though Loki tried to stop him. Od got ahold of Tilarids and swung it toward the wolf. The blade bore into Fenrir's heart, and he sank to the ground, dead. The black disk of the sun was reduced to rubble, clouds slid over the sky, and the giants screamed as they were pulled into the sea.

Serén leaned her head back slightly so she could look into my eyes. "Which future do you prefer?"

"The second one." My voice was barely audible. "It's the fulfillment of the Ragnarök prophecy. The bloodthirsty gods are out of the way, and a new guard will take over."

Hejd spoke, and her words wrapped around us.

Now does she see the earth anew
Rise all green from the waves again;
The cataracts fall
And the eagle flies

*And fish he catches
Beneath the cliffs*

*More fair than the sun a hall I see, roofed with gold on Gimle it stands
There shall the righteous rulers dwell, and happiness ever there shall they have
There comes on high all power to hold
Rule he orders, and rights he fixes
Laws he ordains that ever shall live*

In tandem with Hejd's words, I saw the images. The earth was resurrected with blue skies, mild summer breezes, and green fields. The giants were gone, flushed into the ground. They were still there, but they no longer fought humans and gods. I saw the shining god who descended from the sky.

"Od."

Hejd laughed out loud. *Always have I seen the mighty. Time can pass while the grains grow.*

Serén gave me a grave look. "Od will be the new supreme god in Asgard. The dead will keep their home, and the living their faith."

"What is the price for this future?" There was always a price.

Serén held me tighter. "Our völva powers must be combined to avert Ragnarök. We're holding it off right now. You know what must happen for doomsday to begin."

I blinked away tears. "You've known all along. You said so. You saw one of us die."

"I've searched the future," Serén said. "Every version ends this way. Hejd said:

*O'er Midgard Huginn and Muninn both
Each day set forth to fly;
For Huginn I fear*

Lest he come not home
But for Muninn my fear is more.

My blood ran cold, but I was resolved. "I'm ready."

"I'm the one who isn't going home. I'm Huginn. Hejd is worried about you because you have to stay behind."

"No!"

Ravens. You've figured it out . . . It has to be now.

"Wait," I said desperately. "If we meet, we have the power to alter things. Can't we change course so we aren't separated at birth? So Ragnara . . ." My voice tapered off as I realized it wouldn't help.

"Anna! This is the only way."

I'll carry you, raven, Hejd said. *You'll rest with the other völvas.*

It was time, but I was in no way ready to say goodbye when we had just found each other.

"Let it be the other way around," I said. "Who says which one of us has to die?"

Serén embraced me again. "It has to be me so the future is set free." She inhaled shakily. "Tell Aella I love her." Serén screamed, and like a flower drying in my hands, she faded away until she was nothing but dust. I held nothing, and nothing held me.

"Serén," I yelled. "Serén."

But she was gone.

The membrane around me tore, and I was flung back to Vigrid. Fenrir and the Midgard Serpent lay dead; Hel's disembodied head rolled across the ground; and Od had begun his ascent to the sky.

Everything Serén had shown me happened.

Above me, the ice wall rumbled. It cracked and split, and a tidal wave surged toward me. I swirled in the water with screaming giants and dead gods. Od hovered over me and smiled gently. I breathed water into my lungs, and everything went blurry, but he embraced me, and even though he was up in the sky, I felt his touch. I was immediately filled with life.

"There needs to be a god's child on the earth," Od said, and his voice was soft and strong at the same time. "There need to be witches and giants. And a völva. Will you be mine?"

"Are you sure? I'm really difficult."

Od laughed. "I'm sure."

Mathias swayed toward me. He held the Gjallarhorn in his hand, and its sound still hung in the air from when he had blown it. I fought my way to him.

"You're alive."

Mathias held me with his superhuman strength. I turned my face to the sky and caught Od's eye.

"Thank you," I whispered. I had no problem binding myself to him because it was with love, not by force.

Od raised Tilarids. It flashed, and he breathed on it, causing the metal to melt in his hand. I had to squint against the light, and once I could see again, the metal had been reforged into a plow. Freyja was by his side in the sky, and he presented the tool to her. She nodded in thanks and disappeared. At Od's other side stood Hejd, dark and wild. The two of them would rule Valhalla together.

The ice wall melted completely, and the water swelled farther onto land. If it was the ground sinking or the water rising, I wasn't sure, but I was surrounded by blue-green sea. Mathias grabbed me and pulled us down. Eventually, we were deep beneath the waves. When I leaned my head back and looked up, I saw the bubbles on the surface from below. Light was refracted by the water, and we were struck by a sharp beam.

Sea creatures swam around us, and I saw gigantic silhouettes in the distance, like those of whales and giant squid.

The ground rumbled. The sounds were muffled under the water, but the seafloor cracked open, and bubbles seeped out. Then the bedrock began to rise. Standing on it, I was lifted out of the waves, and eventually, I was standing on the bare sand in front of the placid North Sea. Vinr washed ashore at my feet, and I picked it up. I breathed in fresh, warm, mild air.

The sky was dark blue above me, fading first into an ice blue, then an orange tone. Yellow light streamed over North Jutland, which was so flat, I could see over land for several miles. The trees were scorched, and there were no buildings, but there was a fine green glow over the black earth. Birds chirped, and a gentle breeze ruffled my hair.

Just when I could barely stand the beauty any longer, the golden disk crested over the horizon and, beautiful and glorious, the sun rose.

EPILOGUE

I sat on Odinmont, where my house had once stood. Even though it was gone, the place was still elevated above its surroundings. The air was mild and warm, and not even a breeze stirred. The sky was a striking contrast of blue and pink because the sun—which, for over a year, I had seen only in dreams—was on its way down behind the horizon, coloring the clouds baby pink as it went.

It had been a long day of driving around in electric cars with Niels Villadsen and the surviving civil servants from the DSMA. Most of them had an awful hangover from Mardöll's many layers of hypnosis.

Elias's grain collection would be used to replant the fields, and tomorrow, we would start sowing. Planting crops was so rooted in a belief in the future that the mere thought made my heart feel light. At the same time, sadness gnawed at me. I stroked Vinr, and the many völvas responded with love. One voice in particular rang out. It was Serén's. She was now inside my staff. We would forever be separated, but at the same time, we were together. I would have to find Aella soon and explain it to her.

"Hey, Anna." The voice was so high-pitched that it sounded like the speaker had inhaled helium.

The little myling stood a little farther up the hill. He squinted in the sharp light.

"Hey." I opened my arms, and he ran up to me and leaned his head on my chest.

"I'm lonely in the grave. Mimir is gone, and your dad isn't there, either. I'm all alone in there."

I was well aware I had some loose ends to tie up, so I stood up and thumped Vinr against the ground. I called on two spirits and a demigod, resting my hand on the myling's shoulder. I addressed him first.

"Your time here in Midgard is over," I said. "You were a human sacrifice, so you will go to Valhalla. It's great, and the new guy in charge is really nice."

The boy clung to my leg. "I'm going to miss you."

I was about to thump Vinr on the ground again, but I stopped myself. "Find someone named Varnar. He went to Valhalla not too long ago, and I'm sure he'll take care of you." I lowered my voice. "He'll probably seem a little surly at first, but he's a good guy." I couldn't help but grin. "Tell him I'm coming later, and that I'll take good care of our daughter." I laid my hand on my stomach. "Her name will be Ast. It means *love* in Old Norse." This last part was hard to say, and I squeezed my trembling lips together. Then, I looked at Ragnara's spirit, which was hovering behind him. "You'll go with him."

Ragnara looked surprised. "There is no realm for me. I have to wander forev—"

"Nonsense! We make the rules. Od will take you in. Varnar is there, and even though he won't admit it, he'll be glad to see you."

Ragnara stepped from one foot to the other. "You were Odin's raven. You were Ragnarök. What are you now?"

I pondered this. "I guess I'll find out." I thumped Vinr against the ground, and she and the myling disappeared.

"Ulfberht. Mimir."

The two came toward me. Mimir was in spirit form, and the blacksmith looked at the blue sky in amazement. It was strange to see Mimir so tall in his full body because I was used to seeing him as a head stump.

"There is a realm of the dead that needs a leader. Helheim is vacant. Do you want it, Ulfberht? You would make an excellent goddess of death."

Ulfberht brushed her silvery blond hair away from her eyes. "Me? The goddess of death in Helheim?"

"Hel didn't take great care of Helheim, so it's a bit of a fixer-upper, but with Mimir as your adviser, I'm sure you'll get it into good shape. These days, there are a lot of people who die of old age or illness, so we need plenty of space and good conditions. Can I count on you?"

Mimir and Ulfberht nodded.

I walked up to Mimir, and he hugged me, laughing in his way. I couldn't really feel him, but there was more volume now that he had a rib cage.

"Greet Hejd from me," he said.

"Greet her yourself. There's no need for strict separation between the realms of the dead and the different belief systems. In any case, I'll do what I can to remove it."

"I can visit Hejd in Valhalla?" Mimir beamed.

"If I have anything to do with it, everyone will be able to visit everyone."

Mimir and Ulfberht disappeared, and I sat with a thud. The sadness made it hard to really be excited, even though we were heading toward brighter times. There was a movement behind me.

"Come sit, Elias," I said without turning around.

He chuckled. "I guess your clairvoyance is still working."

I ran my hand over the dirt, which was still black and dusty. A tiny pale-green sprout was reaching toward the sky. Right now, it was only half an inch tall. My first impulse was to pull it up, but I clenched my fingers into a fist.

"Actually, I smelled that it was you."

He sat next to me. Close enough that I could feel the heat from his body, but far enough that we weren't touching.

"I am in awe of your senses."

"Don't interfere with them."

"But I would like nothing better."

I rolled my eyes.

"Od let you go?"

"It was frustrating to sit there while you were in danger, but Od was afraid I would get hurt."

"I think it's more so because you have a role to play after Ragnarök."

"You saw what happened the night you almost died as an infant?"

I rested my chin on my knee. "I did. But you should have just told me. I trust you."

"Really?"

I couldn't look at him. "I promised to, didn't I? It was an honest and fair deal."

"You also once promised to save my life if it was in your power to do so," he whispered.

"I didn't let you out of The Boatman. You would have gotten yourself killed if I had."

Elias didn't reply.

"Are you okay?" I asked.

"I'm normal now."

"You'll never be normal."

"Now that Od is the supreme god in Valhalla, I'll age like everyone else."

I cautiously met his gaze. "And you're not happy about that?"

Elias pursed his full lips and looked toward Kraghede Forest. The trees were still singed, but they weren't dead. Buds protruded here and there. I couldn't see them clearly from here; they just looked like a green blur. Luna, Rebecca, and Mathias were running around down there, pressing life into the trees. Mathias would take over The Boatman in Od's place, and he would have the same function in Midgard that Od had had for centuries.

"Now I'm just like any other twenty-five-year-old man." Elias smirked. "Physically, in any case . . ." He stopped himself but then couldn't help but finish his sentence. "Although no one can measure up to me in one particular aspect."

I ignored this. "I'm sensing a *but* . . ."

Elias grew serious again. "I'm free."

"Haven't you always been?"

He turned his face toward me. "Now I'm free to live."

"You're also free to die." The words flew out of my mouth, and I held my hand up as though to shove them back in. "Sorry."

"It's okay, Anna. You're right. I am free to die."

"I thought you were striving for immortality."

"No!" It came out so quickly, I could tell there were four hundred years of consideration behind it.

"What about those of us who miss the dead?" My stomach clenched.

"They live on because we remember them."

"Hmm." I looked up. The clouds were a jumble of purple and orange bulges and bubbles. If I stared at them long enough, they looked like figures and creatures. "Have you thought about how you want to spend the rest of your life?" I asked.

He, too, looked at the clouds. "I'll keep studying. There's plenty to rebuild after Ragnarök, and I'll happily share my knowledge with others."

"Sensible." I didn't know why, but my words dried up in my throat. I pulled my knees closer and wrapped my arms in front of me.

"What about you? How will you spend your time in this new world with your life ahead of you?"

"The same way as before. I'll see my friends. The ones who are left." This last statement sounded like a whisper. "But, otherwise, I'll live like I always have. Alone." I touched my stomach. "Well . . ."

Elias looked down. "Are you having a baby?"

"Varnar's." I had to take a deep breath, and my exhalation was shaky. I thought Elias would be jealous, but he broke into a huge grin.

"That's amazing. Congratulations."

I slung my arms around myself again and hugged my knees.

"Anna." Elias pressed his fingers into mine, and although I didn't take his hand, I didn't push him away. Tentatively, he moved to close the remaining space between us. I turned my head to the side so my cheek came to rest on my knees. The fabric moistened under my eyes. I remained sitting there, curled up in a little ball.

"You don't have to be alone."

I shrugged. Because I was hunched over, the movement was stiff. "Luna and Mathias have each other." This came out as a squeak. "Monster has his wife, and Arthur and Thora are apparently trying to repair their relationship. Védis and Rebecca are going to live together so that Védis can finish her witch training."

"What about me?"

"Elias. I can't be with anyone. I can only figure out how to be alone."

He looked straight ahead. "I can't figure out how to be anything but alone, either. But maybe we can be alone together."

"That might be the strangest arrangement in history."

The corners of his mouth turned up. "You are who you are. I wouldn't change that for all the world. But we have mixed our blood, after all. There's a very special bond between us."

I couldn't tell if he was joking or serious. I looked at the sky again. It was now a psychedelic mix of yellow and cherry red. The clouds suddenly resembled faces. Benedict's, Od's, Varnar's, Hakim's, Serén's, and the myling's. I stared at them. Elias looked up, too, and I suddenly realized it didn't matter if the dead were there or not. For us, they would always be there.

I gently rested my head on Elias's shoulder while he kept his arm around me. And so, we sat, watching the sunset together, certain the sun would rise again tomorrow. I saw a dark cloud in the sky among the red and orange ones. I snuggled closer to Elias.

"Do you see that dark cloud that looks like a dragon?" I asked.

"I think it looks like a bird." He pointed with his free hand. "It has feathers."

I laughed, my heart lighter than it had been in years. The pressing knowledge that everything would end soon was gone. The future lay ahead of us. I didn't understand it, but even though I was stuck in the past and had a hard time letting go of the things that had happened and the dead who were gone forever, there was a road continuing endlessly over the horizon.

I looked at the edge of the world, and I could make out the horizon through Kraghede Forest. The sun had ducked beneath it, but fiery fingers still reached up behind the trees.

The dragon, or bird, or whatever it was, hovered darkly over us among the clouds. Suddenly, the faces of all the dead were in its tail. Or they were riding on its back.

Imagination. My imagination created that.

I squeezed Vinr, and the völvas pulsated within its wood. My sister was somewhere in there, too.

I heard Hejd's voice faintly inside my head.

> From below the dragon dark comes forth,
> Nithhogg flying o'er the plain
> The bodies of men on his wings he bears
> But now must I sink
>
> Völuspá,
> 10th century

CHARACTERS

AELLA [EYE-ELLA]	Varnar's friend and Serén's girlfriend
ARTHUR	Anna's father
AUGUSTIN ODION	Ben's twin brother, now contained inside a porcelain figurine
BALDR	Odin's son
BENEDICT SEKIBO [SE-KEE-BO]	Luna's father
BODA	a giant wolf, the wife of Monster/Etunaz
BRENDA	a holistic therapist who works at The Healing Tree
ELIAS [EH-LEE-AHS] ERIKSEN	potion maker and Od's assistant, also known as the Brewmaster
ESKILD BLACK-EYE	Ragnara's adviser and commander of her army
FAIDA	a girl Anna met in Ísafold
FINN	a fingalk Anna befriended while traveling through Hrafnheim
FRANK	Anna's friend and would-be killer, owner of Frank's Bar and Diner
FREYJA [FREY-A]	the goddess of love
GRETA	Anna's social worker
GYTHA	a woman who sells clothes near Dyflin
HAKIM [HA-KEEM] MURR	a young police officer
HALFDAN	Frank's grandson
HEL	the goddess of death
HUGINN AND MUNINN	Odin's ravens
INGEBORG	Prince Sverre's wife
JYTTE [YUDA]	a woman Luna knows through Norse Pagan circles

LOKI	a giant
LUNA SEKIBO	Anna's friend, a witch
MADS	Anna's friend, a half giant
MARDÖLL [MAR-DULL]	the prime minister's wife, a witch
MATHIAS HEDSKOV	Anna's friend, a demigod
MIMIR [MEE-MEER]	an oracle who was decaptitated but kept alive as Odin's adviser
MINA OSTERGAARD	Anna's neighbor and classmate
MODGUD	guards the entrance to Helheim
MONSTER	Anna's friend, a giant wolf
NAUT KAFNAR	a murderer; Anna calls him "the Savage"
NIELS VILLADSEN	the director of the DSMA
OD DINESEN [DEE-NE-SEN]	owner of The Boatman, a demigod
ODIN	the All-Father, the supreme god of the Norse pantheon
PRINCE ETUNAZ	Monster's real name and title
RAGNARA	Sverre's mother and predecessor who tried to kill Anna
REBECCA SEKIBO [SE-KEE-BO]	Luna's mother
ROKKIN	Monster's daughter, a giant wolf with black fur
SERÉN [SE-REN]	Anna's twin sister
SKRYMIR	a giant in charge of Utgard
SVERRE [SVEHR-A]	the king of Hrafnheim and Anna's lover
THORA BANEBLOOD	Anna's mother
TÍW	a man Anna met in Ísafold
TRYGGVI	a skald Anna met in Ván
ULFBERHT [ULF-BAIRT]	a giant who forges weapons
VARNAR	was sent to protect Anna, then they fell in love
VÉDIS	a witch
VERONIKA	a bartender at The Boatman
VÖLVA HEJD [VOHL-VA HAIT]	the mother of all seers

PLACES

ALFHEIM	the home of the elves
ASGARD	the home of the gods
THE BOATMAN	Od's bar in Jagd
THE BRONZE FOREST	home of the Forest Folk
DYFLIN	a town in Hibernia
FÓLKVANGR	Freyja's domain, where she takes her share of those who die in battle
FRÓN	a small, flat kingdom
HARALDSBORG	the rebels' castle
HELHEIM	Hel's domain
HIBERNIA	a kingdom
HRAFNHEIM	a world created for believers in the old faith
THE IRON FOREST	home of the Wolf Folk
ÍSAFOLD [EE-SA-FOLD]	a small town in Frón
IVING	a river between Frón and the Iron Forest
JAGD [YAGD]	a coastal town in northern Denmark
JORVIK [YOR-VEEK]	a town in Hibernia
JOTUNHEIM [YO-TOON-HEIM]	the home of the giants
KRAGHEDE [KRAG-HEY-THE] FOREST	a forest bordering Ravensted
MIDGARD	the human world
ODINMONT	Anna's home
OSTERGAARD	the property next to Odinmont
RAVENSTED	a town in northern Denmark
SÉNT	the capital of Hrafnheim
SØMOSEN [SUH-MOH-SEN]	a bog in northern Denmark

SVERRESBORG	a prison in Hrafnheim
UTGARD	a manor in Jotunheim
VALASKJÁLF	Odin's private quarters
VALHALLA	Odin's domain, where he takes his share of those who die in battle
VIGRID	the red plain surrounding Sént
VINDR FEN	a desolate stretch of land in Hibernia

CONCEPTS / OBJECTS

AUKA [OW-KA]	Anna's axe
BERSERKERS	a group of warriors
BLÓT [BLOHT]	a ceremony
CLAIRVOYANT	someone who can see the past and/or future
DEMIBLOOD	the blood of a demigod
DEMIGOD	someone who is half human, half god
FEHU	a rune designating property, adopted as a symbol by Ragnara
FIMBULWINTER	a three-year-long winter that signals the coming of Ragnarök
FINGALK	a frightening winged creature, described as part bird, part ape
GIANT CRYSTAL	a crystal made by a giant; it keeps its user hidden from their enemies but glows red when their loved ones are nearby
GJALLARHORN	a horn that, when blown, summons the gods to Ragnarök
GUNGNIR	a magical spear
HÁLFA	a holiday celebrated in Ísafold to mark the halfway point of winter
HANGADROTT	the sacrifice of a royal

HLIDSKJALF	the throne from which Odin can see into all realms
JÖTUNN [YUH-TUN]	another name for giant
KLINTE [KLINT-A]	a potion that dulls the senses
LAEKNA [LEK-NA]	a healing potion
LÆKNIR [LEK-NEER]	an inferior version of laekna
THE MIDGARD SERPENT	a giant lindworm, also known as Jörmungandr, that wraps around the whole world, holding its tail in its mouth
OSKOREIA [OS-KO-REY-A]	Odin's wild dead. Restless spirits of those who died violently or unexpectedly
RAGNARÖK	doomsday, the fate of the god
SEID [SAIT]	a magic ritual
SKALD	a traveling performer who recites news and poetry
TILARIDS	Sverre's sword
ULFBERHT SWORD	a sword into which the Ulfberht smith puts part of their soul
VÖLUSPÁ [VO-LU-SPA]	a tenth-century poem containing the völva Hejd's prophecies
VÖLVA [VOHL-VA]	a female clairvoyant, also called a seeress
YGGDRASIL [IG-DRA-SIL]	the World Tree of Norse mythology, where Odin was hanged

© Sara Galbiati, Gyldendal Medie

AUTHOR
MALENE SØLVSTEN made her debut in Denmark in 2016 with the first volume of the fantasy trilogy Whisper of the Ravens and was nominated for the Readers' Book Prize in the same year. The series quickly became a bestseller in Denmark, for which the author received the 2018 Edvard Prisen, awarded annually by the Danish Library Association. She published seven books in total. She lived in Copenhagen, Denmark until her untimely death at age 47 in 2024 following a short illness.

TRANSLATOR
ADRIENNE ALAIR is a literary translator working from Danish, Norwegian, and Swedish into English. She studied Scandinavian Studies at the University of Edinburgh and has lived in Sweden and Denmark. She is now based in Charlotte, North Carolina.

Discover how the thrilling trilogy began . . .

Malene Sølvsten
Ansuz
(Whisper of the Ravens Book 1)
ISBN 978-1-64690-026-8

Malene Sølvsten
Fehu
(Whisper of the Ravens Book 2)
ISBN 978-1-64690-027-5

Read Siri Pettersen's first trilogy
—The Raven Rings—out now!

"Will captivate lovers of Bardugo's gritty situations and Pullman's wide mythic worlds." —*Publishers Weekly*

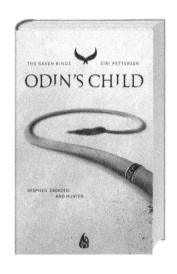

The Raven Rings – Odin's Child (Book 1)
ISBN 978-1-64690-000-8

"An intricate fantasy world . . . Unexpected and intriguing."
—*Kirkus Reviews*

"A satisfying, powerful conclusion."
—*Kirkus Reviews*

The Raven Rings – The Rot (Book 2)
ISBN 978-1-64690-001-5

The Raven Rings – The Might (Book 3)
ISBN 978-1-64690-002-2

Discover the exciting Rosenholm fantasy trilogy!

A paranormal fantasy about love, friendship, and dark secrets.

"This intriguing and intricate story is a winner." —*Kirkus Reviews*

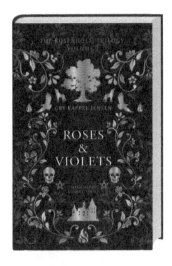

Roses & Violets
(The Rosenholm Trilogy Volume 1)
ISBN 978-1-64690-012-1

Forget Me Not
(The Rosenholm Trilogy Volume 2)
ISBN 978-1-64690-013-8

Nightshade
(The Rosenholm Trilogy Volume 3)
ISBN 978-1-64690-014-5

Four girls are accepted to Rosenholm Academy, a boarding school for those with magical abilities. They unwittingly get involved in solving an old murder case that puts them all in grave danger as they realize that Rosenholm carries a dark secret.